BRIGHT LEAF

BRIGHT LEAF

BY FOSTER FITZ-SIMONS

RINEHART & CO., INC.   NEW YORK, TORONTO

BRIGHT LEAF

PART ONE

CHAPTER ONE

I

H<small>E CAME OUT</small> of the August afternoon and stood suddenly in the big square frame of the warehouse doorway. Young Ralph Lippenstock, drowsing on his elbows behind the paying window, happened to look up and there stood this motionless man, a frail and lone silhouette hard against the brilliant sunlight.

Some ten minutes earlier Ralph had mechanically marked the fact that the 2:05 southbound had arrived at the station two blocks away and then had passed, hissing and clanking down the tracks alongside the buildings. He could hear its desolate hoot—as he had heard it daily for most of his eighteen years—moaning away at the crossing half a mile south of Kingsmont. It made not a ripple on the surface of his private reverie. This reverie was a continuously pleasant succession of fancies dominated by the prideful knowledge that Mr. Ashgood had seen fit to leave him in sole charge of the warehouse for a couple of hours that afternoon.

The dim-spread tunnel of the warehouse interior stretched out before him quiet and deserted. This was in high contrast to the teeming excitement that had filled it for most of the morning when the first sale opened on the floor. The swarm of denim-clad figures shuffling down the six long rows of baskets piled neatly with the pale golden hands of tobacco, the high, ritualized cries of the auctioneers echoing under the low ceiling—it was all over and done with now, leaving an empty and exhausted quiet. The rows had already begun to look ragged and decimated. Down at the farther end two or three Negroes, slow-moving shadows, were piling the empty baskets in a corner and loading a van for one of the factories.

1

Young Ralph's gaze in the moment he looked upon the figure in the doorway was so preoccupied that it was immediately distracted by the feverish battering of a wasp trapped against the grimy glass partition before him. His eyes went up, and when they came down again, the lone figure stood opposite him on the other side of the paying window. While not exactly startling him, this apparently noiseless move gave him a curious sensation. Well, he thought, well . . . and his jaws ceased their tender rumination upon a large quid of rough-cut.

The man stood very still before him as though awaiting judgment. His arms hung limp by his sides. In one bony hand he held a faded mulberry-colored carpetbag. It was not so much that the spare height of the body between the cracked brass-toed shoes and the flat beaver hat was so great as that it gave the impression of having been stretched and elongated on the rack of some long and painful process. He was neither young nor old. The thin neck drooped forward a little from the soiled collar with its limp string tie. The face above it was pale and equine with a big nose falling out of it over an uncertain chin. He looked at Ralph from a pair of faded, unblinking eyes. Ralph stifled an overwhelming impulse to snicker. Well, what now? he thought again. Why didn't this apparition speak up instead of just standing there? Ralph darted another glance of frank conjecture over him. Must be another of those cheap drummer fellows. They appeared out of nowhere when the market season opened and set up little stands about the warehouses to wheedle the new tobacco money out of the farmers' pockets with cheap jewelry and other worthless gimcracks. Well, he needn't come here. Mr. Ashgood wouldn't allow any one of them nearer than the corner of Bay Street.

"Ayehhh . . ." This strange sound broke out of the stranger like a whinny. It startled Ralph again and set his jaws into motion.

"Do something for you?" said Ralph loftily. He shifted his weight with elaborate unconcern from one hip to the other and projected a stream of tobacco juice with neat precision into the cuspidor at his feet.

"Ayeh . . . I—" The queer falsetto sound came again and the man's free hand began to pluck along the trouser seam.

A feeling of bafflement began to come over Ralph. It made it difficult for him to maintain his studied air of polite, businesslike detachment. What in all get-out did this fellow want? Couldn't stand here all day waitin' on him to make up his mind.

"If you're lookin' for Mr. Ashgood, he's gone home to dinner. Most likely won't be down again till late this evenin'. Maybe not then, because we don't have another sale until Monday."

"No . . . no." The strange, naked hand had now begun an agonized journey from button to button up the front of the wrinkled

2

coat. "No, I'm not—uh—looking . . . I mean I'm looking for Mr. Singleton—Mr. James Singleton. They told me down at the station that he wouldn't be over at his factory, but that I might find him down here at one of the warehouses."

"Oh!" Ralph's wide mouth split in a sudden childlike whoop of mirth. He leaned forward with a grin.

"Reason I laughed," he explained candidly, "is I don't think I've ever heard ol' Major Jim called "Mr." since I was born! New here, ain'tcha?"

"Ayeh . . . just got in on the train."

"What business you in?"

There was another long pause while the face before Ralph became blank.

"Not any," said the man carefully, "I reckon."

"Oh." Ralph's curiosity—at best a limited attribute exercised exclusively within a few select categories—began to flicker out. "Thought you might be a drummer. Lots of 'em about this time of year, you know. So you're lookin' for ol' Major, huh? Well, as a matter of fact he was here awhile ago." He leaned farther forward, cupping one hand about his mouth. "Hey, Mason!" he yelled down the building, his voice receding in a muffled echo under the low roof. One of the slow shadows at the far end paused.

"Yassssuhh!" elongated and booming, the word floated back.

"Any you boys seen Major Jim round recently?—Gentleman here lookin' for him."

The far shadow communicated briefly with another and then again came the slow, booming howl.

"Nawsuhh, ain't seed him foh an houah or moah."

Ralph pulled himself erect and turned to the back of the office, where a pair of dusty-paned windows gave on the street. They presented a smudged view of low rooftops opposite. Over these Ralph pointed vaguely.

"Across town there," he said. "You can just about make out the top of the house from here. It's the big one on the hill. Major's most likely there this time of day. If you want, you could try over to the Singleton factory across the tracks, but he don't stay down there much in hot weather, especially this bein' Sat'd'y afternoon—even if it is openin' day! Why don't you go on over to the factory office anyway? They maybe could help you."

"No. I've got to see Mr.—Major Singleton, himself, I reckon."

"Suit yourself," said Ralph briskly. "If you don't mind walkin' round in the sun this time of day. Just light out across town there to the east. Take you about ten, fifteen minutes." He was rapidly losing interest in this interview. "You can't miss it—anybody 'most from here on out can show you."

3

The gaunt specter stood as though it had something more to say. But when it spoke it was in the two wailing syllables with which the conversation had been opened.

"Ayeh . . ." he said, looking beyond Ralph through the back windows as though to imprint the blurred shape of that distant roof-top on his memory. In a moment he murmured again. "Thank you."

And turning, he walked slowly to the doorway. There he paused, blinking out into the furnace of the afternoon like some queer, be-draggled crow blown into an unfamiliar field. Then, stepping forth, he was swallowed up in the light again as suddenly as he had come.

Young Ralph at the window sighed and placed his elbows on the counter again. The encounter of a moment ago was already as blandly erased from his mind as though it had never occurred.

2

The man stopped at the corner for a long time. He stood there as he had done before that boy in the office. Now he was staring up and down at the long, irregular line of warehouses fronting on the street. The bright glare shivered the edges of the corrugated roofs and caused the faded legends and trade announcements to advance and recede crazily upon the brick and wooden sides.

Tolliver Company . . . Ridgetwist . . . his thin mouth formed itself hesitantly about the dusty letters, barely moving. He spelled the words out like a primer, his head following his eyes . . . Single-ton & Sons . . . Fine Domestic & Imported Tobaccos . . . Ware-house No. 3 . . . He stopped still upon these words for a long time.

This was the place. His free hand moved up slowly and brushed carefully across the narrow forehead. Yes, this was the place all right. From all about him there rose a rich, almost stifling odor, as though the very earth were saturated with it. It was compounded of the smell of pine resin and something else far more pungent and heady. Tobacco. His mouth whispered the word with a kind of tremulous satisfaction. Tobacco . . . thousands of pounds of it stored in hogs-heads and bins behind those long walls.

He stepped down into the roadway, where the dust lay rutted and churned with the passing of many wheels, and crossing over, started up the street. At a distance he assumed more than ever the appearance of a scarecrow. But like no old and comfortable inhabit-ant of a field. He carried with him an aura of complete aloneness. This impression was even more palpable since he was the only mov-ing thing along the empty street in a bright, still nightmare of heat.

I guess I'm tired, he thought as he walked along with his pecul-iar jerking stride. I'm tired, but I can't stop now. He began to perform an exercise that he had found himself doing many times as

4

the course of this journey swept him farther and farther into space. He began to repeat his name and origin to himself voicelessly. My name is John Barton . . . John Barton from Wyland in Connecticut. . . . It's a little town up the valley. My name is John Barton. . . . He did not know why, but this repetition seemed to vindicate his presence, to reassure him in an alien and threatening world.

The line of warehouses on either hand broke away, disclosing a series of slattern frame houses. They were scarcely more than boxes, fronted with little disreputable porches, crowded close one against the other. A few of them were set back in minute spaces of baked earth enclosed by fences where dusty honeysuckle and trumpet vines tumbled triumphantly in and out of the broken pickets. Here and there a solitary and gaunt pawlonia or a listless chinaberry tree offered its scanty shade.

There was no more evidence of life and movement here than before. He became increasingly aware that his lone progress was observed from a dozen black doorways and shuttered windows. He sensed, rather than saw, here and there upon the porches, relaxed, sprawled bodies, the limbs heavy and quiet under sleazy cotton. Big, frank breasts resting melonlike upon a window sill, and a quick gleam of white eyeball out of a shadowy interior. From somewhere out of the still air nearby came a slow cry.

"Cal . . . oh you, Cal . . . git on up here wid dat bucket 'foh I gives you mah hand!"

Negroes. Of course he had seen them before. But always then they had been like creatures from the moon. You stared at them curiously across a blank space separating their existence from yours, and that was all. But this was different. This was their place and you were the alien. There was something about it that tightened his Yankee senses. He found himself lengthening his irregular stride, holding his eyes rigidly fixed upon the top of the street.

He arrived breathing hard. Before him lay the town square of Kingsmont, its geography precise and geometric. Superficially it differed in appearance not at all from a thousand others the country over. The same undistinguished architecture was evidenced in store fronts and ugly commercial buildings of brick and wood running along the four sides. The same tin awnings spreading out over the wide walks, the same irregular line of second-story roofs, some frankly flat with a scattering of unrelated cornices set upon them in various styles, others nothing more than the inevitable corrugated iron glittering nakedly under the sun. At the center of this was a little park set about with trees and indifferent shrubbery surrounding an impressively ugly red-brick building. This edifice was topped by a mansard roof and a tower with flat clock faces telling time in the four cardinal directions. From where he stood the man could read, cut into a plain granite lintel set above an entrance to this building, the words GRANGE COUNTY COURTHOUSE. The word "county" was curiously scarred upon the letter N with a deep, round pit, and on the bricks under the eaves and above some of the window openings were black smudges. It was evident that the building had suffered a terrible experience at some time in its history.

To the stranger, John Barton, standing there gazing about him, there came a sense of relief. Here at least were plentiful signs of familiar life and activity. A horse and buggy clattered slowly by, raising little plumes of dust beneath its wheels, and all about him in front of the stores and hitched to the railings surrounding the courthouse square was a crowded jumble of vehicles and animals. Saddle horses and mules, buggies and buckboards, and, here and there, a Conestoga wagon with arched canvas top lent a curious frontier note. And here—instead of blank and empty streets—moved a motley host of humanity: men, women, and children of all sizes and ages. They passed slowly in and out of the stores or squatted and leaned in little groups under the shade of the tin awnings and the trees, conversing and calling out to each other, or just stood looking out with intent eyes upon nothing and spat at long intervals ceremoniously into the dust. In spite of all this the scene seemed dreamlike to John Barton. Completely unreal in a sense that he could not fathom. Even when two men engrossed in conversation brushed against him in passing. One of them murmured "'Scuse *me*, suh!" and then turned back to his companion. He had a feeling that he stood in this sun-drenched place, with its oblivious inhabitants, invisible and bodiless. The conversation of the two men drifted back to him. Their speech fell strangely upon his ears.

"Yeah, we made out fine this year, I reckon. Two hundred pounds o' prime at top price today."

"I reckon you are makin' out all right! Didn't do so bad myself. You sell at Dever's?"

"Naw—Ashgood's my man."

"Ain't much choice 'tween 'em in the long run jest so you git what's acomin' to you."

"Yeah—I reckon!"

They passed out of hearing. With their going John Barton felt a wild sense of loss sweep through him, a sickening nostalgia for the place he had left. How like this it was! And yet how different, with its neat severe buildings lying dappled beneath the elms, all of it shaped by a prim decorum that had no echo here. No one seeing him standing there would have thought that any emotion moved behind his gaunt countenance. Only the pale eyes seemed to deepen and widen.

Blinking, he crossed over to the courthouse square, picking his

6

way between the wagons to a worn marble drinking trough. He set the carpetbag down here, enjoying the sight of the patient animal heads about him, the gleaming hide twitching at the flies. With slow and careful gestures he removed his hat and coat and hung them over the end of the railing. His thin head thus revealed was untidily covered with lank, damp, dun-blond hair. Cupping his big hands, he filled them under the thin spurt of water that fed the trough and dashed the cool liquid into his face. Great Jerusalem, that felt good! At once he felt refreshed. Looking up out of this momentary delight, his eyes fell upon a woman sitting alone in a nearby wagon. She held a fat, limp infant across one arm, her free hand moving monotonously to and fro over the face of the child, brushing at the flies. It was a moment before he realized, with a shock that sent the blood rushing over his sallow temples, that she was nursing the infant, her breast frankly bared through the faded calico of her dress. She stared back at him from beneath her slat bonnet without speculation, then called shrilly to someone beyond him in the square:

"Ella Mae! I done tol' you to leave them things alone now. Come on back here to the wagin!"

He turned quickly to the trough again and began to throw water furiously and erratically at his face until it streamed down over his shirt front, wetting him to the skin. It was as though by this behavior he sought to erase his confusion. In a moment he stopped abruptly and, fishing a large much-used handkerchief out of a rear pocket, began to dry his face. His hands were trembling and he began to say to himself with a sort of blind desperation: Major Singleton . . . Major Singleton . . . I've got to see him right away.

Quite suddenly, without any warning whatsoever, there fell squarely into the midst of the drowsy murmur about him a shocking burst of sound. It was like a blow on the backbone of every living creature there. John Barton stood with mouth agape, the handkerchief arrested before his face.

The outrageous fanfare came again.

This was followed immediately by a flood of brassy sound, a raucous plunking and squealing. It was such a wild and grotesque parody of its intent that only by a special dispensation of the imagination could it be believed. The square seemed to release its breath collectively, to start awake with a grin. Heads turned, necks craned forward, leaned suddenly out from doorway and window. All about —from beneath wagon beds and tumbling out of them, from doorways and steps—surged a little tide of sheer delight, a flashing of small bare legs and pinafores. Every child who could get free had started for the south side of the square. Trailing after them arose a halfhearted chorus of female admonition and protest.

"Jemee! . . . you, Tate! . . . git on back here . . . hold on to yore sister. . . . Pa, *Pa!* make 'em . . . keerful . . . Mareee! . . ."

His mouth still agape, John Barton saw advancing along the side of the square, diagonally across from him, a large van drawn by a team of big chestnut horses. It was a fantastic vehicle carved in scrolls and curlicues and painted in brilliant reds and yellows and greens. On its roof were seated five figures. Three of them matched the van in the fantasy of their dress and the glistening grease paint on their faces. The fourth of this quartet, a tall hat set jauntily upon his perspiring head and displaying a rather elaborate black mustache in a lean and mocking face, was stripped to his shirt and a pair of handsomely tight fawn-colored trousers strapped beneath his boots. He managed to look at once amiable, saturnine, and dandyish while blowing upon a battered cornet. At intervals he removed the instrument from his mouth with a flourish and, displaying a row of even white teeth, bowed ceremoniously to either side of him. In front of the quartet, upon the driver's seat, sat a giant Negro in the soiled and tarnished glory of a braided scarlet coat, his black skull glistening with sweat. He sat, the long reins held almost disdainfully in his huge hands, monumentally erect, a strange and scornful majesty about him.

It was hard to accept the fact that so much hideous sound could be produced by one ancient cornet, one battered bass drum, a fife, and a banjo. It rolled about the place, echoing from the sides of the buildings in waves of monstrous cacophony. There was about it something orgiastic and compelling.

It proceeded along the street before the wide veranda of the frame hotel and turned the corner. As the spectacle bore down upon him John Barton felt its excitement stir timidly in his own belly. The children were swarming about it now, leaping and prancing and screaming with shrill ecstasy. They were not alone in this. Their elders all along its route swayed toward it, their faces frozen in sheepish grins.

As it passed him in a slow crescendo of color and sound, John Barton read, blazoned in fancy letters on the side of the van:

DR. MONACO'S SOVEREIGN REMEDY
GIANT MEDICINE SHOW

And beneath it, on a placard freshly painted with less authority:

At Weller's Livery
8 O'clock Tonight
Free! Everyone Invited! Free!

As the tumult continued to the next corner and turned again, drawing in its wake a train of excited children and dogs, the bitter sense of his being cut off and alone descended upon him again. What

8

was this place, this land to which he had come? What meaning did any of these alien faces, this familiar and at the same time strange little arrangement of dusty buildings, have for him that he should be here? He could not pretend that there was one thing in any of it that offered him assurance. All he had—all he had ever had—was the implacable compulsion underneath that bony frame moving him forever forward along the deserted track of his life. And the nature of this compulsion was so buried, so private within him, that one looking upon him there at that moment would not have believed it existed. He was strange, but even the strangeness was so blurred that it marked nothing upon the memory. He was like a wraith born to roam the earth unrecognized. It was this quality, dim and tenuous, that made it difficult for those who were to know him and work with him even to remember the shape of his face.

He replaced his hat and coat with the same deliberation that had marked their removal and, picking up the carpetbag again, looked about him recalling the scanty directions given him by the boy at the warehouse. It was fairly simple, because the geography of the square rested flatly on the four cardinal directions. His way lay to the east. He crossed the street with his peculiar disjointed gait, and proceeded down to the corner opposite the hotel and turned to the left, up a long slanting street overhung suddenly with many trees. He had advanced but a few steps when he paused. A sudden musical clash and clangor was coming out of the gaping door of a low, barn-like building on his right. Behind him the uproar in the square was retreating into the distance. Whereas that had awakened only a momentary excitement in him, this new sound spoke in his very blood, falling sharp and clear in his ears. Drawn by something far stronger than his profound and painful shyness, he crossed and peered in at the open doorway. Within was a sort of cavern. He recognized the red glow of coals upon a forge in the corner, its blackened hood ascending among the sooty rafters. Nearby an anvil gleamed dully, and here and there upon the earthen floor were several piles of rusting scrap iron. In the midst of this a tall horse stood quiet. A big man with thick, sweat-stained shoulders bent over its lifted forefoot. To John Barton's nostrils came a faint, acrid stench of seared hoof. This was good. An irrational feeling of comfort began to steal over him. This might be the smithy back home in Wyland. The palms of his hands began to sweat with the memory. It cannot all be so strange after all, he thought. I can live anywhere where there's a smithy.

The man before him gave a final, precise tap on the iron shoe and, releasing the hoof, stood erect with a grunt. John Barton felt himself regarded by a pair of child's eyes, simple and piercingly blue. The face was open and pleasant, broadly streaked with sweat and

9

soot. It threw into great contrast an energetic tumble of iron-gray curls on the head. The smith spat generously on the floor and smiled. It was so direct and candid that John felt himself smiling palely in return.

"Afternoon!" The greeting came in a gentle bass.

"Good afternoon," replied John, wondering a little desperately what he was going to say next. But the low rumble continued:

"This is m' tenth horse today." The smith turned and murmured to the beast standing at his side and patted it gently on the shoulder. "These dog days get most folks I know. Not me. Like warm weather m'self. Always could work harder and longer when it was hotter'n the hinges!"

He grinned again, flipping the sweat from his streaming forehead.

"That was . . . that was a good clean shoe you put on there," John Barton heard himself saying, surprisingly. "Couldn't help but notice it."

The smith looked as pleased as a small boy.

"Well now, thank you! Kind of you to say so. Like to do a neat job. You a smith yourself?"

John studied the carpetbag in his hand for a moment.

"I've done some smithin'," he said in the high, wailing voice.

"Well now," said the smith, wiping his hand across the grimy apron front, "I'm glad to make your acquaintance. M' name's Upham —Roger Upham."

The arm he extended was heavily muscled and covered with a delicate sheen of gray hairs. John took it almost gratefully.

"My name's John Barton."

"Not from hereabouts, are you?"

"No."

"Well, to tell the truth, neither am I. Come from Ohio m'self, after the war. Been here goin' on twenty years now. I don't really do much shoein' any more. Just for old customers when they're full up over at Barker's and down to the livery. Mostly make and repair carriages for a livin'. But"—he paused with a look of pride—"I'm a machinist by trade. Can fool with anything that's been forged out of iron. Like to do it better'n anything I know!"

He turned and pointed into a nearby corner. Here was a large worktable supporting a drill press and a lathe and littered with tools, and before it upon the earthen floor an intricate contraption of small girders and supports about a flywheel and a housed valve.

"That's a pump I'm improvin' for Mr. Trenton's place now."

As though irresistibly impelled, John approached the little engine, his vague eyes suddenly focused and concentrated with excitement. He moved about the pump, viewing it from several angles.

10

Then he squatted and gave the wheel a flip with his hand. The valve wheezed softly. The smith stood watching him.

"That's interesting," murmured John at last. "That's very interesting—the way you've got the arm connected to the shaft there."

The smith's blue eyes blazed with pleasure. He took the horse by the head and led it over to a post, where he tied the reins to a nail with quick, economical gestures.

"You think so?" He came to squat on his powerful haunches opposite John. "It's a little idea I've been foolin' with. I know it ought to work"—he ran a hand through the gray curls—"but somehow she don't just do yet."

John nodded, looking closely at the pump. Then he turned the little wheel slowly several times, his long face quiet and concentrated. Then he spoke low, almost as though he were talking to himself.

"Ayeh," he said, and the smith leaned forward to hear him, "I see . . . some trouble with your power drive there. What if you moved your flywheel out a little?"

"You mean extend the shaft?"

John nodded slowly.

"But—" exploded the smith with a vigorous gesture. In a moment the two of them were talking rapidly, their hands going out to point at and touch some part of the machine. Their heads drew close together, and they expostulated in the quiet and amiable tones of two men who had long known each other.

"Look here!" rumbled the smith at last in a loud, enthusiastic voice. "I hope you can stay around for a while. I'm goin' to be workin' on it some later this afternoon."

The excitement washed suddenly out of John Barton's face, leaving again the bleak mask. He stood up slowly.

"Thank you . . . I'd like to, but I can't now . . . I've got some business to attend to . . . some—" The high, thin voice trailed off dismally. "But I would like to look in later on if I can."

"Any time you like, you're welcome, Mr. Barton!" roared the smith, rising to his feet. "I'm pretty near always here in the daytime on weekdays—sometimes in the evenin's too!"

"Thank you," said John Barton, half-turning back but not looking at him. He wanted to respond more adequately to the warmth and generosity in the big man, but he felt powerless to say more, drowning again in a sea of inarticulateness.

"Good afternoon, Mr. Upham," he mumbled, ducking out the doorway, his long legs taking him wildly up the shaded sidewalk. He heard the gentle, muffled roar of the smith behind him acknowledging his departure as though there had been nothing unusual about it.

11

He hurried along, buried within himself, hugging the warmth and strength gleaned from this latest encounter to himself like a precious thing. He began to elaborate upon it like a starved man presented with a crust. He felt—no, he *knew*—that deeper than the impersonal words he had exchanged with the smith there had been present an understanding between them, an immediate recognition that required no discourse. It was something intangible, but he felt it as a sort of bulwark within him against whatever need and stress awaited him this afternoon, a little citadel to which he could return with comfort no matter what darkness hid the course of his experience here.

For a long time he walked thus, implacably putting one foot in front of the other, the street empty and quiet, the houses he passed withdrawn and seemingly deserted in their yards. Then suddenly, looking up out of his thoughts, it lay there before him at the top of the hill. If there had been a banner blazoned in the sky over it, he would not have been more certain. There it was, a large white house looking down upon him and all the world from beneath its trees.

3

Within the personal maze of his incoherence and awkwardness John Barton possessed an authentic, if modest, flame of sensibility. For the form, the precision and balance, that governed all beautiful things he had an immediate, mindless appreciation. So, standing now before the Singleton house, he felt well within him that instant, warm recognition. The deep weariness and loneliness, the long and desperate journey upon which his feet were set, became, for the moment, unimportant. Coming from a part of the country that built its dwellings compactly into the earth against cruel and bitter winters, he felt amazement at the candid expanse of this house. Its quality was not manifest in sheer bulk or showiness. On the contrary, it was rather modest in size and almost austere in its simplicity. And over it lay a subtle patina that had nothing to do with age. Rather it was the evidence of fastidious taste and the product of intense loving pride and care.

It was the most beautiful house John Barton had ever seen, and he knew it. As a small, shy boy he had crouched near the big-bellied stove in Aaron Harbach's store through many a snowbound afternoon, hearing the local veterans of the war talk about the magnificent dwellings they had seen in the South. But there was nothing in these half-remembered fantasies to prepare him for this actuality. Nothing in the shape and style of the houses he had passed most recently had prepared him either. Most of them had been as large, or larger, encrusted in the opulent gingerbread Gothic that had been

12

the architectural style for some years now, but not one of them with the compelling character of this structure. With a craftman's eye he catalogued with deliberate appreciation the physical details that combined to make it what it was. The severity of the square, two-storied form, the modified Doric columns supporting the roof of the porch across the front and down each side, the balanced spacing of the tall front windows, the pure magnificence of the entrance door-way. He noticed that it was set back at just the proper distance on the gentle rise of lawn under the trees like an impeccable and gracious monument, its white surface dappled now with a warm pattern of shadows. John Barton realized with a little thrill of justness that here the street up which he had come swerved suddenly to the right as though in deference to this house, allowing it to look down magnificently over the town.

Crossing, he entered upon a gravel path through the open half of a low iron gate. Ahead of him on the porch there was a Negro man sweeping. He was very tall and very black. John Barton had again the panicky desire to turn then and flee to the refuge he knew did not exist. But his feet kept him moving relentlessly forward. At the bottom of the steps he stopped and cleared his throat weakly.

"Is Mr.—is Major Singleton at home?"

The Negro leaned upon his broom and stared down upon this spectacle that had no precedent in his experience.

"Yessuh. Majuh's heah. Won't you come on in, suh, an' have a seat?"

The richly voweled and elided words came forth in a cadence that was then and remained forever strange and difficult in John Barton's ears.

"No, thank you," he said, setting the carpetbag down on the porch. "I'll—I'll just rest here."

"Well, Majuh's sittin' round to de side." The Negro waited as though expecting something more from John. "Who'll I say's callin'?"

"Tell him—" John paused, marshaling the words carefully upon his tongue. "Tell him that John Barton from Mr. Eli Whitehead of Hartford, Connecticut, would like to see him, please."

The Negro turned from him with a nod, murmuring under his breath, "Mistuh Barton . . . Mistuh Whitehead," as he walked down the porch. John saw him shrug his shoulders as he turned the corner of the house. Well, he told himself, it didn't matter. What mattered was that he had got here finally, and he could never go back. His route lay erased behind him as surely as though it had been a path of mist and smoke. This he had known from the moment he had first set out upon it. And this knowledge perversely added another measure of strength to the small store available to him. All his life the nature of this strength and the strange dogged quality of his progress

13

were not natural to him. They were forced upon him by a crowding desperation and denial, and their very acquisition exhausted him. He leaned wearily against the tall, fluted column nearest him, one of his big, nervous hands moving over the blistered paint in an odd, caressing gesture. The feel of wrought things, the quality of their planes and curves, their mysterious perfection, had always held more than a sensuous meaning for him. They reassured him in a way that was inexplicable. Lulled momentarily, he gazed half-seeing back down across the lawn. He was immediately impressed with the extent of the view commanded from the porch. He could see suddenly very far over the rolling surface of the earth to the west. It opened in a long sweep of endless woods and fields beyond the rooftops and shimmered off into a smoky haze of heat.

The fields interested him. He could see most distinctly the corner of a large one toward the south beyond the last roof. It was marked off in long threadlike rows. And bristling along the rows were ranks of naked brown spikes. Beyond it was an interval of woods and then another corner of a field. He had a sudden sense that these cultivated spaces stretched on either side of him for miles and miles. These he knew were tobacco fields stripped by the harvest. He had seen endless acres of them rushing past the windows of the train coach both yesterday and today. How different it would have been in his own native valley, with the denuded stalks in the compact field reluctantly revealed from beneath the great tents of white cloth that had tenderly and jealously guarded their growth all through the summer. Here it all sprawled fiercely and nakedly in a careless bounty. What a completely strange and incomprehensible land this was in every way. . . .

"*God*frey's Cordial! . . . Simon, you hulking ignorance!"

It was more like a yell of supreme outrage than anything else that burst at that moment upon John Barton. He started out of his musings as though he had been shot. Approaching him down the porch was a small, exceedingly plump man in his shirt sleeves. In that first distracted moment John got an impression of a very red face above a rounded expanse of open vest apparently held together by a heavy gold watch chain. The little man bore down upon him, almost running on his small feet, holding himself beautifully erect and gesturing about him with an enormous palm-leaf fan. The Negro followed close behind him grinning idiotically. The little man stopped short, breathing heavily, and extended his hand in a magnificent gesture of welcome.

"Mr. Barton, is it, sir? Delighted!" He pumped John's hand vigorously. "I don't understand what's got into these damnable black-amoors of mine these days. Times are too easy now. Lost all their manners since the war—addled every bit of sense they ever had, too.

14

Unendurable state of affairs, I tell you—not to be tolerated! Give you my word I have to be restrained from breaking their necks fifty times a day. *Towers of Ilium*, Simon!" He turned his head fiercely toward the Negro. "Stop grinning and fiddling about and go get some more ice." Then, taking a step apologetically toward John: "Come around to the north side of the house, Mr. Barton, won't you? You can at least pretend there's a breeze there even if there isn't a breath stirring in the whole infernal county this afternoon. I tell you these North Carolina Augusts have shortened my life by ten years at least! Lived all my life here—born here. Looks like I'd get used to it, but I never have. Can't understand how I've survived. Hell itself can't hold a candle to Kingsmont in August . . . *no, sir!* But please make yourself at home, Mr. Barton. How is that penny-pinching old *miser*, Eli Whitehead, now? Tell me honestly, how well is he prospering these days? Too well, I bet my ace. Eli could make money at his own funeral! He could indeed, sir!"

The palm-leaf fan went darting and swooping in and out of this avalanche of words like some strange and delicate bird. John felt stunned and shattered more by the continuous flood of sound than by its import. It boomed forth from this little man in a tremendously courteous bass voice. In response he could only feel his Adam's apple leaping futilely along his throat; he could not have answered a syllable in that moment if his very life had depended upon it. He found himself helplessly caught in the swirling orbit of this vigorous and talkative little individual. His carpetbag once more in his hand, he was swept down the length of the porch.

From where they lay sprawled among some rocking chairs and a table two big liver-spotted hounds looked up out of tragically adoring countenances and thumped their tails mournfully on the floor as the two men approached around the corner.

4

Sunk deep into his rocker, listening to the Major's gentle interminable rumble, there came to John Barton a sense of ease such as he had known but rarely during his angular life. Something in this place, and particularly in this energetic little man sitting near him, accomplished it. He didn't know what he had expected in the Major, but it certainly hadn't been this comfortably globular figure—unbuttoned but retaining an air of neatness—nor had it been the really magnificent head under the vigorous mane of gray hair. For the twentieth time during the past half-hour he glanced with covert astonishment at the broad forehead, the long, clean-shaven jowls; the full, sweet mouth, and the lively gray eyes under their iron thatch of brows. None of it should have gone together without being ridicu-

15

lous. However, by virtue of some celestial alchemy they not only met and fused perfectly in the Major, but they succeeded in being impressive. The fact that he was well-bred and a gentleman lay like an easy garment over the little man, and because of it he seemed to have no trouble in accepting the entire universe on the same terms. John was forever to remember this initial interview with an inexplicable sense of gratitude. No human being whom he had encountered before had ever conjured up in him this sense of serenity and well-being.

So far he had uttered nothing more than a few barely audible monosyllables. They were simply polite punctuations. There had been need for nothing more. He realized that the facts of his presence and his willingness to listen constituted all the credentials that the Major desired of him for the moment. However, he felt that this was merely a pleasant preamble. It could not last forever. Inevitably the time would arrive when he would have to step defenseless from this respite and say what he had come all these miles to say.

Before the two men the yard stretched green beneath the trees. Toward the back there were a stable and some outbuildings. A group of chickens absent-mindedly investigated the dust under some fig trees. Beyond them, a whitewashed paddock fence bordering an open pasture swept out of view over the hill. Now and then John could hear the subdued murmur of voices and the squeal of a pump at the back of the house. From a tree covered with great gleaming leaves at the edge of the lawn came the incessant twittering of a host of sparrows. Through this nervous chorus a distant cicada wove a harsh and insistent thread of sound. It all formed a fitting background to the heavy, dreamlike place into which he had wandered.

On the table between the two men sat a decanter and a bowl of melting ice. The Major held a glass in one of his plump fists. It was wrapped about with a moist handkerchief. Another glass sat on the table near John Barton's elbow. From time to time his eyes came to rest upon it with an expression half astonished, half despairing. If his own father could see him at this moment! At first John had protested, weakly, futilely; but the glass was placed in his hand before he could string half a dozen stumbling words together.

"A little bourbon, sir, to drown the heat in your throat!" the Major had said, pouring the amber liquid ceremoniously over the clinking ice.

"Ayeh . . . thank you, no . . . I don't believe—"

"*Towers of Ilium*, sir! In this heat? Nonsense, of course you will. Cool you off. Not extra good bourbon, but it's wet!"

It was no use. John realized that any protest he could muster would not be believed anyway. He held the glass gingerly, feeling the slow bite of the cold in his palm. Somewhere within him a neat,

16

gray Puritan heaven shuddered at its foundations. He sipped, and after a very little while he discovered that it didn't really matter at all. He was lost long before he arrived at this point, irrevocably lost. Then too, this liquid seemed to possess the kind quality of hushing the protesting and incredulous voices from his past. They no longer had any meaning. The drink clawed chilly in his throat, raced down through him and over him, working some kind of magic. In it his tight mind, his imprisoned body, were merged at last in an entity. This was what *they* had meant, then—his Aunt Rheba and those others with their grim and righteous hubbub—when they went to meetings and held fierce conclaves in the closed parlors of a Sunday, talking about those impersonal and foreign horrors, the *Lost Souls of the City* and the *Brew of the Devil*. Meaningless colloquies until *now*. And now they had no more weight or substance than the sound of the sparrows from the edge of the yard. In fact he had a distinct feeling of satisfaction and pleasure. It was astonishing.

"No," the Major was saying—his fan, which was as much an instrument for punctuation and emphasis to his words as it was a weapon against the heat, hung briefly in the air. "Dammit, I don't believe I've seen Eli Whitehead for over three years. Used to get together with him in New York when we were both attending the big Association meetings in the winter. But it takes too much time and trouble to go gallivanting about these days. Have my hands full right here in Kingsmont. Usually just send Ed Raeburn or one of the boys in the office up to report on the proceedings. More convenient from my viewpoint, and gives a promising youngster an opportunity to spread his wings a bit. Broaden his outlook on the tobacco business, you know. Eli's still on my books, though. Must have been shipping him a hundred hogshead of our best every season now for over fifteen years. And every year he protests the quality and tries to make me haul down the accepted market price—the tight-fisted, blue-nosed old rascal! Good business head, though, have to hand it to him. And he manufactures a good-quality product. Can't ask more of a man. You in the tobacco business, Mr. Barton?"

"No," said John, the word coming up out of him with clarity and finality. "No, I'm not."

There. It was out in the open at last—spoken. This was the moment. *Now*. And the dread with which he had awaited it was no longer there. Words were suddenly crowding upon his tongue. He felt released, almost exhilarated, as though he might, if he had need, converse with princes and angels. He leaned toward the Major. It seemed natural at this moment, almost imperative, that he tell this little man all about it.

"No," he repeated, and he was conscious for a fleeting moment of standing apart and looking with amazement upon this strange,

17

confident John Barton. "You see, Major Singleton, I'm not in tobacco . . . ah, exactly . . . myself, but I was born and grew up a man in that part of Connecticut which had always grown tobacco. So I know a little something about it. My father knew all there was to know about growing it, I guess. He raised it up in the valley all his life. So did my grandfather before him. Mr. Whitehead always said that my father produced the finest grade of wrapper leaf that he knew of. Father never had to take his crop down to market. He just dealt direct with Mr. Whitehead at the factory. I used to go down to Hartford with him when he went to sell. . . ."

The round face opposite him was politely attentive, but there was a twinkle in the gray eyes.

"I'll bet ol' Eli got the best of the bargain, sir!"

John smiled wanly.

"No. Mr. Whitehead and Father used to have some pretty smart tiffs about the price, but I reckon it all came out even from season to season. Neither of them gettin' more than they ought. They knew it, too. It's what kept them bein' friends in spite of sayin' hard things to one another's faces and behind one another's backs . . . each hopin' someday to get the better, one of the other."

The Major chuckled appreciatively.

"And you?"

Well, here it was. He plunged.

"You see . . . I was never much a hand at the planting and growing part myself. My brothers were the ones for that. They helped Father and, me bein' the youngest, he let me pretty much alone, to do as I liked, which was mostly foolin', and tinkerin' with things. I reckon I was born with an itch to be takin' things apart and fixin' them. Never was a stalled pump nor a broken thresher about the place I couldn't put to workin' again. Used to make up all sorts o' gadgets, y'know, for the kitchen and house for my aunt Rheba and the womenfolk around Wyland. Then my uncle Daniel taught me smithin', and when I was old enough Father sent me down to the Mechanics' Trade School in Hartford. When I was through there Mr. Whitehead gave me a job in the repair shop at the factory. I was there eight years. I liked it a lot, workin' on all the factory machinery. An' I was foreman of the shop the last three years I was there, although Mr. Whitehead said it was because I could handle machinery—*not* the workers. . . ."

John paused to take an indiscreetly large gulp from his glass. It choked him. The steady creak of the Major's rocker continued through his sputtering and coughing. He wiped his mouth hastily, afraid to stop. Afraid of any interruption that might seal him up again.

18

"While I was workin' in the shop I got a lot of ideas about improvin' the machines that Mr. Whitehead used. But all the time I was workin' on one big idea of my own. I guess it started from seein' things in the other factories and hearin' shopmen and foremen talk. It didn't come to me all of a sudden—nothin' ever did, I reckon. It came slow. But when I had it all worked out in my mind it seemed to me so big I had to talk it out with someone. I had a friend from the Trade School. He listened and came down to work with me nights at the shop after the factory closed. Then I went and told my father. He heard me out, but he said that it would be a waste of good time and money. He always thought I was a fool for makin' things I never got anything for. So finally he told me if I was so dead-set on doin' it, not to come around botherin' him or the rest of the family again till I got sense. Even that didn't really worry me, y'know. I was too full of it. Seemed like it was the thing I'd been waitin' and studyin' all my life to do. I went on thinkin' and workin' and studyin' at it for a long time. I made a lot of false starts. But I expected that. I even worked it out on paper. But that wasn't much good. My friend from the Trade School was the one who had to do all the drawings and figures when it came right down to it. I've always had to do things out with my hands. I think with my hands, I reckon." He paused to glance down at those two rawboned objects clasped primly in his lap. "So I gradually thought out what was in my head with my hands. It took a long time, but even before I was done *I was sure it would work!*"

He uttered these last words with slow and passionate emphasis, his eyes intent upon the Major's listening face.

"It was a good feelin' standin' there lookin' at it and knowin' I was right . . . and knowin', too, that it would make a lot of money for somebody in the tobacco business, if I could make them see it the way I did. I knew it would take money—a whole lot of it—to start with. I didn't have any. When Father heard that I was goin' to Mr. Whitehead with a proposition, he blew up and said that if I was that big a fool I could just keep on goin' to perdition and he hoped Mr. Whitehead would help me on my way. But I went anyway. I *had* to."

His slow voice dropped almost to a whisper and his lank limbs sagged even farther into the chair, as though they were crushed under the weight of the memory.

"So I went and had a talk with Mr. Whitehead himself. I showed him what I had made and how it worked. But when I was finished he just put his hands in his pockets and walked up and down."

The Major's chair ceased rocking. He leaned forward in his chair.

19

"And what," he said with elaborate irony, "was this idea of yours for making money that a pinch-penny Yankee like Eli Whitehead could let pass by?"

John bent farther forward without answering. He undid the strap on the carpetbag between his feet, and fished carefully within it for a moment. At last he drew forth a little package of folded papers. He proceeded in silence to open and smooth them out with tender, deliberate gestures on the table top, moving the decanter and his glass to one side to make room. Thus revealed, they proved to be covered with a series of fine and meticulous drawings of some kind of machine. The precise delineations bristled with hieroglyphic figures and measurements. The Major frowned and cocked an iron-gray brow upon them. Not looking at him and continuing to speak as though no hiatus had occurred between the Major's question and his answering, John Barton said solemnly:

"It is a machine for manufacturing cigarettes by the thousand, cheaper and better than they've ever been made before."

There was an ominous stillness in the erect, round torso opposite him. He knew that if he were interrupted now he would never be able to finish. He lunged on breathlessly:

"You see, I had noticed—and most of the trade journals that I had been studying bore me out—that there were a lot more people smokin' cigarettes instead of pipes and cigars, or chewin', nowadays. Especially around big places like Hartford. Seemed to me there would be more and more people smokin' them as time went on just because it's a cheap and easy way o' smokin'. And if you had a machine that could make them so you could sell them reasonably instead of expensive like all the handmade ones, it would make a good business for somebody. It isn't a new idea with me. I found that out soon enough. I saw a machine working in a Hartford factory. I read about another one that was patented and on the market. But the one I saw was clumsy, expensive to operate, and unreliable. Mine was away ahead of it."

"Yes!" rumbled the Major. "I know about these contrivances. Saw one of the damned things on exhibit the last time I was in New York. Heard it was fancy and unreliable, like you say—"

"I know, I know," John interrupted, his voice keening with urgency, "but this one—*mine*—isn't like that. I know it. It works fine, and I can demonstrate it if I have the chance!"

"No doubt, sir, no doubt at all," said the Major. "But Eli Whitehead couldn't see it, could he?"

"Not exactly. But he told me it wasn't anything he had against my machine. He just said that he was too old in his business to start something new like this. He gave me good recommendations, though, to personal friends of his in New York and New Jersey, and told me if I got nowhere with them I ought to try down here in the old Virginia and Carolina tobacco country. He gave me your name—"

"He did, did he? Godfrey's Cordial! There's a Yankee trader for you!" The Major's countenance was becoming choleric. His voice began to roar in his throat as though he were about to address not only John Barton but an invisible host of refractory listeners about him. "So he sent you on a wild-goose chase all the way down here to me!"

He threw back the leonine head suddenly and a magnificent bellow of laughter gushed forth. The sound echoed about the yard and aroused the sparrow chorus into a frenzy of indignant twittering. John crouched in his chair. The gates were closing in upon him again. Even knowing now he had lost once more, he could not stop the desperate, useless pleading.

"I saved a long time to have the money. I took the letters Mr. Whitehead had given me. I went to New York—" he paused and brushed a hand blindly across his expressionless face—"I went to the manufactories in New Jersey. I even came on down to Pennsylvania and Maryland. Now I've come down here."

The Major leaned forward, brandishing the fan.

"Let me tell you something, Mr. Barton—you're having a very sorry game played on you at your expense. Eli Whitehead knew as well as he knew his own name when he started you out on this that neither I nor anyone else in the business who've still got one grain of sense left to knock against another would be willing or able to help you along with this idea of yours. I advise you to go back to Hartford and tell him so for me! I'll write him myself tomorrow."

"I can't go back," whispered John desperately. "I can't ever go back again." He shook his head like a grave and humorless child. "No, I have a feeling that somehow I'll find someone *somewhere* down here who'll see it the way I do."

The Major's reaction to this was characteristically volatile, transparent, direct. He set his glass down with a little gesture of sympathy.

"Believe me, I'm sorry, Mr. Barton. No hard feelings to you and your machine, you understand. You see, sir, I'm not just giving you a blank refusal. Let me try and explain something to you—in all fairness—about us Singletons and the business we have made—something that Eli Whitehead doesn't know, or didn't bother to tell you when he gave you my name. My family has been in tobacco, one way or another, for the last hundred years or so. We started raising it in Virginia way back before the Revolution. My father—all honor to him—brought it down here with him when he moved here some fifty-odd years ago. All that time we have been talking, eating, think-

21

ing, chewing, smoking, admiring tobacco to a man—why, it's been the very breath of our lives! That kind of association with and feeling for a thing makes for a pretty steady tradition, Mr. Barton. This tradition is built on everything that has to do with tobacco: its cultivation, its marketing, its proper function in the society of man. It's the sort of tradition that is respected in this part of the country and any place where tobacco is understood or admired. My family's business was founded on it. All the warehouses and factories in town were built on it. And it's made Singleton and Sons the largest and most respected manufactory south of Richmond, sir!"

The Major's rich voice trumpeted forth in fuller and more sonorous periods as he progressed through this little speech, covering what was evidently familiar and well-beloved ground.

"And—again without meaning any offense, sir!—I simply can't agree with you about cigarettes." A grimace of distaste flashed over his perspiring countenance. He dabbed about his mouth and the double chins with the moist handkerchief. "I've never been able to see them myself. In fact, I have always regarded their entrance into the business as a distinct step downward toward degeneracy and degradation in the use of a noble plant. A little paper wrapped around some low-grade tobacco sweepings and stuck into the mouths of grown men! It turns my stomach every time I have occasion to witness it. So you can see, Mr. Barton, I could not in all honesty encourage something that might help promote a condition that not only I deplore, but which is entirely opposed to my way of thinking about tobacco. I'm not sidestepping the issue like my friend Eli Whitehead with any fancy sentiments about being too old to begin something new like your machine—or any such beans-and-bacon. No, sir! I'm telling you the truth the way I see it."

"Ayeh . . . I see," murmured John in a voice distant and passive. It committed him to nothing. This retiring into himself was so habitual that it had long since ceased to be merely a blind defense against an adamant world set about his life. It had more the quality of a snaillike withdrawal in preparation for another slow emergence in a new direction.

"I must admit, though—*and* with regret," continued the Major, settling back in his rocker for a more leisurely onslaught, "I must admit that all my colleagues here in Kingsmont don't see exactly eye to eye with me on this. They have seen fit to go into the manufacturing of cigarettes on a small scale. But it's a trifling, piddling part of their business. Not anything that they are particularly proud of or talk about much among themselves. To do it at all they had to import special labor from Russia and such outlandish places, just because these foreigners seem to be the only ones who know how to make the things properly by hand. And *there's* another thing!—

22

all this foreign element brought into Kingsmont, living down there along the tracks with the darkies . . . bad element, bad element. Now you wouldn't believe it, but some of them have been here ten, fifteen years already and can't speak English properly yet! Can't say I like it at all."

John Barton felt completely voiceless and alone again. The interview had long drifted away from any center in which he had any control or interest. He would never be able to make this violent, set little man see this thing with his eyes any more than he had been able to make any of the others see it. How it had had its beginnings; how it had grown steadily within him, had crystallized and become perfect in his brain while he worked through the long Connecticut winters in Mr. Whitehead's shop. Nor could he ever make those intricate lines on the drawings come to life for someone who had not witnessed the actuality. The actuality that had grown with such sureness and tenderness under his fingers. The little forms of steel and wood, the wheels and springs and levers, the delicate gears that had been wedded painfully and carefully together to materialize that single passion in his narrow skull. The heartbreak, the long, stubborn, despairing hours alone experimenting with special papers and scraps of tobacco swept from the factory floor coaxing the machine to yield up at last that final, perfect, continuous cylinder. . . . How could you tell another man of the bitter loneliness that had surrounded your achievement—how, when even your own blood and kin had always looked upon you out of hostile, indifferent eyes because you squandered precious days of your life on this strange, inhuman folly? No, you could not—now or ever. Instead you sat, sunken and silent, with the small, implacable voice crying in you that somewhere—*somewhere* . . . He reached over and began to fold the drawings again with the slow, meticulous hands.

"I'd be thankful if you would direct me to someone else," he managed to say at last as he replaced them in the carpetbag. There was no rancor or irony in his voice. There was in the Major's statement that which he had to respect, just as he felt intuitively that the rotund little man had respected him even in the act of denying him.

On his part, the Major could not escape the naked desperation that looked out of the pale eyes opposite him. What a queer, long-faced individual this was to whom he had been talking for more than an hour! These New England Yankees were a strange breed anyway. He felt a rush of warmth toward this man—generous and unthinking, a warmth not a little flavored with bourbon. This feeling was given no small impetus by the fact that he felt emotionally expansive after having delivered himself in fine style on a favorite subject! Singleton & Sons, Fine Tobaccos! . . . And dammit, there was something strangely appealing and helpless about the man even

23

though he was just another in a long series of peddlers and drummers with whom he had had to deal during his life. There was a difference, though. This man, after all, had come a long way just to see him, hadn't he? There was a compliment implied in that act alone that he had to acknowledge. The Major cleared his throat ponderously.

"Well, now," he began kindly, "I'm afraid that would be a little difficult, Mr. Barton. I wouldn't want to give you any more false hopes in this. You see, Kingsmont has practically grown up around Singleton and Sons—and of course the other tobacco interests here too—and we all think pretty much alike on business policies. No, I think it only honest to advise you that it would be useless to approach any other concern here with your proposition." He paused. It became immediately apparent on his open countenance that something had occurred to him that might relieve him of the awkwardness of the present situation. "No—wait a minute now! There is someone else in town here who might listen to you—though how he would be able to do more than listen only the devil could say. On second thought, the suggestion I had in mind would be an insult to you, sir! But as long as you are here you may as well try it. There's a man—Templeton Royle by name—runs a small tobacco business back of a general store he keeps for the whites and darkies that live and work around the other factories." The Major made a gesture of profound deprecation with one plump hand. "He has for the past several years, I understand, peddled about the county a cheap grade of plug and twist of his own manufacture. Even has the effrontery to put a trade name on his product. He's of no real account. I know. I've had dealings with him in the past, and I have no use for either him or his three boys. Scabby lot. I suppose old Royle himself is a harmless scapegrace. Crazy as a coon. In addition to selling tobacco, fancies himself as a preacher of the gospel and evangelist of sorts—in season. When he can't peddle, he preaches. Understand he cuts quite a figure at all the big local camp meetings. I don't really know much about the boys since they've grown up. I've seen the oldest one now and then hanging around the courthouse and less savory parts of town. But they're all bound to be more in trouble than out of it—a generally no-good lot, you can take my word for it. Royle did some tobacco farming for me years ago and I had to throw him and his brood off the place for general shiftlessness, gross mismanagement, and all sorts of mean, underhanded little tricks!" The pontifical head fell back and again the deep bellow of laughter came forth. "You can see why there's no special love lost between them and me. Although we haven't had occasion to meet in many years, I venture to say they still entertain a lively dislike for me. It's in the breed. I wouldn't advise, in any event, mentioning my name to them by way of recommendation—the scoundrels!"

24

He roared again over some private memory, tears of pleasure joining company with the beads of perspiration rolling down his plump cheeks.

"No, no, Mr. Barton, I didn't really mean it. I couldn't be in my right mind and send you off to them!"

John looked back at him without expression.

"I think maybe I'd better go to see Mr. Royle," he said, fastening the strap on the bag at his feet. Something in his quiet voice brought the Major up short.

"Now, now, sir!" he protested, leaning from his chair. "Forget I ever said anything about it. Royle couldn't possibly have any money to invest in such a project even if he were interested."

"Ayeh . . . I think I'd better see him anyway."

The Major looked and felt sheepish. Somehow he had talked himself out of control of the situation. He began to notice for the first time the implacable bones under the incongruous surface of the man opposite him.

"Well, if you feel you must—I suppose you must," he said lamely. "But don't say I didn't warn you fairly!"

"That's all right, Major Singleton—I thank you."

"I know you'll find yourself of a like mind before you've been with Royle a quarter of an hour. Anyway, when you're done with him, come see me down at the factory on Monday. I'll make it up to you by sending you on to friends of mine in Henderson and Danville. I don't know if they will be any more interested than I, but at least they're gentlemen."

"Thank you," repeated John in the grave, monotonous voice. He picked up the carpetbag and rose to his feet. The interview was over. He didn't look at the Major. Instead, he stared out across the yard with his slow, grave glance, twisting the soiled brim of his hat cruelly in his hand. From below the hill, more distant now, the thin, acid voice of the cicada threaded the blanket of heat. Standing there, he had a sudden desolate feeling that nothing had happened at all. That this scene would lie, motionless and immutable, ten or a hundred years hence, deeply embedded in time.

5

The Major insisted on accompanying his visitor to the gate, walking with precision upon the balls of his small feet. The palm-leaf fan moved like an amiable metronome in and out of the ceaseless flow of his small talk. John walked beside him, hat in hand, the carpetbag hanging listless against his thigh, his long thin face looking down upon the gravel, expressionless.

They had progressed about halfway to the gate when a sudden

grind of wheels in the driveway brought both men to a halt. A surrey drawn by a great, comfortable roan horse drew up before the mounting block. This square of weathered marble stood at the end of a side path that came into the center walk below where the two men stood. It was an elegant little vehicle gleaming with brass appointments and painted a dark green. Fringe of the same color edged the flat canopy. Over the horse's back was a fly net of the same hue. The Negro was assisting two women—one rather tall and one exceedingly tiny—to dismount. The taller one did not pause. She came swiftly down the path toward the two men.

"My daughter," John heard the Major murmur at his side, and over that brief comment the little man hung such an aura of unspeakable pride, admiration, and devotion that John barely heard him as he went on to say "—and my cousin, Miss Jackson."

To John that first sight of Margaret Singleton sweeping down upon him was another unforgettable moment from a day that was already rich with a profusion of images and strangeness. And to say that she swept down upon him was an inadequate and meager word to describe how this woman moved. The mode of her dress was elaborate, a light material in pale blue, rigidly corseted under a tiny basque and richly draped across the hips to a bustle. The elaboration enhanced her progress rather than impeded it. She held her skirt delicately and firmly to one side, subtly disclosing the vigorous outlines of the lower part of her body. She came, head high and erect, sailing over the pathway to them.

Great Jerusalem, thought John in sudden, mindless panic, *Great Jerusalem!* He felt gaping, gawking, and monstrous before her—and he was. But he could not turn his eyes away. He had a vivid impression of dark, dark hair piled under an absurd little bonnet that seemed largely composed of two pale-blue feathers; and as she approached, the cool perfection of the features and two big amber-flecked eyes. Her mouth was a fine echo of the mouth of the man at his side, but it revealed a greater perfection and stubbornness. Her skin was creamy, and flushed delicately now. To say simply that she was beautiful would have been banal and incorrect. John could not have found a word for the quality of this creature's perfection. There was nothing in his experience, either dreamed or real, to prepare him for it. He would have liked to run, to escape, to be anywhere except where he was. But he stood rooted through an endless moment, and while he stood, somewhere at the core of him something untouched and unused stirred and uncoiled in a deep, nameless excitement. So deep and so nameless that he was not even aware of it then. The afternoon appeared to vibrate about this woman, to become tense and alive with her vitality as she stopped before them. There was no acknowledgment of John Barton's presence in

26

her bearing. He might as well have been thin air. Her face, brilliant with some disturbance, was directed completely upon the Major.

"Father!" she exclaimed, and the word, coming like a cry, chimed through John, shivering him. He felt perspiration break out upon him afresh. And with an animal-like sense of relief he found himself able at last to force his eyes out of the trapped and helpless stare.

"Father!" the cry came again. The Major went to her with a grave courtesy.

"Afternoon, Meg. Nice visit?" He turned back politely to John. "Meg, I would like you to meet a friend of Mr. Whitehead . . . you know, Whitehead of Hartford, Connecticut. . . . Mr. Barton —my daughter Margaret."

John raised his head obediently, and felt the dark eyes swing down upon him for the first time. They swept over him briefly and perfunctorily. He knew that she didn't really see him—John Barton —standing there. It was not rudeness. It was simply that whatever was disturbing her at this moment was too overwhelming to include anything incidentally.

"Pleased to meet you, ma'am," he muttered inaudibly, and dropped his eyes again. Great Jerusalem . . . great Jerusalem! he repeated idiotically to himself.

"Father!" There was unmistakable appeal and outrage in this third exclamation. Then she turned abruptly with a small, inarticulate sound, and passing them, went up the walk and into the house. The Major gaped after her, his face a ludicrous mask of shock and concern.

All this had occurred so swiftly that neither of the two men had paid any attention to the approach of the second passenger from the surrey. She stood now suddenly before them on the identical spot in the pathway where Margaret Singleton had paused. It was somehow a bizarre transposition. John, looking up, found her not much more than five feet in height. He was being regarded brightly by a pair of jet-button eyes set in the face of an elderly and amused monkey. She was dressed completely in black, but the effect was rich rather than funereal simply because there was so much of it. A minute black hat perched over a pile of strangely blond hair, long jet earrings dangling, an enormous gold and black cameo bobbing loosely upon the narrow corseted breast, a shiny black dress boned up high upon the wrinkled throat, even black gloves on the tiny hands. The effect was fantastic as she stood, her mouth pursed in a secret half-smile, her eyes darting from John to the Major to the front door through which Margaret Singleton had disappeared.

"Well now, well now," she chirruped in a brittle, tinkling voice, addressing no one in particular, "I never—would you look at that!"

27

The Major wheeled on her furiously.

"Tabby! What in damnation—"

"James!" she tinkled, looking at John. "Now, *James!*" She waited, her eyes bright upon John's unhappy countenance. The Major regained his composure with an obvious effort.

"It must be the heat—hellish heat—poor dear!" he murmured distractedly. "Tabby, let me present Mr. Barton of Connecticut. My cousin Miss Jackson, Mr. Barton." This was all hurried, hollow, and meaningless. At the center of an increasing discomfort John Barton knew that he had bungled into the midst of an affair of tremendous privacy between the members of this family. He wanted passionately to be out of it—to be away from this tense atmosphere of things left unsaid, questions stifled, explanations held in abeyance because he was present. The little woman bobbed her head at him and widened the pursed smile, but before he could muster an acknowledgment of the introduction, the Major continued, "You must let Simon drive you down into town, sir."

John began to back awkwardly toward the gate.

"No, I thank you," he protested in the bleak, high voice. "I don't mind walking."

"To the hotel at least, sir!"

John shook his head and placing his hat hastily upon it, extended a hand in tentative farewell.

"Rather walk—thank you. Good afternoon, ma'am—sir."

The Major took the hand briefly and said with strained heartiness: "Well, good afternoon, Mr. Barton. You must let me know how things go with you now."

"Yes," said John. "Yes, I will."

They stood—the Major fiercely fanning the air a foot from his face, the little woman watching with the set and vacant brightness—while the strange, disjointed figure shambled awkwardly through the gate and into the street.

"Damn!" said the Major under his breath. "Oh damn!"

Then, as though released, he turned and almost ran up the walk to the house; the little woman tripped at his heels admonishing him in a breathless chirrup.

"Now James, there's nothing whatever the matter—it's all a great to-do over nothing—a great to-do—"

She continued to repeat this latter until they had entered the cool hallway, where he turned upon her furiously.

"Tabby, what are you talking about? What's the matter with Meg?"

Her eyes went brightly from him to her reflection in a gold-framed pier glass that stood near them against the wall. One of the little black-gloved paws began to flit about the hat and hair, touch-

28

ing and patting them in an incongruous gesture of coquetry, her mouth pursed shut in the secret and meaningless smile.

"Tabby, for glory's sake!"

"Now don't shout at me. I said it was nothing, didn't I? A great to-do all the way around. I told her it was no use getting you upset —no use now at all."

The Major glared at her speechless, his face purpling with indignation. At that moment the Negro entered the hallway from the back. The little man wheeled on him.

"Where did Miss Meg go, Simon?" he demanded.

"Upstairs, I think, Majuh!" The white eyeballs rolled hugely in the gloom.

Throwing the fan upon a hall stand, the Major turned and began to trot up the long flight of stairs that curved upward from them. The little woman darted to the foot of them and tinkled warningly after him:

"Now James—remember what Dr. Ross told you—no use getting excited. I declare . . . *James!*"

He didn't look back, but he paused midway in the run and, recovering his dignity in a breath, with monumental deliberation mounted step by step out of sight.

CHAPTER TWO

I

It seemed as though she had been walking up and down the length of her room—from the closed door to the windows and back again—for hours, like a caged animal, unthinking. She stopped at the foot of the big bed and grasped a post violently as if to make herself stop this senseless journey by sheer force. The pulse hammered hard in her temples as though she had run a long way. It was the beating of her heart, then, that was making all that noise. She cupped her hands over her ears in an effort to stop it, to shut it out, but it went on and on under some dreadful compulsion over which she had no control. What was the matter with her? Why in one moment had she ceased to be that calm, unshakable entity herself, Margaret Singleton? She glanced about the room with desperation, forcing her attention arbitrarily upon each item of its furnishings in turn: the petit-point chairs with the grape clusters carved in their backs, the gold clock on the mantel ticking secretly away beneath its miniature glass dome, the gleaming rosewood dresser, the familiar, faded shapes of the rugs on the dark floor. Almost daily in her life she had paused for a moment to afford herself the intense and personal pleasure of this catalogue. Now it seemed—not strange, but arid and without meaning, although the pattern was as precisely bland as ever. No, not quite. Something lay forlorn on the floor near the big wardrobe in the corner. It was the hat with the blue marabout that she had got last April in Richmond. It was the hat she had put on after dinner that day. What was it doing *there*? Even as this question formed itself in her mind the answer came to her. It made her recoil with fresh dismay. Why, she had thrown it there herself! She had torn it from her head and thrown it violently on the floor and there it lay, a patch of pale blue on the dark oak of the floor. She could reconcile a good deal, but not the fact that she was feeling and acting like an undisciplined, petulant child. And all this because . . . how had he dared . . . how had he *dared* . . . the creature, the *beast!* She was outraged anew that she had in her vocabulary nothing more adequate than the insipid, stock vocabulary from popular novels with which to brand this situation. She wanted to scream and rage, to throw herself upon something and beat it with her fists. It was even more horrifying to realize how passionately she desired to do this. What had happened to her, what had been done to make this violent stranger out of herself?

She crossed to the dresser and leaned forward staring desperately at her face mirrored there. Her features looked back at her as though from the surface of a dark pool, pale and set. With age the mercury backing the old glass had acquired a blue tint. Images reflected in it swam eternally in a cool and mysterious world. It was one of the reasons she loved it. It was no different now. There was her familiar countenance, unchanged, except it was as rigid as a mask. It afforded her no comfort. It was what was going on behind that mask that mattered now. That mattered terribly. . . .

How long ago had it happened—or had it really happened at all? Yes, she could not escape that. It had happened, irrevocably. She closed her eyes and waited for all of it to come back again and give her some answer. It came slowly and with merciless precision. . . . The wide, shaded stretch of Hill Street and the cobbles under the dust making the wheels of the surrey utter little jarring exclamations. The glossy highlights on Renny's well-groomed rump, the drowsy clop-clop of Renny's hoofs making a sort of duet with the subdued twittering from Cousin Tabby on the seat beside her. Where had they been? . . . To call on Mr. and Mrs. Abbott at the hotel (down from Richmond to attend the market opening) and to invite them to supper . . . and from there to see the Marston girls, of course. Lennie Marston was going off to Raleigh to marry one of the Lloyd boys, and the house was full of trunks and cases being packed and unpacked and then packed again. Mrs. Marston bearing up bravely with eyes red from weeping (although the marriage was over a month off), thrusting glasses of iced tea on everyone. The air had been full of a lot of aimless bustle and chatter. Poor Roberta Marston —so tall and plain—had become quite hysterical over Lennie's intricate and opulent trousseau. Lennie, plump and pretty, reclined on a sofa (like a little blonde cow, Cousin Tabby had whispered wickedly) fanning her face with a bit of handkerchief and munching divinity from a compote as placidly as though nothing whatever were happening, while her sister, her hair escaping from its pins, ran distractedly among the trunks and piles of boxes that had been arriving from Richmond and Washington. . . . O Meg! isn't this jacket with the pompon a dream? . . . Do you really think so? . . . Mama always says you have better taste than anyone we know, *don't* you, Mama? It's all really *too* exciting! . . . I *wish* someone were marrying *me* and taking me to New York and Chicago *both* for a honeymoon. . . . Meg, how can you be so calm about it? . . . I'm simply dying with excitement right now!

All that dear and silly chatter, and she in the midst of it, comfortable and remote as always, like a presiding deity over these familiar human affairs. It was strange how clearly the sound, the burden of Roberta Marston's ceaseless, excited chatter, came back to her. It seemed such a long time ago, something that had happened in another place a long, long time ago. Then quickly it was gone, the pattern torn, wiped out, and with it the sound of Renny's sundrugged hoofs. The surrey stopped with a jolt, the heat and stillness closed down, and out of it the flushed, dark face looked insolently up into her own through a long and astonished moment. Then the deep, male voice, driven and urgent, flowing to her out of the afternoon: "You're high and mighty, aren't you . . . it won't help you . . . someday you'll listen and be proud to step down beside me." He had swayed gently, absurdly, where he stood, steadying himself with one hand on Renny's bit strap. As she looked upon him there the blinding, suffocating feeling had crashed down upon her without warning or preparation, as though it had been waiting there all the time. When she could see again the voice was silent, and the sullen face looked up at her with a terrifying expression of agony and fury, its features marked curiously across the brow and nose with an ugly red streak. In her hand she held the surrey whip. It was trembling. She realized with horror that her whole body was shaking. She reached forward and struck Renny's hindquarters smartly with it then, and the horse leapt forward into an outraged trot. The face was gone. She remembered sitting forward in a frozen attitude, one practical fragment of her mind wondering if any of the windows—with which the street seemed suddenly bristling— had witnessed what had happened. But they remained comfortingly bland and indifferent behind the verandas and blinds. Cousin Tabby

31

had begun to giggle, saying something about its being nothing to get upset over . . . and well now, of all things! Margaret had not uttered a word in response, but she remembered thinking in a precise and detached way that she wasn't upset and that of course it was nothing at all—or was it? The terrible black feeling continued to grow in her all the way back to the house. She hadn't dared speak, and when she had, what a mess she had made of it to Father out there just now on the front walk. And there had been someone else there with him, hadn't there? She could remember bits of it, unrelated and thrown into space. Poor Father. She had clumsily involved him now, too. He would want some explanation—would demand one. And what was she going to say to him when she didn't even know herself?

Margaret found herself longing suddenly and passionately for the presence of the woman who had occupied this room which she had for so long a time called her own. The woman who had been her mother and who had left only a dim cipher in her memory. Now in an instant of recognition she realized her in detail, as though the need Margaret felt summoned her alive and complete out of a child's half-dream. Her mother would have known what to say. She would have looked out of the tired, handsome eyes, breathing about her an austere odor of camphor and Florida water, and the elongated Georgia vowels would have dropped from the drawn and bitter mouth, putting the pieces back into place with acid authority. She would have said: "You are my daughter, Margaret Singleton. This thing is not worth even a moment of your consideration, of your contempt." . . . But Margaret *knew* that. The occurence itself, momentarily unpleasant, she recognized as essentially banal. She could dismiss *that* with ease. But what she could not dismiss was this profound disturbance in herself. For a time all her attitudes and defenses, the bulwarks she had been fashioning about her life since birth with the unconscious industry of a bee, appeared to have vanished. They left her defenseless on a barren plain at the mercy of an enemy she could not see. Never, never would she have believed that she could be made to feel this way.

So still had she been standing, scarcely breathing, in front of the mirror, that the rigid muscles along her arms and across her back began to ache. Her lower lip throbbed with a dull pain. She realized with added vexation that she had been biting deeply into it. Her mouth tasted of salt and when she put her finger tips to her lips they came away stained with red. This was *impossible!* With a little gasp she thrust her hands tightly behind her, and, walking to the bed, lay down on it carefully as though she were brittle and might break into a thousand pieces. Dry-eyed she stared fixedly at the ceiling above her where on the surface of the faded, old-fashioned paper occurred a mysterious dimming and sharpening of shadows reflected from the windows. Deliberately concentrating her attention upon this fantasy as she had when a child, making pictures of the shifting forms, she thought: I *must* get calm inside myself . . . somehow, somewhere. I have lost something . . . I must find it again. But as though to mock her she heard the thunder of her heart and the echoing confusion in her head, a little vortex of fragments swimming about without meaning. She felt herself grasping at them desperately like a drowning person . . . Mother . . . the surrey whip in my hand . . . his face . . . really nothing at all . . . Mother . . . Father. . . .

2

Margaret Singleton knew the necessary history of her family as well as she knew the palms of her well-kept hands. It was part of the equipment of growing up and being a Singleton. Her sources had been the accepted mythology of Kingsmont filled in with anecdotes and stories garnered from her father and her nurse, Aunty Jule. There was no snobbery in this. It was simply incontrovertible fact, like any natural phenomenon, and, as such, subject to neither discussion nor question so serenely and immutably was it fixed in its progression like a minor though superior saga that it had never occurred to her that anything might happen to either the events or the personages encompassed by it to disturb its orderly design.

Margaret's grandfather, Robert Singleton, had really begun it. Margaret had never known him, but thrice a day since she could remember she had sat across the table from his likeness, handsomely framed over the mantel in the dining room. He had been a little man and in spite of the indifferent talents of the painter, something of Robert's foxlike sharpness and brilliance had been caught on the canvas. Margaret had admired it because it was her grandfather, but sometimes, by a trick of light, the small black eyes in the portrait across the room would catch and fasten upon hers with an ironic expression that unfailingly made her vaguely uncomfortable.

Robert had been the youngest of six brothers, all scions of a fairly old midland family in Virginia. The Singletons, as a whole, were more inclined toward comfort than toward distinction. This comfort was of long standing and firmly based on the methodically prosperous yield of a large tobacco plantation. But there had been born in Robert—as distinct from his brothers or any of his remembered forebears—a perverse and subtle spirit, a restless vitality, that outraged his family. Moreover, it was directed by an implike intelligence and a kind of capriciousness that baffled and routed them at every turn. Why couldn't that harum-scarum youngster see that

33

he had a good, gentlemanly life made to hand for him with no more effort or obligation required on his part than to take hold of it? It was simply incomprehensible! He could have taken hold easily. Several generations of Singletons before him had done so as naturally as they had breathed. He observed his father and brothers, fat and sleek as pastured horses, deeply grooved in it. But it was not for him. His chronic escapades and his quicksilver refusal to conform were the cause of a series of special interviews between himself and his parents throughout his youth and young manhood. They were monotonously alike: his mother weeping quietly and ineffectually in her chair, his father stomping up and down the parlor, more baffled than angry, and Robert, impeccably deferential in his bearing, being entirely reasonable and adamant. It invariably ended in tacit victory for Robert, but they never ceased trying.

In his twentieth year a solution offered itself. A cousin came to visit the family from new landholdings in Texas. When he returned home he took young Robert with him. The Singletons, in concert, breathed a sigh of relief and privately congratulated themselves. The rough, hard life out there would knock the nonsense out of him; in six months' time he would be crying to come home. They were wrong. Robert didn't come home again for five years. During that time the news from him was sporadic and spaced over long intervals of time and postmarked from distant quarters of the continent. They heard from him in California, from several places in the great Northwest Territory, from New Orleans, and once even from some unheard-of place in the West Indies. His brief communications, always addressed to his mother and inscribed in his neat copper-plate hand, revealed almost nothing as to his activities or his life. Even at a distance there was a tone of mockery in his elaborately polite generalities.

Then one day he descended upon them with a bare week's warning. He brought with him a wife—a pretty, placid girl he had met in Texas—and a retinue of servants. Outwardly he was remarkably little changed in appearance from the young man who had left five years before. But there was on him the hard and polished patina of success. This had to do, they gathered, with a variety of activities —chiefly concerned with an import and export business in cotton, molasses, rum, and tobacco. But he never bothered to acquaint them with the full details, and they were too stiff-necked to ask. Also, they had discovered that the passage of time had not removed his ability to make them feel like fools in his presence. He extended his visit over a period of eighteen months, during which time, to the family's complete and final mystification, he set himself to learn with methodical concentration all his father and brothers knew about the cultivation and curing of tobacco. They had spent a great deal

34

of time trying to invoke such an interest in the past, but now that he evidenced it so enthusiastically it only made them uneasy. He gave them no explanation for this about-face. But Robert was never in his life to explain his actions to anyone. When, with characteristic lack of warning, he announced that he had bought land in the piedmont region of North Carolina and intended to make his home there, they did not even bother to make token remonstrances. They were more eager to be rid of him again than they dared admit even to themselves. Why, that damned youngster!

Robert made a couple of preliminary journeys to Carolina in that summer to prepare the way. Late in August he, with his wife and a six-months infant son, his servants, and a vast accumulation of household furnishings, departed southward. He never returned to Virginia again except for perfunctory visits that could not be avoided when he came through that state on business.

His new holdings were situated in the rolling, piny country in the north-central part of the state; a thousand raw acres on the edge of a tiny crossroads settlement called Kingsmont for no more romantic reason that that the original settler, an obscure pack trader named King, in the late thirties had set up a small store at the top of a knoll by the crude western highway. What appeared to be sheer eccentricity on the part of a gentleman of Robert's Virginia background in coming to this undistinguished landscape to make a home was far from it. Robert had never been a fool. Under his unpredictable surface and polished manner he possessed an infallible business sense. Besides, he had a profound liking for playing a game for its own sake. Something in the rough, untried Carolina earth he had chosen challenged and satisfied a basic need for irony in him. Then too, he had carefully investigated the potentialities of the chosen gray and yellow soil for producing prodigious crops of tobacco of a type little known in Virginia.

As soon as his first hundred acres were cleared he set about exercising his lately acquired knowledge in tobacco cultivation. His success astounded everyone but himself. He had known it all the time. Beginning simply as a grower, he had shortly moved over into the business of processing and marketing his product. Energetic, calculating each move to a split-hair nicety, he enjoyed—as always— pitting his brains and charm in the questionably genteel activities of business. The big Richmond market came to know and respect him. But business alone was not enough for Robert. His restless intelligence and energy, requiring wider fields of activity, turned to local politics. To this new game—for such it was to him—he applied himself with his usual acumen. In due time he was elected to represent the district in the state Senate. While there during several terms he adroitly used his charm and energy to further projects both for himself and for his constituents. By a series of complicated and dazzling maneuvers, and against the bitter opposition of certain of the more conservative planters who were his neighbors, he induced the railroad people who were building a line through the county to turn it through Kingsmont. Robert was fully aware of the advantages inherent in this arrangement for furthering the development of resources in his region. Also, Robert enjoyed triumphing over opposition of any kind. He disliked the long-unchallenged reign of the Richmond market and Exchange over the Carolina growers and manufacturers. He had determined from the beginning to break that position. Kingsmont had been little more than a sleepy settlement in a wilderness of piny woods opened by a few fields. As Robert built his fortunes, the hamlet began to stir into life and grow as though his imperious vitality controlled its destiny also. With the coming of the new railroad it soon began to look like a town worthy of the name. In due course it was inevitable that Kingsmont should become the market center not only for the immediate county but for a whole section of the state as well. The county seat was moved there. Robert's personal interests flourished along with this as he had expected they would. He established his business properly— Singleton Company—and sold his Kingsmountain brands of snuff, cut, and plug with steadily growing prosperity.

To top it all off he built, with a characteristic touch of arrogance, the finest house in the county on the highest eminence in town. The town was in a section of the Southland that had no history of architectural splendor. It was inhabited for the most part by small landholders and conservative, middle-class businessmen. Their dwellings, therefore, were—when they were not simple, utilitarian farmhouses—solid and substantial with no particular distinction. It was typical of Robert Singleton to construct his house with no reference to anything except his own taste, plus the satisfaction of creating a gentle paradox by placing it in a setting where, by virtue of its position on the hill, no passing eye could avoid seeing it. It created, during its construction, something of a sensation throughout the county. People came from all over the countryside to watch its progress. On Saturdays the roadway before the site was lined with silent rows of farm wagons and even some more affluent equipages, all of them full of a fascinated audience. Each stage in its erection was attended by endless comment and conjecture. Senator Singleton was sure building him a house all right! Mighty smart man, Singleton, couldn't tell what he was goin' to do next. They had early grown to admire and delight in him with the grudging admiration always given a virtuoso. Soon forgotten was the fact that he was an outsider, a smart-alecky Virginian. In a like manner they quickly forgot that his house hadn't always been there at the top of Hill Street. It be-

came a part of the accepted geography of their lives and an unfailing
source of community pride. Together with the growing line of warehouses and factories down by the railroad, it was something with
which to impress visiting strangers and friends. And by the same
token they never realized how much their own lives had been caught
into and affected by all that Robert accomplished. His progress, in
spite of certain attributes of a histrionic quality, was subtle and
oblique in its manifestations. But it was progress, and distinctly a
part of the mighty stirrings in a young nation finding its industrial
and commercial feet, preparing the way for the coming of giants—
although Robert in his secret, aristocratic self would have been the
first to pooh-pooh such a grandiose notion. It would have amused
him.

When that terrible four-year agony—the War between the States
—finally broke out, Robert was a man in his most dazzling prime.
Singleton Company had become Singleton & Sons. Harley, the elder
of Robert's two sons, and then James Singleton, had gone into the
business as they reached their majorities. When North Carolina
came into the conflict, Robert and his two sons enlisted in the first
feverish week. Almost from the outset Robert was commissioned a
major. His early schooling had included attendance at a famous
military institute in Virginia. Also, he had not waited for any organized recruiting to come his way. He had loaded the two boys into
a buggy and together the three of them, during the course of one
mad week, had dashed from farmhouse to hamlet all over the county.
When he went down to the capital on his return he carried with
him in his pocket what was to become a Grange County Brigade.
His commission followed as a matter of course. Harley and young
James went with him. None of them was ever destined to distinguish
himself in the conflict. By some curious and fortuitous design, Robert
and his sons always found themselves with forces arriving tardily
upon the scene of action; or in pursuit of routed armies, as was true
in the early months; or, as in the last two years, in endless and exhausting retreat before an enemy with whom, except for minor rear-
guard skirmishes, they were never permitted the satisfaction of
joining actual battle. Their only personal loss came in the last
months, when Harley fell ill of camp fever and died within the space
of three days.

In the early part of April 1865, the news of Appomattox arrived.
Two weeks later the harassed and weary General Johnston surrendered his forces to Sherman in a perfunctory ceremony at a
crossroads not twenty miles distant from Kingmont. A few days
later, during which time men like ghosts of themselves, unkempt and
ill, began to straggle back into the town and countryside, Robert,
with James beside him in a buggy, both of them thin and worn but

spruce in civilian clothes and no air of defeat about them, drove up Hill Street to the big white house. Mrs. Singleton, somewhat faded, but still composed and gay, waited to welcome them at the top of the porch steps as though her men were returning from a fortnight in Richmond instead of from an inferno.

Singleton & Sons had come through the holocaust essentially unscathed. Robert, with his customary acumen and foresight, had known the conflict was coming long before it arrived and had quietly made provision for it. He had turned his foreign accounts over to an English house and left the factory in the capable hands of his superintendent. By some magic known only to himself he managed not only to keep himself advised as to its condition but to send certain directives as to its conduct while he was wandering endlessly over the South. As a result—not without minor inescapable disruptions—when he arrived home Singleton & Sons was still alive and functioning while almost every business surrounding it had long stood paralyzed. Even the buildings and warehouses had escaped serious physical hurt, although some of the last and most bitter of the fighting had passed through the region. Kingsmont itself had stood for one nightmare day in the path of battle while the courthouse burned in the square and shells screamed overhead through a limpid spring sky and burst among the brick and wood buildings. Even this had passed as quickly as it had come, leaving, miraculously, only a few fire-scarred buildings and a terrible memory of scarecrow men and animals and equipages fleeing insanely northward in the night. On the following morning a neat column of Union infantry under an apologetic young officer had formally invested the town.

In the months immediately following, while most of the state continued to struggle in the toils of that period to be known, euphemistically, as the Reconstruction, Kingsmont escaped all but the most superficial discomfort. A curious and gratifying development came as the result of the six-months perfunctory occupation of the town by the Union troops. Being idle soldiers in a conquered land, they had behaved themselves very well except for breaking into some of the warehouses and helping themselves to the cured tobacco that had accumulated and lain aging there. The gentlemen whose property this was were forced to accept this despoiling—not, however, without futile protest—but it proved a remarkable investment. The soldiers liked the tobacco. The mild, light leaf was a discovery for most of them. They liked it so well that they not only carried away quantities of it when they departed, but sent it home to families and friends. Not many months passed before inquiries and orders for this "light" tobacco began to trickle, then to pour, into Kingsmont from Northern jobbers.

Singleton & Sons naturally took the lead in promoting this new

38

business, and a great deal of the recent rancor and outrage was soon effaced and forgotten in this highly satisfactory turn of affairs. The town and the countryside settled back to grow peacefully and unhurriedly again, as though there had never been any interruption to the process. And Robert Singleton's house looked down upon the proceedings with remote benignity. . . .

Margaret Singleton was never to have the pleasure of knowing her paternal grandparents. They brought Robert up from his factory one noon in the bottom of his carriage. He had suffered a stroke. The war, which he was in the habit of referring to—when he referred to it at all—in a casual and offhand manner, had caught up with his small, secret person at last. For a month he lay speechless and motionless in his bed. Only the sardonic eyes, wandering restlessly about the room, revealed what was left unquenchably alive in him. Then, as though he had arranged it with Omnipotence Itself, a second stroke finished the affair in a brief half-hour during one night. The whole state acknowledged the loss. It was a tribute to Robert's special abilities that his funeral was attended by more dignitaries than the county had ever heard of—much less seen. It was no time at all before everything concerning Robert began to take on the color of a local legend. It was inevitable. Not that Robert had ever really attempted or accomplished anything of spectacular moment. On the contrary, his achievements among them were almost fastidiously orthodox. But he had managed to invest even his most commonplace activity with such an aura of secret and indefinable splendor that men were drawn to observe him like children looking upon a distant and mysterious light burning upon a hill. In spite of a life lived essentially and profoundly within himself, and during which no man really knew him as a friend, his memory became public property in the town he had made simply because he had always done pretty much as he pleased. There was in this final irony something that Robert would have found superbly fitting.

A year after his passing, the gay and modest little woman who had lived contentedly in the background of his life for nearly thirty years was buried beside him in the little cedar-grown lot on the Singleton land about a mile out of town.

It was to a house without mistress or kin that young James returned with his bride some months later. Because his marriage to Miss Louisa Culbert of Georgia had been accomplished with such precipitateness during the course of a leisurely business trip, some of his less charitable friends were constrained to the opinion among themselves—particularly in view of later developments—that James had entered upon this marriage simply because he could not face returning to the big empty house alone.

James would have been the last person in the world to pretend to be anything of the person his father had been. Everything about him was simple, casual, and easy. Before the war he had attended the State University, situated at a conveniently short distance from Kingsmont. There he had distinguished himself by social rather than scholastic activities. His contributions to the Confederacy had merited him no more than a lieutenancy. But after Robert's death people gradually began to refer to and address him as "Major" Singleton as though this title—which had long lost its military implications—had by some natural order of things become the property of the family to be passed on from father to son. Also it was just simpler to think of the head of Singleton & Sons as "the Major."

James inherited a number of his father's more obvious and understandable characteristics without any of the elder man's subtlety or directed energy. The fact that he had been born a gentleman and a Singleton provided an ample code by which to govern his existence. He enjoyed with perfect candor the pleasant things of life. He liked food and drink and people. He liked very much being called "Major." He had no special bent or talent for the business that had been left him. His attitude toward it was one of unthinking admiration in the same way that he regarded any other of the family's accepted attributes. There was no demand for him to go further. Robert had built his house so well that Singleton & Sons ran itself without any too-conscientious attention on his son's part. Often— James suspected—a great deal better! His position as head of the business became more and more nominal with the passage of time. He kept his father's office with its heavy mahogany furnishings, and appeared at its desk for a short hour meticulously every morning of the week. Any visiting business connections or friends he took off to Hill House at the earliest possible moment and transacted what had to be done there in an atmosphere of easy hospitality.

Temperamentally he was as transparent as water. Easily aroused to towering displays of anger colored by a special mild profanity of his own invention, he was as easily aroused to laughter. Profoundly sentimental, he was constantly spilling over generously in all directions. His friends—of which there were many—while not holding him in any awe, loved him. His enemies—or rather those few individuals singled out for his enthusiastic disapproval—were not afraid of him, because there was nothing in him capable of either deviousness or pettiness. In a private corner of his otherwise candid and expansive nature he possessed, however, a profound conviction that he alone realized that the part he was playing in the name of a tenuous tradition was already outmoded and a thing of the past. Before the war? Why, of course, sir! But in these modern days with all the developments and the new machinery for living and getting about—well, he suspected that it was not only pompous but a little ridiculous. It amused and tired him in a breath to realize he must assume a mantle he was ill-equipped to fit with distinction, and one which was often burdensome to live up to simply because he was surrounded by a sentimental conspiracy bent on keeping a splendid fiction alive whether James willed it or no. When it came right down to it he would have much preferred spending his days in heated and violent arguments as to how dead campaigns in the war should have been conducted with old Captain Phillips who lived at the hotel; or else in relaxed, interminable discussion of political and celestial affairs with certain of his gentlemen cronies who gathered of an afternoon in Tom Pate's office across from the courthouse, or on his own front porch. But he was Robert Singleton's son, head of the town's oldest and biggest house of business, and he never let this private view on his situation interfere with the proper discharge of his noblesse-oblige. This realization was perhaps James's sole intellectual and spiritual achievement. He *knew* it, and because he knew it, whenever his comfortable existence was threatened by tedium, he was able to dismiss it with a chuckle.

3

Kingsmont as a small, sociable community was at first highly conjectural and curious, then taken aback, by the woman James married. It took it only a short time to realize that his wife was utterly unlike the pleasant, easily approached James. During the whole of her sojourn they never quite grew used to the idea of her being in the town at all. This was evidently Louisa Culbert Singleton's intention. From the moment of her arrival she conducted herself like an exile, aloof and withdrawn from everyone and everything in this raw, ugly North Carolina country where, through no choice of her own, she found herself. She hated it. Her living in Kingsmont was a martyrdom endured stoically between one visit to her people in Georgia and the next.

In the weeks immediately following her arrival the wives of James's friends and business associates dutifully called at Hill House. Mrs. Singleton either received the visitors in an atmosphere of such cold and hostile formality that conversation withered and interviews were terminated as soon as possible or the callers were informed that Mrs. Singleton was indisposed with a migraine. The visiting cards collected in a neat pile in the hall tray. The calls were never returned. Very soon even the most persistent among the town's ladies had to give it up. For the most part she kept to her room, suffering from a multitude of vague feminine ills, the blinds drawn against either day or night or any glimpse of the despised land outside her windows. There in the still and airless room she lay on the big, disordered bed reading an endless succession of bulky romantic novels. Or she simply lay staring in grim and uncommunicative silence at the opposite wall. As time passed, with increasing frequency the thread of light beneath her closed door began to show all night long.

If James was hurt or embarrassed by this conduct, he never showed it. Nor did the town betray him. People were unfailingly correct in asking him, with just the right degree of solicitude, about Mrs. Singleton's health. This information having been imparted, they pursued the subject no further, as though through the workings of a universal recognition of good form—not by any means consistent with them in all things—they had banded together to protect James.

On his part, James treated his wife with an elaborately grave and ceremonious courtesy as though there was nothing whatever awry in his marital and domestic scene. Quite honestly he was more awed and bewildered by her than anything else, but he never opposed or questioned her mode of life. In this his personal code served him very well. He was a gentleman, and she was his wife. This was as far as it was necessary for him to go in explaining anything Louisa Singleton chose to do quite satisfactorily to his own mind as well as to everyone else's. In the meantime there was good food to eat, good whisky to drink, and a constant procession of people to know and talk with streaming through his life . . . and, finally and miraculously, a small daughter to exhibit with ceaseless pride and delight before the whole world. No, James had no quarrel with God on the state of his existence. On the contrary, he found life an unfailingly pleasant affair. He had no talent for regarding it otherwise.

In Margaret's seventh year her mother had taken permanently to her room. There was no dramatic emphasis in this action. Indeed, it was accomplished with such gradual inevitability that no member of the household was aware of the fact that she had ceased to come downstairs to join them as she had, infrequently, at mealtimes, or for little walks silently performed about the house and yard. Louisa Singleton had never been known to complain audibly about anything to anyone. Nor did she make the usual subtle and intricate demands for attention expected of a female in her condition and situation in life. She had never looked or pretended to look like an invalid. A gradually increasing pallor of complexion could as well be laid to her life in semidarkness as to any organic failure. Otherwise to all intents and purposes the outside physical shell remained intact. It was as though her consuming dislike for her existence, kept fired at white heat within her, had finally worn her down, burned her out. In the face of her somewhat remote amusement, in which there was neither acquiescence nor refusal, James futilely called in a succession of medical gentlemen from Raleigh and even distant Richmond. This he did on the exasperated advice of his friend Dr. Frank

Richardson, who had long washed his hands of the case. The gentlemen arrived, were closeted briefly with the invalid, held baffled discussions with James over whisky downstairs, and departed, leaving directions—which Louisa Singleton made no gesture toward carrying out—and prescriptions for a variety of medicines that merely accumulated in a staggering array, untouched, on the mantel and the bed table among the inevitable novels, imparting to the already dead, still air of her room a faint and sickening odor of medicinal sweetness.

It became apparent that if she could not be quit of them in any other way she would simply die. And she would die *not* Mrs. James Singleton, but Louisa Culbert of Georgia, withdrawn, untouched by any of them.

And then she did. . . .

One morning late, as was her custom, Aunty Jule, the black matriarch of Hill House, took up Miss Louisa's breakfast tray and discovered her lying motionless and unresponsive upon the bed, the lamp still burning and the room thick with the fumes of coal oil. Louisa had departed silently and without fuss, as she had lived her life, alone in the room with the blinds drawn implacably across the windows. . . . James had to be sent for at the factory. Aunty Jule, a loyal party to the protective conspiracy surrounding James, never mentioned, to him or to anyone, the empty laudanum bottle she had discovered beneath Louisa's pillows.

For a decent period following the funeral, James tried to assume the aspect of sober bereavement expected of him. He found it difficult because, while neither he nor any of the town would have dreamed of admitting such a thing to themselves, they were all of them vastly relieved. Everyone had, in a way, shared the strange burden of Louisa with James. He had unquestionably admired the *idea* of his wife, but there was no denying the fact that the shadowy reality of her presence had inhibited and complicated his existence to no small degree. It was with something of a jolt that he discovered at intervals during the months following her death that she had left no deeper mark upon his life, his home, the community at large, than a visiting ghost would have. Beyond the shining fact of his small daughter, all he really had left from his years with this woman was the formal little photograph on the dresser in his room, the frozen, handsome face staring out disdainfully upon him and his world from among the silver-backed brushes and the stud box.

In a special sense Margaret had known her mother, perhaps, better than anyone else. Founded on no definite manifestations of tenderness, there had been between the poised, sedate child and the unhappy, silent woman some bond, some understanding, that ran deeper than blood and bone—close, strong, unvoiced. Margaret's memories of her mother were the sharp, fragmentary, unrelated recollections of a child. But by the same token they remained intact and intensely vivid: the persistent odor of camphor and Florida water, which were so tangible a part of that largely intangible presence; the dark, tired voice with the acid edge; the dim and mysterious room where she went almost daily to sit and take part in a delicate sort of catechism concerning her activities and conduct; Aunty Jule's frequent and fierce admonitions for her to "keep quiet, 'cause yo' mama is ailin' and restin'!" There had also been occasions—somehow of tremendous import because of their infrequency—when her mother had walked in the garden with her, holding her small hand in a cool, impersonal grasp and uttering no word as they paced to and fro among the boxwood Robert Singleton had planted.

Out of this motley of recollections there was one memory that, over the years, recurred with such acuteness of detail, and of implication, that it assumed precedence over them all.

One day when Margaret had been five she fell while playing on the gravel of the walk and cut her knee. It was a commonplace little happening. Aunty Jule had taken her upstairs to the nursery crooning comfort to her while she washed and bandaged the small wound. But Margaret would not be comforted. She continued to cry, outraged. If James had been there he would have had her in his arms, cajoling, quieting her, bearing her off finally to the library to solace her with a peppermint from his desk. But James was away in the country for the day. Aunty Jule had almost exhausted her patience and her long list of blandishments when suddenly her mother came into the room.

"Let me have the child, Jule," Louisa had said. "Come here, Margaret!"

Margaret had gone to her, still shaken with sobs. Her mother, thin and tall in her dressing robe, had reached down and picked her up—something she had never done before. She took Margaret down the hall to her room. There she had walked silently up and down until the little girl's sobbing became a tired murmur and finally died away. Then, placing the child on a chair, Louisa had sat facing her on the edge of the disheveled bed. For a long moment she looked deeply into Margaret's tear-streaked face. Her tired, shadowed eyes burned into the small replicas opposite her. Then almost gently her mother had said:

"You should not cry, Margaret; you must learn not to cry no matter how much it hurts you." Then the woman's eyes seemed to leap into fanatic life: "It *doesn't* matter—*none of it matters*. You'll learn that. You are a Singleton, but you are also a Culbert. And Culberts do not cry. You must *remember* that!"

She never knew why, but she never forgot it forever afterward.

44

She grew up a serious child, not as the result of any catastrophic circumstances but from a natural inclination and an almost complete lack of intellectual curiosity concerning anything outside her own interests. Naturally grave, serene, and meticulous, she could on occasion be wildly stubborn about any idea she had decided to accept or anything she had chosen to like or dislike. James adored her unreservedly. She treated him from the beginning as though he were a heedless, lovable child whom it was her duty to look after and discipline. It developed into a sort of game between them. A game which both of them realized was more than half the truth. As far as he was concerned nothing was too good for her. He did not altogether understand her, but then understanding the mysterious whys and wherefores of humankind was with James largely an intuitive process when it was anything at all. Anyway—Godfrey's Cordial, sir!—she was his own flesh and blood, *his* daughter, Margaret Singleton. What more could a man ask? He did, however, have the perception and the sense of humor to realize early that his daughter had little of either of those two leavening and amiable qualities. He discovered when she was little more than a babe that she disliked his fondling or making over her too extravagantly. He respected this reserve in her by subjecting himself to a long and tedious self-discipline totally at variance with his own naturally warm and demonstrative self. But such an effort did not prevent him from recognizing and appreciating his daughter's good points. On the contrary, he took enormous pride in her unfailing poise, her air of graciousness. Accordingly, he always treated her, from the first day she was allowed to toddle about the house in a minute pinafore, with an elaborate courtesy as though she were a mature and, to him, fascinating woman—which she was. These qualities in her, while they were of a perfection and consistency that could not be denied, were not always the subject of universal approval among those who knew her best. Coupled with her startling beauty they made her, for some reason, unendurable at times. As Lennie Marston, then twelve, had, on an occasion when Margaret came to play at the Roberts house and had quietly refused to take part in any of their games, shrieked at her at last in a voice shrill with utter and complete frustration, "You're *prim*, Meg Singleton, that's what you are—just prim!"

For a week or more after Louisa Singleton's passing, the house was a bedlam of crape-hung relatives come from both Georgia and Virginia. They besieged James. They quarreled acrimoniously among themselves as to which of them was best fitted to take over the care of his motherless daughter. It was unthinkable, as well as impractical, for James to consider undertaking her upbringing without a woman—a lady—in his home. He tacitly admitted the propriety of this. Meanwhile, with all the social skill and tact at his command,

45

he fought a long delaying action. At last he got the house and the town clear of them; that is, all of them except Cousin Tabby. This derelict relative remained by virtue of the fact that, unlike the others, she made no demands on James, and by the simple process of not leaving. At first irritated, James soon discovered to his delight that her innocuous presence satisfied the much-discussed proprieties without disturbing the arrangement of either his or his daughter's life.

Tabitha Jackson was one of those obscure spinster relatives who spend their lives revolving about in the little limbos created especially for them on the outer fringes of large and long-established families. In spite of certain harmless eccentricities—her secretiveness, her mild hypochondria, her insatiable curiosity about everybody and everything around her—Cousin Tabby fitted effortlessly into the scheme of things at Hill House. She was simply omnipresent. She had a genius for appearing miraculously at any hour of the day or night when there was anything "going on about the house," as she termed it. She trotted tirelessly after Margaret or James, flashing like a bright-eyed bird in and out of her room. She bubbled with a thousand interests and managed, somehow, never to intrude upon any of theirs. In short, she was ideal. Not many months passed before James and Margaret forgot that she had not always been with them.

In this atmosphere of set and placid security Margaret's growth into womanhood was simply an expanding and solidifying of the traits she had evidenced as a child. Her poise became more monumental; her physical beauty more rich; her prejudices more colored by passionate intensity—and all of it shaped and controlled by a tremendous store of pride moving deep within her. Sometimes it distressed James that she evidenced no more of his broad social inclinations than she did. But after all, he philosophized ruefully at odd moments, she was her mother's child as well as his. She seemed perfectly content, year in and year out, to move among a small and select group of friends—largely made up of the members of the families of his associates and friends in Kingsmont. Among them she reigned as undisputed queen by virtue of protocol and her own undeniable distinction. On occasion, with James, she took part in various social functions of larger nature in Richmond or in Raleigh— where, during her late teens, she had attended a fashionable Female Seminary for two sessions—at the opening of the legislature. These were times when James became positively incandescent with pride in her because of the attention and comment her presence invariably aroused.

From her fifteenth year there had been eligible and attentive young gentlemen. They were by no means exclusively local swains. They came from all over the state. Even from across the border in

Virginia. They visited, they sat in the parlor or on the porch according to the season, they walked with her or took her driving in elegantly turned-out buggies and surreys. But it always ended the same way. At last they departed entirely or their calls became more and more infrequent. Without one exception they accepted defeat quietly but with a definite air of puzzled anger. The exception was Willie Radford, son of the county solicitor. When he put on his first pair of long pants Willie came calling. He continued to call, doggedly and patiently, over a number of years. Then he created a little scandal by announcing to his father that he wasn't going to stand it any longer. He was observed one midnight weeping furiously and unashamedly as he threw himself on the train going north. If any of this moved Margaret it was in no way discernible even to those who considered themselves her intimates. She continued as unruffled and serene as ever. All of it bothered James a little. Not that he was anxious for some other man to come along and take her away from him, but there was something about it that impressed him as being not quite normal. On the other hand, the town accepted it as perfectly natural. The man hadn't turned up yet, they considered with perverse satisfaction among themselves, that was up to Margaret Singleton!

In the meantime her absorbing passion, beyond the ordered path of her personal existence, seemed to be the place, the home, the house on the hill. With Cousin Tabby chirruping at her heels she had managed it with a terrifying natural efficiency from the time she was little more than a child. There was no detail about it—the kitchen, the garden, the servants (who stood in adoring awe of her), the ordering of meals, the intricacies of the account books—that escaped her strict devotion and care. This included disciplining James tactfully, humoring him, being an unfailingly competent, if unimaginative, hostess to his numerous guests. She loved every moment of the day and night concerned with it, every tree and blade of grass on the lawn, every stone and board and lintel—as though together they constituted the distinguished attributes of some passionately beloved person. They were really more than that. They were the center, the positive and concrete symbols and reason, for her very existence.

4

To Margaret now, lying dry-eyed and motionless on the bed in the still room there came, for the first time, a sense of her own unique aloneness; the frightening feeling that her perfect existence was a façade behind which she lay at the mercy of memories and acts over which she had no control. There were implications whose meaning perversely escaped her. They eluded her just on the point of illuminating the confusion swirling about her. They came and went without her being able to order or halt them.

Out of them now there came unbidden the memory of another summer's afternoon. An afternoon as hot as this one, when she, a prim little figure in fresh muslin, had sat sedately rocking by the side of her father on the porch, enduring the wicked heat that, even in the shade of the yard, fell suffocatingly about them. Cousin Tabby was upstairs taking a nap or writing letters, as was her custom after the midday meal. She, Margaret, had been eleven or twelve? What did it matter? Something had happened on that afternoon, though, and that *had* mattered. She had never understood why. She did not want to understand now. She twisted fretfully on the bed as if by turning to the wall she could halt the inexorable procession of her thoughts. It was useless. They marched in upon her unimpeded.

James napped gently and sonorously at her side. He lolled in the chair, the sheets of the Raleigh paper spread over his short, fat thighs. Into the midst of her own childish reverie the harsh, grating clack of the front gate opening and closing fell like a challenge. The shabby figure of a man was advancing up the walk to the house. Beyond him in the roadway, hitched to a pair of weary, fly-tormented mules, stood one of the familiar wagons used by the countryside to haul tobacco to the market. Its dirty gray tarpaulin was so carelessly roped that the arched roof staves were bared gaunt and riblike to the sun. The man came up the walk with a peculiar, uncertain step. Seeing them sitting to one side on the porch, he cut across the lawn until he stood directly below them, rocking slowly on his heels. He did not remove the soiled, ruined hat, but stood there staring up out of small defiant eyes at Margaret and the unconscious James. Margaret stared back at him with candid outrage—he had walked so meanly across her sacred grass! She remembered thinking him extremely old and hideous with his stubbled face and the thin, scrawny neck rising out of the dirty, collarless shirt.

"Majuh!" he spoke at last. And Margaret immediately disliked the whining resonance of his voice. In fact, this *person*—whoever he was—had absolutely nothing to recommend him. No manners, no *anything!* Margaret's small spine stiffened against the back of the chair. She turned to James. He was just coming awake, his blue eyes blinking open blindly and furiously.

"Eh?" he muttered thickly. "Eh!"

Then his eyes came to focus suddenly upon his visitor. James's body sprang bolt upright in the rocker. The newspaper crackled in a little avalanche about his feet.

"That you, Royle?"

"Yessuh, Majuh."

48

"Well, what in damnation— 'Scuse me, Meg. What in damnation do you want now?"

"I come to see you, Majuh."

"What about, Royle? Godfrey's Cordial! I said all I had to say to you last Friday, didn't I?"

"Now, Majuh—won't take up much of yer time. Jest a word"— the unkempt, angry face made a little inclination toward Margaret —"in private."

"What? Great Godfrey, Royle! Oh, well . . . Meg, excuse me for a minute—go take a walk or something—for a minute, honey."

She arose and left them with a feeling of relief. There was no mistaking that this dirty man was angry about something. It meant that before long Father would be angry, too. She had had occasion to witness such interviews before. There would be a totally inexplicable and uncomfortable conversation full of loud and explosive words. Obediently she got her wide-brimmed hat from the rack in the hall and went down the front steps into the yard. It waited before her, a tranquil design of brazen light and shadow, tree and grass and shrub. It would be nice to have something to do, but it was too early to water the petunias and far too dull to consider a game of hopscotch or to guide her hoop (a blond circle suspended upon a thread of sun) decorously up and down the walks. Anyway she was getting too old for such a silly old thing! The murmur of her father's rumble and the visitor's whine drifted down to her in an ominous crescendo. Without thinking she hurried toward the front gate to get out of earshot. Not that she was frightened or afraid of being upset, but it would have been distinctly improper to have been caught even on the outskirts of this conversation. She was almost upon the gate when she looked up suddenly. There were three pairs of eyes staring down upon her from the rickety wagon. It was too late to retreat with dignity. Trapped in that triple-barreled scrutiny she stood frozen, feeling her face turn slowly scarlet. Belatedly she attempted a heavy interest in the big crape-myrtle bush that swung its thick pink clusters somnolently over the gateway.

On the wagon bench sat three boys. They wore dusty jeans and tattered, sun-faded shirts, and their bare feet and legs sprawled frankly over the front board. Two of them were scarcely more than children—and one of these was obviously a year or so younger than herself. The eldest of them was a gangling, big-boned lad of seventeen, or thereabouts. He had a sullen face under a tumbled mat of black hair. He slumped in an awkward-graceful jumble of limbs against the roof stave arching over his head, his jaws moving with practiced swagger on a mouthful of tobacco.

"Hello, ma'am," he said after a long moment, his voice coming to her in an uncertain bass.

49

"Good afternoon," she answered politely, now staring back at all three of them candidly.

There was another interval of silence. The three pairs of eyes divided their attention rhythmically between her person, the yard, and the house behind her.

"That's a mighty big house," commented the oldest boy quietly.

"Yes," agreed Margaret, "it is."

"You live here?" His eyes, unwavering upon her, burned with a curious and fascinated concentration.

"Yes. It's my home." Even then her child's voice grew heavy with pride.

The smallest boy squirmed on the seat between the other two.

"Who's her?" he demanded laconically.

"Aw, shet yer mouth, Pete Henry!" admonished the next older, scowling and emphasizing this command with a kick at his shins.

"She lives here. Didn't yer hear her say so?" This from the big boy leaning forward to spit expertly between the mule rumps.

"Oh." The smallest boy left his mouth open upon the single, astonished syllable. "It shore is a mighty big pretty white house," he offered after a moment, his clear treble chiming in the hot air. Then he added without emotion: "We ain't got no house a-tall no more."

"I done tol' yer, Pete Henry—shet up!" The middle boy burst out fiercely again.

"But we ain't." There was only faint protest in this.

"Well, shet up!"

"Leave 'im alone, Sammy," said the big boy.

"You mean you have no home at all?" Margaret's voice was shocked and incredulous.

"Naw," answered the big boy. He spat into the road again before turning upon her once more his sullen, defiant face. "We did oncet," he continued, leaning even more deeply against the stave, "but Majuh Singleton taken it away from us come last Friday."

Margaret looked at him speechless. He . . . that boy had said . . .

"No," she protested hotly, "no, he didn't either—he—"

She didn't know what to say, but she knew he was wrong. He must be talking about someone else. Not her father. No matter what they said, he *couldn't*—somebody's *home?* But something in their ragged, dirty intensity silenced her. She saw now that the little one called Pete Henry had begun to cry silently, shockingly, one small hand pawing blindly at his cheek.

"It ain't such an awful pretty house, Pete Henry," the big boy observed with quiet, bitter scorn. His black eyes, narrowed and ablaze, consumed Margaret's face. "We'll have a prettier one some of these days—a whole lot prettier and bigger and *whiter* . . . you wait."

50

Margaret stood rooted and defenseless before them. There was something terrible here that she could not understand. She wanted wildly to run and hide from their faces. But she couldn't. Even then her pride held her still. She stood, silent and troubled, her small head stiffly erect. Then the sound of James's voice came bursting across the yard behind her. She turned quickly, pressing back into the crape myrtle. Her father stood at the top of the steps now shouting down upon his visitor as though he wanted the whole world to hear.

"No, no, *no*, Royle! Dammit, I told you last Friday and I meant every word of it. Do I have to go on listening to you and repeating myself from now till Christmas? Another chance! I've given you another chance so many times it's a scandal—and you've gone right on abusing my patience and good faith behind my back like the two-faced, double-dyed liar that you are. How you have the damn-fool impertinence to come here to my house— I said get out last Friday and I meant it. Now get on with you and stop plaguing me!"

The shabby figure on the grass hesitated briefly and then turned, muttering, and shambled to the walk, the worn hands writhing terribly under the stained galluses. Margaret shrank deeper into the shrubbery as he passed her. Reaching the gate, he opened it and turned to face James down the length of the walk. He raised one fist and shook it.

"Majuh!" he called, the nasal voice taking on an offensive, sing-song resonance. "The Lord in His everlasting mercy forgive what you've done this day to a pore widowed man and his homeless children. The wicked shall be brought down and put to the fire, and the proud shall be smitten low, saith the Book! Repent, sinner, repent! The judgment and the Kingdom are at hand and Satan has yore name on his books!"

"Are you daring to preach Scripture at me on my own premises, you bare-faced, lunatic scoundrel?" James's voice shook and grew hoarse. He strained forward on his small feet as though he were going to project himself bodily across the space that separated him from this tormenter. "If you don't clear out of here—"

He stopped abruptly as though he were afraid to commit himself further to words. The quiet, scornful voice of the big boy in the wagon cut into the silence.

"Come on, Pa—let's start movin'."

The gate clanged shut and in a moment the ungreased wheels of the wagon screeched agonizingly down the hill.

Margaret began to walk, then run, toward her father. His face, when she reached him, was dripping with perspiration and still purple with emotion.

"Who were they?" she demanded breathlessly.

51

"What? Oh, just that no-count Royle and his brood bothering me again, honey," he rumbled distractedly at her. Then he added contritely: "Meg, I apologize most humbly, honey—I thought you'd gone around to the back—sorry you had to hear, but that ol' fool Royle always gets me riled!"

"Father," she went on as though she hadn't heard him, "those boys—out there in the wagon—they said you took away their house."

He looked startled, consternation twisting his fine features.

"Now, Meg," he said gently, "don't you bother your little self about this at all. That man that came here just now"—he searched briefly for an adequate yet seemly word and failed—"was a *bad* man." Then his head with the thick mane jerked up and he rumbled with an echo of thunder, "A thief, that's all he is—a damn thief!"

She looked at him searchingly for a moment and came to a conclusion. It was all right. James was her father. She took his hand gravely and they went into the house together.

But she never forgot. No . . . out there in the hot roadway . . . the big boy's eyes looking upon her and her whole world with scorn and deep, terrible hunger. . . .

5

The careless slam of the summer door echoed dully in the hall below. The murmur of voices and then footsteps, at first rapid and then slow, coming determinedly up the stairs. Father, she thought with unreasonable despair. I don't want to see him now. She got up abruptly and crossed to the windows feeling her eyes burn in her face. If she had to see and talk to him now, she preferred doing it standing. What an idiot she had been to allow herself to go to pieces like this. If only he would give her time to think things out, to get more than this tenuous control over herself . . .

There came a tentative rap at the door and then his muffled voice, apologetic and concerned at the same time.

"Meg . . . Meg, honey, are you all right?"

"Come in, Father." Perhaps the necessity of facing him would serve to steady her, but there was a traitorous quivering edge on her voice.

The door opened and closed softly. She could feel with mounting irritation his upset, insistent gaze upon her.

"I'm perfectly all right, Father." She hated the way her voice sounded upon that simple statement. Completely insincere. Not like her voice at all.

"I thought this damnable heat might have got too much for you. Maybe something I could get for you, you know—a lemonade with a little claret perhaps?"

His words were absolutely meaningless. She turned to him almost savagely.

"No, thank you, Father!"

And even as she said it she thought: How ridiculous I must appear shrieking at him in this high, unnatural voice; and how ridiculous he looks standing there, warm and ineffectual, as though I were seeing him for the first time—shirt sleeves, palm-leaf fan, and all. Why, I've seen him exactly like this a thousand times. My father, James Singleton. . . .

"No, there's nothing, thank you. I . . ." But she couldn't go on. She uttered a little gasp of helpless agony and felt the rush of sobs and laughter begin to tear at her throat. There was no stopping it now. She shook helplessly in this sudden storm of horrifying, uncontrolled sound pouring out of herself. As her hands flew protectively to cover her face she saw James's countenance sag with dismay. He had never in all her life seen her like this. But then, she had never been like this before. Never.

But she underrated James.

"Meg . . . Meg, honey!"

His arms were suddenly about her and she felt herself surrendering willingly to them. He led her, unprotesting, to the bed and sat there on the edge gently and firmly holding her, saying nothing. His embrace was awkward, perhaps, but intimacy of this sort had been sparsely permitted him since she was a small child. It was simply unbelievable to see Margaret like this, crying wildly. The look of dismay on his face was replaced by one of bovine tenderness. Meg's head—the adored, dark, beautiful head—surrendered upon his breast. He felt like a giant—towering over this inexplicable need for his strength. And even as his stature grew in his thoughts his eyes filled with two enormous tears. They spilled over and went leaping down his smooth, pink cheeks. He had missed this sort of thing. He could not help remarking to himself upon the delicious sentiment of the moment. What a truly noble picture they must present—father and daughter weeping together. When had he last offered peppermints as a panacea for this sort of thing? He began to rock to and fro a little with the memory.

The tremors and small convulsions of Meg's body against his gradually weakened and ceased. Raising her head, she released herself from his embrace with a gentle but fastidious movement. She dabbed at her eyes with a crumpled bit of handkerchief. Her eyes, cleared and enormous, lifted to his, full more of irritation than of unhappiness.

"I'm sorry, Father." It was her voice again, low and controlled.

James felt rather rudely recalled to himself and looked back at her with a cocked and outraged brow.

53

"Sorry!" he exploded.

"Shhh!" she answered, disciplining him from long habit.

"But, Great Godfrey, Meg!" he complied, dropping to a hoarse and thunderous whisper. "What's this all about now?"

"Now, Father, please! If you're going to get upset and excited . . . Didn't cousin Tabby—"

"Oh, Tabby!" he interrupted with a snort. "You know Tabby. I couldn't wait around for your Cousin Tabby."

"Very well, but you must listen calmly. I can't talk to you now if you are going to get angry and shout."

"I'm not shouting. I just want to know what all this fuss is about —cool as spring water right this minute!"

She hesitated maddeningly, straightening the crushed folds of her dress with precise little movements of her hands. The corners of her perfect mouth began to turn up adorably in a deprecating half-smile.

"It will all sound silly . . . such a small thing to make me act like this." She grimaced with distaste. "I don't know exactly how to tell you."

"Now, Meg," he said with heavy patience. He patted her hand encouragingly.

"Well, on the way home from the Marstons' a while ago—just as we turned up the hill—Brant Royle stopped the surrey."

James's brows shot up and hung comically vibrating upon his forehead.

"Brant Royle?"

She continued hurriedly but calmly in the tone of one imparting some ordinary bit of information to a friend.

"I think he must have been drinking—you know, market opening and all—or he wouldn't have dared!"

James stood up, his short legs spraddled vehemently to the floor.

"Are you telling me that Brant Royle stopped the surrey?" he demanded in a deliberate voice. This was part of the ritual. This was the role he had played so often that he stepped into it without thinking. Behind it, though, he thought in a flash of honest and growing dismay, *O Lord . . . what's this now? . . . this will mean trouble . . . real trouble, maybe. . . .* He continued aloud, the bull bellow beginning to rise in indignant crescendo:

"He stops my daughter in a public thoroughfare, *and* he had been drinking—you call *that* silly?"

His jowls quivered. With a tremendous inarticulate snort he strode to the door and flung it open.

"Simon!" he bellowed into the hall. "Hob! Damnation . . . come up here!"

54

"Father—" Margaret got up and faced him as he turned back into the room—"you promised to stay calm if I told you."

He brushed past her and began to pace up and down the rug, muttering a furious, disjointed colloquy to himself.

"Damned ill-mannered, ill-bred riffraff . . . town's getting full of them . . . Ed Raeburn was right . . . ought to have railed them out long ago . . . the whole mongrel pack of 'em! . . . blight on any decent society . . . I've a good mind—"

"Father, *will* you listen?" she said wearily. She had known it would be like this.

"*Listen,* Meg! I'm listening. What do you expect me to do when low-down trash like that affronts my daughter?"

"But he didn't do anything so really terrible."

"Didn't do anything! I suppose the way you have been acting just now is because he didn't do anything *really* terrible!" He snorted loudly again.

She looked at him with direct and passionate candidness as though to force him out of these histrionics.

"That was because of something *I* did," she said simply.

James stopped his pacing. Something in her voice swept the mechanical fury out of him like a wind. When he spoke it was almost apologetically.

"Something you did, Meg?"

"Yes—and this will sound sillier than all the rest. He acted like a bad-mannered boy—that's all."

"Brant Royle is in his late twenties if I reckon rightly," he stated with heavy irony.

"When he stopped the horse he said something to me."

"What?"

"He said— It all happened so quickly . . . it was something about my being glad to marry him someday. It's hard to remember now."

"He said *that* to you?"

"Don't you see how silly it all was?"

"Of course it was silly—silliest thing I ever heard of—so silly I'm going to see he gets the whipping he deserves, and right away!"

She crossed to the window and stood with her back to him.

"You won't have to," she said almost inaudibly.

"What?"

"I said you won't have to," she said precisely, "because I've already done it. I hit him with the surrey whip . . . hard across the face. I've never felt like that before, and it was horrible!"

She felt shaken and weak now and very tired. James exploded into delighted and incredulous sound.

"You mean you whipped him yourself? Why, Meg, damn me!"

"I simply lost my mind for a minute. I don't know how I ever could have done such a thing. Oh, it was shameful—unforgivable!" A tremor shook her. "I don't think anyone saw me."

"Well, I certainly hope they did! Has he ever bothered you before?"

"No, of course not!" she said indignantly. "He lives here. I can't help seeing him now and then, but just as I see hundreds of other people around town." Her voice rang false even in her own ears. She knew suddenly that she was lying. But she couldn't explain why it was a lie. How could you explain the strange reappearance of that dark, flushed face come year after year to stare silently from the roadway at her and the house—the unspoken battle waged without words or gestures between two children, and then between two who were no longer children, standing on either side of an iron fence looking with deep recognition at each other?

"Godfrey's Cordial, I'm proud of you, Meg! That's all I've got to say—damned proud of you!".

"No, Father." She turned suddenly and came to him. "It was nothing to be proud about. I've never acted like that before in my life. It was as though I was someone else entirely. It made me ill. I hate it because it did that to me!" She grasped him firmly by his vest lapels. "I'm all right now. Let's not think about it any more. It's all done and over with and it will only embarrass me to try and do more. Let's pretend it really didn't happen. *Please*, Father!"

He patted her hands on his chest. He felt enormously relieved. He wasn't going to have to pretend to do anything.

"All right, Meg, if that's the way you feel about it. We'll just forget it."

There was a timid rap on the door. A muffled voice said, "Majuh —you call, suh?"

"It's Simon," said Margaret.

"Oh, Simon," James called, "it's all right. I won't need you now."

A muted chiming floated across the room to them.

"Half-past three!" Margaret exclaimed in dismay, her hands flying to tidy her hair. "And I haven't said a word to Relda about what we are going to have for supper and the Abbotts are coming up!"

James shook his head fondly at her. She smiled and they walked arm in arm to the door. As he opened it for her she turned to him with a little frown.

"Father, I just remembered—who was the gentleman you introduced to me when I was coming in awhile ago?"

James looked completely blank. He had all but forgotten himself.

"Oh," he said. "Oh, that was some man from Whitehead's in

Connecticut. Queer sort of fellow. Wanted to sell me some sort of contraption or other."

"He looked so tired and ugly." She mused for a moment. "I'm sorry if I seemed rude." She chuckled deep in her throat, a rich little sound of self-deprecation that never failed to delight him. "This has been a bad day for me. I've broken nearly all my rules for myself. . . . Oh, and I haven't even got out the Spode for tonight. The Abbotts would be impressed with the Spode, don't you think? I *must* hurry!"

6

He stood watching her move down the hall. She moved beautifully, with an unconscious physical grace. He lost himself in familiar pride in her. Damn, what a woman she was! She had horsewhipped him with her own hands. Any other woman he knew would have been capable of nothing more than hysterics under the circumstances. What a story it would have made to tell down at Tom Pate's office. In his mind he started to elaborate the fine way in which he would frame it. . . . But he couldn't now. He had promised Meg. It was a shame, though, not to be able to avail himself of a beautiful performance. Anyway she had hit him—herself—with her own hands. Damn!

Behind him in the hall a door opened. He turned. It was Tabby. Her face, beneath the perennially pale mass of hair, peeped from her door. Like a catbird peepin' out of a hedge nest, he thought irritably. He said aloud:

"You were perfectly right, Tabby. A great to-do. . . ."

She pursed her lips and looked long and brightly at him, as though in a moment she would reveal that eternal secret. Then her head pulled back and the door clicked. He stood frowning at the empty space for a moment. How like her to intimate that there was more to be said and then vanish!

"Oh glory, Tabby!" he muttered at last and stomped down the hallway to the stairs.

CHAPTER THREE

I

It had been a bad day. The kind of real dog day that belonged properly in July instead of the end of August. Jim Prentiss, mopping his face on a damp and dirty sleeve for the hundredth time, remarked that it was the kind of day that had to bust out in rain or some worse sort of meanness. This kind of weather, plus its being market opening with the town full of a lot of folks with money in their pockets and a chance to look up trouble for the first time in a year—why, something was bound to happen. Couldn't help it. He remembered saying this to the youngest London boy while he was rubbing down Mr. London's big roan gelding in the hot dusk at the doorway of Weller's livery stable.

He remembered with mournful satisfaction having said it only after what occurred later that evening.

But Tommy London wasn't listening to him. Tommy stood just outside the door. He was watching with absorbed attention what was going on in the weedy vacant lot that lay between the stable and the houses down Maple Street. The medicine-show people were setting up in the midst of the open space in preparation for the performance late in the evening. The big van stood splendid and horseless while its little group of strange inhabitants busied themselves about it. They had removed most of their finery now and two of them were driving tall stakes into the hard ground between the ponderous vehicle and the street front. A third was fetching water in big pails from the pump at the back of the livery. The big Negro who had driven the van through the square earlier in the afternoon knelt in the dust by one of the wheels, carefully filling some crude torches from a coal-oil can. The scene was oddly domestic and placid except for one wrong note. Near the street stood several little groups of onlookers. For the most part they were idling young white workers from the factories, rawboned youths who stood tight and silent among themselves, watching. Their faces were hard and blank, shoulders hunched, hands thrust deep into trouser pockets. There was something at once meaningless and ferocious in their intent attitudes.

Occasionally one among them would exchange a laconic observation with another. This would be followed by a forced explosion of neighing laughter and backslapping. More often than not it would develop into brief eruptions of fists, violent thudding blows on bone and flesh with no evident rancor or purpose other than to release some blind and pent-up protest against themselves, against each other, against they knew not what. They were young, they were empty, and they were sad. One of them called out boldly to the two showmen who were driving the stakes:

"Hey!" he said. "What you got the nigger for? Kin he do the Noo Orleens Fancy? Ain't much of a show if you don't have the Fancy."

The man holding the sledge hammer looked up briefly and smiled without humor, but said nothing.

"Hey, you hear what I ast?" They burst into raucous guffaws. Jim Prentiss scowled down the street at them.

58

"Listen at *that* now, will you?" he said dourly, shaking his head. "Just spoilin' for some kind of trouble, ever' last one of them!"

Night fell slowly, thickly. The air was still, close, and flannel-like. But darkness is a kinder element. It was a relief simply to be delivered at last from the heavy clash of light on light. The stunned blood quickened; bodies which had endured the martyrdom of garments all day strained onward toward little imagined eddies in the still air. Voices became relaxed and friendly, calling back and forth across the interval of a street. Suddenly there was a sort of anticipation in the air. It was Saturday night. And there is some special magic implicit in a small town's Saturday night. It was in the voices of the children still romping in the square, running in and out among the horses at the hitching rails. It was in the hooting of the boys who trailed after old Jack Davis while he lighted the few street lamps at the corners. It was in the mysteriously floating, giggling groups of older girls as they eddied along the sidewalks under the trees. The watchful youths, uncomfortably smart in hats and ties and tight yellow shoes, lolled in little bands about the open front of Tyree's Drug and Refreshment Parlor. They had a sound of Saturday night in their low voices, spoken tenderly and sidewise from their mouths, their eyes searching among the girls with shy arrogance. A few last fireflies bloomed among the trees in the square. They were answered in kind by the lamps on buggies and surreys already pulling up before the brick front of the Grange Hall on Brent Street. Along the dusty length of the Tobacco Planters' Hotel the rockers creaked on the veranda. There glowing cigar ends described eccentric parabolas about a relaxed rumble of masculine conversation. "What's that fool Harrison in the White House tryin' to do now? . . . Looks like we could get a gentleman at the head of the government sometime, b'god! . . . Country never was in worse shape. . . ."

There was a section of Kingsmont that had nothing in common with lawns or prosperous dwellings, nor even proper places of business. As is generally the case, it was loudly regretted by that part of the citizenry who year after year could talk about it from an antiseptic distance without bothering to do much about it; and, as was to be expected, those who were most vociferous in their complaints and denunciations were usually those who had helped most in bringing it into vigorous being. This reverse side of the community was (for rather obscure reasons) known in Kingsmont as Jamaica Town. This title loosely encompassed a sprawling district over the northern and western quarters of the town between the square and the railroad. In it were situated most of the tobacco businesses, the factories and warehouses. This section contained a jungle of rickety dwellings, cheap stores and eating establishments, rutted, odorous alleys and byways. Here lived the Negroes who worked in the factories, chanted about the sorting tables where the leaf was graded, or at the licorice vats where it was dipped for flavoring, or at the great hydraulic presses where the plugs were formed for cutting. Here also lived and worked a disparate scattering of whites who either had forsaken the land for factory wages or who ran poor little businesses and boardinghouses. These latter were, in general, lost men, their roots atrophying in Jamaica Town, hating themselves while they clawed bitterly at their black neighbors in a dull and desperate effort to keep from slipping entirely out of sight. That is, nearly all of them except the *'Krainians*.

In '75 one of the manufactories—the Pendleton Company—had, after much discussion (both public and private), brought down from New York a score of skilled cigarette-rollers and their families. They were immigrants from the Russian Ukraine, with big Slavic faces and incredibly deft hands. With their strange tongue and dress, their solid peasant vitality, they were a six-months curiosity in Kingsmont. After that they were neither formally accepted nor rejected as a part of the community. Because they were thrifty and law-abiding and hard-working and content to stay within Jamaica, they were remembered as aliens only on these occasions when some fretful national issue involving the question of foreigners made the righteous and critical citizenry recall the fact that these people hadn't always been with them. The Ukrainian children grew up and worked in the factories with their parents. Some of them went to the grade school given to Kingsmont by Robert Singleton, and began to lose their strange way of speaking. Never was there any trouble between them and their Negro neighbors. From the beginning there was a deep sense of kinship between them that leapt the barriers of language and color; they were both peoples who had never lost touch with the earth and who had come the long, hard way through sorrow to a profound understanding of what it was to be alive and joyous. And neither of them—the Negro nor the Ukrainian—had lost the gift for laughter nor the gift for the rich songs that were the special property of the heart. In time some of these 'Krainians drifted out to farms they had purchased with their careful earnings from this fabulous rich country. Some went into business for themselves in Kingsmont. And some continued to roll cigarettes all their lives.

2

John Barton came out of the Soldiers' Saloon on the square. The dim face of the clock in the courthouse tower advised him that it was eight o'clock. From one hand the carpetbag still sagged, as per-

60

manent a part of his person as the worn, antique hat. Behind him from the saloon came a buzz of conversation and masculine laughter. Some townsmen and a few farmers were still celebrating the sales of the day. Outside in the wagons the families waited in stoic silence for the time when they could start homeward down the dark roads, a lantern swinging from each wagon tongue against the night.

John stood on the sidewalk, looking more gaunt and tall than ever. His long equine face hung ghastly against the shadowed brick of the building, transfixed in the dim glow of the corner lamp. He stood thus for a moment, then turned abruptly at the corner down into darkness, his long lean legs plunging unevenly over the brick pavement.

All afternoon he had crouched in a corner of the long saloon with its dirty, churned sawdust, drinking glass after glass of whisky and methodically paying for it out of the flat purse with the big clasp. He had done it with the despairing air of a lost soul completing its damnation. He had never been drunk before in his life and he accepted the dizzy and wavering universe that now encompassed him as an extension of the long-familiar nightmare. . . . "Ol' man Royle's place?—Why, sho! Jes' turn the corner down West Street. First store of any account you come to."

His whole life was now completely at the mercy of such random odds and ends of information. They were cast at him like bones to a stray dog. He eddied, forever derelict, between one point in space and another, always going onward, because there was no other way for him to go—and never arriving, because there was no real destination for him. *Down West Street, you can't miss it. . . . No, there is no possible way for you to miss it.*

How good it was to be alone in the comforting dark, a creature of shadows, free of the dead heat of the barroom, the tobacco fumes, the close odor of perspiring humanity, of stale alcohol and hops. The darkness in some way was cleansing. It provided him, too, with an interval of privacy in which his meager personal resources could repair the most recent ravages of time. Always it must be thus. He must manufacture himself anew to meet the assault that inevitably lay ahead. And because of it he must rebuild his tottering fortress from materials that grew more threadbare with each succeeding encounter. It had been so in all the crises thus far in his sparse and arid existence. From the harsh terror that was his father through a host of lesser dangers—from Mr. Whitehead all the way down to this day and the pleasant, fat little man on the porch. *Now* it was someone called Royle. The name meant nothing to him. But then, most of the other names had meant nothing. "Royle" was merely another in a long series of labels applied to the same desperate situation. But always, somehow, he moved forward along the predestined road feeling that somewhere ahead lay that final, transcendent answer to all his wanderings.

3

The goal that John Barton was almost blindly approaching would not have excited any special attention even in the light of day. It was an ugly boxlike building pressed hard against an intersection. Two large windows flanked its entrance on West Street. They were openings which even in the light of noon gave but an obscure view of the interior of the building and of the objects of merchandise half-forgotten and thrown higgledy-piggledy for display within the windows themselves. Over the front doorway, and just beneath the second-story windows, hung a sign inscribed in plain block letters, black on white. Because it had been recently painted its legend stood out in the dim night light with a sort of crude vitality: T. ROYLE GEN. MDS. & TOBACCO. At the side, a flight of stairs ran up to a narrow landing above. In spite of its hard ugliness, there was a distinct air of blank solidity about the building, as though it had been there for some time and expected to remain for considerably more.

It was here, toward the last decade of the century, that an obscure stream of Scottish blood, generated in the valley of the Clyde, had, after long and tortuous wanderings which a hundred years before had seen it cast up on the Carolina shore, had come to rest in a back street. Upon this spot Templeton Royle, driven by a tight thread of madness all his own, had achieved at last a place upon which he could set his feet firmly and raise his head above the level of the earth. Eccentricity alone did not help him accomplish this. There came with it a deep Celtic shrewdness, the only legacy left him from forebears who had long been swallowed up in the maw of time and a devouring and merciless wilderness. His own meager history at this later date was still dominated by the image of that same wide land, an image that, even in his own mind, was defined by the most primitive manifestations. Birth and death, earth, rain and drought. A life shaped by struggle with pure elements—a pattern divided up ceaselessly between those who managed to survive and those who vanished down a dimming vale of futility and poverty.

Cast forth into it, Temp Royle had married and begotten three sons. But he lived always with anger, staring forth upon the Carolina land that held him like a prisoner, battling blindly and without purpose against a destiny that had caught his own father and his father's father in a merciless, impersonal grip. In his narrow, bony frame burned fierce fires. They drove him, foreordained, from one small catastrophe to another. His catastrophes differed only in that his fury would never let him rest among the acquiescent and beaten. They always sent him dashing onward, unregenerate, from one meager disaster to another.

Disaster, when it is of sufficient degree, has a way of negating all barriers, all scales of values. Those who have never breathed the air of ruin and those who have known no other breath are left at last in the mother slime, standing eye to eye. The War of the Secession did this to many men. There were those who simply drowned in the panoply of blood and destruction and the confusion of values, social and political, that washed in its wake. And there were others whose grain was so inherently tough, so resilient, that they sprang out of the common wrack again with no more interruption than the pause for breath, the interval in which the studied and cunning muscle of the spirit tensed itself for the surge upward.

Temp Royle found himself among these latter without knowing it. Temp, with his thin and angry little ferret's face, his bowels eaten with heat, his body clothed in ragged jeans. The war meant nothing to him. It expressed itself in the terms with which his life was long familiar. The only difference being that he took off from a point where most men were just discovering themselves. The point with him was arbitrary and as meaningless as any other place that might have been chosen from his existence. The land, the sun and moon and rain, the perfidy of mankind, banded ceaselessly together in a conspiracy to cast him forth, to grind him into oblivion. Or it might be said that the point was reached when he was turned off the land by James Singleton, another miserable sixty acres that he had been sharecropping in his usual desultory fashion. But he had been turned out a dozen times before. Again the turning point might have occurred mysteriously in the week when he and his three cubs slept curled in a corner of the Adams warehouse following this last dispossession. But it must be admitted that they had experienced homelessness before, under like circumstances, in other people's lofts and empty rooms.

Or it might be said that it was all resolved, that you could see the needle on the graph of his history begin to tremble upward from the long jagged line of descent, on that day when he traded the fly-bitten mules and the rickety tobacco wagon—the last in a long series—for a spavined and aged mare and a scarcely less disreputable buck-board into which he piled the three boys, two stone jugs of green whisky, and a meager assortment of odd household merchandise, mostly needles and pins and buttons, pack junk, that he had talked one of the storekeepers in Jamaica Town into letting him have, on what terms only a kind devil could say. With these he began to roam the countryside through the all but trackless wastes of pinewoods and untilled land. He had wandered all his life, restlessly and furiously, from one tenancy to another. But it seemed that in the admitted rootlessness of this new mode of existence he found some kind of stability. For one thing, it had purpose. It was as obscure to himself as it was to the rest of the world, but it was there. And so from farmhouse to farmhouse and hamlet to hamlet he peddled his way during the days of the week. Sundays invariably found him at some preacherless gathering in little frame churches in forgotten groves or at crossroads, where the congregations, such as they were, would find themselves suddenly addressed by a thin, violent creature exhorting them in as fiery a brand of hell and damnation as had ever swayed them into moaning ecstasy on the hard plank benches. There was that in Templeton Royle which found justification for the whole dark universe when he released a flood of marvelously misquoted Old Testament thunder and apocalyptic splendor upon these gatherings. Over those strained and upturned faces, the dulled gazes and jibbering mouths, he danced, shrieking his incantations at them with such bottomless fury that it seemed as if—instead of opening the Gates of Glory to them—he vented an intolerable burden of anger and spleen upon them for being what they were.

It is to be noted that his most frenzied performance was invariably anticlimaxed by a demand for a collection. Thus peddling and preaching he and the three boys and the wagon with the ruined horse became a familiar spectacle along the sandy, rutted, and lost byways of the county. A lone plowman looking up from between the furrows in the forenoon would hear bearing down upon his isolation a distant, screeching howl that presently resolved itself along the roadway into a wagon careening wildly among the ruts, the mare in a desperate and hopeless lather, and Temp Royle standing precariously braced against the seat, exhorting the struggling beast and the whole echoing wilderness of pine and oak in a torrent of sound. Clinging to the wagon bed about him in attitudes of resigned and silent grimness, or remonstrating in high protesting yells at their sire, were the three boys. In this manner the strange charade would pass, pursued by its invisible host of furies, swallowed up in dust and distance along a tunnel of trees. It left behind it a quaking, shattered stillness. The stunned figure among the furrows would stand in disbelief for a moment before closing his gaped mouth upon a grin. Then, picking up the plow reins again, he would murmur with a kind of outraged helplessness, "Ol' Temp Royle, by dern! Ol' Temp himself."

In the course of his early trading Temp Royle began to acquire increasingly large quantities of low-grade tobacco. Most of it had been discarded as worthless in the curing and the grading and had gathered ignominiously in some barn, whence it had been virtually handed over to him gratis by the grower—just to get rid of the stuff.

64

In Kingsmont, which he used as a sort of base for his forays, Templeton resold it when he had collected enough to realize something on it. Gradually, with the help of his boys, he began to subject it to a crude manufacturing process, packing it by the pound into cheap cotton sacks upon which were printed Templeton's name and SWEET BEULAH LAND TOBACCO. Then back to the piny trails again to sell it sometimes to the very same farmers from whom he had acquired it in the first place. This new development in his activities was attended by uproarious amusement among his acquaintances in Kingsmont. Templeton Royle was sho crazy and funnier'n a monkey in July! Settin' hisself up in business . . . "Looka here, Temp, you gonna invite me an' the missus up to Richmond when you gits you a place on the Ex-change? Hope you ain'ta gonna fohgit yoh friends now." They simply could not take him seriously. No more seriously than the established businesses of the town and the country took him from their acknowledged eminences. They were constrained to admit in due time, though, that he evidently had something to him underneath all that wild craziness. This was especially true when he suddenly turned up owning a store down on West Street and able to hire a few hands to manufacture his tobacco on his premises. Even then they continued to cast a skeptical and oblique eye upon his activities. Not that any of them really cared. They didn't. The regions marking Temp Royle's domain were so far below the interest of either their pocketbooks or their own solid eminences that they let him alone. They thought of him—when they did—merely as a mild curiosity.

4

Templeton's relationship with his three sons was in many ways extraordinary. Unlike what would naturally have been expected of him, he did not try to shuffle them off on any of his relations. He not only held grimly onto his progeny, but insisted upon taking them with him wherever he went. As a result, there grew among the four of them a fierce bond of independence and mutual protection. All during this period, Templeton pridefully believed he was taking care of his pack of cubs; but it was the three boys who really took care of Pa. This they did with an air of savage antagonism toward sentiment. It was a feeling that was the very epitome of sentiment itself—a bared-tooth daring of the whole world to hurt the Ol' Man. In this helter-skelter life they became proficient and learned in various ways. Ways that served to advance their mutual fortunes that would have done credit to men twice their ages and with twice their opportunities. There was never anything placid or even about this course. They were frequently involved in brawls, encounters that grew largely out of the baiting given them by yokels, who saw

65

in their fantastic life something to pillory with laughter and disparagement. In addition, there were occasional early scrapes with the law. But among the four of them they always managed to get themselves free of any entanglement or embarrassment. It was accomplished without too much personal damage to themselves and achieved usually an added measure of universal respect for their shrewd ferocity. Templeton had a fine time whenever these encounters involved the local constabulary. When the gentlemen of the law found themselves at last free of the harassing tumult of the Royle boys, they were left with the uncomfortable impression that they and not the Royles had been caught in some terrible mishandling of justice which had brought them to the immediate attention of a glowering and vengeful God.

On the other hand, the three boys did not share their parent's close and terrible partnership with Deity nor his insatiable appetite for religious gatherings. When Pa was holding forth in a wayside slab-board church, the three of them could be seen drowsing and inert in their wagon tied a little apart in the shade. But in this seeming inertia they were as watchful as cats, ready on the instant to depart when Pa's paroxysm had worn off. Or, if conditions warranted, to leap into the church through the nearest opening—window or door—to rescue him from a congregation that had got completely out of hand, as they frequently did; or from a congregation that evidenced physical resentment at Templeton's bland pocketing of the collection, as he invariably did. In the uproar that accompanied these happenings, they were always confronted by superior numbers, angry, murderous knots of men and shrieking, hysterical women who appeared bent on reducing their wagon to splinters and them to bleeding pulp. Usually it resolved into impotent and seething sound in the face of the Royles' unmistakable, chill willingness to do murder. Not that they escaped entirely unscathed. Not one of the three boys but bore a long and varied history of scars upon his body as a testimony to this period in their lives.

Out of this it was inevitable that a legend of inordinate wildness and disorder should grow concerning the Royles. Paradoxically, it never seemed to affect the warmth of their welcome wherever they went. Those places which sent them on their way down the road under a shower of rocks and howled threats received them on their next appearance as though nothing had happened. In fact, with an air of distinct pleasure. It was easy to understand this when one considered the unvarying atmosphere of monotonous and lonely drudgery that marked most of these lives. The appearances of Ol' Man Royle and his boys spelled a brief release from it. They offered always the possibility of violent and exciting change from the flat bondage of their existence. Then there was the fact that any blame involved could be loaded like unwanted merchandise on the wagon with the Royles and they could see it drive off conveniently down the road. Besides, Ol' Man Royle was sure a powerful preacher when he stood up before a congregation or a camp meetin' or just in front of the kitchen stove. They loved listening to him, their mouths and faces open and grinning at him, feeling the strange magic of his frenzied tongue beat over them—whether it was concerned with endless visions of flaming angels brooding over a mawing hell of awful and immediate proportions or whether he was calling down maledictions upon the heads of that nameless legion of monsters which peopled the world about Templeton Royle, plotting to bring him down, personally and especially, to an ignominious and horrid end by evil and knavery unheard-of.

"I ain't got a chanst!" he would howl. "Nawssuh! Ain't none of us got a chanst long as them mighty devils of pride and injustice—them harlots of the kingdom of man—sit in the seats of the mighty. O Lawd of Vengeance, smite them down in yoh wrath! Do you think them that dwell in the habitations and the palaces of governmint cares 'bout you or me? Nawssuh! They got their noses in a hawg trough fillin' their fat bellies with their feet ready to stomp us in the ground if we so much as look t'other way. Bloodsuckers of chillun and widders and orphans—they'd burn you in yoh own curin' barn if they got the chanst. The milk of mercy ain't in them, plottin' to grab the country right outen from under our feet and make us all less'n niggers. . . . Bring them down to hell-fire where they belong, O Lawd! They are the pledged enemies of all the poh men of the earth like you and me—an' I got the proof—*I got the proof!*"

The proof, as such, was never forthcoming except in a further flood of invective. His gnarled fists beat on his bony shanks and his lined, unshaved little face blazed. When it became more than he could bear sitting down he would leap to his feet and begin to pace up and down the space available to him, whether it was in a crossroads store or a farmhouse kitchen. Like a frenetic animal he would dash about, beating upon a counter top or a barrel, striking at whatever object came within his reach, the words pouring out of him. He worked himself up to a shrieking, gibbering pitch before the entranced audience. Young and old they hung motionless upon his frenzy, drowned, lost, and uncaring, until from the wagon waiting outside in the road or the yard, or from the porch where he had been sitting, would come Brant's clear young bass:

"All right, Pa, come on. If we gonna make Hanson's 'foh dark we gotta get movin'."

And Templeton, without rancor, would bring his discourse to an end, turning it off like a tap. He departed promising that he'd have more to say when he came through again. They didn't care what he was talking about; it was the ritual, the ecstasy, of the performance they hungered for. As he grew older, the magic of it began to wear thin and the attitudes of his audiences took on an air of indulgence, a half-irritated, half-embarrassed sufferance. But they still listened.

5

It has been noted that it was his boys who took care of Templeton Royle. In their collective attitude toward the shifting world of men and weather they presented what appeared to be and was accepted as an unbroken front. Seen together, they produced a consistent effect, as though shaped and hardened by the fires of the same experiences. They seemed to think, act, and even look alike. But this was merely the superficial product of their common struggle for survival; observed closely, they resembled each other physically only in a most subtle and fleeting sense, and emotionally not at all.

Nominally it was Templeton who guided their destinies, but it was Brant around whom they rallied, upon whom they leaned, willingly or unwillingly, at every point in those early years—as well as later.

He was the eldest. From birth he had been physically the biggest of them and possessed of almost terrifying strength. He was large-boned, broad, and heavy. There were those who thought his face handsome. It had a kind of crude power under its thick mop of black hair. Moody, sullen, and taciturn, he was capable of turning on his father and brothers without warning in unreasoning rages. But it was by virtue of that same dark and unspoken drive and energy in him that they were held together. It was he also who, when Templeton lay sodden with green whisky on the wagon bed for as much as two days at a time, saw that they got the bare necessities of food and shelter. It was Brant who extracted them from their frays, dispersing their assailants by displays of sheer brute power. And it was Brant, too, more than any of them, who revealed the final shrewdness in the handling of their affairs. He saw to it that no matter how small the transaction, it was the Ol' Man in particular and the Royles in general who emerged with the edge of the advantage.

Over the years it was this infallible and innate business sense as much as his strength in physical combat that gained him the grudging admiration of those with whom he dealt. He had a widely scattered host of acquaintances, but no friends. The warmth that was in him was not of the sort to awake intimacy or regard in others. His father and brothers held him in pretty much the same kind of fear and respect as did the rest of their world. But over them he

68

exercised a brooding and careful guardianship, a sort of deep, inarticulate tenderness that was as likely to reveal itself in a roar and a cuff as it ever was in any voicing or act of affection. They skirted him warily when he was in one of his capricious black moods, keeping themselves prudently out of his reach until the storm had blown over. Often they snarled and yelled impotent irritation and disagreement at him from a safe distance, fleetingly opposing his tyranny, but they always fell in with his decisions. More than anything else this was because—without understanding him any better than did anyone else—they respected the deep and ordered drive, the purpose, in him that was larger than anything they possessed. No matter how trifling or how great their difficulties, they knew Brant would find the best way out for them. In this he never failed them.

It was he who bullied Templeton, at last, into buying and stocking the store in Kingsmont; who pushed Templeton's little tobacco manufacturing beginnings with the crude Beulah Land Rough Cut into something like a business with six Negroes working in the big room at the back of the store. In doing it, though, he had to agree to a compromise with his father. Templeton had been too long conditioned to his wandering existence. Confined to the limited horizon of the store and the town, he grew restless and querulous, so Brant wisely let him continue to take the loaded wagon out and do the selling. One of the boys always accompanied the old man while the other two remained to tend the store and the little factory. In this fashion they prospered, not with any brilliance, but with the fierce and watchful industry of creatures who have known the world only as an impersonal and ever threatening force ready to blot out the weak and the careless.

Samuel, who was younger than Brant by four years, came in time to take over most of the affairs concerned with the running of the front part of the establishment known as Temp Royle's place. This fell naturally to his lot. He had aptitude and liking for small trade and, as his father said, a nose for a nickel. He was a stringy, weedy young man with small eyes and a mouth full of bad teeth. An air of mingled craft and complaint, a sly and whiny manner, characterized him. And while he evoked a feeling of contempt in the store's customers—black or white—at the same time he held for them the fascination of a slightly unclean animal, a creature not subject to the same kind of law and regulations that they were. He had a way of leaning over the counter and whispering a confidence sidewise from his mouth. While he measured out a piece of yard goods or weighed some groceries, his little eyes darted secretly about him, never looking at anyone or anything directly. It was a procedure that unfailingly produced a zany tittering or a weak guffaw from his customers. They were never sure afterward just what he had said

69

or what had made them laugh, and each time they returned it was with the feeling that they would find out. He was entirely capable in his position as storekeeper, but it by no means was the extent of his activities. On the side he found time to conduct a series of shadowy little businesses mostly having to do with petty interest on small loans. He also represented several cheap-jewelry companies whose wares he palmed off on the Negroes and factory workers by a payment system all his own and a personal bookkeeping that bulged his pockets with the records of innumerable complicated transactions. These activities kept him a familiar figure in all the twisted byways and corners of Jamaica.

He stood in mortal fear of Brant. Their fierce sessions over the books held once a month in the little office between the store and the factory room invariably ended in hysterical and gibbering defense on Samuel's part over some not entirely clear entry in the big red ledger. He lived in the perpetual hope that someday he would succeed in putting one over on Brant. But it was with the foreknowledge that, no matter how ingenious his device or how small the sum in question, it was doomed to discovery under Brant's adamant and infallible examination. There had been brief periods during which Sam had been more or less free of this tyranny. These were the times when Brant disappeared from Kingsmont on what he called one of his "learning trips." He would be around the place for a year or more and then he would get moody and restless and announce that if they were going to get anywhere in the business somebody in the family would have to go learn more about it than they did. Then he would take himself off to work at a factory in Danville or Oxford, and once he was gone for six months at some kind of job on the Exchange in Richmond. Each time Sam had a wild hope that Brant's big ideas would keep him away for good, leaving the store and a blissful unsupervised life to Sam. But Brant always come back to Kingsmont. And after each return he seemed worse than when he went away, more exacting, more morose, more unpredictable.

Pete Henry, the youngest of the three, survived his rough upbringing with complete equanimity. He was a pleasant, happy-go-lucky boy with a quick grin and a careless mop of blond curls. Frankly lazy and easy-going, he showed not the faintest signs of Brant's driving, dark ambition or of Sam's rodent industry. He evidenced no inclination for furthering himself in any direction. Brant had tried furiously and earnestly to make him realize that he had to find him a place in the harness and pull with the rest of them if he expected to get along.

"Aw, Brant," he would tease with his disarming candor, "why do you want me to get underfoot when you know I ain't a bit o' good? I'd jes' get in the way, an' you know it. You an' Sam tend to the knittin' an' I'll set by an' be pretty!"

The best thing he did was to look after Templeton, accompany him on selling trips, and get him back safe with the money and not too drunk. He had a clear and musical baritone which he cultivated assiduously with the aid of a battered guitar. He employed this talent among a host of admiring females, old and young, scattered over the county. He became a decorative and valuable addition to his father's sermonizing and religious activities. Sitting at the front of the church, his instrument held lovingly across his knees, he was ready at any moment, when the feeling was ripe, to take the lead in a good roof-raising hymn, his voice soaring melodiously above the fervent caterwauling about him. He loved an audience and a changing scene almost as much as did Temp. A gathering of any kind was his most natural environment. He could pass the time of day or night endlessly and effortlessly with a group of customers or acquaintances. People found themselves putting up with Templeton for the pleasure of having that bright, laughing scalawag of his about. Pete Henry was sure of a warm welcome in any of the isolated tobacco farms they visited, or at the big sectional revivals held in a hot grove of trees among the wailing of sleepy infants and the debris of lunch baskets. Brant fully realized the value of these qualities in his younger brother. He was, in his way, as susceptible to the careless charm of the boy as any of them. So he let Pete Henry more or less alone to do as he pleased as long as he looked after Templeton properly and didn't get into too much trouble.

The security they thus achieved in the ugly frame building in the back ways of Kingsmont, the feeling of a strong foothold upon the shifting earth, seemed to bring to all of them a measure of peace except Brant. Just why it did not to him they could never understand. But then no one of his family had ever understood Brant or what made him act the way he did. The dark angel that presided over his energies and drove him onward in a black frenzy with himself and his surroundings; the thing that made him intelligent and reasonable one minute and then sent him roaming about the streets of Kingsmont like a blind, caged animal the next. The spirit that after months of ascetic sobriety could force him forth without warning to drink himself into a murderous, destructive mood, inevitably ending in some fantastic melee at one of the town's three saloons and as inevitably followed by a night in the jail, a perfunctory fine, and admonition from a harassed justice of the peace.

It was this thing in him that would drive Sam to scream impotently at him during one of their monthly accountings—particularly when Brant had forced another agreement to apportion more and more of their profits to the purchase of larger quantities of tobacco for the manufactory instead of investing it in safe merchandise for the shelves of the store.

"But godamighty, Brant," Sam would shriek, a creature driven beyond endurance, "what's the matter with you? Ain't we got more tobacco on hand now than we know what to do with? We ain't even got rid of last month's make and here you want to go and git twicet as much. *Twicet as much!* What we gonna do with it, I ast, what we gonna *do* with it? An' me needin' yard goods in the store I could sell in a minute if I had 'em. You're just crazy with this idea of a tobacco business. You're actin' like you can compete with all the big boys up the street, and you cain't—an' you know it! If you don' stop this foolishness you're gonna lose the store right out from under us, that's what you're gonna do. You always said we was gonna have a place. Well, we got it—but you ain't gonna let us keep it at this rate. If this don't suit you, why don't you go somewhere that's got room enough for you? Ain't you never gonna be satisfied?"

Sam's eyes would dart about the little office where they were as though they could find some refuge. But in a moment they would swing helplessly back to the black gaze opposite him. The endless moment of heavy silence dragged on. Then Brant would speak in the terrifying voice he had for such occasions, cold and deep and quiet:

"No, Sam, I ain't gonna be satisfied—and neither are you. It ain't this town's too small for me . . . it just don't know that it's big enough for me yet. But give me time . . . I'll show it, I'll show it, *I'll show it!*"

And Brant's huge fist would begin a slow pounding on the scarred top of the table that served as a desk, a continuous gesture that would increase in violence until Sam, watching fascinated, would think that either the flesh or the wood would have to disintegrate under that rhythmic and terrible emphasis.

6

In the dim and shifting light where he stood, the store front took on the semblance of an inscrutable and waiting face. Its two lighted windows, its door like a mouth ready to swallow him into some further and nameless obscurity. John Barton hesitated as though there were another choice open to him if he moved on. But he knew there wasn't. This was the end, the final reach. And so he stood for a long moment, unable to move, hearing himself repeat alternately: Royle . . . Barton . . . Royle . . . Barton. It was a last little incantation against the nightmare world that swam about him. The distance across the clay sidewalk separating him from the steps seemed a yawning space beset with dangers.

The inside of the building was a shapeless and pleasantly odorous cavern. Stalactites of harness and hardware hung down into it from the ceiling. The floor was crowded by the shapes of seed bags and barrels, and hemmed in by innumerable shelves along the wall. At the long scarred counter Samuel Royle was waiting on a Negress.

"Did you say two pounds now, or three?"

"Two'll be plenty, I reckon. Better let me have 'bout a nickel's worth of that Red Boy snuff too. How much does I owe you now?"

He calculated swiftly, his eyes mechanically tabulating the purchases on the counter.

"Fi'ty-five cents," he snapped out peevishly between tight lips.

She plunged a hand down her dress front between her breasts and drew forth a soiled bandanna with a knotted lump in one corner. She jingled it calculatingly upon her palm for a moment, then replaced it, giving the front of her dress a pat.

"I jes' guess you better put it down in de book an' take it outen Ben's pay when he leave tonight—" her husband was one of the Negroes employed by the Royles in the little factory at the back—"I don' guess I got enough."

"All right," he said impatiently. Then as he moved toward the big ledger under the till he whispered back at her: "You know it's gonna cost you a nickel more if I have to put it down in the book. Y'all never get rich thataway."

She giggled as she swept her parcels under one arm.

"Nawsuh . . . don' reckon so!"

She started for the door. Before she reached it she turned back. Sam, watching her, snorted. What in Jehoshaphat now?

"You goin' to de big show tonight, Mr. Sam?"

"What show?" His upper lip twitched over the discolored teeth. He knew as well as she did what she was referring to, but his irritation drove him to dissemble.

"De free one wid de fancy wagin they's havin' down to the livery lot nex' to de Maple House."

"Did you say the Maple House?" he whispered, his countenance assuming in a flash the secret and indecent mask. They looked at each other grinning.

"Yassuh, dat's what I say!"

She turned then with a throaty gurgle and went out. With her going Sam's face reverted to the scowl, the ferret's look, half nausea, half guile. Even alone now in his acknowledged domain there was something furtive about him. He bit savagely into the remnant of a plug and thrust what was left of the tobacco into his shirt pocket, where it had left an indelible brown stain like a badge on his meager chest. Moving to the ledger, he closed it and opened the till drawer,

73

glanced within, and then shut it with a bang. His eyes darted about the room, making a ceaseless and fretful inventory of its contents. He sighed and moaned and rubbed his thin nose sidewise with his fist. It had been a long, hot, trying day in every respect, what with it being Saturday and market opening. He'd been looking for Pete Henry or Pa to turn up all afternoon. It wasn't like either of them to miss a market opening. They'd been gone for nearly two weeks now. They'd oughta have been back this afternoon, and him with no help! Looked like that Pete Henry was gettin' more flighty and no-count as he grew up. And Brant lettin' him go gallivantin' along with Pa without earnin' his keep.

As for Brant . . . Brant was soaked up to his eyebrows again! He scowled, flashing an apprehensive glance toward the rear of the store before leaning forward to spit over the counter into the scuffled sawdust. Brant had come in earlier that afternoon looking like Ol' Nick himself, and had gone into the little back office and closed the door. He hadn't said anything and he hadn't showed any signs of coming out yet. Drunk again. Damn Brant! He could see his way to spending their money on a drunk but couldn't spare him, Sam, enough to order that new line of ready-mades that the Richmond man had made him such a good proposition on last week. Sam moaned to himself in torment. It wasn't right. There wasn't anything right about it! If it wasn't for him keepin' store, slavin' night and day, they'd all be right back where they started five years ago—in spite of Pa and Brant and their foolishness with tobacco! Now look at tonight—everybody goin' down to the fun at the medicine show and here he was stuck. There wasn't anyone to take over, and he didn't dare close up till he was sure that no more of today's money market would wander his way. He might even have to stay open till midnight.

He leaned forward resignedly upon the counter. As he did so, a woman entered the street door. She blinked and tossed her head. Her body was small, round, and trim in a bright-green dress. Her face, broad and high at the cheekbones, had a generous rouged mouth and small lively eyes set at a slight slant. It was a young face possessed of an attractive ugliness. She was hatless, and the most arresting thing about her was a great coiled mass of red hair that flamed above her face. She stood for a moment while she adjusted the heavy silver rings in her ears.

"Hello, Sam," she said, her teeth gleaming white and perfect. She set one hand on her hip and sauntered to the counter opposite him. "First thing I thought no one was here. But I shoulda known *you'd* be!"

Her voice was low with a little velvet hoarseness, and the words as she said them had an elusive accent, a subtle cadence, almost for-

74

eign. The rodent grimace that passed on Sam's face for a smile twisted his mouth.

"I'm always here, Sonie," he whispered, looking at her with appreciation. "What I want to know is what you're doin' here."

The slant eyes, now green under the light, looked at him steadily with an expression of good humor and scorn. She shrugged.

"Where's that Brant?"

"You talkin' 'bout Brant?" he said with elaborate vagueness, "Why, I reckon he's out back there some'rs."

"Go get him here for me." On one bare wrist she wore a series of loose bracelets and these now jangled impatiently. Samuel eyed them, licking his lower lip unpleasantly. Then he looked up apologetically.

"I think he's drunk," he whispered sidewise.

"Ach!" she exclaimed with a little grimace. "I might have known it. And me at the house waiting while the beautiful supper spoiled—the borsch, the blintzes, all going bad. Oh, I am a big fool, Sam, I think." She reached into the candy jar and helped herself to a piece, placing it delicately between her beautiful teeth as if it were a rare fruit. "Go root him out for me, Sam!"

Sam didn't move. He gave her a furtive, insolent glance.

"Go get him yourself, if you're so all-fired anxious," he whispered. "I wouldn't touch him now no more than I would a polecat on Sunday, and you know it!"

He was thinking: She's got style—plenty of gall to her, too. Guess that's why that hellion keeps nosin' round her. Only woman I ever did see him take more than two looks at. There'd be hell to pay, though, if Pa should happen to walk in now. Take a pitchfork to her more'n likely—the old lecher! Sam began to grin thinly and idiotically. She looked at him, removed the candy from her mouth briefly, and then snorted as she replaced it.

"No more blood in your whole body, Sam Royle, than in a jack rabbit!" She snorted again and threw the candy into a nearby open grain sack with the contemptuous flick of a wrist. She licked her fingers and gave her crown of flame a reassuring pat. Then she strode to the door at the back and flung it open. Sam watched fascinated.

"Come out here, Brant!" she called into the passageway. "It's me—Sonie Lipik—you bad child! Come out so I can give you the whippin' you deserve."

She turned, winked broadly at Sam, and strolled back to the counter. She stopped dead at the sound of a piece of furniture crashing on the floor in the room beyond. They both turned to face the dark little passageway.

When he appeared in it he seemed to fill it completely from sill to lintel and from side to side. His hat was still on, crumpled and pushed back over the tousled, vigorous black hair, his face pale, heavy, and sullen. In one hand he held an empty glass and this he pressed against the door frame as though for support. He loomed over the entire room imminent and terrible. Even in the smoky, inadequate light, from where they stood the woman and Sam could see the angry diagonal marking the brown down across the strong bridge of the nose and the left cheek. He stood quietly looking at them without rancor. Sam, finding the silence more than he could bear, coughed nervously and braced himself against the shelves awaiting the onslaught. The woman patted her hair again and stood looking at Brant fearlessly.

"Hello, Sonie," said Brant at last, his voice thick and deep and emotionless. "What are you doin' here? Go on away."

"Ach! Is that all you have to say to me? I have waited two hours already, and now I have had to come for you myself." She leaned toward him slightly. "No, it's not so easy as that, Brant Royle, even if you don't know how to behave like a gentleman." Her arm flashed out demandingly at him. "Where've you been all this afternoon while I've been waitin'?"

Brant's hand holding the glass brushed slowly at the air before him.

"A little waitin's never gonna kill you, Sonie. Go on now." He sounded tired, as though her presence was immaterial—an annoyance over the surface of a deeper, more painful concentration.

"Where'd you get that thing on your face, now?" she flung at him, crisp and adamant.

The hand with the glass came up deliberately, as though remembering, and touched the angry mark on the cheek. Then his face flushed deeply and with an explosive, savage gesture he dashed the glass downward, shattering it upon the floor.

Samuel started and tittered hysterically. The woman did not move but stood shaking her head from side to side with an expression half mocking, half tender. Then she uttered a hoarse little chuckle.

"You've been fightin' again—drinkin' and fightin'."

He stared back at her, the black brows meeting in one stormy line over the nose. But when he spoke it was still in the quiet, tired voice:

"Yeah, I've been drinkin', but I ain't been fightin'—if it's anything to you."

"Where'd you get the pretty mark on your face then—playin' with kids?"

He looked at her as if she were not there.

"Sometime, Sonie, you're gonna make me take that fine little neck of yours and squeeze it hard just to shut you up—and maybe then you'll know to mind your own business."

76

She chuckled again, goading him deliberately. She looked malicious and pleased with herself—and completely unimpressed by him. *She* understood him, all right!

"Oh, excuse *me!* I'll stop asking the questions. But you must come here and let me fix your face for you." She started toward him, but he pushed roughly past her and leaned toward Sam.

"Where's Pa and Pete Henry?"

"How do I know?" whined Sam. "They ain't come in yet."

Brant began to grumble. He scowled toward the ancient clock ticking rustily above the shelves.

"I'm gonna skin Pete Henry alive bringin' Pa in this late. He ought to know better . . . damn easy-goin' little fool. Pa's gettin' too old to be travelin' after dark. I've told him and told him! Next time—"

He didn't finish because someone had come in through the street door. It was John Barton. He stood before them dazed, dusty, and fragile as a leaf.

Sam whispered automatically: "Somethin' for you?"

"I want to see Mr. Royle, please."

The words came to them like the crackle of dry corn shocks. Sam tittered again, because no one else seemed to be doing anything.

"Drunk," he muttered hysterically. "Guess everybody in town's drunk tonight."

The woman made the little tinkling gesture toward her hair again and regarded this newcomer, as she did everyone, with candid speculation. It was Brant, however, who stood looking at John Barton steadily and soberly.

"What *Mr.* Royle you want to see?" he demanded quietly.

"Major Singleton sent me."

The words seemed to wash the room with silence. Brant said carefully: "Did you say Major Singleton sent you?"

John's pale gaze caught and hung on Brant's countenance desperately. His thin throat convulsed and then the dry and broken words began to come out of his mouth again.

"Cigarette machine," he gasped, "very interesting proposition . . . Major Singleton said . . . Royle . . . you can't miss it . . ." He swayed before them and then quietly fell bonelessly to the floor, his hat slipping over his face in the sawdust as though to shield him. One long arm was thrown forward through the sawdust like a supplication. At the end of it, under the gaunt hand, lay the handle of the ridiculous carpetbag.

77

CHAPTER FOUR

The thing that most people who had known him remembered about Sonie's father was the hat. Jascha Lipik was never seen without it. When he first appeared in Kingsmont he was wearing it, and the day they came to pay their respects at his open coffin in the front parlor it was still in place. It was worn indoors and out without regard to season or temperature, whether it was the sultry Carolina summer or the raw, damp winter. It would have been easier to imagine Jascha completely naked than without that hat. Whether Jascha had bought the hat new no one ever thought to ask. It had undoubtedly once been a good black bowler, high-crowned, and narrow-brimmed, but it had already acquired a venerably gray-green patina when Jascha first appeared in Kingsmont. This changed subtly with the years until it seemed to have no color at all but a strange, dull iridescence.

Other than the hat there was very little that the world at large remembered about Jascha Lipik.

Even Sonie remembered him not as a unique and personal outline, but more as a feeling, a little warming about the throat and heart. It was the sort of vague tenderness that one retains intact and is arbitrarily associated with the odds and ends of the past. A cracked dish, an old tree, or a chair against the wall might evoke such an emotion equally well, not because such bric-a-brac brought to mind specific happinesses or occasions, but simply because they pertained in some special and forgotten sense to oneself a long time ago. Out of this amorphous jumble little of Jascha Lipik protruded to preserve his memory. Such self-effacement was characteristic of him in life as well as death.

Even physically there had been something self-effacing about him. He was a small man with narrow shoulders permanently hunched from the long hours spent at the rolling table. He had narrow, warm-yellow eyes set slantwise above flat bony cheeks, and a droopy, generous mustache that appeared to be suspended from the short stub nose. But it was his hands that Sonie remembered best. They had long delicate fingers. How nervously alive they could look even when they lay at rest in his lap! And how comforting they could be when they touched her, and what marvels of precision and competence they were to watch at work! Like most of the children of the Ukrainian rollers, Sonie had been taken at an early age down to the factory to learn to roll cigarettes. Most of one winter she had sat

78

perched on a little wooden box on the bench beside him, endlessly watching and endlessly trying to do as he did.

"Na, na, Sonia!" he would say gently, dwelling richly upon the vowels. "Na; you must have patience. Like this, like this—see . . . so . . . and so!"

Again he would demonstrate slowly and patiently as he had done a thousand times already. The slender fingers again flashed magically between the little bin of tobacco and the delicate paper wrapper, placing her own stubby hands now here and now there until the cigarette was completed.

But Sonie's career as a roller was brief. The fall following her initiation into the factory she came of school age. There were not one but *two* public schools for the children of Kingsmont. It seemed that the bounties of this new land were inexhaustible. Jascha was determined that his daughter should go to school and be educated like the children of other citizens. His decision was a radical one and created a scandal of several days' duration among his neighbors and in his home. Sonie's mother instantly set up a loud and continuous lamentation. She pursued Jascha about the house. She protested to her sympathetic friends and the world at large that this unheard-of move would precipitate the Lipiks into dire poverty while others of the 'Krainians, blessed with large families, waxed rich. Jascha characteristically said nothing. Having stated himself, he rode out the storm, his eyes looking, if possible, a little more slant and warm, his face a little more bland and uncommunicative. So when September came he took Sonie down and entered her in the first grade in the square brick school building on Peters Street.

There were other odds and ends that Sonie associated with her father. She had liked being the only child of the acknowledged best among all the rollers in the factories. It gave her a certain position among the other Ukrainian children, a taste of eminence that, with her unfailing taste for the theatrical in anything, she enjoyed and used to the fullest. She had liked the rough, warm feel of Jascha's clothes and the rich aroma of cured tobacco that breathed from him as though his entire fragile body had been steeped in it. She had loved the soft, slurred sound of his speech. He had always talked to her in his careful English, sparsely, in a way that gave everything he said an aura of gentle and laughing wisdom.

Jascha had brought as an indivisible part of him to Kingsmont, along with the bowler hat, a cough. The hard little hacking noise of that cough had been as much a part of the familiar sounds in Sonie's childhood as had been her mother's voluble and banging progress through the housekeeping. Sonie remembered the apologetic and disparaging way Jascha had of hiding his mouth in his faded blue bandanna when one of these frequent attacks struck him. Often he

79

had to stay away from the factory for a day or so, the sound of the coughing subdued under her mother's voice, raised now in expostulation, now in sympathy. But, as in everything else, he was so private, so reticent, about this that no one, least of all his family, considered it in any way remarkable—except perhaps his wife, Genia. But toward the end of the winter when Sonie was nine he lay finally exhausted upon the bed upstairs, the slant hazel eyes brilliant with fever, and apologetically coughed his life out on the counterpane.

But Jascha left his affairs in good order. He had prospered well during his life in Kingsmont. Five years following his arrival he had been able to purchase, after long and subtle bargaining, a narrow lot down on Maple Street. Maple Street ran for five ugly blocks along the western edge of Jamaica Town. It was so named for no reason that anyone could recall. It was an ugly little thoroughfare lined with warehouses, a few tottering Negro rentals, and hemmed about by factories. It was almost completely devoid of greenery. Only fierce weeds and indomitable Johnson grass thrust up through the rubble, and a few stunted chinaberry trees along the board fences and the backs of buildings. Jascha's lot was purchased from a hideous strip of land left open along the side of the last block. The strip had been used for years as a casual dump for refuse and offal from both the factories and the town. It had long been dismissed as worthless by its owners, but Jascha's purchase and subsequent building of a house started a modest real-estate boom. Several of his Ukrainian friends, following his example, bought lots and built houses until the old strip disappeared. In its place appeared a half-dozen almost identical boxlike dwellings crowded close against one another. These had scant front porches and steps flat against the sidewalk. Their back yards were narrow enclosures full of clotheslines strung between the back stoops and the walls of the warehouses that bordered the railroad tracks beyond. The only open space finally left was a somewhat larger lot lying at the south end of the block between the Lipik house and the livery stable. Jascha had, in time, bought this too, and although he never did anything with it it evidently satisfied some old need in him to own land.

Jascha's house—of which his Ukrainian neighbors' houses were more or less duplicates—was a square, two-storied dwelling unrelieved by any architectural fancy except a tentative fringe of jigsaw work hung modestly under the eaves and along the top edge of the narrow front porch. When it was first completed it had been painted a serviceable, hideous mustard-brown. Time and the smoke from factories and trains together with the sun and rain succeeded in changing this to a permanently mottled liverish color. But aesthetic considerations never bothered Jascha. He loved it with a quiet passion that recognized no defects simply because this house was *his*.

80

His quiet and profound pride in it led him to call it Maple House after the street.

Maple House had not been designed simply to house Jascha and his wife and child. It had five rooms upstairs in addition to two that the Lipiks used. Soon after they moved in, Mrs. Lipik began to rent this extra space to itinerant workers from the factories, to farmers and traveling drummers whose businesses kept them in town overnight. It was not long before she began to take in regular boarders, serving them richly odorous meals of her own preparing. The dining room was papered in a bright green and hung about with a set of garish lithographs of the Philadelphia Centennial. Long festoons of flypaper dangled permanently in the windows. In time there was rarely an empty chair at the long table.

In this manner the Lipiks prospered. When Jascha died he left his wife and daughter well off. There was a solid sum of money in the bank. The house was not only clear of any mortgage, but a going enterprise, with two new rooms added over the back porch.

If Sonie inherited her honest self-reliance and warm sense of humor from her father, she got her strong histrionic flair and her shrewd business head from her mother. She also got her luxuriant auburn hair. Genia Lipik was a Polish Jewess with a thin, harassed face dominated by a pair of dark, expressive eyes forever shadowed by the ghetto. She was as different in temperament from the quiet, secretive little Jascha as white is from black. Rarely silent, her shrill, emotional voice was heard in a continuous flow of comment, commiseration, or malediction. The unvarying tenor of her talk and her endless hints was that they might all at any moment find themselves without a penny in their pockets, a crust of bread for their mouths, or a roof to put over their poor heads.

Following Jascha's death, affairs at Maple House underwent a gradual, almost imperceptible change. This was due largely to Genia's personal obsession. The rooms in her house had to be occupied by paying guests at the expense of any other consideration. There were other boarding and rooming houses in the neighborhood now and it was no longer so easy to maintain a full house. The old clientele had been largely masculine, but now the pale young clerks from the factory offices, the dry-goods and machinery salesmen, and the occasional silent farmer were replaced by a more or less permanent group of single ladies. They were remarkable only in that they were almost all of them uniformly middle-aged, and their otherwise comfortable and respectable exteriors occasionally revealed a taste for the eccentric and the exotic in the matter of dress. There was, too, the fact that they usually arose late and retired later. Their origins were as obscure as their destinations. But their conversation revealed a variety of experiences and travels, and a good-humored, oversen-

81

timental attitude toward life. At nightfall with the appearance of a succession of masculine visitors, the house would suddenly come to life, full of giggling and footsteps up and down the stairway and in the upper hall, the opening and closing of doors.

Even on Saturday evenings, when this activity reached its climax, there was about it always a curious air of decorum. Only rarely was the placid surface marred by an explosion. Sometimes late—usually a Saturday night when Mama's roomers had a large number of callers, and long after she was supposedly asleep in the room she shared with Genia—Sonie would be startled out of a doze by a discordant outburst somewhere in the house. Sitting bolt upright in the big creaking bed, her heart beating with excitement, she hugged her knees tight in the dark and strained to hear. From somewhere down the hallway or below her there would come a high, indignant female shriek that she would identify as the voice of Mrs. Violet or Mrs. Pearl. (All of Mama's ladies seemed to possess either floral or jewel-like names, and they were always addressed as "Mrs.") Often there followed a muffled crashing about as though furniture were being violently used. Presently she would hear the light sharp sound of her mother's feet coming up the stair and the high piercing sound of her voice cutting through the general clamor. The picture of Genia then was always more impressive in her mind's eye than at any other time. She would advance upon the disturbance in the house with a kind of distracted ferocity. At such times she was a compelling and irresistible little figure, not only because of the flow of indignant sound that came out of her but because there was a remote and impersonal quality about her actions as though her mind were really on a half-dozen other more important things. Sonie, listening in the dark, would hear her mother's voice rise to a long scream as she came upon the scene of the disturbance. The other sounds would quickly die out, leaving it to soar angrily and alone like an undammed flood. It would continue as Genia drove the object of her wrath before her down the stairs and out into the street; it poured out into the night, following the fumbling sound of the offender's footsteps as they died away down the empty sidewalk. A tingling and nervous silence would then fall over the house and Sonie would lie back with a delicious sense of satisfaction, as if she had taken part in the rout herself.

It cannot be said that Genia was unaware of what her establishment had become, or that she was blind to the true nature of her boarders' activities. She appeared to accept it as frankly and uncritically as the rest of the neighborhood did. As far as she was concerned, it was of minor importance. What was of primary consideration was the fact that her roomers were unassuming, ordinarily well behaved, modest in their demands, *and*, most important of all, they

82

always paid on time. The neat, advancing columns of figures in the little dog-eared bankbook attested to that. There were other things about her guests that held her esteem. They took care of their own rooms and linen. They were always generous with a helping hand in the kitchen and at table whenever there was a rush on at mealtime. In a way she was really fond of them. She felt an unspoken sympathy for their lone and defenseless state, their air of simple gallantry in the precarious business of living in the world.

The truth of what had come about in the ugly frame house on Maple Street seeped gradually into the consciousness of Kingsmont. At no point was there an opportunity for a sense of outrage to develop. Anyway, it was much easier to allow such things to remain, out of mind as they were conveniently out of sight down in Jamaica Town. After all, what else could be expected? Down there among all those darkies and foreigners! One couldn't be surprised at anything. Then too, you didn't have to do anything about something you did not admit existed—that is, in public. Privately, if you were a man, you guffawed among some of the boys and recalled the haymow and back-barn lusts of your youth. In a way it even provided you with a sneaking sense of assurance that your world was not so small and rigid that it could not afford at least one or two of the attributes of Babylon.

As for the young bucks of the town, the farmers' and tradesmen's sons in the sad daring and violence of late adolescence, a visit down to Maple Street on a Saturday night, conducted usually in an atmosphere of whisky bravado, constituted a sort of shamefaced accolade of swaggering adventure, a last cry of defiance from whatever little measure of hot blood they possessed to the gulfing amenities and platitudes that awaited them in the geographical and spiritual confines of Kingsmont's horizons. No matter what these episodes resulted in for each of them, what dark disappointment or what discovery about themselves, their pride invested it with all the trappings of an Oriental debauch. In thus telling it the wild and hungry pride that had driven most of them to Maple Street in the first place seemed somehow assuaged.

Now all this had by no means been ignored by those citadels and adornments of society, the ladies of the town—no matter how humble or how exalted their position in the hierarchy of respectability. Most of them became fully aware of it sooner or later. They discussed it with one another, subtly and indirectly, to be sure, but with a finely relished indignation and horror. Since it did not touch them but, on the contrary, furnished them with an unfailing opportunity for self-congratulation, they went no further than private exclamations among themselves. On one occasion only did they ever feel moved to act positively. It was Sonie who, early and innocently, provided them with cause. Typically, she would have loved knowing that she had their attention. There were innumerable little hushed conversations that broke out in the meetings of church societies or in the parlors on Hill and Elm streets. They were all similar.

"That *place* down in Jamaica Town, you know—I understand there's a child, a mere·babe, living in it."

"My dear, it's absolutely true—poor little thing with all of those dreadful women!"

"It's simply awful! She can't help being corrupted. My Amanda says she's in the fourth grade at the Peters Street school, and that little Martha Rosen saw the little thing engaged in a regular sidewalk battle with some of those rough little mill children."

"We *really* ought to do something about it, you know."

"Can you imagine a woman with any feeling allowing such a thing to happen to her child? I don't care to what extremities she has been driven, she must be a perfect monster of iniquity!"

"I think it's our duty—I really do. We ought to make up a committee and go see Reverend Harris before it's too late. He's a man of God and he ought to do *something*. See that poor babe is taken away from those women and placed in some charitable institution where she would at least have Christian surroundings!"

Thus they would proceed in an atmosphere distinguished by sentimental clichés. However, only once did any of it succeed in focusing an attack on Genia Lipik's fortress, and even then it proved an abortive effort.

In the spring that Sonie was twelve the representative of a missionary temperance society appeared in town to conduct meetings on the hospitable premises of the Methodist church. The representative in this case was female, a stern-faced, craggy woman who wore pince-nez and spoke in a ringing, nasal voice with a kind of overpowering refinement of tone. The ladies of the town were fascinated by her. They flocked to her lectures in the afternoon. There she told them of her adventures in the slums of New York and Chicago and flashed a lurid series of lantern slides on a sheet. These sessions invariably ended with a passionate and evangelical exhortation the burden of which was that it was up to womanhood to deliver the world from the clutches of alcohol. So successful was she that early in her stay she bound to her, in a hysteria of dedication, a select band of the town's ladies. Captained by the temperance lady, this intrepid band set forth to do battle. For five days they embarrassed Kingsmont with their activities. Uniformly and funereally clothed in their most sumptuous black, they conducted highly emotional and impromptu "salvation meetings" at a series of strategic points about the town. Their husbands and families were helpless while the frenzy was upon them. They were so strongly armored in

84

self-righteousness that the mildest and most tentative protests from husbands, sons, or brothers only produced more intensely martyred attitudes.

At first Kingsmont's three saloons received the brunt of the attack. A pall was cast over these normally genial masculine premises by the daily descent of the formidable little army of females. Upon arrival the ladies would raise their voices in thin and doleful hymns. They knelt embarrassingly in the sawdust on the floors, their faces strained upward in saintly attitudes toward the embossed tin ceilings. Meanwhile the temperance lady, in her flat, refined Yankee voice, invoked the mercies of the Deity. The saloons, however, soon provided too limited a field for the enthusiasm of the crusaders. They daringly invaded Jamaica. Particularly they directed their attention to the factory yards around noon. There they invoked the dubious mercies of an angry God upon the astonished white and black workers where they leaned in the doorways or squatted against the brick sides of the buildings, munching their fat back and corn bread and drinking innocent buttermilk.

It was on their way home from one of these sorties into the factory yards that the ladies paused one early afternoon on the sidewalk at the foot of Genia Lipik's front steps. Dinner was almost ready and the house was quiet. There was only a subdued clatter in the region of the kitchen and dining room. Sonie, just in from school, was upstairs in Mrs. Lily Mark's room, visiting. Mrs. Lily's windows opened on the street and the stiffly starched lace curtains stirred diffidently in a lazy spring breeze. Mrs. Lily, half-reclining, freshly powdered and corseted, on her bed, was buffing her nails and keeping half an indulgent eye on Sonie. Sonie stood preening herself before Mrs. Lily's dresser mirror. She was engaged in one of her favorite occupations of the moment—investigating with delight the contents of one of the jewelry boxes possessed by Mama's roomers. She had just put a pair of elaborate earrings in her newly pierced ears. Striking various fancy attitudes, she regarded her reflection in the mirror with affection. Suddenly from outside there arose a thin, concerted wailing, an anemic and protesting sound of soprano torment:

"Wash us clean, dear Say-vee-or,
  Wash us with Thy blo-o-od!
Bring the lowly sin-n-ner
  Where Thy feet have sto-o-od.
Wash us clean, dear Say-vee-or, wash us wholly cle-an,
  Bring us to the glo-ree . . . "

Sonie and Mrs. Lily looked wide-eyed at each other and rushed for the window. Brushing the curtain aside impatiently, Sonie could

85

just see a group of upturned faces over the edge of the porch roof. The eyes were closed, the mouths open. They appeared framed in black: black hats, black dresses, black gloves—in fact, black everything! And they weren't all old ladies either, Sonie observed swiftly, and added, characteristically, for future reference: Black is the ugliest color there is. I'll *never* wear black even when I'm dead. From the window the group below looked like a bed of nightmare flowers sprung up abruptly from the red brick of the sidewalk. Sonie gazed upon them with fascination. As she watched, a group of the neighborhood children gathered along the opposite side of the street. There they began to make horrible faces and to caper fantastically. In a moment they were joined by a group of the big boys who hung around the livery. They snickered openly as they watched. Sonie's quick green eyes narrowed and she grinned to herself derisively. She heard footsteps on the Vitchek front porch next door. Faces began to appear in the dark, open holes in the Negro shacks down the way.

"For goodness' sake!" breathed Mrs. Lily, gazing avidly, "Whatever in this wide world—"

At that moment the door burst open behind them. Mrs. Pearl, her hair half-done and her mouth full of pins, and Mrs. Rose, wheezing, her washed-out blue eyes wide-open, burst in. They crowded to the other window.

"My heavens, Lily," Mrs. Rose said hoarsely, "what is it?"

"Don't ask me!" tittered Mrs. Lily over Sonie's head.

"Why, it's them salvation ladies we been hearin' about," said Mrs. Pearl through her pins. Then they all three giggled nervously as the wailing swelled outside. Then it ended as suddenly as it had begun. In the abrupt silence Sonie heard the kitchen door slam below. (Mama always slammed every door in the house behind her.) There followed the hard quick sound of her mother's heels coming to the front door. Bang! went the screen door. In a moment she heard Genia's voice on the porch, sharp, breathless, and a little distracted as always:

"What iss, pliss, ladees? What iss!"

The tallest and plainest of the black figures on the sidewalk—the one with the hideous hat that wobbled and with the glasses pinched high on her nose—detached herself from the group and mounted two of the porch steps. There she paused and raised one black-alpaca-clad arm in a slow portentous gesture.

"Dear sister!" she cried toward the porch in a harsh and domineering voice. "Dear sister, come down from this house of sin and shame and pray with us. The Lamb is all-merciful. Let Him make your soul and your house be clean—"

Genia's voice interrupted plaintively:

"What you say? My house dirty? What you want, pliss, wit' my house?"

"Oh, dear sister, come—bring the innocent child out of the black sin of this wicked house. Come before it is too late and the wrath of Jehovah is visited upon you and yours. Suffer the little children, saith the Book. Bring out the sweet child and let Jesus put His arms about you both and save you!"

"What you say now?" Genia's voice was rising shrilly. "You mean this house a bad house? You make for trobble, eh? My house is good house—costing t'ree thousand dollar, all paid for. I'm keeping it fine yat—I'm not needing halp from nobody, pliss! An' what you mean about my lit' girl, eh? She all right—she does good at school, so what now? I'm not complaining, she's not complaining, so what you want? Go away, pliss! I'm good woman—I pay the taxes on time—I want no trobble. . . . I call poleece, I gat lawyer. Pliss, queek, you go!"

"Dear sister, the Lamb is all-loving," the lady on the steps began intoning patiently. She got no further. Her voice was drowned in a screaming torrent of Polish from Genia. Its force was so overwhelming that it appeared to paralyze the group on the sidewalk. They froze in ludicrous attitudes of dismay. The lady on the steps started to raise her black arm again. But this action was never completed. Instead she beat a hasty and awkward retreat down the steps before Genia's advance. And advance Genia did. Craning her head outward, Sonie could see the top of her mother's agitated head, blazing and untidy as usual. In one hand Genia held a big saucepan. Evidently she had not stopped to put it down when she was interrupted in the kitchen by this visitation. She brandished it now in wide sweeping arcs over the heads of the women on the sidewalk. Under the dire threat of this weapon, Genia's visitors hesitated briefly, clutching briefly at a vanishing nobility. Then as Genia's voice rose even higher and the pan swung out over them in a particularly threatening gesture they broke with little shrieks of fright and departed precipitately down the street in disorder.

Genia's imprecations pursued this rout with undiminished fervor, full-voiced. It continued until they were well out of sight around the corner of the warehouse on Trent Street. Then it ceased. Once more she brandished the pan, muttering to herself. Then with a supremely final and contemptuous gesture she spat on the sidewalk in the geographic center of the spot lately occupied by the visitors. Then she went back into the house. Her voice rose again as she went. The doors slammed like exclamation points marking her progress back to the kitchen. There they could hear her continuing indignantly to herself, banging the pots and pans in angry emphasis. Mrs. Lily drew her head back into the room with a snort.

"Mercy!" she gasped. "Well now, I really *do* declare!" Sonie looked from her to Mrs. Rose and Mrs. Pearl. Mrs Pearl took the hairpins out of her mouth and they all grinned suddenly and warmly at one another with an air of secret triumph.

This encounter with Genia proved both climax and deathblow for the reform movement. The blight of religious fervor, the scenes of public martyrdom, vanished overnight. A gale of ridicule briefly rocked the town. The local ladies disappeared abruptly from the public scene while the storm of laughter blew itself out. The temperance representative departed for fresher fields in an atmosphere of frigid amenities. No one was fooled, and everyone who was not immediately involved enjoyed it shamelessly and thoroughly. In returning to their comfortable haunts the men were filled with a vast sense of relief and a profound, if secret, respect for Genia Lipik. That damned little 'Krainian woman could sure stand on her own two feet all right!

By this one act Genia earned for herself and her establishment a permanent indulgence from Kingsmont. Never again during her lifetime was she troubled with any open hostility or interference.

2

It was in this half-world, threaded by alleys and back streets, forever closed about with factory and warehouse as though the open world of forest and field and stream did not press upon it on all sides —it was in this corner of a sleepy and landlocked island, set off by invisible boundaries, and soaked deeply in the rich smell of tobacco, that Sonie Lipik grew up. For her the boundaries did not exist. She had no ability to feel that she was set off or had any fewer privileges in the business of living than the rest of humanity. She relished every moment of the rough-and-tumble, the garish sprawling, the unexpected excitement. The circumstances peculiar to her home provided her with an oddly sophisticated environment in which to flower. Life had held no mysteries from the beginning. It only produced an endless succession of incidents and people. She had an insatiable appetite for everything, and she had in her small, quick body a boundless store of energy and laughter with which to satisfy that appetite. Nothing was too great or too small to be worthy of her notice. She discovered early that she had the ability to attract and hold attention merely by her presence. This unerring appreciation for the theatrical in any situation she exploited to the full, frankly and with enormous ability. Almost from the beginning she was allowed free rein. She took advantage of every circumstance and she did it knowingly. She was spoiled, and she knew that too.

Between her and Genia there existed a haphazard relationship

88

not marked by any great degree of affection on either side. But underneath there was a solid mutual respect. Genia, preoccupied, immersed in her private battle with insecurity, let her daughter grow up pretty much as she pleased. It was not that Sonie lacked affection. She had it from all sides. The boarders, those childless and derelict women, lavished affection and attention on her. It was as though she had several mothers instead of one. They petted her and scolded her. They showered her with little gifts of castoff finery, dressed her up like a doll, taught her little songs, and provided an unfailingly appreciative audience. Once home from the bondage of school, Sonie was forever in and out of their rooms, observing their toilets, asking them innumerable questions about the world beyond Kingsmont. In addition she was always running on dozens of little errands for them up in town.

With the children in her school she was at once their most imperious and most interesting companion. They never knew what she would turn up being and doing next, or what wild tale she would have to regale them with. She feared no one, and if she encountered teasing or bullying she was quite capable of changing into a spitting, biting, scratching fury that earned for her the profound respect of all her associates. It was not a gentle world, but Sonie did not expect it to be. She was not pretty like some of the limpid-eyed, soft-bodied little 'Krainian girls who lived about her. In fact she was scrawny and ugly. But she had something beyond exterior beauty that made every eye turn to look at her with a sort of grudging admiration. One moment she could be artfully feminine and glowing and the next yelling capable vituperation. She knew she was different; she knew that she could take care of herself, and that knowledge was like a flaunted banner in her slant green eyes, in the broad expressive mouth, in the fiery tumble of her hair.

And so in the geography of Kingsmont and Maple Street, the space bounded by warehouse and livery stable and railroad track, the world of factory workers and the smell of greasy cooking and the back entrances to saloons uptown, of drying wash and cheap perfume—the world that included the school on Peters Street, where they let her be Columbia in the Columbus Day celebration, and the vacant lot next door, where she played under the pawlonia and the single struggling chinaberry tree with the other children—both white and black—Sonie Lipik grew up, resourceful, self-reliant, on her own two feet, looking out upon the universe with eager speculation.

She was shrewdly cautious, but she had a hard head and was utterly fearless. Early she exhibited a sharp gift for mimicry, which, together with her love of strong color in her dress, was shamelessly encouraged by Genia's ladies. They screamed with delight when she was showing them how old Mr. Duncan, the school principal, waddled when he walked. They also squealed and hugged her delightedly when she revealed one of their own foibles and mannerisms transfixed for them in brilliant pantomime. There was no doubt about it in their minds that Sonie was made for bigger and better things than Maple Street. They vied in tutoring her out of their own checkered experiences and histories. Mrs. Lily, the scrawny one with a cast in her eye and a foolish sad grin, taught her to play a decrepit banjo. All of them contributed to an enormous repertory of songs and sentimental ballads recalled from long-defunct traveling companies and forgotten music halls. Sonie was a deceptively pliable and voracious pupil. She thrived on this lavish and loving attention, but she always managed to pull away and declare herself in no uncertain terms when things did not go to suit her. One season the ladies devoted themselves to teaching her something they broadly termed "manners." Among other arbitrary procedures this called for sitting straight in one's chair, eating one's food in tiny mincing bites, and talking in a high, mannered voice. Sonie submitted so placidly to this new and radical instruction that after a while even Genia began to examine her curiously. One day she came screaming down Maple Street, fresh from school, her cheeks flaming with high spirits, her red hair flying and disheveled. She flung herself breathless and laughing on the front porch right at Mrs. Rose's feet, and began to squeal and kick her heels on the floor.

"Why, honey!" cried Mrs. Rose in alarm, panting up out of the chair. "What on earth's the matter with you?"

Sonie flung her arms wide in delight and grinned at the ceiling.

"I raced Tony Griton," Sonie said breathlessly, her child's voice already clouded with the soft hoarseness that was to characterize it all her life. "I bet him a pencil I could beat him home an' I did, I *did*, I DID!" Mrs. Rose looked shocked.

"Honey," she said, "honey, get up off that floor this minute and stop makin' that awful noise. After all the things Mrs. Pearl an' I've been tellin' you. Well, honey, did you hear me? Don' you want to be a *lady*, now?"

Sonie shrieked again. She sat up suddenly hugging her bare knees, not even trying to pull down her petticoats.

"No, Mis' Rose—I don' wanta be a lady—I jus' wanta be *somebody!*"

She leapt to her feet and flew into the house laughing, banging the door behind her and singing mockingly: "My mother was a lay—dee!" as she ran loudly up the stairs.

But that was Sonie. They couldn't hold it against her. They loved her far too well to hold anything against her.

Genia was the only one for whom the precocious, knowing child ever showed any awe or respect. When Sonie got to queening it

90

about the house too blatantly, or when her attitude became too elaborate after some success in the parlor or dining room, she would find herself suddenly in the hallway confronted by Genia. There would be a moment of silence while Genia swept her with the sharp, distracted glance. Then the older woman would say:

"Ach! What iss on the face now, Sonya—eh?"

Sonie would bridle defensively for a moment, then shrug. Unconsciously she had already begun to imitate both her mother's tone and attitude.

"Ach, Mama, it's nothin'! Just a little cheek rouge. Mrs. Ella let me put it on me."

"Washing it off with the soap then right avay now, queek!"

"Ach, Mama!"

But she would go and do it. And without resentment. She knew that the rest of her world, perhaps, could be shaped and handled as she saw fit, but not Genia's tired, detached glance. Genia would often say to her as though she were stating a perfectly reasonable fact:

"It is hard thing, Sonie, to keep from looking like the fool when one gats old. Why you gotta start before you have to, eh? Someday, Sonie, you get to theenk you too big for how you belong—then you won' gat the leetle slap to tal' you—you jus' gat the beeg slap, an' then you be sorry!"

Aside from these encounters with her mother she let no one tell her how to conduct her life. The gibes and attention she attracted from all sides she accepted as homage due. Rather than resenting it she adored the excitement. Even if it ended—as it often did—in a physical encounter. When she went uptown on errands for her mother or one of the boarders, to buy some thread or liniment or to get a pail of beer, she was not afraid of the comment from the male idlers about the stores and the saloons. She had a quick, free tongue and could exchange gibe for gibe. She knew that they admired her profoundly. Her appearance represented a note of utter and untrammeled freedom among them. They, all of them, had to subscribe to some sort of code or caste which bound them in an arbitrary pattern willy-nilly. Sonie had no precedent to live up to. She was as free as a bird.

The foreordained, the inevitable, happened just after Sonie was sixteen. Although there had been no dearth of material for Genia's darkest conjecture long before that, it was not, surprisingly enough, one of the local males. From the time Sonie turned fourteen, those who had fought with her at the school or climbed trees and scaled fences, together with those who had merely engaged in verbal passages with her, the older men at the saloon and the young men about the livery stable, began to regard her with entirely different eyes.

Sonie's tense and vibrant little body suddenly blossomed. It flaunted itself as boldly and frankly as the gaiety of her apparel. On the slim stalk of her person appeared a generous bosom, almost incongruous in its proportions. But it was undeniably beautiful. It made her look distractingly attractive and appetizing even when she was chastely buttoned clean up under her chin. Her skin was translucent in its dazzling whiteness. This was in contrast to her hair, which had always been beautiful, like a banner, and the secret, oblique set of her rather small green eyes added up to a sum that spelled violent turmoil and savage frustration in a whole wake of males, old and young, who now spun about her. They crowded her, importuned her, wagered shamelessly among themselves. Which of them would have her first? She swam through them with a mocking air of triumph, treating them all impartially with the same spirit of rough give-and-take. Provocatively she acted as though she were blandly unaware of any change in either them or herself. On Saturday evenings the parlor and front porch would be so crowded with Sonie's admirers that Genia had to keep her in the kitchen or send her uptown to keep from seriously interfering with the normal procedure of the house. However, never had things prospered so well for all of them. Sonie knew this as well as Genia. Whenever Genia would haul her out to the kitchen, hissing fiercely at her for being a little fool, Sonie would look back levelly and mockingly at her mother. They both knew that the men who came to see Sonie remained, defeated, to go upstairs finally with Mrs. Rose or Mrs. Pearl or one of the others.

This does not mean that Sonie commanded nothing but a wolfish slavering or had become merely a walking aphrodisiac. There were those among the youths and men who besieged her desperately to enter an honorable state with them on any terms. Sturdy Willie Vitchek, the eldest of the sons in the house next door, was a good, solid boy. He had a good steady job in the boiler room at the Pendleton factory. Together with his friend Johnny Weiss, who was doing well at Graham's feed store, he besought her patiently and continually from the fringes of the crowd. It was as though by stubbornness and persistence alone and the best intentions in the world the two boys believed they could finally break through to her. Willie climaxed his silent courtship by taking Sonie to ride in the most expensive rig from Weller's livery—the surrey with the yellow tassels and the red spokes—on three consecutive Sundays. His mother and sister were so outraged at this extravagance that they refused to speak to Genia or Sonie for a month. Sonie went, and loved it. But it did Willie no good in his suit. When Willie came back after the third fruitless outing he and Johnny Weiss went down to the Soldier's Saloon and got very drunk. Then they took themselves off somewhere behind the warehouses and solemnly and savagely beat each other up so badly that both of them were absent from their jobs for nearly a week.

No. When the inevitable happened, it was, on the face of it, banal and shoddy. Not like Sonie at all. It was not because she lacked more exciting and rewarding opportunities. But there is no law operating finally in these things. They are done. Sonie's doing had more object in it than most—at least from Sonie's standpoint.

He was an ugly, loud-voiced little drummer representing a wholesale hardware house in Chicago. His clothes were cheap and flashy, as were his loud laugh, his black-button eyes. He obviously considered himself a devil with the ladies. He kept Genia's parlor in an uproar with his tales and off-color verses and songs. He also kept both button eyes cocked upon Sonie from the moment she came into sight. The two of them engaged in acid and continual warfare. Sonie, on her part, was openly scornful. So much so that Genia finally yanked her upstairs and told her to hold onto her tongue or she would lock her in. Sonie played meek, but when he left it was discovered that Sonie had left too. Gone also was Genia's old portmanteau from under the bed, together with a considerable wardrobe. Sonie left behind her a brief and cryptic note. Mrs. Rose read it in a tragic and trembling voice to Genia and the household:

> Dear Mama,
> I have gone to New York now with Mr. Edwards.
> Respectfully,
> Sonia Lipik

Genia immediately set up a loud cry and sat—as she very rarely did—in one of the green-plush chairs in her parlor, moaning and rocking herself. The ladies plied her with handkerchief and sounds of sympathy to no avail. It became apparent almost immediately that Genia's display of emotion was not governed by the profound anxiety of a mother for the safety of her daughter's physical or moral person.

"Aieee!" Genia wailed. "Going off now with the beeg market opening next week yat! All the peoples coming, all the beezness—an' me with no help in the kitchen. She shouldn't have done it with me. Aieee!"

Mrs. Rose sniffled into her handkerchief over Genia's head. She stared dewily at the others.

"The poor young thing—an' she don't know one single little thing about life. She'll find out, though—I can tell you—the *hard* way —the poor young thing!"

They all nodded direfully and solemnly at each other. Genia let out another wail. She yanked at her hair. A strand of it came loose and fell over her face.

"I'm hoping she's gatting the beeg slap now!" screamed Genia. "I'm telling her all the time she's gonna gat it. Aieee! I'm giving it to her myself when she come home!"

Two weeks later Sonie walked into the house at noon, just before dinner. She had evidently come in on the twelve-o'clock train from Richmond. No one asked. She was blatantly empty-handed, but she wore, somewhat travel-stained, a smart outfit that bore the mark of more sophisticated centers than Kingsmont. She offered no explanations nor did her attitude reflect either defiance or regret. There was, however, in her usual matter-of-fact, straightforward bearing an indefinable note of newly acquired poise. It was as though she had received at last some sort of answer to a question that had long been bothering her. Mama's ladies engulfed her in cries of welcome. They surrounded her with a babble of curiosity. It was cut off abruptly by Genia's appearance, pot in hand, from the kitchen. She and Sonie looked at each other briefly.

"Coming to the kitchen, Sonie," said Genia flatly. She turned and went out. Sonie grinned briefly, the wide, big-mouthed grin, and followed her mother. The ladies huddled, whispering and giggling, in the parlor. Listening, half-fearfully, they heard the long crescendoing scream of Genia's voice above a tumultuous, emotional clatter of cooking ware. It died away at last.

At dinner Sonie appeared washed and scrubbed. As usual, she served at table, her face a mocking mask of meekness and self-pity, the slant green eyes sparkling with secret laughter. And that was the end of it. No amount of oblique and persistent questioning, no bribery on the part of the ladies when they lured her to the privacy of their rooms, was able to extract one morsel of information concerning her recent experience. Whatever she had done or seen or learned she chose to keep to herslf. But now they no longer treated her like a child. A subtle difference in their attitude toward her began to appear. Their conversations and exchanges with her became full of innuendoes. They resorted to an air of camaraderie as though what she had done had moved her into the circle of those who knew about life. Life, endowed in their minds and in their speech with a special and mysterious capital *L*. Sonie simply grinned maliciously out of her ugly, attractive little face and went on energetically saying nothing and enjoying herself. She observed more carefully now the world beyond Maple Street. That world which encompassed the big houses, the town's big names, those other girls, now removed to a more rarefied and separate world. No rancor and resentment at the ease and security that accompanied their movements about their world, but with an air of candid interest and something like mock-

94

ing pity. Sonie envied nothing about them except the *kind* of attention *they* could command. She observed their actions carefully. And what she saw she salted away for future use.

During a particularly merciless and damp winter following the escapade of Sonie, Genia fell ill. Doc Saunders, the unkempt old reprobate who administered blasphemously to the ills and physical misfortunes of Jamaica Town, diagnosed it as pneumonia. For the first time in the fifteen years that she had dwelt in Kingsmont, fifteen years of relentless slavery in the service of her demons of avarice and insecurity, Genia was confined to bed and given up for lost. But the tight, fanatic energy that had seen her through so much enabled her to survive even this. But the effort cost her a great deal. When the struggle was over she was left emaciated and skeletal, confined to her room with a terrible, racking cough. This did not prevent her from watching jealously over Maple House and its occupants and activities like a worn spider at the center of her web. Sonie now became Genia's legs and arms and eyes. Scarcely more than a child, she took over the running of the establishment with a gusto that surprised no one. Overnight she ceased to be simply self-willed and indulged. She became at once a strong-willed resourceful young woman commanding respect and attention that had nothing to do with her years. It was no time at all before the household was taking all crises and disputes directly to Sonie's arbitration and judgment instead of to the ill and wasted little woman upstairs. If anyone ever considered taking advantage of the situation, he was soon rudely disillusioned. The slant-eyed girl revealed qualities of shrewdness and sharp dealing that allowed no nonsense. She permitted Mrs. Rose (the senior of the quintet of permanent residents) to help her in the chores of running the house, but all final decisions were referred to her. The fact that they were all years older and thought of her as a child inhibited her not a bit. She ordered them peremptorily about. She cajoled and pacified them as specifically and adamantly as Genia herself had ever done. All those years, she had missed nothing that would stand her in good stead now. She was as good a cook as her mother and her liking and talent for meeting and dealing with people made the little world of Maple House run with even greater ease and success than ever.

With Genia's physical removal from the picture, mother and daughter found themselves drawn together in an intimacy and understanding they had never enjoyed before. Genia leaned desperately upon her daughter now, and Sonie returned the confidence with tenderness. Several times a day Sonie ran upstairs to go through the form of referring a decision to Genia. It was a gesture of pure tact designed to keep the sick woman feeling alive and necessary. Any real decision would have already long been made and put into action. Every evening, when the house lay finally quiet and the world outside shrouded in dark and sleep with no sound but the thud of a hoof on the wooden floor of the livery a few yards away or the wail and clatter of the late freight passing on the tracks beyond the warehouses, Sonie would come into their room. While she undressed and made ready for bed, she would relate carefully and patiently in detail all the happenings of the day. The tense and sleepless little figure under the covers in the big oak bed watched her. Genia's black eyes stared out of her face, little and gaunt like a monkey's.

"Sonie," she would say every night during Sonie's preparations for bed, "Sonie, the house and the land—they'll take it from you if they can yat. Don' lat them, pliss, *pliss!* You be alone in the world without food for your mouth or a roof for your head, poor child. Aieee!" And Genia would begin to moan and babble and rock her head terribly upon the pillow.

"Now, Mama, you know nobody's going to get this house away from me. I'm lookin' after it fine."

"But you run off again one these days an' leaving me all alone. Then *they* come and gat it from me an' I'm lying in the bed a sick woman an' alone." Genia would begin to whimper. "Don' leave me, Sonie, don' leave me!" Sonie, combing her blazing hair at the dresser with long loving strokes, would answer calmly: "Now, Mama, what are you talking about? You know I wouldn't leave this house or you for anything. Where would I go?"

But her slant green eyes would catch the image of herself in the mirror floating goldenly in the light of the oil lamp. It formed little flames about her head as she stroked the hair; it glossed the white roundness of her breasts and shoulders flowering above her corset. There was her whole body inexhaustibly alive with youth as though poised to leap laughing into space. And a shrewd and secret look would come into the slant eyes turned away from Genia, and the big mouth would assume a deep curl at its corners.

Sonie stayed. She stayed even after Genia had been buried fittingly in the cemetery up Judson Street in a plot of ground adjacent to the grave of the lady boarder who had been interred some years before. It gave Sonie a comfortable feeling that the two of them must be having an endless gossip over some other worldly boarding-house. Somehow she could not imagine her mother being comfortable and happy under any other circumstances.

Sonie stayed in Kingsmont for reasons that had nothing to do now with her comparative prosperity. Partly it was because of habit. A sort of inertia becalmed her with Genia's death. But long after this feeling had disappeared she stayed on. At market time the following fall, in the dim exciting haze, in the heat and sweat, the clamor of the auction floor, she looked up across a row of golden cured tobacco waiting on baskets, and her eyes met head-on the black and storm-ridden ones of Brant Royle.

3

For perhaps a half-hour longer she moved with the jostling, friendly crowd opposite the auctioneer and the buyers, never once returning the look that had discovered him on the other side. Her emotion was one of excitement strangely mixed with antagonism. She resented the force of that dark and violent gaze leaping out upon her from the group beyond. It was fierce, lone, and in some way she could not fathom, challenging. It disturbed her. It made her presence automatic. She was no longer aware of the familiar din. She moved and answered talk about her without thinking what she said, and without knowing or caring what she had said after she had said it. It was an entirely new sensation for Sonie. At the turn of a row she stopped and pulled Lydia Vitchek to one side, letting the crowd amble by them.

"Lydia, who is that big black ugly-looking fellow over there?"

"For heaven's sake, Sonie," whined Lydia. "Which one do you mean? There must be a hundred."

And then Lydia tittered nervously as though Sonie had made a joke. She was afraid of Sonie.

"The biggest one of them, Lydia. He's walking behind Aaron Hartwell now."

Lydia peered, her face goggling forward in the helpless near-sighted way that Sonie found distinctly irritating.

"Oh, *that* one! Don't tell me you don't know who *he* is. That's that awful Brant Royle. He's back in town again."

Lydia bridled and peered at Sonie as though she expected some comment. Sonie was silent. Her face was expressionless as she adjusted the hang of the gold circle in her left ear. Why, thought Lydia, she isn't even looking at the man! The green eyes were half-closed, staring at the maze of beams above them. Lydia hesitated for a moment, giggled uncertainly. Then she skipped off awkwardly to catch up with the slowly moving crowd.

Brant Royle. Of course that was who it was. She should have known. She knew about him, had seen him, a legendary figure, walking at a distance, many times before. But it seemed now, suddenly, as though she were seeing him for the first time. In some way the thought irritated her. She shrugged. What difference did it make? Not any at all as far as she could see. But he had looked at her. He had kept on looking at her. But then she was accustomed to having men look at her. She expected it. This was just another man, and a

97

sour brute of a man at that. Why should she feel as though she had been challenged in a special way? She shrugged again. Someone called her name from a group that was passing.

"Hi, Sonie, who you waitin' for?"

It was Arthur Tyree, son of the druggist. She had known him since school and he was a rather regular visitor to Maple House. Sonie grinned.

"What difference would it make to you, Art?"

"Sonie, you *are* a card. Always the last word, eh, Sonie!"

They jostled around her laughing, a group of the familiar faces, all male.

"You call that a last word, Art?"

They roared appreciation and she allowed herself to be swept back on the floor with them. It was all friendly. She felt herself going along with the crowd unthinking. At the top of the row near the big, gaping entrance upon the street, she detached herself, exchanging a gibe or two in the friendly caustic way that they expected of her. Somehow they seemed unbearably thin and tasteless to her. She felt that she had to get clear of them for a while.

There were people milling in and out from the street. She picked her way easily through them. In the door she stopped dead. At one side, apart and alone, stood Brant Royle, and he was looking at her with that lowering, half-angry, half-challenging gaze. Sonie looked coolly back at him this time, her head high, unafraid, her hands on her hips, a mocking, questioning smile on her wide mouth. Suddenly he smiled at her. He walked over. His head and shoulders plowed him through the crowd like a giant among a lesser and frailer breed. At her side he stood looking down at her for a moment. Sonie's gaze did not falter. He removed his hat, revealing the full, vigorous tumble of black hair. It was a commanding head, Sonie thought instantly, a really magnificent head in many ways. And he was not so ugly. She realized that the face, with its stormy torment, its bare violence and energy, looking down at her was not only handsome but one she would never forget. There was a fleeting look of sadness in the half-smile that he bent upon her now.

"You're Sonie Lipik, aren't you?" he said quietly, directly. It did not bother her, that directness. Somehow it was no more than she had been expecting all the time.

"And you're Brant Royle."

He nodded, the strange half-smile coming and going on his face. The dark eyes, now that they were close to her, seemed sad and withdrawn.

"I guess I've been away from home too long," he said in the quiet booming bass. "Things have been happening around here, I see, since I left."

She accepted the compliment implied in this with her most characteristic gesture. She patted her glowing mass of hair with an air of ageless coquetry.

"Things do," she said. "Where have you been?"

"Richmond. Three years working on the Exchange."

"Richmond's a fine place," she said, "I was there once." He said nothing for a moment but stood looking into the street, ignoring the crowds that swept to and fro about them. Then he turned back to her suddenly.

"You've grown up, haven't you?" he said, looking slowly down from her face. It was a look she was used to and expected, but this time she felt her whole body brace and lean against his glance, frankly oblivious of the place, the time, the noonday roar of the warehouse.

"You didn't expect me to stand still," she said, the green eyes narrowed and mocking. "Can't say I remember what you looked like, or how you've changed—if you have."

She laughed suddenly, the hoarse, throaty, attractive little sound of amusement. He smiled back, the fleeting expression that was so at variance with the violence implicit in him, because it was somehow sad like the look in his eyes.

"I think I'm glad you've grown up, Sonie Lipik," he said. "I think you and me could get along."

"Much obliged," she mocked him. "Honored, I'm sure!"

"When can I call around and see you?"

"Any evenin' you like. I'm usually at home. If you don't know where that is, I think you'll be able to find out." She paused. "In fact, I'll be at home this evenin', I think."

"Thanks," he said, almost harshly, the smile gone, his face dark and preoccupied again. "Not tonight. But I'll be around sometime." And giving her one last look, he turned abruptly and plowed back through the crowd into the warehouse.

She stood waiting to feel angry while she was jostled and pushed by the slow herd of people moving in and out of the doorway. But she didn't feel angry. She laughed the hoarse laugh again once and stepped out into the street and started homeward. Never in all her life had she been so treated, and she found the experience not only novel, but full of a kind of vibrant excitement. She found herself smiling broadly as she walked along. The crowd, the heat, and the press and excitement of market opening, the season that she had always loved best, drifted past her forgotten. She heard, as from a great distance, the clamor of it, the strange, high-pitched wailing chant of the auctioneers, the cries of hawkers, the laughter, the clatter and rumble of the laden wagons down the street. Now it did not move her. She even forgot that she had intended getting a half-dozen more fryers for tomorrow's dinner. They were expecting a big crowd. She went directly home to Maple Street.

The house was empty. Everyone would still be uptown and it was an hour or so before dinner. She found Mrs. Rose, in a soiled dressing gown and cap, her generous bulk comfortably sagging in a rocker in the kitchen. That plump lady sat fanning herself futilely against the early September heat and superintending Jimmie, the black spidery Negress they had in to help at the cooking and serving during market time.

"Why, honey," said Mrs. Rose, her kindly face flushed with the heat, "what you doin' back so soon? You gave me quite a turn comin' bustin' in here like this."

"Mrs. Rose, what do you know about Brant Royle?"

Mrs. Rose stopped fanning her pendulous bosom.

"You mean that awful boy that used to make so much trouble around town? Why, honey, I haven't seen anything or heard anything of him in a long time, thank the Lawd! He went away, or they ran him out of town. I've forgot which."

"He's back in town now all right."

"Mercy, honey, I hope not! Because it'll mean trouble, unh-unh! He's rough and mean as a striped snake. Always gettin' himself and other folks into trouble. Course, I've never known him personally, if you know what I mean! He's never come down here that I could remember, an' neither me nor any of the girls ever associated with that rough, hell-raisin' type—"

"I've just been talkin' to him."

Mrs. Rose groaned and rolled her round, childish eyes.

"Well, don't do it again, honey, that's all I've got to say. He's pure poison from what I know."

"I'm not afraid of him," said Sonie calmly, examining the nails of her right hand. "I think I might even like him."

Mrs. Rose threw up her hands.

"Mercy, honey, I hope not! 'Course, it's none of my business, an' I wouldn't be one to interfere, but—"

"Now," said Sonie, "tell me all you know about him."

Mrs. Rose gulped, then leaned forward licking her lips with relish.

"Gawd, honey!"

During the succeeding days Sonie questioned all of them adamantly and relentlessly, garnering odd information and stories, apochryphal as well as what she could shrewdly recognize as truth. When she had drained her household dry, she asked casual and oblique questions of all the men—Jim Prentiss at the livery, Doc Saunders, even Alton Richardson, the cashier at the bank. Upon all

100

of this information she made no comment. She did not see Brant. She did not even seem interested in seeing the market out. She stayed away from it and its attendant excitement for the remainder of the week. It worried Mrs. Rose and Mrs. Lily and the rest of the house. They tried with all sorts of little blandishments to get her out. She was friendly and bullying, but she was not fooled. And they dared not interfere. They depended upon her too much. And they were all a little frightened of her now. She was not apathetic during this period. In fact, she seemed rather cheerful and more full of spirits than usual. But there was something a little too tense and over-wrought in her manner. They were extremely sensitive to it. It made them all nervous. The atmosphere of Maple House was vibrant with her poised waiting, unbearably suspended and taut.

But Brant did not come down to Maple Street, nor did Sonie lay eyes upon him until two weeks after that first brief meeting in the hot, crowded doorway of the warehouse.

It was late on a Tuesday evening. Sonie was out in the kitchen setting some bread to rise overnight. Mrs. Pearl, who had been en-tertaining a caller in the parlor, suddenly thrust her face in at the door. Mrs. Pearl's eyes were big and scared, the silly fringe of bangs over her wide powdered forehead seemed to stand on end.

"Sonie—honey," she faltered in a piercing whisper, "Sonie, I think there's someone at the front door to see you!"

And then her face popped back as though she were afraid to commit it to more. Sonie knew instantly. She did not, however, do as she was accustomed to do, call cheerfully to Mrs. Pearl: "Send him in, Mrs. Pearl!" or "What's the matter with him? Is he bashful? Tell him to come back here to the kitchen."

Instead she stood for a moment grinning the fine wide grin. Then she carefully covered the dough in the bowl with a cloth, rinsed her hands at the tap, patted her hair once, and opened the door into the front hallway. As she passed the parlor she heard a muted and breathless whispering from Mrs. Pearl, and then silence as she came to the open front door.

Beyond the screen he loomed gigantically, as she had known he would, a huge distinct outline in the darkness. She could just make out the pale smudge of his face, indistinct and blurred.

"Hello, Brant," she said. "Come in."

He did not answer for a long moment. Then he said with a deep rumble, slowly, almost carefully: "No, I can't come in there. I want to talk, Sonie. I can't talk in there."

She waited. But he was silent.

"All right," she said. She opened the screen door and stepped out on the dark porch beside him. He did not move and she could

not tell whether he was looking at her or not. She waited, feeling
excited, and mocking her excitement to herself. She wondered at the
unfamiliar passivity that had come over her. She could hear him
breathing slowly and heavily. He was bareheaded and in his shirt
sleeves and there was a faint, but unmistakable, aroma of whisky.
He had been drinking, but he was not drunk. At least not drunk in
a way she was accustomed to seeing. It was very still there in the
dark. The quiet she found appropriate. She did not mind standing
there waiting. Exhilarated and suspended, she felt that she could
wait till day came if necessary, without hurt or embarrassment. It
was he who must make the next move. He reached out and took her
roughly by the elbow. It hurt her, but she did not mind. She did not
wince. She felt the pain as something she had been awaiting and
now welcomed.

"Come on," he said. "Let's walk."

"Where are we going?"

"Nowhere. Just walk."

He started to move toward the steps, taking her with him. But
she pulled herself free of him and laughed.

"Must say politeness isn't your strong suit, Mr. Royle," she said.
"Wait a minute."

She could almost feel him glower in the dark.

"Nobody's makin' you come." His voice was sullen, withdrawn.

She laughed the throaty, hoarse little sound again. It indulged
him, but it had an edge on it. She felt a heady anger coming into
her excitement.

"Well, if you aren't as touchy and bad-tempered as a July mule!
I just wanted a minute so I could take off my apron. I don't fancy
myself walkin' out in public with it on. It's not my style at all."

He was silent while she untied it from about her trim waist with
deliberate movements and flung it into one of the porch rockers. She
straightened her dress, pulling the full flounces over her hips. Then
she patted her hair and stepped to him. He took her arm again and
they went down the steps in silence. He turned up toward the livery.
They walked past it and down into the dark tunnel of warehouses
beyond. He did not speak and neither did she. He strode forward
so violently into the darkness that she felt herself being almost pulled
with him. With her free hand she gathered up her skirts in front to
keep from tripping. Again she marveled at the unfamiliar passivity
in herself that allowed her to be hurried along without question or
protest by this rude stranger. And while she wondered in bemused
amazement at herself, he stopped along the blank black wall of wood
that rose beside them and, pulling her to him, kissed her.

Sonie was no ignorant child, and the act of kissing was neither a
mystery nor a curiosity to her. But no experience of that various and

102

pleasurable caress had ever been like this. There was no trace of tenderness in it. No giving or asking. It was like a blow, hard, hungry, direct. Even while she reeled under its impact she had a strange sense of loss. It did not include her. It merely used her mouth in assuaging itself. She was shocked by it beyond breath or protest. Never before had she been unequal to any man or to any occasion. She felt completely at a loss and was silent when he released her at last and stood looking down at her. Then he laughed, and the laugh somehow had in it all that she might have expected from the kiss.

"Sonie—Sonie," he said, and he reached forward and touched her face. It was a rough, hesitant gesture. She had no anger in herself for him at that moment. In her strange confusion and amazement she did not know what she felt. "Yeah—I think you an' me'll get along all right."

"You're not much of a by-your-leave fellow, are you?" she heard herself saying with some of her accustomed asperity.

He laughed, pleased. He sounded relaxed all of a sudden. "You suit me all right, even if you ain't no doll-baby."

"Well, you're no beauty yourself," she said crisply, "you big, black, stuck-up brute!" She slapped him then, a hard sudden blow on the cheek. He laughed again and caught the hand tightly and easily in his own. She was tense and furious, neither straining to or away from him, breathing hard. They stood looking through the space of darkness directly into each other's faces. Then she smiled, the sudden, wide smile. He answered it with the little crooked half-expression on his own full, closed lips.

"Come on," he said, and turned her down the street again.

As before, it did not occur to her to ask where they were going or why. She found herself merely waiting for his next move, braced and excited because she did not know what to expect from him now. She was still half angry and half curious. Whether because of her own actions or his she could not tell. But as they walked along, wrapped in silence, she knew with finality that she was caught up in him, bound by his strangeness and violence to clash against him, to crouch waiting always for his next move, to lash out at him in fury, to withdraw only to come back again to the thing she sensed in him and could not escape, the dark and plunging magnificence, the ruthless, blind drive toward a destiny she could not fathom, only feel. Here was a mettle at last equal to her own, dangerous, capable of wrecking itself and all that lay in its way. She had known it from the moment their eyes met in the golden clamor and gloom of the warehouse two weeks before. Maybe it was what she had been waiting for all her life. Now moving forward quietly in the darkness she could not tell whether she was happy or angry, or whether what she was feeling was not something akin to sadness.

The last black outline of warehouses dropped behind them and with it the thick, almost oppressive tang of tobacco. It gave way to a fresh clean smell of resin. Sonie realized with a little amazement that they were already passing the lumberyards. Why, they had walked over a mile already! Nothing but fields and woods lay beyond. But she did not pause or turn to Brant. She had not even glanced at him for a long time. Only felt him. All of him complete in the hard touch of his hand on her elbow.

The September night seemed to loom toward them, to envelop their lone advancing figures on the shadowed road. The brave chirruping of late crickets in the dry blackberry bushes along the way arose deafening in the stillness. The dark air was warm with just an edge of frost in it. Sonie felt it breathe sensuously along her face. The bitter scent of goldenrod and loam came up into her nostrils like something new and undiscovered.

Somehow she was not surprised when he stopped at the top of a little rise and turned to look back in the night toward the town. She could hear him breathing deeply and strongly by her side. His hand still held her tightly, cruelly, including her in the orbit of the mysterious emotion that possessed him. She waited, looking up at the dark head above her thrust heavily forward against the sky. It was a bullish and magnificent attitude that she was to grow accustomed to. She could divine nothing from the tense outline of those heavy features. They were directed against something away from him, beyond them both. He shivered suddenly and a sound broke out of him.

"Goddammit, look at it!" he whispered. It was an agonized hoarse ejaculation. "Asleep, *asleep* . . . shut up in itself, an' it doesn't even know it! The town, the land, the whole damn state—they've got it locked up like a hogpen, all of 'em. They won't let me in. I could do somethin' with it, I could make it belch fire for 'em. It belongs to me, to *me*, goddammit. I hate it, how I hate it. . . ." The whisper trailed away. For the first time in her life Sonie felt as though she were going to faint, a quick weakness in her knees and a thickening in her throat. She was almost surprised to hear her voice say calmly:

"Why did you come back, then? You didn't have to."

He swung her roughly to face him, his hands holding her helpless, arching body to his. Her head dropped back and his bent over it.

"I did have to come back," he whispered. "I always have to come back. I can't help it!"

His mouth came down upon hers again in the hard, devouring gesture of hunger and sadness. As the night reeled about her Sonie thought, He's crazy . . . crazy . . . but I don't care. He released

104

her mouth as abruptly as he had taken it, speaking again with his lips almost touching hers.

"An' I'll stay this time, Sonie. There's a way, an' I'll find it. Do you hear? I'll find it this time!" He shook her slowly and terribly, as though she were some instrument to hold and carry his meaning.

"Yes, yes," she whispered, not knowing or caring what he meant, drugged in his violence. "I know you will, Brant, I sure know you will."

Her hands came up slowly and clenched themselves upon the bare flesh of his big forearms. They stood locked and swaying like two opponents who had met in the dark of the roadway, staring blindly into each other's faces, their separate breathing coming quick and heavy above the little insect thunder that rose about them in the still night. Then his big hands began to move upon her, tearing at her body and her dress as he pulled her into the deeper shadow of the roadside.

It was accomplished there in the dark between them, less like a love-making than a passionate struggle. Each met the other as an equal physical entity, neither asking nor giving quarter, with no words or thought, direct, demanding, ruthless. Somehow Sonie had known this was the way it would be, and she gloried with all of her complete and animal honesty in accepting it. It was no time to weigh and question meanings. There was no meaning other than the act and the moment. Later there would be plenty of time.

He lay at last breathing deeply and quietly in the grass at her side, withdrawn, with a kind of gentleness and gratitude in his stillness. Sonie lay silent, too, her intelligence and good humor stirring to life through her body's drunken content. Now that it was done she did not know exactly what she expected of either herself or him. Certainly not a fumbling, shamefaced protestation. She was glad of his silence, and yet there was something in it that piqued her. There was more in this for her than the simple meeting and appeasing of hunger. Just what it was she could not define at the moment. But what about him? Could she be in love at last with this dark, crude stranger upon whom she had laid eyes but twice before? No. That was too easily said. It explained nothing. As she lay there, intensely aware of him yet cut off from him, she was profoundly puzzled and annoyed with herself. And at the core of her annoyance there was the same little aching sense of loss that she had experienced when he had turned her to him and kissed her under the dark shadow of the warehouse wall. Why did she find herself now lying at the side of a country road like any silly, addleheaded bitch pulled under a hedge in a spring night? She, Sonie Lipik, the smart little girl who lived on Maple Street and thought she knew everything? Well, she didn't have to stay, did she? She could just get up and go any time she

105

liked. Neither *he* nor anyone else could stop her. But she wouldn't go. She knew that now. She was held by the thing that she could not name. It had held her from the first, the sense of mystery and power and excitement in this man. Oh, you're sure a big fool, she thought, a big fool!

She sat up and began to put her disheveled hair into place. Her dress, she thought ruefully, was going to look a sight after wallowing in the dew. It was her prettiest silk muslin, too, the one with the yellow and brown stripes and the nice, high-style drape about the hips. She began to smooth and straighten it with her hands. Why, that heavy-fingered ox had torn the neck of it almost to her waist! Oh well. . . . She grinned and stretched like a cat in the darkness. Her trim body felt lazy, swollen with content. One thing, he *was* a man. No weedy, hesitant stripling or seedy oldster leering and pinching and groping. She reached over and laid her hand playfully in the thick black thatch of Brant's hair. For a moment he did not move, then he reached up and took her by the wrist and sat up looking down at it. The night was empty about them. Even the cricket voices sounded lulled and remote.

"You're a good little gal, Sonie Lipik," Brant said quietly. For a moment Sonie felt as though she were going to throw herself into his arms again. But he did not move or speak further. The perverse sense of antagonism began to flood through her.

"Much obliged," she said tartly, pulling her hand away. "It's nice to know that you *can* talk. An' since we're feelin' complimentary—you'll do in a pinch yourself."

He got up heavily and stood looming over her, staring down the dark road toward Kingsmont.

"Come on," he said. "I'll see you back."

She felt sulky and annoyed, whether at him or herself again she did not know.

"I'm not so sure I want to go back right now," she answered petulantly. "You brought me all the way out here to talk, you said. Well, I can't say you've had much to say for yourself yet. Why are you always in such a big hurry?"

"Suit yourself," he said, and his voice was again withdrawn, almost weary. "I'm goin' back now."

He meant it. He turned and walked away from her. She was immediately furious. The emotion gave some focus and relief to the sense of bafflement that had been nagging at her. Darting to her feet, she picked up her skirts and ran like a boy—ran as she had as a child, heedlessly and wildly. As she overtook him and passed him she screamed, "Go to hell, Brant Royle!"

She heard the sound of his feet running after her, overtaking her. When he came up beside her he was laughing, a deep, delighted

106

sound. It was so strange and new from him that it almost stopped
her. He took hold of her elbow and pulled her, struggling, back to
walk with him. She jerked at the restraining hand, clawed and beat
at it with her free hand. She refused to look at him. Then she bent
her head and bit him on the arm, hard. He took her by the hair and
pulled her off, and laughed again. Then he kissed her, and for the
first time it was gentle, undemanding. All the fight drained out of
her. She felt hollow and weak and blind again.

"Oh, Brant," she cried in a strange yearning voice, "Brant—"

"You're my gal now, aren't you, Sonie?"

"I don't know. We'll see about that, Brant Royle."

"I told you I thought we could get along, didn't I?"

"Yes, you did." She glanced down at her hand holding together
the torn bosom of her dress. "But if it's gonna be like this you're
sure gonna cost me money, you big black careless brute!"

She grinned up at him again and slipped her free arm compan-
ionably through his.

"I'll buy you a hundred better dresses one of these days if you
want 'em."

"Big talk comes cheap, *Mr*. Royle. We'll see about that too."

"You stay around, Sonie," he said. "You'll see. This whole damn
town's gonna see!"

She laughed. The velvety, hoarse little laugh. It was a friendly,
skeptical sound.

"All right," she said. "We'll see."

Linked thus they walked down the empty road, leisurely and
in silence, back to Maple Street and the house. They met no one and
there was no sound but the ring of their footsteps in the clear, cooling air. As they crossed under the dim glow of the street lamp by the
livery Sonie heard the 1:15 freight to Salisbury passing southward
down the tracks a hundred yards away. As the low roaring clatter
of it died away in the night she thought: Lawdy! Is it that late? Well,
who would have thought it?

Maple House looked as dark and blank as the rest of the street.
But when they stopped at the foot of the porch steps she saw a low
glow through the transom over the front door. It was somehow an
accusing and fretful light. Sonie pulled the front of her dress together
and shrugged. Mrs. Rose and the rest of them were very likely in
there waiting and having a fit. Oh well, they might as well start in
gettin' used to it. She turned back to Brant expectantly.

"Will I be seein' you tomorrow, Mr. Royle?"

The dark, almost handsome face stared broodingly down at her.
But it was not seeing her. She felt it locked away within itself again
almost as if she were not there.

"Tomorrow?" He frowned as though the question were an in-

107

trusion upon his thoughts. She was to get used to that look. "No, not tomorrow. I've got to go up to Reidsville to look into some business for Pa."

She waited. "Well?"

"I'll be around soon."

"That's nice to know. I'm a busy woman, Mr. Royle. I've got things to see after myself."

"You'll find time for me, I think."

"Ach, so!" She sounded like Genia, as she often did in moments of stress and excitement. "You're all-fired sure of yourself, aren't you?"

"Yes!" The word exploded out of him upon her. "I am." Then he got very still again. "Well, g'night, Sonie, much obliged."

He made no move to touch her. Turning, he pushed his fists deep in his trouser pockets and walked away down Maple Street. In the half-light his shirt stretched against the hunch of the powerful shoulders, the big shaggy head thrust forward bullishly into the darkness. She stood looking after him until she could no longer see him, hearing the steady pound of his footsteps fade away around the corner. She shook her head grimly, her eyes narrowed. Somehow it was no more than she had expected. For the first time, while she stood there alone, a feeling almost like tenderness for him came over her. She shrugged it off impatiently.

"G'night, yourself, Mr. Royle," she murmured to the night. "We'll see."

She turned and went briskly up the steps. The front door was unlocked. She closed and latched it behind her. Inside, the hallway was quiet, but it was not the quiet of sleep. As she bent over to blow out the lamp she heard a stir of movement above her at the head of the stairway.

"Honey, is that you?"

Glancing up, she saw over the banisters a row of chalky faces framed in curlpapers and frilly nightcaps. Mrs. Rose, Mrs. Lily, and Mrs. Pearl stared owlishly down at her. Sonie could not suppress a giggle.

"Yes, it's me all right."

"You sure had us worried," said Mrs. Pearl, "runnin' out like that without sayin' boo to anybody. Lily was about to get dressed and go after the sheriff. Weren't you, Lily?"

"I cer'n'ly was," nodded Mrs. Lily, two of her curlpapers bobbing with her. "Honey, where *have* you been?"

"I've been out with Brant Royle," said Sonie flatly. "Now here I am, so you all can just run on back to bed."

She saw Mrs. Rose's moon face float out beyond the others' over the stair well, her pale eyes goggling avidly at Sonie's dress.

108

"Sonie," she wheezed, "Sonie, are you *sure* you're all right?"

Sonie felt oppressed suddenly with the familiar odor of the house and the hallway, the smell of talcum and faded flesh and musty carpeting. She dropped her hand from her bosom and faced them squarely and shamelessly. She put her hands on her hips and yelled up at them furiously:

"I'm here . . . I'm all right! Ach! Now go to bed quick before I throw somethin'!"

The three masks above the banisters withdrew precipitately. Sonie waited, grim-mouthed. She heard the retreating shuffle of slippers, the prim, elaborate closing of doors in the upper hallway. They were hurt and disapproving sounds. She turned to the lamp again and blew it out with one clean and angry puff.

"Am I all right?" she muttered fiercely, then giggled irrepressibly as she started up the stairs in the dark. "Of *course* I'm all right."

4

That fall and winter marked a change in Sonie and with it a change in the atmosphere of Maple House. A sort of temporary disintegration set in. It echoed directly the struggle Sonie was having with herself in her relationship to Brant Royle. As was to be expected, the news was all over town in a few days: Sonie Lipik had taken up with Royle. While no one dared to mention it openly, everyone waited around with one eye out for the fireworks. It was a match too good to be true. As for Sonie, she did not care what they thought. She never had cared. Now she flaunted it like a banner in their faces. However, she seemed, underneath her familiar, coarsely bright exterior, distracted as though turning some problem over in her mind. Before this she had always been completely shrewd, openhearted, and generous. Now she became moody and unpredictable. Often she would sulk in the kitchen or upstairs and refuse to come out and entertain the Saturday-night callers in the parlor. She did not seem to be much interested in the establishment any more, though she kept a sharp eye on it. There was still sure to be a row whenever anything got out of line or anyone tried to take advantage of her. Between her and Mrs. Rose and the other four roomers there came to exist an unfamiliar tension. She could be her old sweet, jolly self one moment and the next turn flatly rude and bullying. She seemed driven to it.

At first they were bewildered by it. Then they grew resentful. Not one of them dared mentioned Brant, but they were all sure he was at the bottom of it. Little scenes, unheard-of in Genia's time, exploded now almost daily between one of them and Sonie over the most trivial and inconsequential of causes. There were tears, shrieks, recriminations, and slamming of doors. It climaxed in a particularly bitter little encounter between Sonie, Mrs. Daisy, the tall one with bangs, and dumpy little Mrs. Ruby. It concerned a missing dressing scarf that none of them really cared a hang about. They knew it even as they quarreled. The upshot was that Mrs. Daisy (trailed by Mrs. Ruby) went upstairs to pack, indignantly shrieking down to Sonie in her high, pinched voice:

"I don't know what's come over *you,* Miss Sonie Lipik, but you ain't fit to live around any more, and *I* for one am leavin' this house!"

"Nobody's beggin' you to stay, Mrs. Daisy—neither you nor Mrs. Ruby," Sonie yelled up after them. "An' you'll please leave those rooms clean when you go!"

With this final, unheard-of rudeness she went into the kitchen and threw herself into the making of a cheesecake. Like Genia she needed something active to ease her anger. She banged the utensils and muttered to herself exactly as her mother had done. A little later she heard footsteps coming down the stairs and a sound of whispering and sobbing in the hallway. Then the front door opened and closed. Sonie shrugged and beat fiercely at her batter. Presently she stopped. She could still hear muffled weeping in the front of the house. After a moment she put down the mixing bowl and untied her apron. In the front hall she got her mackintosh off the hall tree. It was drizzling outside in the late October afternoon. Mrs. Lily sat alone in the parlor on the sofa, her dress pulled high exposing her thin calves in the tea-colored lisle hose, her face buried in her handkerchief. She was sobbing tragically.

"Where'd they go?" demanded Sonie, buttoning up the front of her mackintosh with quick fingers. Mrs. Lily lifted a countenance puffy and ruined with weeping.

"They went up to Weller's—to get one of the boys to—to drive them down to the station. Rose—Rose and Pearl went with them." She hiccuped through her sobs. "They wanted m-m-me to go, too. But I could'n'—I simply could'n'!" Mrs. Lily's voice rose in a desolate wail. "Sonie, how—how *could* you talk like that to them, how could you?"

"Oh, for goodness' sake, Mrs. Lily, you look a fright!" Sonie's voice was rough and terse, but not unkind. "Run upstairs now an' bathe your face in some cologne before you get clean hysterical."

She closed the front door behind her and went swiftly down the steps into Maple Street. She headed north instead of toward the livery stable. The light raw rain felt sharp, almost pleasant on her face. Breathing in the bite of it, she made her way swiftly and decisively down Maple Street, past the blank rows of warehouses. She knew a way to get to the station in ten minutes' time without any help but her own two briskly moving feet. And ten minutes was about all the time she would have if they had any silly notion of catching the 5:15 northbound.

Her shoes were wet and muddy by the time she came to the bottom of Peters Street in view of the station. It squatted familiarly by the tracks in the drizzle. A smoky, dismal gleam came through the waiting-room windows. She saw with instant relief that the tracks were still empty. Expertly she skirted puddles and made her way through the wheel ruts to the platform. There they were, almost as though they had been expecting her, a little lone huddle of four just outside the telegraph office, their hats bent together beneath an umbrella. They turned at the sound of her running feet, four pale blotches of faces. They all looked so utterly forlorn, so deserted. She stopped a few feet in front of them and flung her arms wide.

"Mrs. Daisy," she cried, "Mrs. Daisy!"

There was a moment's breathless hesitation. Then with shrill cries and sobs all four of them fled into Sonie's embrace. They clung and swayed together weeping—Sonie as loudly and unrestrainedly as the others—and through it babbling protestations and endearments. When the storm had subsided they all collapsed exhausted upon a bench and plied their eyes with handkerchiefs. When they discovered Sonie was without one they crowded about her like foolish hens, touching her with loving hands and making her blow her nose as though she were an injured child. Then they all looked at each other moist-eyed and giggled. Sonie said brightly, if a little hoarsely:

"Now that bygones are bygones, let's all go home and have a cozy gab and some hot spiced tea like Mama used to make!"

Mrs. Daisy, who was sitting close on Sonie's right and patting Sonie's damp sleeve with a gloved hand, looked down at her lap with a dissembling, simpering expression. Her lean, horsy face, under the indestructible fringe of frowsy bangs, and the mauve traveling bonnet, looked suddenly girlish and secretive. They were all silent, as though each was waiting for the other to speak. Sonie looked at them expectantly. In the spent clarity of the moment she experienced a fresh pang, as though here on the deserted platform she were seeing them all for the first time. My God, she thought, they're all really on their last legs, poor ol' things. I've been acting like a regular hellcat. I'll make it up to 'em . . . I will. . . .

"Honey," began Mrs. Daisy, still looking down at her lap, "I hope you won't get upset, but we ain't comin' back." She paused, then went on hurriedly: "We've got our tickets and everything. We're all packed and got our minds set on goin'. I expect we'd better keep right on now that we've started."

Sonie looked at her aghast. "But, Mrs. Daisy, what'll I do? All of you up and leavin' like this!"

"Why, honey," exclaimed Mrs. Daisy, leaning to her full of concern, "we ain't all goin'! Just Ruby an' me. Why, poor little thing, did you think we were *all* goin' off?"

She clucked and shook her head, glancing across at Mrs. Rose, who was snuggled close to Sonie on the other side. Mrs. Rose goggled the pale-blue eyes and squeezed Sonie's hand.

"Gawd, honey, me an' Pearl here aren't leavin'—wouldn't think of it without tellin' you—would we, Pearl? We just came along to see the girls off in some sort of style. Couldn't have them go off like this after all these years. We've tried to make 'em change their minds —haven't we, Pearl? But you know Daisy when she gets set. Just plain hardheaded. I couldn't feel worse if my own flesh an' blood was leavin'. . . ." Her voice broke and trailed off, the eyes opened rounder and swam in moisture.

Mrs. Daisy leaned across Sonie and interrupted in a brisk, matter-of-fact tone. "Now, Rose, it ain't so bad as all that!"

"Don't cry, Rosie," added Mrs. Ruby, pulling at her bonnet and waddling to and fro before them. "Don't cry."

"I can't help it, I'm just a sentimental ol' fool!"

"The way I see it, honey," continued Mrs. Daisy, "it's time we were all leavin' anyway. I've had it in the back of my mind for a long time. You don't need us round no more really. You're growed up an' can take care of yourself. Why, you'll be wantin' to leave this dinky little ol' town yourself soon—now you *know* you will! We've talked about it before. You won't want us around when that day comes. We've all been here too long as it is. We've jus' got the habit of stayin'. An' the longer we hang around, the longer it'll be before you'll make up your mind. An' when you do you don't want a lot of ol' extra baggage like us around to bother about—"

"Now, Daisy, that ain't a bit fair!"

"Rosie, don't try to fool yourself. Every word of it's true, an' you know it. We're long past our prime in this business—Lawd knows we've been lucky to hang on like this as long as we have. We've done all right in the last eight, ten years. Sure. Ain't a one of us hasn't been saltin' away a nice little ol' roll of change in the top of our stockin's for that rainy day. Well, the way I see it, that rainy day has come!" Mrs. Daisy tossed her head emphatically at the four of them. She was pleased with herself and what she had said. Looking at her, Sonie thought: I've been livin' with her all this time an' I don't know anything—not one thing—about her. How'd she ever come to be like this? Was she ever pretty when she was young?

"But Mrs. Daisy," she protested aloud, "where're you goin'— what'll you *do?*"

The simpering expression appeared on Mrs. Daisy's face again.

"Don't you worry about Ruby an' me for one minute, honey," she said, squeezing Sonie's arm. "I'm going up to Illinois to live with

112

my sister. She's been tryin' to get me to come for a long time. She's a widow with no children an' a nice little bit of property—she ain't got no financial worries, if you know what I mean—an' she's lonesome. Ain't laid eyes on one another in years. We're both gettin' on, an' it seems like a sensible thing to do. Ruby'll come along with me an' then go on up Wisconsin way. She's got some folks in Madison an' an ol' beau—ain't that right, Ruby?"

"Ach!" said Sonie, "but it's so sudden-like this way—I can't get used to it."

"You will, honey," Mrs. Daisy continued in her pinched voice. "You'll see it's all for the best—so will Rosie an' Pearl an' Lily. Anyway they'll be stayin' on for a while. We'll just run out on you gradual-like. So you're not to worry. We'll write for our trunks after we get settled. They're all packed an' ready."

"Here it comes, here it comes!" screamed Mrs. Ruby from the edge of the platform. They all turned desolate and silent as the single monstrous eye of the headlight lit up the curve of the warehouses and the approaching train came clattering, brakes and wheels squealing, toward them. Mrs. Daisy stood up and walked to where the two handbags rested. Sonie watched her with a desperate feeling that something more, somehow, needed to be said. She had been very thoughtful in the last few crowded moments. It was as though Mrs. Daisy, in speaking her mind, had put her fingers on a lot of things.

"Mrs. Daisy!" she cried, jumping to her feet. But her voice was drowned in the sound of the cars laboriously groaning to a halt. So she ran to the thin, spare figure bending over the luggage and threw her arms around it. There was no time for any more to be said that made sense. Everything was torn and scattered in the confusion of getting them on the coach. They called little half-statements to one another above the clamor. Warnings, admonitions, endearments, that continued after they stood looking up at the two faces pressed against the inside of the dirty coach window. In the smoky glow from the car lamp, Mrs. Daisy and Mrs. Ruby appeared remote, already irrevocably separated from them. Mrs. Rose and Mrs. Pearl were sobbing again and waving their handkerchiefs. Sonie stood very still and tried to grin, feeling her mouth tremble. She was suddenly frightened. She wanted to say: "Don't go away, Mrs. Daisy—Mrs. Ruby. Please stay. Let's let things go on being like they used to be."

She was very thoughtful and silent on the way back to Maple Street. It had begun to rain in earnest, so she blew them all to a ride in Old Jim's surrey. Old Jim met the trains and took passengers—when there were any—up to the hotel. But no one had got off the northbound and they had the rackety little carriage to themselves. None of them had much to say.

Sonie remained silent over supper while Mrs. Rose and Mrs. Pearl gave a detailed account of the leave-taking to Mrs. Lily. They set the table for four rather self-consciously. They had all repaired the ravages of emotion and dampness on their countenances and were beginning to feel themselves again. Sonie looked at them with the new recognition that had come to her that afternoon. While they were clearing away the dishes she said suddenly, addressing them all:

"How much do you think I could get for this house?"

They turned to her, arrested.

"Do you mean, honey," faltered Mrs. Pearl, who had been clearing off, "do you mean you're—you're really thinking of selling?"

Sonie frowned. She leaned forward on her elbows, cupping her chin in her hands. "I'm thinkin'," she said. "It's gonna take money to get me started on the stage like we always said. I'm twenty years old an' not gettin' any younger."

Mrs. Rose gasped.

"Honey, do you really, honest-to-Gawd mean it? Why, I hardly know what to say all of a sudden like this. Why, we've been hopin' and hopin' you'd make up your mind soon—haven't we, girls?" Mrs. Pearl and Mrs. Lily bobbed their heads enthusiastically and beamed at her. "Why, I'll set right down first chance I get tonight and write my old friend George Hallett in Chicago. George'll know a good thing when he sees it, I'm tellin' you! An' I'll stick around to see that there's no monkey business. Why, Sonie, you'll have your name up out front before you can turn around twice. Honey, you jus' don' know what this means to us."

"Well, don't get too excited yet," said Sonie, narrowing her eyes. "I'm just thinkin'."

"Why, sure, honey, sure," said Mrs. Rose carefully. She glanced at the others. "Didn't mean to be pushin' you at *all*. It's just that all of us here know you need to get out an' show 'em what you really can do. This ain't no place for you. . . . Kingsmont! You wanta get where a higher class of folks can have a look at you." But she had gone too far. She realized it instantly. The specter that had been at the back of all their minds leapt to the fore in that moment.

"If you mean," Sonie said, looking hard at her, "better than Brant Royle—"

"No, no, honey, I never meant any such of a thing!" Mrs. Rose looked about wildly for help from the others. But they were already studiedly piling dishes on the tray preparatory to carrying them to the kitchen. They would not look at her.

"Just one thing, Mrs. Rose," said Sonie slowly. "When I leave Kingsmont it'll be because I want to go. Not because anybody's makin' me go!"

114

"Of course, honey, of course."

"We'll talk about all this some other time maybe." Sonie got up abruptly and pushed her chair under the table. "We'd better get cleaned up in here. It's nearly eight o'clock. A rainy night like this is usually good for callers. Remember now there are only three of you to do the receivin'." She turned and went into the kitchen, leaving them to stare after her.

None of them dared to mention it for a long time after that night. Things settled down placidly enough to adjusting themselves to the loss of Mrs. Daisy and Mrs. Ruby. Sonie was more like her old self, singing and joking and humoring them. But it was only a lull, and it was a lull because Brant didn't show up till two weeks later. As usual, he appeared without warning. He peremptorily sent one of the others for Sonie, and when she came to the door argued bitterly with her for a long time. But finally she disappeared with him and did not return for nearly three hours.

It was this lack of control over their meetings that spoiled Sonie's temper as much as anything else. It endangered the freedom and independence that she had enjoyed all her life. *That* she found particularly unendurable. She twisted and turned in the toils of her captivity like a cat. She tried to explain it to herself a hundred times a day without success. She swore she hated the sight of that big tramp, that no-good, that stuck-up so-and-so, but irrationally she would tolerate no criticism of him from anyone else. Her associates soon learned this and carefully avoided any reference to the subject.

Sometimes when Brant appeared at an odd hour of the day or evening, and refusing, as he had from the first, to set his foot inside the house, stood at the door demanding her presence, she would scream down at him from the upper hallway or from the kitchen:

"Go. away, *go away!* Where did you learn to be so choosy that you're afraid of dirtyin' your feet in my house? We're not good enough for you, eh? Well, go away before I throw somethin'—and *don't come back!*"

Or, just as unpredictably—she did not even seem to know how she herself would act—she would run breathless to the door, her face vivid with pleasure, to plead with him in soft undertones. But always it ended by her going away with him. Sometimes it was merely a walk up to Tyree's for some ice cream. Sometimes there would be a buckboard at the foot of the steps and she would be gone all day with him while he was taking care of some tobacco purchase at a farm or a warehouse in the near countryside.

It was a relationship without precedent, and while those who had known Sonie all her life—the 'Krainians on Maple Street, the whole turbulent world of the warehouses and factories—grew used to it, as they had grown used to and accepted many things, they

115

could not understand its premises nor where it was leading either of the two principals involved. Some declared with satisfaction that it was Sonie who was getting the worst of it and making a none too flattering spectacle of herself. Others felt that that troublemaker Royle had picked himself more than he had bargained for. But none of them could see what held them together. Beyond the evidence, arrogantly admitted on both sides, of a shameless physical attraction, they acted either like a pair of disreputable old cronies or like rivals engaged in an acrimonious and endless contest. There was no vestige of sentiment or tenderness, none of the more recognizable aspects of passion. It made a scandalously good show for a while, but before long they all began to grow weary of it. The only real change was effected in Sonie's life and the lives of those immediately about her. Her old suitors, to a man, cleared the field respectfully for Brant. They left her strictly alone. Deeply wrapped up in this private contest, she did not even notice it. On occasion she was as sociably inclined and talkative as ever, circulating among neighbors and acquaintances as before. But a certain restraint colored her encounters now. It had not been there before. For one thing, like Maple House, they all forbore any mention of Brant.

It was not all going so smoothly with Sonie, however, and she knew it. Perversely, as she could not bear the encroachments on her freedom represented by Brant, her vanity was fiercely wounded by the fact that she could never somehow bring this one man into line. Up to a certain point she grew to understand him as well as how to handle him—which was more than anyone else who had ever known him could say—but beyond that point, the reasons for his perverse and black humors, his capricious actions, the thing that made him tick so violently, remained as deep a mystery to her as it did to everyone else who, willingly or unwillingly, knew him. She had no great powers of analysis to bring to bear upon the problems he presented, but she was shrewd and stubborn and she used every female art and artifice that was hers, either by careful observation and education or by intuition, to get at the core of him, to bend him to her in some way. It became almost an obsession with her, and she seemed able to do nothing to halt it.

Early in the struggle she became convinced that Brant was hiding a liaison with some other woman. When once she screamed the accusation at him he grew very white. Then, coldly furious, he ended the interview by stopping her mouth with his hand. She fought against him like something possessed. They were at the time on their way back from a trip to Leesburgh, ten miles away. Finally, when he could not quiet her, he dumped her unceremoniously out of the wagon and rode off leaving her to limp back three furious miles to Kingsmont. This in no way taught her a lesson. Rather, the

116

incident only made her more certain that he was keeping something concealed from her. She became even more madly determined to prove her suspicions right. She haunted the places about town where he was seen most often, the warehouses, the saloons, the Grange Hall, pacing feverishly outside till he appeared. Then she dogged his progress. Shamelessly she even bribed one of the black urchins who inhabited the dirty rentals across from Maple House to spy upon him. This got her no more satisfactory information than that he seemed given to wandering pointlessly over the town, particularly in the eastern quarter around Hill Street. They were meanderings that apparently had no goal, in which he stopped to speak to no one, and they ended only when he returned to his quarters above the store in West Street. It was the most frustrating and near-humiliating experience Sonie had ever undergone. When she could no longer bear trailing him at a distance she would run and catch up with him. Whether this action was in broad daylight or decently covered by darkness, characteristically, was no concern to her. Sometimes Brant knew that she was following him and would stop and wait for her to come up with him, glowering silently at her approach. He would either permit her to accompany him or would turn about and, against all protest, escort her forcibly back to Maple Street or the square, and then leave her.

It was at the height of this particular phase of their relationship that she began visiting the store on West Street. This was sheer defiance. Brant had early ordered her to stay away from his father's establishment no matter where else she might choose to come after him. In the meantime, she had become acquainted with Sam and Pete Henry. Sam she delighted to tease and taunt. It somehow eased her gall against Brant. Pete Henry she enjoyed as she would have a weaker and younger brother of her own. The two Royle brothers were frankly fascinated by her. They both started sneaking round to Maple House. Mrs. Lily in particular made up to Samuel. Sam, in spite of his ratty conservatism, was highly flattered. Pete Henry, with his almost feminine blond good looks and his unscrupulous charm, became easily the darling of them all. The three older ladies spoiled and petted him every time he appeared; and he and Sonie joined forces in impromptu musicales, she performing on Mrs. Lily's battered banjo and Pete Henry on his guitar. These occasions were the only happy ones that the ladies experienced during that disrupted period. The shadow of Brant hung over all of them.

Through all this, Sonie, either by design or by good fortune, had avoided meeting Templeton Royle. When she brazenly visited the store Sam became hysterically uneasy until Pete Henry would cajole her into leaving. She never really expected to corner Brant there. She stayed only long enough to make them thoroughly un-

117

comfortable before departing. But the day finally came when she did meet Templeton. It was a head-on, and it was at the store. She dropped casually in one afternoon, and the minute she set foot into the familiar oniony, grain-dusty, leathery atmosphere peculiar to the store she knew that this was the day she should not have stopped in. She was not avoiding this meeting, but neither was she seeking it. She had a healthy respect more for what she had heard of Ol' Temp himself than for any consideration for his sons' peace of mind.

As she came in, point-blank before her in all his scrawny, ugly majesty, was Templeton talking to a farmer. It was too late to withdraw, and it was against Sonie's principles to retreat from a situation once she had committed herself. She was dressed in her new taffeta plaid that afternoon, blazing in reds and blues and greens with the hat and coat to match. It showed off her red hair and complexion at their best. They, plus the gold-loop earrings, the gold-chain choker, and the plaid parasol, gave her an almost barbaric magnificence of which she was well aware. Too, the occasion was attended by a certain drama. In it she immediately found herself one of the central characters, and that she could never resist. She relished the tingle of excitement that ran along her veins. There was also in this for her an element of frank curiosity. Here at last was Brant's father, then. This peculiar little man about whom she had heard many a crazy and improbable tale, the lone person in the world whom she had ever heard Brant speak of with any special affection. She stood looking at him insolently, the green eyes narrowing. Then with elaborate unconcern she closed the parasol and tucked up her gloves. Templeton stopped short in the middle of his conversation with the man beside him and turned to her. Immediately his narrow face crimsoned under the fierce lines and the eternal gray stubble of beard. The store became quiet. Templeton's scrawny neck twitched convulsively. He raised one hand and pointed squarely at her. Calmly and unflinchingly Sonie looked back at him.

"Woman," Templeton spoke at last in a hoarse, strangled voice, "take yoh'self from my house."

Sonie raised her eyebrows and twisted a corner of her wide mouth upward.

"Beg pardon, I'm sure," she said crisply. "Am I interrupting somethin'? I thought you were open for business. The door's open—"

"Woman," continued Templeton as if she had not spoken, shaking the extended finger slowly, "wear no look of piety an' innocence. I know yoh face. It is the face of sin an' Sodom!"

"For heaven's sake," said Sonie, rolling an elaborate eye about the store, "who is this ol' gran'pa anyway?"

Templeton grabbed the edge of the counter, one hand clutching the familiar tall glass candy jar. His face was contorted.

118

"*Woman!*" he howled for the third time like a soul in torment. "I am the avenger of the Lawd an' you are an abomination—you an' all yoh sisters in scarlet that dwell in our midst. You corrupt the innocent of the land an' feed them on the fleshpots of Egypt. Do you think hell mouth doth not maw foh you? Do you think that yoh day of judgment approacheth not? Do not try to hide yoh face—you cain't hide from the judgment, sister! I know yoh dwellin' place— that house of filthy abominations. I will seek out yoh dwellin' place and tear it down. It stinks in the sight of the Lawd God of Righteousness too long, too long. . . . I will seek ye out. . . ."

His voice strangled in a retching cough. Sonie, surveying him with growing amazement, thought: Why, he's crazy as a bedbug— like they all been sayin'. Aloud she said:

"I'm not hidin' from anyone, you ol' fool!"

Templeton caught his breath in a shriek of rage. He began to look about him, sobbing and slobbering horribly through his breath. At that moment Sonie saw Pete Henry appear in the back doorway, his face flushed and concerned as he took in the scene. She became conscious of shufflings and snickers at her back. She turned her head. The doorway was crowded with faces. They were massed flatly against the glass of the front windows. Before she could turn back she heard Pete Henry yell:

"Pa!"

She turned just in time to see Pete Henry running down along the counter. What happened next happened so swiftly that it was a blur of movement and sound. She heard Templeton shriek:

"*Whore of Babylon!*"

Then there followed a splintering and shocking crash at her feet. Looking down, she saw a confusion of glass fragments and the bright-colored shapes of hard candy bounding across the floor. For a moment she could not believe what had happened. Why, I mighta been killed, she thought slowly, if that ol' fool had hit me! She became instantly and coldly furious. Before her the sound of struggle continued. Sam had reached across the counter and caught Templeton from behind and Pete Henry was holding the struggling and gibbering little figure of Templeton. Sonie coolly raised the hem of her skirt and, grasping her parasol firmly at its middle, picked her way across the floor through the glass and candy to them. Pete Henry was crying, pleading over and over, "Now Pa . . . now *Pa!*" Seeing Sonie almost eye to eye with him, Templeton renewed his struggles with his captors, straining against them as though once free he would claw her to death. She raised the point of her parasol and planted it sharply against his heaving soiled shirt front. She pushed upon it disdainfully. Templeton's scream continued.

"Ach, shut up!" yelled Sonie. The sound of her voice in the

119

tumult was so clear and definite and so full of pure rage and scorn that Templeton stopped short, his head craned forward toward her, his mouth open like a raw hole in his face.

"Go away, Sonie," said Pete Henry in a muffled, desperate voice. "Please!"

Sonie ignored him.

"You go around throwin' things at people an' you'll get in trouble, you ol' windbag," she said directly into Templeton's face. "Try it again with me an' you'll wish you hadn't. I'm not one bit afraid of you. Get that into your crazy head. I didn't come in here lookin' for trouble, but you just bring that turtle face of yours around my house an' I'll show you what *real* trouble's like!"

Templeton turned green. He no longer looked human. He began to scream again.

"Goddammit, Sonie!" Pete Henry's young voice was driven beyond endurance. "Get out of here!"

Sonie removed the parasol point.

"He ought to be put in a bughouse," she said. "Well, just keep him away from me, boys, that's all I've got to say—just keep him away from me!"

She turned with a toss of her head and picked a passage through the mess on the floor to the door. Behind her Templeton became articulate again.

"Whore of Babylon . . . *whore of Babylon!*" he screamed over and over again. The sound of it rushed after her as she pushed her way through the grinning faces in the doorway and out into the street. She ignored the crowd and carefully putting up her parasol, sauntered deliberately up West Street to the square.

She moved through the rest of the day with an air of glittering triumph. She went out of her way to stop and talk to people in corners about town she had not bothered to visit for many weeks. She seemed full to overflowing with high spirits, all her old verbal give-and-take, all her loud and brash charm. A broad wake of masculine backslapping and appreciative guffaws followed her progress. But it was play-acting and she knew it. Inside herself she was maddeningly depressed by the encounter. All through the day, beneath the bright exterior, she moaned crossly and despairingly to herself: This is no way for you, Sonie Lipik, this is no way. Brant, you black devil, it was you I wanted to beat . . . it was your black eyes I wanted to scratch.

Back at Maple House Mrs. Rose and the others sensed her black mood the moment she set foot in the front door. They carefully effaced themselves. News of the West Street incident had preceded Sonie and they all felt miserably apprehensive. They did not know what to expect, but they felt with a dismal certainty that what had

120

happened was only a preamble. They wanted passionately to be out of it, but a tenacious loyalty to Sonie as well as a hysterical curiosity kept them rooted. It was this latter emotion that had held them in thrall. Like a hutch of rabbits watching a weasel. They tiptoed about the house, they spoke in whispers, they started nervously, and laughed in forced unnatural voices at supper. Sonie continued full of wild, loud talk almost as though she were intoxicated. Mrs. Rose, as soon as she decently could, excused herself and went upstairs to her room complaining of a headache. Mrs. Lily and Mrs. Pearl insisted on doing the dishes alone. They were vastly relieved when Sonie did not protest, but sat chin in hand banging childishly with her fork upon her plate. She remained silent, her eyes unnaturally brilliant beneath a frown, while they cleared off and retired to the kitchen. They were just putting away the last of the dried dishes when she came in. She tied an apron carefully over the plaid taffeta and threw some coal in the range. Then she shooed them out, saying she felt like making blintzes. Without protest they retired to the parlor and nervously began to straighten what was obviously—as always—straightened and correct to perfection, because they vied all day long in keeping it that way. Mrs. Lily began to feel as though she could scream. She burst into a fit of coughing.

"Pearl," she managed to say finally in a strangled voice, "I just think I'll go to my room for a minute and freshen up."

Mrs. Pearl was alone in the parlor when Brant came. Without ever mentioning it each of the four women in the house had known that he was coming—that he had to come—and they had been waiting for his coming unbearably.

Sonie in the kitchen looked up from the lifting the last of the blintzes from the hissing fat in the pot. She heard the heavy tread up the porch steps. Then the fist thundering on the front door. Her face was colored by an expression at once inscrutable and triumphant. She put the spoon down on the table, wiped her hands slowly on her apron, and patted her hair. Ach, so he had come at last! It was about time! She could hear through the half-open door into the front hall the rumble of his bass and Mrs. Pearl's voice in response, strained and breathless.

"Sonie," Mrs. Pearl's voice came down the hall hysterically coy. "Gentleman here wants to see you."

Sonie was both irritated and amused at this temporizing.

"Who is it?" she called back clearly and sharply. It had all fallen into a pattern, she realized in a moment, as formal as a pink tea, the introduction, the response, the exchange. She grinned and did not move.

"It's—uh—it's Mr. Royle, I think, honey." Mrs. Pearl sounded as though she were trying unsuccessfully to hide behind something.

Sonie snorted. "You think!" Why did they all have to begin acting like scared mice the minute *he* showed his face? "Well, tell him I'm not in the mood for callers tonight. Some other time maybe."

She turned to the stove again. She had just picked up the spoon when she heard the front door slam. There was a little whimpering gasp from Mrs. Pearl, then deliberate hard footsteps coming down the hall to the kitchen. A shock of fear and delight swept over Sonie. For a breath she could not move. Why, he had come into the house —he was coming where she was! She turned to face him almost triumphantly. He did not stop till the table at the center of the room barred his way and there he stood towering over her and the whole room. He had not removed his hat. His clothes looked disheveled and the big, heavy face wore a two days' beard. Sonie looked at him and shook her head. He looked something awful! He'd been off somewhere drinking again. Surveying him coolly, she wondered, with a mixture of rage and despair at herself, Why did she bother? He wouldn't ever be anything but this big, oafish man full of strange power and violence, fooling himself and her into thinking he was going somewhere, blurring himself in drink like any tramp. This was a road that led nowhere for both of them. She shrugged. I'll just put a stop to all this right now, she thought. This will be a good time to call it quits. But when she raised her eyes to his it all went clean out of her mind. He was looking at her with the hot concentration that had always puzzled and maddened her, because it seemed to be *at* her and yet there was in it that other part of himself looking out withdrawn and full of sadness. It angered her but it never failed to twist a sharp knife of compassion in her. It was a feeling that she was utterly powerless to subdue or deny, and she found in some way it included herself as well as him.

"Sonie," he said. And although he said it quietly, the sound of it crowded the big warm kitchen. "Sonie, damn you, I told you to stay away from Pa, didn't I?"

"Did you think I went down to the store this afternoon looking for *him?*" She stepped up to the table facing him defiantly.

"You didn't have to come there a-tall, an' I could break your neck for it. That's the one place I've told you to stay clear of—"

She whipped up anger in herself.

"Ach! I didn't go there lookin' for trouble. You have a store to sell things, don't you? I thought I might be as good as the niggers I see tradin' there. You don't throw *them* out. Anyway yo're not too proud to return the visit tonight, I see. First time those big feet of yours have ever dirtied up my kitchen, an' I can't say I like it too well!"

She thought, I'm talkin' like a ninny, just babblin', an' I can't stop myself.

"Sonie," he said in the slow angry voice. "Pa's a sick man—"

"Well, he just about killed me this afternoon. I should've gotten the sheriff down—"

"He doesn't understand about things, Sonie, an' I won't have him troubled by you nor anyone else." There was a terrible, smoldering patience in his voice as though he were holding himself in very carefully. "We had a helluva time quietin' him after you left this afternoon. When I came in Pete Henry was having to hold him down in the back room under lock and key to keep him from grabbin' an ax and comin' down here." Brant frowned and shook his head. "He goes plain wild sometimes, an' he don't forget once his mind gets on somethin'. He'll try to come down here and make trouble one of these days."

"Well, let him," said Sonie fiercely, "just *let* him. If you can't keep him where he ought to be, I'm not afraid of him, an' I told him so. Goin' aroun' with axes choppin' at people's houses and throwin' things. Who do you Royles think you are anyway? Nobody!" Her voice rose shrilly. She flushed and leaned angrily toward him, flourishing the spoon. "Just nobody, *nobody*—an' you never will be anybody at this rate!"

His face seemed to drain of all color and expression. It became set like stone under the black shadow of the unshaved beard. He looked as though she had struck him. In that moment, as they strained toward each other across the table, she was sure he would hit her and she waited, almost welcoming the blow. But instead, after a suspended and endless moment his clenched right fist slowly came down heavy and hard upon the table top. It leapt under the blow and she felt the force of it jar her to the toes. A mixing bowl that she had been using fell to the floor with a sharp clatter.

"I will," he said in that strange, agonized whisper that she had heard—how long ago it seemed now!—on that first evening when they walked out the road into the night together. "I *will* be somebody, Sonie Lipik, I *will!*"

And then a terrible thing happened. The face that she could not look away from, the mask of stony features, suddenly crumpled like a child's. The hot eyes widened and swam with desperation. He reached up blindly and made a brushing motion across his forehead. His hat fell to the floor. He did not seem to notice. Clasping both hands across his face, he slumped slowly into the kitchen chair, his face coming to rest upon the table top. The big fists lay clenched and still upon the scrubbed wood. In the shocked silence Sonie stood looking down at the tumbled black hair, the big shoulders now hunched and motionless as though he dared not breathe lest that breath betray him. I love him, she thought simply and honestly at

123

last. Ach! God help me, I love him. There's no use tryin' to beat around the bush any more.

She put down the spoon and walked around the table to him. Taking his head between her hands, she pulled it against her as she would have a hurt child's. He reached out and encircled her, holding her tightly and awkwardly as though he dared not let go. Desolation swept over her as she stood there in the silence rocking him gently to and fro. She knew as certainly now as though someone had spoken the words to her. I love him, yes; but he doesn't love me. He loves somebody, *something*, that he's gotta have—but it isn't me.

After a while she said, "When did you eat last?"

He looked up slowly, still holding her with his hands. His face was quiet, almost boyish, as though the hurt had washed it clean. His mouth curled in the crooked half-smile as he looked at her.

"I always said you were a good gal, Sonie."

"When did you eat last?" she insisted. Her voice sounded to her calm and old. She removed his hands from her hips gently, not looking at him.

"Ah, I don't know—"

"Not since yesterday or before that from the way you look," she said briskly and matter-of-factly. She thanked God in that moment that she wasn't one to waste time beating her breast once she had faced the truth. Like Genia, she had a great sense of the world going on. It didn't do you any good to sit down and let it roll over you. In fact, she felt rather peaceful. This honesty had given her back to herself. Now that she knew, she wouldn't have to bother about *that* any more. It was simply a fact. It was a senseless waste of time to fight a fact. She moved around him to the stove.

"There's cold meat from supper and I've just finished making a batch of blintzes."

"Thanks," he said, his eyes following her; but already she could feel that they were looking somewhere else. "Don't go to no trouble, Sonie."

"An' there's plenty of coffee on the back of the stove. Coffee's what you need. Coffee and food. Somethin' hot in your middle. Wait'll you put your teeth in one of these blintzes. I won't have to ask you a second time."

She moved busily from stove to table, clearing off, setting plates and cutlery before him. Suddenly he reached up and took her by the arm.

"Sonie," he said, "you've got a good head under that carrottop. If you was a man with ambitions for startin' a business in this town —a business that would get you ahead, away ahead of all of the boys that own the town—what do you think you would do?"

"I don't know." She frowned. "I've never thought about it. I

124

wouldn't want to get ahead here, anyway. What's there to get ahead in anyway except tobacco?"

"Exactly!" he said warmly, and pulled her down into his lap. He looked contentedly at her as though she pleased him a great deal. "I like to talk to you, Sonie. Better than most any man or woman I know."

"Eat your supper, you big bear," she said, ruffling his hair.

"That's the reason I keep comin' back to you, even if you're hell an' all to handle. You've got sense."

"It's a pity," she said, with a toss of her head, "I haven't got a good tobacco warehouse along with it."

He laughed for the first time.

"Come here!" he said, and he pulled her down again and kissed her.

5

Things eased between Brant and Sonie after that night. Not that their meetings were no longer tumultuous. They were both possessed of energy and could not keep from feeding with a strong delight upon the violence in the other, any more than they could keep from glorying in each clash as it came. But they clashed as intimates now; they were like two old antagonists who had come to an understanding. For one thing, Sonie, once she had cleared her status in their relationship, typically ceased to struggle in the blind female way. She accepted everything casually now without losing any of her relish and warmth. She prodded and mocked and spurred Brant endlessly almost as though he were a relation, a member of her family. He came to the house freely now, but it was again in his own way. There was still that strange reticence and scorn in him that prevented him following the accepted conduct of any of the other visitors who came to Maple House. It was typical of him both then and later. His manner was fiercely individual, separated, and unpredictable. Although Mrs. Rose, Mrs. Lily, and Mrs. Pearl were resigned to his presence and he maintained a coldly formal speaking acquaintance with them whenever he met them in the house, he would never come into the front parlor. Sonie always received him in the kitchen. There she outdid herself cooking meals for him, and while he ate ravenously the storm of their voices would echo muffled through the doors and walls. Everyone within hearing would stop and listen fascinated to the sound of it. Brant found a direct solace in talking endlessly to Sonie, arguing out a host of schemes, pouring out his hatreds and dissatisfactions. She was a shrewd listener; but she was by no means always sympathetic. She could never quite understand his obsession with Kingsmont, his endless diatribes against the tobacco country as though it were peopled with ranks of antagonists, set with dark giants whom he was always besieging. Often, out of patience with him and his talk and with herself for listening, she would yell at him:

"Ach! Why do you bother, then, if it is what you say—this no-good town, this rotten state, where a man can't get ahead? Why don't you go somewhere else? Why don't you go north, east, west —*anywhere* where the big opportunity is—the big cities, the big money? If you want to do it, those are the places—not this little one-horse tobacco town. Believe me, when I get ready, I'm not going to waste time here!"

She would always get the same answer, always passionately pronounced, so that even though she could not understand it she began to believe it as she believed that there was something fateful working in him that would someday break itself through.

"Sonie," he would say, "this *is* the place for me—no matter what I say about it, *this is the place.* Don't you see—every damn thing's already been grabbed and cornered in the places you talk about. But nothing's been done here—not only Kingsmont, but the whole poor bleeding South's been on its knees, asleep since before the war. Here's the place to do things for somebody who wants to do 'em, by God! It only needs some man to grab hold of all the things they haven't touched, all the things they haven't used, all the things they don't even know they've got, to make a bigger thing than anybody ever heard of. Look. My pa was born raisin' tobacco, I was prac-tically born in a tobacco field, I've broken my back suckerin' tobacco plants many a time, I've tried to learn everything I could about to-bacco—an' here we live in an ocean of it, fields, acres of it, stretchin' every which way as far as you can go. An' what happens to it? They pay the poor devil who grows it a penny, sell it an' make a couple of more pennies for themselves, an' send it all away for somebody else, who's got sense, to make a killin' on it. You an' me live on it, because we can't help it, but that's all. Sure, we've got some factories here— little two-by-four businesses that any real money-man would laugh at. But why aren't the big boys here where it is? Why isn't that money made and poured out all over this state, goddammit!"

"Tobacco, tobacco, tobacco," she would answer crossly. "Can't you talk about anything else? I'm sick an' tired of hearing about it. Sometimes, Brant Royle, I dream you've turned into a basket of prime bright-leaf an' the bright-leaf isn't just yellow but all turned to pure fourteen-carat gold. Well, I wish it would, so you'd be satis-fied."

"But it *is* gold, Sonie, every leaf of it—if somebody just had sense enough to see it and use it like it ought to be used."

"Well, you run a business, don't you? Why can't you do it in-stead of just always talkin' and talkin' about it?"

126

"Oh, Pa's business—Sweet Beulah Land—ten cents a bag!" He would shake his head bitterly and mockingly. "He's tried, an' look what he's got. He's satisfied—or thinks he is—he's done all right. But that's not for me. There's got to be some other way. All the old ways are cut-and-dried, closed-up, finished. You can't win fightin' with them. It's just a waste of time. I've beat my head bloody against them an' got nowhere. There's got to be somethin' new, somethin' different that nobody's ever even dreamed of before. Folks have been smokin' an' usin' up a power of tobacco since those old fellows first grabbed it away from the Indians, an' they'll use a power more if somebody finds a way, a different way, to let them use it. Well, I'm gonna find that way before I call it quits if it's the last thing I do."

Sonie sighed patiently. "Papa used to say there isn't nothin' new. It's all been here before."

"Sure, an' your daddy spent his life rollin' cigarettes for Mr. Pendleton—rollin' cigarettes!" Brant's mouth curled with scorn.

"Now don't go throwin' off on Papa, Brant Royle," Sonie yelled. "You can talk all you want to about anything, but leave Papa alone. He was a good man!"

"I'm not talkin' about your papa. I'm talkin' about what he had to do to make a livin'. Rollin' cigarettes. Think of it; they bring a man all the way over here from Europe to set him down at a bench to roll a hundred cigarettes ever' so often. Now, why hasn't somebody done somethin' about that? Men rollin' cigarettes! Why haven't they got a machine that would roll a million? We're still operatin' like they did a hundred years back."

"Oh, you're just plain crazy, Brant. Who'd you ever find to smoke that many cigarettes?"

"By God, if I had 'em, I could find a way to make people smoke 'em! That's just one thing I'm talkin' about—"

"Oh, have another cup of coffee. You talk like you're drunk!"

And so it would go. Other times he would not mention it for a week. But he was always looking, caught in his dark search. Sonie followed him with the patience of resignation, bullying and blustering, but sticking with him. She saw him through a try he made the following spring at beginning a tobacco brokerage. He was full of plans for a month, making trips around to the various outlying towns and markets. She went with him often, dressed in her best seasonal outfit, sitting like an interested child in the buckboard while he talked business in some warehouse or with a farmer at his barn. But the new venture died stillborn. It went to pieces overnight. Brant disappeared. When next she heard of him they had him down in jail again for drunken and disorderly conduct. She got hold of Pete Henry at the store and together they went and got him out. She knew the sheriff well. He was an old visitor down on Maple Street.

When she paid the fine she told him if he ever mentioned what she had done for Brant, he need never come her way again.

"Good Lawd, Sonie," he said, "you're just throwin' yoh money away."

"It's mine, Sheriff. You let me bother about it."

She watched Pete Henry load the sodden Brant into the store wagon with the help of the courthouse janitor and drive away. Then she went across to the grocery store on the corner and bought two pounds of cottage cheese. She would make up a whole batch of blintzes! She knew Brant would be around that night or the next, when he had pulled himself together. That was the way it would go until something—what, she did not know—happened to change it. She seldom even questioned her own actions as a part of it any more. It was still in some way more exciting than anything she had come across so far. Just being in the same place with him made her feel sufficiently alive not to want anything else—for the present, at least.

It was Mrs. Rose who finally took the initiative. It was abortive, but she took it. One evening she met Sonie at the foot of the stairs in the hallway. Sonie had just come in from a search for Brant with Pete Henry. It was a hunt that had taken them all the way to Reidsville. They had found him in the saloon there and it had been a long and tiring struggle to argue and bully him into coming home with them before he made more trouble. Sonie looked so utterly weary and somehow childish in that moment taking off her bonnet in the dim hall light that all of Mrs. Rose's motherly bosom ached to comfort her. However, she restrained her emotion and putting on a guise of excitement that had worn thin with waiting all day, she approached Sonie flourishing a piece of paper.

"Honey!" she cried. "I'm sure glad to see you. I thought you'd never get here. Guess who I heard from today?"

"I—I don't know," said Sonie listlessly, as if she didn't care.

"You'll die when you hear. Remember I said I was gonna write that friend of mine up in Chicago? Well, I did. An' look, just read what he's written back!"

Sonie took the letter, placing one foot for support on the bottom stair, and began to read carefully with a frown, as she always did. Mrs. Rose watched her face eagerly for some sign of response. But Sonie read to the bottom and then looked up and shook her head.

"That's mighty nice o' your friend thinkin' he can put me right in a vaudeville act an' all. But it's no good, Mrs. Rose. Later maybe we'll all go, but not now. You know that."

She handed the letter back. Mrs. Rose looked as though she were going to weep. She stuck the piece of folded paper back into her capacious corsage and patted Sonie's hand where it rested on the balustrade.

"I know, honey," she said hoarsely and earnestly, "I sure to Gawd understand."

"I wish I did, Mrs. Rose," said Sonie.

"Well, don' you worry, now," said Mrs. Rose. And then she burst out as though she couldn't stand not speaking any longer: "Honey, don't waste your time on that riffraff trash!"

Sonie's head came up and some of the fire flashed back into the green eyes. "Who says I'm wastin' anything on *him!* I know what I'm doin'."

"Sure you do, honey, sure you do," soothed Mrs. Rose, "but there must be a hundred others better'n him would really set you up handsome, roll out the red carpet for you if you'd give 'em the chance." Her bulging, baby-blue eyes rolled expressively. "My Gawd, honey, he just ain't good enough for you!"

Looking down at her, Sonie flashed a sudden grin. "Of course he isn't good enough for me, Mrs. Rose. But that isn't the point."

"You're jus' wastin' yourself, that's all—jus' throwin' yourself away," Mrs. Rose pressed on. "An' he won't know nothin' but trouble, I'm telling you—never will know! You—why, you've got a future ahead of you if you'll just let loose and let it be!"

Sonie was silent for a moment, biting her lower lip.

"I think he's got somethin' ahead of him too, Mrs. Rose," she said slowly. "That's why I'm stickin' around. I want to be here when he gets there and the fur really begins to fly."

A little later she stood before the mirror in her room, undressed to her camisole and combing her hair with long, slow strokes. She stared at the image of herself without really seeing it. She was feeling utterly weary and low in her mind. Suddenly she pulled herself erect and grinned defiantly at herself, shaking her head mockingly.

"You're sure a fool, Sonie Lipik," she whispered. "Just one big fool!"

And then she combed a long, thick lock down over her eyes and began to hum one of Mrs. Lily's tunes in her throaty, delightful voice. The comb kept time, flashing through the burnished curtain of her hair.

CHAPTER FIVE

I

She stood in the doorway, fascinated. Almost breathlessly she watched the faces of the two men in the light. The chimney of the lamp had been smoking unnoticed for some time, but neither she nor they made any move to trim the wick. She wondered what held her there in the hot, untidy little box of a room that served as the office for Templeton Royle's store, listening to the talk between these two. It was a conversation she only half understood and which concerned her not at all. In fact, she, Sonie Lipik, with all her best silver bangles on and wearing the new dress she had ordered especially from Richmond, might as well have been in any of a dozen other places for all the notice they gave her. She had not meant to stay. There were a dozen other things she ought to be attending to at this hour of the evening. But she remained, caught in the tense and terrible excitement. It was a feeling that crowded the space from wall to wall—the scarred roll-top desk in the corner with the dirty glass and the empty whisky bottle lying among the scattering of old papers and bills, the plain wooden table, the chairs. She stood watching the two faces as though her life depended upon every flicker of expression, every movement of the heads and eyes as they looked from each other to the papers covered with strange hieroglyphics and drawings. These lay spread out between them on the table. The two faces were taut and sober now. You would never have guessed that a little while . before they had both been men blurred and heavy with drink. At least *she* found it remarkable! Brant had seemed to wipe out all signs of alcohol in him the moment this stranger had slumped, a lifeless and ludicrous bundle, to the floor. But neither he nor Sam was able to do anything practical about it. It remained for her to work —with Brant cursing and deviling her like a wild thing.

Hot coffee and ammonia, the simple miracle she had performed countless times before at her own house when one of the callers had arrived carrying more than he could handle. But had Brant thanked her when she had at last brought the stranger around so that he could sit up and talk sense? No! Not he! You'd have thought she'd never even come into the store—Ol' Temp's sacred premises—for all the notice Brant gave her once they got this ugly, tramplike creature on his feet. Brant just hauled him and his silly carpetbag back to the office and plumped him down opposite him and there they had been at it ever since. But she was used to it. She couldn't even feel angry. There was neither time nor room for anger now. All she could do was to watch and listen, to try to feel that it didn't matter as long as she could catch the drift of what was going on.

The strange man, once he began talking, seemed unable to stop. He spoke endlessly and pleadingly, referring with a gaunt and trembling forefinger occasionally to the papers. Brant sat listening with a still intentness, occasionally leaning forward to ask some question in a low rumble. Samuel had been there at first, but had had to leave, protesting, when the factory hands came in to be paid. Sonie tried to remember that she had been away from the house far too long for a Saturday night. Things were very likely in an uproar there, with the medicine show holding forth in her vacant lot that very minute. But even with this concern at the back of her mind she could not tear herself away. Deeply and intuitively she felt that something was happening here between Brant and the horse-faced stranger, in this little room reeking with the smell of coal oil and spilled whisky. Some conclusion was being reached, some decision formed, as the result of this meeting that she could not afford to miss even if Maple House were being devoured by flames.

"And you could build one of these here—*now*—in Kingsmont?" Brant was asking in the heavy, careful tone that had marked all of his part in this conversation. Sonie recognized the sound. He always spoke that way when he was most excited. She knew that behind it his thoughts were flashing and running in a dozen different directions.

"Ayeh," answered the strange man. "I can get a lot of the parts tooled in a place I know up in Hartford. The rest I would have to machine myself—with some help. But I *could do it*, Mr. Royle!"

"There ain't a machinist shop closer than Richmond."

"That smithy just off the square has a lathe. I was in there this afternoon."

"Oh, Upham—I forgot about him. You think you could do it with what he's got? You think he'd be some help?"

"Ayeh—he could, I think." John Barton's voice had grown thin with excitement. In that moment his Gothic face looked transfigured, fanatic, like the face of a saint approaching at last some long and desperately sought spiritual consummation.

"An' you say ol' Singleton himself sent you down here to us." Brant shook his head slowly.

"Ayeh—yours was the name and the place."

"You know why he did, don't you?"

"Reckon he was tryin' to get rid of me easy as he could—like everybody else."

"Yeah—an' he thought it was mighty funny, too, to send you off to us. He felt pretty sure we wouldn't be able to be interested in your proposition—a dinky little store down in nigger town!"

Oh for heaven's sake! thought Sonie, here he goes again—off on that ol' song and dance about the Singletons, the Pendletons, the Tollivers. What difference did it make? She looked intently at Brant's face and wondered what lay in it that could always hold her even when she felt he was acting like a hardheaded fool, charging blindly ahead. She wondered again who had given him the red slash on the cheek. He won't ever be able to love anybody or anything, she thought in a blinding flash of illumination, he won't ever have time! It's got to be the whole world for him or nothin' at all.

131

It was the second occasion on which this rare detachment had come to her. It seemed always to arrive at a moment of real import, whether the moment concerned her or not. I don't even know now if I really love him any more. I don't hate him—I've tried, but I've gone right on lettin' him get away with more than I'll ever let any man get away with again. An' here I stand watchin' him like I couldn't stand to miss anything he did. It *does* matter. I don't know why, but it does! Maybe I'll never know. . . .

At that moment Samuel came in from the front. He brushed past her rudely, and pulling another chair up to the table, sat down between Brant and John Barton. He was breathing hard as though he had been hurrying desperately to get back. He seemed driven by the thought that the worst had happened while he had been absent. He thrust his chin forward combatively toward Brant and sucked his teeth. Brant did not even look at him. He studied one of his hands lying quiet on the edge of John Barton's drawings.

"Is your title to this thing clear?" he asked mildly.

"Ayeh," said John Barton, watching Brant's face. "The patent's applied for in my name."

"An' how long do you think it would take for you to build and install one o' these machines?"

"If I can get the parts on time—an' the help—about two months."

Samuel hitched his chair frantically and muttered: "What's this all about now, Brant—what's this all about?"

Brant ignored the interruption and continued to look at his hand with an expression of cold concentration and purpose. It was a look that Sonie recognized, and one that many men who were to know him later also would come to recognize with both fear and helpless fascination.

"What kind of arrangement would you want to make for building one now?"

John Barton's hand pawed at his cheek. He seemed afraid to speak.

"Well," he exploded hesitantly, "I hadn't exactly figured—"

"Come on now," interrupted Brant, staring compellingly at him. "You must have some sort of proposition in your mind. If I get the money to build your machine, would I get first rights to its use on a partnership basis—or what?"

Barton's face worked wordlessly, his inescapable Yankee caution holding him in check, as always, before any commitment. Samuel broke into the pause almost with a scream.

"Brant! What damn foolishness are you talkin'?"

Brant turned his eyes slowly to his brother and then back to John Barton's face. Barton looked back at him with that sudden candor, so like a defenseless child, and nodded his head.

"Ayeh." He pronounced the words carefully as he continued, "I think we could work it that way."

"How much capital will you need to finance it at first—you know, to buy your materials, pay for the parts you will have to order?"

"I've figured it will take five, maybe six thousand dollars to build it from scratch—providing I don't find any snarls I haven't counted on."

"All right," said Brant in the same heavy, deliberate voice, "I'll get it for you."

"What are you sayin', Brant!" Sam screamed as though he had been struck, jumping up from his chair so suddenly that it fell over with a crash. "Who you think's gonna give you five thousand dollars? You sure to God ain't got it, an' nobody with a nickel's worth of sense is gonna lend it to you. Look what you've done wasted already with all them schemes of yourn. . . ." His voice died away under Brant's terrible glance.

"Pick up that chair an' sit down, Sam." Brant's voice was quiet and deadly. "An' you can either shut up an' listen or get back to your storekeepin' where you belong."

Sam made a whimpering sound and retreated toward the door. He craned his neck over Sonie's shoulder toward the storeroom.

"It's all right," said Sonie, watching him scornfully. "Nobody's come in in the last five minutes."

Sam ignored her. He turned back into the room and snarled at John Barton.

"Don't be fooled by no big talk, mister. We ain't got no money."

"I can get four thousand that I know of," said Brant to John Barton.

Sam leapt to the table with a gasp of horror. He leaned across and screeched at his brother:

"You can't have that four thousand, Brant! That belongs to Pa and me an' Pete Henry an' by God we ain't gonna be talked into lettin' you have it this time!"

"You'll let me have it," said Brant, and Sonie shivered deliciously. "You'll let me have it an' I'll get the rest if I have to beg, lie, an' steal from here to Richmond an' back—if we have to mortgage the store, the factory, and everything we own. But I'll get it!"

Sam just leaned there looking at him aghast. Words bubbled incoherently in his throat. His neck stretched thin and cordlike.

"You're crazy," he managed to gasp. "Always thought so before, but now, by God, I know it!"

Brant waited until he finished. Then mildly, placatingly, he spoke, as though to a child:

"Maybe so, maybe so. Sam, you're always sayin' I couldn't fight

133

with the big boys up the street, because I didn't stand on the same kind of ground they did. Well, I've got the one thing now, I think, that's put me on equal terms with any and all of 'em. I've got an idea now. I've got something new that I can work with. They haven't had anything new, no ideas about what to do with what they've got, for a hundred years. They've gone to sleep an' let everything go to sleep with them. Well, this cigarette machine an' me's gonna wake them up. It's just what this town, the whole damned country, has needed for a long time. You wait. It's gonna make Kingsmont the biggest place in the tobacco business. An' you know why? Because this time I know I've got somethin'. They're too set in their ways, too dumb to see it, but not me, Brant Royle! I've told all o' you I was just waitin'. You wouldn't believe me—thought I was some kind of a wild hellion of a fool who couldn't get his sights straight on anything. Well, this time I've got 'em straight, an' I'm not gonna let you stop me just because you were born with the guts and nerve of an ol' woman, Sam. You're too careful. You'll never get where you'd like to be by yourself, but you'll get there because you'll come along with me. When Pa comes in tonight I'm gonna have a talk with him. First thing Monday mornin' you an' me an' Mr. Barton are gonna find us a lawyer an' then go up to the bank. Maybe this bank here won't listen. I kind o' think it would be better if it didn't. But we'll find a bank—Danville, or Richmond, maybe. You can't stop me, Sam! You ought to know that by now. Nobody in the world's gonna stop me!"

Listening to that quiet, steady voice fill the room, Sonie felt as though she were being hypnotized by the look on Brant's face. He's never sounded like this before, she thought with amazement, an' Lord knows I've heard him talk plenty. He's like somebody new an' strange I haven't seen before! He sure believes what he's sayin' this time—I almost believe him myself. And she grinned the wide grin for no one but herself. Her hand patted her hair with the little prideful gesture. A heavy stillness fell over all of them as Brant finished. Even Samuel was quiet. Under the sound of their breathings she heard approaching the hard pound of running feet. It burst in with a hard clatter on the wooden floor of the store. Sonie turned. Pete Henry exploded into the doorway. He was streaming with perspiration, his babyish face flushed and wide-eyed, his breath coming in gasps. He looked across the room, past her and the others.

"Brant!" he yelled as though he could speak no softer. He caught at the door frame and leaned into the office. Brant got up out of his chair.

"Where've you been?" he demanded. "Where's Pa?"

"Don't ask no questions now, Brant. Come on! Hell is about to pay off down the street. Pa's stopped that show down by Sonie's

134

place. He's preachin' fiery furnace an' all get-out. Couldn't do a damn thing with him. He's gone plumb crazy—he'll have everybody else crazy 'fore long. You gotta come an' get him away before somethin' *really* happens. Never saw anything like it before!"

His voice broke hysterically as if he wasn't sure whether he was going to laugh or cry.

"You let him get hold of liquor again, Pete Henry? I ought to—"

"God dern! Don't stop to jump on me now, Brant. Come on! I don't know where in hell he got hold of it, I swear I don't. He seemed all right till we pulled into town, but he must've been foolin' me all the time. We was just passin' Sonie's place with all that crowd of folks at the medicine show an' all of a sudden he was gone before I could lay a hand on him."

Brant pushed the table out of his way.

"Come on, then."

He brushed through them at the door. No one said anything. Pete Henry and Sam followed in a rush. In the moment before she joined them, Sonie caught a glimpse of John Barton kneeling on the floor. He was carefully folding the papers that had fallen there.

Then she picked up her skirts and ran.

2

West Street was dim, close, and deserted. There was no sound in it but that of their own hurrying feet. John Barton came up by Sonie's side, walking with a loose gangling stride. She saw that he had brought his carpetbag along. Ahead of them strode Brant, flanked by Sam and Pete Henry. Pete Henry's voice floated back exclaiming, pleading.

"Had to leave the wagon an' mules hitched at the livery . . . never saw so many people . . . couldn't get past . . . weren't no time to do nothin' but push through an' run!"

Brant made no answer. His tall bulk moved urgently and powerfully ahead. Sonie began to wonder with growing anxiety what was happening at her house. O Lord! whatever made me think I could leave 'em this long on a Sat'd'y evenin'? I *am* a big fool! She pulled her skirts higher and broke into a run, leaving John Barton behind her.

They turned the corner into Maple. At first it seemed as ominously empty as the street they had left, the warehouses higher, the wooden walls leaning over them. They had not more than three blocks to go, but it began to stretch endlessly in the empty darkness. Ahead of them a big wavering glow spilled out into the street, throwing monstrous shadows on the side of Weller's livery and on

135

the warehouse opposite. Sonie knew it was coming from her lot, where the show was in progress. There was not a light in any of the other houses as they passed them—the Gorons', Altmanns', the Vitcheks'—and next them her own Maple House was as devoid of illumination as a tomb. What, for heaven's sake, had come over them! As she approached, running as hard as she could, she saw that the whole street beyond was packed with people, a whole milling, flickering sea of faces turned toward the light. The whole end of her narrow front porch toward the lot as well as her front steps was packed with them, and across the way they stood upright in wagons. She recognized a few better-dressed young blades from the other side of town, but most of them were farmers and their families mingling with the inhabitants, black and white, from Jamaica Town and the warehouse section. Pete Henry was right. She'd never seen so many people, all sizes, shapes, and ages. Excitement raced together with her concern at the sight of them. Something sure must be goin' on and she was missing it! She recognized that there was a sound coming from them now, a steady murmuring noise with sudden bursts of high raucous laughter and catcalls. It was the sound of a lot of people having themselves a time. Above it she became aware of a lone, long, babbling shriek. It sounded as though someone were in the last stages of intolerable agony. Reaching the fringe of the crowd, Sonie began to push and worm her way in among the backs. She succeeded only in becoming swallowed up in a close press of hot perspiring bodies and could see nothing. She had lost Brant and the others. She turned irritably to a tall young farmer next her. He was holding in his arms a wide-eyed little boy.

"What's happening?" she yelled, wishing she were ten feet tall. But the child began to cry and the young man became absorbed in comforting him, dandling him and lifting him high on his shoulder. Sonie could hear that hideous inhuman shriek rising and falling. What a mess! she thought grimly, and began to fight her way out of the crowd again. I've got to get in the house. If that isn't somebody already being hurt, I bet somebody will be before this evenin's over. Anyway I want to see what's goin' on!

As she pushed her way on again, tramping upon feet, boring up through the crowd on her front steps, she began to think, irrelevantly, that she hadn't charged that fellow with the gold teeth enough rental on the lot—ten dollars wouldn't begin to cover the damage that was sure to come from all this. She had been taken in by his insolent, flattering eyes, the highbrow manner. . . .

"If you don't mind," she said aloud, addressing two masculine figures who stood between her and the front door, "I'd like to get in my house!"

They moved aside, making way for her. One of them spoke.

"Sho, sho! that you, Sonie?"

She recognized the voice of Willie Edwards. Willie worked in the hardware store off Main Street.

"It's what left of me," she answered crossly and turned the doorknob. It was unyielding. She banged on the wood and turned the handle of the bell. She could just hear its muffled tinkling inside.

"Mrs. Rose—Mrs. Lily—somebody, let me in!"

At last it gave under her hands. But only an inch or two. A scared whisper came through the crack.

"Go away, please, an' stop knockin'. We're not receivin' callers tonight till after the show."

"For heaven's sake, Mrs. Rose," said Sonie. "It's *me!* Let me in!"

"Thank Gawd, honey!"

The door opened at last. She slipped inside and closed it behind her. There was no light except a glow on the parlor walls. It came through the bay window overlooking the vacant lot. She felt herself enveloped in a massive, excited hug and smelled Mrs. Rose's strong carnation talc.

"Are you all right, honey? We've been worryin'—"

"I had an awful time gettin' in," said Sonie, disengaging herself in the dark. "Where are all the lights?"

"I turned them out. That rough crowd was foolin' 'round out there on the porch. I was afraid they might try breakin' in."

"I've just got here. What's happened?"

"Honey, you wouldn't believe your eyes!" gasped Mrs. Rose. Sonie waited for no more but ran past her to the bay window. All three of the casements were open and Mrs. Lily and Mrs. Pearl were leaning on their elbows, fanning themselves and looking out with all the aplomb and attention of ladies in a theater box. They made room for her.

"Just look!" squealed Mrs. Pearl, squeezing her arm enthusiastically. The window was the perfect vantage point for observing everything. Sonie took it all in at a glance. The crowd stretched below her almost solidly from the side of her house to the livery. Toward the back of the lot, just in front of the chinaberry tree where she had watched them set it up that afternoon, was the medicine wagon, its red and gold scrollwork glowing magnificently in the light of half a dozen oil torches. The torches were set on poles along the sides of a little platform resting on trestles. This platform normally served as a side to the van and was hinged to it. Let down thus, it revealed a miniature baroque proscenium framing the interior of the wagon itself. The opening was closed now with a red curtain, draped and hung with gilt tassels and fringe. Appliquéd across the face of its folds in shabby gold letters were again the words DR. MONACO. Upon the platform chairs were set up in a little

137

semicircle facing the crowd, and in them were the same gentlemen with their battered instruments who had made the air up in the square hideous with sound earlier in the day. Immediately behind them, against the red curtain, stood the giant Negro, dressed in a purple robe. A silver turban topped his head. He stood, arms folded, like a carved figure. On the platform near the front was a small table. On its gold-fringed cover stood some bottles colorfully labeled. Behind the table, one hand resting lightly on the tops of the bottles, the other elegantly placed on his hip, Sonie recognized the tall gentleman with the top hat and the mustache to whom she had rented the lot that afternoon. Against the towering dark, hung low with heavy stars and pressed about on all sides by the thick sea of upturned faces, the scene glowed with such a pure theatrical magnificence that she caught her breath. It was even better than the circus years ago at Reidsville! She felt dizzy. What a lot I've been missin'! she thought impulsively. I could be a part of this, too. I ought to have been long ago. . . .

But it was only for a moment. She sensed immediately that something had gone wrong with the scene before her. The crowd was not looking toward the men on the platform at all. Everyone, including the costumed figures, was turned toward her house. The crowd swayed and crude yelling sounds broke out of it. She realized that the lone screaming voice was still going on, had never, in fact, stopped. So enchanted had she been by what she saw before her that for a space she had not heard anything. Now as she listened she knew that all of them out there were listening too, with a curious, bestial intentness. Of course she knew who it was now! She had known almost before she heard it at all. It was the voice of Templeton Royle. She leaned out the window farther, turning her head until she saw him. On the little landing at the very top of the back steps leading to the second floor of her house stood Templeton, a hatless, bristling, terrible little figure clutching the flimsy handrail. He was leaning dangerously out over the crowd below him. As she watched he swayed and rocked, and began to make strange tearing gestures at the air above his head as though he wanted to rip the sky asunder and pull it down. The high, maddened sound of his voice resolved itself into words.

"Sinners ye are—every man, woman, and babe of ye!" he bawled in his hoarse high screech. "That ye stand in the sight of the Lord gazing with lustful eyes an' hearts upon the pleasures of Babylon an' the fleshpots of Egypt. The fiery pit gapes foh you—down on yoh knees an' beg foh His mercy on yoh blackened souls!"

There came a burst of scattered yells, whoops, and whistles. A man's voice called out above it:

"Get that ol' fool down from there! We want the show!"

138

Templeton stopped. Sonie saw his pinched gray face freeze in a grimace of hate. A woman laughed, a high, clattering nervous sound. Scattered voices from all over the restless, shifting herd of humanity began to call out.

"Put it away till tomorrow, Granpa—tomorrow's Sunday!"

"Let 'im be—he's better'n the show!"

"We don' need no hell-fire tonight, do we, boys? Haw haw!"

"Come down offen there an' shut up befoh we have to haul you down!"

There was something ugly and edgy, not festive and exuberant, in the sound of this. Sonie felt her chest constrict. What had happened to Brant? She searched below her for a sight of him. But in the wavering light she saw no face that she knew, although she felt certain that at least half of Jamaica Town must be out there. She had a wild thought that she might be able to persuade that crazy old man to come inside if she ran upstairs. . . . At that moment, however, the elegant figure of the gentleman in the top hat advanced to the edge of the platform. He raised his arms for attention, his smile flashing golden beneath the mustaches. He looked like a tall and glittering insect. Sonie could not help admiring his poise at the moment. Beneath his brash, theatrical exterior the man had something about him that interested her. In a back corner of her mind she decided that she ought to have a little talk with him before he left town.

"Laideees and Gentlemen—one moment, please!" The long vowels rolled out sonorously over the tumult. "*If* the gentleman holding service on the steps could be persuaded that he is, perhaps, in the wrong pew—"

The crowd interrupted him with a burst of laughter. He waited, the mocking, golden grin including them all intimately in his little joke. He sure knows what he's about, Sonie observed to herself.

"If the gentleman on the steps could be persuaded to let me interrupt his interesting dissertation for a minute—just one short minute—I think we could get on with our entertainment. It will be climaxed by a little lecture I have especially prepared on the ills of mankind, a dissertation which I have delivered before distinguished audiences all over this great continent, and which I am sure that you ladies and gentlemen out here tonight will not want to miss. You will not want to miss it because not only will I discuss the ills, but in due time I will bring to your attention a marvelous cure—"

He was interrupted again by a splatter of mocking applause and whoops. Sonie began to notice that most of this ferment seemed to originate from a clot of young men near the middle of the gathering. Whoever they are, she thought grimly, they're spoilin' for trouble tonight.

"Yeah, that's right—get on with the show, if you got one!" one among them yelled out. Try as she might, Sonie could not tell who any of them were. Everything seemed to be happening too swiftly, and yet she could not see anything happening on the surface at all. It was in some way sinister and frightening. Her thoughts were cut short again by Templeton Royle. He began to scream down, singling out the speaker on the platform for his full wrath.

"Sinner! You sly-mouthed son of Baal—you and yohs cannot stop the word of the Lawd, an' you know it! Tremble, tremble! Foh His avengin' angels are breathin' hot on yoh heels at this moment, reachin' to drag all of you down to flames an' everlastin' torment—down on yoh knees, you honey-mouthed minion of hell! I tell you on the Day of Glory there ain'ta gonna be a houn' dog even that'll stan' up to answer foh you."

Templeton paused to gasp for breath. A curious and deathly stillness gripped the crowd. Then Sonie saw Brant at last working through the packed bodies toward the stairs, furiously pushing everything out of his way. He must have had to inch slowly, all the way from the other side. Sonie wanted to call down to him, but she realized he couldn't hear her. Her attention, as well as that of everyone else, was seized by a strange, moaning cry proceeding from the van.

"O Lawd! . . . Sweet Jesus, save us!"

It came from the huge Negro in the silver turban. His black face thrown back, the eyes rolled upward, he sank slowly to his knees behind the seated players, clasping and wringing his hands. Bedlam broke loose. Screams and howls of delight rose from all sides.

"The nigger's got religion, glory!—Preach, preach, Ol' Temp Royle! You got 'em licked—give us the show, the show, the show! Throw the nigger out. . . . Throw the ol' fool out with 'im! Let's get the gals out of the sportin' house—I bet Sonie Lipik could use a little fancy preachin', eh, boys?"

At the sound of her name out of the babbling storm Sonie froze with anger. She heard Mrs. Rose moan over her shoulder.

"Oh Lawdy . . . I knew there was gonna be trouble. Where's the sheriff? He ought a be here. Oh Lawdy, what'll we do?"

"Keep quiet!" she hissed fiercely. Mrs. Lily and Mrs. Pearl had disappeared suddenly from their positions on either side of her. Angrily, she continued to look. Events outside were now developing so rapidly that it was difficult to focus and comprehend just where they were leading. She saw the man on the platform turn to the players with a sharp gesture of command. They raised their instruments and instantly blaring, raucous music joined the confusion of sound. Below her, where Brant was struggling toward the stairs, a fight had broken out. It spread in a mad contagion of writhing

140

bodies and falling fists throughout the crowd. The scene was one of magnificent and utter insanity. It was as though every man there had been seized on the instant with a madness to destroy whatever lay closest to hand, to release all the pent-up wildness, the cruel pressure of the hot night, in a mindless anarchy. Above her Sonie could see Templeton dancing on the landing, flinging his arms, his mouth opening and closing, but she could hear no sound of his voice.

It was then that the first rock was thrown. It struck with a sharp, tinkling crash among the bottles of Dr. Monaco's sovereign remedy on the platform. It signaled a perfect hail of odd missiles. They exploded out of the night. The musicians ceased playing and ducked behind their instruments. An assortment of stones and rubbish rattled all about them on the platform and against the show wagon. Only the man in the top hat remained unmoved. He stood coolly caressing his black mustache and looking about him with the fixed, saturnine grin. Sonie could not help feeling a thrill of admiration for him at that moment. The van, however, was not the only target. Blows began to clatter all along the side of Maple House. From the far side of the parlor Mrs. Rose gasped.

"Honey, get away from that window!"

Sonie shrugged and yelled over her shoulder, "They wouldn't dare hit me!"

But she moved slightly so that her face at least was protected by the window frame. Meanwhile she followed Brant's progress below. Glancing up at Templeton Royle, she saw the little man stop suddenly in the middle of his frenetic dance. His arms raised over his head were frozen in a final awful gesture of rage and hate. Something in his attitude made her hold her breath. He swayed and tottered at the edge of the top stair and then began to fall end over end like a thin bag of grain, terribly. It seemed an endless time before he stopped, twisted limply, face downward, about halfway down the stairs. The bundle did not move. Everything paused to watch that grotesque plunge. In the little silence that followed Sonie heard the hoarse, deep bellow of the Negro again. "Lawd Jesus!"

She saw him rise to his feet on the platform. The splendid turban had fallen off, leaving his ebony skull naked and glistening with sweat. While every eye followed him, he leapt from the platform and with arms outstretched before him in a gesture of pity and despair, he plowed unresisted across the space between him and the stairs. Reaching them, he leaped up to Templeton in one incredible bound. He made no move to touch the inert figure there, but, falling to his knees, he began to sway and moan, his purple-clad back turned to all of them, oblivious. It had happened so quickly, and was an action of such strange power and mystery, that every eye seeing it was held suspended and incredulous. A man's voice howled:

141

"The nigger's gone crazy!"

A roar then arose as though out of the bowels of the trampled, hard-packed earth itself. Sonie at the window felt her fingers bite into the sill. The whole crowd swept toward the stairway. At the foot of it Brant's big figure, the shirt half-torn from his back, exploded out of a knot of tossing arms and bodies. Hands reached and clawed at his legs as he caught the handrail. He turned swiftly and kicked himself free, his face set and white with rage. Seeing him caught briefly in the leaping, wavering light, Sonie felt both relief and fear sweep over her. If they don't watch out he'll kill one of them, she thought. She saw him leap up on the steps to the Negro and push him aside. For a moment, as he leaned over Templeton, hiding him from view, it looked to her as though the big white man and the huge black bent their heads together in an attitude of mutual graciousness. It was a moment she was to remember long after out of all the insane kaleidoscope of that evening. The two of them seemed utterly unmindful of the men who were crowding up the stairs after them. Then with a strangely tender gesture Brant stooped and picked up the body of his father as though it had no more substance than air and began to climb upward. The Negro rose and turned, an awesome and gigantic figure in the purple robe, blocking the path of the men struggling below him. Then Sonie saw the railing sag and give way. She turned from the window and dashed past Mrs. Rose and the others into the dark hallway. Behind her, something smashed through one of the parlor windows. She heard Mrs. Lily squeal with fright. She did not stop.

"Get some light—all of you," she called back curtly to them as she sped up the stairs. At the top she stumbled in the hem of her dress. "Oh holy Joe!" she muttered in exasperation. "The first time I've worn it, too!" She ran on down the hall to the upper back porch. Here the roar of sound from below broke upon her anew. Beyond the screen door she could see the dark loom of Brant where he stood on the little landing. She tore impatiently at the latch. His back was to her and she had to scream to make herself heard above the noise.

"In here, Brant—*in here!*"

He stood looking below him, without moving. She caught at his arm impatiently. Then she saw that he was watching the struggle on the stairway. The Negro was still there as she had last seen him, only now he was throwing off a succession of raging assailants, one by one, calmly, almost indifferently, like a great bull beset by terriers. Then, as though tiring of the game, he turned suddenly and without a breath of hesitation leaped out into the darkness toward the back of the house. The great thud as he hit the ground could be heard distinctly.

"Get that damned nigger!"

142

The stairway emptied instantly. They tore after him back toward the warehouses and the railroad tracks. The whole lot was covered with grotesque, struggling knots of humanity. The center of activity still raged around the van. It looked now like a strange vessel tossed and shaken in a storm of moving bodies and faces. The platform and the players had vanished in the midst of it. One of them still remained in view. He had climbed to the roof of the van, where he squatted laying about him at the clutching, leaping figures with the banjo. Then he too was caught, pulled down, and swallowed in the general melee. It was difficult to tell what was happening. Three of the torches had gone out. The others were dashing weirdly about the space, in the hands of yelling, hooting boys. It was like a hideous dream. Across the street a team of horses began to neigh in terror and to rear in their traces. There were some women screaming hysterically and continuously. The crowd in the street began to scatter in all directions, getting away from the plunging hoofs. Another wagon, piled with figures, pulled out, its driver cursing and cracking his whip over the straining team. Individuals leaped on and off it as it was swallowed up in the darkness beyond the livery. Suddenly a voice rang out clearly: "The law! Here's the law, boys!"

It was followed instantly by cackling laughter and a general flight. The torches disappeared, dropped to the ground. Listening to the laughing, cursing exodus in the darkness, Sonie thought grimly, Well, it's about time! Then a boy's voice screamed hysterically, "Fire! fire!" Caught up by other voices, it echoed up and down the length of Maple Street. Someone had tossed the last of the burning torches on top of the van. Little tongues of flames were already creeping down one corner, licking up the spilled oil. Seeing it, Sonie cried out in rage, "The fools, the damned ol' fools!"

She left Brant and ran back into the hallway. They had lit a lamp below. She leaned over the stairwell.

"Mrs. Rose!" she called. "You-all go get every bucket and pan you can lay your hands on down there and fill 'em with water."

"But honey—"

"Don't stop to argue. Just do like I say."

Brant came into the hallway behind her.

"Wait a minute." She was calm again. "Till I get a light." She went to the hall table and lighted the lamp there with steady fingers. All the crazy excitement that she had been a part of for the past quarter of an hour had left her. Brant stood quiet in the back doorway looking down at the little sagging figure across his arms. It was a strange look, half pain, half wonder.

"Is he hurt bad?"

He shook his head. "I don't know," he said slowly. "He's still breathing, so I guess he ain't dead."

143

He came down the hallway to the head of the stairs.

"Where are you goin', Brant?" Sonie crossed and opened the door to her room. "Put him in here on my bed. I'll go get Doc Saunders."

He turned to her with a frown. "What are you thinkin' of, Sonie? I can't leave him here in your house. I'm takin' him back to West Street."

She started to speak, but checked herself, shrugged, and closed the door again. This was no time to fight with him.

"Sonie, did you see what that damned nigger did?" There was still the slow note of wonder in his voice. He did not wait for her reply, but started down the stairs shaking his head. She followed him. Below, the hall and parlor were brightly lighted, and deserted. She heard a great clatter in the kitchen and the thrum of water pouring out of the sink tap into a bucket. There was still noise outside. Running feet, the rattle and creak of wheels, a few shouts. But it had a dying, exhausted sound. Through the parlor window she could see the leaping, angry glow of the burning van. She could also see figures hurrying to and fro from the livery. Well, they were doing something sensible at last! Brant paused before the front door waiting for her to open it. Suddenly she felt tired and depressed, all the vitality gone out of her. Before she could move to the door, however, it began to echo with a steady determined knocking. The hysterical tinkle of the little bell joined it. Through the din came a hearty, masculine roar.

"Sonie, Rose! Somebody, open this damned door—it's me!"

It was too good to be true. Doc Saunders! He must have been in all the mess out there and seen them bring Templeton in. Behind her she heard Mrs. Rose, Mrs. Lily, and Mrs. Pearl come breathlessly into the hall from the kitchen.

"It's Doc Saunders," she reassured them, releasing the latch. A tubby little figure shot in and confronted them. He was coatless. One sleeve of his shirt hung in shreds. Over a perspiring countenance like that of an inebriate mastiff—a great bulb of a nose plastered squarely in the middle of sagging cheeks and chins—he was wearing an enormous crumpled black hat pushed low on the forehead.

"Sons of fame and glory!" he shouted, slamming the door behind him. His little pig eyes surveyed them. He rubbed the palms of his fat hands together, cut a little caper with his feet on the hall rug, climaxed it with a click of heels in the air, and swept the hat from his head. "Sonie—you an' the gals all right? Did you ever see anything like it? Everybody tryin' to kill everybody else for no reason 't'all, far as I could see, 'cept for the fun of it. Sheriff showed up just in time. Ain't goin' to stop 'em though. They've just cut loose

144

all over Jamaica Town, chasin' every poh dahky they find out of doors. No sense to it. Hot openin' for the market, lotta hell to be raised. Gets worse every year. Gonna be a lotta cuts and bruises huntin' Doc Saunders 'foh the night's out. Thought I might as well begin here."

This poured out of him in a breathless, staccato roar. He turned to Brant.

"Let's have a look at 'im, Brant." He stepped forward, laid a hand briefly on Templeton's ashen forehead, took one of the limp arms at the wrist, pulled back the lid of Templeton's eye, shook his head, and barked: "Stroke!"

Brant did not move. "I'm takin' him back to the store, Doc," he said quietly. "You come along. Go get your things."

The little man looked at him aghast, the sweaty cheeks quivering. "Back to the store!" he exploded indignantly. "You wanta kill what's left of him? Put him down—"

"I'll get him there all right, and you'll come with me, Doc." There was no emotion in Brant's voice. It was calm as iron. Sonie, watching him, felt the little, irrational rush of tenderness for him flood her again. He'll always be able to make them do what he wants, she thought through her weariness. *They* don't know it yet, but I do.

"Open the door for me, Sonie."

He walked past her and out into the darkness. It was still full of the shouts and commotion going on about the fire next door. She had a wild impulse to step forward and hold him back. It was a desolate feeling, a feeling that had been growing in her ever since he had brought his father off the landing upstairs. He was walking away from her, from all of them forever, tonight. But she stood there, her hand holding the doorknob hard, and watched him go down the front steps. Behind her Doc Saunders growled and threw up his arms in exasperation.

"Blamed young mule!" he ejaculated and jamming his hat over his ears, stomped angrily to the door. There he whirled with a comical, leering wink and roared good-humoredly: "You gals take care of yourselves—you're still all too young and pretty to be gettin' into trouble!"

Mrs. Rose, Mrs. Pearl, and Mrs. Lily, standing wide-eyed at the foot of the stairs, bridled in unison.

"Go on, Doc!" giggled Mrs. Rose. "You *are* a sight!"

He uttered a single bark of amusement and went out. Sonie, leaving the door open, ran into the parlor and looked out the window. The van was now a glowing pile sending up a thin cloud of acrid smoke. The whole hot night was full of the smell of scorched paint and charred wood. Men were still bringing buckets from the livery pump; but most of the remaining onlookers stood about at a respectful distance talking in subdued tones. Satisfied, Sonie ran back into the hall and seized Mrs. Rose's plump arm.

"Look, I'm gonna run over to the store for a while, too. They've got the fire out over there. You won't have to worry about that. I think we'd better just close up for the night. There might be some o' those fools all liquored-up who'd wander back here lookin' for trouble. Don't let *anyone* in. You all just go on up to bed, now. I'll be right back soon—soon as I see that Brant—"

She faltered and looked away. Mrs. Rose's careful mask of discreet rouge and powder was no longer heavy and slightly silly. The blue eyes hung on Sonie's face full of wisdom and a tired sadness. She patted Sonie's hand. "You run along, honey. Don't worry for a minute. We ain't been livin' this long without findin' out how to take care of ourselves!"

Sonie hugged her briefly and blindly and went out. Even with the group standing up the way, Maple Street seemed unnaturally dark and quiet. At the foot of the steps she paused. A man sat there. His head was buried upon his knees. It was an attitude of such utter dejection that she said:

"You hurt?"

The figure lifted its head. Her eyes were becoming accustomed to the dark now. It was John Barton. His lank hair was matted on his forehead and a dark streak of blood marked one cheek. His hat was gone, but she saw the inevitable carpetbag clasped tightly between his feet.

"No, ma'am," he answered in the bleak nasal voice. He looked down at a smear of blood on his hand, puzzled. "I reckon I'm just lost."

Sonie shook her head. The poor fool—the poor, helpless ol' fool.

"You'd better come along with me, then," she said, not knowing exactly why she did so, except that somehow now he and his precious carpetbag belonged to Brant.

As she stepped lightly down the brick sidewalk she heard his footsteps following unevenly, a grotesque, slow echo of her own.

3

It was after midnight and dead-still when Brant stepped out alone upon the little porch landing above the store. The alley below was a dark, bottomless trench. At least it was cooler here than within. The little rooms inside were like ovens, husbanding the heat. About him Kingsmont lay tranced under the warm stars. He welcomed the calm like a new friend. The violent and disconnected happenings of the day lulled within him. He could hold them all. He could hold anything! There was a difference, though, between him and all of

146

it that rested out there beyond his eminence. He felt above and separated from the familiar spreading jungle of the town. It lay there about him, quiet and tired, like a creature licking its wounds in the shadows. He, on the other hand, stood free and clean within himself, full of a pulsing sense of power and release. Tonight he had come to the end of a sum, had opened a door upon a vista within himself that he had always known was there. Only now, this day, had he found the key. He did not speculate upon the mystery of it. He was too impatient for any mystic consideration of the shape of the world as he now found it. All his life he had viewed it with fury, a caged animal, weighing all that he saw or felt or voraciously learned to the end that it should destroy the bars between him and the need for power over all his actions, over the actions of others.

He would have been the last to realize it, but there was in him that which had to grasp, to hold, to shape. Until this day it had lain within him without any goal or purpose. It had been more like a sickness, blocked and pent-up, eating at his vitals until it became only a black need to tear and rend all about him, to strike blindly, to drink hard and deeply and without relish, just to still briefly the agony in his soul. It was all gone now. Wiped out. He could not think how it had been done. But what had been done added up irrevocably to just that. He felt the certainty in his very bowels. Although they were not arranged yet in sequence, the cards lay in his hands ready to be declared. It was going to be a big game. The kind of game he had been seeking. It was cut at last to suit him, and him alone. The pointless violence that marked the events of that evening did not touch it. He viewed them impersonally. They were, however, part and parcel of the more profound realization. The town would forget, absorb, what had happened tonight. It would become embedded in the common sediment of events that holds the history of any community of men. He knew that he himself would always remember it no matter what else lay in store for him. It was a day marked especially for him. For the first time he stood alone and knew he was going to hold the world by the tail.

He tried to be moved by the fact that Pa might be dying. But it was a distant, a mathematical supposition. It was only one more cipher in the design that had shaped itself for him.

When he had brought Pa at last from Sonie's house and put him in his own bed, he had stood impatient at the foot of it. He watched Doc Saunders, working to the accompaniment of a constant stream of comment and blasphemy, bending over all that was now Templeton Royle.

"He ain't dead—he ain't very likely gonna die, in spite of himself. Sometimes I believe the ol' devil's permanently preserved in alcohol and bile—God dern him! Guess it'll take somethin' more than a stroke an' a little concussion to haul him before his Maker, damn him! Looks like you three boys together could hold him together, keep him out of trouble. I'm tired of havin' to patch up the lot of you. At his age he oughtn't to be loose plaguin' mankind. This time anyway he'll have to rest quiet for a while, whether he likes it or not. If he's lucky, he'll come out of this with nothin' more than little paralysis of some sort. Blast him! he doesn't deserve it."

Brant scarcely heard him, standing there. He kept looking tenderly at the raddled, cadaverous countenance of his father. The breath came and went harshly through the thin, blue mouth. He looked with a kind of recognition, as though he saw in those familiar features, permanently molded by burning violence, some reason at last for Templeton's twisted, driven wandering through life. Some reason for his having kept his sons bound closely about him, for his having clawed and yelled himself toward that mysterious goal lying beyond the sight and comprehension of those about him.

While Brant stood there, Sam and Pete Henry came in. He heard them first below putting the wagon in the shed at the back of the factory. Their voices were joined in bitter quarrel. But when they came at last into the room where their father lay, Sam stood aside gnawing silently at his fingers and Pete Henry, bursting into tired, childish sobs, fell on his knees by the bed.

"Pa!" he cried. "Pa!"

"Oh for God's sake!" said Doc Saunders, wiping his bulbous nose with disgust and glaring fiercely. "You big ninny—yoh pa ain't dead by a long sight. Get out of the way so I can do my work properly!"

Pete Henry turned to him a face smudged with dirt and battle, and then buried it in the bedclothes. He went on sobbing, too worn-out with emotion to care.

"Oh for God's sake!"

Doc Saunders turned back to his patient furiously. Brant said nothing. After a moment he turned and walked out into the hallway. He was confronted by a breathless Sonie. Behind her was John Barton.

"How is he, Brant?" Sonie's husky familiar voice was low and grave.

"Doc says he thinks he'll be all right."

"I thought I might be able to help a little. . . ." She faltered, looking beyond him into the room.

"Thanks, Sonie." He wanted it to sound grateful. But he could feel nothing because she was there, that she had never been in his house before.

"I brought your friend," she continued breathlessly. "He didn't seem to know where to go."

148

She waited for some comment from him, but he was silent. So she brushed past him into the room where Templeton lay. Brant looked at Barton.

"You got those papers all safe?"

"Ayeh."

"Where you stayin' tonight?"

"I don't know."

Brant stood silent for a moment. "All right. You'd better stay with us. I can bed you down here till you find some place."

There was no warm hospitality in his voice. It was clear command. It expected no protest and received none. He motioned to Barton to follow him. They went down the dark, narrow little hallway. It smelled of resin and greasy, careless cooking. The sound of Doc Saunders's voice complaining above the noise of Pete Henry's hoarse and muffled weeping followed them. Brant flung open a door into a little airless chamber normally used for storage. He lit a lamp. In the light of it Barton saw a rickety cot. His eyes fell upon it gratefully.

"Sure I'm not puttin' you out any?" he questioned.

Brant shook his head. He was looking steadily at the carpetbag. "Naw," he said, almost roughly. "You're welcome."

There was a sound of footsteps coming up the steps outside. In a moment Sam bawled down the hall.

"Sheriff Tom's here, Brant. Wants to see you."

Brant looked piercingly at Barton. "I'll see you tomorrow," he said, and closed the door.

The sheriff was waiting in the bare, ugly little sitting room, which was seldom used as such because Templeton and his sons only slept and ate in the house. The sheriff was a large man with a congenitally lazy and somnolent countenance. He stood, hat in hand, shifting uneasily from foot to foot. With him was Hugh Ridges, who acted in emergencies as a deputy. Both of them seemed embarrassed and awkward.

"Well, Brant—" The sheriff mopped his streaming face with a dirty bandanna. "For once I'm sorry to come bustin' in on you like this. Leastways, I ain't comin' to git you *this* time!" He guffawed nervously. Brant waited in silence. He and the sheriff were old acquaintances. They had met many times under unvaryingly violent circumstances. Usually they ended with Brant accepting the hospitality of one of the cells in the dirty, verminous little jail up behind the courthouse. In spite of this the sheriff held a special regard for Brant. There was something about this young giant that puzzled and troubled him as much as he ever allowed anything to puzzle the fat, inert course of his existence. Not that Brant had ever made any effort to be friendly. On the contrary. But still a kind of tentative

149

understanding had sprung up between the two men based on familiarity if on nothing else.

"No," continued the sheriff. "I really come to find out how yoh daddy is—an' to tell you we got all those show folks that started the trouble locked up—that is, all 'cept that damn nigger, who's vanished off the face of the earth's far as we can see. They're sayin' he's the one first began throwin' things. I wanted to know if you was there when it all happened so's you could give me an idear—"

Brant shook his head. The sheriff rocked on his heels.

"Never saw such a market openin' in all my bawn days! There's some hellions—they must be from out o' town—wanderin' 'round tryin' to beat up niggers. I've had to call out all my extry deppities —haven't I, Hugh?" The deputy nodded. "The jail's plumb full of drunks an' rowdies now. Don' know what I'm gonna do if I have to haul anybody else up!" He shook his head sorrowfully. "Them show folks, now—I don't know whether they's to blame—or who's to blame —but that feller with the mustache who's in charge of 'em's been raisin' hell, talkin' slicker than a Raleigh lawyer—ain't he, Hugh? Says he's gonna sue the whole damn county for assault and batt'ry and destruction of property. Can't much blame him, either. They sho ruined his business tonight. But I'm tryin' someways to find out how it all started—you got any idears, Brant?"

"No," said Brant. "An' you'll just waste your time tryin' to find out who was the first to begin, because it wasn't started on purpose. It just happened that way. An' Pa just happened to set it off."

"How is yoh daddy?"

"He'll be all right," said Brant. He wanted the sheriff to go.

"Well, I'm sho glad to hear it! 'Fraid for a while I had murder on my hands. The Mayor'll be on my tail as it is—he's already runnin' round in his carriage raisin' hell. Ain't he, Hugh? . . . Well—" the sheriff put on his hat—"come on—we gotta find that nigger dead or alive 'fore we rest easy tonight. Real sorry 'bout yoh daddy, Brant. Hope he gets all right. An' thanks for givin' me yoh views on the subject an' not enterin' no complaint. Lord knows I'll get enough of 'em as it is!"

Sam saw them out. Brant sank into a chair in the airless, close little sitting room. He heard Sam return, go to his room down the hall, and close the door. A little later Sonie and Doc Saunders came out of his father's room. Brant, half-listening, heard Sonie cajole the old, swearing man to the head of the stairs and out into the night. Still he sat thinking and thinking—not about any of them. They were all far away. His mind was on tomorrow and the next day, and the day after that. He was studying it carefully. He didn't even hear Sonie when she stopped in the doorway behind him and stood smiling at his back, her vitality undimmed by the night, her whole

150

bearing proud and awake. He looked up finally, hearing the bracelets tinkle and clash on her arm. She was fooling with her hair as usual.

"Guess I'd better go now, Brant. He's asleep an' I got Pete Henry to go to bed. Doc says he'll stop by first thing in the mornin'. You gonna sit here all night?" He didn't answer. "I'll slip over myself tomorrow—don't worry, I'll do it on the sly so it needn't worry anybody. I have an idea you boys'll be as helpless as babies."

"Thanks, Sonie, for everything you've done tonight," he said, then added, turning to her, "I'm sorry 'bout the food. Did you make blintzes?"

"Yes," she nodded, scolding him gently with the green eyes, "and a pot of Mama's borsch too."

They would be on the stove as she had left them, with the table set for him. She had forgotten all of it too. What moved her now was his attempt at an apology. It was the nearest he had ever come to one.

"Forget it," she said. "There's always more where they came from."

"Yeah, I reckon."

His mouth twisted in the half-smile. They looked at each other, bemused. A dog was barking in the distance.

"Brant," she said at last, "do you really think this man has something that you can use?"

"You mean Barton's machine?"

"Yes."

"Sonie, it's the kind of opportunity I've been waitin' all my life for. It's a gamble, sure, but it's a gamble for a big thing. If he's not just a crackpot—an' somehow I have an idea he's not—an' if this thing of his will do half he claims for it, then I'm thinkin' it can be made into the biggest thing that's hit the tobacco industry since they first found out how to flue-cure. They've all thought he was crazy, an' they'll all think I'm the same kind of a damn fool when I start, but they'll find out different!"

His jaw set, big and lean and hard. Sonie looked down, fiddling with the gay row of ribbon bows in the low neck of her dress.

"I was pretty sure you felt that way when you were talkin' with him," she said. "I just wanted to hear you say it." She paused, considering something carefully before she spoke again: "It's gonna take lots of money. Startin' something new always does."

Brant nodded. "It's got to be big. I've learned a lot in spite of my foolin' around, an' one o' the prime things I've learned is you've got to start bein' big where everybody else's left off, an' then keep on gettin' bigger. The money? I'll get the money no matter how much it takes."

"I think you will, Brant." She looked shrewdly at him. "I've got ten thousand dollars in the bank."

151

He frowned unbelievingly.

"What do you mean, Sonie?"

She laughed the hoarse chuckle and jingled her bracelets.

"It's a business proposition, pure and simple. I gamble too, when I like the looks of a game an' who's playin' it."

Exultation pounded in him. And this was only the beginning, here in this little room above the store and factory he had always hated. The place, the store, would be enshrined in him forever now. He would never forget it. He got up and crossed to Sonie, his black eyes blazing with emotion. He had never looked at her that way before.

"You're a smart gal, Sonie—always said you were! You stick with me."

Never since she had first known him had she felt so close to him as she did in that moment. And never, at the same time, had she felt that he was so much a stranger. She could not help saying, mockingly:

"Where do you think I've been all this time?"

He moved to embrace her, but she pushed him away.

"I said this was a business proposition, Mr. Royle. I'll want you to put it all down in writing properly, just like you would with anyone else. And I'll expect my investment to pay plenty." He grinned crookedly at her, but did not protest. She said crisply: "You draw up your papers by Monday, an' when I've agreed to them—an' I'm warnin' you, if you don't know it already, I'll be fair, but I'll be a hard bargainer. Don't ever forget I grew up in Jamaica Town too."

"I don't think I'll forget, an' I'll take you up on it."

"Good! When that's done we can go up to the bank together." Her tone was quite direct and unemotional. He took her arm.

"I'll see you home. It's late."

She looked at him unbelievingly. Then she reached up and patted his cheek affectionately. Her fingers just brushed the dull, long bruise of the welt. I wonder who gave him that, she mused again. He's already forgotten he has it. Aloud she said: "Oh no, you won't do anything of the kind. Ach! it's real nice of you, but I'm not used to it. You stay here where you're needed. I've done all right takin' care o' myself so far. I don' want to begin gettin' any new ideas now. I'll get back to the house all right."

Grinning, he followed her out on the landing and watched her go down the steps.

"Evenin'," he called softly after her. She did not answer but raised an arm and waved. The jingle and tinkle of the bracelets came up to him out of the darkness of the street. He leaned on the banister looking long after she had turned the corner of the building. It was so still now that he could hear nothing but the sound of his own

152

beating heart. And while he leaned there he only half saw a shadow detach itself from the side of the warehouse opposite and cross soundlessly to the foot of the stairs.

"Boss!" A deep whisper hailed him out of the darkness below. "Is dat you?"

Brant raised his head frowning. "Who's that?"

"Sweet Jesus! It's me, boss, de poh niggah what helped you in de fight."

It was him all right. Brant could see the tall robed figure now half-crouched down there.

"What in hell you doin' down there?"

"Dey didn' catch me yet. I was hidin' over 'cross de way when I seed you go up dere wid de preacher man—oh, boss, don' let 'em get me now! I wanta stay neah de preacher man—he's gonna save my poh soul. I knows it, boss, I knows it—I'll wuk, I'm big an' strong. I'll do anything you say, but please, boss, don' sen' me 'way now— dey'll get dis sinner foh sho—jus' let me stay where I can be neah de preacher man!"

The whispered pleading was desperate, but there was an odd dignity in it. Brant felt touched. He did not know whether to curse or laugh.

"What's your name?" he called down.

"Maryland, boss!"

"Well, Maryland, I haven't forgotten what you did for me tonight." He leaned over the banister and gestured toward the back of the building. "You go back there now an' you'll find the door to the wagon shed open. You can stay there tonight. Nobody'll bother you. I'll talk to you in the mornin'."

"Ah thank you, boss, thank you. Praise His name!"

As Brant watched, the tall shadow slipped away down the side of the building. It was an odd finish to the evening, but it pleased him in a way he could not fathom. Well, poor Pa had turned one sinner to glory that night, at least. He almost laughed aloud standing there, with the wild exultance running through him. He turned to the night again as though he could force all the sleeping roofs, the fat and privileged, the poor and mean, alike that had hemmed him in and throttled him—yes, the whole wide, dreaming tobacco country out there, harvested and sleeping among the empty furrows—all of it to look at him standing there upon his threshold. He threw his head back in a gesture full of sensate power and gazed eastward across Kingsmont, as though he could pierce through the darkness to the hill and the great white house. It lay there, the enigmatic symbol, remote beneath its trees—the thing that he could never escape no matter how far he fled. And together with it there floated the arrogant, beautiful face, a part of it. The two—the house and the

153

woman—were inextricably bound up in his desire. He leaned out tensely in the darkness as though he would reach and touch them where they lay. Then he raised one clenched fist against the stars and shook it slowly.

"Wait," he whispered. "*Wait for me!*"

4

Sunday morning found the reverberations of the preceding night rocking staid breakfast tables up as far as Hill and Elm streets. Market openings were really getting out of hand. Another year with no better control than this and there was no telling what might happen. It was not only demoralizing, but it was bad for business. There was a great deal of solemn conferring among the heads of families meeting in their Sabbath best along the sidewalks on the way to church. Respectable farmers and out-of-town buyers would be taking their business elsewhere if Kingsmont was going to get a name for rowdiness and lawlessness. The Mayor himself had driven down to his offices in the courthouse right after breakfast and Sheriff Tom, as he had anticipated, had experienced an uncomfortable hour. After church, however, everyone felt a little calmer. The sermons delivered that day were unusually colorful and satisfying. Their character was wonderfully denunciatory and soothing, the texts on which they were based so thinly disguised and so immediately applicable to the state of affairs that everyone who attended them had the sensation that the burden of responsibility for action had been shifted from them to God. Sunday dinner could be approached with equanimity.

Sheriff Tom was not in a position to accept absolution so easily. He had the whole damned mess still sitting in his plump, unhappy lap. With the Mayor's heated words still fresh in his mind he did the best he could under the circumstances. To relieve the outrageously crowded state of the jail, he made a hasty review of a large number of cases and dismissed them peremptorily with no more than a blasphemous warning. Next he ordered the unhappy medicine-show people released with the suggestion that they remove themselves from Kingsmont as quickly as possible. But here he hit a snag. Instead of showing a proper gratitude for this generous treatment the fancy, slick fellow with the mustache insisted on an interview. His finery, not his manner, much dimmed by events, he confronted the sheriff in that worthy's office. He gave the harassed officer of the law to understand that he, Mr. Christopher Malley, was not to be put off so easily. Hadn't the sheriff himself signed the performance permit? Hadn't a perfectly respectable enterprise been ruined for lack of ordinary protection? This fellow, then, had the gall to add that if anything had happened to his nigger Maryland, he would invoke the

154

powers of a superior court of justice. Sheriff Tom found this man very difficult indeed.

"I don't know where your damned nigger is! We've been huntin' him all night—haven't we, boys?" He bellowed for sympathy from two sleepy deputies who slumped in the window behind him. "Hell, man! He's very likely taken to the woods! Any nigger with sense would. I'm not hidin' him—I don't *want* him! Look here. Be reasonable. It wasn't my fault what happened last night. I don't admire seein' anyone in trouble, but you act like you wanta make more trouble than you've already been in. Why don't you go see the Royles if you think somethin's owed you? After all, it looks like Ol' Temp started it—if you can 'cuse anybody of startin' it. Pity the ol' fool didn't do a proper job an' kill himself good while he was about it!"

He glared helplessly at the man before him and thought dismally about his lost sleep and the breakfast he hadn't had. Christopher Malley, sometimes patent-medicine doctor, did not seem unsympathetic.

"My dear Sheriff, I have no intention of making trouble. I only desire the fundamental rights accorded even the humblest of citizens in this fair land. I came here in all innocence, prepared to dispense balm and healing as I have done in cities throughout the length and breadth of this country. If you will recall, yesterday I secured your gracious permission to present in public the matchless product I represent."

Sheriff Tom grunted.

"Not only that," continued Malley with asperity, "but I paid a pretty penny for the use of the mean ground on which I was allowed to set up my peerless presentation. It was equipment and a presentation representing a large investment, as was obvious even to an untutored eye. Scarcely had the audience assembled to witness the entertainment offered by myself and my fellow thespians—five gentlemen, Sheriff, five accomplished gentlemen—when we were interrupted by a madman and a crowd of ruffianly inebriates who soon showed signs of needing the offices of an asylum. And you, the representative of the law, imply that you can do nothing about it! Well, let me assure you, Sheriff, that I have every intention of doing a great many things about it. I should warn you that I am not entirely ignorant of the due processes of law. You see before you a man who at one time practiced before the bar. I am fully aware of the legal grounds for this complaint. I shall engage a lawyer and start proceedings immediately."

"Go ahead, go ahead!" exploded the sheriff. Trouble, trouble, he moaned inwardly; I wish to God there warn't a Sat'd'y night in the whole week. "I ain't tryin' stop you doin' anything. Make up a

155

bill of damages 'gainst the township if you want to—but clear out o' here now before I git mad."

Malley smiled, bowed, and sauntered jauntily out into the dirty hallway. His companions awaited him there, slumped disconsolately on a bench. Even in the tired morning light they looked as bedraggled and whipped as any riffraff he had ever seen. Malley examined them with disgust, and stroked his mustache.

"Well, boys," he said at last, "let's go back and see what's left of the wagon."

Silent and bleary-eyed they followed him out into the square. He paused in the shade to look about him appreciatively. Then, sauntering easily ahead of them with the air of a man taking a pleasant walk, he set out for Maple Street. He could hear the others limping after him and cursing wearily among themselves. Oh well, he thought with philosophical detachment, here you are again, Chris Malley, right on your holy uppers! You'll have to do some fast thinking, some fancy wriggling, to get out of this one, because it's really rock bottom this time, m'lad. The only thing that really bothered him at the moment—and he called himself several kinds of a sentimental idiot for it—was the disappearance of the Negro Maryland. Having that great, imperturbably majestic animal about had delighted him. It had invested the whole shoddy venture with a note of barbaric splendor. Not only did he add color to their performances, but his gigantic strength had proved invaluable in more than one instance along the road. It had delighted Chris Malley having him about, in a very personal way. It had given him a rich and princely feeling entirely to his taste. Yes, he would, out of the whole thing, regret the loss of Maryland most. In view of the highly uncertain nature of his immediate future, however, it was, he had to admit, for the best. He felt assured that the Negro could take care of himself if he had managed to escape last night.

In silence they came upon the scene of last night's disaster. The team of horses, they knew, was safe in the livery, but the show wagon was a complete ruin. It lay, a shattered and charred skeleton, in the middle of the trampled lot. Malley, after a moment, crossed to Maple House, rang the bell, and was admitted. He was gone for half an hour. When he appeared again, walking jauntily across the churned ground, his company stared at him open-mouthed. Instead of the remains of the costume they had last seen him in, he now, by some miracle, wore again the natty, fawn-colored suit and the tall black hat set at its customary cocky angle. His lean, saturnine countenance was freshly shaved and the black mustache, though still elegant in shape, had been drastically shorn of its histrionic length. He paused before them grinning.

"Well, I'll be damned clean to Halifax!" Dave, the fat drummer, found his voice at last. He looked at Malley accusingly out of his bruised face. "Chris," he demanded, "where in hell did you find 'em?"

They crowded about Malley, excitedly asking for an explanation.

"Well, boys," Malley held up a hand for silence—"things are not quite so bad as we thought. It seems that the ladies who live next door took it upon themselves last night to rescue what they could for us. You'll find enough of your personal belongings left to cheer you. I've also arranged with the lovely owner of the establishment, Miss Lipik, to give us breakfast. I am also pleased to find out that Miss Lipik knows of Maryland's whereabouts, and that he's safe. Now, no more arguing and discussion. Wash up and we'll all put something into our stomachs and then we can discuss more intelligently what we are going to do. Come along!"

There was a noticeable change for the better in their attitudes as they followed him back to Maple House. There, surrounded by the warmly solicitous and maternal attentions of Mrs. Rose, Mrs. Lily, and Mrs. Pearl and Sonie's good-humored bossing, they removed the grime of the preceding night and sat down in the dining room with the green wallpaper and hungrily and gratefully consumed an enormous breakfast. After the last fried egg, the last pile of wheatcakes, the last cup of steaming coffee, had disappeared they remained at the table, presided over by Malley, talking long and violently as to what would be the best course—either separately or collectively—for them to follow. They arrived at the conclusion, proposed by Malley, that since the team of horses was their only remaining asset, it should be sold immediately, the proceeds divided equally among them as a stake. After that each of them could go his own separate way.

"All right, boys," said Malley, rising from the table, "if that seems fair to you, that's the way it shall be. We've had some rough and rare old times together and you've stuck with me. No one has ever accused me of not doing the best I could for my friends. I regret that we had to endure this final indignity and catastrophe together, but there's no use fooling ourselves. You know as well as I that the show wasn't doing very well." He paused and looked about at them. They all nodded in solemn agreement. "Now you know I'll get the best price I can for the team. You are all men of considerable resources, as I have reason to know, so I feel confident that you'll get yourselves successfully into some other gainful employment. I wish you luck. As for myself—I haven't made any plans yet. For the present I think I'll stay here and have a look around. There are several things about this city—if you can believe it after last night—that interest me."

Then he went back to the kitchen to see Sonie. She was piling dishes at the sink and clearing up at the stove. Jimmie, the little spidery black Negress who generally assisted in these duties, she had sent over to help at the Royle place until she could get there herself. It was hot in the kitchen. But in spite of this and in spite of the fact that she had been up through most of an active night, she looked as freshly groomed, as brightly alive, as ever. Malley saluted her with admiration.

"Miss Lipik, if I may be permitted to say so, you are a paragon among women! Allow me to express again my profound appreciation for your hospitality and kindness to six weary castaways wrecked on these inhospitable shores."

"Don't mention it, Doc. It's been a pleasure." She surveyed him with a slanted green-eyed look, half amusement, half shrewd speculation. He grinned at her. It was a friendly, knowing grin. She was calling him "Doc." From the advertisements, she had taken for granted that he was Dr. Monaco himself. It was not at all unfriendly. On the contrary, there was a great deal about this flashy, elaborate gentleman that both pleased and attracted her. But she was not fooled by him. She could not help admiring the self-possession with which he faced adversity. She recognized in that bold, theatrical front a lot that she and he had in common. Too, in spite of the gold teeth, he was not hard to look at. His taste in clothes and the way he wore them pleased her. He was a refreshing and exciting note in the masculine world of serge and denim that she had known all her life. Yes, she decided, in more ways than one it might be useful to know this man better. She reached into the pocket of her apron and taking something from it, extended it to him.

"Here's your ten dollars," she said. "You didn't get much use out of the lot last night, and I guess you could use the money now."

As she had expected, he appeared not in the least nonplused by this offer.

"Miss Lipik, you overwhelm me! But I couldn't think of it."

"Oh, come on, Doc, you don't have to pretend you don't need it. I've got eyes in my head an' I don't have to look twice. Call it a loan if you want to. You can pay me back later."

He stepped forward and took her hand warmly.

"I do not have to tell you that you are a gem among females!"

With a graceful gesture he bent over her hand and brushed the back of it with his mustache. Sonie enjoyed the entire maneuver thoroughly. She responded immediately. She mocked his attitude by assuming one equally theatrical herself.

"Really, my gratitude knows no bounds!" he said, brushing delicately at his mustache and regarding her ardently. It was a look that fooled neither Sonie nor himself, but they both enjoyed it as part of the game they were playing. "Circumstances and yourself permitting, I think we shall see more of each other. My companions in the

158

next room will be leaving shortly, but I expect to stay on, for a while at least, to examine some possibilities I have in mind. I understand that in the past you have let rooms here. Do you think you could put me up in your establishment for a few days till I get my bearings?"

Sonie considered this for a moment, frowning and pursing her lips. She was examining this man now, reducing him to practical terms of red and black for the personal and instinctive ledger that she kept upon her life. Then she nodded.

"I stopped takin' in roomers quite a while ago, but I think I could accommodate you if you want to stay." She extended a hand and looked him mockingly in the eye. "Rent money in advance, though. So I think you'd just better hand over that ten dollars again."

He looked at her for a moment of undisguised admiration. Then he laughed and placed the bill in her upturned palm.

"Miss Lipik, you astonish me! You add wisdom to beauty—I tell you I must afford myself the pleasure of knowing you better. I think we will understand each other."

"I'm sure we will, Doc."

They both laughed.

"Now," he said, "I must reluctantly turn to business. Is this place where you say my nigger is far from here?"

"No. It's Temp Royle's store. One block north and two to the right."

"Temp Royle. That name has already been called to my attention once this morning. I believe he was the gentleman who misguidedly interrupted my performance last night. Strange coincidence that Maryland should find his way there of all places! Hmmm—you're sure they're not holding him, that he's all right?"

"He looked all right to me when I was over there this morning. Havin' his breakfast in the kitchen. Brant told me he wandered in lost last night and begged to stay. He's been cookin' and cleanin' up and makin' himself useful."

"Extraordinary," murmured Malley, shaking his head. "His refusing to leave, I mean. Not the cooking, cleaning part. I think I had better go see about Maryland. Thank you a thousand times again, Miss Lipik."

5

For nearly an hour that morning in the hot room where Templeton lay, Brant had insisted on talking to his father. He waited until after Doc Saunders, red-eyed and drunk as much with lack of sleep as alcohol, had paid his call and departed. He was not impressed or moved by Sam and Pete Henry's horrified protests against this invasion of the sickroom.

"He's eaten breakfast, hasn't he?" he demanded coldly of them. "He's got enough life in him to do a lot o' cussin' so far this morning. He'll talk to me, all right."

"But wait, Brant! What's the hurry? Tomorrow—"

"I can't wait. Tomorrow might be too late." And he pushed past them into the room and closed the door, shutting them and their protests out. The Negro Maryland bent over the head of the bed in an attitude of massive tenderness, slowly waving a piece of newspaper tirelessly over the old man who lay there. He had been performing this office since early that morning.

Brant sat down by the bedside and began talking in a low voice to his father. Sometimes his tone would be soothing as though he were addressing a child, but always with an adamant concentration he would return to the business he had in mind. Often the figure on the bed would jump spasmodically and the maddened and ravaged face turned from side to side on the soiled pillow as though desperately seeking escape. One side of it was drawn down and frozen in a paralysis. When he spoke it was in a halting, jerky tone. Sometimes he uttered a tormented halting yell, calling on his God—that awful presence of doom and vengeance who had for so many years been a familiar and boon companion—as though he were calling Him to account for some inexcusable misdemeanor.

"Leave me be!" he shrieked at Brant. "O Lawd—O Lawd, why have you struck me down in the presence of mine enemies?—What are you a-talkin' 'bout, Brant . . . cigarette machine? . . . plaguin' me about money . . . the root of—all—evil . . . an' me laid low, a poh dyin' man. . . . O Gawd—I'm a-dyin', I'm a-dyin' . . . where's the doctor . . . go git the doctor!"

Patiently Brant waited till the yells became moans. When they died away, he would continue quietly, implacably.

"Now, Pa, you ain't dyin' any more'n I am. Doc Saunders tol' you you were gonna be all right, didn't he? You just rest easy an' try to understand what I'm tellin' you. All I want you to say is I can use that money . . . I've got to have that money. . . ."

It seemed to go on for hours. Sam paced the hall outside the closed door and gnawed frantically at his fist. Pete Henry had gone up to the square to find some other solace and companionship around Tyree's drugstore. Sam occasionally paused in his pacing to glare in at the door of the parlor. John Barton sat there, unaware, quietly looking out the front windows.

When Brant came out at last he wore a look of sober triumph. He had changed subtly in the night. Not in any way that could be neatly labeled, but there already were signs in his bearing of that

160

ruthless glacial certainty which was to mark and set him apart later on. His face was pale under a fresh shave. His expression of complete self-possession infuriated Sam. Something always happened in their lives when Brant got that look on his face. He was used to the raw, black humors and violence that had been a familiar aspect of Brant. But it was this cold, immovable mien, this tyrannical stranger who moved arbitrarily along a course of his own choosing, sweeping them with him, that made him feel frightened and impotent. Always he was moved to rage against it, no matter how futilely. He burst out now.

"What have you done? What have you made Pa say?" he demanded, thrusting his yellowed face toward Brant. "What have you gone an' done now? An' Pa in there a sick man! You better tell me—"

Brant looked at him. "Where's Barton?" he said.

"Waitin' in the front room. Look, I gotta right to know what you did in there, Brant—I gotta right to know!"

"You'll have plenty of time to find out."

Brant swept him out of the way and walked to the door of the parlor. "Mornin', Mr. Barton."

Barton started and turned in his chair. "Ah—good morning, Mr. Royle."

Brant nodded, noticing that the carpetbag rested on the floor nearby. "Bring your papers, Mr. Barton. Let's go downstairs to the office." As they started out Brant turned to Samuel. "You stay up here with Pa."

"But I gotta right to know what you're doin'."

"You stay with Pa!"

They left him whining and gnawing his hand and went downstairs to the empty store and the airless little room where they had talked the night before. There the papers were spread out upon the table again. A square of dusty sunlight fell slantwise upon them. They began to talk. The conversation today was terse and economical in both questions and answers. Occasionally they would bend their heads over one of the drawings and Brant would scrawl some figures in its margin. The excitement was still there in both of them, but it was more considered and sober.

It was about an hour later that Sam broke in upon them. He was fearful, bursting with malice.

"Somebody out front to see you, Brant—and I think you'd better have a talk with him."

"Who is it?"

"Looks like the feller who ran the show Pa broke up last night."

"What does he want?"

161

"How do I know? Wouldn't talk to me. Wanted to see Pa first. When I told him Pa couldn't, he said he'd talk to you."

"All right. Bring him on in here."

In a minute Sam ushered the visitor through the store. Chris Malley entered with the easy aplomb of a man who had been welcomed into much more splendid offices. His expression was polite and well-bred. He appeared warmly pleased with what he saw. Perfectly at ease, he removed his hat and inclined his head briefly toward the two men at the table. He seemed to recognize Brant at once and measured him with a glance.

"My apologies, Mr. Royle, for this intrusion on a Sunday. My business is pressing. However, I will only take a moment of your time, if you will permit me? First of all, I understand from Miss Lipik that you have given refuge to one of my company who managed to escape the attentions of both the law and the lawless in the night's debacle?"

Brant nodded. "You mean the nigger?"

"Mr. Royle, it was very kind of you under the circumstances."

Brant laughed. "It wasn't much kindness. He just came and wouldn't leave, Mr.—?"

"Malley's the name—Christopher Malley, Mr. Royle—although you might have been misled by the advertisements in connection with my late lamented enterprise." Malley grinned intimately at Brant. "Being a businessman yourself, Mr. Royle, you must understand the value of a good trade name properly presented."

"I think I do," Brant said. This fellow was interesting him. He felt that there was an active, razor-sharp intelligence working behind all this fancy folderol. Also he was sure now that the man hadn't come this morning just to see about Maryland. "The nigger's upstairs with my father."

"Regrettable business last night, Mr. Royle, entirely regrettable," said Malley. "I hope your father is recovering satisfactorily from his accident. As for Maryland, I shall see that he doesn't impose any longer."

"He's not imposing exactly." Brant smiled faintly. "He just wants to stay with Pa. Seems he got a powerful dose of religion last night. He thinks Pa's the last prophet of glory or something. Crazy, I reckon, but he's not in the way."

"Ah—I see. Well, I should like to talk with him presently, if you don't mind. You are in the tobacco business, Mr. Royle?" continued Malley politely. "I find that very interesting. I have been a businessman myself, of sorts, for a good many years. I might say, without undue exaggeration, that I have been a fairly successful one"—he looked levelly and pleasantly at Brant—"until last night. Which brings me to the second reason for my intrusion this morning."

162

Brant regarded him unblinkingly. "Are you tryin' to tell me, Mr. Malley," he said quietly, "that you think Pa was to blame for what happened to your outfit last night?"

Malley looked pained. "Mr. Royle, you leap to conclusions! I have seen enough in my life to know that the business of placing blame is usually a very slipshod and unrewarding activity. A great deal of time, effort, and money is wasted upon it that could be used more effectively otherwise. Let us say that last night's affair was most uncomfortable and unfortunate for both of us. Mr. Royle, permit me to be frank. Putting it bluntly, there is a disparity in the extent of the losses suffered by each of us. You still have your business. I find myself this morning, through no fault of my own, suddenly and entirely without material resources. Beautifully cleaned-out!"

"Is it money you want?" Brant watched Malley's face keenly. It was a face that interested him more and more. By God, the fellow had nerve, lots of it. And he had, too, a quality of personal distinction that Brant could never resist, because he had always wanted it for himself.

"I'm afraid you're jumping to conclusions again, Mr. Royle. You may not believe me, but monetary aid is not precisely what I had in mind. However, don't misunderstand me—I have a profound respect for money, particularly in large quantities. But I am also of a realistic turn of mind. I am also a gambler. I am always looking for wider and more rewarding fields in which to exercise my knowledge and talents."

"It's a job you want, then?"

"Let us call it a position, Mr. Royle," protested Malley. "I find myself stranded in your city, which from my observation is throbbing and bustling with affairs. It interests me. With a little aid, let us say, it shouldn't be too difficult for me to find a place for myself. You are a man, I can see at a glance, who could wield a little influence. Surely, in view of the circumstances of last night, you cannot say that I am unreasonable!"

"No," said Brant. He looked at Malley for a long moment. "You're a good talker, Mr. Malley. What do you know about the tobacco business?"

"To be perfectly frank—absolutely nothing. But I learn quickly. Particularly if I find the proposition interesting and there is an element of chance involved."

"Who do you know in Kingsmont?"

"Aside from my presumption upon you this morning, Mr. Royle," he said, "I should say no one but a few of your worthy officers of the law—who I am sure would be pleased to forget me as soon as possible—and Miss Lipik."

"Sit down, Mr. Malley." Brant leaned forward slowly across the table. Malley seated himself. The two men looked at each other. Malley's mouth was shaped in a questioning, metallic smile. Brant's face said nothing. It was again glacially keen and concentrated.

"How would you like to work for me, Mr. Malley?"

Behind them in the doorway Sam sucked in his breath with a moan.

6

It was on an afternoon some days later that John Barton stood in the open door of Roger Upham's smithy looking out upon an empty sun-struck section of Hill Street. His face wore an expression of calm abstraction. The interval since his arrival in Kingsmont had worked a remarkable change in him. He still looked gaunt and strange and his clothes hung listless upon his bones. But while he moved in a gangling, tentative way toward all things, there was an indefinable expression of content—almost happiness—on his ugly, long face. He had attained some measure of peace, and he showed it.

Near him, beyond the horse stalls, Roger Upham bent over a lathe. The big cavern of the smithy was filled with an intermittent scream of metal cutting metal and the constant chugging gasps of a small steam engine that powered the machine. Above this clamor rose the happy, ponderous sound of Upham's singing. No words, and only snatches of melody, came through the general humming and clanking and hissing, but together they made a pleasant and melodious racket. Occasionally the smith would turn and, waving a micrometer in his big fist, shout some comment to Barton through the din.

John Barton held in his hand a freshly sealed letter. It was the last of a series that he had been writing and mailing all week. They contained drawings and minute specifications and were directed to various machine-supply and hardware jobbers in the East. One of them was to his friend Rainey Williams in Hartford. It was Rainey's good mechanical and engineering mind that had seen him through from the beginning. Now he had written him to drop whatever he was doing and come south. With Rainey there with him things could not help but go successfully. He sighed. Now all he had to do was sit back and wait.

Then, too, there was Roger Upham. Except when he slept he never left the big, comforting man's side now. He had called on the smith with Brant the Monday following his arrival in Kingsmont. Brant had handed the smith the drawings and begun asking more questions. They were reasonable, intelligent questions. John was still amazed at Brant's ability to grasp essentials and absorb them, even when it was evident that the subject was new to him. At last he had asked the smith, "Well, Roger, what do you think—can it be built?"

164

The smith looked at John Barton, his blue eyes sparkling, and then he said quite simply: "Sure. Why can't we begin right now?"

And forthwith he had. From that moment John had begun to be happy.

Altogether it had been a strange week. But he had accepted it as passively as he accepted all things now. Events were developing too rapidly. He did not attempt to understand all their portents any more. He had sat in on dozens of conferences with Mr. Royle and his brother and the suave Mr. Malley. They discussed, endlessly, drew up scores of plans on paper, discarded them and began anew. It had been exhausting. He only knew that certain decisions had at last been made. The versatile Mr. Malley had composed a long and legally technical paper which he had signed in the presence of a notary. He had not bothered to understand all the implications of this act. But he knew that he and they were now committed to the enterprise. Out of it all the only thing that he clung to or cared about was the fact that it was going to be possible for him to build his machine. If nothing further came of it than that, *that* would be compensation enough.

While he was rolling down his sleeves he wondered why, when he was in the smithy, he continually turned from what he was doing to stare out into the street. But he knew why. In spite of any evasion he knew why, and the blood rushed up into his face with the realization. Always he looked with the hope that *she* would walk past, or that the green surrey would roll sedately by.

As he stepped out on the sidewalk he saw Sonie Lipik coming toward him up the other side of Hill Street. She carried a red parasol over her bare head, and when she saw him, she waved. Then, glancing up and down, she gathered her skirts from the dust and crossed to him.

"Hey, Mr. Barton," she called to him, "wait a minute!"

Her green eyes were friendly and excited. She made a little face at the noise from the lathe. "Mercy, what a racket!"

Even in the noise the little hoarseness of her voice came pleasantly to him. He thought that of them all she had been the kindest to him. He liked her and was grateful, but he didn't know how to tell her.

"Well," she said with satisfaction, "I've just come back from the depot. They took the two-o'clock to Richmond."

"They?" He looked puzzled.

"Brant and Mr. Malley. They got a letter this morning that decided them. They may even have to go to New York—think of that!"

"Ayeh—I know."

"Well, aren't you excited?" she demanded. "Seems to me things are happening mighty fast for a beginning, Mr. Barton—don't they to you?"

"Well, ma'am, I don't know. . . ."

She shook her head in mocking despair and grinned. "Mr. Barton, I don't believe you could get excited about anything!" Then she patted his arm consolingly. "Well, don't let it bother you. You must have enough on your mind as it is. I just thought I'd stop by and see how things are goin' up here. Since I'm a partner now in this thing —signed papers and everything—and particularly since I've got money in it, I've got to keep my eyes open, you know. . . . I hope you're right about your machine, Mr. Barton."

"Ayeh, ma'am, I hope so too."

"Ach! I must say I'm havin' a lotta fun, though." She cocked her head and looked him squarely in the eye. "Tell me honestly now—do you think Brant's really goin' to be able to do something for us with this thing?"

Barton blushed furiously, but for once he answered her in a voice so steady and clear that she heard it distinctly above the noise in the smithy.

"Yes, ma'am, Miss Lipik, I think he is."

PART TWO

CHAPTER SIX

I

UNTIL THE DAY he died old Captain Phillips, whenever the subject arose, would remark loudly to anyone within hearing: "The Grand Columbian Tobacco Company, sir, was founded by a blackguard, financed by a tart, and promoted by a mountebank!" Thus stated, it expressed the sentiments of a large group of people in the beginning. It was a group that under the fierce wash of time and events gradually wore away and scattered until there remained nothing but senile and peevish complaint. For Captain Phillips the passage of the years only increased the intensity of his feeling. Somehow the Grand Columbian gradually assumed the position of personal archfoe second only to the ghostly Union Armies whom he had fought in his youth. When the Grand Columbian encroached upon his life, he felt he was the last champion of decency and gentility in a world gone to pot. It found him at the end of his days still embattled in the solitary citadel of his room in a boardinghouse. It was a neat, bare room with faded regimental colors draped on the wall over lithographs of General Lee and Jefferson Davis, and a bottle of cheap bourbon whisky on the washstand. Of course it was nothing like the room he had inhabited for over a decade at the Tobacco Planters' Hotel.

Captain Phillips and the old hotel were only two of the many things that had been changed or set aside. What John Barton had prophesied to Sonie Lipik as they stood in the doorway of Upham's smithy on that August afternoon came true in the following three years. It came true in such a way as to make John's declaration seem naïve and oversimplified by comparison. His concern and belief was limited solely to seeing his machine a reality; to have it recognized and used as he had meant it to be. He had no way of knowing that it would serve as the catalyst for an empire. Brant Royle did. He had seen it as the first tangible key to power that had come to his hand—power over men, over machines, over money. And, in the end, simply power itself. Power was for Brant the hunger and the drug in one, and when he first tasted the true elixir he became a creature complete, focused, and invincible.

The time conspired to make him a phenomenon. It was a period sown with dragon's teeth for a new race of giants. They sprang up over the landscape of a country recovering from the illness of civil struggle, and sensing its vast energies. These figures were ruthless wielders and shapers of men, machines, and the fruits of the earth on a scale beyond the comprehension of any group or individual. It was beyond their understanding because, being lesser creatures, they were caught fast in the clamor of this vast commerce, blinded by the smoke of huge factories, deafened by the din of new machines. Entrapped more and more in this gigantic maze they could only feel, not see, the terrible and inhuman battles of the giants above them, their inhuman ascendencies, their equally inhuman falls and disappearances. It all happened in another world.

But Brant Royle was of the new race. All the dark and violent power implicit in him, which had for so long set him apart, flowered into a kind of genius. He had at the outset the advantage of springing from a land benumbed and unused. A country drained by passion, traditionally and historically limited in its range of exploitation. It lay fallow for his plowing. Other men had touched it. But he dug deeply and exultantly into the very earth beneath his feet, hauling its riches in a new way out into the open air. It was a thing so astonishing that it stunned not only the South but shook that fastness of the giants, Wall Street itself.

Of the two men—John Barton and Brant Royle—the historian might say with some truth that it was Barton who was the real creator. He made the cigarette machine. But Brant Royle made an empire. He made the Grand Columbian Tobacco Company.

But what is of importance to this immediate account is the microcosmos of Kingsmont. The little, slumberous collection of dwellings and businesses—in no way unique. What was brought to bear upon it was not unique. It had occurred to many a lesser hamlet and crossroads. The difference here was that Kingsmont was used to a much gentler metamorphosis, a more imperceptible change. It was not educated to revolution. War it had recognized and endured. But war was a hiatus only. Progress was expected to take up after the interruption and continue along the same road. Anything else was beyond the community comprehension.

168

And so when Brant Royle began with Barton's first completed cigarette machine they had no precedent upon which to base an understanding. It was simpler to pass it off as a fad, something curious, of course, but not worthy of any serious attention. Meanwhile the world continued very much as they had shaped it. There were normal business habits, good meals to be eaten, families to be raised. And because an upstart was disposed to folly, there was no cause for alarm. Brant had counted on this. He knew them. He had made a long and bitter study of their habits and minds. The granite shape of their own thinking and security he now turned against them. He had not lived among them, envied them, hated them, studied them, for nothing.

During that fall and winter following John Barton's appearance Brant and Christopher Malley traveled a great deal. Joe Lawson, the agent at the station, reported that they went often to New York and Chicago and even as far south as New Orleans. It was also noted that various gentlemen began coming to Kingsmont from out of town. They were obviously and uniformly of prosperous and businesslike appearance. They always put up at the Tobacco Planters' during their brief stays—two or three days at the most—and spent most of the visits closeted with Brant Royle and Chris Malley. Occasionally they were seen in a little group walking about the factory section of Jamaica, listening silently and gravely while Brant talked in an enthusiastic, earnest undertone. All this was a little mysterious and curious, but it was nothing beside the change in Brant himself. At all times now when they saw him he was neatly dressed, silent, and dignified. His old haunts, the saloons, the livery stables, the Saturday-night brawlings about the warehouses, knew him no more. Met by old companions of these places, he was abrupt and bewilderingly formal. There was for a while a deal of head-scratching and cussing among them over this transformation. Not only did he never take a drink in public any more, but he showed no signs of any drinking at all! And no signs of hell-raisin' any more, either—they just couldn't understand it. After a while their curiosity wore thin and they ceased to bother.

Whatever it was, they knew that Chris Malley was deeply involved. He and Brant were as thick as thieves. By means of a very subtle process Chris had gained a place for himself in Kingsmont. Very early he had taken a room at the Tobacco Planters'. He was very much in evidence when he was in town and not with Brant. He went to some pains to make himself agreeable to all the businessmen of Kingsmont. It was convenient that they used the hotel as a daily meeting place and informal club. They were cool with him at first. But he was so well mannered, so engaging, that even the crustiest of them finally succumbed. He had an endless stock of amusing and

169

interesting stories, which he told well. He was a sympathetic listener and his political views, when expressed, seemed even more conservative than their own. Before they knew it, he was an accepted and welcome member of the groups meeting in the bar or in the lobby of the hotel (when the weather was bad) or on the veranda (when it was mild). They did not invite him to their homes, of course, but the man obviously had come from a good background, was educated, and in spite of his association with Royle—damn it!—seemed perfectly all right. Malley let them conjecture what they liked about him. In the meantime, while making himself agreeable, he learned a great deal about them, their business methods, and the tobacco industry.

When it came at last, the sound of the explosion that Brant had been setting all that winter was so huge that very few in Kingsmont even heard it. They had known for long that Roger Upham and the Yankee fellow were working on some sort of contraption or other in Upham's shop, but not until Brant set up Barton's first machine on the floor of the warehouse he had rented down on West Street did they realize there was any connection between what they had been doing and what Brant was about. So that was what it was? A cigarette-manufacturing machine! Here was the final madness of the Royles. Brant was setting himself up in the cigarette business! Well, let him. He'd find out soon enough. When good solid businessmen like Walter Pendleton and Dick Watts had been manufacturing cigarettes for years with only reasonable success, what did this fool ruffian think he was going to do? Who was going to buy any more cigarettes than were already being made?

They were human enough to want to know what this machine looked like. There were various rumors immediately running about that it alone could make as much as an entire week's output of both the local hand manufactories *in a day!* Ridiculous, of course. However, they sent, on the sly, various representatives down to Royle's place to have a look. These clerks, foremen—or whoever they chanced to be—found themselves cordially received and conducted about the big, humming monstrosity in the makeshift factory by either Brant or Chris or Pete Henry. Now that it was up and running they, the Royles, seemed to want to make a point of what they were doing. This even extended itself to all the town's curious, the factory workers themselves, the courthouse square loiterers, the polyglot of Jamaica Town. Anyone, in fact, who wanted to see. They came, looked on while it spewed forth its miracle, and were as fascinated and incredulous as children. They regarded it as a nine-days wonder. A month's wonder at the most. Since none of them really believed, inside of them, that anything would come of it, the novelty of it wore off.

But Brant had more in store for them. It was soon noised abroad

170

that, not content with the single machine, he had ordered half a dozen more and that John Barton and Roger Upham had gone to Chicago to supervise their construction. Meanwhile workmen labored all that summer reconstructing the big warehouse as a temporary factory to receive them. In addition, offices were set up in a nearby building. A sign in sober black and gold over the main door of this place advertised the fact that it contained the enterprise of ROYLE & COMPANY. It became immediately full of every sign of activity common to a businesslike firm—clerks, stenographers, all the usual office paraphernalia and personnel. Brant and Malley were in and out of town more than ever. When they were in Kingsmont the office building received a growing stream of jobbers, agents, and out-of-town businessmen.

As if this weren't enough, the final blow came in the September issue of the August *Tobacco Journal*. A whole page of that estimable monthly—the unofficial Bible of the whole industry—was taken up by an advertisement announcing a new cigarette on the market. CORPORAL SMART—*The Best for Less;* Manufactured by Royle & Company.

In the face of this lavish display the heads of the town's other manufactories speculated crossly and frustratedly. How and where was Brant getting the money for all this? They knew that none of them had been approached. Even Josiah Randolph of the Kingsmont Bank had to confess that he was in the dark. But wherever and however he was getting money, there was no denying the fact that Brant was managing to finance what he was about. Although they all knew that if they had been approached they would never have considered it, they felt a sense now of pique that they were so noticeably being ignored and by-passed. However, a partial answer to their question came when they discovered that shares for Royle & Company were being listed on the New York Exchange. This they somehow found more shocking than anything that Brant had managed to do till now. It was just sheer effrontery and nothing else. Why, the foolhardiness of Royle! They waited for what they felt was bound to occur.

But it didn't. Instead, there blossomed on the sides of buildings in the town, and on the sides of barns in the country, a big gaudy poster. It was reported as far north as Richmond and as far south as Charlotte. The biggest and most inescapable of these occupied the whole side of the warehouse Royle & Company occupied. Large or small, they were all more or less identical. Over a big box, opened at one end to show the tips of ten gigantic cigarettes, there marched the jaunty figure of a smiling grenadier in full regimentals. On the picture box itself in big bright letters was again the legend CORPORAL SMART CIGARETTES. And under it the slogan *The Best for Less.* It caught the eye everywhere in the landscape. They began to feel that it was a blight falling on everything. There was a good deal of indignant talk about how common in taste and ruinous to the general appearance of things this was. But they had to admit its force as advertising. Brant was evidently going all out with his venture, and advertising on a scale that had never before been seen in the business.

In all this, while angrily agreeing that, whatever it was, Royle's business couldn't survive the year, James Singleton found himself curiously pursued by a sense of guilt. He felt as though he were in some way responsible for what was happening. It was a feeling that he confided to no one but himself. Damnation and Godfrey's Cordial! who would have ever thought that his chance recommendation to that Yankee fellow would have produced this turn in events? In suggesting the Royles as a bad joke at the time, he had intended nothing more than that rather heavy-footed quip implied. Certainly he had not thought to be taken up on it. And most assuredly he had not foreseen any such development as this, even if he refused to believe that it was anything more than a temporary condition.

However, even he had to admit, reluctantly, that if Kingsmont was any indication of the success of Brant Royle's persistent advertising elsewhere, this new cigarette business was succeeding pretty well for the present. Every day he was confronted by the evidence on every hand in the public places of the town. Youngsters who had never thought of smoking before, and older men who should have known better, now openly displayed the yellow boxes containing the Corporal Smart brand. These same boxes, empty, stared up at him from the gutters, from the usual trash in the grass of the courthouse square—in fact from a hundred odd corners and crannies wherever he went. Edgar Bason, James's manager at the factory, reported on his return from a routine trip up East that Royle's new cigarette was displayed for sale in every tobacco store he had entered along the way. No, James was not happy. But he was not unhappy because he felt personally endangered. On the contrary, none of it seemed to be affecting him or his business, although he had been getting various vague complaints from the Pendleton and Watts interests.

It was in this somewhat vague spirit of guilt and confusion that he accosted John Barton late one afternoon that following summer. James was in the buggy on the way back to the factory after the midday meal and nap. John was coming out the door of Roger Upham's smithy. The two men met at the foot of Hill Street. James drew up at the curb. He did not know exactly what made him stop then, because he had spoken to Barton only in passing on a couple

172

of occasions since the year before and the Yankee had never called at Hill House since his unique visit that hot August afternoon.

"Good afternoon, Mr. Barton," James bellowed.

Barton stopped short and flushed crimson but managed to return the greeting without dropping his eyes.

"Ah-h-h . . . Good afternoon, Major Singleton."

James remarked the change in him since the year before. The Yankee was still as lank and plain as ever, but there were certain notable differences in his exterior. For one thing, gone were the antique garments he had first appeared in. His present clothing, while it refused to fit him any better and hung awkwardly on his lank frame, was recently tailored and well-cared-for, giving him an incongruously prosperous air.

"Had a letter from Eli Whitehead the other day," continued James in a hearty, booming voice. "He asked me if I knew how you were getting along."

"Mr. Whitehead askin' after me?" said John. "That was real good of him."

His long face lit up with a thin smile of pleasure. It made him look suddenly younger—years younger. The Major noticed a kind of dignity and confidence in him that had not been there a year before. He felt the little tug of sympathy and warmth pull at him.

"Well, Mr. Barton, I suppose I can inform Eli that you seem to be doing all right—eh?"

"Ayeh," admitted John, nodding gravely, "the machine seems to be doing all right."

"Well, I'm certainly glad to hear it, sir! Guess I was wrong, eh?" James laughed the deep, roaring guffaw and slapped his plump thigh. "Don't mind admitting it. Never hurt anyone to admit the truth. My congratulations that everything worked out so well for you. Should have got around to telling you before!" The big, handsome, perspiring countenance assumed an expression of mock severity. "You haven't been around to see us, Mr. Barton."

"I know." John studied the sidewalk between his big polished brogans and flushed again. James wagged a chubby finger at him.

"Not very neighborly of you, sir! Not very neighborly."

"I'm sorry, Major Singleton. . . . I've had it on my mind. You were very kind to me, and I am grateful. But I've been kind of busy recently, you see—"

"Busy? Ha!" James looked his most waggish. "Well, I expect you have been busy, from the evidence hereabouts recently." John Barton made no reply to this. "Well, there's no reason why you shouldn't remedy matters now," the little man roared on pleasantly. "You must come see us soon. In fact, why don't you come up for supper tomorrow evening?"

173

John Barton stood very still. His eyes seemed fastened on a spot in the air near the horse's head.

"Thank you, Major Singleton," he said at last in a voice so low that James could scarcely hear him. "I'll be glad to come."

"Good! About seven-thirty, then, eh? We'll be looking for you. Afternoon, sir!"

James clucked to the sleepy roan horse and flourishing the little buggy whip, drove off smartly down toward the square. As he turned the corner he suddenly thought with dismay: Now what in the devil ever made me do that? I had no thought of doing any such thing when I stopped. Just meant to exchange a greeting. That invitation popped out of my fool mouth before I knew what I was saying. Hope Meg won't be upset. Well, it won't hurt a thing—just this once. I kind of owed it to him after the way I treated him the last time we met.

Back on the shaded sidewalk John Barton had not moved. He stood tranced, looking toward the square. It made him look as though his feet had grown downward into the earth and rooted him there.

2

James imparted the news of his invitation to Margaret and Cousin Tabby at breakfast the following morning. He blurted it all out at once in a roaring, defensive manner and then glared at them. Margaret set down her cup and looked at him placidly. She seemed merely a little surprised at his vehemence.

"But of course, Father. Why not?"

James did not know whether to feel relieved at her calm acceptance or irritated by it. He glanced across at Tabby.

"It will be nice to see a new face," she tinkled. "I'm getting awfully tired of all the old ones."

"Indeed!" snorted James. "I take it, then, that you need some new sort of diversion?"

"I do—we all do," said Tabitha. "We're all going to seed. Need something to perk us up."

She darted a malicious glance at Margaret, who was sipping her coffee again. Her face was smooth and gently preoccupied. Her rich beauty was at its best in this morning light. She always looked well then, as though the adjustment from the world of sleep and dreams to one of besetting reality offered her no problems at all. The skin was softly glowing, the eyes wide and luminous, the hair impeccably sleek and black.

"Indeed!" repeated James lamely. His eyes were caught for a moment by the painted eyes of his father's portrait. He looked angrily back at his plate. He had a sudden sense that they were all making fun of him—the portrait included. It was a frustrating moment.

That evening John Barton appeared at Hill House promptly on the hour. James was pleased to notice that he was even more fittingly dressed than he had been when they met on the preceding day. His lank blond hair was neatly barbered and combed and the air of new dignity was even more marked. What James had anticipated as a rather awkward occasion that would somehow have to be seen through did not turn out so at all. The man had somehow acquired some poise in the interval. He was still shy and had very little to say, but he was quiet and agreeable. When he asked a question it was intelligent and brief and he listened attentively and well. In fact, the evening went off very satisfactorily from start to finish. Margaret, as usual, had said little, but her air of graciousness had been, if possible, more warm than it ordinarily was. Later when she and her aunt had joined the gentlemen she had been easily persuaded by James to give them a few songs, accompanying herself at the old-fashioned square mahogany piano that had been James's mother's. She had a pleasant small contralto that lent itself well to the sentimental songs that constituted her repertoire. For once John Barton seemed impelled out of himself. He went and stood by the piano with his back to James and Tabitha, but where he could stare unabashed and hungrily at Margaret's profile bent toward the music. Between songs she consulted him charmingly over her next choice. She seemed to want to erase all memory of that strained and awkward first meeting by a generous outpouring of herself.

That evening proved to be only the first in a long series of widely spaced visits to Hill House by John Barton. They became quite used to his turning up on one occasion or another. Sometimes they would not see him for several months. And then he would appear on three successive days. He never intruded. He seemed to know when his presence might be awkward for them. It was a curious sort of relationship that sprang up between them and this man who seemed to belong to no one. He called on Margaret and went driving with her. He went on little errands for Tabby. He listened endlessly to James or accompanied him about the house and grounds. His association with Royle or his work was never mentioned, although each of the three knew more or less what he had done and was doing. When he appeared they received him with cordiality. And after he had gone they scarcely ever mentioned his name or thought of him till he turned up again. If he was aware of this, it made no difference.

It made no difference because John Barton was happy for perhaps the first time in his life.

CHAPTER SEVEN

I

Even in that first year Kingsmont began to lose its calm and settled dignity with a terrifying rapidity under the impetus of what Brant Royle was doing. It began to stretch painfully out of its accustomed torpor and to spill out geographically over its familiar boundaries. It was not a pretty process. Violent upheavals seldom are. It was marked outwardly by a new air of teeming business, hundreds of new faces about the streets, the sudden and shocking disappearance of old landmarks, the erection of a dozen new places of business. It had all the distressing, formless vitality of a small town becoming a much larger one. Real estate was suddenly becoming a very good business. New streets began to push out into what had been open countryside which till then had been untroubled by anything except the raising of tobacco. People began to speak of the new residential section growing up to the south of town. To the west of the square a whole block of old shops bounded by a warehouse was razed to make way for a new, big hotel, named the Carolina. No one was greatly surprised, because the old ramshackle Tobacco Planters' had long been inadequate. Old inhabitants had a painful feeling of loss—although no one was much surprised—when that antique hostelry was pulled down to make way for a long four-story brick building announced as the home of Lawson & Royle, Finest Store South of Richmond. The Royles were not confining their interests to cigarette-manufacturing alone. Sam Royle had swallowed up—with his brother's help—the old Lawson General Merchandise, which had catered to the county for over a quarter of a century.

The biggest results of that initial eighteen months was the news that Brant had acquired two whole blocks of warehouses and dwellings—all the property including Weller's livery to the Pendleton factory—between the tracks and Maple Street, and was going to erect an enormous new factory. Sonie and her household moved out of Maple House to the fancy big house Sonie had rented near Elm Street.

It was perhaps peculiar that during this period, when there was so much building going on and so many new people moving and constructing new houses for themselves on the new wave of prosperity that was engulfing Kingsmont, of all the new hierarchy rising in the world the Royles alone showed least interest in expressing themselves in the construction of a dwelling fitted to their new eminence. Their combined energies—except for Pete Henry, perhaps—

seemed concentrated solely on their spreading affairs—Samuel with the new store up on the square and Brant with the new factory and the promotion of sales for the cigarettes that were pouring out of his makeshift factory in a fabulous stream.

When they moved out of the old store down on West Street to make room for John Barton's machines they had rented a modest, shabby dwelling on the fringe of Jamaica Town and moved in. There, attended by a cook and Maryland, they moved with the sick and querulous husk that was Templeton Royle. And there they appeared content to stay for the time being. They did not entertain at home and they did not encourage visitors. No one thought it was particularly remarkable, and if they did they put it down to the perfectly permissible eccentricity attendant on success. In the light of developments all the Royles—particularly Brant—were rapidly losing the outline of individuals with lives of their own. They were figures, massive without definition, dominating their surroundings, and like all monuments, becoming public property. Brant Royle was shaping and changing the life of a whole community, imprinting himself upon a whole era, but in the process he was becoming the property of the whole world that teemed about him and ran to do his bidding.

2

And what of the old bastions? The ancient fortresses of factory and bank and business, those impregnable family keeps that lined the tree-arched reaches of Hill and Elm streets? What was happening to them and their owners and inhabitants in the rush and surge of this period?

After the shock of the initial impact the tight little hierarchy appeared outwardly—for a while, at least—to face the flood of new changes unruffled. It fell upon James Singleton, as titular head, to express best this attitude of stubborn equanimity, to preserve an unbroken front of apparent indifference in spite of the unmistakable and ominous tremors that were shaking the foundations of their position. James was by no means so stupid that he was blind to the evidence of what was happening. It unavoidably confronted him at every turn. But of them all he was uniquely fitted by several factors to play the ostrich most successfully. The security of his position was so deeply ingrained in him that he had neither the talent nor the desire for speculating upon the obvious. The premises for his conduct had been formed and set forty years before. Now, even if he had wanted to, it was too late to change. That, too, he knew. But the little balm of familiar irony somehow failed him this time. There was no longer even the faintest whisper of private laughter at himself. The capacity for it had atrophied completely somewhere along

177

the road of his fantasy until the fantasy itself was all that remained. With this alone he faced the enemy. He knew it was expected of him. His belief in that regard chained him to the spot beyond any escape —even if he had ever for a moment entertained the thought of escape. Which he had not.

However, during the summer that saw the completion of the new Royle factory there had occurred two incidents of entirely different character but equal magnitude that struck at the very core of his position. Heretofore everything that had happened had taken place at a convenient distance and involved impersonal elements. These were different. They directly invaded his own domain, where he could neither avoid nor gainsay them.

Late one warm afternoon he was returning across the back garden to the house. He had been down at the stable paddock discussing with Simon the question of the disposal of a new foal born to old Jenny, the elder of the two mares that were Hill House's carriage horses. It was with his usual sense of serenity and well-being that James had started back to the house to freshen up a bit before supper. The thought that there might just be time to enjoy a little whisky on the side porch beforehand stirred pleasantly in him. He would have to tell Relda to crack some ice before he went upstairs. A sprig of fresh mint wouldn't hurt even if there wasn't time for the elaborate ritual of a julep. He turned aside toward the mint bed that lay on the shady side of the summerhouse. The miniature pergola of that structure came into view as he rounded the fig bushes. Its architecture reflected in small the severe beauty of the main house. Pergola and roof surmounted four little Doric columns over a brick floor. Robert Singleton had built it for his wife and James and his brother had played in it as boys, as had Margaret when she was a child. Otherwise its function had remained purely decorative and sentimental. It was half-obscured from James now by the luxuriant growth of an althea.

Suddenly he stopped midway down the stretch of grass, balancing on the balls of his small feet. Into his musing regard of this pleasant scene came an alien and curious element. So tenuous and ephemeral was his first impression that he was not sure as he stood there whether he had seen anything or not. But it came again. There was no doubt about it. A thin gray thread of smoke floated out on the calm afternoon air from beyond the althea bushes. The sight of it did not fill James with any alarming vision of a conflagration in the summerhouse. On the contrary. He knew instantly two things: that someone was in the summerhouse, and that whoever was there was making some use of burning tobacco. He could smell it distinctly now. Now, who in the devil? . . . Very likely one of Relda's brood experimenting on the sly. Wouldn't it give the little black scamp a fright now if he confronted him without warning? He crept forward carefully over the grass, a smile of childish anticipation curving his mouth. Then he strode suddenly around the althea. But it was not the spectacle of a startled little darky that greeted his eyes.

It was Cousin Tabby.

She sat prim and erect in one of the iron chairs, the toes of her diminutive black shoes barely reaching the bricks of the floor. One elbow rested nonchalantly on the table, and in the hand, clasped precisely between forefinger and thumb, she held what was unmistakably a lighted cigarette. On the table lay a small yellow pasteboard box open at one end. The confrontation was shockingly mutual. There was no possibility of retreat. For a long moment they held this absurd attitude. Then Cousin Tabby coolly put the white cylinder to her lips, pursing them to accommodate it, and puffed a little cloud of smoke deliberately toward James.

"Tabby!" James found his voice at last in an explosive whisper. "What in damnation—" But he could not go on. For once words failed him. She swung her feet like a child and smiled the bright, secret smile.

"Oh bother, James!" she tinkled in the small, doll's voice. "Don't stand there looking like a ninny. You can see very well what I'm doing. No harm in it for anyone—no harm at all. I knew you'd have to know sometime. Tried not to fuss you with it any sooner than I had to. Guess this is as good an occasion as any. I know what you're going to say. Waste of breath. Don't say it."

She puffed at the cigarette again. She was completely at ease and frankly enjoying the situation. James darted a glance back over his shoulder toward the house and was immediately cross with himself for doing so. He turned to her fiercely.

"But this is preposterous, Tabby! You don't really mean—"

"I most certainly do, James, and there's no sense making your usual to-do over it and yelling and roaring at me, because then everyone within hearing will know. Everything is perfectly all right as it is if you'll just let it be. And don't try to tell me that only fast women smoke. Whatever else I may be at my age, I couldn't possibly be called fast. I've been discreet about it, too. You see I came way out here in the back. Usually indulge only in the privacy of my room. Tired of my room this afternoon. Besides, it was too warm."

"And how long, may I ask, has this been—"

"Oh, weeks," she interrupted flatly and blithely, waving the hand holding the cigarette in a gesture that he found both mocking and insulting. She continued: "Weeks and weeks. Mr. Barton introduced them to me. Not on his own, of course—he's distinctly not the forward type, you know. No, I was the one who asked him to accommodate me. I was curious to find out what all this cigarette

179

fuss was about. You're always saying it won't amount to a hill of beans. Well, I think you're wrong, James. I think you're wrong!"

"This is ridiculous, Tabby!"

"Not at all. Just the thing for a genteel lady of my years. I always wanted to feel wicked and dangerous. This way I can do it without harming a soul."

A long ash fell from her cigarette to the table beside the open box. James could no longer ignore the fact that imprinted on it was the figure of the omnipresent grenadier.

"But those are Royle's cigarettes," he protested lamely, and knew immediately that he wasn't making very good sense.

"Why not?" she said. "They are everywhere now. If I'm going to be wicked, I want to be fashionable."

"Does Meg know about this?"

"Wouldn't be at all surprised if she did. But I suspect she's got enough common sense and good manners not to let it bother her. After all, James, I haven't taken to drink or drugs. I think I've been very careful. No one knows except Relda and Simon."

"Relda and Simon!"

"Well, you didn't think I would be so foolish as to go traipsing about the stores buying them for myself, did you? James—you *are* a ninny! Now run along and stop gaping at me. It isn't becoming in a man of your years—not at all. I'll be in to supper when I've finished. I don't think there's any use in your trying to say anything more."

And he knew there wasn't. He mumbled incoherently and slapped irritably at a little swarm of gnats that had appeared out of the approaching evening.

"Godfrey's Cordial, Tabby," he expostulated weakly at last, "but I find this *really* incredible! . . . All right, all right, if you're going to do it, you're going to do it and that's all there is to it, but for heaven's sake be careful. It would make me out a pluperfect fool if this ever got out around town."

"It won't. Wouldn't harm a soul if it did. But if that's what's bothering you, you're the one that's got to be careful, not me." She nodded her head at him and delicately withdrew another cigarette from the package. "Now do run along, James."

He started to stomp back across the lawn and then midway changed to a cautious, almost furtive manner of progress to the house. He felt confused, as though he were in danger of being found out. That he was the guilty one. Insufferable. That's what it was! He just didn't know how to handle or to understand Tabby. Never had. Well—best to leave well enough alone, he supposed. Small comfort in that. He realized that his sense of outrage was the result not of the fact that he found her smoking, but that she had been smoking that damnable Royle product. It would not have been so bad, some-

180

how, if it had been one of the cigarettes that Walter Pendleton put out. He had to admit that. Anyway, she would very likely tire of it before long. He determined not to refer to it again or to bother his thoughts with it. What he needed was a good strong whisky toddy.

He had long ago forgotten the sprig of fresh mint.

3

The second incident occurred toward the end of that summer. It made a breach in James's wall that could not be ignored. Beside it Cousin Tabby's little eccentricity paled into insignificance. Later he was to admit in the privacy of his darker moments that the two things were rooted and related in the same thing.

In the middle of a rather cool afternoon a day or two before the market opened that fall a buggy containing Walter Pendleton turned into the driveway at Hill House. Walter and James were old acquaintances, although they had not been intimate of late. Their two families had been casually connected in the same spheres of social activity, and the two men were nominal heads of two of the town's oldest tobacco concerns. They had both grown up in Kingsmont together, and although Walter was a year or so James's junior, they both looked much the same age. On this particular occasion his thick, rather undistinguished features under the brim of his good panama were as expressionless and stolid as ever. The only expressive note in his face was a cigar, unlighted. This he shifted—without ever touching it with his hand—from one corner of his thick mouth to the other. James had always maintained that Walter never smoked a cigar—he *wore* it.

Walter refused any refreshment, but accepted a chair on the porch beside James. He was not an effusive or brilliant conversationalist, but James liked him. He was pleased to see him now. It struck James that he had not been seeing much of Walter lately. But then he hadn't been seeing much of anyone for that matter. Not that he didn't always enjoy company, but a vast inertia seemed to be falling over him this year, a reluctance to bestir himself in any direction except the close and comfortable one that demanded the least effort of him.

For a while their conversation was desultory. It was concerned in the main with an exchange of amenities about their respective families. Having exhausted the possibilities of this, they sat silent for a space creaking comfortably in their rockers. Then Walter stopped and shifted to turn himself slightly toward James. He removed the cigar from his mouth and looked at it for a moment. This action alone should have warned James that something was in the wind.

181

"Well, James," said Walter in his heavy, flat voice. "I really came up here this afternoon to give you a piece of news."

James cocked his head politely but continued to rock slowly back and forth bemused.

"What is it, Walter?" he asked, only half listening.

"Everybody'll know it tomorrow," said Walter, continuing to study the chewed end of his cigar. "I felt you ought to have it from me first."

"Trouble?"

"No—no trouble." Walter shook his head. A long sniffing sigh escaped him. "I've sold out. I've sold the Pendleton Company."

James's chair stopped moving. Walter went on in the flat, un-emotional voice, his pouchy eyes staring out into the yard.

"I'm stepping out. I'm through. Time I retired anyway. Stella and I've wanted to do a bit of visiting about among the children up East, and—well, there's nobody left in the family that cares a hoot about taking on the business anyway."

"Walter," said James, finding his voice at last. "Walter—this is a shock. . . . I had no idea—"

"There's no use in my not being frank with you, James. We haven't been doing so well lately. Business began getting thinner and thinner all winter. Well, we were in pretty bad shape. You see we had more tied up in cigarettes than anyone knew about and we just couldn't meet the competition any more. Too stiff. And I'm too old to want to tear up everything and start all over with new pro-duction methods. We're out of date. Been getting out of date all this past year faster'n you could talk. We've sort of known it was coming for quite a while now, but we didn't know it was coming this quick. So it seemed just sensible to get out now without any fuss. Got a good price for it. Cash, and I get a block of the new stock when the company is organized."

James felt hollow and sick in his middle. It was as though Wal-ter had dealt him a physical blow. But there his friend sat saying he was finished as calmly as though he were talking about the most inconsequential thing in the world. Walter cleared his throat and replaced the cigar in his mouth. He settled back in the chair.

"I guess this'll come as a shock to a lot of people. I'm sorry. You have to move with the times—or move out. I'm moving out."

"Well, Walter," said James at last, "all I can say is I appreciate your telling me this first—good of you." Then he burst out sud-denly: "Why didn't you come and talk to me about this before? We could have gotten together with the Tolliver people and some of the others and tided you over so you wouldn't have had to do this!"

Walter shook his head again.

182

"You couldn't have done anything but hold off for a little while what was bound to happen. And the way things were going I'm afraid your help would've just been thrown down a rain barrel."

Then James asked the question he knew he was afraid to ask: "Who bought you out?"

"Royle and Company," said Walter bitterly, almost as though he were talking to himself. James felt that he had known the answer all along, but he hadn't really wanted to face it till Walter himself said it aloud. "There was no other way," continued Walter, his voice more colored by some emotion working up in him. "They offered a damn good price. I'd have been a fool to refuse it." His big pudgy hand suddenly pounded the chair arm. "I just can't understand where that crowd is getting all their financing. Doesn't seem possible they could be doing as well as they seem to be. It's been less than two years, too! And I remember I joked about it at the beginning along with the rest of you. Less than two years—"

Walter squirmed ponderously as though his seat pained him.

"You know the thing that got me the worst about this whole thing? Brant Royle never once came to see me during the negotiations. Perfectly evident he didn't think it was worth his time and trouble. Sent that Malley fellow down to do all the talking. Oh, everything was perfectly in order, but it made me feel like a little two-by-four shopkeeper. He's a damnably shrewd businessman. I think we've all been underrating him from the beginning, but you sure wouldn't have thought this of him on the basis of his past history. But he knows what he's about now all right, and we'll just have to admit it. He's shrewd, and he's a different breed in the industry than you or I've ever met up with before. He's not going to let anything stop him. And I tell you this—I know just as sure as I'm sitting here today that his sights are set considerably higher than just buying the Pendleton Company. That's small potatoes the way he's headed. He's out to corner the whole damned industry!"

"No!" roared James, finding his full voice at last. "No! Not as long as I'm alive, he won't. Why, Walter, you don't think we're all just going to take this lying down. By Godfrey, we'll give him a fight!"

He fell silent as abruptly as he had begun. There suddenly seemed nothing else to say. The pause extended awkwardly between them. Finally Walter got up ponderously and stiffly.

"Well, James, guess I'd better be running along."

"Good of you to come," said James, and shook Pendleton's hand overemphatically. They avoided each other's eyes. "You haven't seen the last of this yet, Walter—not by a good stretch!"

After the buggy had disappeared down the drive James sat for a long time on the porch without moving, his plump hands folded

183

over his paunch. Inside he was a tumult of confused emotion. His heart beat fast and hard. It just didn't seem possible. It was exactly as though someone near to him had died—or had violence visited upon them without his having raised his hand or done his duty. He felt as frankly futile and impotent in that moment as he ever had in his life. And there was nothing at hand upon which he could release himself in rage.

He was silent and distracted that night at supper and displayed a notable lack of interest in his food. Margaret was puzzled and a little concerned. In a very real maternal sense, from long habit and observation she was acutely aware of every slightest change in him.

"Would you like something else, Father?" she asked, watching him with the grave, dark eyes.

"No," said James. "No, thank you, m'dear. Doing perfectly all right with what I have."

"But you're not eating, Father," she protested gently. "You've scarcely touched your bacon. If you'd prefer, there's some cold chicken from dinner today—"

"I reckon I'm not as hungry as I thought I was—that's all. . . . Did you two have a nice time this afternoon?"

Margaret fell upon the opportunity. She did *so* hate an uproar at the table.

"We called on the Howells. Mrs. Howell's not been well all summer. Poor dear, she can hardly get downstairs any more, but you wouldn't believe how patient she is. They're such nice people and they have had their troubles since Mr. Howell passed away."

"That young Judson is a bright young man," said Cousin Tabby, pursing her lips and looking sagely at the ceiling. "Fine figure, too."

"They're quite excited about Jud," said Margaret. She lifted the table bell and rang it for Simon to clear off. "He's not going back to finish at the university."

"Not returning to the university?" said James, only half listening. "Why not?"

"He's had a very fine offer to travel for those—" her hesitation was so brief that James did not notice it; she continued deliberately and calmly "—for the Royle people, I understand. Jud seems to think it's a wonderful opportunity. Says now he never wanted to be a lawyer anyway. It was only because of his father having been the judge."

But James wasn't listening any more. He didn't want to hear. He felt as though there were no escape from this thing. Everywhere he turned there it was in some form or another. He had an intense sense of relief when they got up at last from the table.

Usually after supper, when there were no guests, he read his copies of the Raleigh or Richmond papers brought up from the factory and drifted off into a little nap. But he had no stomach for the

184

usual tonight. Mumbling something about needing a breath of air, he took his hat and walked down into town to call on Captain Phillips. He hadn't seen much of that fiery old war horse since they had torn down the Tobacco Planters' Hotel the previous winter. He had some vague idea that a discursive evening spent in the Captain's company might ease his state of mind.

But even that failed him. Captain Phillips was not interested in discussing the finer aspects of the Shenandoah campaigns. For two miserable hours James had to listen while the old soldier delivered himself of a vitriolic discourse on how Kingsmont was being taken over by thieves and trash and the world going rapidly to the dogs—no place for gentlemen and decent people any more . . . just look at the kind of people you saw on the streets nowadays! James excused himself as soon as he decently could.

In bed he lay tossing. He felt sweaty, although the late August night outside was cool with a first hint of fall. He could hear through the open window sharp little plunks of falling acorns in the yard and the idiot cheeping of frogs back in the pasture. He groaned and tightly closed his eyes. Insomnia was a new and terrifying experience. He had all his life been able to slip off into sleep almost as soon as he had got his head settled upon the big pillow. But not tonight.

The interview with Walter Pendleton kept haunting him. Try as he might he could not bring himself into any clear objective relationship with it. Always before he had been able to remove himself comfortably when things forced themselves upon him too critically.

"Damnation, damnation!" he groaned aloud in the dark. "It's Walter's affair. It's not mine."

He clenched his hands hard on the sheet. It wasn't just Walter's affair. . . . It pertained to all of them—himself, Tolliver, Marston—all of them who had built this town and county and made it what it had been. What that had meant and stood for mustn't be jeopardized and wiped out overnight. . . .

"We'll just have to show them," he said aloud again. "We *will* show them. We're not just a bunch of old ninepins! I'll do it—I'll do it alone if I have to."

CHAPTER EIGHT

I

With the passing of the Pendleton Company the business structure of the town began to change with increasing rapidity. Walter Pendleton's removal from the scene seemed to have precipitated it.

185

If there had been any doubt before about Brant Royle's intentions, they became increasingly clear now. He was going to absorb them all. One by one during the succeeding months the remaining names in the tobacco business were swallowed into the maw of his plan with almost monotonous regularity. The Watts Company followed Pendleton in December—and then the Freedleys and the old Tolliver Company. They were like a house of cards. And they were helpless. They were faced with a ruthlessness of a quality so bloodless, so monumental, that they found the weapons with which they were normally armed to fight back completely obsolete. The force opposing them was shaped by no business morality that they knew. No methods or means seemed too petty or too involved for its use. No matter how hard each of them fought back they found themselves at last hopelessly enmeshed in a web of Brant's fashioning. At times they sensed a special, almost personal malignancy in it, as though he sought their individual humiliation beyond capitulation. It was almost impossible to pin this down because always it was cloaked in what they had to admit—however reluctantly—was a masterly and brilliant business maneuver.

During this painful period James Singleton moved in and out among them like a man demented. He who had never actively concerned himself with the affairs of the industry now seemed to be taking it on as a personal battle, although his own position was unassailed as yet. He cajoled, he exhorted, he held endless meetings, laid elaborate plans. He traveled so much to Raleigh, to Richmond, to other tobacco centers of the state, that year that his friends felt embarrassed by his activities. He seemed possessed. He began to look pale and sick. Again they found themselves, because of old loyal and sentimental ties, having to conspire together to preserve the illusion that his efforts were valuable and effective. In the midst of their own troubles he became an added burden. They could not ignore it, because he preserved in himself the appearance of all the old, safe, comfortable tradition that they knew was dying. It was a new day in the tobacco business for a new kind of man, and they all felt very old. Individually and collectively they all wished passionately that there was some easier and more dignified way of retiring from the field. But there wasn't. Dying—no matter of what kind—was an inescapably painful affair.

Not only the town but the face of the whole tobacco country was changing. Kingsmont, sprawling and growing, losing all its old simple definitions, seemed with all its new factory buildings, its new blocks of warehouses, its new clamor and din, to be pushing out into the sea of tobacco fields washing up to meet it. All year now, it seemed—instead of just in season—the cobblestones rang with the sound of wheels. The big loaded vans snarled the streets, moving

186

eternally to and from the packed warehouses. The bright golden leaf, cured and piled in hogsheads by the hundreds of thousands of pounds, was a thing to conjure with as never before. Gas was the fashionable illumination in the new houses now, although the new electric lamps had replaced the old oil lamps that had hung for so long at the corners of the square. It was a new Kingsmont, a hub for its own particular universe, and enthralled with its growing.

And over it all loomed Royle & Company. Behind it, behind the phalanx of offices and hirelings, behind the bills plastered across the countryside and the smoke of the factories, was Brant Royle, a figure of towering and enigmatic power. He was seldom seen in town now. The company had its head offices in New York. His local appearances were attended by no ceremony. Like as not they would see him alone, soberly dressed, heavier in figure and wearing the black bowler hat in season and out, striding along the streets on his way to the factory or to the bank or to his brother's store. At other times when he was in town he was seen riding in his carriage driven by the enormous black Negro. But he was withdrawn from them now. It was hard for those who had known him to remember what he had been. He moved among more restricted circles—bankers, out-of-state businessmen, lawyers, and national politicians.

His interest in politics was evidenced that year when he came out supporting Harry Bonner, a county son, for North Carolina Senator to Washington. There were interviews and articles in the *Kingsmont Herald,* the daily paper that had newly sprung up in town, as well as evidences of his opinions in other state journals. Locally this was climaxed by an event long advertised in advance. Royle & Company was presenting candidate Bonner at a big barbecue outing to be held at Seller's Grove on the outskirts of town. The whole county was invited.

On the afternoon of the day of this festival—but in no way connected with it—Alton Devers and Rance Hokins met with James Singleton at his office in the Singleton factory. The three men represented the last of the independent owners still operating in Kingsmont. Their meeting today was only the latest in a long succession of like ones that had been held over the recent months. Defiant councils of war, conferences of strategy that had resulted in fewer and fewer attendants. There were only three of them now, and on this particular occasion their meeting seemed more glum than usual. Devers and Hokins had come burdened with the now familiar story. They were going to have to sell out to the Royle interests. This they had all known before they had assembled. But somehow they had to go through the ritual of getting together and voicing their bewilderment and indignation—as though it hadn't been voiced many times before.

187

Alton Devers, who had a sour and dyspeptic countenance, kicked the foot of the empty office stove as he passed it on one of his laps up and down the room. In some way its squat presence appeared to outrage him. The loose draft door, finally dislodged by this assault, fell to the floor with a clatter. He ignored it.

"What's Royle after?" he demanded in his thin, furious voice. "I just can't make it out. You'd think owning practically the whole State of North Carolina lock, stock, and barrel would be enough for any man. But he's got to ruin and have *us* too."

Rance Hokins sat in a chair near the windows. He was a stout man with a pale and flaccid countenance. He wore a glum expression as he studied the floor between his feet through pince-nez glasses. These had no ribbon to guard them and at intervals they came loose from his flat nose and fell to the floor. Hokins would then replace them carefully with a hand that noticeably trembled. James, sitting at his father's old mahogany roll-top desk at one end of the room, found his procedure unbearable. His resentment widened to include both visitors. James's face bore the mark of the past difficult months. The flesh had lost its definition. The jowls sagged flatly, the pouches had thickened under his gray eyes, and the lines in his forehead were creased into an expression of violent concern. Only the mouth remained undamaged. It was as incongruously curved as ever. The old vigorous thrust of the gray mane of hair looked somehow unkempt, as though James were getting careless about his appearance. He watched the tall figure of Alton Devers walk back and forth across the worn and faded Axminster rug. The room felt close and airless in the late summer heat.

"Brant Royle isn't an ordinary man," said Hokins mildly as he continued to study the floor. "You can't try to judge what he's doing or what he wants by your standards or mine."

"But you'd think that our little property wouldn't mean a drop in the bucket to him now. Lord knows we're not threatening him, and he sure doesn't need us. We've never come near stepping on his toes. Never made or sold a cigarette in my life. Furthermore, don't intend to!" Devers gritted his teeth as he walked.

"I don't think that has anything to do with it, Alt," continued Hokins, still in the mild voice. "Seems to be perfectly clear that he doesn't give a damn about us really. Not as a business threat anyway. He got out of our class a long time ago. It's something else he wants to do—to us. I'm convinced of that. He wants to show us he's had us in the palm of his hand where he could brush us off at any time he chose. He just chooses to do it now. It's like it was a personal point with him."

"Personal!" exclaimed Devers acidly. "I haven't spoken to the man twice in my life."

188

For perhaps the twentieth time since he had arrived Hokins's glasses slipped to the floor. He bent to retrieve them.

"I'm afraid that's not the point," he said, sitting upright and wiping them on his handkerchief. Then he added meditatively to no one in particular "—or perhaps that *is* the point!"

Devers snarled over his shoulder.

"What nonsense are you talking now, Rance?"

James swung from his desk to face them, dropping his fist hard on the desk top.

"The point, gentlemen," he roared, and he sounded hoarse, "the point is that Brant Royle is an unprincipled blackguard. Always was, always will be. You can't expect decency or honor from that blood. I know it from experience if you don't. The way he's gone about cutting the ground out from under your feet is a perfect example. No action is too low or mean for him to stoop to in his dealings. You can follow it through everything he's done so far. He's succeeded in making the whole industry a fat preserve for rogues and thieves. I almost feel ashamed to be in it still. He's a disease, dirtying the whole countryside—everything he touches. All that advertising mess on every barn side in the state! I understand from my manager that his latest inducement to the public is the inclusion of pictures of actresses and pugilists in every package of his filthy product."

"I know," nodded Devers. "My youngest grandson—Roger's boy—was at me last night for not smoking the Royle cigarette. He's making a collection of those pictures. Seems that all his friends are doing it now."

"There you are, there you are!" The close little net of veins showed purple on James's cheeks; his jowls shook. "Getting at us by corrupting the young. I tell you it's getting where a gentleman feels embarrassed to have to admit that he's in any way connected with the tobacco industry nowadays!"

He glared at his two visitors. Alton Devers halted and faced him, his legs spraddled, his countenance grim and angry.

"Well, Major," he said dryly, "it looks like after today you're going to be the only gentleman left in the county that'll have to bother. You're the only one left at large."

"Now wait a minute, wait a minute!" blustered James. "I'm coming to that. I've been thinking since I got your news. If you've got to sell out, why don't you sell out to me?"

"You?" spoke Hokins from his chair, almost with a sigh. "James, you don't have any use for our business."

"I tell you I'll take it on any terms rather than see Royle get it."

"Major, be sensible." Devers stood and shook his head. "I appreciate the gesture, but it doesn't make sense."

189

"It isn't a gesture, damn you, Alt!" roared James. "I mean every word of it."

"I'm sure you do, but let's be frank for a moment. Even if you do mean it, who's going to finance such a transaction? You know what an involved state we're in—pluperfect mess. I told you all about that."

"Doesn't make a bit of difference as far as I'm concerned. If you haven't got friends still, I have." He arched an eyebrow at them and paused dramatically. "Why don't we all take a little walk over the bank now and have a talk with Jo Randolph?"

Devers and Hokins exchanged a glance. Then Devers turned to James and shook his head again.

"Major, that won't do. Jo's not even at the bank this afternoon. The bank's closed!"

"Closed! Isn't this just Wednesday? He'll open up for me."

"I mean right now Jo's out at the barbecue for Harry Bonner along with the rest of Kingsmont and the county while we're talk-in'." He added sardonically, "Didn't you get an invitation?"

James didn't answer for a long moment. He gripped the arms of his chair hard.

"So Josiah Randolph has gone into the camp of the enemy too."

"Oh, let's not be unfair to Jo," said Devers. "After all, the Royles have an awful lot of money in that bank now. I wouldn't be at all surprised if they didn't own stock in it too."

James didn't seem to hear him. He chewed his underlip.

"When did you say you had to meet with them for the final arrangements?"

"They have suggested," said Hokins, "that we come around to the offices at the Royle factory in the morning."

"You mean that you can't put them off for a few more days till I get my arrangements completed?"

"We mean," said Devers flatly, "that tomorrow morning around ten will find us humbly presenting ourselves at the gates of the tyrant's establishment."

James banged his fist on the desk again.

"Jo Randolph will see me this afternoon! I don't care where he is or how deeply you think he's obligated, he'll see me this afternoon if I have to run him to earth. He'll listen to me. After all, I've known Jo for forty years! He can't just walk out and leave us. I'm—I'm going out to that barbecue."

His voice was shaking with emotion and his countenance had taken on some of its old familiar leonine impressiveness. He thought as he looked imperiously at the two men: This will show them! This will show them there's one left who doesn't know how to knuckle under! But great Glory! I've got to calm down—can't get all upset

190

like this. I've got to be more careful . . . can't get this mad . . . too much effort . . . makes me hurt all over. But damnation, what are you going to do? Somebody's got to do *something*. . . . They know I'll do it. It's expected of me. He disliked the way Alton Devers was looking at him, his thin mouth twisted in a little grimace.

"*Morituri salutamus*," said Devers with a little mocking bow.

"Eh?" said James. "Oh—of course, of course. Have your little joke. But I'm going to see Jo Randolph somehow this afternoon."

The close room was suddenly heavy with their silence. Each of them felt suddenly that the office floor of pine boards on which they stood was eggshell-thin over a yawning abyss. There was nothing more for any of them to say.

Presently there was a sharp little clink. It was Rance Hokins's pince-nez. They had escaped him completely this time and lay shattered near the edge of the rug. He didn't appear to care. He made no effort to pick them up. There was no exclamation of annoyance. He merely sat and looked down at the little wreckage of glass splinters. James and Alton Devers looked too. They looked for a long time until their trance was broken by a tap on the door to the outer office.

"Come in!" said James, looking up.

It was Irv Bason, his head clerk, who thrust his head in apologetically at the door.

" 'Scuse me, Majuh, but Miss Singleton's outside in the surrey. Says she'll take you home when you're ready."

"Ah—thank you, Irv," said James. "Tell her I'll be out in a minute."

The door closed on Bason and James turned to Devers.

"Where is this damned barbecue?" he demanded.

"The usual place out near the river," said Devers, turning with a shrug toward the window. "The bills advertising it said Seller's Grove—you know, the old picnic grounds."

James got up and took his hat from the tree in the corner.

"Gentlemen," he said with the old pontifical ring in his voice, "if you will excuse me, I think I'll go out to Seller's Grove—*now!*"

2

Margaret Singleton sat in the green surrey at the curb in front of the factory. Mr. Ed Bason had come out of the office to invite her in while she waited. He always did when Margaret came to pick up James, and Margaret always courteously refused. Although the two of them rarely met on any other occasion, they had carried on a highly formal little relationship for a number of years, he standing on the sidewalk and she sitting in the surrey. Almost as long as

Margaret herself could remember. Bason was the manager of the Singleton factory, a polite, methodical, unimaginative little man whose sons, Irving and Scott, also worked in the factory office with their father. It was generally understood that the Basons were the ones who really ran the business. James had begun almost from the time he had to assume the nominal position of owner to turn over more and more of the humdrum tedium of the company's affairs to this devoted and hard-working man. Whenever he had to know anything he only had to ask good ol' Ed Bason. Why, he wouldn't even know what was going on in the factory if Ed didn't keep him posted! It was a sentiment he had publicly expressed loudly and frequently during the past twenty years. Mr. Bason was saying now to Margaret in his eager, breathy voice: "Irv says the Major will be out in a minute, Miss Margaret."

Margaret smiled and nodded. "Thank you so much, Mr. Bason."

At that moment the street door from the factory office opened and they both turned. James emerged with two gentlemen whom Margaret recognized. Mr. Devers and Mr. Hokins. They were not talking and they all looked rather grim. Seeing her, however, all three of them paused and tipped their hats gravely. Margaret bowed. They did not come over to the curb, but after a brief exchange with her father tipped their hats again and walked off toward town. James came over rapidly to the surrey. Margaret thought his color unnaturally high and the whole expression on his face rather strained.

"Thank you, Ed," he said almost curtly to Mr. Bason, and climbed up into the seat beside Margaret, untying the reins from the whip socket. "I won't be back at the office this afternoon. Look after things, will you?"

"Certainly, Major."

They drove off leaving him standing there. They had rattled and bumped across the crossing by the depot before James spoke again.

"Sorry to keep you waiting, Meg," he said, looking ahead of him. "Something has come up that I've got to attend to this afternoon."

"I'm in no hurry, Father."

He turned to her then, abruptly. "Look, Meg, do you mind if I take a little trip before we go home? It'll mean a little drive out into the country, but I've got to see about something."

"Of course not, Father. It's a lovely afternoon. I've got nothing at all to do at the house. I'd enjoy a ride."

He grunted and turned away. His face again took on the expression of grim preoccupation. She was accustomed to his whims, but he had been more than usually arbitrary of late. Margaret was worried about him. She had begun to wish that he would talk to her.

192

But when he talked it was always in the old roaring cadences that had ceased to mean anything. She felt that he had grown away from them into some private concern of his own. He had always been so open. It was painful to find him distracted and set apart from her. It had made her realize how much she had centered her life about him. She knew that he was more than ordinarily concerned about the things that were happening in his business. But that wasn't so bad as the fact that he didn't seem to want to talk much about it any more. She found him somehow very touching these days. More so than ever before. It aroused all her fierce passion to protect him. Was it all this change going on about them? She found much of it as distasteful as he did, but again he would say little about it. Well, let them change, she thought, looking at his concentrated profile now beside her, I won't let them change us! Whatever is bothering him, I shan't let it hurt him. We can go on just like we are. Well, she wasn't going to let it upset her now. The afternoon was too nice and she was going to enjoy the ride. She sat a little more erect than usual. She felt a vague sense of defiance—against whom or what she did not know. It was a feeling that she had grown more and more aware of recently.

They drove on in silence. James impatiently flicked Renny into a trot. There was a quality of urgency in his stillness.

They drove up through the center of town, passing the square. It seemed more deserted than usual. There were people passing, but many of the stores were closed and there was none of the crowded hurry and bustle that had become common of late. They came into the old residential district at the foot of Elm and Oak streets. Margaret noticed again how badly kept all the old familiar houses were beginning to look. Many of them had become rooming houses. Little signs advertised their changed status. It all had begun to have a dilapidated, forlorn look, the paint peeling, the yards untended. She was relieved when they had passed through it down into the new section. She turned to James.

"Where are we going, Father?"

James came out of his silent study with a start.

"Oh—sorry, Meg. Should have told you. Hope you don't mind. I've got to go to Seller's Grove."

"Oh!" she exclaimed, and then caught herself. "Why, I haven't been out there in years!"

"Do you mind?" he said, turning to her with a frown of concern. "It won't tire you now?"

"Of course not, Father," she protested. "It's not as far as all that. Anyway, it will be a lovely drive."

"We won't stay long," he assured her. "I've got to see Jo Randolph about a little matter. He's at some kind of rally or other that they're having for Bonner, the candidate for the Senate, this afternoon. Guess you've heard about it."

"Oh, the barbecue?" she said. "It's been in the papers for weeks. I called by the Tollivers and Marstons this afternoon. They weren't any of them there. They'd all gone to the barbecue."

James said nothing for a moment. His face was grim and uncommunicative. "The Marstons too," he grunted, and then closed his mouth tightly.

No, he's not looking at all well, thought Margaret. I've seen it all winter. Maybe we ought to try to get him away for a while. If he wasn't so stubborn, so difficult. . . . She shook her head and began to look about her again.

They were out in open country at last. The road was dusty and the air stirred warm-cool along her face. The afternoon sun fell goldenly on the fields that stretched on either hand. She saw that the blackberry tangles were becoming brown in the ditches and all the greenery just beginning to turn. It hadn't achieved the dusty, resigned look of early fall. There was still a freshness and sparkle about it, the last remnants of spring. She delighted in it.

Presently they passed through a long tunnel of trees and came out near some fallow fields. Beyond this was a solid line of woods that Margaret recognized as hiding the sluggish, muddy little stream known in the county as the Parr River. James turned the surrey into a narrow track leading to the left. Presently they came upon a couple of saddle horses tethered to a sapling, and beyond them scattered among the tree trunks were more horses, buggies, and wagons standing quiet in the cool gloom. It had a curiously deserted, empty look. James pulled Renny up short and the surrey stopped. He looked about, frowning. Margaret heard drifting back to them, as though from some hidden distance beyond, a high chattering buzz. Then she heard quite distinctly a burst of laughter and a man's voice shouting. Concealed not far ahead there were evidently a lot of people enjoying themselves.

James clucked to Renny. They pulled off the track to the left and stopped between two towering sycamore trees. He tied the reins carefully about the whip holder again and descended to the ground. He stood for a moment, removed his hat, and mopped his forehead with a distracted gesture. Looking at him in the diffused light, Margaret thought again how pale and ill he looked. He turned to her.

"If you don't mind," he said, "I think I'll leave you here and walk on up ahead. I won't be gone long." He searched her face anxiously as though he wished to reassure her about something—almost as though he wanted to apologize. "You'll be all right, won't you, Meg? You won't mind waiting?"

"Of course not, Father. Don't you worry about me." She closed the little parasol and smiled down at him. "What on earth could happen to me here?"

He looked comforted.

"Good girl!" He reached up and gave her knee a pat. His face preoccupied, he crossed to the road. Watching that familiar square back disappearing among the trees she was suddenly swept with a wave of blind feeling. There was something so lone and defenseless, so vulnerable, in the sight of him going away from her. She almost cried out after him: "Father, wait! Don't leave me . . . let me go with you!" But she sat frozen and silent, an element of panic mixed with her emotion. It was almost as though she herself were deserted in that moment as well as he.

3

The moments dragged slowly by. A squirrel dashed between the trees nearby. Renny, startled, snorted, and returned to investigating the thick mold beneath his hoofs with big crunching teeth. A horse nickered and stamped somewhere beyond. Each sound, each movement, seemed to intensify the stillness, the emptiness, of the place.

Sitting there she could not shake off the feeling of melancholy. She had never been given to introspection. She found little joy in brooding over herself. It was confusing and got her nowhere. She didn't like to be confused. Whenever she felt moody it had been her practice to turn herself energetically to some objective problem. It had usually been successful. But here she found she could turn to nothing but her thoughts. A lot of isolated things that she had been ignoring seemed to be taking advantage of her disturbance. She could not ignore them now, or turn away. Maybe it was because her smooth and polished existence, so carefully fashioned for so long, had recently begun to seem empty and without meaning. More often than she liked to remember during the past year she had, while following the long-familiar pattern of her activities, stopped with a sudden blank shock and asked herself: What am I doing? Why am I doing it?

Recalling them now, she tried to examine them with honesty. Was she trying to hide something from herself? If she was, it would be better to have it out in the open. Perhaps it was because she was getting older. She was twenty-six now. But it was too simple just to let it go at that. Maybe it was because time was not changing her so much as it was changing everything about her, that what she was no longer fitted. So many faces had disappeared from the scene—familiar faces, accustomed voices. But you had to expect that. Marriage had eaten away at the comfortable little circle, of course, and death too.

So many old friends had moved to new homes or had gone to live in other places. How narrow her social activities had become! She could number the people she called on nowadays on the fingers of one hand, and even they had other preoccupations, other activities, now that did not interest or include her. Was it something lacking in her, this feeling that she was slowly being deserted? Sometimes she had a half-humorous sensation that of all her old friends there was now only Roberta Marston left. And she had always known that Roberta, bitterly locked in her plainness and growing spinsterhood, didn't like her. She had never really disliked Roberta, but then she had never felt particularly intimate with her either. They had grown up in the same group. They were accustomed to each other. Roberta flattering her with words that contained a feverish, envious sting. And she accepted it as she had always, unruffled in her security, her knowledge of her own person and its power. And now there wasn't even Roberta this afternoon. The Marstons had come out here to attend this big, vulgar gathering with everyone else. She supposed she was a snob, but she couldn't help it. There were so many things that people were doing nowadays—things that it would never occur to her to do—that it was always with a little shock of surprise that she realized that they no longer considered the same things important that she did. It only served to make her cherish more stubbornly what she had.

Perhaps marriage—that distant thing which she had always put aside to consider later—was the answer. She was not afraid of it. That wasn't the reason for this continuous procrastination. On the contrary, she had always considered her marriage as one of the accepted elements in the design of her life. But she thought of marriage not as a disruption or a sudden change. It was always in terms of a continuation of her life at Hill House. She could not imagine it otherwise. It included the addition of someone very like James, whom she would look after and bear children for while she continued her close meticulous guardianship of the big white house and its grounds and functions. And it wasn't because she had lacked opportunity. There had been a number of men who had passed through Hill House who had interested her. They had taken her to dances, driven her about the countryside, had passed in a continuous succession through the parlor under the interested regard of her father and the obvious machinations of Cousin Tabby. When she tried to think of them as individuals they seemed a ghostly series, all with the same face and the same voice. There weren't very many now. Besides John Barton, who in spite of his silent attention when he came on his occasional visits had never protested anything, there were only Albert Cole, who worked at the bank, and Judson Howell, who had taken her to an occasional function during the winter. But even Judson was gone now. He was out of town indefinitely with his new job. The trouble was that no single one of them had ever made her pause and consider him especially. She had been waiting—for something, for someone . . . for she knew not what.

Sitting there alone in the silent shade, twisting her gloved hands in her lap, she felt no satisfaction come of her thoughts. They only grew more confusing and painful. By a conscious effort she turned them from herself to the problem of her father. James was not at all well. It had become increasingly obvious all winter. But she could not pry him away from the business and Kingsmont.

The sense of stillness and isolation was suddenly intolerable. She could not bear sitting there alone in the surrey another moment. She must get out and walk about, if nothing else. She lifted her skirt and climbed over the side, stepping lightly from the little stand to the ground. The thick carpet of leaves was soothing underfoot. She decided to walk toward the river. She wouldn't go far. Just a hundred yards or so and then come back so that James, if he returned, would not be alarmed.

She knew the place of old. Many times she had come here on picnic parties when she was younger. All that atmosphere of boiled eggs and pickle and wading in the shallows swept back to her pleasantly and nostalgically. It was really a shame that one had to grow up! She hadn't been out here in years. Picking her way among the trees toward the left, she took a sudden pleasure in knowing what she was about. It all came back afresh to her. Beyond, screened by the trees, lay the open grounds where the great crowd of people was gathered. She caught a glimpse of them walking and sitting on the grass as she passed through the thicket.

Walking on, she came upon a little path worn bare underfoot, tunneling through honeysuckle thickets. Progressing down this, she heard at last the purling murmur of the river close at hand. After a moment, sunlight glimmered and flashed upward through the screen of leaves from the surface of water. She couldn't see it yet, but it couldn't be far. She went on a few yards farther where the path, skirting a huge green wall of vines, dipped to the edge of the bank. She stopped by an old elm leaning out over the river. The water ran smooth and quiet below. No rocks, no little rapids, to disturb the opaque, clay-colored surface. It mirrored nothing but a dun-colored image of the arching green over it. She leaned a hand against the elm trunk as she stood, half-content, and dreamily followed the fairy flight of two dragonflies. They skimmed the surface of the water under the tree in tandem and vanished.

Then she heard something. For a moment she was not sure that it wasn't just a high cadence in the voice of the water deceiving her. But across and above it came the unmistakable high, giddy laugh

197

of a woman, from somewhere nearby. It was followed closely by a man's protesting voice. She could hear no words. The murmur of the water covered any definition. Whoever they were, they were just beyond her, concealed by the honeysuckle. They might have been there for an hour or just arrived. She could not tell. But if they had not seen her she did not want to be discovered now like an interloper or an eavesdropper. She turned swiftly to go back. But another cry from the hidden woman arrested her. There was something compellingly familiar in the sound of that voice. She found herself turning back inadvertently. And then she stood rooted to the spot. In plain view, just beyond the bend of the path, a man and a woman were locked in embrace. And as she watched they broke apart and she saw the woman's face. It was Roberta Marston. Roberta laughing, her plain features flushed and excited. Whatever was happening, she was not protesting it. The man, whose back had been to Margaret till now, reached out and took Roberta caressingly by the arm, and turned. It was the thin, unpleasant countenance of Mr. Samuel Royle, owner and manager of the new department store.

If they had seen her in that moment Margaret could have done nothing but stand looking back at them. But they continued to laugh, absorbed in each other. Margaret felt the blood drain out of her face. Her whole body turned rigid. Then she turned and ran blindly back down the path. Branches whipped across her face and the sting meant nothing. Vines caught at her feet and dress. She stumbled and went on as though she were pursued by death itself. She could not think or feel. Her only desire was to get back to the surrey, away from where she had been. Anywhere. But anywhere seemed miles away. The green world swam about her and her breath began to sob and clutch at her throat. She stumbled again and felt the parasol slip from her hands. She did not care or look back as she sped onward. If she could only get to the surrey before . . . Her legs gave way beneath her again and she pitched forward cruelly. She uttered a little moan as she saw the path rush up to meet her. And then she was caught, suspended. She felt herself lifted up slowly and gently and held close to a warm and living body. She heard a voice, deep and slow and surprised, utter her name.

"Miss Singleton!"

She looked up, dazed, half-fainting, blindly clutching and holding to the strength thus suddenly offered. And the face she saw bending over hers was the one that haunted the background of her life, shadowy and unrevealed. The violent face. The passionate face. The hated, inescapable face with the black unruly hair and the stormy, demanding eyes. She knew now that she was in a nightmare.

"No, no, no!" she gasped and pushed away from him, hiding her face in her hands. They stood thus apart for a long moment while

198

the trees and the river whispered about them. Then Brant Royle spoke again quietly, unhurriedly.

"I'm sorry, Miss Singleton. Is there anything I can do?"

For a mad instant she felt as though she must run to him—not away from him. Here, without thought or sense, was all security, all the answer that she needed to the poignant confusion she had felt this afternoon. But she could not. She could not then any more than she would be able to till the day she died. She knew it in a flash, and knowing it, recognizing its inevitability, erased the hysteria that she felt choking her. She would not weep before him. She forced her hands away and looked up.

"No, thank you," she said. Her voice was cool and strained, separate from her. "I was on my way back to the surrey."

He stood blocking the path, looking down at her. And there was a naked tenderness in his eyes. He did not attempt to conceal it, as he had never attempted to conceal anything in their meetings. His solid bigness had a kind of dignity, although he stood in his shirt sleeves and carried his coat over one arm.

"Permit me to accompany you," he said, and stepped a little to one side.

"Thank you," she replied rigidly. "Don't bother. I can go on perfectly well alone."

She wanted to break into wild laughter then at the two of them, speaking so formally and meaninglessly there alone. Words that in themselves said nothing—and yet words that uttered a whole wild torrent of meaning. I have not even addressed him by his name, she thought; I will not. And because she would not it thundered through her mind. I must get away . . . I cannot stand here . . . I must run, run, run. And she knew now that she had been running all her life. She caught her skirt in one hand and walked stiffly past him. But he came with her, not touching her, but she could feel him like a wall at her back, moving quietly with her.

"It is foolish," he said in the quiet, musing voice, "for us to behave like this to each other. We've met before—we'll meet again. You can no more help it than I can. There's less reason than ever for all this now. I've been busy, as I think you know. It ought to be possible now for you to look at me without feeling you have to spit on me."

He did not sound angry. His tone was contemplative and without a trace of the old bitterness. She did not answer. He continued after a moment, almost to himself:

"I never thought you'd be here this afternoon. Everyone else— yes. They had to come. But not you."

She spoke tersely without looking back at him. "I did not come to the barbecue. My father had to ride out on some business—"

199

And then she could not continue. It sounded too unbearably stupid and meaningless. Would she never reach the surrey!

They walked in silence and came at last to the park of trees where the horses stood and she could hear again the background of voices beyond in the distance. She saw with relief that James had not returned. She stopped now and turned to him.

"If you please," she said, looking through and blindly beyond him. "I would rather—"

He interrupted her, compelling her to look at him, the little half-smile on his mouth, his eyes reaching out to her with understanding.

"All right," he said, "I won't annoy you further. But if I may, I shall call on you in the proper way, one of these days. I think I can come recommended by the best now. I'll even present credentials if you need them." For the first time there was a note of irony, a little echo of the old anger, in his voice. "Because I've got them now—the most fashionable and expensive recommendations that money can buy."

"Good afternoon!" she said and walked swiftly away, leaving him there. When she got to the surrey she climbed woodenly to the seat and sat erect, looking before her. He was no longer there where the path made a break in the thicket. There was no more sign of him than if she had never left the surrey, never walked down to the river, never seen Roberta. . . .

She sat there longing passionately for James to come. And after what seemed ages he appeared, walking rapidly. He looked deflated, diminished, as he came toward her down the leafy road. But she found she could not look at him or be concerned about him as he climbed tiredly in beside her. He seemed locked in some private concern of his own. Wordlessly he turned Renny back toward Kingsmont. She was grateful then that he did not speak. She felt that if he had she would have screamed.

4

She remembered nothing of the drive back. Nothing of what he had said to her or what she had answered. She felt enclosed in ice as the landscape, unrecognizable and meaningless, drifted by. Only when they turned up Hill Street at last did she feel some of the frozen tension leave her. Even then she could not turn to him and pour out upon him what was tumbling about within her mind. Looking at him sitting sunken by her side, she knew that she could tell him nothing. It was long past that for both of them. She could never tell him anything again.

CHAPTER NINE

I

Roberta Marston's marriage to Sam Royle that fall was the final evidence of the rise of the new hierarchy in Kingsmont. The Marstons as an old family were—with the exception of Mrs. Marston—completely eclipsed in the event. Not many paused to mourn over their passing. If anything, they thought the Marstons were doing a smart thing, that Roberta—whom everyone had resigned to spinsterhood long ago—was incredibly lucky to have captured one of the Royles at her age! There was envy as well as pure wonder in this. But no one could deny that the Royles were doing right by the situation. The affair was preceded by the most expensive preparations ever witnessed by Kingsmont. The caterers came from Richmond, the orchestra from New York, and the guests from not only all over the state but from Baltimore, from Pittsburgh, even from as far away as New Orleans and Cincinnati. There were some of the Marstons' old friends and relations mixed up among them, but they were, for the most part, hard bright men and their families with the glitter of new money upon them. They all had one thing in common, too. They were either connected with the Royle enterprises or were in line for some such good fortune.

Brant himself was little in evidence during all the social hullabaloo that preceded the event. He was in New York and only arrived the day of the wedding. It was Chris Malley and Pete Henry who were omnipresent and in their glory. Pete Henry particularly enjoyed everything—the parties, the people, the arrangements. In the past couple of years he had been rather lost in the sudden rise to glory that had come to him as a Royle. He had no place in it. Brant had tried him in all sorts of jobs—even made positions for him—in the factory and in the offices. But in each case he had begged off after a month or two, or got himself into some scrape that necessitated his removal. He dressed like a peacock, haunted the saloons, dashed about the streets in a carriage always spilling over with noisy young bloods, and spent money carelessly in every direction among an ever more numerous and catholic selection of acquaintances.

Brant never hauled him up short or took him to task for this. On the contrary, he seemed to enjoy indulging the younger man's caprices now that he had the means to do so. It was as though he were compensating for a son or a younger lost self—a self who had been starved and deprived of all these things. He got an almost perverse satisfaction out of flaunting the near-scandalous spectacle of

Pete Henry's gilded, frivolous existence in the face of the town. It was in such startling contrast to his and Sam's concentrated and tremendous industry.

Sonie Lipik, also, was heavily involved in all the wedding festivities. As *the* Miss Lipik, she was the acknowledged center of the new society and certainly the richest individual woman in town by virtue of her holdings in Royle & Company. Everyone recognized her importance in the higher councils and deferred to it. She enjoyed it with every fiber of her being, but it had not changed her a bit from the old shrewd, common-sense Sonie. She was merely playing the part expected of her. She appreciated the power of her new wealth, but she never let it interfere with her understanding of the true nature of the deference paid her.

When they had left Maple Street she and her three indestructibles, Mrs. Rose, Mrs. Pearl, and Mrs. Lily, had taken rooms in one of the more elegant boardinghouses near the center of town. But Sonie was restless. She missed Maple House and she wanted a place of her own. So she was one of the earliest to buy a lot and build a big elaborate house in the newly developing section out on Bay Street. This occupied her energies for nearly a year. She buried herself enthusiastically in it, hounding the architect and the builders, making trips to Raleigh and Richmond for its furnishings. She enjoyed having money to spend, but she spent it as carefully now on the new scale as she had spent it in the past. Every purchase had to represent good value. All this activity helped absorb the period of change and adjustment for her. She talked often and vaguely about going away, but committed herself to nothing definite. Although she had every reason to, she could not seem to bring herself to take the step. Brant was a creature separated from her life now. They met only at wide intervals, but the quality of their relationship had undergone a change. There was still the old familiarity, the old energetic clash, but it was no longer personal. He seemed to be withdrawing—as he was from everything else—behind the widening curtain of his activities. It was a region in which she herself felt less and less interested. She had been excited by the newness of it at first, but as he became less a factor in her connection with it, she became less interested. She found herself accepting him only when he appeared formally, or when she sought him out in the panoply of his offices at the factory.

She quarreled frequently with her three companions, but she was immediately contrite. She could not let them go. She had accepted them as her responsibility as she had from the beginning, and they were her last solid hold on the past. She was almost glad when poor Mrs. Lily, who had been increasingly troubled with arthritis, became so crippled that the doctors advised taking her to

202

a sanitarium. The arrangement of this and the sending of Rose and Pearl to accompany the invalid to an expensive watering place in the mountains of Virginia occupied all of one summer. But Mrs. Rose and Mrs. Pearl had returned. They could not leave their baby alone any longer and Lily was so comfortable and so grateful in the new place! She didn't need them any longer. And so the old round began again. The ladies had taken to the new scale and comfort of their lives with the placid alacrity that was the result of their long dealings with the vicissitudes of life. They were grateful. They were so smotheringly grateful at times that Sonie, in her irritation and growing sense of frustration, found relief in yelling at them and quarreling with them on the flimsiest pretexts. But this got her nowhere. They were hurt and resentful, as they had always been back in Maple House, and she always capitulated, overwhelming them anew with some silly and lavish gift to make things right. Then it started all over again.

So she was grateful when Sam's marriage was announced. With her accustomed energy and interest she threw herself into all the activities. She had never witnessed or been a part of such a ceremonious and elaborate function before. In the Maple Street days there had been weddings among the Ukrainians attended by all the feasting and visiting and the turmoil of a peasant holiday, but this was entirely different. This was surrounded by all the appurtenances of a different world and life—the world and life into which she was now drawn.

The marriage came off with all the expected splendor on a crisp day in October with the cool sun brilliant among the turning leaves gracing the oaks and maples along Elm Street. It took an hour for all the carriages to disgorge themselves in front of the Baptist church. The sidewalks were lined with curious townspeople, tradesmen and factory workers, who had come to see and comment upon this pageant of the swells. The wedding party were appropriately splendid in dress. The Royle brothers in formal black were not one whit less correct than the figures in the Marston carriage just ahead. Roberta, swathed in white, looked like a thin, tall doll, her face a feverish mask of triumph, staring straight ahead of her with a fixed smile. She had looked like that for weeks—dazed, mannequin-like, but still triumphant. No one could blame her. No one could feel sorry for her. They could only envy her. She was going to be one of the omnipotent Royles now, wasn't she? The name already had magnificent connotations. The fact that she was a Marston and that there were Tollivers and Randolphs and a fine old Virginia contingent in the procession—a lot of the venerable old names came out of hiding for the event—seemed only piquant on consideration.

And when it was all over, the crowds on the sidewalk saw the bride come out on the arm of the grinning Sam and pose on the steps with the wedding party for old Albert Jenkins, who had been Kingsmont's photographer for years—and another photographer with elaborate paraphernalia and several assistants, who it was said had been brought down all the way from Washington for the event. This over, they watched the whole procession form again. A great part of it wheeled on off to the Marston home near the head of the street for the big reception. Following this they knew that the bride and groom were taking the train for Cincinnati. The pair were to spend a week's honeymoon in Chicago and attend the World's Columbian Exposition.

Brant arrived, as has been said, the morning of the affair. He appeared at all the events of the day, a figure of glacial correctness. He wore, like his brothers, a handsomely tailored Prince Albert appropriate to the occasion. But unlike them he refused to wear the accepted silk hat. He wore, instead, the black bowler which was now associated with him. And because of the association it did not appear strange. His expression was sober and completely uncommunicative. They could not gather from it whether this marriage pleased him or not. Or whether, indeed, he found it a matter of any concern whatsoever. This did not prevent all eyes from following him with a kind of awe and admiration everywhere he went. It was almost impossible to see the rough, disheveled, violent hoodlum of the old days in this austere, impersonal man of thirty-five. Closely attended by the ubiquitous Mr. Malley and constantly in terse conference with some gravely efficient young man from the factory office (they came and went like couriers all day), he progressed through the crowded events. With the guests who sought him out he preserved a distant and unbending politeness. Only once did he seem to warm up. At the reception Sonie pushed her way to him and they exchanged some words that made him smile for a moment. But that was only for a moment.

Brant's wedding present to his brother had been the huge old Pendleton house just across the street from the church where the wedding took place. The Pendletons had long since departed from town and the big, ornate house with the mansard roof and the iron stag on the lawn had remained untenanted for months. Brant had informed Sam of his intentions several weeks in advance of the wedding. And when Sam came to Roberta with the news she had burst into tears. The Pendleton place, secondhand, did not represent at all any part of what Roberta thought the position of being Mrs. Samuel Royle, wife of one of the city's leading citizens and businessmen, required. She had privately cherished visions of something new and magnificent, built especially on one of the more desirable locations down Bay Street.

Sam didn't tell her then that there were conditions attached to the gift. He revealed them to her when they were safely away in Chicago, and then it was too late for her to do anything about it—except to indulge in brief hysterics. The house not only was to be theirs, but was to provide in its ample rooms a home for Pete Henry and for the sick old husk that was Templeton Royle. In addition Brant was to use it as his domicile whenever he came to Kingsmont. If this was more than Roberta had bargained for, she knew by then that there was nothing she could do. It was part of the price, inconsiderable really in view of what she knew she had gained. And then she was terrified of Brant himself. His presence was enough to reduce her to a figure of gibbering nonsense. She solaced herself with the meager knowledge that her old home was only a block away and that Mama would always be comfortingly available.

So Roberta stopped crying. She was Mrs. Sam Royle now.

2

Brant was with the big party of guests who went to see Roberta and Sam off at the station. But once the train had arrived and taken the bridal pair off he did not linger longer than was required of him to take a decent leave of the Marstons. He and Chris Malley walked down to the factory and remained to look over the sales sheets and talk over some wires that had arrived from the New York office. This occupied the time till dark. He said good-by to Malley and, refusing, as he generally did, the services of any conveyance except his own two feet, walked back across town through the early evening alone to the house—the house that was now the Royle house. Although Sam and Roberta had not taken up residence, Brant's orders concerning it had already been carried out. The preparations had required the services of painters and decorators for weeks. Not only was he to sleep there tonight, but his father had been moved there, together with the devoted Maryland and a practical nurse, newly hired, to look after the failing old man. He knew that Pete Henry, still involved with some lingering part of the festivity, would be in later. He had a sudden poignant sense of his isolation, a ghostly feeling as he traversed the familiar street. Jamaica humming in the evening with the noise of the restless factories, the square with the old courthouse, an anachronism at the middle of all the new buildings rising about it. Somehow tonight it held none of the satisfaction that he had enjoyed observing the town's change and knowing that he was the cause of it. It seemed empty. He felt more depressed than he wished to admit as he strode along. He wanted to see his father. He hadn't seen him at all except for a few moments at the beginning of the day while he was dressing for the wedding. When this blank mood descended upon him he always felt that seeing Templeton, soothing him, talking to the mad, irascible figure in the bed or in the wheel chair by a window assuaged the unrest in him.

Turning up Elm Street, he saw with distaste the dark mass of the house come into view. There was a light in an upper window and a dim glow lit the glass in the front door. He felt no joy in the sight of the house. What if it had been one of the landmarks of the town? The Pendleton house! Well, what of it?

He let himself in and stopped in the hallway to hang his hat, smelling the new varnish and seeing the gleam of the new furniture and fittings spread out in the rooms about him. He walked stonily through them and up the broad curving stairs. At the end of the hall he knocked on the door of the room where Templeton lay. He was glad that none of the new servants had heard him come. He didn't want to see anyone. He was even glad that Pete Henry hadn't arrived. He wanted to be alone with his father. The door opened on the plump face of Miss Sprend, the nurse.

"Is he asleep?" he asked.

"No, Mr. Royle." She glanced back over her shoulder into the room behind her. "But he has been excited all day. Real unmanageable, I would say. He sat at the window during the wedding where he could see. I couldn't make him lie down."

"All right, Miss Sprend," said Brant. "I'd like to see him alone."

"Of course," and she glided past him almost as though she were escaping.

He entered the room. It had an antiseptic odor of sickness and old age. The gaslight burned in the central chandelier hanging over the big bed where Templeton lay, a tiny shape at the center of pillows and covers. Brant regarded the skull-like face on the pillow with compassion.

"Hello, Pa."

The eyes in the face flickered over him. He waited and then pulled up a chair and sat down.

"What do y'want?" Templeton's voice was like a whisper.

"Nothin', Pa. I just came up to see if you're comfortable."

There was silence. Brant smoothed the covers awkwardly.

"Well, the wedding's over. Did you have a good day?"

The thin bones twitched under the covering. "Where's Sam?"

"Gone to Chicago, Pa," Brant's voice was patient. "He's married now."

"Gone with the whore of Babylon!" said Templeton, and fixed him momentarily with a wild glare.

"It's all right, Pa. He'll be back."

206

"We're all given over to the devil. Sinners sunk in the deep—Jesus save us!"

"How do you feel, Pa?"

"They can't git me, Brant—don't let 'em git me!"

The sheet was suddenly snatched and pulled up to the little burning eyes: They searched the room frantically.

"How do you like the new house, Pa?"

"What new house? Brant, you hellion—someone's below. Call Sam—call Pete Henry. Tell 'im to git the wagin out. Gotta git that tobacco out to the corner 'fore dark!"

"Sure, Pa, sure." He felt a terrible sadness sweep over him. Suddenly he hated where he was. It seemed ghostly and meaningless—all this rich paraphernalia. He wished he had never come, that he were back in New York, where he belonged. That he were anywhere. But he continued in the deep, patient voice: "You want me to read to you some, Pa?"

"The Book—ah, yeh—the Book, let me hear. . . ." The figure on the bed grew still. The eyes were closed. Brant took the ever-present Bible from the table near him and opened it. . . .

He read on and on—as he had done many times before. He read till he knew that there was no sense or hearing in the waxen face on the pillow. He read on beyond that till he heard below him the front door open and close. Then he got up quietly with a wild sense of release. He had to get out of here. Go down to the factory, sit in the office, do anything. It was pain to cross the floor, open the door, and close it behind him. Below in the big empty rooms he found Pete Henry. Flushed with the day and drink, lighting the gas brackets in the enormous cavern of the parlor.

"Got home early," said Pete Henry, sprawling boyishly in the big chair. "Funny thing for me." He looked admiringly about him. "Sort of wanted to, though. Had to have a good look at this house again and make sure it was ours."

Brant stood in the doorway looking at him. "You like it, Pete?"

Pete threw back his head and stretched his arms. He looked all of sixteen in that moment. Something in the sight of him pierced Brant to the core.

"Like it? It's pluperfectly dandy! Think of it—us ol' Royles bein' in a house like this—think of it!"

Brant said nothing for a moment. Then he spoke softly. "It isn't a white house, Pete. A big white house."

Pete turned a questioning, mocking face to him. "What the hell're you talkin' 'bout, Brant?"

"Nothing," said Brant. "Nothing at all."

Then he turned suddenly and, taking his bowler from the hall tree, opened the front door and walked out into the night.

207

The autumn night rustled softly about him with the sound of the first leaves falling. They whispered beneath his feet on the sidewalk. When he had stepped from the house it was with no definite goal in mind. He could not bear the big empty splendor, the rich furniture, the feeling of being an interloper, another moment. The knowledge that he possessed it, that it was his, came no closer to stilling the old, central torment than if he had purchased a toy for children. He started walking and found, without thinking, that instead of toward the lights of town, his feet were taking him in the direction of Hill Street. And the moment he turned into it he knew with a savage and despairing recognition where his feet were taking him. He knew, too, that he had to go tonight, at this moment, whether he willed it or no. He had to make this lonely, meaningless pilgrimage up the long hill as he had done so many times before.

So at last he stood again in the darkness clinging to the gate of Hill House. Leaning upon it like a drowning man, he stared through the shadows toward that dim and gleaming presence under the trees. He moaned in agony. What was it? *Why* do I have to come here? he whispered. I'm going where I always intended to go . . . I'm getting there fast. The whole damn world knows it now . . . everything but you, *you!* You have no right, no right at all. . . . I paid Walter Pendleton a sight more for his house than you ever cost . . . and it's bigger, much bigger than you . . . it's the biggest house in town . . . everybody knows that!

But this was no balm to the pain in him. He had said it so many times before and his words came back to him mockingly. Then he did something he had never done before. He opened the gate and entered. He stood for a minute and then walked up the path, the gravel crunching sharply under his tread. He did not hear it. His eyes were fastened on the front of the house as though he could force it to come down and, as a living, sentient thing, submit to him. Near the foot of the front steps he paused again, his feet planted apart, his fists thrust hard against his thighs. It was an attitude of challenge, rock-hard and ungiving, and one that the world of his activities was coming to know. He stood thus for a long time, rigid and frozen, and then something went out of him, as it always did. I'm a fool, he thought tiredly, I'm a damned-to-hell fool. But he continued to stand there helpless.

The bitterness of his sentiments was interrupted by the grind of approaching wheels in the driveway. There was no time to retreat. He stepped aside into shadow. The vehicle stopped and he heard a man's voice clear in the night and then a woman laughed. They came across the porch and stopped at the door. There was a moment while they opened the door and then they stood silhouetted and framed. He could hear their words clearly now.

"Thank you so much, Jud," said the warm, dark, and haunting voice. "Won't you come in for a moment? I'm sure Father's still up."

The male figure bent to her. "No, Margaret, I've got to run along. Busy day, you know. Got to be on the job tomorrow."

That voice, he thought, standing there unseen—it works for me. He can stand there now and laugh and talk to her and she will listen. I can throw him out—I can destroy him if I just say the word. . . . The dark stretch of the yard about him seemed so silent with a kind of crystal quiet that he could hear the crackle and fall of a twig from one of the elms above him, the lorn and peevish voice of a last feeble katydid scratching at the surface of the night. Then he heard Margaret Singleton laugh again.

"It's a shame, Jud, the way you and everyone nowadays seems to feel they've got to slave at something. I don't understand it. Well, good night."

The man murmured something in reply, his head bent intimately to hers. The door opened and was shut. Brant heard the departing footsteps ringing on the porch, then the wheels down the drive again. Still he stood for a long time. Suddenly he turned to the path and plunged, heedless of the grate of his feet, down it and out into the street.

As he approached the corner and the hard, bright glow of one of the new corner lights, a figure stepped forward to meet him. It was as though someone had been waiting there for him. It was a woman.

"Hello, Brant." The hoarse, derisive voice was unmistakable. It was Sonie.

4

He looks something awful, she thought, staring up at his face where it hung in the bluish glare. Like he'd been on a week's toot. But he hardly touched all that fine champagne at the reception . . . I watched him. . . . I haven't seen him drunk in years. Inside herself she felt all humming and strumming and hollow and not making much sense. . . .

"What do you want, Sonie?"

His voice was harsh. But she could not feel offended. None of the old relish for a battle with him rose in her. She felt only sad and drowned in compassion for both of them standing there alone under the street light, oblivious, farther apart than all the changes, the complexities, that had mazed them in and engrossed them during the past three years had placed them. She knew now. She had begun knowing from the minute she saw him go in at the gate, and then the buggy enter the driveway and emerge, and then Brant appear again coming toward her like a drunken man. Four such simple and inconsequential things considered apart. Placed side by side they answered a lot of things. In fact they answered the whole mystery that had tormented her from the time they first came together down on Maple Street. She could not face even yet what that answer was. She only knew—and knew hard—that she had it at last. She heard her voice, hoarse and calm, answering him, the most natural sound in the world:

"Want? I don't want anything special. I haven't seen much of you today. There was all the fuss and folks. I didn't even see you get away at the station. For a man of your position you sure managed that slickly. At home tonight I got tired telling Mrs. Rose and Mrs. Pearl all about what everybody wore and who was down for the weddin'. I thought I would just run over and call on you an' Pete Henry at the mansion. I didn't want anything special. Just thought we might sit down quiet-like and talk without havin' to bother with a lot of people. . . ."

She paused. He hadn't moved. He wasn't even looking at her. Lord, she thought, I wonder if I look like he does. He looks sick. But, as always, she was honest with herself. She didn't feel ill at all. Only empty, released, and very calm. So she continued in the hoarse, bright voice, talking, talking—it helped.

"Finally I slipped away in the carriage, an' when I got to your house I pulled up on the side instead of the front. I was just gettin' ready to get out when I heard your front door open an' saw someone go down to the gate. It was you. You couldn't see me, because I was in the dark. First off I was gonna call, but when you started walkin' up the street I decided it might be fun to follow you and slip up on you like—" she faltered and grinned, but she felt her mouth shaking—"like I used to do. But you lit out like all hell was after you. I tried to catch up, but my skirt kept gettin' in the way. I sure like the new styles, but they weren't ever made to run in!" She chuckled. "I made all kinds of noise. I even cussed once or twice, but you never heard a thing. I kept rememberin' how many times I'd trailed you before, an' I had to laugh. I even liked it. Made me feel good. I got this far when I saw you go in the gate up there and— well, I just stopped."

He reached up and rubbed his face slowly, pushing the bowler to the back of his head.

"Sorry, Sonie," he said. "I don't feel much like talkin' tonight."

Again she did not feel affronted. It had all the old familiar sound. It came back to her with an ache how many times it had hap-

210

pened before when she had tracked him down like a relentless fury on just such a night. Only now the words were lifeless, as though they came from a stranger. They had no power to move or touch her any more.

"Oh, that's all right," she said. "I won't bother you any more. But I guess we oughtn't to stand out here like this the rest of the night."

She turned. They began walking down Hill Street together under the trees. She did not slip her arm through his nor did he offer it. The sound of their feet on the bricks was the only thing that came together. About them the old familiar houses gleamed from their windows. They were as withdrawn in their places as they had always seemed to her, but they filled her with nostalgia—fragments of that other night, months ago, kept coming into her mind with a peculiar poignancy. She had never known what it was to feel this way. Any other time she would have scorned herself. Would have said, What an' ol' mush you've got to be, Sonie Lipik! That other road was dusty in the dark—and the sound of crickets . . . the smell of crushed grass . . . and the warm, hard arm under her. . . . But she understood now. That was two other people. That wasn't him now, nor her. It would never be *them* again—that was what she knew; it had never really been them at all—not him anyway. She was glad that it was dark, that he couldn't see her face if he looked. Mama was right, she always said I'd get it sometime—the big slap. I guess this is it.

"Brant," she said, not looking toward him. She didn't have to. She could always feel him when he was there. "Brant, there's one thing I want to tell you tonight. I'm goin' away."

She could not tell whether he had heard or not, but he answered at last in the tired, toneless voice.

"Goin' away? Where?"

"Oh, I don't know yet. I want to take a little trip. Been meanin' to for a long time. I'm tired of Kingsmont. I don't have to stay here any longer. Should have got out a long time ago. After all, I'm not gettin' any younger!" She managed to chuckle again, and felt better for it. "I've got more money than I know what to do with. Guess I'll spend it in a few places. Go to New York. Just think of it, all this time an' I've never been any farther north than Baltimore—an' that was a long time ago. I might even take a boat to Europe. I need a change—to see some new faces, see what the world's like."

She wished she didn't sound so giddy and silly spilling it all out in this hurried, forced voice as though she wanted to keep him from saying anything.

"I'm goin' back to New York tomorrow," he said. "Why don't you come along?"

211

He didn't sound convincing, but he was trying. She felt a rush of the old, traitorous tenderness well up in her for him.

"Ach! are you crazy? I couldn't get packed up and away outside of a week, an' you know it. We aren't all as used to jumpin' in a minute from here to there without stoppin' to catch a breath as you are, Mr. Brant Royle!" She chuckled again, feeling almost easy.

"Well," he said, "when you do decide to come, have them wire me from the factory. We'll do the town together. Haven't had much fun lately. Haven't had time."

Time. Time. Time. She could feel it rushing out, a relentless track, before them and behind. There would never be enough time now for either of them. But she was grateful.

"All right," she said, "I'll take you up on that."

But what they were saying sounded strange to both of them. There was no ground between them now to stand upon. They walked on in silence and came at last to the iron gate. Here she put out a hand and stopped him.

"I'll just run along. Don't bother to come to the carriage."

" 'Evenin', Sonie," he said.

But she didn't go. She stood looking at the great pile of the Templeton house facing them at the end of the walk. She shook her head in wonder.

"My, you'd never thought it, would you? You Royles all grand now in the Templeton house and me out on Bay Street in that elegant place that's too big for me. Sometimes I think there wasn't any Maple Street ever."

He didn't answer. And in that moment it came out of her. She couldn't have stopped it if she had tried. It had to be said to take away some of the sense of loss, of waste.

"Brant," she said, trying to find his face, "it was ol' Major Singleton's girl all the time—*wasn't* it, Brant?"

His profile was cut in stone, turned hard away from her.

"Go on home, Sonie," he said, "go on home."

Then he plunged through the gate and stalked up the path and into the house. She did not move for a long time. Just remained standing there, feeling the emptiness and the cool, desolate sense of freedom.

Late that night Pete Henry woke up in the strange new bedroom at the back of the house. He didn't know whether he had dreamed it or not, but he had heard a noise, muffled but distinct, somewhere below. He could not get back to sleep. His head throbbed a little and his mouth felt dry from all the drinking and eating at Sam's wedding. He got up and lit the bracket near the bed and went to the washstand. The pitcher was empty. All those fancy new servants and they couldn't even fill the pitchers! He cursed and yawned. He had to have some water, and anyway he couldn't sleep. He'd just slip down to the kitchen. He threw a robe over his nightshirt and slipped out into the hall. It stretched like a tunnel to the night light at the other end. He knew that Maryland would be asleep on a cot there just outside of Pa's door. Pa wouldn't have that fancy new nurse about at night. But it *was* a sight how that crazy big nigger took care of the old man. Never leavin' him whenever he was in the house, sittin' for hours patiently listening to all those crazy sermons and talks that Pa made. It was like a two-man revival meetin' every day. And neither of them ever seemed to tire of it—Templeton doin' the savin' and Maryland gettin' himself saved.

The floor creaked and Maryland lifted his head. Pete Henry hissed at him: "Just me, Maryland. I'm goin' down to get a drink."

The white eyeballs gleamed at him and a smile split the black face. Maryland nodded and put his head down again. Wide-eyed, Pete Henry descended the broad gloomy stairway. He didn't know whether he would ever feel at home in this big place that Brant had bought for them, but being in it excited him childishly. The rich, strange feel of it. The smells of varnish and new plush. He almost had a feeling of awe, like a kid.

He proceeded back through the lower hallway, running his hand along the wall. It was as black as the pit. Then he saw a thin gleam of light under the door at the end. Someone was in the kitchen. Maybe some of the help still up celebratin' on the quiet. That was the noise he had heard up in his room. Might be fun to give them a fright now. He grinned and tiptoed carefully forward.

He flung open the door. But it was Brant he saw, sitting heavy and sunken in one of the kitchen chairs by the big central table. Brant with his elbows on the marble top, holding his face hidden in his big hands. On the table were a glass and a half-empty bottle of whisky. Another glass lay shattered against the big gleaming range across the room. Pete Henry felt awkward seeing his brother surrounded by all these bright pans, the cutlery, the gleaming tile. Something that held him silent, too. He could not say a word. And then Brant dropped his hands and revealed features so pale and tormented that the younger man felt as though he were looking on the face of a stranger. He had seen Brant drunk many times in the old days, but never looking like this. The exclamation of derision and cajolery that had risen to his lips was never uttered. Brant just sat there looking at him, a terrible stranger, with eyes that stared blindly. It made him shiver. Then Brant spoke in a voice, slow and full of infinite weariness:

"Go away, Pete Henry, go away; leave me alone."

And Pete Henry closed the door carefully. Without saying anything he stumbled back through the house to his bed. He didn't turn out the light. He felt suddenly afraid, troubled by what he had seen. He was a little boy now, completely alone. It was a sad feeling and one that he did not like. It belonged to the unrest that had been growing in him for a long time. He didn't know whether he was cut out for all this high-powered living. Of course there were plenty of nice things that came with it. All that pocket money—the mandolin he had changed for the battered old guitar—all those fancy clothes hung in a long row over there in the big wardrobe. He wasn't just Pete Henry any more. He was Mr. Peter H. Royle, brother of the biggest man in Kingsmont. The man with a whole flock of folks runnin' ever' which ways just because Brant lifted an eyebrow. He had always worshiped his older brother, as only a small boy can. Brant was the big strength, the thing he could always turn to for help when there was trouble. What if he had slapped him about a bit? It didn't make any difference. He knew Brant would take care of him. But he didn't know this lone fierce stranger sitting in the kitchen below him. He couldn't get that out of his mind. It left him bereft, prey again to the feeling of being cut loose and alone—lost in this new life.

He got up and turned off the gaslight and lay down again. But he couldn't sleep. He lay thinking about Brant and himself and feeling terribly sad. And he didn't know why . . . any more.

CHAPTER TEN

I

Promptly at a quarter to ten on the evening Sonie Lipik was due to take the train for New York, Ed Huggerston, proprietor of the Soldier's Saloon, called out from behind the long bar to the usual evening clientele sitting about the tables.

"All out, boys! Take your business down the street. I'm closin' early this evenin'. Sorry. Got an important conference."

They knew he meant it, so there wasn't any protest. They drained their beers, settled up, and strolled out. One or two of them jokingly made a bawdy reference to his "conference" as they passed the till, but that was all. He laughed and shooed them out, closed and locked the front entrance, and untied his apron.

In the washroom he carefully parted his graying hair, combing it down flat. His tongue worked against the inside of his round cheeks as he critically examined his image in the cracked mirror. Then he reached behind the door and removed the coat to his best suit from its hanger and donned it carefully, patting and smoothing it along his shoulders and arms. Satisfied at last, he cocked his gray derby jauntily over one eye, gave his cravat a final hitch, gave the ensemble one last glance in the mirror, turned out the wall bracket, and stepped forth.

Outside he paused under the light at the corner and pulled a heavy, old-fashioned watch out of his vest and looked from it to the courthouse clock. It was, perhaps, the twelfth time during the past hour that he had performed the identical action. The Washington train up from Atlanta wouldn't be due for another half-hour at least. He had plenty of time. He waited for a big dray, its driver a sleepy huddle on the street, to clop ponderously by. Glancing down the block, he could see the yellow side lamps of a carriage winking in the darkness. It was drawing away from the lighted entrance of the Carolina Hotel at the corner.

He turned briefly down a side street and stopped before a darkened store. He knocked at the entrance and waited. Funny thing to be banging on the funeral parlor at this hour of the night. Something almost indecent about it. But he had arranged it earlier that day when Cary Alston, the mortician, had stopped in for a beer. Someone had opened the door at the back now and was coming to the front. The door was unlocked and Cary's voice called out in a heavy undertone: "That you, Ed?"

"It's me, all right," Ed whispered in return. He wished Cary wouldn't use that conspiratorial tone. Made it seem like they were doin' somethin' they oughtn't to be doin'. "You got 'em for me?"

"Right here!" whispered the face showing pale in the doorway. He thrust out a bundle. It crackled faintly with crisp paper when Ed grasped it. "I did it up with my best goods, Ed. No cheap stuff."

"I'm much obliged to you. How much do I owe you, Cary?"

"Dollar and a half sound like too much?"

"Nope."

Ed fumbled in his trouser pocket and found a bill and a fifty-cent piece and handed them over.

"Thanks. Well—night!"

The door closed and Ed, grasping his bundle tenderly, went back to the street with a feeling of relief and satisfaction. He turned down once more toward the depot, now only a matter of a couple of blocks away. Still had plenty of time. Well, he sure hoped Sonie liked 'em. They weren't exactly what he wanted, but it was the wrong time of the year. He was glad he had been able to find anything for his purpose. He felt proud that he had been able to solve what had presented a real problem. Of course Sonie would like them! He reassured himself and immediately began to feel a little sad and sentimental as he approached the depot. He had been feeling that way

215

off and on ever since he had learned that Sonie was going away. Couldn't expect any different. She might have gone away a long time ago. She had all that money now, could move among the swells, but it hadn't gone to her head like it had with a lot of people. No, sir, Sonie was just as friendly as ever. Nothin' cheap or stuck-up about her. No pretendin' that she didn't know you because she lived out Bay Street. But then, she had always been that way. She wasn't the sort to put on airs, no matter what happened to her. Well, here she was going away—guess that had to be counted as part of the big change. A town became a city and people kept right on growin' up and marryin' and dyin'. And people kept right on comin' and goin' too. That was part of it.

At the end of the street he came at last to the depot. It was a bigger, newer edifice now. It had been enlarged and almost completely rebuilt last year. They'd outgrown the old one, like so many old familiar places had been outgrown. But he liked it, liked what it represented in the way of Kingsmont's coming to amount to something while he was still alive and kicking to watch it.

He crossed through the usual waiting line of cabs, their Negro drivers squatting and leaning about the street door, and entered the waiting room.

2

There seemed to be quite a crowd down to see Sonie off. There were a lot of other people just sitting on the benches waiting under the sickly glare of the gas chandelier. But you could tell the difference immediately between them and those who had come to see Sonie. They made a distinctly festive group there in the corner between the ticket windows and the door to the platform. Ed Huggerston felt suddenly shy and a little self-conscious as he moved toward them holding the tissue-paper bundle stiffly in front of him. He began to recognize some of them. Pete Henry Royle dressed like a dude was there with a whole bunch of the younger men who worked in the offices down at the Royle factory. And near them and mixed in among them were Phil Randolph, the banker's son, and Miss Edna Ross of the tobacco-broker Rosses—a whole contingent of the Bay Street crowd. They were laughing and talking like all get-out. Ed saw Sonie now. She was standing by the door. Nearby Mrs. Rose and Mrs. Pearl clung to each other smiling and wiping their eyes. Sonie was talking to a dumpy, overdressed woman who held a fat sleepy little boy by the hand. Ed recognized Mrs. Lucas, one of the Ukrainian crowd who used to live down on Maple Street before the factory was built. It was a good scene; it warmed him up inside just to see it.

He felt proud of Sonie. Proud that he knew her. It was a testimonial to her whole life in Kingsmont that she could bring together such a group—delegates from every part of her life, past and present —a tribute to her essential generosity and honesty, her lack of shame. He thought Sonie herself looked radiant with her hair all piled up and gleaming red under the big hat. She had always known how to make the best of whatever she wore and she never showed to better advantage than when she was in a crowd. He remembered now with a pang the picture of her when she used to come flying in the saloon unafraid among his customers. Just a little birdie thing with earrings and a lot of red hair falling down, come to get a pail of beer for someone at the Maple House. Ed sighed. And now she was going away to New York. And when she went away tonight—even if she was coming back—somethin' was sure goin' outta this town with her. His eyes misted over and he had to stop and blow his nose discreetly. Damned sentimental old fool! He was glad that no one had noticed him yet. Well, no use puttin' it off. . . . He pushed sturdily through to her, a big grin on his face.

"Why, Ed Huggerston!" she cried in the hoarse, delighted voice. "I haven't seen you in a coon's age."

She reached out and hugged him right there in front of everybody. She smelled good. Expensive, like a real lady. Good perfume. He blushed furiously and held out the bundle.

"Bone voyage—an' all that, Sonie."

She took the package. "For me, Ed? Why, you sweet ol' thing!"

They were all watching. She took off the wrapping and held up the bunch of stiff pink wax roses. He didn't care now if they all could see that they came from the funeral parlor. None of *them* had thought to bring her flowers. And if she knew, it made no difference. She held the bouquet proudly up for all of them to see.

"Had to see you off in proper style, Sonie." He grinned again and winked broadly.

"Ed, you sweet ol' goose!"

Then she grabbed him around the neck and kissed him right then and there. No, sir! Nothin' stuck-up about Sonie. She wasn't ashamed. She never had been, God bless her! He hugged her enthusiastically, now feeling all teary. He'd have to blow his nose again quick or really disgrace himself in front of everybody. He was glad to hear them all laughing warmly about him. Somebody slapped him on the back. He was even more glad when an interruption fortuitously occurred at that moment when things might have become a little difficult. Somebody uttered a little shrieking sob and threw herself on Sonie. It was Mrs. Pearl. Mrs. Pearl older and thinner but still with the wall eyes and the silly dyed bangs peeping out from under the hat, and her rouge a little smeared. But it made no difference to Sonie. There she was hugging her and talking to her as sweet as anything and Mrs. Pearl raising all kinds of fuss. More like it was a funeral and Sonie was dying instead of just going away to New York. There was such a babble of sound, all of them crowding around and talking at once and patting each other as well as Mrs. Pearl. Nobody was acting embarrassed or superior. Sonie did that to people who wouldn't be speaking to each other when they met on the street tomorrow. You couldn't act mean around Sonie!

Sonie and Mrs. Rose, with Mrs. Pearl between them, moved to a nearby bench and sat down. Everyone else crowded about them.

"Now, Mrs. Pearl honey," Sonie was saying, grinning over Mrs. Pearl's head at them. "Now, Mrs. Pearl, don't take on so!"

"Now, Pearl," echoed Mrs. Rose from her side in a voice hoarse with weeping. Then she too buried her face in her handkerchief and said in a muffled, crying voice, "It's only for a month or so, Pearl."

"Honey," sobbed Mrs. Pearl against Sonie's bosom. "I don't mean to do it. I really don't. We've been together so long and I feel all broken up inside. You've been like my own baby, honey—my own little girl—an' here you are goin' off."

She wailed and Sonie patted her and made a delicious little grimace at the others. She wasn't making fun of the silly old woman. They knew that. She was just telling them, too, that it was all right, and not to let it bother them.

Between consolations Sonie continued to exchange banter with those about her as if it were all the most natural thing in the world. She was obviously enjoying every bit of it. She was the center of attraction and she could no more help responding to it than she could help breathing. It was instinctive, and she handled it with a practiced hand. She looked almost beautiful now in the stylish, becoming traveling suit, her green eyes sparkling, her big mouth so red against the brilliant pallor of her skin. It had a special radiance that even the unflattering light could not dim. She knew she was putting on a good show, and not one of them there could tell what an effort it was. Every moment or so she glanced toward the platform door. She wished that Chris Malley would come on back from seeing after the luggage. He seemed to have been gone for hours. She had been grateful during the past week for his sharp, elegant presence, the bite of his sardonic attention. It had been a help to have him around for a change. She had needed his particular flavor, had grown to depend on it to fill up the space that continued to grow around her no matter how busy she kept. She had liked him for a long time, but she didn't feel that she had really appreciated him until now. She was deeply grateful when his slim, impeccable figure appeared again in the doorway, his lean dark face unnaturally pink from the chill.

He took in the scene at once, smiling at her, the insolent, knowing, familiar smile.

"Well, here she comes, Miss Lipik," he announced in a clear, mocking voice. "Precisely on the hour—all in honor of you, I'm sure."

Everybody seemed to stir with relief. They laughed. Sonie hugged Mrs. Pearl and lifted her up. And then Pete Henry and some of the young men crowded about her joking among themselves. She began to feel better. She felt even better when Chris came and took her neatly by the arm.

3

Outside on the platform the air was clamorous with the sound of the approaching train, a great din that swept down upon them. It drowned their voices out so that their mouths opened and shut, specterlike in the dim lights, giving them all the appearance of wailing masks. Sonie, waving to them and shrieking first to one side and then the other at them, felt the nameless desolation steal into her throat again. She kept remembering the night Mrs. Ruby and Mrs. Daisy had gone away so long ago, when they had all huddled, lost and cheering one another, on this same platform. They had gone away—but this was no time to be thinking about that. That was all past, dead, gone. It was she who was going away now. She knew it now, standing alone again, because Chris had gone to find their car. Standing alone and grinning, grinning at them all.

Then Chris was back and helping her past the porter up the steps, Mrs. Rose had already gone inside the car with Pete Henry and the luggage. Chris held onto her hand as she turned again in the vestibule and looked back. He pressed it before he released it.

At that moment there was a disturbance at the edge of the group at the bottom of the steps. A tall, hatless man plunged through them heedlessly. It was John Barton, his ugly face paler than ever, his lank hair all awry. He looked blown-about. He made no excuses for his rudeness but pushed past Chris up the car steps to her. He seized her hand in both of his as though he were drowning. Sonie heard the long call down the platform: "Boaaard!"

"Hello, John," she said, "I thought you'd forgotten me."

"No—no," he gasped for breath. "Out in the country—buggy broke a wheel. Had to walk a couple of miles to borrow another one —afraid I was going to be too late."

"Well, here you are, and it was nice of you."

"Had to get here," he said in the labored, thin voice. He was looking at her with that peculiar intentness which had always been his since she had known him. "Wanted to tell you before you got away—thank you for *everything*."

Sonie squeezed his hand hard and felt warmed.

"Don't mention it, John; anyway, I'll be seein' you again soon."

"For everything," he kept saying, *"for everything. . . ."*

The train gave a lurch under them. He released her hand and stumbled back down the steps with Chris helping him. Sonie braced herself against the lurching car and waved the bouquet again. A wailing chorus of good-bys came up to her from the platform. And then they began to drift by the frame of the door like a display of dolls, grimacing, frozen, motionless. She caught sight of Mrs. Pearl supported by Mrs. Lucas and someone else, her head thrown blindly back and her hands clutched tragically to her bosom. And then they were gone and the dark warehouse sides, flat and lonely, began to rush past. She remained standing, still feeling warm about John Barton. Then she turned to the door and as she struggled to open it she felt such a sense of loss and desolation sweep down upon her that she had to stop. *Brant,* she thought with helpless and traitorous recognition. She bit her lips. She had been holding this off for a long time. And now that she was alone she couldn't keep it at bay any longer. It was a moment of supreme agony for Sonie as she stood there clinging to the handle, her body pressed desperately against the half-opened door. It was not a moment for weeping—even for crying out. She could only stand there feeling—and think through the feeling: I'm a bigger fool than I thought I was. Nobody, *nothing's,* ever going to hurt me like this again—because I won't let 'em. She pulled herself erect and gave her hair a pat with the hand holding Ed Huggerston's flowers. "Well, I guess you're on your way, Sonie," she whispered. "On your way at last—and it was true all along. They didn't know it, but you really are goin' away tonight. Somebody'll come back—sure—but Sonie Lipik won't ever come back again."

Putting a smile on her mouth for Mrs. Rose and lifting her head high, she entered the car.

CHAPTER ELEVEN

I

In the spring of 1897, four years after Sonie Lipik left Kingsmont, the Grand Columbian Tobacco Company came into formal being. It was the logical climax to the sequence of relentless activities begun by Brant Royle on that day when he told John Barton to go ahead and construct the first cigarette machine. The machine itself represented only a starting point in Brant's colossal scheme for an empire. And it was an empire now whose domains stretched throughout the industry in America, and was heavily involved in the vaster world markets. It was a monster that not only poured forth some score of brands of cigarettes from over forty factories, but it controlled the making of virtually every other tobacco product on the market—snuff, plug, cut, and cigars. By dint of imaginative and continuous advertising on a scale never before attempted, and by threat, coercion, and lavish inducements to the outlets, furthered ceaselessly by a huge and active sales force, Brant had all but cleared the field of any rival—and had virtually changed the smoking habits of a nation in the process. He never forgot that America by tradition was a nation of chewers and that while he might eventually create a tremendous demand for cigarettes, the big money was still in the plug market. And so he invaded and conquered that side of the business as thoroughly and as ruthlessly as he had begun to with cigarettes. His creation now included not only the whole industry and its markets, but fostered the activities of several subsidiaries—factories that produced nothing but the tinfoil that lined his cigarette packages, factories that made licorice paste for flavoring his plug products—and he was ceaselessly on the lookout for new machines for packaging his products, or for making any part of their manufacture more efficient.

And when he was done he had ruined a thousand men and made the fortunes of ten thousand more. He had spent hundreds of thousands of dollars and made millions. And in less than six years he had made out of an old and formless industry a huge empire. The empire was his.

He arrived late in a world of big business already organized around a narrowing circle of powerful interests. His almost meteoric ascent to a place among them was accelerated not only by his own particular genius, but by the fact that the resources he exploited with such magnificent shrewdness, with such a dazzling display of innate business acumen, did not lie in the special provinces of the older giants. It was fortunate also that these almost legendary gentlemen were so deeply locked in mortal combat among themselves for control over the monetary and natural resources of the nation that Brant emerged among them almost full-blown before they took notice of him and what he was doing. By that time, their own activities had attained such a degree of monumental unsavoriness that the country was being rocked from the Atlantic to the Pacific by a series of major industrial scandals. Scandals so outrageously cluttered and meshed with the political scene, with high persons in the administration, that something had to be done about it. The editorial hue and cry had been going on for some time. The newspapers were full of revelations, charges, countercharges, attacks, and counterattacks highly colored by the frenetic journalistic vituperation of the day. It was on a wave of this feeling that the Sherman Antitrust Bill, long pending, had been finally passed. A series of trials followed. But so ramified and ponderous were the proceedings that the country at large soon lost its first fine sense of outrage.

So, while the Grand Columbian was aided into being by the particular conditions existing at the time of its emergence, it was almost immediately jeopardized by those conditions. Rumors began to fly about the tobacco world that the Royle business was in line for a going-over by the Office of the Attorney General and the Investigating Committee. There were embittered individuals not only in Kingsmont but in many other places who watched these developments with passionate interest. They read the accounts of Brant's appearances in the capital, they saw the fluctuations in the Grand Columbian stock, with profound satisfaction. They waited and prayed. Some of them waited and planned to reap a profit the moment there appeared any breach in the structure that towered over them.

But, as usual, they underestimated the central figure. The summer passed and nothing came of it. Instead the papers were full of the examination of the Sugar Trust.

Then in September, for the first time in over a year, Brant Royle came back to Kingsmont.

2

It was a crystalline morning, everything sharp and distinct. A morning cut out of cool gold and blue. Christopher Malley, Special Promotions Manager of the Grand Columbian Tobacco Company, stood with Mr. Peter H. Royle on the Kingsmont station platform waiting for the arrival of the 9:05 from Richmond. The two men were dressed smartly for the weather in beautifully tailored topcoats and expensive derbies. Of the two, Pete Henry's ensemble was the more elaborate. His shirt collar was a hair more extreme in height, his cravat pale lavender in color instead of black like his companion's. His attitude was one of nervous, apprehensive dignity. From time to time he self-consciously removed a thin gold watch from his waistcoat pocket and studied it. He was enormously proud of that watch. Sonie Lipik had sent it to him all the way from Paris, France. He had displayed it all over town as though having a watch was a wonder to him—and was not simply another in a long succession of expensive timepieces that he had lost or discarded. This direct and childish delight in every new possession was still one of Pete Henry's most charming attributes.

"She's four minutes late already," he remarked with satisfaction.

Chris cocked an eyebrow and smoothed his impeccable mustaches.

"My dear Pete," he said, "you can't expect that Brant's presence on this train is going to change its bad habits of some dozen years' standing!"

"Why not?" Pete Henry sounded cross. "Brant seems to be able to make anything else run the way he wants it to. Isn't he the one that's always sayin' to everybody—whether they work for him or not—'A minute lost is a dollar lost' . . . isn't he?"

Chris was not to be ruffled by the younger man's bad humor.

"Your brother," he continued coolly, "among other things has developed a marked taste for homespun sayings. But I must agree: I feel quite confident that if he set his mind to it he'd make the Carolina and Central Railroad mend its ways."

Studying Pete Henry's half-averted face, he was struck with the change it had undergone since he had first known the younger man. There was still the boyish quality. That would always be there. But it was no longer fresh and open-eyed. There were unusual signs of strain clearly evident in the tight jaw, the too-nervous movement, the capricious, restless roaming from one interest to another without design or object. He had a feeling that Pete Henry of them all was the least well equipped to handle the weight of wealth and attention now fallen upon him. Of late he had looked more and more baffled. Like a man opposing an amorphous, enveloping force he could not understand. So Pete Henry bought new clothes, got into some wild brawl, made some near-scandal with a girl—and emerged empty-handed, more desperately, gaily searching than before.

Chris had returned to town only the day before. He had been on a long inspection trip over the far-flung interests of the Grand Columbian, a journey which Brant had terminated with one of his usual abrupt telegrams merely instructing him to meet him in Kingsmont on this morning. From long experience now, Chris understood that Brant wanted to talk over something at first hand. Brant was great for that. Never from the beginning had he trusted much to paper. He had always preferred to carry endless details and complexities in his head.

"Here comes Roberta with the baby," said Pete Henry mockingly. He gestured toward a carriage that had just driven up back of the platform. They watched as Maryland handed out Mrs. Samuel Royle and a Negro woman carrying a small child. Roberta saw them and waved. She turned and gave some instructions to the nurse and came down the platform. Chris doffed his hat. Marriage to Samuel, he thought, watching her approach, had not particularly improved Roberta. She was as gaunt and graceless and as full of nervous bursts of laughter as ever. Even having the Royle money could not give

223

her any distinction. And here she was coming down to meet her brother-in-law, the tobacco baron! Poor Roberta, caught like a piece of crazy flotsam between that redoubtable matriarch Mrs. Marston and the bewildering pressures of the Royle dynasty. And now that the little girl had been born and was two years old, she seemed no more happy in the fact of motherhood than she was in any of the rest of her life. Chris almost shook his head in despair. He managed a smile of welcome instead.

"Goodness, Peter," she screamed, and pecked the younger man on the cheek, "I thought I was going to be late. And Mr. Malley—how do you do? It's been months—simply months, hasn't it? Well, you are looking well."

"You're looking very handsome yourself," returned Chris. "I want to see that good-looking baby of yours."

"I sent her into the waiting room with Dicey. Much too chill out here, you know. I maybe shouldn't have brought her down. But Brant has never seen her. Think of it—Tina's almost two years old and her own uncle has never laid eyes on her!"

"I'm sure he'll be pleased, Mrs. Royle," said Chris in his most unctuous tones.

"Where's Sam, Roberta?" Pete Henry scowled. Roberta darted a glance back over her shoulder and smiled the frightened smile, not at them but around and between them. She pulled desperately at her gloves.

"I don't know," she screamed, "I simply don't know! He said he would come from the store and for me to come straight from town. Such a morning! I've been positively distracted getting everything ready for Mr. Royle. The house in a mess and none of the servants able to find *anything!* Then something's gone wrong with the boiler in the kitchen again, and—well, I *do* hope Brant isn't going to find everything too awful. He hasn't been in the house now for over a year and I was away in the mountains then. . . . Well—" she looked desperately around and between them—"I suppose I'll just run in and see if Tina is behaving."

She didn't wait for them to make a move to accompany her, but turned and walked stiffly and awkwardly down the platform and disappeared into the waiting room. The two men were silent. They had been enormously uncomfortable, as always, in her presence. Roberta had no gift for putting people at ease, so tormented was she by her own lack of it.

Chris was glad to hear at that moment the long wail echoing among the outlying warehouses to the northeast announcing the arrival of the 9:05. He had found the last few moments with the Royles markedly uncomfortable. He hoped devoutly that it bore no omen for his coming meeting with Brant. The two men moved leisurely up the platform, placing themselves strategically at its center. Others were pouring out of the station now to join them. With some of these they exchanged the sort of distracted and noncommittal pleasantries common to people trying to be polite and still watch the approach of a train at the same time.

And then the train roared into the station. As they stood watching for Brant, Roberta joined them with the nurse and the baby. The child was crying. In the general hubbub Roberta shrieked remarks indiscriminately at her daughter and the two men.

"There he is!" yelled Pete Henry, and darted away toward the car just below them. Chris saw him run and embrace the big, unmistakable figure descending the steps to the platform. Brant was laughing, his face smooth-shaven, the jowls delicately blue. He looked in high good humor as he greeted his brother. Chris observed that he was putting on weight. But with that tremendous frame he could afford to. The inevitable black bowler sat on his head and the equally inevitable Prince Albert flapped about his big legs as he strode toward them, talking to Pete Henry. Directly behind them followed a slight gentlemen of indeterminate age, who was fussily directing a laden porter. He wore rather thick spectacles which gave him a gnomish, prim look. Chris recognized Mr. Fenton Banks, Brant's personal secretary who traveled everywhere with him. Brant paused for a moment to exchange a few words with someone who had greeted him from the station crowd. Chris could not see who it was, so interested was he in observing Brant himself. The old boy was certainly radiant with good spirits, voice booming, face smiling and animated! It was a manifestation in Brant that Chris, who was a cynical and perceptive student of the human animal in general and of his employer in particular, found continually interesting. In the seven years of stormy association with Brant he had never ceased to wonder at the mysterious springs in the man, the quality that revealed him one moment a creature furious and dangerous, the next glacially inhuman. Now it was this warm, gusty, vulgar person, brimming over with animal spirits. Whatever the manifestation, there was always behind it the merciless and insatiable drive. Chris shook his head wryly. The creature was a complex one, to say the least!

Brant swept down upon them.

"Well, look who's here! Hello, Chris. . . . And Roberta!"

He shouted and embraced the frozen and shrinking woman. She uttered a little scream of laughter. Brant held her at arm's length.

"You're lookin' all right except you need a little meat on your bones. Sam been starvin' you? Where's Sam?"

"I don't know, Brant. He said he'd be here. Something important must be keeping him." She looked anxiously, following his gaze, then shrieked, "But I brought Tina—here's Tina!"

225

She snatched the baby from the grinning nurse and thrust her at him. The child began to wail again. Brant took her suddenly from her mother and held her up before him, laughing.

"Well, well, so this is the little lady I've been waitin' to see—well, honey, don't you cry. At least you don't favor your daddy an' that's a blessing." He threw back his head and roared with laughter. "Now, now, don't you take on so. Your Uncle Brant's got some pretties for you in his bag. Wait'll we get to the house."

He thrust the baby back to Roberta, who held her awkwardly, alternately shushing her and watching Brant feverishly.

"Maryland's here with the carriage," she shrieked, and began to walk down the platform. They followed her, Brant chuckling and looking happy. Pete Henry and Mr. Banks were directing the disposal of the luggage on the front seat. When Maryland saw them coming he jumped down and stood in an attitude of monumental servility, bobbing his head slowly up and down, his mouth split by a wide grin, his eyes fastened on Brant.

"Hello, Maryland—you black scoundrel!" Brant greeted him. "How's my pappy?"

The giant man continued to bob his head and grin.

"Mr. Temp's fine, Mr. Brant. He told me to bring you on home. He wants to see you bad."

Brant turned to Roberta.

"I got to go down to the factory for a while, Roberta. I'll walk. Want to get the cramp out of my legs. You just drop Banks by the hotel for me and I'll be along around dinnertime. Chris here'll come with me."

"Certainly," said Chris. "Have you had your breakfast?"

"No. I'll have some coffee sent in at the office. Let's go," said Brant, stepping down into the roadway.

3

They walked briskly along the street, Chris a little to the rear of Brant. Not because he was observing some fine shade of protocol in their relationship, but because, even with his own long legs, he found it difficult to keep pace with Brant's purposeful stride. He reflected wryly that their walking position was quite consistent with every other aspect of their relationship. He, like everyone connected with Brant, would always find himself following just a little behind. He knew Brant as intimately as any man alive, he supposed, which was not saying much. But the intimacy had been based only on certain superficial experiences shared in common. He could not say that he knew the man behind all the things they had done together any better. The final knowledge—if there was a final knowledge—was as

226

closed off from him as it was from any casual passer-by. The two men had complemented each other from the beginning. It was Brant who had sensed the large design, the intuitive, breathtaking daring. To this Malley contributed his own hard knowledge of men and the world, his talent for dealing with details, his cynical and acute estimation of the difficulties inherent in any projected plan. He had no illusions about Brant's regard for him. It went no further than his usefulness. Brant exploited that usefulness ruthlessly. And Brant had a frightening talent for choosing men. It was one of the marks of his particular genius. It was also a mark of that genius that it had no compunctions whatsoever about getting rid of a man who at any point showed signs of weakening or an inability to toe the mark. For those who were able to fill the requirements the rewards were rich indeed. Brant always paid well for what he wanted. But the pace was a terrible one and the list of casualties long.

Chris often thought, ironically, how condescendingly and patronizingly he had first entered upon this relationship. It had been intended simply as a steppingstone when he had entered the Royle store that Sunday morning so many years ago. He certainly had not expected to be caught in the vortex. He had come to realize his error during those first months. But it was too late to extricate himself then, even if he had wished to do so. He had been swept along—and the central fascination was Brant himself. If Chris had ever thought he knew what the world of men was like, his association with his boss had opened his eyes. Here was boldness, ability, capacity for the most astounding conceptions, side by side with a complete disregard for moral means. All on a scale that he had never imagined possible—and he had been familiar with all the chicanery and intricate double-dealing practiced by the human animal. No matter how involved he had become he had always managed to maintain his equilibrium. He was a born tightrope walker. He knew he exercised this ability sometimes for the sheer pleasure of doing it. It suited his temperament. He had learned how to manage Brant. He even liked Brant. Not warmly, but with the liking engendered by continued amazement. Sometimes he felt that the real hold Brant had upon him was each further revelation of consummate greatness or pettiness appearing endlessly out of the man. His was the respectful admiration of one born gambler for an incredibly superior player. Then, too, he had done very well for himself. He, Christopher Malley, was feared and respected on his own account as one of Royle's closest associates. And he had become materially rich in the process. He could easily afford now the sort of life he had always pretended to. No, he had no quarrels with his lot. He was doing all right. . . .

He became aware—as he had done often before—of how quickly the news of Brant's presence got around. As they passed, people quite noticeably were pointing Brant out with an air of mixed awe and curiosity. There was something of fear in their attention, too. It was a force on Chris's back. A carriage bore down upon them containing an older woman and two younger ones. Chris identified the wife and daughters of Hinton Turner, president of the King National Trust Company. The three women bowed and smiled from the carriage as they drove past. The two men tipped their hats. Chris elaborately and Brant almost curtly.

"Looks like the Turners have come back from gallivantin' 'round Europe," said Brant, dropping back to Chris. "Bet ol' Hinton had a sorry time of it with those three women on his neck."

Chris smiled obediently.

"Kingsmont's getting quite cosmopolitan these days," he said, watching Brant out of the corner of his eyes. "Sonie Lipik arrived in town last week, too, I understand. I gather that she was a great social success in Italy and on the Riviera this past season."

If Chris had hoped for some special response from the other man he was disappointed. Brant's face looked merely pleased.

"Yeah—trust Sonie to cut a wide swath for herself! She'll always get along all right. I knew she was back. She came by the Manhattan office while I was in Washington. She'd left New York by the time I got back. You knew she'd bought herself a fine house up on Fifth Avenue?"

"No. But I've been rather out of touch with things for the past six months, and Miss Lipik is chary with correspondence."

Brant's mouth curled.

"Sonie's no better than I am with letters. She's generally too busy. Haven't set eyes on that red head of hers in a long time. I'll have to see her while I'm down here this time. Bet she's got a lot of tall and fancy tales about what she's been doin'!"

Brant strode ahead again immersed in his own thoughts. This abrupt beginning and end to a conversation did not astonish Chris. He was used to it.

As they passed along the square and turned down West Street by the new hotel, Chris heard the old enveloping factory hum, the thick warehouse smell of cured tobacco close in about them. . . . As they came under the shadows of the block-long building housing the Royle factory, the machine hum from the open windows filled the street. Brant stopped and shook his head, smiling. Whatever hundreds of other factories he might now own, Chris knew that this one was closest to Brant's heart. If any spot on the face of the earth could be called his home, this was it. Opposite the factory, across the street, stood a more elegant brick building. This housed the company offices. Brant stopped and turned to Chris.

228

"You go on over," Brant said, raising his voice above the pervasive hum. "I'll join you in fifteen minutes."

Chris nodded. He watched Brant stride a hundred feet to the entrance of the factory. He knew where Brant was going. This was so typical, too. The boss was going on a swift tour through the factory rooms. Chris had accompanied him on such tours in the past more times than he could remember. Brant would enter the blending room where the workers were placing the correct mixture of North Carolina, Virginia, and Kentucky leaf together with the imported strong sweet Turkish tobaccos on the long belts that fed the cutting machines. Walking along it, he would pick up a handful of the tobacco, hold it, smell it, and throw it back. Maybe he would speak to one of the workers. Then he would walk up to the next floor—or ride on the freight elevator—where the big whining machines, a hundred of them, poured out an endless stream of cigarettes. He was sure to look over one of the holding racks and find an imperfect one. This would produce a talk with the machine's attendant, scaring the worker half to death. By that time the news that Brant was in the factory would have spread like wildfire to the farthest reaches and to the ears of the most menial shipping boy in the factory. Having done this, Brant would frown over some daily countsheets and walk into the packing room, where the new packaging machines had been installed last year, and ask a lot of questions of the foreman. Then he would go on down to the shipping room and simply stand and watch them pile the big cartons on the drays loading at the door. Chris knew every step of the procedure. He had seen Brant go through every gesture of it a hundred times over. It had assumed the nature of a ritual. A ritual that Brant punctiliously performed no matter in what factory of the Grand Columbian he happened to be. There was something about it that Chris found quite touching over and beyond the close attention Brant paid to every smallest detail involved in his business. Here, he appeared, for a brief moment, naked and human, happy with his creation. He was not simply that august and invincible figure, Mr. B. Royle. Chris always could see the ghost of the big hungry country boy—calloused hands, earth-stained, the dark eyes burning with wonder and delight —walking among those miraculous singing machines. . . .

Chris shook his head, smoothed his mustache, and crossed the street to the office building.

4

The central foyer, surrounded by private offices, contained a waiting place for visitors. It was expensively but uncomfortably furnished and beyond it a series of desks, filing cabinets, and type-writers presided over by the usual battery of busy stenographers and file clerks. Chris proceeded through these, acknowledging their various good mornings, and knocked on the door of the manager's office. There was no vocal response, but the door opened in a moment and the portly figure of Mr. Ellery Benton himself appeared.

"Ah, it's you, Malley!" Mr. Benton looked a little harassed under his habitual, well-fed, brisk surface. "Everything all right?"

"The train was a little late. I just stopped by to say that Royle is here."

"Ah—already!"

"He's over in the factory now, but he'll be over in a few moments."

"Good, *good!*"

Mr. Benton stepped out and closed his door behind him. He made a grimace of despair.

"Things are popping this morning all right, Mr. Malley. I've got Senator Richards in my office now. He's been raging like a lion for the last half-hour."

"What does *he* want now?"

"That grower unrest I was telling you about the other day. It's really assuming serious proportions. They're hot on the Senator's tail now because of the way we're controlling the market price. And of course all that night-rider business—burning warehouses over in Kentucky. It's getting some of the boys on edge. The Senator seems to feel that it might spread down here to Carolina."

"All right," said Chris coldly. The man was quite evidently unnerved by Brant's approaching visit. "Let's not discuss it here. Hardly the place. Mr. Royle will see the Senator later."

Mr. Benton mopped his face with a large handkerchief.

"There are two gentlemen down from the Richmond Exchange waiting out there, too. Absolutely refuse to see anyone but Mr. Royle. I don't understand how they find out he's in town. I certainly haven't said a thing to anyone!"

"They'll have to wait their turn," said Chris curtly. "Mr. Royle will send down when he wants to see you."

"Of course, of course."

Chris turned irritably on his heel and went to his own office. He stopped only for a moment to dispose of his coat and hat, take a fat file of papers from the desk, and look briefly over the elegantly furnished room that was kept solely for his use. It afforded him a moment of sardonic pleasure to realize how little real use he had ever been able to make of it. Leaving it, he went up the carpeted staircase to the second floor. There Brant's office and that of his secretary occupied most of the front, the windows opening on the factory across

230

the street. Chris wondered whether Brant, when he came over, would arrive by the front door or come up the back way through the less public entrance. He rather thought the latter. He knew it pleased Brant to appear suddenly and without warning among the office personnel.

In Brant's outer office he found the correct and superior Mr. Banks conferring at a desk with a nervous young lady stenographer. They both rose formally. Seeing that he was alone, they relaxed.

"I have copies of both the sales and the morning's market reports on Mr. Royle's desk," Mr. Banks announced primly. Chris nodded.

"Thank you, Mr. Banks. I wonder if you would send someone out for coffee. On the way down from the station, Mr. Royle said he wanted some."

"Of course, Mr. Malley. I'll see to it immediately."

Chris entered the inner sanctum and closed the door.

Brant's Kingsmont office was almost identical in size and appointments with the Grand Columbian offices off lower Fifth Avenue. A big, bare chamber. No rug on the plain, oiled floor, no draperies at the tall windows. Its furnishings consisted of an undistinguished flat-topped desk. Near it sat the homey, barrel-back chair Brant preferred to a swivel. In one corner there was a hat tree. A brass cuspidor, a water cooler, in the other. Against the near wall, a couple of barrel-back chairs for visitors and a deal table with some trade journals spread on it. That was all. It was somehow exactly right.

Chris could never quite reconcile himself to the honesty expressed in this severity. He knew only too well what his office would be like were he in Brant's position. But Brant was funny about his wealth in relation to himself. Having acquired it in staggering amounts, he did not seem much interested in flaunting it. Even his clothes, while of the most expensive materials and tailoring, were plain and conservative almost to the point of looking old-fashioned. At the same time he lavished money on his family and in spectacular entertainments. He was equally generous where charities were concerned. But then he could afford to be. And when old bedridden Templeton had expressed a desire to see a more splendid church from the windows of the house on Elm Street, Brant had contributed the money that rebuilt the Kingsmont Second Baptist Church on the opposite corner. A ponderous Romanesque pile stood there now in place of the once-familiar wooden tabernacle. Chris recalled, too, the vast acreage recently purchased along the Hudson fifty miles north of New York. There Brant was keeping a small army of architects, contractors, and workmen busy creating what he boasted, in exuberant moments, would be the finest estate in America. All these diverse elements added up to something. What that *something* was eluded him, as so many things did in his ceaseless study of Brant.

Brant simply was not predictable. The man followed his own course and it was open to no one but himself.

The door opened and Brant entered. He nodded and hung his bowler on the tree.

"I've sent out for coffee," said Chris. "All the reports are there on your desk."

Brant grunted. "Good." He seated himself energetically in his chair. Before looking at the papers he lighted a cigar and puffed hard. Immediately it filled the room with an overlayer of rich tobacco smoke. Chris turned to the window again. He knew he must wait until Brant wanted to talk. Behind him he could hear Brant puffing at the cigar and turning the pages methodically one by one. Occasionally he grunted, a little unemotional sound. The beehive hum of the building across the way seemed gradually to muffle the room in an all-encompassing blanket.

Brant grunted again. This time it was a sound full of satisfaction. "Well, that just about completes the picture, doesn't it?"

Chris turned from the window, attentive now.

"You've done a damn good job, Chris," continued Brant, pushing his chair back and spreading his big legs under the desk. He clasped his hands behind his head and grinned at the ceiling, sucking at the cigar. "Yeah, we've done it now. That just about makes the Grand Columbian *it* in this neck o' the woods. No loose ends—not a single one. They can go right on hollerin' but we've got 'em where the wool's short. They've got to come along where we go whether they want to or not. They'll all want in now. Can't help it."

"Even Ogden?" Chris asked. The Ogden Company, situated in Old Bethel, North Carolina, and headed by shrewd, aggressive Philip Ogden, had been the only serious new competitor in the cigarette-manufacturing world since the founding of Royle & Company. Ogden had steadily encroached upon the field, employing quite as effective methods as Brant. He was resourceful and not to be intimidated. He had been an increasing thorn in the side of the Grand Columbian and had won Brant's grudging admiration as a mettlesome opponent.

"Yeah," continued Brant. "Even Ogden. That surprise you after all the backing and filling we've had to do? Well, you know what I've always said—if you can't beat 'em, join up with 'em. That's what we've done. Phil Ogden came up to see me in New York. We've worked it out very nicely. He's satisfied because we're letting him operate as his own boss and I'm satisfied because we're going to refinance him and expand him under the Grand Columbian. How does that strike you?"

"As usual I offer you my congratulations," said Chris, making a little half-mocking bow in Brant's direction. "Then that does really

232

complete the picture, doesn't it? I can think of but one fly in the ointment. What is the Federal Government saying these days? They've been sending me routine reports on your sessions in Washington while I've been on the road, but I found them meager and unrevealing."

Brant slapped his hands on the desk top and frowned at Chris through the cigar smoke.

"Meager and unrevealing—that's what they were." He grinned the half-grin. "Hell-fire, Chris, those dumbheads in Washington don't know what they've got into. We've got them in such a tangle in their investigations this past year that they'll be years getting around to us seriously. By that time the big noise ought to have quieted down. Anyway, you don't believe that I spent all my time in the nation's capital dancing attendance on the committee, do you?" He fixed Chris with a cynical, black-browed glance. Chris shook his head in reply. "Hell, no!" Brant guffawed a short roar of amusement. "The company's got a lot of new little friends among the bigwigs. It's a little project I've been working on gradual-like for a long time, as I think you know. Looks like we're gonna have us a right nice effective little lobby working for us from here on out whenever we need it."

"Money," said Chris, "is a remarkably persuasive substance."

"If you're not afraid to use it, know what you want to buy, and what to pay for it."

"I've always admired the way you manage to handle it, you know."

"And you know why? Because I've always used *it*. It's never used me."

"I agree. A very rare talent among the general run of men."

They fell silent. Brant regarded the ceiling, his face relaxed and bemused. When he spoke again it was in a warm and intimate voice almost as though he were addressing himself.

"You know this is a pretty big day for me, Chris. We've done it. We've done every damn thing almost that I wanted us to do. I feel pretty good. I guess I feel as good as I ever have in my life. When I think how I used to be half a dozen years ago! How I hated this place! Hated the state, the people, every hand of tobacco that was sweated out of the ground by some damn fool and brought into the market—hated what I was, in particular. And I broke my heart and bloodied my head battin' against all of them. Now look at me. Six years and it's all mine. All of it to do with as I damn please. Now it's all of *them* and all of *it* that's hatin' me to the guts"—he chuckled deep in his throat—"an' there's not a thing in this world they can do about it. Most of 'em thought I was trash, rubbed my face in the mud. Now the trash is rubbin' theirs. By God, I like 'em hatin' me!

233

Sometimes I think I've done everything I've done just because of the way I felt about the people who once held the whip hand over me. The ones that *had*. They made me mean. That's where I've got it on all of 'em. I can't stop feelin' the way I do about them. It's in my bones, an' I'll keep right on after 'em, doin' everything I know how and can do now—*everything*—to squeeze and push them out till there isn't anything left for them to stand on, not a damn thing!"

Chris listened fascinated as the deep voice grew more quiet and more intense. He's really speaking out now, he thought. I've always known this, but it's different hearing him say it. I may never see him as naked as this again. . . . Brant suddenly leaned down across the desk toward him, his face cold and businesslike.

"Well, I didn't call you here to meet me just to talk about this," he said. "How would you like to take a little vacation across the Pacific Ocean and have a look at China for me?"

Chris's face betrayed no surprise at this sudden shift. He merely looked politely interested.

"An Oriental journey might be very pleasant. What are the odds?"

"A lot of people may think I'm through just because I've got things sewed up on this side and have a good toehold in Europe. I've got bigger things in mind. I'm not through by a long shot. I particularly don't like the way the British tobacco combine is tryin' to keep us out of China. The Manchu Government raised the tariff on all American imports again last month."

"So I noticed."

"Well, a blind man could see the British boys are behind it. We'll have to get at 'em another way. We'll fight 'em from the inside. That's the only way. I want to know which o' those gents has a price in mind for his business. That's for you to find out. No matter what it is, we'll buy it. They're scared to death already. This will really bring them to heel. It'll all have to be done strictly on the q.t. You're good at that. When you've got something definite, cable me and I'll slip over myself to close, as usual. I want it all done before anyone can find out what's happening."

"All right. When do you want me to go?"

"As soon as we clear up the business before the board meetin' tomorrow. I wanted to let you know what was up before we broke it to them."

"I'll be ready as usual."

"Good!"

Brant leaned over and spat into the brass cuspidor by the desk and began shuffling through the papers on the desk again with the familiar concentrated, oblivious expression. Chris crossed to stand before him.

234

"There are a couple of things," he said, "not included in my reports that may or may not be on the agenda for the meeting tomorrow. I found out about them since arriving yesterday. I thought I'd check them over with you anyway."

Brant lifted his eyes from the papers and removed the cigar from his mouth. It was astonishing how the cold, attentive mask now could have been a face warm and lusty just a few moments ago.

"O.K.," he said. "Let's have 'em."

"I saw Benton for a moment before I came up just now. He's in something of a sweat as usual. The 'Friend of the North Carolina Farmer' is beating on the front door again."

Brant's mouth drew down slightly on one side.

"So the Senator's in town, eh? Well, what does the fat ol' possum want now?" He spat contemptuously again.

"He's been making Benton's morning miserable demanding to see you. It seems his rural vote is giving him hell about the way we are holding down the market price."

"So that's it. Well, we'll fix that all right. I've been prepared for it. Can't have any stink like they've been making over in Kentucky right now. Do us no good. I think we've squeezed 'em tight enough. No use killin' the goose anyway. I left instructions with the purchasing department to ease up gradually on the market through the summer. By fall it will mean a ten-cent rise on the pound. But with business like it is we can absorb that without knowing the difference. And then"—he paused to push back from the desk again—"the Grand Columbian will throw a big shindig for every mother's son in the county—barbecue, eats and drinks, maybe a dance in the biggest warehouse—a real shebang at market-opening time. Between the two, the poor hayseeds will forget we've still got the price in our hands. I want to play it along easy now, anyway. Be damned good publicity to boot." Brant nodded with satisfaction at the ceiling.

"That should work admirably," agreed Chris. "Anyway, as you say, we've still got plenty of slack to let out."

They looked at each other for a moment in complete understanding.

"Sure, plenty." Brant turned the hard mask to him again. "What else have you got on your mind?"

"Oh—Barton dropped by to see me yesterday. We had quite a long talk."

"Anything special?"

"He's putting his shares on the market. Everything. Including the patents. He didn't say so but I think he wanted to give us first refusal."

Brant shook his head.

"That queer fool! Isn't he doin' all right for himself with us?"

"It seems that he and Upham have gone crazy over some sort of internal-combustion machine. They want to start a company. Got some people up in Ohio interested enough to go in with them. Barton needs the cash now, all he can lay his hands on, to finance his share."

"Well, let him go," said Brant, and relit his cigar. "There was a time when I wouldn't have let him out of my sight for a million dollars. I think he's through as far as we are concerned. Funny how a man's got the imagination to make a thing like that cigarette machine and then never be able to do another thing. Look at the money we wasted while he was tryin' to make us that packaging machine last year. No. He's just a one-shot gun. You wait and see. He'll never do a damned thing with this internal-combustion affair he's got on his mind except lose the shirt off his back. He's thrown money away on just such foolishness before. It isn't that the ideas he's got aren't good. I've made it my business to look into every one of them. They'll all be done one of these days, but somebody else will do 'em. Somehow he can't seem to bring that wonderful know-how of his together again on anything else. He's shot his bolt as far as I'm concerned."

"You know," said Chris, "I've always felt a sort of sneaking pity for him, like I might for a stray dog. He was born lost. Certainly he was never cut out for a big business like this. I had a feeling yesterday that he wanted to be out from under, would really be relieved to cut himself loose."

"Sure. He belongs back on some farm where he came from. Never had got the dirt out of his fingernails." Brant reached over and ground out the stub of his cigar in an ash tray.

"Funny you should say that," mused Chris, looking toward the window. "Did you know he owned some land down south in the county?"

"Nope—I didn't, but I wouldn't be surprised."

"About three years ago he bought an old five-hundred-acre farm that hasn't been worked in a decade. It's somewhere between here and Carlton Springs. I don't know what he's done with it since."

"Well, don't bother your head about it," said Brant tersely. "Did you make him an offer?"

"I discussed a proposition for taking over his shares pending discussion with you. He accepted it. I've had the papers of transference drawn up. You can have a look at them whenever you want to."

"You're right smart, Mr. Malley."

"It's my business to be, Mr. Royle."

Brant opened the file again. The matter was closed. Hail and farewell, Mr. Barton, author of the Wonderful One-Horse Cigarette Machine! Chris allowed his fancy to wander as he looked out the window. The big hum embraced him again.

"There's one thing more," said Brant in a low voice behind him. The sound had such a peculiar timbre that Chris turned, startled. Brant's face was expressionless. Only the dark eyes burned with a black intensity. "What about the Singleton company?"

"I followed your instructions and had Benton send them another offer last week. The old boy made no more acknowledgment of it than usual. He's crazy of course. Our latest reports show that he hasn't really had a leg to stand on for over a year. The business is a joke. He's even had to mortgage his personal property, including his home, to make a pretense of keeping the factory going last quarter."

The peculiar fixity of Brant's gaze upon him at that moment he found embarrassing. He didn't like it.

"So he's mortgaged Hill House." Brant's voice sounded as though he were holding the words down carefully by a terrific effort. "Who to?"

"The Richmond Trust. Typically, he didn't approach anyone in town. I think if you'd have let me handle it personally in the usual way we could have finished up this farce a long time ago."

Brant's face turned dead-white. "I didn't want you or anybody else to touch him," he said in the slow, thick voice. "That's to be my little party. It's one of the main reasons I made this trip. I've waited a long time. The time's come."

The tension in the room was distinctly uncomfortable. These incomprehensible, startling manifestations in Brant had always made Chris feel that under all the complexity and power in the man there was something out of balance, something completely out of control and obsessed. Looking at Brant now, he sensed it keenly. He did not like it, and to ease the feeling he removed a handsome cigarette case from an inner pocket and withdrawing one of his expensive hand-made Turkish cigarettes, slowly lit it as he spoke.

"If you will forgive me, this extraordinarily long campaign against Singleton has always puzzled me. It's so out of proportion. Any special reason, Brant?"

"Yes," said Brant.

"Something personal?"

"If you want to put it that way. Sure, it's personal. It's been personal all my life. Something I'm paying back the Singletons for—them and every one of their kind. You think I've gone to all this trouble just for the fun of it? You think I couldn't have brushed him off the map a long time ago?"

"It's been perfectly obvious that you could have for some years." Observing him through the curtain of cigarette smoke, Chris thought: He looks completely mad now. I should never have gone into this. I should have known better.

237

"I didn't want it that way. I've surrounded him, taken away his props one by one, left him hangin' high and dry looking alive and knowin' he was dead. He doesn't know how to crawl, but that's what I've been makin' him do for a long time. It's been long enough now. It's time for me to go see him. I'll go up to Hill House this afternoon —Mr. Brant Royle to call upon Major Singleton!"

The man behind the desk had just completed the establishment of an empire, but the uncontrolled hate in his face had nothing to do with the Grand Columbian. It was as though someone else, someone cruel, ferocious, and animal-like, had come into the room and sat in the chair. For Chris it was a dreadful, frozen moment. Then one of those lightninglike, subtle transformations occurred in Brant's face. It relaxed. He looked suddenly tired and not a little puzzled. Chris felt his own breath loosen and ease.

"Yeah," said Brant, and the word came out on a deep sigh. "Sure I can see how it must puzzle you and maybe a whole lot of other people. It's bothered me all my life the way I feel about Singleton's. I know just as well as you do that the Major and the company aren't worth a drop in anybody's bucket now. I've told myself that a million times. But that doesn't seem to have anything to do with it. I've tried to get away from it, but I always find myself comin' back to it eternally no matter what else I may be doin'. I *have* to come back, you see. Something inside makes me. Sometimes I have a crazy feelin' that every goddam thing I've ever done in this wide world was done just to show the Singletons I could do it. Funny thing how somethin' like that can get hold of a man so that he can never get rid of it. Maybe it got hold of me before I was born—I dunno. . . . Yeah," said Brant in the tired obsessed voice. "I'll go up to see the Major this afternoon."

Someone knocked at the door. Chris heard the little precise sound with a feeling of profound relief. Brant growled out of the corner of his mouth without looking, "Come in."

Mr. Banks entered bearing a tray with a coffeepot and some cups. He closed the door and crossing to the desk, set it down with an air of self-conscious precision. Brant nodded and shoved the reports out of the way.

"All right, thank you, Banks."

Mr. Banks drew back a step and regarded his employer owlishly through the thick glasses. It was an expression that managed to be at once superior and servile. Chris turned away in irritation to the window again.

"There are several gentlemen here to see you this morning," said Mr. Banks in the prim, clipped voice.

"Yes?" said Brant, pouring some coffee into a cup. "Coffee, Chris?"

"No, thank you."

"Senator Richards has been here since nine waiting to see you, and there are a Mr. Howell and a Mr. Thomas of the Richmond Exchange."

"Make my excuses to the Senator and tell him I'd like him to have dinner with me tomorrow. And I reckon Mr. Malley here will take care of the boys from Richmond."

Mr. Banks did not move. He cleared his throat.

"Well?" said Brant, eying him over the rim of the coffee cup.

"There's someone else," said Mr. Banks, lowering his voice discreetly. He glanced over his shoulder toward the closed door. "It's Miss Lipik—"

"Here at the factory?"

"It seems she came down to have a look over the plant this morning. Mr. Allers has been conducting her about across the street. But she heard, somehow, that you were here, sir, and insisted upon coming over. Mr. Benton tried to reason with her and I did my best" —Mr. Banks paused, shrugged slightly, and looked disapprovingly down his thin, nervous nose—"but she's in the outer office now."

Brant threw back his head and uttered a short bellow of laughter. Chris turned. They smiled across at each other almost intimately.

"Well, Banks, don't just stand there!" yelled Brant. "Open the door and let Miss Lipik in!"

5

She stopped just inside and looked from Brant to Chris and then back again. Mr. Banks went out and closed the door on them. Then she grinned, the old familiar, wide grin full of beautiful teeth, and laughed the husky, deep-throated laugh—half derision, half healthy animal spirits. She felt their eyes upon her, and loved the moment. She was beautifully dressed in a shade of her favorite green. It made the cat eyes sparkle like emeralds. It was also a dress that bore the print of more subtle thought and hands than any to be found on this side of the Atlantic. It was enormously becoming to her and she knew it. She carried a gray fur muff, and there was some more of the fur about her neck and on the hat above the piled red pompadour. Chris shook his head in complete admiration. What a girl! She's just the same. Something indestructible about her. She'll carry that vitality to the grave. He thought in a flash for the hundredth time since he had met her that she was the one woman in a long, confirmed state of bachelorhood who had ever made him consider matrimony. She would be worth any man's changing if he could have her! She had always been friendly, flirted with him as she did with all of them. And that was all. He could never get beyond that.

239

He had been discreet enough in this instance not to try. He had long ago given her over to Brant as part of his property, untouchable. He had observed their intimacy without being able to understand it. It was obvious that there was something between them—strong, hard, electric. He felt it whenever he saw them together. He felt it now. But what it was that kept it alive, what hold each had on the other, what it was that forever kept their relationship unresolved—that he could not get at. The longer he lived, the more diamond-cut his cynicism became, the more he had come to realize how mysterious the essence of the human animal and its relationships were. He shook his head again.

"Well, Mr. Royle!" she said, cocking her head at Brant. "It's getting to the place where even your old friends can't find you or get anywhere near you these days. Pretty soon we'll have to get a permit from God! Don't blame your young man out there. Don't blame any of them. They did their dead-level best to keep me out. But I said that as a director of the Grand Columbian Tobacco Company I'd see you or else. Looked like the only way I was going to get to see you while I was here anyway—right smack in your office with a lot of flunkeys and secretaries about. Ach, how times have changed!"

She chuckled. Brant's face was delighted. He crossed around the desk, came to her, and took her by the hands.

"Hello, Sonie."

"Hello, yourself, Brant. Hello, Chris."

She released one hand from Brant's and extended it to Malley. He crossed elegantly and took it.

"It's been a long time, Sonie!"

"Too long. My, it's good to see both of you again! Stand back a minute and let me see if you've changed. Chris, you've put on a little weight—it looks good on you. But Brant here's gettin' just plain fat. Too many desks to be sat behind, too many people to run around and do for you, eh, Brant?"

And then they all laughed. It was a good moment. They all felt warm and friendly and gay.

"Sit down, Sonie," said Brant.

"Thank you. I've walked miles over that factory this morning."

Chris brought up one of the plain chairs and set it before Brant's desk. She seated herself in a manner that made the ugly piece of furniture look immediately comfortable and rich. Admiring her, Chris thought: Essentially she hasn't changed, but the old vibrant hoyden is a woman now. The exterior is polished and perfected. She's made good use of her time. Aloud he said:

"I can see your travels have agreed with you."

"Europe?" she said. She was not looking at him but at Brant, studying him out of narrowed eyes. "Why not? I had a good time. But I got tired. It was time I came home."

Brant was pouring more coffee.

"You're gettin' out of our class, Sonie," he said. "Haven't any time to do any fancy gallivantin' myself. Too busy. Have some coffee." He extended one of the thick cups to her and she took it and held it delicately. "I didn't get any breakfast on the train this morning."

"No time to eat properly any more either, eh?" She shook her head mockingly at him. "I remember you used to eat well when I did the cooking."

"Sure, I remember too. Can't find any blintzes like you used to make."

"I can still make them any time you can stop long enough to come around." She was teasing him, but there was a definite edge in it. Not far under this elegance and poise crouched the little girl who screamed and kicked. She turned to Chris.

"How do you happen to be in town too?"

"Little business, as usual."

"Of course," she said, and lifted the cup to her lips. "I should have known."

"You're bein' hard on us workin' men, Sonie," said Brant.

"Am I? Maybe I can't get used to running my friends down in offices every year or so, just to see them." She drank the coffee and set down the cup on the edge of the desk.

"Well," she said, suddenly bright. "I didn't break in here this morning just to make a social call. I know you're busy, but I thought I had better catch you while the catching was good. I'm leaving Kingsmont, Brant."

"What do you mean? You haven't been around any more recently than I have."

"I mean I'm closing up here. I might even sell the house. It's been empty ever since Mrs. Pearl decided to go back to Indiana. Mrs. Rose doesn't mind. She'll go wherever I go. She's in New York at my new place up on Fifth Avenue. You knew I had a house there now?"

Brant nodded. "I walked up by it one afternoon after I got back from Washington. Nobody was in. Just a lot of painters and decorator people. You're steppin' pretty high, aren't you?"

"Well, why shouldn't I? I've got money to burn, thanks to you gentlemen. I've met a lot of people and been a lot of places in the last two years. I don't have anything here to hold me any more. I like plenty of things goin' on, as you ought to know. There's always a lot goin' on in New York. I like people, and ach! God knows there are enough of *them* there to suit anybody's fancy. Yes, I think I'll

241

like New York fine. Europe was fun. You wouldn't believe the number of proposals from very fancy gentlemen I got while I was gadding about. They're all crazy to marry American girls—'specially if they can smell a little money!"

She threw back her head and laughed. Brant roared with her.

"Hell!" he said. "Don't tell me. I wish I could have been along just to see it, Sonie. Must have been a picnic. You've always been able to pretty much make monkeys out of anyone you wanted to. Just the same—" he shook his head, elaborately looking her over—"I wouldn't say it was just because of your money."

Her face became very still looking at him. For a breath she said nothing. Then very quietly:

"Did you hear what I heard, Chris? Brant Royle, that's one of the nicest things you ever said to me, whether you meant it or not."

Brant flushed suddenly and sat down. He thrust himself back in his chair looking almost flustered under her direct gaze. The powerful handsome face looked almost boyish for an instant.

"Come on, Sonie. I'm not all that bad."

"And I've got something else up my sleeve," she said, toying elaborately with the muff, frowning at it. "I don't know how it will strike you two. It's going to raise a pretty little noise among all the snobs who've had to choke me down the best they could since I became the rich Sonie Lipik. It's also gonna please a few poor ol' dodos who'll think they've got me where I belong—I'm gonna have me a career."

She swept them with a slow, casual glance. Chris leaned forward attentively. Brant frowned at her and ran his hand impatiently through his hair.

"A career, Sonie? Come on, let's have it. You're dyin' to tell us."

"I like being different," she said, returning to her preoccupation with the muff. "Always have. I guess most people have a career first and then get money. Not little me! I've got the money, so now I'm gonna have a career." She paused and looked up again. "I'm going on the stage."

Chris stepped forward with a delighted exclamation. "Bravo! I knew it, I knew it! You've kept me waiting a long time for this, Sonie, but I always knew you'd come around to it."

She inclined the pert head toward him, but her eyes were on Brant. He slapped his hand on the desk top and leaned over it.

"Godamighty, Sonie," he said incredulously. "You mean you're gonna be an actress?"

She shook her head at him, her face grave, almost pitying.

"Does it seem so strange to you, Brant Royle, after knowin' me all these years? Yes, I guess it does. Yes, I'm goin' to be an actress. Do you mind so much?"

242

"Hell, it isn't that," he protested. "I—I just never thought of it."

"It's real easy and simple," she continued. "I've had a very good time traveling about in the last four years. I've learned a lot. I've learned one thing sure. When I left Kingsmont I was twenty-two and full of hayseed. I thought I was just tired of *Kingsmont* then. Needed to go someplace else, see some other things for a change. But after a while I began to feel just as restless. And the more restless I felt, the more crazy, wild things I'd do." She chuckled. "You should have seen me! I got quite a name for myself in the fastest, fanciest circles. London, Paris, Cannes, Rome—all the society columns full of what Miss Sonie Lipik was doing and who she was doin' it with. Mrs. Rose kept a scrapbook everywhere we went. She thought it was something wonderful! I'll show it to you when you're around sometime. I'm saving it for the time when I'll be wandering around with a cane. It'll give me some laughs to cheer me up. Well, anyway, it was no good. I should have known it was no good quite a while back. This past June I was down with a big party to spend a month at a villa in Deauville. I was at the casino one evening as usual with some of them—I've even forgotten who, it doesn't matter. But there I was playin' chemin-de-fer and feelin' bored. I looked around me all of a sudden like I was just seein' where I was for the first time. And I said, 'Sonie Lipik, you're twenty-six years old—and you're still a big fool! What are you doing here? This fat, rich business trying hard to do nothing isn't for you. You need to be *doing* something!' And it was true. I always have. I left the casino without so much as a fare-thee-well and went back to where I was staying and woke up Mrs. Rose. 'Pack up, Mrs. Rose,' I said. 'We're leaving.' We took the train back to Paris the next day. While I was there buying some clothes I met Willy Shadner at a party."

"The darling of Broadway, no less!" exclaimed Chris, smoothing his mustache and rolling his eyes in mock awe. "It all becomes increasingly clear."

"Wait a minute—back up!" Brant held up a restraining hand. He looked amiable but a little baffled. "I'm losing out in this. Who's this Shadner fellow, now?"

"Brant," said Chris, "I'm afraid you're too hopelessly devoted to the holy temples of business. Mr. Willy Shadner is the author of such frivolous but wildly successful ventures in the theatrical world as *The Bon-Bon Girls* and *Rat-Tat-Tan*—do you mean you have even escaped hearing that omnipresent ballad of the past season, 'My Little Yaller Honey'?"

"Afraid I have." Brant frowned. Then he added almost apologetically: "I've never had either much of an ear or much time for songs. But you say this Shadner is the big boy in his work? He's a big success?"

243

"Incredible!" Chris threw up his hands in despair.

"Ach, keep quiet, Chris," Sonie said tartly and then grinned like a gamin. "Sure, Brant, he's enough of a success to be able to charge me five thousand dollars for a show he's written for me. I've bought it, Saul Ellers producing it for me, Tony Parsons is playing in it; it goes into rehearsal at the end of the month, and sometime in November the boards in front of the Blackwood Theater will go up saying: 'Sonie Lipik in "The Girl from U.S.A." '!"

She rattled this latter off, finishing with a flourish. Then she leaned back in the chair and laughed.

"Shadner . . . Ellers . . . Parsons," repeated Chris in a reverent whisper. "*And* Lipik! Sonie, you astounding woman—I have been on my knees before you all these years. Metaphorically speaking, I am groveling at your feet at this moment."

Sonie laughed again, glancing at Brant. "Don't," she said. "It's not becoming to you."

Brant beamed at both of them uncertainly. He rubbed his big hands together.

"Well, well!" he boomed enthusiastically. "Our little Sonie going to be a big star on the stage, what do you know about that! We'll have to do something special when you begin—give you a big send-off. Show the folks in the big town what we feel about her, eh, Chris?"

"I should say so. I for one wouldn't miss this opening—" He cut off with a grimace of pain. He was remembering. "I am the most miserable of earthly creatures! Brant, couldn't the Grand Columbian postpone China for a few weeks?"

"Oh, don't worry about that. You very likely will be back in plenty of time," Brant assured him. His face was concentrated upon the celebration he was arranging in his mind. Sonie turned her head to Chris.

"So, you're going to China?"

Chris thrust his hands deep in his trouser pockets and lifted his shoulders. "Business." He shrugged. His face was suddenly blank, masklike.

"I see. Of course, business." She turned back to Brant.

"Yessiree!" he continued energetically, as though they had not spoken. "We'll have to make a damned big thing of it. Big supper at Delmonico's after the show . . . champagne—lots of champagne . . . everything of the best for Sonie!"

Looking at him she felt a pain. He's trying, again . . . trying real hard, because he thinks it's the thing he ought to do . . . but he doesn't know how . . . he's never known how. . . .

"It's nice of you," she said, "but don't get all excited about it too soon. It may all turn out to be terrible. It's just something that way back in me I've always wanted to do. I'm not getting any younger. Twenty-six isn't doddering, but it isn't exactly sweet sixteen either. This just seems like a good time to do it if I ever am goin' to do it. If it's a fiasco, I can afford it, and no one else will be hurt. I'll work hard at something I want to do—and I'll have fun."

Brant glowered at her. "Now, Sonie, what are you talkin' about? You're gonna be great—we all know you are."

She stared back at him calmly, directly. "Would it make any difference, Brant?" she said quietly.

He shifted protestingly in his chair and pushed at the papers on the desktop. He lowered his eyes.

"What are you gettin' at now, Sonie?" he said furiously, then stopped dead. She waited tense in her chair for him to say something more. But he was silent, withdrawn, staring moodily at the papers. The room became very still. It slowly filled with the deep, monotonous factory hum. Chris was the first to move. He walked softly to the door.

"If you'll excuse me," he said in the suave professional voice, "I think I'd better go see about the gentlemen from Richmond."

He was fooling neither of the other two in the room, and he knew it. Sonie smiled at his infallible tact. Good ol' Chris! He always knew when it was time to leave. He thought she wanted to be left alone with Brant. Maybe she did. She shrugged at herself and swung around to face him partially.

"I'll drop by your office before I go," she said, and patted the back of her hair with the coquettish gesture he remembered so well.

6

They sat silent, each in his place, and a thousand miles apart. Brant had not looked up. His face was still preoccupied, the black line of the brows that she knew so well drawn tight over his nose in the familiar expression of concentration. She watched him candidly as she had been watching him from the first moment she entered the office, as she seemed always to have been watching him since she had first seen him. It was as though always she hoped to find some answer there. I've known him—ach! how long now?—in all sorts of weather and places. I've fought with him. I've been kissed by that big, sullen mouth until it was like my own; I've hated him and been in love with him and taken myself away from him to many far lands. And now I see him again and he's more a stranger than when I first saw him that day in the warehouse standing like a giant knee-deep in golden tobacco. He looks tired, too. He never used to look this kind of tired, she thought sadly, like he was getting old. He's only thirty-nine or so, but he's changed. I've changed, too. All

245

of us have changed. Changed so fast we haven't taken time to sit down and look at one another and see what it means.

She got up suddenly from the chair and walked to the window. The tall factory stretched across her vision like a bastion, shutting out everything save its own solid, implacable self. She found herself trying to spot the place in the long wall of brick and windows where Maple House had once stood. But it eluded her. It was gone. Brant's monument had effaced even memory. It was as though the impersonal physical fact of the building had obliterated a part of her too. The ugly little girl with flying red hair, running down a vanished Maple Street, yelling with laughter. . . . Well, the child had stayed, but she, Sonie Lipik, had gone away. And now here she stood at a window in a green Worth dress, and nothing was left but the enigma —and even it could no longer now evoke anything in her.

"You know," she said quietly from where she stood, not turning or caring whether he was listening or not, "when I was in Austria a year ago I got terribly homesick one day for the sight of Kingsmont. I wanted to smell tobacco in warehouses, I wanted to walk down West Street and hear the niggers quarreling and singing, I wanted to see the kitchen the way Mama used to have it—I thought I'd die if I couldn't. I didn't just come back here to close up my house and see about all that business. I had to come flying back to make sure that Kingsmont, that *something*, was left like it was. Well, not very much is, is it?" She turned to him from the window, pulling herself erect, her fine resilient energy welling up in her again. "It doesn't matter. Now that I've come and seen it like it is, I know it doesn't matter."

He was looking at her somberly from the desk. He had been looking at her for a long time.

"Ach, Brant!" she cried. "I didn't mean to do this to you this morning. I've eaten it all up, haven't I? And just talked and talked my fool head off."

"Why shouldn't you, Sonie, if you want to?" He got up from the desk and came to the window. "We're old friends, aren't we?"

He looked down gravely at her, his hands clasped behind his back.

"I guess it was the sight of you and Chris after all this time," she mused. "Do you know what I really came up for, forced my way in on you?"

"No. I can't say I do."

"I started to write you from Paris when I read it in the paper. Yes, they even had it over there." Her eyes sparkled maliciously at him. "But I'm no good at letter-writing. I tried to catch you at the office in New York. I just wanted a minute eye to eye with you to say something about the Grand Columbian." She reached out and

246

caught him by the arm. "You've done it—everything you said you wanted to do—at last, haven't you?"

He nodded gravely. "Yeah, Sonie, I reckon I have."

"My, when I remember all the times I used to sit and listen to you talk about what you were going to do, *had* to do, until I thought I'd scream. And now you've done it!"

Neither of them said anything then. They stood looking out the window, side by side, not touching, each buried in his thoughts. When she spoke again her voice was so low he could just hear it.

"I've been wondering a lot about you since I came in here this morning, Brant."

"About *me*, Sonie? Now—"

She turned on him swiftly and angrily.

"No, not that way any more. You needn't worry. That's finished. I can't finish being worried about you, though."

"Why—what's it now?"

"Brant, now that you've done what you set out to do, where are you going with all of it? I'm talking about you—*you*. Not the Grand Columbian. When are you going to get all you want? You haven't, because I can see it as plain as day in your face. And I don't like it. I don't like what it's doing to your face, what it's done to you already. You look like a man with a sickness."

"Ah, come on, Sonie! I'm in my prime. Don't worry. One of these days I'll stop tryin' to grab the world. . . ." He hesitated. "Right now there always seems something else for me to go on to."

She shook her head, her eyes bright upon him from under the green hat.

"I don't like that, Brant. I think you've started something you can't stop—even if you wanted to. And that'll be bad for either it or you. This morning walking about town and seeing your name staring at me from every wall side—the old buildings as well as the new. And seein' the wagons always rolling, rolling in from the countryside, pouring out a river of bright leaf tobacco just for you. I had a strange feeling that you weren't flesh and blood any longer, but just a name—a *thing*. A terrible thing that no one could touch any more, just feed, feed endlessly. It scared me, and I hated you then. I hate you now for having made me feel this way about you. Ach, Brant," she cried out suddenly, "what is it you want? *What is it?*"

His eyes were cold and mad, pressed against the building across the street. But his voice when he spoke was so utterly desolate that she felt it like a knife against her heart.

"I don't know, Sonie," he said. "I really don't know."

CHAPTER TWELVE

I

After midday dinner on that September afternoon, as was his invariable custom, James Singleton retired to take his nap. In clement weather he generally performed this amiable exercise upright in one of the rockers on the shady side of the porch, palm-leaf fan tightly clasped in one plump fist, a decanter, a glass, and a pitcher of ice within easy reach, and a handkerchief thrown over his face against the insects. With the coming of fall and the chill, raw days he occasionally went upstairs to his room, but usually he took himself off to the little library-den back of the second parlor. There in the rather airless and musty chamber redolent of the old leather bindings of his father's books, he would stretch himself out upon the ottoman under the one window. This ancient and comfortable piece of furniture had long accommodated itself precisely to fit his physical peculiarities. Once disposed in its embrace he would draw up over his plump knees a faded afghan that had been crocheted by his mother over half a century before. Across the room a small coal fire would glow and crackle in the grate, and on the open secretary against the near wall sat the inevitable decanter with its accompanying glass and pitcher of water. The setting, the properties, and the time had not varied by a hair over some thirty years.

On this particular afternoon it was only James who was different. He closed the door behind him with a tired sense of relief. The click of the latch was a signal that for a while the world and its irks were closed out. Even the small world of Hill House. Meg had gone down into town on some errand after dinner, and Tabby was upstairs in her cluttered room industriously occupied with some one of her minute and multitudinous activities. The rest of the household lay muffled and sealed about him. For an hour or so now he would not have to face anyone.

With a little grunting sigh he stretched himself upon the ottoman. His vest felt intolerably tight across his paunch and in unbuttoning it he saw that its lapels were spotted and soiled. He stared at the stains for a moment and realized that he didn't really care. Hadn't cared for a long time. All his life he had had a passion about his personal appearance. He adored the feel of good, clean linen, the sense that he was impeccably turned out for any hour of the day. Now he didn't want to be bothered. He didn't even want to think about it. He put his head back and closed his eyes, longing only for sleep. All his life he had been able to approach sleep as guilelessly as he approached all activities in his life, slipping down into unconsciousness with the simplicity of a child, and coming out of it again with no sense of shock, his body healthy and comfortable. But over this past year—like many other things—sleep had been eluding him, both day and night, with such frequency that he looked on it now as a luxury. He hated to admit it, but he didn't feel at all well. Hadn't, in fact, felt really well for months. It had occasioned the violations more times recently than he liked to think of the rule he invariably followed in his consumption of liquor. It followed his father's dictum that no gentleman drank until after his nap. James had never considered himself a heavy drinker. After the first relished drink of the day—sometime in the afternoon—he was likely to sip comfortably on through the evening varying quantities, depending on interruptions and in whose company he found himself. But lately, feeling none too well, the struggle for sleep often saw the level in the decanter drastically lowered before he was able to drop off. And when he wakened now it was with no sense of refreshment or well-being. He only felt heavy, torpid, and unhappy.

He groaned now upon the couch and decided that he must take himself in hand. He would *not* touch the decanter this afternoon if he never closed an eye. His head ached dully, as it had all day. His dinner lay like lead in the middle of him. He should never have eaten that confounded fried eggplant. It always disagreed with him. He shifted his body again. I really must be getting old and in a bad way, he thought despairingly, even my victuals are going back on me. Ought to see a doctor—but what good would it do to have Frank Richardson tell me again that I ought to slow up? He had been told that long ago. Now it was no longer a question of slowing up at all. He had to keep going, going somehow—holding his head up, seeing this thing through. I'm not done by a long shot!

But it wasn't just a matter of his digestion, nor was it that he felt bone-weary, nor that his heart was in none too good shape. Nor was it the sense of guilt that he had had to raise money on Hill House and had never told Meg—although that had bothered him considerably.

No. None of these things, gnawing and irksome as they continually were, lay at the real root of his trouble. It was in his increasing recognition of the fact that the pattern of his existence with all its starched little fronts, its comfortable little legends, had changed hue and texture. It was merely a shabby picture of disintegration in which he found himself trapped. All the people and things that he had valued had either grown away from him or he had cut himself off from them. Take this year's market opening, for instance. All his life it had represented a personal festival. This year only by the exercise of much effort had he been able to appear at all. It had been a humiliating experience. He had felt himself looked upon indulgently as an anachronism, a harmless and eccentric curiosity. This feeling of being condescended to had hurt more than anything else. And yet he had to keep on going, completely obligated to the role he had assumed. He was the last champion. Not a champion *for* anything any more. Simply a champion *against*. In the beginning he had assumed the position with enthusiasm. It had pleased him to think of himself in the vanguard of a shining host, armored with honor and tradition, and arrayed against the enemy. He had never dreamed that the day would come when he would find himself left alone upon the field, ignored by friend and foe alike. It was not an enviable position. He felt dismayed that he had managed to maneuver himself into it, and now, willy-nilly, had to hang on whether he wanted to or not. What a lot of damned nonsense he had uttered in his time!

He squirmed upon the ottoman. The afghan slid to the floor. He let it lie. It was hideous what life could do to a man of good intentions. All he had ever wanted was to exist comfortably in his corner of the world and be let alone. He didn't want conflict. Godfrey's Cordial! he had avoided it as much as possible all his life. It was palatable only as long as he could roar out magnificently about what he was *going* to do, or what *ought* to be done. Any real opposition had always dismayed him. Not that he was a coward. It was simply that he did not want to be bothered with all the hurrah, when it came right down to it. Now the ultimate irony had placed him where he could not budge one way or another. He, the lone, last survivor arrayed in tattered splendor upon a battlefield that was no longer a real battlefield at all, but a place full of new magnificent monuments and a few frail ghosts. And it was not where he wanted to be at all.

Anger rose in him blindly, that he should be so used by himself and the world. The feeling had no focus. It made him feel hot and wild, a lump of raw, peevish nerves writhing upon a couch in this room full of tangible memorials to his father pressing accusingly about him. Even here there was really no escape. Not even sleep would come. He glared, red-eyed, about him over the dull sleekness of leather bookbinding. The feeling of despair and oppression grew upon him. A dull ache throbbed in his temples. He got up with a groan and started toward the decanter on the secretary. Then he paused and sank back again, hiding his face in his hands. Can't go on like this . . . I must really be sick to feel as I do . . . I'll go see Frank Richardson tomorrow . . . I've been saying I will, but I really mean it this time. . . .

He let his head fall back and closed his eyes. Sleep did not come, but gradually his thoughts dulled and clouded, giving him a kind of peace. In this suspended half-dozing state he found himself hearing, as if from a great distance, the casual sounds of the living house about him. . . . He didn't know how much later—he must have really dozed off—he heard footsteps in the parlor approaching the library door. Then there was a careful, soft rap.

"Yes?" he growled, without opening his eyes.

"Majuh, suh." It was Simon's voice. "I was afraid you was still nappin'."

"No. Come in, Simon."

Simon, stoop-shouldered, stood in the open doorway. "Gen'man to see you," said Simon.

"Well, who is it, Simon?"

James sensed rather than saw the queer strain on Simon's face.

"It's Mr. Brant Royle, suh," said Simon, scarcely above a whisper.

James sat up slowly, his hand straightening his cravat with a blind, bewildered gesture. Beyond Simon through the open door he could see the cool afternoon sun streaming palely into the parlor from the west. In the empty still feeling of that moment all he could hear running through his mind was: *It's getting late.* . . .

2

James stepped from the hallway into the main parlor and paused. Across the room his visitor faced him. Brant stood on the rug in front of the fireplace, his strong legs astride, his head lowered. With the Major's entrance a curious expression of pain, almost of uncertainty, flashed upon his face. It was gone almost immediately, leaving the face heavy and impassive. Only the eyes smoldered beneath the dark brows. He did not move to meet James. He simply stood looking across the room at him.

Meeting that gaze, James did not at the moment know what he felt. His senses seemed still numbed and dazed. He could feel only that his hands were shaking, and prayed that it was not conspicuous. He was poignantly aware of his disheveled state. Even as a wild sense of relief flooded over him he felt decidedly at a disadvantage in this meeting. Here it was at last. He recognized instantly that it had been inevitable for a long time. Neither of them could escape it. There was a kind of triumph in the moment for him. He raised his face, somewhat puffy but still polite, and advanced toward his visitor. He extended his hand.

"Afternoon, sir."

His voice had that subtle impersonality that made a question out of the greeting.

Brant did not move to meet him. He let the little man come all the way across the room to him.

251

"Afternoon, Major."

Then he took the proffered hand briefly, scarcely touching it before letting it drop again. James looked up at him unflinchingly. He thought, with satisfaction: I'm not scared of him at all. He's got them all scared, but he can't scare me! He has the look of a gentleman now—I must say that for him—but it can't have improved the grossness of the blood.

"Won't you sit down, Mr. Royle?"

James indicated one of the chairs nearby. It was an icily correct gesture and his voice came briskly and unfalteringly out of his mouth.

"Thanks," rumbled Brant, his eyes never once leaving James's face. "I'll stand if you don't mind."

"Of course," said James, with a little smile. "As you wish." He turned and seated himself elaborately. Inwardly he hoped that he wasn't overdoing it.

"This isn't a social call, Major."

"I see. Then wouldn't it have been better if you had come down to my office?" James said.

"I don't think so," said Brant abruptly. His voice was hard and without coloring. The sound of it made James feel as though the skin of his face were being drawn back over his scalp. His upper lip felt stiff and cold. He leaned back deliberately in the chair and crossed his hands over his stomach. No sense in getting riled right here at the start, he thought rapidly. I mustn't get riled. Deliberately he calmed himself, but the effort cost him something. He concentrated on the physical fact of Brant. He saw that the man had not troubled to remove his topcoat and still carried his hat in his hand like a tradesman. But instead of indicating servility it was a gesture somehow insulting and contemptuous.

"Let's not waste time cutting fancy capers around each other," continued Brant. "You don't even have to pretend to be polite to me if you don't want to. You don't like me any more than I like you, but I've been looking forward to this meeting for a long time. And I've always intended that when it came it would be here in this house with just you and me. None of that folderol down at your office."

In all his life James had never been so addressed. He felt the peculiar tightness in his face spread down like a vise. His face, pallid before, now became a deep red as though it had received a blow. The dull pain at the back of his head spread sharply across his temples, striking upon them with regular hammerlike blows. I will not lose my temper before this man, he thought desperately. It's what he wants. I won't give him that satisfaction if it's the last thing I do!

"Very well," he said in the slow, controlled voice, its usual rumble a little thin. "If that is the way we are to understand each other,

252

I may speak freely. I see that your change in fortune has not markedly changed your manner. Apparently money won't buy you good breeding nor make you a gentleman. But since you have come to my house this afternoon I cannot help but extend you the common courtesy that I am in the habit of offering the humblest visitor entering my doors. . . . You say you want no folderol. Good. I shall appreciate your stating your business as briefly as possible. We can then cut short this interview, which you must find as distasteful as I do."

Over Brant's face there flickered something like admiration. But the mouth remained stonily set. He shook his head.

"You're wrong, Major. I find this interview very much to my taste! I have no wish to cut it short. I've waited too long for the day when you would have to sit there and listen to me because you couldn't help yourself."

"What do you mean?" James did not move. The once-clear eyes were muddy and bloodshot.

"You know exactly what I mean, Major. It wasn't very long ago—was it?—that you Singletons had the world the way you wanted it. You'd have thought every hand of tobacco grown in this county was cured for you, every pound of it auctioned in the warehouses for your own special benefit. You sat up here on your hill in your fine big house"—Brant's eyes traveled casually about the room as he spoke—"and let the rest of us squirm where we belonged down below. You're still trying to feel that way, but it's a damned sight harder now, isn't it, Major? Maybe you've forgotten, but I haven't. I haven't forgotten one damn thing about the way you and the rest of the big boys here in town tried to keep me down—to count me and the others out because we didn't start off having it easy. You never thought anyone could take that away from you, did you? Well, I have. I've done it a-purpose. You don't think I really needed the decrepit little two-by-four concerns here, did you? Hell, no! I didn't even need to look twice at any of 'em six months after I'd got my foot on the ladder. But I've eaten you alive one by one and in my own sweet time. I've made you sit by and watch me do it, too. Oh, you've tried, all right; I have to hand that to you. I've watched you try. Sometimes I've almost felt sorry for you, because there wasn't one little ol' damn thing you could do, Major—*not one damn thing!*"

Brant's tone was quiet, deadly. James looked as though he were suffocating. His face was splotched with red, as though the blood were trying to burst through the quivering, sagging jowls.

"Is this why you came to see me this afternoon—just to say this to me?" he burst out hoarsely. Looking down on him, Brant continued calmly:

"Yes, partly. It's something that I wanted to have you hear from

253

me, to have you know I knew. But I came on business too. I've about closed my books in Kingsmont." He looked out the front windows. The declining sun now slashed into the room, cutting the space between the two men like a blade. It left each of them in half-shadow. Brant continued without looking at James: "I've saved Singleton and Sons till the very last. I don't usually bother about little details like this any more. I don't have to. I've got people hired to do this kind of job for me. But this was one time I wanted to do it myself. I somehow felt I owed it to you. You were top dog for so long—I'm top dog now."

James's body seemed to writhe in the chair. His hands clutched its arms desperately as though he feared he was going to fly into a million pieces.

"Get out of this house," he said carefully. His voice was so strangled in his throat that the separate words came forth thick and blurred. Brant turned to him again, his expression almost pleasant.

"I've already made you several offers, I think. For some reason you didn't have the courtesy to acknowledge them. Maybe they didn't interest you. I could just sit aside and let your business drown in its own dead weight. But no. I've paid good money for all the rest. So I've come today to offer you again a damned good price for Singleton and Sons. Maybe it's less than my last offer, but I expect it's still a sight more than what you're worth. You ought to be glad to accept. I don't think you're in any sort of position to refuse anything any more, are you?"

"Get out!"

James's shaking voice sounded as though he were pleading rather than commanding. He seemed to be controlling himself with one last supreme effort. His body swayed in the chair like that of a man gone blind, reaching forward for support. "I'm not for sale, Royle . . . you can't buy me . . ."

Then he stopped. But his body went on swaying. It rocked in a kind of agony upon the chair. His eyes seemed to search the air above Brant's head. He got slowly to his feet.

"Royle," he said, "you're still scum, still an unprincipled black-guard, and I still say *no* to any dealings with you if it's the last act of my life!"

Brant watched him for a moment in silence. Then he brought his hands from behind his back. One of them contained his black bowler hat. He looked down at the familiar headgear and gave it a flippant, ironic little twirl between his fingers. Then he walked slowly to the hall doorway. Reaching it, he turned once more to James, the down-curved half-smile on his mouth.

"Well, Major, I see you haven't any more sense than you ever had. Still proud-mouthed and stiff-necked as ever." He paused and cocked his head a little. "You called me some pretty fancy names just now. They don't make me mad a bit, because you're perfectly right. I guess I'm all those things. The only difference now is that being scum and a blackguard, I can get what I want. I don't have to bother about any highfalutin sentiments standin' between me and what I'm after. Whether you know it or not, you helped me be what I am, and I'll go right on being it. An' one way or another I'll have Singleton and Sons the way I want it. I won't come to you again. But you might as well know now that no power on earth can save your little business for you. It's been as good as mine for a long time. Funny thing is that I don't want it. But I'll take it away from you, and when I do, nobody will know it but you and me."

James felt as though the big familiar room were revolving slowly around him. The band of iron about his head was constricting slowly and terribly. Dimly he heard the front door open and someone come into the hall. When he looked beyond Brant through the doorway he saw that it was Margaret. She stood arrested at the foot of the stairs, one hand on the newel post. Brant had turned to follow James's look. All three of them stood thus immobile. Margaret was not looking at her father. Her face, white and transfixed, had the expression of one looking upon a specter. Brant's body tensed. Like figures spaced widely in a dream the three of them remained. Then Brant spoke softly, breaking the spell.

"Afternoon, ma'am."

Margaret did not answer but continued to gaze back at him helplessly. Then she turned her head sharply away, raising it high upon the proud neck, and slowly began to mount the stairs. That deliberate progress upward and out of sight seemed to James only a further extension of the nightmare that held him. There was neither time nor spatial limits to it. It simply existed endlessly as a buzzing vortex. Brant's face turned back to him. In the blur its expression of lost agony was meaningless. And then when it changed from agony to cold fury James scarcely heard Brant say, "Good-by, Major."

James started toward the doorway, his right hand raking the air before him in a slow awkward gesture. He moved ponderously, like a man pushing through heavy, darkening waters.

3

To Margaret slowly ascending the stairs, a creature turned to ice, there came first the sound of the front door closing. Then, as she set her foot upon the upper landing, she heard a hoarse animal-like cry come up out of the hall below her. Something in it caught at her throat and terrified her. Even before she could think she found herself coming back down the stairs. As she made the turn she saw

255

James in the doorway beneath her clutch wildly at the frame and fall forward slowly into the hall. Then she started to run, heedless of her skirts, her voice coming out of her high and faint. It was more like a whisper than a summons: "Relda! . . . Relda! . . . Simon!"

CHAPTER THIRTEEN

I

It was a little after midnight when the Negro Maryland stepped out of the carriage house at the rear of the Samuel Royle place on Elm Street. Whenever they let him, he slept in the upper hallway outside of Mr. Temp's room. But he had a little room here above the stalls where he kept his coachman's uniform and his few other personal effects.

He stood for a minute sniffing at the frosty air, then buttoned his coat about his throat. The January night was brilliant with stars. A breeze blew gustily out of the east, stirring the old leaves in the yard. It made the naked branches over his head creak plaintively. It was a good night. Jes' right. Jes' like Mr. Brant had told him it would be. All afternoon he had been looking forward to this hour with a feeling half excitement, half foreboding. He tried to scorn himself out of it. Hadn't he done things for Mr. Brant before—dark things that no one but him and Mr. Brant would ever know about—an' hadn't Mr. Brant always told him jes' what to do and when to do it? And hadn't Mr. Brant always told him they would come out all right? And hadn't they? Mr. Brant sho had the Lawd and Mr. Temp on his side. Still, looking about him in the crystalline and familiar darkness, he could not quite shake off the feeling of uncertainty.

He grunted derisively under his breath and stepped out across the yard with long, noiseless strides. Passing down the shadowed side of the house, he paused in the driveway and looked up. A dim light glowed behind the curtains of one window in the second story. Mr. Brant must still be up there with Mr. Temp readin' to him outen the Big Book—or jes' sittin'. Mr. Brant had got in town that mornin' and except for an hour or so he'd been up in that room sittin' with his daddy. It was a wonderful thing the way Mr. Brant would do that. It made Maryland feel good, standing there looking up at the window. Nobody but Mr. Brant could make him leave Mr. Temp at night now. For the past few weeks Maryland had been uneasy about the strange, wild little invalid to whom he devoted every free moment. Sometimes there'd be days now, one right after another, when Mr. Temp never preached none, never said a word. Just lay in his big bed with his eyes closed, hardly breathin'. Looked like most all that stirring, fiery spirit had already gone on to Glory, leavin' a little of him behind to follow after. Well, it wouldn't be long now. Maryland had known that for a long time. Maybe that was what was makin' him feel uncertain about tonight. He didn't want Mr. Temp to leave without . . . Maryland swept his eyes along the house. Except for that one lighted window the rest were blank and dark. He whispered up toward the glow in the lone window: "Git de Lawd to movin' wid me now, Mr. Temp—git de Lawd to movin'!"

He continued down the driveway and turned outside the gate toward the dark and sleeping town. He moved swiftly, his big shoes padding noiselessly upon the brick sidewalk. He was like a part of the night, black, silent, and swift. He did not turn toward the square and the business center, but cut aside into a crooked alley running back of a block of stores. From this he crossed a street into another back way, and still another, following an intricate and shifting route. He met no living thing.

This seemingly formless route brought him at last into the maze running in and out among the warehouses and factories along the edge of Jamaica Town. He traveled through these expertly, feeling the rutted mud hard with frost beneath his feet. Never once did he pause or break the long stride. It was as though he did not need to see where he was going. And indeed he didn't. In dark or light this was a way as familiar to him as the palm of his hand. He knew it almost without thinking.

He emerged at last on the line of tracks a little distance away from the back of the Royle factory. He paused here, breathing deeply and glancing warily up and down the sudden openness. The thin lines of tracks, gleaming dully in the faint light, ran endlessly into darkness above and below him. About a quarter of a mile to the south he could see the winking glimmer in the yardmaster's hut near the crossing. He knew no one could see him at that distance, but Mr. Brant had told him to be extra careful tonight. Mr. Brant, standing in the doorway of the carriage house that afternoon while he was grooming Josie, and talking to him in the particular quiet voice that made his spine curl and his muscles knot in blind excitement along his big shoulders. It was like Mr. Brant had reached out and put a cold hand on him. He did what Mr. Brant told him to do. He had to. And it had always worked right like Mr. Brant said. Even if Mr. Brant scared him more than anything walkin' on two feet he'd always looked out for him, hadn't he? Mr. Brant's a big man. Yessuh! A big man. He'll take care of you—don't have to think about nothin'. Jes' do like he says. It'll come out all right.

He crossed the tracks, putting his feet deftly in the intervals of ties and gravel and keeping a couple of empty freight cars on a siding between him and the distant glow in the yardmaster's hut.

Beyond, set back on the margin of some ragged fields, ran a sparse line of little shacks. Toward one of these he made his way, crossing the bare, beaten little yard before it. He stepped swiftly around to the side of the shack. Flattening himself against the weathered, whitewashed boards beneath a small window, he reached up and scratched softly on the sagging shutter. Whitewash flakes showered down upon his face. He pushed his mouth against a crack.

"Etty!" he whispered. And there was both demand and caress in his voice. "Etty honey!" He waited a long moment, listening intently. His fingers moved again, insistently scraping against the clapboard. "Etty! . . ."

He felt, rather than heard, her stir at last in the darkened room within, the creak of the cot under her wakening body, the crackle of the flooring as her feet stumbled to the window.

"Who dat?" Her voice cautious, half-frightened, came to him through the shutter.

"Come on, let me in, honey!"

"Maryland!"

He heard her grumble happily, then he slipped away from the window to the door at the back of the shack. He grinned while he waited for her to open it for him, feeling his body warm with his walk, the deep, hard beat of his blood rising in his ears. The door finally opened cautiously. There was utter darkness within, but he did not wait. He sprang up the two rickety steps and entered, closing the door behind him, catching her body to him at the same time. She uttered a little startled cry, but he stifled it against his chest. She spoke crossly against his coat, her hands moving eagerly along his shoulders.

"What you mean comin' heah dis time o' night?"

"Honey," he said, "you got dat jug I left foh you to keep safe?"

She grumbled impatiently, released herself so that she stood touching him only with her hands.

"Jug . . . jug? What you wanta talk 'bout a jug now for?"

"I needs it now. I got business to attend to tonight."

"What kind o' business?"

"Go git me dat jug!"

"Now?"

"Git it foh me."

She moved sleepily to the bed, scratching her haunch as she went. Squatting, she searched beneath it briefly, grumbling to herself, and drew out a stone jug stopped with a cob.

"Deh it is." She gave the jug a little shove toward him.

He made no comment, but reached forth one huge hand and laid it—almost caressingly—about the neck of the container.

When he stepped forth into the night sometime later and closed the door carefully to behind him, he crouched back against it. A monstrous roar was approaching him out of the crisp blackness. The wind curled about his ears, distorting the gathering rush of this sound. Then the wind sound was swallowed up and the world was full of gigantic hissings and steely squeals as the train passed and roared off northward into blackness. He waited until the noise of that fierce progress died away beyond him in a confusion of empty echoes among the warehouses. Then he crossed the yard to the pathway between the field's edge and the nearest track. His movements were still relaxed and unhurried, but they moved him forward with the same intent and steady purpose. He went in the direction the passing train had just taken, following a great curving rim along the edge of Jamaica Town. It was the longest possible route to his ultimate goal, but he would be least apt to meet anyone there at that hour of the night. To cut across the sprawled maze of warehouses, factories, and hovels would have been quicker, easier. But there was no special hurry. He knew there were still some hours of darkness left him.

His path was soon closed about by buildings. For half a mile or more he continued looking to neither left nor right, his big head lowered. The jug, hanging easily from the fingers of his right hand, bumped comfortingly against his thigh.

He stopped. Down the long tunnel before him he could see a dull square of light. This he knew was the station office a hundred yards beyond. Between him and it, suspended in black above the invisible tracks, hung the round unblinking green light of the signal lamp. He glanced quickly into the darkness behind him, his body suddenly alert. No sound or movement came to his ears. Then, turning quickly, he entered a narrow interval between two of the buildings. It was a passage barely two feet wide. At the farther end of it he stopped and looked out into the sudden open space. It was a wide, shadowed yard enclosed by buildings except for a rutted passage that he knew gave on the street. Nearby were piled some empty hogsheads along a loading platform. He slipped silently over to them. Across the dim yard from him one of the windows in the lower floor of the factory was lighted. It was a sleepy glow, blurred behind dirty panes, completely innocuous. But toward it he began an elaborate and cautious journey, slipping from shadow to shadow, sliding flat along the wall. Finally he reached a position where he could peer in. What he saw within brought a smile to his face. It was an expression compounded of both contempt and satisfaction. Inside there was a lantern set upon a table in a cubbyhole of the room. In a ruined chair beside it, his head thrown back in snoring oblivion, sat an elderly Negro, his toothless wizened jaw gaping. It was ol' Marcus, a-sittin' like he had for the last twenty-five years—snug as a coon in a hollow stump . . . hadn't had an eye open on the premises after midnight in Lawd knows when. Ol' Marcus, us gonna warm yoh sleepy toes foh you tonight—Mr. Brant an' me!

He slid away from the window, passing down the length of the wall till he reached another joining it. There was another loading platform. He pulled himself upon it noiselessly. The length of the building was marked by four closed sliding doors. Maryland passed from one to another of these. He pulled at each one in succession with a soft and terrible effort, feeling the muscles across his shoulders strain at the seams of Mr. Brant's old coat. The first two resisted him completely. The third yielded. He grunted with satisfaction. The locking chain had been left slack. He pulled slowly again. It gave, the wheels on the track squeaking rustily. He pulled slowly and steadily, an inch at a time. When he had made a gap of nearly a foot he stopped. Out of the inky darkness within came the thick warm smell of stored tobacco. This was enough room for his work. Lawd, more than enough! Reaching down swiftly, he pulled the cob from the mouth of the jug. Then, thrusting the container through the opening, he tipped it. He could hear the gurgling sound of the contents emptying on the floor. The smell of coal oil rose into his nostrils out of the chill air. Behind him the wind swooped into the yard again, stirring up the dust, whining under the eaves overhead. Everything's jes' right! Keep de Lawd wid me, Mr. Temp! He continued tipping the jug till he felt it light and empty in his hand. Between his feet, even in the light that was no light, he could see it seeping under the door and staining the platform on the dry splintery wood.

He pulled the empty jug out, and setting it down, reached deep into his pants pocket for a sulphur match. He scratched it against the inside of the door. He heard it burst into flame and felt the quick lick of the flame against his thumb and forefinger. He dropped it. For a moment he waited breathless. Then he saw the light glow slowly within, defining the opening in the door. He seized the door desperately and started pushing it back into place. He must shut it against the betraying flame. But in the eager exultation of having done what he had come to do he moved too swiftly and the little wheels in the track above his head suddenly let loose a thin protesting screech. He finished closing the door and stooping, picked up the jug. As he did so the light in the window across the yard wavered and shifted. Ol' Marcus had come to life. He dropped from the platform, crouching on his haunches. At that moment the door in the factory building opened and a sudden wavering glow spilled across

260

the space. Without thinking he fell back beneath the platform, lying flat on the earth between the supporting timbers. Watching the old Negro stand blinking with the lantern, Maryland's breath came forth in a slow hiss. Ol' Marcus in the doorway stretched and shivered with the sudden cold of the night. Then, grumbling to himself, he shambled to the center of the yard and looked about him, a slow, blind inspection. It lasted an endless moment. Maryland could hear now, like a rising whisper, the faint and ominous crackling in the wood over his head. Already he could smell the smoke.

The old man with the lantern seemed satisfied. He turned, scratching his head under the ruin of a hat, and returned to the building. Maryland leapt from his hiding place and sprinted across the yard. He did not stop to look right or left but rushed heedlessly through to the tracks and the cinder path. There he paused and assumed a more deliberate pace, not running now, but walking casually and swiftly with no thought but to put as much distance as possible between himself and what he had left behind him. Not once did he turn to look back. He had no thought now for what he had done or for its success or failure. His mind seemed full of sorrow and pain. He was certain now of disaster; something had happened in his act this night that he had long dreaded and he did not yet dare name it. He moaned to himself as he hurried along back toward Elm Street, toward the house and the room upstairs. Only once did he pause when he became conscious that his forefinger was still crooked in the ear of the jug. Then he lifted his arm with a cry and flung the empty thing from him out into the dark fields. . . . Mr. Temp! Sweet Jesus, Mr. Temp!

And then he began to run.

3

In the weeks following her father's attack Margaret found a feeling almost of gratitude growing in her. Here at last was something to do. She had done nothing really for a long time. It frightened her to think that she had merely been going through the motions of living for months—maybe years. So she threw herself with passionate purpose and energy into the business of taking care of James. Dr. Frank Richardson had held a serious conversation with her belowstairs after he had examined James in his room. James lay there looking defenseless, his face blue and sunken with pain, his breath coming and going in a stricken and terrifying manner. Dr. Frank paced up and down on the rug before Margaret. Under no circumstances must James be allowed out of his room or his bed. No visitors, no business, absolute quiet, rest and simple food. He had warned James about this a long time ago. He shrugged his shoulders.

"Any more excitement of any kind," he said in his dry voice, wagging a precise and delicate forefinger direfully at Margaret, "will serve to finish this business completely. I'm depending upon you, my dear, to keep your head and a strong watch upon him. I've been telling your father for years about this. . . . Admirable fellow, admirable! But as heedless and hardheaded as a mule. You'll forgive me if I say that Jim Singleton has never paid much attention in his life to anyone but himself. Well, he's got to now, and you're the one to see that he does."

And so with all her competent energy she had taken charge. It was nothing new, because she had really taken care of his comfort since she had been a little thing in pinafores. It had always been a tactful and understanding mothering that had left James's sense of masculine independence and dominance completely free. The difference now was that he could no longer pretend that he was anything but helpless. For the first two or three days he lay like a terrified child. Margaret had never seen him so stunned and deflated. Somehow she found this more poignant than the fact of the illness itself. All the old roaring life and false energy seemed blown out of him. He lay on the bed watching her with humble eyes, making no demands, only thanking her in a strange fragile voice when she had done something for him. His besetting terror seemed to be that of being left alone. He grew almost hysterical if he found himself deserted for a few moments in the room. Margaret arranged the household so that one of them was always in attendance during the twenty-four hours of the day—Cousin Tabby, Relda, Simon, Hob, or herself. Each in turn sat in the chair by the bedside or at the window, Relda humming softly and reassuringly, Simon answering little questions put to him about the horses or the dogs, or telling him that he had seen a covey of quail feeding like chickens in the lower pasture. James did not even seem to find Tabby irritating any more. With Margaret he was silent for the most part, thanking her with something of the old ponderous courtesy for her attentions or suffering them passively and without protest. A constraint had grown between them, as though they could not trust themselves to words. Not since the day of James's attack had they mentioned Brant Royle's visit. But it seemed to loom portentously behind every gesture, every trivial exchange made between them in the sickroom.

Once, late in the afternoon, as she sat quiet beside him he stirred from a doze and turned a desperate and haggard face about the room. It was as if he did not know where he was. Then, seeing Margaret, he uttered a low cry and grasped her hand beside him on the counterpane.

"What is it, Father?"

"Meg!" His voice was hoarse and naked. "Meg, he's a madman

—but we won't let him scare us, will we, Meg? No sir! He'll try, but we won't let him. He wants *everything*—this house. But we won't let him have it, will we, Meg?"

He reached his free hand to her, raising himself from the pillow, pulling her down to him like a drowning creature. In that terrible moment, leaning over him, she felt such a wave of awful darkness and chaos sweep over her that she barely restrained herself from crying out. But even here the discipline of her great pride saved her. Gently releasing herself, she pushed him down on the bed again. She heard her voice, low and calm, as though it were addressing a child:

"Don't worry, Father. I won't if it's the last thing I do."

He relaxed with a sigh. And even though she felt dizzy and faint as if for a moment she had balanced precariously over the yawning abyss of some personal disaster, she knew that she had spoken the truth.

4

The subdued but insistent knocking on her door had been continuing for some moments, she realized, when she started upright at last in the dark room upon her bed, fully awake. With a certainty that brought her heart into her throat, a cold and choking lump, she thought instantly, Father! The knocking continued.

"Miss Margaret—Miss Margaret!"

It was Relda, whom she had left sitting with James. She flung back the covers and swung her feet to the floor, feeling the dead chill of the room fasten upon her body. Without pausing to find her wrapper she crossed swiftly to the door and opened it. Relda stood there in the dimly lit hall, her good round face at once apologetic and frightened. "What's the matter, Relda?"

"Mr. Scott Bason is downstairs—says he's sorry but he's got to see you quick."

"Mr. Scott Bason?" Margaret turned back into her room again. She seized the wrapper off the foot of the bed and reached for her slippers. It was too dark to see the face of the French clock on her mantel.

"What time is it, Relda?"

"Don't jes' know, Miss Margaret—reckon it's around three-thirty in the mornin', though."

"Is Father still asleep?"

"Yes'm."

"Well, get back to him quick, now. He oughtn't to be left alone for a minute. You know that!"

Watching Relda waddle away toward James's room, she had a

curious feeling of breathlessness under her relief. She had a sensation of being hollow from head to toe, as though she were about to meet some final crisis. As she tidied the ribbon holding back her hair she heard Cousin Tabby's door creak open behind her. She turned to see Cousin Tabby. She blinked expectantly at Margaret.

"Is it James?" she hissed, with a kind of macabre relish. Margarent took no notice of it. She shook her head.

"No, Father's all right."

"Well, what's all the to-do?"

"Scott Bason's downstairs about something. Go on back to bed, Cousin Tabby, before you catch your death. I'll tell you about it tomorrow."

She made herself wait until Cousin Tabby's door was closed again before moving swiftly down the hallway to the head of the stairs. At the turn of the landing she stopped. Below her the hallway looked like a deep pit lit faintly by the table lamp. At the foot of the steps stood a youngish man with tousled hair and behind him at the front door loomed Simon. Her visitor turned a face wild and distraught up to her.

"I'm sorry to have to break in on you like this, Miss Singleton," he began in a shaking, breathless voice. He sounded as though he might have been running and hardly knew what he was saying. "But Daddy sent me up to tell you—I've got to get right back to see if I can help, you know. It's awful! Never saw anything like it. Knew we couldn't bother the Major, but Daddy felt you ought to be told right away."

"What is it, please, Mr. Bason?" Margaret's voice was crisp and businesslike.

"You won't believe it, but the factory's on fire. Worst thing I ever saw—worst thing I ever saw," he repeated, with an awed and stunned disbelief. "I've got to get back right away. Excuse me, there may be something, you know—"

He began to back toward the front door, muttering wildly to himself. Reaching it, he bowed to no one in particular and let himself out. Margaret, standing quite still on the landing, heard herself murmur almost as an afterthought, "Thank you, Mr. Bason."

From where she stood she could see now a faint and rosy glow along the panes of the fanlight over the front door. Then she spoke again in a precise, unmoved voice:

"Simon, go hitch up the buggy quickly and bring it around front."

"Yes'm!"

He disappeared toward the back of the hall below her. Still she stood motionless on the landing; then a violent tremor, whether of cold or something else, shook her. She turned and ran back up the stairs toward her room. At the top she almost collided head-on with Cousin Tabby.

"I heard!" she whispered triumphantly up at Margaret. "Every word—where are you going?"

"I'm going down to the factory," said Margaret flatly, not looking at her.

"Mercy! What on earth for? What could you do?"

Margaret brushed past her. "I think I'd better go," she said.

She went into her room and lit the lamp on the dresser with quick, efficient gestures. From the wardrobe she selected a warm coat. She buttoned it up close under her neck, and taking a silk scarf from one of the dresser drawers, wound it close about her head and shoulders. She blew out the lamp and stepped into the hallway. At the top of the stairs she hesitated and started toward James's door, then decided against it. As she turned back again she heard a hiss and Cousin Tabby, an ancient black cape thrown about her and one of the glittering black bonnets tied under her chin came running on tiptoe behind her.

"I'm coming along with you!"

Margaret started to protest. Outside she could hear the crunch of the buggy wheels in the driveway.

"But, Cousin Tabby, don't you think—"

"I don't think anything except that you can't go alone. Now don't try and tell me that I'll catch a cold or that James needs anybody beside Simon and Relda to look after him. I don't care—I couldn't miss this."

Margaret nodded. It didn't matter. She went down the stairs, letting Cousin Tabby follow as best she could. As they stepped out upon the dark front porch the strange light to the northwest of town hung ruddily over them, bathing them and the front yard in a sinister glow. The wind, chill and sharp, tugged at their garments. Margaret suppressed a tremor. The sense of being caught irresistibly in a tide of culminating events grew strongly in her. Somewhere at the bottom of it was a feeling of anger, a strange and final feeling that the world was set against her. Simon waited at the mounting block.

"You stay here with Relda, Simon," Margaret addressed him firmly. When he hesitated she added in an impatient and furious voice, "I can drive perfectly well myself."

"Yes'm, Miss Margaret," he mumbled under his breath, and helped first her and then Cousin Tabby into the seat. She leaned back toward him.

"Simon, don't let Relda leave the Major for a minute while I'm gone. And don't let anyone see him or talk to him till I get back—not *anyone*. Do you understand?"

She did not wait for his affirmation, but slapped the reins across old Renny's back. They creaked down the driveway and into the street. Once there she hitched sharply at the reins again until the horse broke reluctantly into a shambling trot down Hill Street. The night closed about them full of darkness and stillness, as though it held its breath against the cancer of flame eating at it there in the distance. She realized that in his haste Simon hadn't lit the buggy lights. But again it didn't matter. She could see well enough. Hadn't she been up and down Hill Street all her life? Only now it looked unreal and completely strange. Time and change had taken even this away from her. It wasn't the same old street at all any more.

Cousin Tabby began to cluck monotonously at her side. The sound provided a slight distraction for the moment.

"What a time they must be having!" chirruped the little woman. "Both the fire departments will be out for it, and all the men in their new uniforms having a fine time dashing about."

It occurred to Margaret that Cousin Tabby was conceiving all this in terms of a spectacle. To most of the people witnessing it, it would be. The fact that the firm of Singleton & Sons was disappearing in a stupid holocaust did not affect them. The whole world seemed indifferent. She recalled now that they were almost at the square that no window they had passed had showed a light in alarm. All was indifference. She had a sudden savage impulse to stand up in the seat and scream at them.

"Henry Poplar's up, I see," said Cousin Tabby, almost as though she were answering her. In the last residence on their right—a house hemmed in by buildings fronting on the sidewalk—a light streamed from the front door. Margaret caught a glimpse of two figures huddled indistinctly at the edge of the porch.

"I'll wager Mady's trying to keep him from coming," rattled on Cousin Tabby. "His rheumatism has been awful this year. But Henry's hardheaded. He'll come. Mark my words. And Mady'll come too. It would kill Mady Poplar to miss anything going on, day or night."

Cousin Tabby clucked a period to this. Margaret made no response. They turned at last into the square. At first it seemed as empty as the street they had left, but from the distance now they could hear the wild clangor of bells. Somewhere over toward Jamaica Town another bell began to answer with a slow tolling. One of the churches. Fire and calamity had always been accompanied thus in the days past. As they rolled along she became aware now of the scattered pounding of feet on the pavement about her and blurred voices shouting to one another against the gusty wind. A figure suddenly darted out in front of Renny. It was a boy.

"Warehouse . . . Singleton . . . sh' won't . . . care!" His

266

words beat back to her separated and meaningless. A buggy burst up behind them and went careening past down the street toward the station. She saw men clinging to its back. The strange light was growing more intense now. It cast a still, ferocious glare along the faces of the buildings as they passed. There were more flying figures along the sidewalks here, and the bend of their hurrying bodies, the pounding patter of their feet, lent the scene an air of sinister festivity. Above them in the sky an enormous and terrible blossom was gradually revealed swaying against the night. Immediately it became a monstrous black plume, its billowing edges rosy. Out of it came strange and violent flashes as though it contained a succession of silent explosions. As they reached the foot of the street they were slowed by a dense clot of carriages, buggies, rolling vehicles of all kinds spilling over with insanely shouting humanity. Margaret adamantly guided Renny through them, saying nothing, but lashing out with the buggy whip at the backs of other horses, at nameless figures that blocked her wheels, dragged at the horse's head, and cursed at her. Her eyes were on the plume. She could see it now balanced on a column of blinding light beyond the black outlines of the station and the freight warehouses.

Renny skittered and balked between the poles, but Margaret held his head firm and lashed his rump. As they fought their way around the station they could feel a wave of heat wash across their faces. A thick smell of pine and tobacco smarted in their eyes and throats. Margaret felt her eyes dim and spill over with the agony of the smoke, but she paid no heed to it. The heat as they turned the corner of the station and started across the street across the tracks seemed to engulf them. Voices screamed at her, but she was deaf to them, her eyes fastened ahead.

Across the tracks the walls of the Singleton warehouse seemed to present an unharmed front, gently retaining the great roaring column of smoke, flame, and glittering sparks that shot above it. Almost dispassionately she noticed that the old painted letters along the side seemed gleaming now with a renewed life in the enormous glare. Even as she looked, a little caressing tongue of flame shot out between two of the old boards and licked at the big familiar S of "Singleton." For the first time the violent hollow feeling that had possessed her came to life with pain. She tore her eyes away. Men were pouring back and forth across the tracks on all sides of them. Beyond she saw the gleam of red paint and brass that announced the presence of the fire engine; and about it the figures of men, transfixed and grotesque in the leaping glare. Through the sea of hissing and roaring she could hear yells and screams. Suddenly someone darted out of the crowd before her, caught fiercely at Renny's head, and turned a screaming face up to her.

"Back!—get back! Are you crazy!"

She looked down at him blankly. Then the madness of his face—a young face blazing with excitement and streaming with sweat and soot—changed. It crumpled with recognition.

"Miss Singleton! Sorry, didn't recognize you." He waved a conciliating hand at her. "Better get back on the other side of the tracks. They're doing all they can."

Still she did not acknowledge him. She sat erect, looking beyond him into the flame as though it held some answer for her. The young man yelled again and, releasing Renny, wormed his way back into the crowd. In the midst of it he accosted someone, pulling at his arm, screaming something into his ear and pointing back at Margaret. The man thus addressed disengaged himself and staggered blindly back to the buggy. It was Bason, manager of the factory. He lifted a stunned and haggard face to Margaret. He was hatless and with one hand he smoothed at his sweat-matted gray hair apologetically. He shook his head slowly and called up to her in a thin wounded voice, "Too late—too late!"

She leaned down to him and said in a slow clear voice: "How did it happen?"

He shook his head again, a slow blind wagging.

"Nobody knows," he keened. "Nobody knows anything. 'Fraid it's a total loss. Insurance ran out, y'know. I've been telling the Major—no insurance."

The flaming wall behind him seemed to hold nothing at the moment that could match the enormity of this fact. He continued to shriek it weakly up at her as though it maddened him. "No insurance—*no insurance!*"

The mask on Margaret's face remained unchanged. She looked once more long and blankly into her handkerchief. Then she pulled abruptly on the right rein, turning Renny and the buggy about, heedless of the swarm surrounding her. Mr. Bason was swallowed up as though he had been blown away. Inside her the sense of cold rage and hollow pain seemed to crystallize as they progressed through the sea of meaningless faces. She felt that not the factory but she herself had in some way been consumed in those flames. All the soft and rich contours that had been her life as Margaret Singleton were gone forever. And as she drove back through the empty streets to Hill House she knew that she was irrevocably cut off, that in the ashes of her being there was nothing left but the diamond-hard, unyielding core of pride. A pride without reason, or object, or humanity. Never again could she look at her life or the universe with the same eyes. She had nothing left now but the weapon that she had been forging unknowingly all her life. This night had unsheathed it, and with it she would face any catastrophe. Nothing would ever touch her again.

So completely possessed was she by this realization that she left the buggy at the block without turning to help Cousin Tabby. She had forgotten her. As she came up to the front door Simon flung it open. He stood before her, blocking her way. In the light of the hallway his face contorted. Then he seized her by the arm—something he had never done before in all the years he had known her.

"Miss Meg—" He fumbled, employing the address he had not used since she was a child. "Miss Meg, Hob's done gone down the hill for Dr. Richardson."

Even then she did not run. She walked deliberately past him and up the stairs. She thought, in the same dispassionate way she had been thinking for the past hour or so, Dr. Richardson . . . too late . . . no insurance. It was gibberish, but it somehow added up to terrible and appropriate sense. As she arrived outside James's room she had another moment of clairvoyance. It seemed that from the moment Relda had awakened her she had been making a strange, tortuous journey from her bed to this door. As she opened it and stood just within she knew already what she was going to see. Against the farther wall Relda huddled, rocking and weeping. In the big armchair before the windows where they faced north was James. He sprawled grotesquely in it as though he had come to it by some special effort and had been thrust back into it by a dark hand. His head, thrown back in a grimace of final and complete agony, not all physical, was bathed in the rosy and insistent glow. It gleamed from the night upon him, touching the tossed and rumpled mane with a final and terrible aureole.

CHAPTER FOURTEEN

I

By an irony that continued grotesquely consistent, not only did James Singleton and Templeton Royle pass from life on the same night within an hour or so of each other, and not only did their eulogies as prominent citizens of the county appear simultaneously side by side in the *Kingsmont Journal* and the state papers, but they were doomed to go to their final resting places on the same afternoon. It was by no one's special planning. It just happened that events were so arranged. One drizzly, cold November afternoon a large and elaborate cortege departed from the portico of the Methodist church on Elm Street bearing Templeton's remains to the old town cemetery on Judson Street. And within the hour another, more

269

sober and modest as to aspect and numbers, left the little Presbyterian church to bear the mortal remains of James to rest beside the graves of his wife and his mother and father in the little grove of cedars two miles out of town. Templeton's cortege was full of newly prominent faces from the realms of both politics and finance, personages who would have been utter strangers to him under any circumstances, but who had come to do homage to the powerful name of Royle in death as well as life. James's small following was made up mostly of old faces, faces with names long prominent, but old and faded, faces that had not all been seen together in many a year.

It was not completely a personal tribute to James that these people had come together to honor his passing. It was more a collective recognition in the ramified social strata they represented—from Captain Phillips, wispily erect with his cane, through the Harmon brothers of the Richmond tobacco firm, right on down to some of the Singleton factory employees and black Simon, who was allowed to drive the hearse—that they all were in this event bidding farewell to the last vestiges of a way of looking at life. A special regard that had been kept alive purely on the basis of nostalgia and sentimentality, by a desire to look fondly backward upon a never-never golden life that had not existed in reality but had been constructed out of their fancies. There was no longer any point in pretending that life now wasn't quite a different thing from what it had been even half a dozen years ago, that Kingsmont itself was not just a comfortable and undistinguished little Southern town but a young, ugly, sprawling city where the streets were being lighted by electric arcs and the houses and buildings contained telephones and a great deal of elaborate indoor plumbing. How easily they all had permitted and accepted the metamorphosis! And so it was with a sense almost of guilt that these people who had known James closely for most of his and their lives or who had done business with Singleton & Sons now followed him to his grave as though to assure both him and themselves that they had not forgotten, while most of them privately realized that they were here burying a host of fragile ghosts that should have, in all honesty and decency, been laid away long ago.

A great many carriages and buggies lined the driveway and the street before Hill House in the three days between his death and his burial. Old friends and acquaintances from abroad in the state who had neither been in Kingsmont nor seen nor spoken to James for years appeared now at the door to pay their respects and offer formal sympathy to Margaret. Margaret entered the barbarities attendant on the situation with an air of frozen detachment. She looked very handsome and pale in her mourning as she moved about performing the amenities, managing the enormously complicated household situation with the grace and efficiency that was by now an automatic and mindless activity. Her face, white and set, the dark eyes looking even darker by contrast, moved graciously and correctly among the visitors seeing to their welcome and comfort precisely as though nothing whatever were altered in her world. It was the source of much admiring comment now as it had been in the past.

Mrs. Marston had come up for a quarter of an hour one afternoon. She had slipped away from the funereal uproar down at the Royle house on Elm Street. It had been over a year since she had set foot in Hill House. A coldness had grown between the two families after Roberta's marriage to Sam. Now she sat pressing Margaret's hands between her own, the tears rolling down her fat, raddled cheeks, looking at Margaret wordlessly as though she wanted to explain something that she could never explain. Both of them were thinking of the days long gone when Margaret had been almost like one of her own daughters—in and out of the house every day. But that was a lost world, and at the moment Mrs. Marston, the energetic, ambitious, pushing mother whose daughter was a Royle, mourned selfishly and richly over her part in breaking it up. She could not see that Margaret's head, correctly inclined, was neither hostile nor sympathetic.

"I had to come just for a moment, Meg dear," she managed to say at last in a strangled voice. "Mr. Marston would have come, but he hasn't been well and all these terrible blows at once—you know. He was very fond of your father. This is a sad time for us all. Poor Berta is prostrate, simply prostrate, with Mr. Royle's death. Although it isn't exactly the same. He's been sick for so long. Almost a blessing, you might say, but sad—terribly sad. We old friends must comfort each other in times of trouble. We mustn't ever drift so far apart again. Never, never! . . . Oh dear, I must be getting back to help Berta!"

"It was good of you to come, Mrs. Marston," said Margaret. And that was all.

On the tide of rich pathos that flooded her Mrs. Marston sped back to her daughter on Elm Street. The lower floor of the house was still crowded with long-faced visitors, but she sailed majestically through them and went upstairs to Berta's room. Berta had a sick headache. She had had one all day. She lay now with the shades down, flat upon her bed, a handkerchief soaked with cologne across her forehead. Mrs. Marston drew up a chair and without preamble launched into an emotional report on Margaret Singleton.

"You wouldn't believe it! Just the same as ever—a perfect old-fashioned lady, Berta. No word of complaint. Didn't break down for a minute, and goodness knows she's got troubles enough ahead of her to make any really gently reared person want to break down and weep for days." Mrs. Marston wagged her head admiringly.

271

"She's always been like that since I can remember her, and I've never understood how she did it. Such poise!"

Roberta groaned and put a hand to her sallow temple.

"Oh Mama, you haven't come in here just to tell me how grand Margaret Singleton is, have you? I thought I was done with that when I married Sam Royle."

Mrs. Marston was shocked. "Why, Berta!" Mrs. Marston tightened her mouth disapprovingly. "How on earth can you say such a thing—and about a bereaved friend, too!"

On the bed Roberta suddenly clasped both hands over her face —its plainness drawn deeper by pain—and began to titter weakly and hysterically.

"We're all bereaved friends," she gasped, "bereaved, bereaved— but she's still got her poise and I've got Sam!"

Mrs. Marston could not make head or tail of this gibberish, but she found it most offensive. Obviously, Berta was completely unstrung by events.

"Well, Roberta," she said, rising. "I was only telling you because I thought you might like to hear. . . . I don't suppose in all the confusion anyone has looked in on poor dear little Tina to see how *she's* getting along in all this. I don't trust that new nurse you've got at all. Looks lazy and irresponsible to me."

A sharp sound, half cry, half groan, coming from the figure on the bed interrupted her.

"Go away, Mama! Please leave me alone!"

Mrs. Marston threw up her hands and went out of the room without saying anything further. She closed the door rather sharply. For a long moment Roberta lay completely still, her face still hidden in her hands, her breath held tight and locked within her. Then it rushed out of her and she turned her head deep into the pillow and began to cry like a lost creature, in long, desolate, racking sobs.

2

And so James was buried, and within a month his death and the destruction of the Singleton factory were old news. For a week or so after the fire ugly, half-spoken rumors flew about. They were confused and grotesque, as is the nature of such things. One story had it that it was a discontented worker at the factory, discharged by James in a typical angry scene, who had perpetrated the outrage. Another—most farfetched of all—had it that James himself had in some way been behind it. They had never been able to make any revealing sense out of Marcus, the ancient watchman, who had come bursting into the depot that night screeching the alarm. The experience seemed to have thoroughly addled what was left of his senile brain. Afterward, even the most gentle and careful questioning by the examiners was able to extract from his toothless babble only something to the effect that he had heard a noise in the factory yard shortly before the fire broke out. But in many men's minds, supported by no evidence, the whole occurrence left a sinister residue. Many of these had done business with James Singleton or been his friends. Like a persistent echo there recurred to them the idea that Major Jim's long and insane defiance of the Royle interests and the final destruction of the Singleton factory—that landmark of the past— were in some way connected. There was no rational basis for this. There was only the fact of Brant Royle. Their own individual experiences, added to the legend of voracious power that had become synonymous with his name, were precedent for any act. It constituted a paralyzing realization, impossible to admit, of the terrible web in which they all now lay enmeshed—the city of Kingsmont and the whole empire of tobacco. It was an unendurable thought, and being men who valued their self-respect, they erased it out of their thinking as swiftly as possible. The uninterrupted pressure of their own affairs and Kingsmont's teeming life made it easy for them.

It remained for Captain Phillips, characteristically, to speak an epitaph for both James and themselves. Standing in the muddy country road outside the Singleton burial ground on the chill November afternoon after James had been laid to rest, he had turned suddenly to the little group of gentlemen with him.

"Well, sirs," he had growled in the loud, commanding voice that was not modulated even for this occasion, "mark my words! We've officiated at the end of honor and gentility as I have understood them in this county. From now on we are delivered over to the hounds and the hogs, and we may as well admit it—God help us!"

Trim and erect, he had swung his cane about him like a saber and stomped fiercely down the roadway toward the waiting carriages. No one answered him. They all stood looking solemnly at the ground and shaking their heads. There did not seem to be an answer.

3

It was on an afternoon some three weeks after the funeral that Margaret Singleton went down to Mr. Pate's office over Tyree's drugstore. Ordinarily Tom Pate would have gone up to Hill House, but she requested that she be allowed to come down to his office instead. If he found this a little eccentric, Tom passed it over as some personal delicacy on Margaret's part in not wanting her home and privacy invaded at this time by business matters. Besides being an old friend of the family, he had handled most of James Singleton's legal affairs, and he had been named executor for the estate.

273

With him in the office on this particular afternoon was Mr. Edgar Bason. The former general manager of the Singleton factory looked worn and dazed with the shock of the preceding weeks. His eyes were obscured behind the usual pair of thick-lensed spectacles and his stubby-featured face wore an expression of puzzled and frowning concentration. This was habitual and in no way indicative of his true state of mind, which was fumbling and stunned as though it could never comprehend what had happened to his world. It had been a world securely and comfortably anchored between two poles —the factory and James Singleton. And now neither existed any more.

In contrast to him, the lawyer was a tall, thin man in his early sixties, confident and suave in action or repose. There was something histrionic in both his manner and his dress, which was a little old-fashioned but proper to his profession and the shabby comfort of his office. He had looked and acted in the same manner for the thirty or more years that he had practiced in Kingsmont.

When Margaret's knock sounded on the door the two men stood up and Tom escorted her ceremoniously to a chair opposite them. While she was seating herself after the brief exchange of greetings the lawyer could not help remarking to himself how becoming her mourning dress was. Although they had never in any sense been intimate, he had known Margaret for a long time. What a fine pair of eyes she had! The appropriate pallor of her face set them off handsomely. Something had changed in that face, though he could not quite put his finger on it at the moment. Perhaps it was the mouth. Its chiseled perfection, so like her father's, had lost its richness and sweetness. It looked stern and set, and there were down-drawn lines at the corners. Ah well, she was no longer exactly a girl and she had been through a difficult experience. Enough to bring a few lines to anyone's face. Still, looking at her now he wondered irrelevantly how in the devil James Singleton had ever managed to sire so magnificent a creature.

Drawing his coattails aside, he sat down and turned to the desk. From a folder he selected a document and flipped it open between his long fingers. He frowned, pursed his lips, and cleared his throat. He turned to Margaret and began speaking in the soft, drawling voice.

"As an old friend of the family my duties this afternoon are not so pleasant as I could wish them to be, Margaret. But I'm sure that you understand the necessity of conducting practical affairs during a sorrowful time as well as I do."

Margaret nodded. "I think I do, Mr. Pate. I should only like to ask that we finish what has to be done as soon as possible."

"Of course, my dear, of course," the lawyer protested. She was

274

cool, all right! He was prepared to be the soul of diplomacy, to bring all his talents to bear to soften the blow—he was even prepared for tears. Certainly they would have been more fitting than this dry, almost peremptory response.

"I asked you to meet with me this afternoon not only to begin formally my duties as executor of your father's estate, but to offer you some advice. This advice I hope you will accept as coming not only from a family counselor but from a friend as well. Now—" He glanced at the paper in his hand and tilted back his chair to look at the ceiling. Now that he had started he began to feel better. "Now you must realize that your father left his entire estate to you. Normally this consisted of the manufactory as well as the family stock in same, the house and property in Kingsmont as well as the property consisting of the two small farms near Rowenville, and certain shares held in the Southeastern Railroad and the Angelico Shipping Company of Virginia."

Margaret inclined her head again, but there was no change of expression on the fixed mask of her feature.

"Mr. Pate, I'm afraid I know nothing about these things at all. Father never discussed them with me."

The cool, impersonal voice was neither polite nor impolite. The lawyer had a disconcerting feeling that he was being put in his place. He felt vaguely insulted. Undoubtedly there was something queer in Margaret Singleton. It gave grounds for the woman talk that had flown about the parlors for years. Handsome or not, she *was* difficult. It would be easier to understand this cool, opaque exterior if only for a moment it would show signs of breaking. He had been prepared to be his most sympathetic and kindly self, to be extra warm and charming in her behalf, and here, by her manner, she was bringing him up short before he had even got started. When he spoke again it was with some asperity.

"Well, that is more or less the substance of the will as it was drawn up some years ago by your father. However—and I regret to have to be the one to inform you of these matters—we must face the facts. Time and events have considerably changed the shape of things, as they have a way of doing."

Margaret leaned slowly toward him—the merest inclination of her whole body. Her eyes looked fixedly at him as though he sat at a great distance.

"Let us not waste time, Mr. Pate. What is it you wish to tell me?"

Tom Pate's long face reddened. It would be unthinkable to get angry at a time like this. He continued rather more hurriedly than he was accustomed to speaking:

"Mr. Bason and I have been holding some extensive discussions

275

during the past week or so regarding the whole matter. Your father's business had unfortunately fallen into a very bad way quite a while before his death. Like the true gentleman he always was, he quite naturally wished to spare you any anxiety, so he never mentioned it to you. Also I'm sure he felt that he would be able to put his affairs back into order in due time. But fate intervened. The tragic and scandalous burning of the factory left outstanding indebtedness which will, I'm afraid, complicate and tie up the settlement of the estate for quite a long time."

He paused, cleared his throat again, and set the paper down upon the desk.

"What you are telling me, then," said Margaret, "is that I cannot really expect very much—if anything—after all these things have been cleared up—isn't it?"

"I wouldn't go so far as to say you were destitute, my dear!" protested Pate with a jocularity that rang false even in his own ears. "But it is on that score that I wish to offer you some advice which may be of assistance to you. Mr. Bason here—as your father's devoted steward—has had the unpleasant duty of informing me more precisely as to the unpleasant details of the truth. He agrees entirely with what I am going to suggest. Am I right, Ed?"

The little man, pinioned thus under their gaze, seemed to shrink in his chair. He gulped, nodded bleakly, and a vacant smile creased his dry, precise mouth.

"Now," said Tom Pate, looking at the ceiling once more, "you have some modest investments from your mother held in trust till now by your father. They do not represent any large sum, as I have said, but they are something and will bring in a modest but steady annual income—you perhaps already knew about them."

"I believe Father did mention to me the fact that they were mine, but since I have never handled them I have never thought about them one way or another."

"I see. Well, what I am coming to is that I do not think you will find them entirely adequate for your maintenance unless you add to the principal they represent. So what I wish to suggest is that as soon as the mortgage on your home here can be cleared up—"

"Hill House mortgaged!" It was only a whisper from Margaret that interrupted him, but it was so clear and so agonized that he paused to look at her. For a moment her composure seemed on the brink of shattering into a thousand pieces. Her eyes stared wildly and unbelievingly at him and one hand flew to her mouth as though to suppress a much more unseemly demonstration. But it passed in a flash. The mask regained its position. The hand dropped again to the lap. Her body remained rigid, braced for a further blow. Tom Pate felt an instant's satisfaction. Something had got at her finally.

But her concern was so naked that he immediately felt sorry for her.

"I'm sorry, my dear," he said warmly, "but your father found it necessary at one time recently to put a small mortgage on the town property. But I think we can clear that up very satisfactorily by the sale of the farms. That brings me to the heart of my suggestion. When the title is clear once more, I strongly advise that you sell it. You could realize a very good sum on it now. It is the only large piece of land left on Hill Street and, as you know, business is moving up that way."

"You mean sell Hill House, Mr. Pate?"

Margaret did not move. In that moment she looked like a sumptuous doll fashioned of wax and ebony and set upon the edge of the chair. Tom Pate nodded.

"That is precisely what I am suggesting, my dear. I know it is a hard thing for you to consider—your home and all. But we must be realistic and face the facts. Real estate is demanding a very fancy price in this town now and the Hill House property is highly desirable in many ways. I am sure you could realize a considerable sum in its sale. And with what you have from your mother reinvested you could hope to be very comfortably settled."

"I will not sell Hill House." Her voice came flatly, almost colorlessly out of the waxen face. The lawyer, who at the moment had been basking comfortably in the sound of his own round periods, opened his long palms toward her in a gesture at once pleading and remonstrating.

"But, my dear," he protested. "I know this is very distasteful—I might say as distasteful for me to have to advise such a step as it is for you to hear it. I am in complete sympathy with your natural reluctance in having to face such a thing, but we must look at the facts—yes indeed, the facts!"

Margaret stood up suddenly and looked at him as though he had become her bitterest enemy.

"Mr. Pate," she cried, "*I will not sell Hill House!*"

The lawyer's countenance flushed slowly over its lined length. It was with an effort that he kept his composure intact.

"My dear Margaret," he said, "let me be frank—if you do not, I cannot see how you are going to manage."

"I shall find a way!" Her eyes, now blazing and contemptuous, swept from him to Ed Bason, who studiously avoided her and shifted miserably upon his chair. "I am not as helpless or entirely without personal resources as evidently you and Mr. Bason think."

"Now, now," soothed the lawyer, "let's not get upset."

"I'm not upset at all, Mr. Pate. I'm sure that you have advised me with the very best of intentions, but I cannot accept that advice. I'm sorry. I will not sell Hill House."

An awkward silence fell upon the room. Tom Pate hunched his shoulders in a half-shrug.

"Well, of course, my dear," he said, "it's your property—"

"Yes."

The monosyllable cut him short like a bullet. She stood fastening the button on one glove as though it were the most unemotional encounter in the world.

"Now, if that is all you wish to discuss with me, Mr. Pate, I must be getting home."

The red on the lawyer's face deepened as he rose lankily to his feet. "But, my dear, we haven't even read your father's testament," he protested.

"I don't think it will be necessary. It would only be a formality now. From what you have so kindly told me I think I understand all that I need to know. If there are papers that have to be signed, please send them to me at the house."

"Of course," he replied, looking patient with a great effort. "As you wish, my dear, as you wish."

He crossed to the door and opened it for her. She came to him, took his hand briefly and then turned to Ed Bason.

"Thank you, Mr. Bason. Thank you both. I'm sure Father would have been pleased with the way you have taken care of things for me."

Ed Bason had risen. He stood smiling blindly at her.

"The best I could do, Miss Singleton." His voice and face crumpled as though he was going to weep. "Only too glad, y'know."

Margaret turned to Tom Pate again.

"I want you both to know that I deeply appreciate everything you did for my father and everything you are now trying to do for me—in spite of what I feel necessary to say to you." Her tone was formal, distant—meticulously correct.

"Of course, of course," murmured the lawyer.

"I will be grateful, Mr. Pate, if you will continue to handle my affairs—what there are of them."

"A pleasure, my dear, a pleasure!" He was feeling warm toward her again. He had to admire her in spite of all. "I'll see you down."

"Please don't bother. I'm perfectly capable of getting myself down. Thank you again . . . and good afternoon."

She stepped into the dim and chill hallway and the door closed behind her.

4

She had no sensation of passing down the stairs and out upon the sidewalk into the early winter sunshine. She simply felt frozen.

278

It was a feeling that she was becoming more and more accustomed to, and it had nothing to do with the temperature of the afternoon. It was a feeling that locked her, her blind determination, and her seething pride all together and permitted her head to hold itself high but to look to neither the right nor the left as she made her way down to where Simon stood with the surrey. The old beloved green surrey that had carted her about over so many countless journeys, still green, still polished, but somehow shabby and down-at-the-heel, standing at the curb. It was a part of the universal pitying glance that she felt directed upon her. Poor Margaret Singleton—poor green surrey! It became like a pain, this feeling, while Simon assisted her into the rear of the surrey and tucked the carriage rug tenderly about her knees. It was part and parcel of that frigid sense—not of sorrow but of stubborn will not to lower her face, let drop a tear, or allow them to see her at any point vulnerable. Who *they* were was not exactly clear, but she had a growing sense of them—real or not. In the meantime she would meet them with the refined essence of her nature. Hard, crystalline, adamant.

"Home, Miss Margaret?"

"Yes, Simon."

What a valued word, a delicious word that monosyllable "home"! She savored it.

As she sat there, frozenly erect in the back seat, she thought passionately with every bitter revolution: Let them look! All of them. I'll not permit them the pleasure often—nor will I subject myself to this kind of indignity again. It made not the slightest difference to her that of all the casual passers-by, the usual population of the street and square, no face was turned in her direction. She knew what they were thinking, what they were *really* feeling. The whole world now harbored a thousand chirruping, mean whispers and snickers. It had been so since that night of violent smoke and flame. Well, they need not feel sorry for her. She could face them down to the last!

At the corner of the square—full of this sense of defiance—she made Simon stop and go into the stationer's for some note paper that Cousin Tabby had requested. Then they drove on up Hill Street. Every foot of the way the sense that she was being followed by a host of derisive eyes grew upon her, so that when they came into the driveway of Hill House it was with an effort that she restrained herself from leaping down and running into the old safety of the house.

In the hallway at last she stopped, breathless, transfixed, in front of the familiar pier glass and looked at herself. The carved gilt frame stretching up and over her two images—the one standing on the carpet breathing rapidly, the dim one in that other world of glass beyond, the white face staring without expression mysteriously back at her. It had no meaning any more, that face. It might have been the face of a phantom—and a phantom that did not interest her. As she began to remove her gloves her eyes fell on the tray resting on the little table set against the mirror. In it was the afternoon mail, arrived while she was away. The usual miscellany. Most of them notes, still arriving and still burdened with meaningless condolences. Among them was a letter from one of the Virginia cousins. She picked it up absently. Below it lay another envelope, long, flat, and white. Her name leapt out at her inscribed in a bold and at the same time careful hand. Almost as though it had been written by a school-boy. She picked it up. It had a New York postmark. She frowned for a moment before running her nail under the edge and opening it. Inside was a single sheet and when she unfolded it it was covered with the same heavy scrawl, vigorous and intent. She began to read it slowly—almost uncomprehendingly.

Dear Miss Singleton,
    Our mutual bereavement prevented me from paying my respects at the proper time. Since then the press of affairs has occupied me to such an extent that I have been unable to sit down and take pen in hand to write you properly.
    There was no love lost between Major Singleton and me, either as men or as associates in the tobacco business. This you very well know. I will not be hypocritical and try to make as though it were otherwise. But this I must say. He was a worthy antagonist. He just happened to belong to another time. He had the misfortune to outlive that time. You cannot help feeling sorry for that, everything else being considered.
    Let us now let bygones be bygones. You and I have no reason for acting as we have had to act toward one another for all these years. I do not feel that I am presuming or being forward in writing this. You and I can meet face to face without making any pretenses.
    It will be my pleasure to call upon you and express these sentiments in person when I return to Kingsmont in a month or two.
    I do not express myself well on paper.
                                        Respectfully yours,
                                        B. Royle

She stood for a long time staring at the words. They were incredible and at the same time touching. Gone was the icy, static feeling. Her blood seemed to run hot and cold. Her knees felt hollow. She welcomed the feeling and at the same time could not bear it. It was too much. She leaned suddenly and heavily against the little table. I will not faint . . . it is only a letter . . . words badly written on a paper. She closed her eyes and pulled herself erect again, turning her face away. The sense of fate, of something uncompleted, swept over her. It was all connected, deeply embedded in what she had become. It must be met finally and concluded. That she knew —as she had always known.

When she opened her eyes she saw dimly through the narrow window at the side of the front door someone coming up the front walk. It was part of the design, as though she had summoned this wavering image precisely at that moment. It was a man. His figure wavered and came to her distorted as though he were underwater. It was John Barton.

Very deliberately then she tore the letter in her hand to bits and dropped the scraps into the tray. Then with a curious cold little smile on her lips she ran to the front door and opened it.

"Why, John," she cried in welcome and held out both her hands to him. "John Barton!"

He stood before her with the afternoon behind him—precisely as she had seen him so often—the unchanging, tortured, ugly face lit now with her welcome. He took her hands and held them still and looked at her.

"Miss Singleton—Margaret, I wrote you, but I had to come after I heard—"

The same bleak voice, trembling now with feeling.

"You've been away for a long time, John," she said in the warm, unnatural voice. "Come into the house!"

He came in.

CHAPTER FIFTEEN

I

But Brant did not return to Kingsmont until the next spring and his coming was occasioned by quite a different personal concern.

All that winter he stayed in the North occupied with the final details of the Grand Columbian. With the inclusion of the Ogden company the bastion was complete. He had all of it now and was immediately moving out for more. Christopher Malley had left for San Francisco in November to embark for Shanghai to survey the field for the coming battle with the British tobacco interests in the Orient. His frequent reports showed that he was doing his work well. Being now the hub of the cigarette industry—because Brant had made it so—Kingsmont and the tobacco regions of the state were shuttled by rumors of what Royle was up to. There was both a kind of grudging pride in him and his enormous success and a very real concern as to how each of the rumored moves might affect them—

from the farmer looking over his fields right on up through the workers and the managerial hierarchy in the factories. They found that he had subsidiaries set up in the pulpwood business owning vast tracts of timberland in the North, the Midwest, and even Canada. This had begun for the practical purpose of making the millions of paper containers for the score of tobacco products and their hundred or more names, but the Western Paper Corporation was beginning to grow out into fields that did not touch on the tobacco world. Also, there was pretty well substantiated talk of Brant's being in the process of forming a public-utilities company that would embrace not only North Carolina but its bordering states. It surprised no one to learn that the Seaboard Electric Corporation, which was laying out two long-needed streetcar lines through Kingsmont that winter, was largely financed by Royle money. All through the cold, rainy months of the year the streets were torn up and the construction attended by the fascinated attention of a host of small boys. It was a different generation of boys from those who had followed after the street-light man not many years before; those were all nearly grown men now, wherever they were. But then, Kingsmont was no longer what it had been. The little band of 'Krainians down in Jamaica had long since disappeared or been scattered. Their places in the factories had been taken over by a drab myriad, both men and women— mostly from farms. Whole families escaping the old slavery of the fields became slaves to machines. They lived hopefully in the sprawling tenement and shack sections—that other inevitable by-product of factories and big industry. Kingsmont was the big, coming city of the state. Kingsmont was where a man could always get a job. Kingsmont was where the money was!

And Kingsmont—among other things—belonged to the Royles and the men who worked for them.

But while the machinery of the Government moved slowly, it moved at last against the Grand Columbian. And in spite of Brant's influence in Washington, the investigation of the tobacco trust was reopened in February. Brant remained in New York during the preliminary legal skirmishes. After a month or so the Government began to tighten its case so that he found it necessary to appear personally in the capital. In spite of all the witnesses and experts giving evidence for the prosecution, it was ironically only Brant who could answer questions that added up. Particularly when it came to trying to unravel the complexities and intricacies of the crisscross empire he had created. The country's newspapers were full of it. With the approach of spring, distraction was provided by the growing tension and hullabaloo over the Cuban question. The sinking of the *Maine* in Havana Harbor in February nearly succeeded in pushing the investigation off the front pages. Not that Brant minded. He was satisfied that his luck was still of a very special nature when in April Spain declared war and the country forgot the tobacco trust and Brant Royle in the resultant hysteria. The investigation continued, but it had lost a great deal of its impetus. He returned to New York. There was a telegram awaiting him there from Samuel.

PETE HENRY HAS NOT BEEN AROUND FOR A WEEK. DON'T KNOW IF THERE IS ANYTHING WRONG. THOUGHT YOU OUGHT TO KNOW. BERTA MUCH UPSET.

SAM

At first he experienced the old mixed feeling of irritation and tenderness that anything concerning Pete Henry aroused in him. Since Pa's death Pete Henry had been unusually quiet. He had taken a job down at one of the warehouses and hadn't got himself into any scrapes. He acted as if he might grow up. But here he had flown the coop again. Brant found it almost reassuring. His brother was just no good, damn the young hellion! Brant had to grin to himself. Pete Henry out on another toot. Eventually he would turn up and then that silly Roberta could stop her hysterics. What a whining nambly-pamby Sam had got himself hitched to! Well, every man to his own taste. He shrugged and put the whole thing out of his mind.

The next day, however, he was forced to consider it again. There was a second telegram from Elm Street.

PETE HENRY IN THE ARMY. WRITES US HE IS STATIONED AT CAMP GRIMES NEAR RALEIGH.

SAM

Brant took the train south that afternoon.

It was a strange journey for him. For the first time in many years now he was beset by a terrifying feeling of loneliness. It was an emotion compounded of rage at first at Pete Henry and then of fear for Pete Henry—the damned, scatterbrained young fool! What had he done this for? The ultimate in all his follies. At the same time he had to admit that there was no reason why his brother couldn't do with his life as he liked. He had never done anything except be pleasant and useless. He had encouraged him in it. Why? Was it because Pete Henry was so honestly and consistently himself? Was it because time and money had not changed him essentially from the pleasant small-town boy he had always been? And Pete Henry, of all of them, was the only person whose devotion to him as a human being had never wavered or changed. In all the world Pete Henry was the only person who really loved him. It was a devastating realization. He spent a sleepless night by the window of the club car staring out at the black and rushing landscape, chewing on an unlighted cigar. His

283

thoughts were scattered, an unending and pointless series of emotional odds and ends—places, people, little occurrences in which he had taken part, lost and embedded in a past that had slipped away from him. All his life he had gloried in his personal battle with the world. He had not been afraid of any opponent. Now he had the majestic forces of the Federal Government opposing him. No matter how bruising the experience was proving, no part of it ever frightened him. It was merely part of the old conspiracy against him and his achievement. He was accustomed to that. But this feeling engendered by Pete Henry's latest escapade made him hurt. . . .

Lloyd Bowen, representative from the local sales offices of the Grand Columbian, met him at the Raleigh station and drove him to the hotel. He was a hearty young man impressed with the grandeur of his charge. He talked briskly and continually in a tone of voice that was at the same time faintly obsequious. Brant contented himself with an occasional grunt by way of reply. He was not even listening. He knew many men like this youngster. The Grand Columbian was full of them.

At the hotel he sent Bowen off rather curtly to find out the name of the commandant at Camp Grimes. Brant went to his room, bathed, changed his shirt, and had some coffee sent up. While drinking it he scribbled telegrams to Sam and to the office telling them he expected to arrive in Kingsmont sometime later that day.

When he came down Bowen was waiting. Not only did he have the name of the commanding officer, but a letter of introduction. Brant thanked him and thrust the letter into his pocket. He didn't want this young cub along on this journey. He wanted to be alone. But the youngster was obviously eager to be of service, and since he knew the way it would save time. Brant decided to endure him.

The encampment—a new one—was set in some fields on the edge of the city. Long rows of peaked canvas and beaten earth, all with the raw, unlovely precision peculiar to military installations. When they reached the entrance they had to pause to let a small detachment of uniformed men come out. The faces were all so young, the uniforms so ill-fitting, the precision of their marching so self-conscious, that Brant felt another swift pang as he watched them pass and march off down the road. In a field beyond, more men were drilling and the sound of shouted orders and the bleat of a bugle came to them through the clear air. Before they could proceed an empty supply wagon dashed up and came clattering through with a great deal of dust and jingling of mule harness. The driver saluted them jauntily as he passed. The whole scene had a quality of impersonal yet devoted activity. And Pete Henry was in there somewhere now. The damned fool! Brant was blindly hostile to all of it. Well, no matter what it took, he would get him out of here and quickly.

It might take a letter to Washington and a bit of official folderol, but he could and would do it. He was Brant Royle and he had the power. . . .

The guard at the gate directed them to headquarters, a group of tents on the other side of the drill space with a flag drooping from a nearby pole. In front of the largest of these tents they were stopped again by a sentry.

"I want to see the commandant," said Brant, and handed over the letter of introduction. The sentry saluted, took the letter inside, and returned. They sat waiting in silence for a matter of minutes. Then an officer, grim, young, and meticulously courteous, came out to the buggy.

"Mr. Royle, sir?"

"Yes."

"Will you come with me, please."

Brant climbed down. "I don't think I'll be long," he said to Bowen.

"Take your time, Mr. Royle," that young man replied with undiminished heartiness. "Don't worry about me for a moment!"

Brant followed his guide into the tent. It was furnished with several desks all occupied by busy uniformed men. They eyed him curiously as he passed through to the far end where the officer opened a small door and announced:

"Mr. Royle, sir!"

He saluted again as Brant entered, then closed the door quietly. Brant found himself in a smaller canvas-ceilinged chamber austerely furnished with only a desk. A stout man with a beefy face, a brush of iron-gray hair, and a bristling mustache to match rose from behind it and extended his hand.

"I'm Colonel Drazer," he barked. "Mr. Royle, this is a pleasure!" Brant nodded and shook the proffered hand briefly. "Please sit down, Mr. Royle."

Brant sat down in the camp chair. This military puppet didn't know him from Adam, but already his name was bringing all the old invisible force to bear. He didn't need an army behind him. It afforded him a momentary satisfaction.

"Sorry to break in on you like this this morning, Colonel."

"Not at all, Mr. Royle. What can I do for you?"

"My brother is stationed here."

"So—your brother! Why, I had no idea, sir!" The beefy face glistened with professional pleasure.

"Since he must be among the rawest of your recruits, I'm not surprised. I know my request may be highly irregular, Colonel, but I have come out here this morning to see him."

"Of course, of course! Not irregular at all." The officer crossed

285

to the door and barked an order to someone in the entrance tent. Then he turned back. "I've sent for Private Royle. If you will be so good as to follow Lieutenant Patterson he will take you to a place where you can talk in private. Have to apologize. Not many comforts around a military camp in wartime, you know."

Brant rose. "Very kind of you, Colonel."

"Not at all. A pleasure, sir, to accommodate you, Mr. Royle." He shook Brant's hand again. "When you've finished your visit please drop back by. I'll be glad to show you about personally if you like!"

Brant murmured his thanks and found himself following the same young officer who had brought him in. In silence he stalked after his escort. They went down a sort of track from which endless little streets of tents debouched. At the foot of one of these the officer stopped and flung aside the flap of a tent. It was unfurnished and unoccupied. He turned to Brant.

"If you will wait here, sir."

Brant growled his thanks, but he did not enter the tent. He was getting impatient with all this formality.

"Is there anything more I can do for you, sir?" inquired the officer with the same impersonal politeness.

"No," said Brant. "This is fine."

The youngster saluted, turned briskly on his heel, and walked back toward headquarters. Left alone, Brant began to pace up and down before the tent in the sunshine. The cigar was going to pieces between his teeth. He spat it out and drew a fresh one from an inner pocket and bit off its closed end. Everything about him looked deserted. No moving figure in uniform anywhere outside the long silent row of tents. From the distance he could hear the same monotonous shouted orders on the drill field. He scowled grimly. In the remote spring sun it all seemed so childish. Like a game. . . . Then he saw Pete Henry.

He was approaching alone and there was nothing in the slouchily uniformed figure to indicate that it was Pete Henry except the familiar swagger of the walk. Brant stood still, overcome again with that sense of inchoate emotion. Rage, love, and loss all swarmed together.

Pete Henry had seen him now, but he did not run or wave. He continued to walk deliberately toward him. It was Brant who felt like running, but he held his place. Pete Henry came up and halted at arm's length and took off his hat. The two men stood looking at each other in silence. Brant with his feet spraddled, his head thrust forward, Pete Henry with the old boyish smile, the ageless and impish gesture of the mouth that had never changed. Brant surveyed him. Pete Henry had changed, though. The face, reddened by the sun, was graver, the eyes bluer and clearer than they had been in many a year. Gone were the blond curls so carefully greased and lacquered into place. The head was close-cropped. The only vestige of the dandy was the carefully groomed mustache grown in emulation of Chris Malley. Brant felt as though he was looking at someone he had never seen before—or was it someone he had seen without ever troubling to recognize him? It was somehow a shocking moment. He brushed it aside.

"Pete Henry," he said at last, his voice rough with the nameless emotion, "Pete Henry, you damned fool!"

"Hello, Brant."

Then Brant did something he had never done in his life. He reached forth and hugged the youngster tightly and awkwardly to him. It was a curious moment for both of them and terminated as abruptly as it had begun. They stood holding each other by the arms. Pete Henry threw back his head and laughed.

"Hell's bells, Brant! I knew it would give you something of a shock, but then I knew a lot of people would be surprised. I bet there was one helluva row back in Kingsmont. And I thought I'd hear from you soon, but I sure to God didn't expect you'd come in person!"

"Listen," said Brant, his voice gaining control of itself. "This is the craziest thing you ever got yourself mixed up in. But I've been getting you out of scrapes all your life. It'll be more trouble and'll take more wirepullin' this time, but I'll do it again. You gettin' yourself all done up in a uniform and marchin' around like a kid. You don't have to do that."

Pete Henry released himself and stepped back. He laughed again, but it was a short laugh and he looked at Brant suddenly with the stranger's face. Only the eyes were bright with the old mischievous mockery.

"No, Brant, not this time you won't."

"What do you mean?"

"I mean you're not getting me out of anything. This isn't just a joke. I did it because I meant to do it."

"Look here," said Brant. He removed the cigar from his mouth and spat on the ground between them. "Look here, Pete Henry, let's not waste time. I'm a busy man. I'm goin' back to Kingsmont as soon as I get through here. And you're comin' out of here as soon as I can get in touch with some people in Washington. After that I've got plans for you—"

"It's no good this time, Brant." The blue eyes were still mocking but there was a remoteness in the mockery. Pete Henry shook his head. "You've taken care of me all my life. You've been a good big brother in more ways than one. But I've decided to do something on my own, and this is it. I'm sorry, but all the wirepullin' in the country isn't goin' to change my mind. It may sound funny, but I've sorta got some plans of my own. No. You go on back to Kingsmont and tell 'em I'm all right. Tell 'em—" He paused and the eyes were no longer mocking. "Yeah, tell 'em that little Pete Henry has gone off to help the poor Cubans gain their fool independence—and maybe pick up a little independence for himself along the way."

Brant felt stunned. It was as though this sudden stranger, his baby brother, had struck him. The sense of outrage grew in him, choking him, and with it came a wild and unspeakable sense of loss. It was as though the dark phantoms that pursued him from the moment he had received Sam's telegram and begun this journey were here stating themselves.

"You mean that?" he finally managed to say in a strangled voice.

Pete Henry looked at him out of the old-young face already a thousand poignant miles away. "Yes, Brant, I do."

Head outthrust, Brant stood looking at him in silence. Then he pushed the cigar into his mouth again and, without another word, turned and walked off.

The younger man remained standing, hat in hand, his body in the indefinable attitude of jaunty grace, and watched Brant out of sight. Brant never stopped, nor looked back.

2

The period following Brant's return to Kingsmont that spring was one of the bitterest and most confused of his life. No matter how dark his personal daemon was, the issues between him and the world had always been well defined. There had always remained the consciousness of his achievement in any moment. Now that was shaken. The bare, eye-level encounter with Pete Henry had created a bruise of uncertainty in himself that no amount of opposition in the world of mankind, the world of cutthroat business, of law and order, had ever been able to do. The case of the Federal Government now in progress against him and his work paled beside it. That he could understand, could deal with, calling to his aid all the innate genius and talent for battle that had been born in him and had finally come to flower. It was an achievement rooted in him, but one which he was able to deal with in practical terms outside himself. This blow was buried deep. He could neither understand it nor deal with it. It challenged him and accused him and he had no answer to it. It tormented him with the additional thought that it had always been there and what he had done before had all been an avoidance, a putting-off of this meeting with Pete Henry.

When he arrived in Kingsmont from Raleigh he stayed only two days at the house on Elm Street. His report to the hovering family—Sam, Roberta, the voracious Marstons—was brief and curt. He had been to see Pete Henry. Pete Henry evidently knew what he was doing. And that was all he would say. He retired into a black and growling silence. He insulted Mrs. Marston, quarreled bitterly with Sam, and found the trembling, hysterical Roberta unbearable. On the second day he took a suite at the hotel. There he virtually locked himself in for days. There also he summoned the aristocracy of his business for quaking audiences. He was peremptory, harsh beyond measure, unreasonably demanding, as he had never been in his relations with them. They tried to mark it down to his concern with the case against the Grand Columbian. Summonses from headquarters in New York left him unmoved. Since the committee in Washington was not demanding his presence, he replied in fiery, curt messages admonishing the New York force to fend for itself. After all, what had he hired them for? Kingsmont was electrified, as usual, by his presence. He abjured all importunities to social life, refused all hostesses who would enthusiastically have made him a pet lion. They all had to accept it as the right of power and majesty. And he knew it. He sallied forth only in the evening. He wandered restlessly about the dark streets under the trees or down the wandering byways among the factories and warehouses. Here everything he had done was made manifest in the night, teeming even in sleeping. He drew scant and bitter comfort from it. It was finished. And having been finished, it was something separate and impersonal, affording him little comfort. Everything except the fact of brick and stone and steel and the implacable machines seemed to withdraw from his path, to clear the way for him—to leave him utterly alone.

Pete Henry had done it. Pete Henry had thrown him off and rubbed him raw. He could not forgive Pete Henry nor the implications of their meeting. He brooded over it ceaselessly. And in his brooding finally he began to erect his defenses in defiance. It was typical. No man, no event, could do this to him. He took another tack. He began to appear in public as a figure—not in the tony world of South Bay Street with all the fine houses built on tobacco money, but in the more certain world where sweaty, denimed men brought their tobacco. The world of the courthouse square and the warehouses. He would suddenly appear on the worn granite steps of that ugly public building and talk in forced heartiness to little groups of loiterers. Or he would squat in his Prince Albert coat at the wide doorway of an empty warehouse, chew a bit of straw or an unlighted cigar, and try to talk the old talk of weather and crops. But it did not work. They all knew him. His presence cast an iron restraint over their intercourse. No matter how much he knew their language, they could not hear him or what he was saying. He embarrassed them. Although he no longer had a place with them, they would go home and boast among their families and friends that they had seen Brant Royle and he had sat down and talked with them just like he was anybody! But privately they did not mean that. He was not like anybody else. Had never been. They remembered the big granite face pierced by the cigar, the rumbling, deep voice, making talk and concerned with the topics they understood—but it was not the same. They recalled the dark and brooding eyes, the black mane of hair that would never look groomed. Oh, he was a one, all right, that Brant Royle! They felt awkward, constrained, in his presence. In some way they could not fathom or talk about, they felt sorry for him. He sat there trying to talk to them and yet he was lost to them and their concerns. They could feel him reaching out toward them, but they never felt touched.

No. They knew it and Brant knew it. He found himself again as he had always been—an alien among those he had sprung from.

In desperation he resorted to something he had not looked to for a long time. He began to drink. What admission this constituted he would not face. For years now he had drunk deeply of a far more potent brew: power. But for once it was lost to him. He had to resort to something more simple and undemanding, and it was the bottle. He began to drink terribly and alone in his rooms at the hotel, refusing the company of any man, the interruption of any demand. In it he achieved no oblivion. Only a blurring of nonessentials and a sharpening of essentials. It had always been that to him in the past. It was even more so now. In particular it reassured him in the basic fact that he was a man and a big one. He had always needed that assurance. He needed it acutely now. Out of it emerged the outlines of his old personal concerns. The dominating factors of his obsessions were few, simple, but terrible. They were known only to himself. He had never had any talent for understanding them, nor, what is more, denying them. He could only put them off, as he had done all his life. Drink simply brought them to the fore.

They began now with an essentially inconsequential fact. He had removed himself from his long association with the household of Sam and Roberta. He knew now that he had held to that arrangement out of his deep tribal feeling for his own. With Pete Henry gone, it was no longer there. Here in Kingsmont he needed a place. Everyone else, his underlings, the men who had risen in the business he had created, had established themselves in the solidity of dwellings and grounds. He alone had no private share of Kingsmont earth that was set aside and marked as his own. What had held him back all these years? The question was more complicated than the answer. He had known the answer since he could remember. There was one place and one place only for him in Kingsmont—and that place was Hill House. It had long since ceased to be a structure of wood, an expression of grace in architecture and grounds. It was a symbol that had dominated his whole life—something far in the background of his activities, but always there. He had long beaten at the invisible walls that surrounded it. The need for bringing that long siege to a close grew into him till it dominated his every thought. The answer was so simple that he almost laughed when he realized it. He could have anything he wanted. Why did he hesitate at this? He had put it off long enough. Now was the time to finish this long business. Here was positive action on a positive thing. An old house on an old street on a hill. He had been too long inactive. That was the trouble.

So one afternoon, completely sober, he dressed himself more carefully than he had for a week or more, and full of a sense of fresh confidence, set out across the square for Hill House.

3

When he got to the gate he stopped and looked up the remembered walk to the remembered doorway, and the old familiar pain and exultation cut through him. It seemed only yesterday that he had first stood on this very spot eating it all hungrily with his eyes. More than that, it seemed that his feet had never left this spot no matter how far he had wandered, so often had he stood there in reality and in his dreams. And here he was once more.

The old Negro who answered his peal at the bell told him fumblingly that Miss Singleton was not in the house but around in the garden at the back and that if he would care to wait he would go and find out if she would see him. But Brant, full of the moment and the clear purpose surging in him, brushed this aside.

"Thanks," he said, "don't bother her. I'll just go around myself. She's expecting me."

He walked off down the porch and left the old servant blinking in the doorway. If he was going to do this thing, he would do it in his own way, without any hedging or sidestepping.

He left the porch and went up the driveway toward the back. Never had he dared come so far before. He noticed that the yard looked shabby, the grass mangy and ill-kept. And the side of the house as he passed showed desperate signs of needing paint. He felt it almost as a personal affront that it had not been kept as he always visioned it—gleaming and richly white. Shabbiness did not become it. He thought with a pang of fierce tenderness and possession that at last it needed him—somebody who could really take care of it. Well—here he was!

He crossed from the driveway toward a barrier of boxwood with an opening in it. Without hesitation he strode through into the garden beyond. Just inside he stopped, though, and took off his bowler slowly and held it behind his back. He knew in that instant with a pang of despair that the house was not all he had come for.

291

She was kneeling a short distance from him by a bed of thick white and pink phlox. She wore an apron and an old flop-brimmed straw hat and gloves. She was weeding—and still her attitude was one of grace and dignity. None of those awkward articles of apparel could affect that. It was as unconscious as the way the folds of the light-gray cotton dress arranged themselves richly about her.

As his feet had made no sound on the grass, she was unconscious of his presence. He stood thirstily drinking in the woman. And as if she felt at last the force of that gaze upon her she looked up and saw him. She was not startled nor did she cry out. The pale face under the absurd straw hat flushed slightly. Then she sat back on her heels, folding her hands like a child in her lap, and looked directly back at him. It was somehow a moment naked and breathless for both of them, as though each had in an instant received an identical blow. The old and familiar blow that had come out of the space between them for so many years. It had in it, too, for those few seconds, the truth: that here, behind the fierce and obscure history of their relationship, they wished, each of them, to call a halt, to declare a final and sensible truce. Each could feel it palpably in the other. But it was intuitive, tenuous, and was gone in a flash. Margaret's face retained its immobility. Her eyes held none of the old denial. They were questioning and puzzled. She began to draw off the soiled gloves and to smooth them against her lap. Her face was thinner than when he had last seen it, more set and fined-down, as though its features had been sharpened and honed against the hard stone of experience. As he looked at her, his emotion almost choked him—not with the old possessive passion, but with a rush of tenderness and sadness; not pity for what had been done to her, but a feeling that enclosed them both. What each was now and what those lost children had been who had looked upon each other over a closed gate.

"Miss Singleton."

"Mr. Royle?" Her voice was low, bemused.

"Your darky told me you were back here," he went on in a gentle voice as though he were addressing a child whom he did not wish to frighten. "I took the liberty of coming around unannounced. Reckon I should have let him come and find out if it would be convenient, but I didn't."

"It's all right, Mr. Royle. I have been expecting you for some time."

He flushed with pleasure. "You mean my letter?"

She nodded her head, a slow, grave inclination. About them on the air arose a little ecstatic humming of insects. A yellow butterfly dashed erratically between them and plunged into the phlox. She raised her arms then and removed the old hat. It was a peculiarly intimate gesture at the moment and cut him keenly. The sight of the dark hair so sleekly parted along the skull and gathered in the rich knot at the nape of the neck gave him a feeling of drunkenness. It looked exactly as he had always remembered it, unchanged by fashion or time, a perfect symbol of all the immutable mystery and desirability that she had eternally represented to him. A desperate longing to go to her and place his hand on her head swept over him, but he stood where he was, feet apart, immobile.

"You will forgive my not acknowledging that letter, Mr. Royle," she continued, smoothing the brim of the hat in her lap. Her voice was so calm, so smooth, that it gave a lie to the extraordinary quality of this meeting.

"Oh, that was all right," he protested. "I didn't expect an answer. I hope you didn't mind my saying what I did. I have never been a man to say what I didn't mean. I meant every word I wrote in that letter."

"I'm sure you did, Mr. Royle. I'm grateful for what you said, and because I am grateful and because I did not answer it, I am seeing you here this afternoon. I have always liked people to say what they mean, because I have always tried to do so myself."

His eyes, usually so somber, glowed darkly upon her. The set, heavily handsome features assumed suddenly a kind of youthfulness. The grim lines around the big, full mouth softened.

"I'm mighty glad to hear you say it, Miss Singleton, because I've always felt you were that kind of person." He took a couple of steps toward her and looked about the garden, breathing slowly and deeply. He wanted desperately to preserve and extend the formal intimacy of this moment. "You know, it's funny that after all these years—and it's been a long time, hasn't it?—after all this time we, you and I, can meet like this without any pulling and tugging and just talk like people."

"What do you mean?" Her head remained bowed toward the hat.

"Let's keep on being honest, Miss Singleton. We've really known each other for a long time for two people who have never been introduced, haven't we?"

"Yes." Her voice was so low that he barely caught the reply.

"And most of that time I've acted like a fool—a mean, rough, unmannerly fool. I admit it. But most of my life I've been backed into a corner. And when we happened to meet you got snarled in my fight. I'm out of that corner now. Have been for a long time. So I can come here and we can talk to each other."

"Is that why you came?"

Her head was still lowered, her voice low, drugged. The informality of her position there on the grass was the attitude of someone becalmed and utterly passive.

"No, not exactly. I didn't come up here this afternoon to make a social call." He smiled the rare, bitter little half-smile. "You should know better than that. I've always been too busy to learn any drawing-room manners. I reckon I've been too long in harness to try now. No, I came on a little business matter, Miss Singleton."

He had the satisfaction of seeing her face turn once more to look full at him with the puzzled, dreamlike expression.

"Business, Mr. Royle? I don't think I understand."

"It shouldn't be hard for you." In spite of himself a harshness came into his voice. It spoke from the hurt he had been experiencing alone for the past week. "Isn't it pretty well taken for granted that business runs in my veins instead of blood? You said a minute ago you liked people to say what they mean. Well, I came here this afternoon to buy Hill House from you. I want it."

She stood up then, slowly. But it was more as though she had been awakened from her daze and grew up straight from the grass, a tall and rigid flower, all the passive and curved lines erased from her body. He moved to aid her, then stopped. The fragile, remote essence that had enclosed them for a few moments was shattered. The sunlight on the grass, the boxwood, the butterfly dancing above the pink and white phlox like a little yellow flame—they were the same. But the giddy feeling of recognition between them had fled. He felt the loss desperately. He felt almost that he could strike this woman who now stood looking at him. Always they were doomed to meet in this dark swirl of violence. He regarded her curiously, trying to command his thoughts, examining them dispassionately: What is there about this woman, of all the women I have known, that holds me in such a way that I can never escape? I have never known whether it was love or hate. Is it simply because it always eludes me that I must have it—buy it at any cost? The questions turned with maddening familiarity in his head. He had been for so long free of their immediate torment that having them rush upon him now drove him to further harshness.

"Now don't tell me that Tom Pate is handling your affairs. I know that. And I know that you have refused to discuss the sale of this house with anyone. But I'm not just anyone, Miss Singleton." His voice, forcibly restrained over the desperate black passion he felt taking hold of him, was still low, but it began to take on the furious, cold tone that had cowed a legion of boards of directors and earned the respect even of a committee of investigating Senators. "I also know—because it is my business to know everything about what I am interested in—that it is no longer reasonable for you to try to hold onto it. I am prepared to pay whatever price you wish to set on it. I am used to paying for what I want."

This was not the way he had intended to say it. It fed the growing rage in him to know that the intangible thing in her presence was forcing him again to reveal himself at his worst. The shadow of mindless pain clouded the black eyes staring hard at her from beneath the thick brows. She looked back at him unflinchingly, her face unmoved and remote. The struggle was there, too. The powerful and strange thing that lay under all their words and all their attitudes hung like a vibrant and palpable presence in the few feet of physical space that separated them.

"Hill House is not for sale, Mr. Royle."

"That doesn't mean anything." He brushed it aside, protesting. "Let's be reasonable. You don't need such a house." He glanced back toward it. "You can't even afford to keep it up any more!"

She blanched at this. It had hurt her, and he had not meant to hurt her.

"It was built by a Singleton," she said. "I am a Singleton."

Again that name rising to mock him.

"You mean because I am a Royle you will not sell to me?"

"Yes."

Her eyes had never wavered from his face and her voice remained at the same low, colorless level as though she scarcely knew what she was saying. He shook his head slowly with the careful gesture of one in the extremities of pain. He had grown very white, the muscles ridging hard and white about his mouth as though the effort to keep down what was rising in him was almost too much for him. He walked slowly and stiffly to her, so that she could feel his breath beat upon her face.

"Miss Singleton," he began, his voice harsh as if it choked him to utter this formal address again—"Margaret!" And this time her name burst out of him like a cry. He dropped the black bowler from his hands and reached forward and took her slowly by the arms and pulled her up against him. She did not resist. There was something terrible in her passivity at that moment. And then she seemed to warm and soften helplessly under his touch. Something broke in him at that, and the words came tumbling out in the harsh, trembling voice.

"Margaret, Margaret!" Having uttered it he could not stop. "Look at us all these years. Why have we done this to each other— *why?* I've known . . . you've known, too. You know what's inside of me don't you—*don't you?*"

He did not wait for an answer. His face was flushed and blindly intent. He shook her a little, gently, between his hands. She made no response, but her eyelids fluttered and closed and her head dropped back with the expression of someone lost and damned. He continued in the harsh voice:

"What has been the sense in all of it? It's not just the damned house I want—it's you, *you*. You're the only woman for me. I've made myself stay away all these years trying to believe it wasn't true. But it *is* true. I've made a big place in the world for myself—and all the while I was making it I knew it was to show *you*. You can have that place now, all of it. I'll give it back to you and more."

"Do you know what you are saying?" Her eyes opened upward to him, lucent like a child's, and full of a burning joy.

"Of course I know what I'm saying. I've waited years to say it, and you've waited years to hear it, haven't you—*haven't you?*" His hands closed cruelly on her arms, but she did not wince. She seemed to welcome it.

"Yes," she whispered, "yes!"

For a long and timeless moment they stood thus locked and motionless. Shadows filled the garden about them and the green space seemed to close warmly about them. He bent his head and set his mouth on hers. And in that deliberate caress were mixed anger and the hunger of an old longing. Her mouth received it without response, but he scarcely noticed it. With something like a groan he released her suddenly and slid down, clasping her awkwardly about the knees, pressing his face against her skirts. Then he turned his face, eyes closed, up to her and said:

"I love you, Margaret Singleton."

She did not move, and for a moment she did not speak. Then she bent over him, not compassionately, but as though she were coiling.

"And I hate you, Brant Royle." She uttered the words separately and distinctly. There came over her face such a flood of relief that it was as if some unbearable pressure had been lifted from her—as if in the saying of those six words she had at last released herself from some long and awful bondage. He did not seem to hear her. What she had said only brushed the surface of his own consuming emotion. He could hear no one but himself.

"It has been so long—so long—and we have been such fools. But we're young yet, Margaret—we'll make it up. I don't want your house. I'll build you any kind of house you want—hundreds of them!" He sounded like someone in a delirium, babbling incoherently against her as he groveled. She straightened herself above him. The expression of frightening happiness on her face gave way to one of profound distaste and scorn. She released herself from his clasp, stepping away suddenly and strongly. It left him kneeling grotesquely on the grass before her, dazed and blind. His hair was tousled and his mouth hung open.

"Get up, Mr. Royle," she said crisply. "You look ridiculous. A young man could perhaps be excused, but what would all those factories, all of Kingsmont, the whole world that you own, say if they saw you like this?"

Her face was calm and set again. Only the eyes burned with a fierce triumph, the slim brows above them arched mockingly. Then she walked to the opening in the hedge and stood with her back to him. He got to his feet then with slow, dazed movements. His face was haggard. And when he stooped to pick up the bowler hat he did it falteringly, like an old man. For a moment he stood, his arms hanging heavy at his side, looking at her straight stiff back. Then he walked to the hedge and stood beside her. She turned slightly to him then, waiting. But he would not look at her. It was almost as though he was afraid to look at her.

"You do not mean this," he said thickly. "You can't—"

"Good afternoon, Mr. Royle," she said in the inhumanly crisp voice.

Still he did not look at her or go. Then he straightened the big shoulders and placed the bowler carefully on his head, looking always beyond and through the dying afternoon. When he spoke again his voice was drained and tired, but it was steady.

"If this is what you wanted to do to me, I hope it has made you happy," he said. "I will never in your life trouble you again—I promise you that."

And leaving her standing stiffly there, he walked off under the old trees down the driveway, his hands thrust deep into his pockets, his coattails flapping about the big legs as they moved him with growing strength toward the street.

4

She stood pressed tight against the boxwood and watched that broad, heavy back—not an energetic back any more, just a solid back under good broadcloth, an implacable back, undefeated—diminish under the slanting shadows of the familiar trees. And as she looked she smelled the indefinable fragrance of the box—something immutable and apart from this happening. She recalled as from a distant vista another time when she had watched—not the back but the dark and energetic, haunting face that had looked at her from a roadway while she cowered beneath a safe and odorless hydrangea. She could dismiss this happening in a spirit of intense and final triumph, but she could never erase the other.

The back, topped by the heavy head and the bowler, turned at the street. Cut off by the old paling fence, he moved across it like an automaton, framed by the trees. And as the round black crown of the bowler disappeared, she gathered up her skirts and ran to the

297

house. Not to the kitchen door. No. To the old back-hall door, so seldom used that it creaked when she forced it to open. Then through the hall under the stairway and out into the broad space, dim and polished, between the two parlors to press her face against the slim panes at the side of the door. Was it still in sight? Yes, there was the minute black mound lowering down the hill beyond the old fence, descending into the approaching spring evening. She watched it till it was no more, avidly—like a creature who sipped poison from the sight and gloried in it. Then she turned from the window with a clenched gesture of proclamation, flattening herself against the panels of the door. And as she waited there in the obscurity of the hallway there crept upon her gradually a feeling that the familiar and besieged structure that stood about her—the house—was dissolving into the gathering shadows. The afternoon was drawing swiftly to a close. Dimly, as though from an imponderable distance, she heard the sounds of supper being prepared in the kitchen. For the first time, standing there against the door tensely still and waiting, she felt utterly alone and defenseless.

It was not what she had expected. It did not rationally follow the surge of triumph that had intoxicated her. She put out a hand and touched the nearest wall like a person lost and in a strange land. In a little while, she said to herself, we will sit down—Cousin Tabby and I as we have always sat down—to supper. And Simon will pass the plates as he always has . . . as though nothing had happened . . . and it will be the same as it has always been. But this seemed suddenly so bleak, so empty, that she turned sick inside. The strange and drunken feeling that had borne her along till now drained out of her. Isn't this what I wanted, she cried silently to herself, what I have always wanted? And then she was flooded with panic such as she had never experienced before. Not all the meetings with Brant— scant as they were—not the burning of the factory nor the death of her father, had left her with this. I cannot, must not, feel like this, she thought, writhing against the tall wooden panels of the door; this is one of the supreme moments of my life. . . . I made him crawl—like an insect—and I sent him away, beaten and abased, as I always wanted to do . . . and he knew it! . . .

With an effort she pulled herself together in the increasing obscurity of the hallway. But she felt cold. Little tremors seized and ran over her body. She thought: We should still have a fire in the house. Simon is getting careless—I shall have him build a fire in the parlor this evening. She had to set her teeth against a threatening chattering.

Overhead she heard a sibilant movement in the upper hallway. Cousin Tabby shuffling along in her slippers. She had been nursing a late cold in her room for the past few days. Margaret heard her cough. A fussy, lonely sound that echoed cheerlessly down the stairs.

"Relda—Simon!" Cousin Tabby's voice, absurdly inadequate because it was so frail and tattered, quavered downward. Cousin Tabby is getting ancient . . . and I am getting old. I feel older than the world at this moment. . . .

"Do you want something, Cousin Tabby?"

"That you, Margaret?" responded the hoarse tinkle from above. "Yes."

"I just wanted a little hot tea to take after my medicine, dear—that's all. I napped too long—but I think my cold is a little better. I do wish my room felt a little warmer!"

It's cold where you dwell, too, thought Margaret. A flashing image of that cluttered and airless chamber, full of mementoes, came to her. It's like my life. A magpie's life and nothing more. And there she is and here am I, two polite magpies—guarding our separate hoards. She hers and I mine, and neither of us knowing or caring what the other has got.

"I'm sorry, but Simon is getting so deaf, Cousin Tabby—deaf and forgetful."

There was a faint sniffling and then a delicate trumpeting as Cousin Tabby blew her nose.

"Have you been having callers, Margaret?" she called down in a stuffed voice. "I thought I heard someone going down the drive a moment ago."

Dear Cousin Tabby! You never miss anything, do you? Cold or no cold. You would hear the dead walk. . . .

"Oh, that," she called upward. "That was Mr. Royle. He came to pay a call about Father." Her voice careful—oh, so careful. She listened painfully to its echoes.

"*Mr. Royle?*" called the stifled, disembodied voice from above. "My soul and body—isn't he a bit *late* with his calling?"

"Yes—late," she replied, and did not know why she had said it. It was beginning to irritate her past bearing. "I'll tell you about it at supper."

"Oh, all right. Is that nice Mr. Barton coming tonight?"

How tired, how terribly, emptily tired she felt. Her limbs were made of lead. She could not move. Then she called up desperately—to herself as much as to the presence above her:

"Yes, I think he is—I'll send Simon down to remind him." Then she added as an afterthought, as though grasping at something: "He ought to come, you know—he *usually* comes. . . . I'll send Relda up with your tea."

The wheezing, throat-clearing, tired sound from above. "All right, dear—good of you. I feel a bit low, you know. Cup of tea sets me up."

She waited tensely while the shuffling whispered away and then heard Cousin Tabby's door click shut. Even then she did not move for a long time. When she did it was to walk only as far as the empty dining room. She stopped there and stood in the center of it by the long bare table. She could go no farther because she felt weak and hollow. She pulled the nearest chair from the table and sank into it, sitting stiffly, waves of realization sweeping over her. She did not know how long she had known it—since she had run into the hallway there, since she had leaned against the door, perhaps—but now she knew it. This room with the table and the sideboard and the yawning fireplace with the portrait of her grandfather above it—this room and the rest of the house that she had cherished for so long were as devoid of meaning and importance as an empty shell. Why, I don't care any more, she thought, amazed and frightened at the same time, I don't care at all. If Hill House were to disappear from under my feet at this very moment I would not feel a thing. Not one thing!

Above her on the wall, crisscrossed in the fading light, Robert Singleton's face glowed palely down upon her. The painted eyes drew hers to them, as they had a thousand times. She could no more deny them now than she had been able to do as a child, swinging her short legs petulantly beneath the table, she had tried to avoid them by sulking at her plate. They seemed to stare at her now with the ultimate, devastating irony. She stiffened defiantly against their portent. Then she rose quickly and started toward the kitchen door. She had forgotten Cousin Tabby's tea. All that ran through her head now—a panicky reiteration—was the name of John Barton . . . John Barton. . . .

CHAPTER SIXTEEN

I

History, even in its immediacy, is a distant and impersonal concept to the majority of mankind except when it affects the life of the individual in the place where he stands and breathes. It also has a prodigal and perverse way of crowding its events helter-skelter, one upon another, without regard for their importance. So it was with Kingsmont in that eventful summer. Two developments alternated upon the stage of public attention. First, there was the progress of the war with Spain. Kingsmont had its quota of men—husbands, sons, brothers—involved. Not many understood the exact issues in question, but all were joined in the welter of romantic rhetoric and violent sentimentalism that was the traditional Southern approach to any conflict. Then there was the development of the case of the

Federal Government versus the Grand Columbian Tobacco Company. When military information was scant or slow, this ponderous battle took the front of the stage. In May the news of Dewey's victory over the Spanish fleet at Manila was the subject of a week's celebration and rejoicing. Hard on its heels, muffling it, appeared the news that Brant Royle had been summoned again to Washington. This was important to the whole tobacco country. Its implications outweighed Cuba and Spain. The attention was drawn away only in June when General Shafter engaged in battle at Las Guimas. It was held by Cuba until the destruction of the Spanish fleet at Santiago at the beginning of July. Then the fluctuations of the stock of the Grand Columbian and its subsidiaries on the New York Exchange frightened many men—and not only in Kingsmont. In one day it dropped ten points. It recovered five the next. Then the qualified news, hedged and obscured in journalistic prose, appeared that the Government—that majestic and equally distant force—had ordered the dissolution of the tobacco trust. This was a matter of deepest concern, on the one hand for speculators and investors and on the other, for men and organizations who had suffered at the hands of the combine and now had cause for bitter rejoicing.

It continued throughout the season, swinging from one thing to another, like a giant pendulum. Between them the matters of weather, of death and birth—the constants of life—were relegated to the background, and summarily.

And so it was that the announcement of Margaret Singleton's approaching marriage to John Barton appeared only as a small item in the *Kingsmont Herald* toward the end of July. At any other time, in any other season, this news alone would have sufficed to set the whole county by the ears. Particularly among the tenacious old circles of Kingsmont. As it was, only a few individuals gave it more than passing notice. They were people who could still be swayed and moved by their roots in the past. After all these years, they thought, Margaret Singleton! And marrying that Yankee. Of course he had been mixed up with the Royles in some way at one time— something to do with the machine that made all the cigarettes. None of them was quite sure. There had been something lately about his connection with a concern in Detroit, some matter of machine manufacturing—internal combustion, or something of the sort. He had been about town all summer . . . owned some land down south in the county a few miles out of town, someone said . . . curious thing for an outsider . . . must be well off, though . . . couldn't help it if he had had anything to do with the Royles!

As for Margaret Singleton, a little note of subacid comment ran under the immemorial woman talk circulating among the parlors where the name of Singleton still conjured up memories. Outwardly

301

they maintained the politely enthusiastic mien traditionally demanded by such an announcement. It gave some who still considered themselves friends of the family the opportunity and the excuse to break in upon the silence that had wrapped Hill House since Major Singleton's death at the beginning of the year. But if any of these bold intruders, moved more by curiosity than anything else, had hoped to glean some special information that they could later report in elaboration among themselves, they were disappointed. Mrs. Marston, meeting her old friend Mrs. Hinton Turner outside Lawson & Royle, remarked after an introductory exchange of amenities:

"Have you been up to call on Margaret Singleton lately?"

Mrs. Marston, monumentally corseted, smoothed the beaver collar of her coat as she asked this question in a deceptively mild tone. Mrs. Turner, redoubtable matron herself, shook her head.

"No, I *haven't*," she replied. "I declare, I've been meaning to, but you know how easy it is to let things slip these days. So much going on—my Frances getting ready to go off to Sweetbriar and all. Anyway, to tell the truth, I've almost felt like I didn't want to intrude."

"I know exactly what you *mean*," said Mrs. Marston, bobbing her head massively. "I felt the same way—reticent, you know—particularly since we hadn't heard a word from Margaret or Miss Tabby on the subject since that very brief notice in the *Herald*. I've been up a couple of times with Mr. Marston to call since the Major's death. Charlie was terribly upset because Major Jim passed away before they could patch up their little differences. They'd been friends for so long, and Margaret practically grew up with my girls, you know. But they had both been a little at odds from the time Charlie sold the business to Mr. Royle and retired; nothing really serious, but you know how stubborn men are, and the Major just would not give in about the cigarette business, when *everyone* knew it was the coming thing. Well, as if that wasn't enough, he and Margaret literally cut us dead after Berta's marriage. As if *we* had done something criminal—can you imagine!"

The ponderous velvet flowers on Mrs. Turner swayed from side to side as if pushed by a slow and shifting wind, and her tongue sucked at her teeth politely, although this was old news to her.

"I do declare, Mrs. Marston," she said, opening her eyes wide.

"Well, Charlie and I were willing to let bygones be bygones— and I certainly never harbored any resentment. I knew that they had suffered a comedown and it must have been hard for Margaret, but she certainly hasn't made it any easier, shutting herself up like that and cutting herself off from everybody. Well, when I read the news of her engagement to Mr. Barton and not a sign of personal word from her I decided that I at least would try to do something.

302

With no close family of her own it just seemed the *least* I could do."

"Of course, of course," agreed Mrs. Turner, almost too eagerly.

"Well, I just said to Berta one day last week, 'Berta, we've just got to do something about Margaret Singleton's wedding—we can't just sit by like this without turning a hand.' Berta was very difficult about it. She's never got over the way Margaret ignored *her* wedding, but I insisted that we, at least, could afford to be generous and show Margaret that she still had well-wishing friends in the world. So I persuaded her to come with me—last Monday afternoon, I believe it was—to pay a call."

Mrs. Marston paused briefly to adjust her collar again and take the opportunity to glance about her to see if there was anyone among the passers-by who might be overhearing her. She lowered her voice. Mrs. Turner leaned toward her avidly.

"Well, we went up. And everything was just as you would expect it to be. The house is beginning to seem old-fashioned now, you know—and the outside is *definitely* shabby and run-down. But inside everything is still beautifully kept—all that handsome mahogany and silver simply gleaming! I must say this for Margaret, she has never let altered circumstances make her cheat one inch on her housekeeping. But do you know it made me feel quite queer to think of all that polished perfection kept shut up there just for the two of them—Miss Tabby and herself. We didn't see Miss Tabby— she's had a catarrh since spring. But I talked to her a minute up the stairway. She sounded a little feeble, but still as bright as ever. Then we went and visited with Margaret in the parlor—the big one with the rosewood piano. She looked all right—a little pale and thin, perhaps, not as handsome as she used to be, but still elegant. You have to say that for her. She's always had style since she was a little thing. And her manners were perfect—a little stiff and old-fashioned perhaps, but perfect. But anyway, she was cordial, if rather distant. Gave me a distinct feeling at times that she wasn't even listening to half we were saying—almost as if she didn't really know we were there, or that *she* was there herself, for that matter. Very queer. I had to do most of the talking, but I simply couldn't get her around to the subject of the wedding. She avoided it every time. Changed the subject whenever I gave her an opening—or was just short of being rude. Berta wasn't a bit of help. Just sat looking at her cup and drinking simply quarts of tea. I was really *very* put out with Berta.

"Well, finally I decided that I couldn't work around Margaret, and I wasn't going to leave until I found out something definite. So I just asked her point-blank: where were she and Mr. Barton going to be married? She had to answer me then, but she did it in the most offhand manner imaginable—she said that she supposed they would be married at the Presbyterian church, or at home. She hadn't talked it over with Mr. Barton definitely yet, and Mr. Barton was away on business up North right now. Can you imagine! As though it were the most inconsequential thing in her life! And when I went on to say that I wanted her and Mr. Barton and Miss Tabby to come over for dinner someday soon, and that I would so like perhaps to arrange a quiet little reception for after the ceremony—just a few of her old friends, you know. It seemed the very least I could do. Well, she just didn't say *anything* for a moment—just sat there looking at me in a chilly, positively *hostile* way. Why, you never saw anything like it, my dear. For one awful moment I positively had the feeling that she would get up and walk out of the room leaving Berta and me sitting there. Then she replied, very short and cold-like, as if I were a perfect stranger, that it was good of me, but she would have to consult Mr. Barton. And that was all! You would have thought I had tried to insult her."

"Did you ever!" said Mrs. Turner, leaning ever closer and nibbling at the tip of her glove. Mrs. Marston straightened herself in her stays as though she still found an affront in the memory.

"When I got home, I must say I felt quite upset. Berta absolutely refused to talk about it and said it was no more than *she* had expected, and that she hoped I would leave well enough alone now. . . . But it worried me. I'm perfectly willing to admit that the shock of the Major's death and his leaving everything in such a mess was enough to do something to Margaret. But this was just too strange. The more I think about it, the more I have come to the conclusion that there is something more to this, my dear. Do you know what I *really* think?"

The two ladies leaned forward again so that the brims of their hats almost touched. They stared hungrily at each other.

"I think," continued Mrs. Marston in a hushed and portentous tone, "I think Margaret is simply going into this marriage for practical reasons. I don't imagine any of us really *know* how bad off she and Miss Tabby are. It's hard to come down, you know, after what she's been used to all her life. And Margaret's always been a shade too proud for my taste, entirely too choosy for her own good. I think that now she is being *forced* to make the best bargain she can under the circumstances." Mrs. Marston straightened again and added almost as an afterthought, "After all, she's certainly not getting any younger."

"No," agreed Mrs. Turner, bobbing the hat and frowning at the chewed tip of her glove, "she certainly isn't. I must say it was a great shock to all of us at the house—Mr. Turner, the girls, and me—when we read the announcement. We had got so *used* to the idea of Margaret Singleton *not* marrying that we all realized we had already begun to think of her being—well, an old maid. And after all her opportunities to suddenly up and decide to marry this Mr. Barton—not even a North Carolinian!"

"You know, my dear," mused Mrs. Marston, "the more I think of this last experience with Margaret, the more I think back to her mother. I never met Mrs. Singleton except on a few occasions—but she was queer. Definitely queer. I suppose it's coming out in Margaret now, after all these years."

"Yes," said Mrs. Turner sagely, "blood is bound to come out."

"Well," said Mrs. Marston, pulling up her chin with a gesture of finality, "we must not be unkind, my dear. We can be sympathetic even if Margaret will not let us do anything else for her. We must stand by, you know, for the Major's sake. We owe it to him at least, because he certainly adored Margaret. And what with all the fine old traditions being swept aside nowadays, everything changing before you can catch your breath, all of us who are left and know must stand by one another—don't you think so?"

"I certainly do, Mrs. Marston, I *certainly* do!"

2

But Mrs. Marston was not to be allowed to stand by, as she put it, that summer. It was an emotional season by anyone's judgment. Full of news, rumors, and counter-rumors. All of them contributing to the general feeling of tension and unrest. Even the weather reflected this. It was blastingly hot and dry. The tobacco farmers were worried about their crops. Many of them had been forced to replant whole fields. In less than a week during early June the first transplanting of the delicate young tobacco had withered and died. As the summer wore on, the drought was broken by violent rainstorms and even hail—all of them ruinous to a crop that had to be slaved over and nurtured tenderly even in the best of weather. And what affected those miles of green rows spread out on the land affected everyone in Kingsmont. It added to the pressure implicit in the unremitting heat. And then there was the war, of course. Everyone was stirred up and excited about that. When the news that the Government had passed judgment on the tobacco trust spread throughout the tobacco land, the pent-up feeling, the bitternesses, against the weather, the state of the war, the uncertainty of the crop, broke out. The anger focused on the Grand Columbian. The tobacco farmer had long felt that no matter how good his crop, no matter how carefully cured, the reward for his labors was controlled down to the last penny by the buyers for the Grand Columbian. It was an old grudge. And now with the giant humbled and forced to divide its strength, the grudge began to break out—not in any concentrated or effective force, but in little spurts of unrelated violence. In the next county some storage warehouses used by the Grand Columbian were burned to the ground. Rumors of a band of masked horsemen were reported from various parts of the countryside. There was talk of night riders like they had had in Kentucky not so long ago. The farmers gathered on the farmhouse porches in the hot evenings and talked. They talked in bitter little knots about the warehouses in Kingsmont when they came to town for supplies.

In Kingsmont there were echoes of all this. Crude invective was discovered painted across the sides of warehouses belonging to the company. It extended itself even to the disfiguring of the sidewalk in front of the Lawson & Royle building. The police force had its hands full with gangs of hoodlums from the oven of Jamaica, out of the tenements and the rows of squalid little boxes where the factory workers existed. A rock smashed into the parlor window of the Royle home on Elm Street one night and Sam began getting threatening letters. It was all fretful, uncomfortable, and potentially dangerous. Sam, in mild hysteria, closed up the house and hurriedly sent Berta off with a nurse and the baby to stay at an old and fashionable watering place in West Virginia. Characteristically he remained in Kingsmont, but it was in the comparative safety of the hotel, where he had to expose himself for only a hundred yards or so in order to reach the store. Mrs. Marston would not have Berta going off by herself. She and Mr. Marston went along to West Virginia. And so things went until the middle of August.

On August 12 the peace protocol was signed with Spain and on the thirteenth Manila was taken by the United States forces. The news did not get to Kingsmont until a day or so later, but the city was flooded with excitement. The recent troubles were forgotten in a spontaneous outburst of enthusiasm. There were impromptu parades. Bunting broke out on the store fronts. The old Grange band and the new firemen's band joined to supply a musical din at a big rally and speechmaking. It was held in the courthouse square on the evening of the fifteenth. It was a noisy and enthusiastic occasion and everyone felt exhausted and relieved by it.

The following day Brant Royle arrived from Washington. And it was characteristic of the kind of shrewd arrogance that had become a dominant trait in him that he did not slip in unheralded. It would have been understandable if he had, since he and the Grand Columbian had been receiving such a drubbing in the public eye. But he arrived full-panoplied on the train, accompanied by a large party of officials and guests. His attitude was that of a completely successful man. With that lightning change of manner—also characteristic of him—he was all enthusiastic joviality, loud in his talk, joining in the spirit of the town's celebration as though he himself were the author of it. He entertained the Mayor that evening at a sumptuous dinner given in the hotel dining room. At it he announced that the Grand Columbian (and he accompanied his use of the name with enough innuendoes to set his listeners roaring) would like to show its appreciation for a long and mutually profitable life in Kingsmont and the county by making the opening of the market at the end of the month the brightest and most memorable in years. Let every man, woman, and child who could get to Kingsmont on August 30—the date of the opening—prepare to have himself a time as guest of the tobacco companies who had found a home in Kingsmont. There would be a king and a queen of tobacco elected by popular vote. On the day of the opening there would be a big free barbecue, followed in the evening by the biggest dance ever held in the section, to be staged in one of the company warehouses. He was roundly applauded, and by morning the news was everywhere. It was announced by word of mouth as well as by innumerable placards nailed on posts, barn sides, store windows, the county over. You could not escape it even in barbershops and saloons—this omnipresent announcement. The surrounding countryside developed a fever of anticipation. Preparations and plans galore. People coming down from Richmond and Danville. People coming down from Raleigh. The opening of the market had traditionally been an exciting time, but this year it was accompanied by an even more gala and festive atmosphere. And all because of Brant Royle. They had received him back into their bosoms after the summer storm. One would never have known that a week or so before his name was anathema and the subject of censure on practically every tongue. But they had forgotten—or never recognized—that Brant, whatever else he was, was no fool. He was managing them and public opinion with the intuitive hand of genius, the knowing opportunism, that had marked his rise from the beginning. He knew them. After all, he had been one of them for a long time. The rumor that this year's crop would command the highest price known in a dozen years washed like a healing balm over all men. Everything, every sin of the past, was forgiven and forgotten in that alone. And no one would ever know whether it was just sheer luck or whether Brant had planned it so that this new turn in affairs rode the crest of high spirits engendered by the news of the war. But it crescendoed daily from the excitement on a mounting wave of good feeling.

No one ever thought to connect, either, the little notice that appeared on the back page of the *Herald* three weeks before the Spanish-victory celebration. It modestly announced that the Singleton-Barton nuptials would be held at the home of the bride on Hill Street on August 30. It was also the day set for the opening of the market and the Grand Columbian tobacco festival.

But Brant had known. The *Kingsmont Herald* was sent him

daily wherever he was. And it was a mark of both his particular genius and his capacity for relentless vindictiveness that he was capable of planning the Grand Columbian's popular action to coincide with and cover the effect of something that was purely personal to him alone.

People began to pour into town some days before the event of the opening. The hotels were crowded, every spare room was filled, and farmers and their families were sleeping in warehouses or in big wagon encampments at the edge of town. Among the fashionable houses out along Bay Street there was held a series of social functions attended by a dazzling array of prominent names in the state. Brant continued to be omnipresent, in the same energetic spirits with which he had descended upon the town. He was indefatigable. Surrounded by a coterie, he personally conducted notables through the big Royle factories, through the warehouses, delighted hostesses by his sudden appearance, attended to all the preparations for the barbecue and the ball.

The night before the big day he stayed up until dawn superintending the decorations being put up in Warehouse 81—the largest in Kingsmont, a wide flat building that roofed nearly three acres of floor. Betweentimes he went out to the big loading lot next to the warehouse to see how the barbecue cooking was progressing. Long shallow pits had been dug across one side of the yard. They glowed infernally from a constantly replenished bed of hickory coals shoveled along their bottoms. Over them, spread on frames, hung the crisping carcasses of sixteen prime hogs, four sheep, and three steers. Presiding about the edges of the pits was a little band of Negro cooks and attendants, their faces and bare torsos gleaming with sweat. They squatted, turned a frame, or swabbed a carcass with basting liquid applied with a piece of cloth wrapped at the end of a long stick. They jogged to and fro between the pits and a row of cutting tables that had been set up nearby. They laughed, they shouted, they sang. In the wide yard, under the velvety August night, it was like the scene of some ancient sacrificial rite, barbaric and splendid. There was a crowd of onlookers—white as well as black—that swelled and diminished as the night progressed. And over it all drifted in warm waves the succulent, smoky odor of roasting meat, redolent of vinegar and pepper. Brant walked about like an emperor, pausing to speak with one of the cooks or stopping to accept a tidbit handed him at the end of a long fork. He appeared to be enjoying himself immensely. They all watched him, the eyes in the shadows following him. There walked ol' Brant Royle hisself!

August 30 dawned hot and clear to the sound of tobacco vans still rolling in from the countryside. They clogged the streets and stood hub to hub about the warehouses down in Jamaica Town.

Never in all the history of the county—in spite of the short crop—had there been such an opening! The Kingsmont police force, struggling to clear the traffic for the parade at noon, agreed fervently and blasphemously. Mayor Roberts had acted as auctioneer for the first row of piled baskets. Perspiring and chanting away very creditably, as everyone present agreed. They congratulated him. He had started things off auspiciously by selling some prime lugs at an all-time high price of forty cents a pound. The information flew swiftly along the grapevine to the farmers waiting at the other warehouses. A frenzy of happy anticipation possessed them. They danced in the streets, where fiddles and guitars held forth at crossings. They crowded the saloons. It began to have somewhat the air of a rustic, sweaty, denimed saturnalia.

At noon they swarmed to the square to witness the crowning of the king and queen of the occasion. This royalty had supposedly been chosen by a poll conducted the preceding week throughout the county. The king was none other than the son of the sheriff —a grinning, embarrassed young man on the eve of setting off for his first year at the state university. The queen was—and no one was particularly surprised—the youngest daughter of Congressman Everett, Miss Mary Lou Everett. She was a rather plump, poutingly pretty young lady, whose golden coronation dress (by courtesy of Lawson & Royle) was richly appliquéd with rhinestone tobacco leaves. She looked very like an encrusted, mustard-colored dumpling standing on the courthouse steps. But no one cared. Everyone cheered and applauded wildly. When the Mayor made a long incomprehensible oration—in which "the grreeat staate of North Carolina," "the mahv'lous bounty and beauty of bright leaf tobacco," and "the magnificent benefactor of this city and this county, Mr. Brant Royle!" were inextricably mixed in about equal portions—they all applauded vociferously again. Then the combined Grange and firemen's bands began to play. The king escorted the queen to the throne on a huge loading dray pulled by four stolid Percherons. It had been converted for the occasion into a float suitably decorated with huge papier-mâché tobacco leaves. It was followed by two lesser floats. Headed by the band, this procession made its glittering and festive way twice around the square to the accompaniment of enthusiastic applause. Turning down West Street, it was accompanied by a great milling crowd, which threatened to attain suffocating proportions before Warehouse 81, the goal, was reached. But reach it they did in spite of the blazing heat and the crowd.

At Warehouse 81 the floats and their inhabitants were instantly forgotten in the rush for the yard and the barbecue. In spite of the numbers the gathering was reasonably orderly as all pressed about the long row of tables laden with hot biscuits, tubs of barbecue, platters of pickles, and bowls of tongue-searing sauce. With stuffed mouths, the crowd shouted and laughed and clapped one another on the back. The yard was a bedlam of masculine bellows, women's shrill shrieks, and the piercing yells of children. Brant along with the king and queen and a hundred-odd specially honored guests lunched at a table in the comparative privacy of the warehouse. Although he had been up most of the night, Brant still presided over the conversation with undiminished energy. He laughed uproariously, gave orders to the servants, was gallant to the Mayor's wife sitting on his left, and to Mrs. Marston opposite him. He was the center of all eyes. He was still the kingpin. If any had thought otherwise, they ceased to think so then. They were fascinated by him. In different ways, they were all still afraid of him.

By three o'clock the barbecue was over. The guests went away to rest and to prepare for the evening's festivities. Brant remained to consult with the nervous caterers from Richmond and with the leaders of the two orchestras engaged to play for the ball.

Outside a sated quiet fell over the big yard. The street was still thronged, but with a subdued humanity. They squatted in rows and clots against the sides of buildings, sprawled along the curbs, among the wagons, chewing ruminatively and spitting on the cobbles. A drowsy hum of contentment rose over them. The tired Negroes, still grinning, were clearing away the debris and the remains of the feast. From the open door of a warehouse came the long, keening, continuous chant of an auctioneer. It was a reassuring, familiar sound, a sound of harvest and accomplishment resting goldenly in the ears of all. The sales were continuing.

At eight in the evening carriages and surreys began to draw up at the Rice Street entrance to Warehouse 81. The tired farmers with their families, factory workers, and grinning Negroes crowded to watch. Like children they enjoyed the sight of the fancy people with candid, open-mouthed pleasure. Lights blazed from the building. The scrape of fiddles and a nervous trial cornet cadenza shrilled forth. There was no resentment in the crowd watching these privileged and special guests—the finery, the pretty ladies, the smartly tailored young men, the dowagers and the dignified, portly gentlemen. They felt only delight in the scene. Anyway, they were invited guests to this party, too. It was for everybody. And after a while—some of them with bravado, others sheepishly—they began to drift into the vast shed, to line themselves shyly along the walls or to promenade in and out among the long wooden colonnades.

By nine o'clock—with the guests still streaming in—the warehouse presented a brilliant spectacle. Brant had arranged that an orchestra at one end of the floor play only square dances, breakdowns, and polkas. At the opposite end was another orchestra. Its members in tail coats, the conductor with white gloves, playing in a rather watered-down style some figure dances, but for the greater part of the evening saccharine waltzes. Here the special guests assembled. Chairs were provided along the walls for the less active and more mature, those who wanted only to look on and gossip. The refreshment at this end of the building, provided at a table covered with damask and centered by a huge silver bowl, was champagne punch. Over the huge floor hung swaths of white and yellow bunting. It was twisted in spirals about each pillar and hung in streamers from the rows of suspended lights that illuminated the scene.

There was no conflict between the two centers of activity. Brant had arranged that the orchestras alternate throughout the evening. Consequently, there was no feeling of division or any self-consciousness between the two groups. Early in the evening members of the amorphous group of factory workers and young farmers drifted up to watch the notables. They mingled, and no one tried to make them feel out of place. In a like fashion some of the town's young blades and one or two of their more daring young ladies slipped away in the general melee, from under the lulled eyes of mamas and other chaperonage, to join enthusiastically in a square dance at the other end of the building. There was a rising roar of coming and going, of conversation, music, and perspiring energy. All of it was saturated, soaked through and through, perfumed, with the departed presence of the new tobacco sold on the floor that morning. By eleven the festivities had reached zenith and showed little signs of abating. Everyone present was having a fine time and showing it. That is, everyone except perhaps the host of the occasion, Brant Royle.

But no one knew that but Brant.

3

He was standing by the refreshment table. Earlier he had circulated among his guests, greeting them as they entered, stopping to chat with those whom he knew best. He had taken a position where he could be seen and where he could watch the dance floor. Then they had come to him—the aldermen, the bankers, the postmaster, the warehousemen, with their wives and families. The daughters, bright-eyed, bridling young fillies, the sons going up North to school or receiving their degrees next spring. Grave, hopeful striplings, stiff and sweaty in their finery and purple, with self-consciousness here in the presence of *Mr.* Brant Royle. He smiled and bowed and could not tell where one presentation left off and the next began. But it didn't matter. He wasn't even seeing any of them or talking to them. Finally he began to realize that Mayor and Mrs. Roberts—

311

like a pair of identical pouter pigeons—had been standing quite a long time engaged in what they thought was an animated conversation with him. Brant stood monumental and grave in his evening clothes. They were not only well cut but they suited the added weight that had come on him during the past few years.

"An eminently successful celebration, Mr. Royle," shouted the Mayor above the amiable din, "eminently successful! Thanks to your acumen and generosity, they'll be talking about it for months."

"I think the idea of a king and queen of tobacco was just wonderful, Mr. Brant," shrieked Mrs. Roberts, interrupting her spouse and continuing to look brightly and greedily about her. "How on earth did you ever think of such a thing!"

The Mayor mopped his pate, smiled at his wife, and ignored the interruption.

"You know, I've been thinking, Mr. Royle, that this would be a fine way to start every market opening. Get things off to a fine start—good psychology, good business, y'know. Now why couldn't we get together with the warehouse association and the merchants every year and organize to advertise and finance—"

Brant cocked his head slightly and thrust his unlighted cigar into his mouth. He was not hearing the Mayor. He looked grave, pleasant, attentive—as he had all evening. But his eyes and his thoughts plunged with bitterness under the low ceiling and over this scene of his own making. Who were all of these bright figures? He had the feeling that while they were mannequins of his own creation—clean blue denim, broadcloth, or mousseline de soie—every one of them was tainted with his factory smoke, the clamor of his machines, shaped by the golden weed that he had grasped and held to a purpose. They were all strangers to him. It was not a new realization. He cried silently against it now. Why always, in the midst of his arrogant sense of accomplishment, must there be this feeling of bafflement, of loss? Here in the midst of the trappings of acknowledged adulation and success he had to face again the fact that he had once more merely surrounded his private failure with common symbols of grandeur. And he knew that always till his dying day he must continue that maddened, frustrated pursuit of phantoms. The white house . . . Margaret . . . Pete Henry . . .

He heard Mayor Roberts's voice—that minion, that fat and silly little man—coming to him insistently. He looked at the man almost with surprise. Could he continue like this till doomsday? Brant began to search for some convenient platitude. But he was saved. Someone touched his arm. He turned savagely, jerking the cigar from his mouth. It was one of the waiters.

"Beg pahdon, Mr. Royle—sorry to interrupt you, suh. Yoh carriage man jes' sent in word he would like to see you."

312

"Where is he?" Brant replaced the cigar carefully, as though his mouth was tender.

"He's waitin' outside the office doah. . . . If you'll come this way, suh—"

He felt cold and still. He had been waiting for this all evening. But he could not help but feel rise in him a senseless anger against the messenger. He held himself tightly together. He bowed to the Mayor and Mrs. Roberts.

"If you will excuse me."

"Of course, Mr. Royle, of course." They murmured and bobbed in unison.

Brant turned and plunged back of the milling crowd. He made his way heedlessly along the wall to the door leading to the business part of the building a few feet away. The office was empty, although the light of the warehouse came through the glass panes of the partition. It gleamed palely on the tops of tables and desks, cabinets—all the dusty office impedimenta. Impatiently he crossed to the street door. He put his hand on the knob and stopped. He felt a vast reluctance to open that door. He waited, breathing heavily, and then with an abrupt movement flung it open. It was cooler outside. Above and below him there was movement in the street. But here was a little space, a little island of darkness and privacy, hidden and separated from all interest and attention. Maryland was no fool. Maryland had always known. The tall black bulk of the big Negro confronted him now, waiting respectfully on the sidewalk below. Neither could see the face of the other. They stood in silence for a long moment.

"Well?" rumbled Brant at last in a bitter voice.

Maryland bobbed his head—a black outline moving slightly in recognition.

"I waited around till it was all ovuh like you said." Maryland's voice came to him soft, diffident. "There was only foah carriages of folks that went with them when they left the house, an' one of them turn off 'foh they got to the depot. I think it was the preacher."

"Never mind," said Brant, "did you find out where they were going?"

What did it matter where they were going? he thought, in the extreme of agony. She was gone. All of it was gone . . . all of it had been gone far beyond him since before he was born.

"I hung around after the northbound pulled out with them on it," continued Maryland's voice mildly out of the darkness. "I hung around and talked to Mr. Jim Bell in the baggage room. He said they was checked through to Washington, but he didn't know how much further they was goin'—an' I didn't dast go right up an' ast Mr. Renfrew in the office."

313

"All right, all right!" said Brant harshly, cutting him off impatiently. He waited a moment and then went on almost in a tone of pleading, "Did you see them—while they were waiting?"

He felt that this question implied some further degradation, some further crawling abasement in himself that he could not prevent. The wound was open, raw, and bleeding, and he must rub salt in it in spite of himself.

"Yassuh," came the Negro's voice, so quiet, so gentle. "That part was real easy, Mr. Brant. I stopped the carriage right up against the platform where I could see them standin' there real easy without gettin' out. Wasn't more than two or three other folks gettin' on the train tonight an' they mostly stayed in the waitin' room, so you could tell jes' who was in the pahty. They stood out there on the platform under the light—with 'bout five or six others. I couldn' tell jes' who —except Mis' Berta's ma. She was there, an' foh a while I was sure she would see me sittin' there—but she didn't—" Maryland paused to chuckle—"she was too busy talkin'—you know Mis' Marston!"

Brant felt a black hatred rise in him at the mention of that bustling female who paraded about on the fringe of his life in the house on Elm Street. So that was why she was so noticeably late to the festivities tonight. He would not forgive her easily for this—the meddling old harridan!

"I'm not interested in Mrs. Marston," he said, biting the cigar almost in two.

Maryland was silent, and then continued: "Mighty little celebratin' foh a weddin' far as I could see."

"Never mind. How did the bride"—Brant faltered on the word, then continued—"how did Mrs. Barton look?"

"Why, she look same as always, Mr. Brant, far as I could see. 'Course the light wasn't so good an' all. But she stood there still an' ladylike, you know. 'Ceptin' she wasn't holdin' onto the groom's arm like you would expect. An' Mr. Barton looked right scared an' long-faced to me. But you know how Mr. Barton always looks! An' they warn't sayin' nothin' to each other. Jes' listened to the others. Jes' standin' there all apart an' listenin' in. I declare—"

But Brant could not let him go on. This was more than enough. He felt as though he was out there in the shadows of the gutter writhing in the street's filth.

"All right, all right," he said in a choked voice. "You've told me enough. You've done all right. That's all I wanted to know."

He thrust his hand into his pocket and pulled out a bill—he didn't even care what denomination . . .

"Yassuh—thank you, suh!"

"Hang around here till Miss Berta and Mr. Sam want to go home. I'll walk back to the hotel."

Neither of them moved, although Brant had reached back for the doorknob behind him.

"When was the last time you were good and drunk, Maryland?" he said.

Maryland received this in silence, then giggled. "Why, I don' rightly know, Mr. Brant."

"How would you like to have some real high-class champagne— like they drink at weddings?"

"Why, I guess I'd like it all right, Mr. Brant."

"Then you go round to the door up there where they're mixin' the punch and tell 'em I said you're to have as much as you can put down straight out of the bottle. You hear me?"

"Yassuh!"

"This is a big night, Maryland—no damn reason why you shouldn't make somethin' of it too. Just be sure you don't take on so much you fall off the seat takin' Miss Berta home!"

"Nawsuh, Mr. Brant!"

Maryland waited docilely for the figure on the steps above him to move.

"Well, go on!" said Brant curtly. "What are you waitin' for?"

"Much oblige, Mr. Brant, much oblige," Maryland protested in a whisper, and backed off. There was the old frightening note in that voice. The tone that could always make him shiver and tremble inside his skin. He did not want to hear more of it. He turned and went rapidly toward the warm light pouring from the doorway a few feet away.

CHAPTER SEVENTEEN

I

It was almost eleven o'clock. The long inky canyon of Broadway glistening with wet pavement stretched before him. At intervals an erratic raw wind burst about the corners and rattled the signs, throwing little gushes of rain vindictively upon impersonal sidewalk and defenseless creatures—human and animal alike. He could see the cab horse's head drooping resignedly under the oilcloth. It was an attitude that irritated him. He could not look at it. He himself didn't mind the weather. To hell with it. What did a little rain more or less matter? He had made the cabman remove the weather curtains from the front because he wanted to see. Besides, it suffocated him to sit back in the hansom's close odor of carriage polish, dankness, and faint perfume—ghostly effluvia of past fares.

How many times during the past hour or so had he regretted

315

the impulse that had brought him all the way up town from the dinner and the late meeting with the directors down on Wall Street? Because it had been an impulse, pure and simple. When he had come out of the offices he had intended going back to his apartment, but he had ordered the cabman—refusing other offers to take him where he willed—to drive up Broadway to the Blackwood Theater at the corner of Twenty-fourth Street. He knew then that he couldn't face going back to his rooms. He had to see Sonie. It was strange how through all the complexity of this tumultuous autumn his thoughts had irrelevantly returned to her. There was no reason for it. He had seen her only once or twice since they had talked in the office that November morning in Kingsmont almost a year ago. That meeting had ended on a strange note of restraint. Nothing at all like the old familiar warm tumult of struggle that had been the life of their relationship for so many years. This was something cool and separating, as though they had not only grown apart, but each had become a different person. He hadn't thought about it much then.

Nor had it worried him when he had come up briefly for the opening of Sonie's show, *The Girl from U.S.A.* He had been too preoccupied. Now, after the big boys in Washington had brought the bludgeon down, forced him to unmake, unravel, disperse, his web, it was the only satisfaction that he gleaned from it. Because he was the only one who knew how they had been *forced* to let him do what they had commanded done. Now he felt exhausted, empty and bruised, with a pointless and seething rebellion washing about inside him. He had no one to turn to. Not one damned soul—and that was what hurt worst of all. Now he found himself on a foul night skulking at the curb across the street from the theater where Sonie was playing in her new comedy *The Countess from Elm City*. He felt vaguely that it must have been running for a couple of months now, and he hadn't even seen it. Hadn't even troubled to see it, often as he had been in town this fall. He couldn't even remember if he had telegraphed her on the opening or if Banks had remembered for him, and had sent flowers. Well, the theater and all that fancy glitter had never been his meat exactly. But here he was on a rainy fall night waiting in a common hansom cab—not even able to bring himself to go inside to wait—crouched against the worn leather, the rug over his knees, his bowler pulled down low over his forehead, his teeth clamped on a cigar (the third since he had stepped into the cab)—just stubbornly, blindly waiting for the doors under the marquee to open and the crowd to spill out into the street.

Across the street a line of hansoms and curtained phaetons had begun to form during the past quarter of an hour. He grunted. It couldn't be long now. A policeman, his buttons gleaming, the tall, rounded helmet glistening wetly, strolled up, paused to lean from the

316

curb and caress the bowed head of the horse. He called something unintelligible up to Brant's cabman. They began to talk. This warm and simple exchange, outside and beyond him, Brant found unendurable. He started to knock on the little roof trap and order his driver to go around the block again. But at that moment he saw a stir under the marquee across the street. People began to gush out and there was immediate confusion around the carriages. Well, it was over at last! He threw the rug off his knees and dug awkwardly into his pocket for his wallet. Finding it, he banged on the trap. It opened.

"Yes, sir?" The cabman was a head and a hat in outline.

"Here," said Brant brusquely, and handed him a bill. "I'm getting out now. Don't bother about the change."

"Thank'y, sir!"

Brant opened the gate and stepped down into the street. He started across, stepping heavily and erratically. Midway he had to pause when a carriage pulled out from the line and cut across in front of him. Standing there he swayed a little and the lights on the marquee swirled crazily for a moment.

By God, he thought, I *am* drunk!

2

He was in a black rage when he finally got into the dressing-room corridor, rudely pushing through human bodies. Figures—men and women—who giggled or uttered exclamations and hurried on past him. The air was close and dusty and sweet, full of the sound of voices and the opening and closing of doors. He felt damp about the shoulders. A little rain coursed down his nose. He suddenly hated it all, and most of all himself being there in it. That fool at the door had wanted to make him wait while he sent in a message to Miss Leonard. *Miss Leonard!* Hell, he could never get used to this fancy business of people on the stage changing their names. What was the matter with Lipik? But he hadn't stopped to argue. He didn't want to make a scene there at the stage door in front of all that gaping, ratty crowd of hangers-on.

"Miss Leonard is expecting me," he had kept saying. But it was the five-dollar bill that did it. You could get through most of the world's doors if you had five dollars. That was one thing he had learned that he had never had to unlearn. And if power was all he would gain from it, he still had *that*. That they never could take completely from him. He had been solacing himself fiercely with that knowledge, because now he knew he had little else.

He stood in front of the door, not hesitating, but just standing, recalling where he was with a certain surprise. Some of the anger

317

was draining out of him. He felt tired but a little eager as he read the plain lettering painted there. *Miss Leonard.* That was all. He almost grinned then. He did shrug his shoulders. He turned, removed the bowler, and smoothed his hair. He thought ruefully, I'm gettin' a little thin on top. Then he rapped with his knuckles on the door. In a moment it was opened a crack. A sharp female face with bright bird's eyes and a maid's cap set precariously on tight mouse-colored curls confronted him. A warm wave of perfume and femininity breathed out upon him from the room. He heard a man speaking and then another man laugh, an intimate sound of amusement.

"Yes, *sir*?" The maid's voice was as pert as the cap.

"I want to see Miss *Leonard*," he said, flatly emphasizing the name as he removed the cigar from his mouth. The voices within grew silent. The maid continued to look at him.

"Who is it, Lise?" It was Sonie's voice, husky, warm, unchanged.

"It's me, Sonie—Brant."

There was another pause. Then the door was flung open, the maid pushed aside, and Sonie stood there before him in a bright-green dressing robe, her face vivid with make-up, her red hair piled up out of the way. She seized him by both arms and drew him in.

"Brant!" she cried, looking up at him. The maid closed the door behind them. He felt suddenly hot and close. It was a disorderly room. A littered dressing table with a mirror and lights crowded one wall. Some glittering costumes were flung about over chairs and on a screen across one corner. There were two other gentlemen present. One, a heavy dark middle-aged man, had a sagging olive-colored face and a little fringe of curly black hair about a glistening pate. He sat forward on one of the chairs, leaning over a frail cane that stood between his fat thighs. The other was younger, slim, elegant, with a kind of weak blond handsomeness. He lolled carelessly against a corner of the dressing table and turned a hairbrush over and over between his hands. The two of them looked at Brant. One pair of sharp black eyes in folds of flesh, one pair of pale-gray ones. Brant looked from them down at Sonie. Her face was animated but inscrutable. It was warm with the excitement of seeing him—that he felt—but it seemed withdrawn. She started to say something impetuously and then seemed to think better of it, and began again.

"Well, I must say this is a surprise, Mr. Royle." Head on one side, she looked at him mockingly and then turned to the other two. "Brant, this is Mr. Ellers, our producer." The dark fat man in the chair nodded and blinked his pig eyes.

"How d'y do, Mr. Royle," he said in a thick, breathless voice.

"And this," said Sonie, grinning toward the young man with the brush, "is Mr. Talbot Graham."

318

Mr. Graham set down the brush and came over with an extended hand to Brant. He smiled pleasantly.

"I don't think you remember me, Mr. Royle, but I had the pleasure, I believe, about a year ago when *The Girl from U.S.A.* opened."

Brant shook his hand. It was a weak, tense, nervous hand. He remembered now. One of that crowd of tony society fellows who had attached themselves to Sonie and had been present at the supper at Rector's. . . .

"Sure—Mr. Graham," he said, and released the hand.

"Sit down, Brant."

Sonie took a costume off a chair and threw it to the little maid, who was busily hanging up things in the corner. Brant did not move. He watched her sit down before the mirror again and then catch his eyes in the reflection. It was a curious glance. Puzzled, cool, strange. Not like Sonie at all. It wasn't exactly what he had come for, and because it wasn't he brushed it aside stubbornly.

He had a sharp sense of his intrusion, of his being out of place. Sonie belonged to these people now. Not to him. And they were all inhabitants of still another world, and looked secretive, superior, looking upon him with condescension. The slim Mr. Graham had moved back to the side of the mirror and picked up the brush again. It was an oddly familiar and intimate gesture. He looked perfectly at home. The dark fat man had settled back in the chair. He regarded Brant speculatively from beneath half-lowered lids.

"Maybe I shouldn't have come bustin' in here like this tonight without warning," said Brant, looking straight at Sonie's face in the mirror. She was unscrewing the lid from one of the many little jars before her. She stopped.

"Oh go on, Brant!—don't bother for a minute. I'm tickled pink to see you. It's been a long time, you know." She unscrewed the top and gestured with it toward the other two men. "As for bustin' in—well, Saul there has just dropped in to report on business as usual, and Tal is waiting to take me out to supper. That's all."

She shrugged and dug into the jar with her fingers and began to plaster grease on her face.

"Sonie," said Brant, still looking at her, "I'd like to talk to you for just a few minutes. I won't take up much of your time." .

His voice was harsh, almost pleading. He felt then that he did not mind being a suppliant. His stubbornness was greater than any pride. The green eyes looked swiftly at him from the frames of mascara.

"Sure, Brant, make yourself at home."

"I want to talk to *you*, Sonie."

Her hand paused against her cheek and a glance passed between

319

her and the slim Mr. Graham leaning above her. She shrugged, ever so slightly.

"Of course, Brant," she said coolly, and swung in her chair to the others. "You don't mind, Saul—Tal? Mr. Royle is an old friend."

"Sure, sweetheart," said the fat Mr. Ellers as he rose to his feet. "After all, I ain't got no bizness sittin' around like this. I oughta have been uptown half-hour ago. That fool Mason's got another play he wants to read to me at his hotel. Well, what a life it is!" He sighed and patted Sonie's shoulder. "Good night, sweetheart, you did pretty tonight. Saul was pleased. Saul is always pleased with his sweetheart, though.

"Pleased to have seen you, Mr. Royle," he said in his thick breathy voice. He thrust the cane under his arm, nodded, and pushing a rather oversized bowler low over his forehead, covering the shining dome, went out into the hall. The slim young gentleman watched this exit blandly, then straightened himself with a studied movement, reset his lapels, and picking up an expensive-looking gray hat from a chair behind him, walked to the door.

"It was a pleasure, Mr. Royle." Coolly he looked at Brant.

"Thanks," said Brant, trying with all his soul not to burst out at him—at all of them.

"Sonie," said Mr. Graham in the doorway, "I'll have a cab ready and I'll wait down the hall. Either with Perkins at the door, or in Bob's dressing room—when you're ready."

"All right, Tal," she said, busy at the mirror again. "In about ten minutes."

Mr. Graham withdrew, and with his going a heavy silence fell over the room. Brant did not move. He stood looking first at Sonie's back and then at the maid in the corner. Sonie noticed this at last.

"Oh," she grunted, and the mockery was there again. "Lise—"

"Yes, mum?"

"Take the blue sequin dress from the second act down to Mrs. Redding's and see what she can do about that hook."

"Yes, mum."

"And Lise, don't hurry back."

She caught the maid's bright eyes in the mirror again and they looked at each other with quick understanding.

"Yes, mum!"

The door closed and the little room fell silent again. Brant felt suddenly stifled by its closeness. He walked heavily to the chair beside the table and sat down. It was still warm from its recent occupant. He settled into it, wearily, but not at ease. There was no ease at all, and he desperately sought ease now. He had to have it, as a starving man needs food. It was why he had come. He looked at

320

Sonie, the square profile with the fine short nose, still provocatively tiptilted. Time had been good to her. It could not change or efface her essential bright strength. He was both gladdened by the realization and flooded with a sense of poignancy as he sat there looking at her. He needed that hard, independent, honest strength.

"Well, Brant?"

She did not turn to him but went on removing the make-up from her face with swift, practiced gestures.

"You're not very glad to see me, Sonie."

"It's been a long time, Brant. I've got out of the habit."

"I've been pretty busy, Sonie."

She smiled faintly then, but still did not turn to him. "You always have been, Brant—as long as I have known you."

"All right," he said. "I didn't come to fight with you. . . . You're looking mighty well."

"Never felt better. Wish I could say the same for you. You're not looking well at all."

It warmed him profoundly to hear her coming back at him. It had been a long time and she—like so many things—had drifted nearly out of his sight. But here she was still as he always had known her.

"I guess you're right," he admitted. "I haven't felt too well."

"You can't expect everything to hold out forever, Brant Royle," she said, working with her hair. The flash of those white arms made him remember other times buried in a past so distant now that it might have happened to another man. The milky elbows evoked a feeling of intimacy which he realized was no longer true here tonight. It was just the appearance of intimacy.

"You've spent yourself pretty freely always. It was bound to catch up with you," she continued dispassionately. "When did you get into town?"

"Last week. Came up from Washington."

She started to say something and then stopped, letting her arms drop. Picking up a hand mirror, she turned toward him, looking at her hair. The green dressing gown was cut low at the neck and it fitted her still trim figure beautifully, rounding over the firm and generous bosom. He looked at it with frank admiration.

"Well, they got you across the barrel at last, didn't they?" She raised an eyebrow at her image in the mirror.

He flushed at the implications of this. It made him a little angry, but he delighted in it. She had always done this to him. No one else had ever dared. And it was for that, too, that he had come tonight.

"You've been reading the papers too," he said.

She dropped the mirror then and looked squarely at him.

"It's the only way I've kept touch for a long time, Brant, with what you have been doing. You know I've always had an interest in you one way or another." She chuckled then, the good, friendly, remembered sound. "And you've never been—heaven knows!—very free with information to anyone, friend or enemy."

"I guess not. But I didn't come here to talk about that, Sonie. That's all over now. Through, done. They ganged up on me there in Washington, and they've won—for the time being, anyway. But they don't know me. The world's a whole lot bigger than this country. I've just started."

He stopped. She was looking at him curiously again, as though she only half heard what he was saying.

"You've been drinking, Brant," she said flatly, and shook her head.

He nodded and glowered at the bowler lying in his lap. "A little —but why the hell not?"

"Nothing." She shrugged and got up. "Seems like old times, you know. That's all. You always hit the bottle when things got too thick for you. Or have you forgotten that too?"

She moved beyond him and went behind the screen.

"No," he admitted, still looking at his hat. He could hear her dressing. She was hitting him hard. He was not going to let it break him up in anger. He had to keep reminding himself that there was not time for that. Neither of them spoke for a long time.

"How are things back home?" she asked suddenly, her voice bright and distant behind the screen.

"Oh, humming along, humming along," he replied. "They had a big market this year. You should have been there. Big doin's, big celebration."

"I read about it. I *do* miss it at the end of summer. Get an itch to be back there every year—and then somehow I don't go. I don't know why I keep the house any more. Just silly sentimentality, I guess. . . . How're Sam and Mrs. Sam?"

"Oh, fine, I guess. I didn't see very much of them. I lived at the hotel this year."

"Oh?" He could almost see her eyebrows go up. "Well, I've often wondered how long you were going to be able to put up with that. . . . I heard from Chris about a month ago—just after the opening of the new show. He seems to be doing all right out there in China. Likes the life. He said I would, too. Wants me to come look over the Orient with him when I get tired of the theater. You know Chris."

"Yes, Chris has done all right for himself. Done a damned fine job for the company, too."

"He sounded happy anyway," she said casually. He could hear her struggling with some garment. "He didn't have much to say about the tobacco business."

"Well, in spite of all the fool laws they've thought up to keep a man from gettin' too big here," he said bitterly, "there's a wide field out there for a lively man and the tobacco business. I'm going out to look over things myself."

No sound came from behind the screen for a moment. "You—you're going to China?" She asked it almost too deliberately.

"Yeah," he said. "I should have gone months ago if it hadn't been for this damned trial and the reorganization of the business. We've got those British boys on the run out there."

"When are you leaving?" she said in the careful voice.

"Tomorrow. Chicago, then San Francisco. Ship from there."

He was speaking more carefully than he had ever spoken to her. But he felt so tired, so drained, so deeply filled with desperation, that he dared not do otherwise. Through all that they had been saying he had not once felt that he was really talking to someone he knew. He waited a minute and then continued very quietly.

"Why don't you come along with me, Sonie?" He rubbed his hand hard against his thigh, watching it move up and down. "Why don't you drop all this play-acting? We could have a good time together. It's been a long time since we've been together, y'know." He paused for breath and then went on almost as though afraid she would say something before he finished. "I need to get away from here for a while. See some new places—do you know I've never been anywhere in the States except where there was a tobacco factory? Well, I'm sick of the States—I'm sick of this damned regulating Government messin' into everything an' legally lynchin' any business setup that organizes more efficiently than it does, I'm sick of Kingsmont and the whole damned tobacco business. I need to go where they'll let me breathe without passing a law against me. A new place with new problems that a man can face and handle." All the rage in him that had boiled for weeks seemed to catch him in the throat then. It did not speak of the bruise and the hurt, but it helped. He snorted a little half-bark of laughter. "You know I know lots of folks, Sonie. Millions of 'em. They think I'm still a big man—yeah, millions of 'em, because I've buttered their bread good for 'em. But there's not one of 'em I know who I'd ask to come along with me, just for *me*—except you, Sonie."

He waited. Then he heard her come up behind him and stop. He raised his face to her, and his mouth was twisted in the little disparaging half-smile. Her face did not turn to him. She was looking behind him at the opposite wall. But the slant green eyes were wide and she suddenly looked very pale, the skin drawn tight across

323

the wide cheekbones. He could hear her breath come quickly as though she was straining against something. It was Sonie's face all right, but again he felt the steely removal.

"Ach, Brant!" she burst out suddenly and then she just looked full at him. He could read nothing from that look. The wide generous mouth closed on itself and he could see her biting the lower lip. She stepped in front of him suddenly with a swishing sound of skirts and turned her back on him. She began to pull at the hooks at the lower end of the placket open down the back. After a moment she muttered with vexation:

"Hook me up, Brant. You'll have to, since Lise isn't here."

He stood up and began to hook her up, almost humbly, his fingers awkward and fumbling. He didn't mind. He could feel the warmth of her, the tight straightness of her under the stays, and it moved a whole layer of his life into his memory. Little fragments of those old days together—the trips in the buckboard down the dusty county roads . . . their fights, their love-making . . . her room with the big oak bedstead smelling always faintly of kerosene and the heavy scent she had used. . . . There surged in him all the vigorous, demanding want of her that he had experienced then and had been away from so long. It would be good to bury himself, drug himself, in her again, to forget everything. He trembled when his fingers at the top hook pressed against the warm, naked skin of her back. . . . There had been other women—sure. Many of them. Faceless, meaningless bodies. But there had always been Sonie to come to when his need ran deepest.

He raised his eyes to her face in the mirror. She was looking at him with a queer expression, half-tormented. Something in it gave him a heady feeling of exultance. He placed his hands on either side of the trim waist—as trim as it had been eight years ago. He looked at her with the half-smile, questioning, waiting.

"This isn't just any trip I'm askin' you to go on, Sonie," he said softly. "I'm askin' you to marry me."

He dropped his mouth to her shoulder and kissed it lingeringly, and fiercely. But she twisted suddenly and rudely out of his grasp and turned to face him, her face white, the eyes narrowed and blazing. They confronted each other almost breast to breast and each was breathing heavily. Then she turned from him and began to pace up and down the short length of the room, one hand on her hip. She kicked some shoes out of the way. She looked as he had seen her many times when she was angry and upset. Even this did not bother him. He could deal with her anger. That was familiar. It was the coldness that made him feel strange and inadequate.

"Sit down, Brant," she said after a moment, and went on pacing. He lowered himself into the chair and waited. She stopped at one turn and looked at him again and shook her head. With one fist she struck against the side of her leg, as though she could not trust herself to speak. And then she went on walking up and down in silence. Suddenly she began to talk, her voice low, but sharp with emotion.

"Ach, Brant Royle! How angry I am with you at this moment! You are the biggest fool I have ever known—or the meanest. I cannot decide which."

"Sonie—"

"No. Keep quiet! Let me talk now. Maybe this isn't the place or the time to say it to you, but you have needed so long to hear it that I must before I change my mind. Ach, Brant, Brant—when you knocked on the door awhile ago and when you spoke, my heart turned clean over like it always has since the day you first spoke to me. You won't even remember, but it was in Mr. Weyman's warehouse . . . you won't remember a lot of things, because it isn't in you to remember a thing—unless it's meant something to you. I've waited a long time to see you. Sometimes I think I've spent half my life just waiting to see you and hear you speak. You didn't know that —or if you knew it you didn't care. I've never said this to any man and I may never say it again. But I was in love with you for a long time—maybe I still am. I used to like you because you were the biggest, strongest, meanest, stubbornest man I'd ever seen. You were going to get somewhere. I knew that from the moment I saw you. And when I saw you I said right then and there that you were the man for me and someday I'd make you admit it. Well, you got going all right. I helped you get going. But if I had it to do over again now you'd never get a red cent out of me, because the only reason you didn't ride roughshod over me as you have over everybody and everything else that got in your way is because I've had enough sense always to keep my head about me. And I've kept my pride too, although it's been hard at times over all these years. Because you favored me—sure—good little Sonie Lipik. You used to say I was a good gal, remember? I was convenient. I was around when you wanted a good row or someone you could have who you knew was on level ground with you. I've stood for a lot from you, Brant Royle, but all the time I kept telling myself there were good things in you. I let you drop me, forget me, pick me up as though nothing had happened. I used to be crazy with happiness when you would come back to me after a long time. Then after Sam got married, you remember I went away. I went and stayed away for a long time for a lot of reasons, and while I couldn't let myself admit it then, one of the biggest reasons was you."

She had stopped pacing and stood looking at him furiously. He sat in the chair not looking back now—just staring at the floor, his face gray and expressionless. My God, she thought, he's got old—

325

old. His hair is twice as gray as when I saw him last year. He looks sick. But this flash of compassion only fired her more. How many times had he been able to melt her without even knowing he did it. Not now! Her mouth drew down in scorn—whether at herself or him she could not tell at the moment.

"When I first saw you tonight," she went on in the tense, furious voice, spitting out the words, "it was just like it has always been when I first see you after a long time. But just for a minute. I knew I was free of you when you came into the room. That I would never have to bother about what you could do to me again—and you've done plenty. You've had your life. You've made it and gone after the things you really wanted, and got them. Well, I've made my life, too, and it doesn't mix with yours any more, Brant. You're not the same black-haired brute of a boy, and I'm not just little Sonie Lipik from those dirty 'Krainians down on Maple Street any more either, ready to come running when it pleased you. Oh, I've seen you do plenty of dirty things, all right, and I've heard of others that I could believe. They didn't use to matter very much to me, because you still had something in you that I loved with all my crazy heart. But you've killed that thing in you—the big, hungry, crazy thing in you —and what you are I don't know any more. I just know that I don't like it and will never like it. I tried to tell you when I saw you that time down at the factory, because when I came back from Europe I had hoped—as I have always hoped—that you would have found what you wanted and would be at peace at last. But you hadn't. You looked like someone who had been sick for so long that you couldn't do without the sickness. I knew then, but I didn't want to believe it. You see, I buried a lot of me in you those early days, Brant, and it hurt me to see what had happened to it. You'll always have that part of me. I couldn't get it back even if I wanted to now. . . . Who are you—who do you think you are that you think you can live in a world with people and have a heart all choked up with nothing but money or what you can do with money so that it doesn't even beat and run with blood any more, but is just a still thing inside you like a sick stone? You may know what's the matter with you and why you have made yourself into this, but you've never given anybody else who might have helped you a chance to know. Ach! no, no, *no*, Brant Royle, you had to do it *all by yourself!*"

Her face was white with fury as her last words spat out upon him. He looked up at her now with bloodshot eyes under the fierce brows.

"All right, Sonie, all right," he said in a quiet, hard voice.

She dropped into the chair before the dressing table and half-hid her face in one hand as though she had been spent. The storm in her as suddenly gone as it had come. They both sat in silence, each

326

hearing the other's breathing. It was not a catharsis, but a sound of loneliness and despair. Then she began to speak again in a hoarse, choked voice.

"I used to dream about the time when you would ask me to marry you—no, not even that, just ask me to come stay with you or go with where you were going. But you had to wait until now when there isn't anything left in me but being angry with you, and feeling through—completely through. I guess I knew it a long time ago—but I hadn't said it till tonight. I didn't think I could ever say it. No, Brant, thank you, but I won't marry you."

He put the dead, chewed cigar back into his mouth.

"All right, Sonie," he said. "Maybe everything you've said is so. I don't know, but there's no use talking about it any more. You know that as well as I do. And you know me well enough to know that when you've said *no* to any offer I make, I'm not the kind that will ever give you the opportunity to say it again."

"Yes," she said wearily, without rancor. She shrugged her shoulders and raised her head. "You never could forgive anything in anyone that stood against you or wouldn't give in to your almighty stubborn pride. That's what's the matter with you now, whether you know it or not. They've slapped you down, had you across the barrel, as I said awhile ago. You can't stand that. You never could. That's part of what's wrong with you—really wrong." She turned in her chair and sat upright looking squarely at him. He met her eyes for an instant and then dropped them.

"You know," she continued in the calm voice, almost gentle, as though warmly amused, "you don't *really* want to marry me. I'm telling you this because I know, if you don't. You see, Brant, it's no good. I'm playing second fiddle here as I always have when you thought I would make a good one. I've got pride, too—a terrible pride. As much as you have. And I never liked playing anything but first to anything. I haven't always been able to, but I haven't liked it and I kept on trying till I could find the place where I could. I'm not used to it any other way, when it was due me. I stopped being your second fiddle a long time ago. . . . You said a while back that I must read the papers. I do. I still get the *Kingsmont Herald*. I still have an interest in home. It's the way I keep up with what's going on with all the funny people there. Who's died and how they are liking the new electric trolley cars—*your* trolley cars. It may seem silly, but I like it. I also find out who is marrying whom. I saw a while ago—" she looked fixedly at him as though to force him to look back at her, but his glance was hard upon the bowler in his lap—"just a short notice—on the back page, I think—where our old friend Johnny Barton had, of all things, married ol' Major Jim's daughter, the one everyone talked about and didn't know anything about.

Well, Brant—" her voice was icy hard now—"I'm not playing second fiddle this time."

She could see the big tired face, the face whose every contour she knew, flush slowly and then go pale—almost green—again. She knew she had got him there. The knowledge went through her like a drunkenness. But still he did not respond. There was something terrible in his silence. She went on hurriedly, crossing one leg over the other and brushing at the violet taffeta with one hand. She could not stop now.

"There's something else I must tell you, now that we are settling up old debts—in a manner of speaking. I can't be a part of you or anything to do with you any longer, Brant. I decided that last year, halfway—but I didn't do anything about it till last week. It may seem flighty and mean of me, but when I do a thing I do it thoroughly. I am no longer a stockholder in the Grand Columbian. All my shares went on the market last Monday. It was a bad time to sell. My broker thought I had gone out of my head. And whether you believe it or not, Brant, it had nothing to do with money one way or another."

He raised his head then and slowly picked up the bowler and ran his hand caressingly around the rim, flicking off a drop of moisture that had been left from the rain.

"Sure, sure," he said. "I believe you."

He got up heavily and slowly, still without looking at her. He squared the heavy shoulders under the overcoat with the velvet collar and walked carefully to the door—careful because he was still drunk. It pierced her a little even then, to see him stubborn and adamant against his own body, even at that moment. She watched him because she could not help herself, although she felt beaten and utterly weary with the past quarter of an hour. He opened the door and turned to her. His face was pallid, a mask of hard, set, enduring pain.

"It's funny," he said, still looking at his hat and turning it in his hands, "but you know I didn't come here tonight to say any of the things I have. I came because I wanted to tell you something else I thought you ought to know."

She waited and watched him turn the hat round and round in a kind of blind agony.

"Sonie, I got a telegram from Washington today." His voice faltered so slightly that it could be accounted to the liquor in him. "Pete Henry's dead, Sonie—fever—somewhere down in Cuba . . . thought . . . you would want to know—"

He said it carefully. Each word calmly set forth in a voice that was more terrible because of the struggle behind it. Then he put the bowler carefully on and turned and went out the door and down the hall. She could not move. She just sat at the dressing table looking at the empty door, hearing him go. Then she leapt to her feet and ran.

"Brant!" she cried into the empty hallway. But there was no one. At least not for a minute. Then Talbot Graham, like a jack-in-the-box, impeccable and resplendent, stepped suddenly from a dressing room down beyond her.

"You call, Sonie?" he drawled pleasantly. She leaned hard against the door frame looking at him. Good ol' Tal. Nice man. Warm, willing slave.

"Oh, Tal," she called, and her voice broke. "Tal, come here quick, you crazy fool. I've been waiting hours!"

He sauntered over to her and looked down with the lazy, hesitant smile on his handsome face. He was a nice boy. Nice. She drew herself up and patted her hair.

"Sorry, Sonie. I've got a hansom waiting outside."

She laughed then, huskily, and cleared her throat, hoping that she did not sound as strange to him as she did to herself. She turned her face at its most bright and glittering—the one she saved for the big scenes and the finale—on him. She took him by the lapels of his coat and pulled him close.

"Listen," she said, "do you still think you would like to marry me?"

His nice, thin features contracted and then he grinned.

"Miss Leonard," he said, "I think you have known my sentiments for a long time. I can think of nothing nicer."

"All right—let's get married. Let's get married right away."

Her voice was feverish and she pulled, pulled at his coat. She was sorry for that. She was sorry that she should appear thus to any human being, male or female. But she couldn't help it. The room behind her was still full, poignantly, overpoweringly full, of that other presence. She could not bear it. Tal looked down at her, his face warm, cynical, honest.

"If you really want it, Sonie," he said calmly. "I've always thought we could make a good thing of it—you and I."

He didn't try to kiss her. He simply gathered her close, and she buried herself in the embrace. Not with passion, but as a refugee.

Years afterward she was to remember that moment as one in which she had liked Talbot Graham intensely—liked him profoundly, because something lost, ignored, unspoken in him had rushed sadly and knowingly to meet her need then.

3

It was a mild winter in the South. The equinox had introduced it with violent storms at the tail of the summer; but afterward came clear, placid days, without violence. Only the falling of a leaf—the yellow maple, the brown oak, the red sumac—betokened the slow coming of autumn. It was a gently fading season. A season for the old, the sere and the dry, empty of movement, empty of strife and immediate meaning to all save the crow, the fallow field, the farmer sitting behind the window looking out upon the tired earth. It was chill, damp, and cold. It was for the old. The old who brought to it the ghosts of all seasons—childhood, youth, manhood—woven into a private and separate fabric. So it was in Kingsmont. . . .

Captain Phillips in his dusty corner of the rooming house down on Elm Street felt it and knew it as a sympathetic time. He pulled forth the malacca cane, the broad-brimmed hat, the thin suit—the nap long gone, nothing but shiny surface—and went out into the land that he had called his own and had abjured. He had not taken his customary walks for many a month. But now he was full of the wine of the year, so clean the sun, so still the air. It made his veins run with remembered echoes, his creaking joints leave off protesting.

At first he went toward the familiar haunts of the city as he insisted upon remembering it. The square in particular. At least nothing—not even time—had modified the trees, the impudent sparrows on the pavement, the dull and dingy architectural horror that was the county courthouse. He only cursed mildly at the trolley cars as they rattled past. Sometimes he went to the hotel and sat in the lobby and read the newspapers. It made him feel quite venturesome and alive. Sometimes he had a beer at old Huggerston's saloon. And then, when he was feeling particularly spry, he would wander out Redmond Avenue to glare at the new hospital being built by those parvenus, the Royles. To salve their bad consciences no doubt! For having robbed mankind in the name of tobacco. . . .

But finally he found himself wandering up the painful incline of Hill Street, a discredited byway now, full of the sound and noise of business. Machine shops, a laundry, an eating place, a tailoring establishment, had crept up that sacred incline, swallowing up most of the remembered places. The rest were shabby ghosts. Passing them he found it hard to remember who had built and lived in those peeling, grass-grown jumbles. Everybody gone. Only he was left. He began to build a sort of insane pride in his remembrance, muttering to himself the litany of their names—Colberts, Greens, Renfrews, Lansings, all gone. Deserters! Only he remained. He was a living repository for all these forgotten things. It gave his being alive some meaning, and he cherished it fiercely, the childless, wifeless, friendless old man.

The thing that made it still worth while was the end of the journey—Hill House. There it stood, a mark of all that was enduring, gray and unkempt. The windows blinded, the yard overgrown. But

330

he leaned on the rusting iron fence and saw it only in his memory. The thing that it had always been. The last keep, the bastion against all that he hated and that he felt had submerged the past—dreadful word!—in an indulgent miasma. This at least remained. He cherished it. Even with the heart out of it. James Singleton was gone to his reward. His daughter gone up North there with her husband, and no one was left to care about the house or attend it.

His first shock came one afternoon when on reaching the closed iron gate he saw a sign posted on one of the sacred oak trees. "For Sale" it read. He did not believe it. He *could* not believe it. He was in a fever of fret and worry for a fortnight, making the journey up the steep street each afternoon to make sure that the sign—horrible as it was—still remained there. But this repeated indiscretion caught up with that brittle and indomitable assemblage of old flesh and bone that he commandeered about as though it had been a ghostly company. It caught up with him at last and laid him low with a fierce grippe in the drab little room that was now his domain. All through February he had to deliver himself over to the ministrations of Mrs. Crofts, his landlady, a devoted female whom he endured only because she would listen to the long and violent monologue of his reminiscences.

With the coming of March, he began to feel himself again. He had a great urge to bestir himself, to get out and away from the austere captivity of the boardinghouse—if nothing else, away from Mrs. Crofts's increasing air of ownership in him. And so on the first day possible he sallied forth. Spruce, brushed within an inch of his skin, and feeling shaky and weak. He did not feel equal to anything but the square at first. Just to go there and sit on a bench and observe the sparrows, to glare balefully at the trolleys, at the cyclists wildly darting in and out of the noisy traffic circling the sacred space.

Finally he felt equal to the journey up Hill Street. He had thought about it a great deal. It and the sign that said "For Sale." . . . He came to the turn of the street at last. But there was something different and unbelievable in the scene confronting him. In place of the polite old iron fence there arose a shockingly new barrier. And it seemed like the fence of a prison because, nine or ten feet high, it surrounded and cut off the whole roadway from the house. There was a gate, but what a terrible gate!—high, with iron spear points along its top, closed fast against any intrusion. It represented an unmistakable expression of possession and arrogance, and the sight of it was like a blow on the frail body of Captain Phillips.

He leaned on that gate weak and shaken and stared through its base at Hill House. Hill House, a prisoner, possessed and shut off from any communication now. Up on the porch he could see some men. They were busy painting the porch with fresh, brilliant white paint. It gleamed down under the still bare trees like a cry for help. Captain Phillips clung to the gate. He stayed there a long time with no thought of opening it. He stayed until at last one of the painters came down the pathway to get something from a cart parked up the street. Captain Phillips let him pass without a word, but when he came back and opened the iron lock, he caught the man by his arm.

"Sir," he said, "sir, where is the 'For Sale' sign?"

"Hell," the painter replied without emotion, "this place's been sold for a month or more."

"Who is the new owner, if I may ask?" said Captain Phillips, drawing himself fragilely erect.

"Don't you know?" said the man.

"I've been away," said Captain Phillips with crisp formality.

"Oh," said the painter, and spat again before continuing. "That Mr. Royle that owns all the factories and the cigarettes bought it awhile back. Funny, too, 'cause he's puttin' a mint of money in it. Look at this fence, fer instance, made in Noo Orleens. Genuine wrought iron, made to order. He hasn't set foot on the place—out in Chiny somewhere, they tell me—but he's havin' it all painted up and refurnished—an' he puts a fence like this around an old house." The man shook his head. "You can't tell about these millionaires."

He spat again and went in the gate, clanging it shut. Captain Phillips stood there, stock-still, leaning on his malacca cane and watching the man return to the long, columned porch. He stood there a long time before he noticed that he was shaking. Then his shoulders slumped, and he tottered blindly down the hill to the last haven on Elm Street. When he had gained the little room he locked the door with an air of finality, of fierce and unregenerate resignation, and laid himself down carefully, like a thing that would break, on the creaking bedstead. He got up only once and that was to grope for the whisky bottle beneath him and place it with the glass on the washstand at the side. Then he lay back with no sound and stared out his window watching the day depart grayly.

He could hear the clang-clang of the trolley sounding at the corner of Bay Street. It went past, following its immutable course down the distance like a condemned thing, ponderous and lasting. Captain Phillips listened to it tensely.

"Mountebanks! . . . whoremongers! . . . unprincipled trash!" he mumbled to the dimming, empty little room. "Own the earth—and still they must defile the temple!"

And then he turned his frail, fierce face to the wall. . . .

PART THREE

CHAPTER EIGHTEEN

I

Brant Royle did not return to the United States for nearly twelve years. And it was almost twenty-five before he set foot in Kingsmont again.

When he shook the dust of the United States from his feet and got aboard ship in San Francisco that day, he was not so much going into exile as removing himself from further personal hurt. But no one was fooled—least of all himself. The vast workings of his creation, its intrinsic nature and impetus, had not been destroyed. Like a giant kaleidoscope which had been turned a fraction, the design fell apart only to assume a new form. But the separate brilliant parts were still identical, if newly juxtaposed. The Grand Columbian Tobacco Company itself was now a name applied only to a small segment, but it remained. As did Pendleton & Ransom, Royle & Company, the South Eastern Tobacco Corporation, the Richmond Company—and a score of others. All standing apart. But the ghostly and invisible hold of the matrix, the mother lode—the vanished hand of something that for a season or two had been called the tobacco trust—stripped by law of its sinister connotations still hovered over all of them, powerful, ineradicable.

And in removing himself from the sight of the American tobacco industry, Brant Royle merely placed himself in a sort of Olympus when he went to China and remained there to live. His affairs were well ordered. If he had occasionally made mistakes, he also had the virtue of never repeating them. His name took its place inevitably among the Great Successful Businessmen. In Kingsmont they cherished him for that. He was the native son, no matter where he went. They incorporated his achievement—now that they had not the pressure of his presence—into the body of the local legend as well as into the industry's body of apocrypha. It was a legend told and embellished in board meetings, in smoking cars, over the after-dinner Havana and brandy. "Now back in ninety-eight, sir, when I was just beginning in the business, I met Mr. Royle at the factory. Scared to death of him, but inside of five minutes felt I'd known him all my life, b'God!" The bitterness, the hate, the bleeding ruins that he had left in his wake, faded behind the irresistible aura of canonization.

In those twelve years Kingsmont went right on growing, in the midst of the vast, rolling tobacco fields. A whole coterie of lesser manufacturing towns had developed out of the same impetus, but Kingsmont was still the center, the richest, the biggest. They knew it. Its citizens proudly said, "More different brands of cigarettes go out in those boxcars, sir, than from any other place on God's earth!" They were proud of it. They were proud of the Royles. *The* leading citizens and public benefactors. Mr. Samuel Royle of Lawson & Royle had given the money for the building of the big First Methodist Church out on Bay Street. Handsomest and biggest church building in Carolina! Must have cost half a million if it cost a cent. And then, in recent years, the new Agricultural and Mechanical College situated between Kingsmont and Raleigh had received a handsome endowment and buildings for the express purpose of research for both the industry and the growing of tobacco. Mr. Royle was that kind of man. Big. His gifts took on new luster when they read that the Chinese Government had also honored him for his generosity to the Chinese people. Yes, sir, big man by any count wherever he was.

They read about him in the *Herald* and the other papers. He was omnipresent in the trade journals. They read how he had freed the industry from dependence on Spain and Turkey for the licorice needed to flavor the tons of plug tobacco manufactured yearly still, by promoting its growth in China. They read the elaborate accounts of his engagement and marriage to the daughter of one of his British associates in Hong Kong—the Honorable Elizabeth Inverloch, daughter of Lord Inverloch, chairman of the board of the American & Orient. The home-town boy had risen so high in the world that nothing less than the "aristocracy" was equal to him. It spread a patina over all the new tobacco families. It became their conquest, too. No, no one could blame him, or hold it against him. . . .

They did not hold it against him when they read that he had returned at last to the States with Mrs. Royle and an infant daughter named Helen, and that they had taken up residence in the costly Gothic pile he had built up on the Hudson. There were long and glowing articles concerning that dwelling. Pictures of the elaborate grounds that it had taken ten years to landscape. It was said to have a series of fountains rivaling that French palace, Versailles. There were accounts of the luxury of the furnishings of the interior, too. Mostly Oriental, collected by Brant at vast expense and shipped home during his years in the East. Samuel and his family went up to visit the summer after his return. And there were some lucky few of the higher-ups in the business who received the royal summons to visit Brant. The estate was named after his wife's family, Inverloch. No, they couldn't blame him for not coming back to Kingsmont when he had something like that to live in.

Perhaps a few recalled curiously the old-fashioned house at the head of Hill Street that he had bought years ago just before he left the country and in which he had never—so far as anyone knew—set foot. There it stood, a pure anachronism in its surroundings now that the town had grown beyond it. A tall wrought-iron fence about a little island in the midst of a business and manufacturing district— machine shops, a feed warehouse, printers, wholesale grocers. They spread all over the hill, full now of the sound of clattering wheels on the old cobbles, the hum of machinery, the dingy smoke and fuss of a city's small businesses. But it *was* an island. If Mr. Royle had never entered the house, then neither had anyone else except the two Negroes who kept the grounds the year round. Lord knows how much money Mr. Royle had spent just keeping up that old place for the last ten, twelve years! Well, what did it matter how much money he spent on it, or if he never came around to look in it? He was a millionaire. He could afford it. He could afford anything he wanted.

2

It was pouring outside the train drawing room. It swished and splashed against the window, making the thick green of the summer landscape rush past as though underwater. Sonie had been up since dawn to see that landscape. She hadn't slept very well. She never did on trains. Anyway, she was far too excited to grudge sleep at this time. She hadn't known that she would get this feeling so intensely. But then twelve years was a long time. And what she thought she had forgotten was not forgotten at all. Never would she have believed it if anyone had told her that she would be pressing her face against the glass searching for a break in that rushing wall of green outside that would reveal the first tobacco field that she had seen in more time than she liked to remember. It came at last, a long slope slanting up from the gully along the tracks and the tobacco standing high in rows that ran away from the progress of the train. They wheeled past like gigantic spokes of green. But at least she had seen it before another interval of forest rushed over the windows.

"A good stand," she said to herself, smiling against the glass like a child. "They'll be priming before long."

She wished suddenly that she could raise the car window and let some of that green wetness come in to take the place of the stuffy, plush-smelling air in the drawing room. Maybe she might be able to smell the tobacco growing where they passed the next field. She couldn't remember whether growing tobacco had a smell or not. But it ought to! she thought fiercely. It ought to because I hadn't seen it in such a long time, and I'm coming home. . . . I'm through with this gallivantin'. Got it all out of my blood for good—and I'm tired. I was tired in San Francisco. I've been tired for years. I came running back here to Kingsmont like a fool homin' pigeon—three thousand miles! She grinned at herself and watched the sheet of rain splash over the window. Well, it takes a lot of livin' around and a lot of time to make up your mind. You've made it up again, and I guess you'll stick to it, Mrs. Graham, as usual. The thought of Tal's name made her a little sad—not unhappy, but just sad in a weak, warm little corner of herself. What a lot of sentimental nonsense one managed to get cluttered up with to carry through life! She shrugged and shifted her position on the rumpled berth. Although she was still slim—even a little thin under her corset—she reflected with good humor that it was highly flattering still to be taken for thirty when she was over the gate of forty. But it constituted an effort in many little cramped and complaining joints and tissues. In spite of her good, unfailing store of vitality, it made her trim off the corners of her activity at times. Anyway, she had recovered from the long bout in the hospital. The vitality was still there. It had pulled her through —as it had pulled her through so many things in her life. Only now it was drawn a little thin. It would take the period of stolid, staid quiet that she had craved for so long without knowing it.

Tal hadn't had vitality. He'd never had a great store of anything but amiability. He had had to draw on her store of vigor, as he had had to depend on her resources in many other things. But it wasn't his fault. That was one thing about Tal: he had never pretended to be other than what he was. He and she had understood each other perfectly from the beginning. Thinking back, she reflected that it had really been a very good marriage. Much better than most in the world in which they had moved for nearly twelve years. At any rate it had lasted, which was more than you could say for most. Of course she had determined from the beginning, once she had taken the step, that it should last. It was the old peasant sense of propriety and honesty toward a real commitment—plus her strong sense of pride— that had seen to it. The question as to whether she had been unwise was never allowed to enter; she was too bent on making the best of what she had at all times. Of course it hadn't all been smooth sailing. But nothing in her life had ever led her to believe that any part of existence was smooth sailing. One employed one's common sense and tolerance to see that things did not get out of hand. That was all.

No, she could not quarrel over her life with Talbot Graham. Nor with Tal himself. She supposed that he had been unfaithful to her, in the technical sense, countless times, but he had been unfailingly considerate and good-humored. If there was anything to be forgiven she could cancel it out on the basis of those two rare virtues alone. She thought of the years of their wanderings, of his endless schemes fomented by the passion of gambling rooted so deeply in him—and he was such a bad gambler! He always lost. All those theatrical ventures during the period when he was trying to be a producer. . . . They had accomplished one thing certainly: getting him out of all his expensive muddles had cured her, after her own modest personal success in that field, of her own appetite for the theater. She had always been willing to indulge him when he came to her with a new scheme—indulge him lavishly—because it amused her and she no longer thought of wealth as something astonishing. But there was at the same time part of her that was forever out of the past, and the vanished house on Maple Street and the little red-haired girl who had tasted the food of poverty, which kept a shrewd and cautious hand on the reins. She had no passion for money. She never had had. But she had never made the sentimental mistake of holding it in disrespect. After all, she was still Genia Lipik's daughter. So Tal had never been permitted to bring her to ruin. He had come close to it, of course, more than once.

They had gone to San Francisco for a few weeks and they had lived there for nearly seven years. They both found San Francisco a good place. The urbane, bustling city suited them. His connections and her wealth opened the highest hospitality to them there as it had in most places in the world. Although they kept the house in New York and the one in Kingsmont and they made an occasional trip back East, she had begun to think that she was settled down at last. She had learned a great deal in the years since she had first gone away from Kingsmont. She had weighed in the balance much of that experience. She had made mistakes—many of them—but she had never been one to waste time weeping over them, and she had done most of the things she had wanted to do, whether they measured up to her expectations or not. After all, that was the chance you took! You couldn't complain about it. You just went ahead making the continual Grand Compromise that was the business of living. In the process she had become a woman of poise and distinction who commanded attention and admiration wherever she chose to go. She often realized, with acute self-knowledge, that the feeling of dissatisfaction with her experience in the theater of real footlights and velvet curtains and grease-paint make-believe was that it had confined her. The most satisfactory role she had ever played was the one she had been playing all her life wherever she went and whatever she did—and that stage had been a big one! The décor and the drama had often changed, but not the leading character. One invaluable trait had prevented disaster. She had always known when the curtain should come down. . . .

It had come down finally on the act called Sonie and Tal—rather banal for all its painful and pathetic trappings. They had been to a rather commonplace dinner at the Delmontes' and coming home they had both got soaked to the skin while trying to get a cab. Well, pneumonia is always waiting for fools, no matter how well heeled—not that either he or she had considered it when Tal, coming home early the next afternoon from Market Street, complaining because he had the grippe, found her already in bed and the doctor there. She had never been inside a hospital in her life and it was hard even now to think that she had spent three desperate weeks delirious and fighting for breath without even knowing where she was or that her husband was in the next room. It was only after she lay exhausted and spent, but knowing that she was all right, looking at the flowers and staring at the big bare ugly room from her pillow that they came and told her about Tal—poor Tal. Amiability was no weapon with which to fight off death. She had tried to feel shocked and bereft, but it was no good. She would do what was expected of her, but she could not be dishonest. She just felt sad and terribly tired. And beyond that a sense of relief, deep relief, that he no longer needed her and she could turn her face away now. She was done with San Francisco. It held nothing more for her. That act was finished. It was time she went home—*really* home.

As she lay there in the hospital room letting her strength grow back into her all she could think of was Kingsmont. She kept remarking to herself in a kind of wonder, Why, I must have been thinking about Kingsmont for years without knowing it! She had done her duty by Tal up to the end—the big, rich, dignified funeral. She had always sworn she would never wear black, but she found the smart mourning extremely becoming to her convalescent pallor and her red hair (she had discreetly been touching it up for years even then!). She attended patiently to the endless somber delegations of friends and business associates, but when she thought she had done enough, she escaped, going to New York to attend to some business. She left the house on the Nob in the hands of Tal's lawyers. It was to be closed up and sold when the estate was settled. Her personal things she left to travel with Lise across the continent direct to North Carolina. Lise was much upset at first. She hadn't been separated from Sonie for nearly fifteen years. But somehow Sonie didn't even want to bother with Lise then. She had need of being absolutely alone for a while. And then Lise had been vastly mollified (how it would have amused Tal!) when she discovered that she was to travel in company with O'Brien, the chauffeur. She and Tal had bought a Chalmers motorcar the preceding year. It was the only thing personally associated with Tal that she was sending back to Kingsmont, and she knew that if she took the car she would have to take O'Brien. He worshiped and cared for the machine with a mad Celtic devotion. So Lise and O'Brien, with all her personal trunks and the Chalmers, had gone on to Kingsmont. In New York she received a telegram saying that they had all arrived safely and that the house was ready for her. Well, it had better be ready! After all, a month was quite long enough for anything, and Lise at least knew the house in Kingsmont—and both Lise and O'Brien knew *her*. They, the three of them, had a perfect understanding. They liked one another. . . .

The coming of day, gray and subdued as it was, seemed to have slackened the rain outside the car window. She could see clearly now. She shifted again for comfort in her good tailored suit—not black, but a gray light wool that fitted her perfectly. Kingsmont was near now. Something was near. The scattered cabins, the roadway clustered with buildings in the pearly, streaming light, the crossroads with the figure waiting, bowed, patient, subdued—no face, no tag to name it—made her sit up in expectation again as they flashed past. Well, this was arriving—this was coming to any spot on God's earth. Kingsmont, home, it made no difference. It was all caught in the dross of memory, the heart of loneliness and mystery.

The first buildings began to crowd against the track, hovels with trees. Then the signs—hieroglyphics on walls or a billboard on top of a warehouse—"Randolph for Feed and Fertilizer" or "Mellow Bar, the Choice of Gentlemen." Her eyes caught at them greedily as they flashed by. So common, so ordinary, so bare of any distinction except their own honesty. Walls, wooden walls, dingy and deserted in the gray light. Warehouses. Tobacco warehouses. The ciphers of her youth swept past her eye. Leaning against the cool damp glass, she felt almost a child again—open and eager-eyed. This was, after all, a home-coming in a special sense. She got up, straightened her hat and skirt, and examined herself critically in the long mirror. It was a satisfactory examination. Being on the threshold of forty became her almost as much as being twenty had—and that in spite of having to wear glasses! She pressed the button for the porter. Her bags were all ready. Rich leather baggage locked and waiting there on the green plush. The knock at the door—"Yes, ma'am . . .

right away, ma'am"—it was all a part of the happiness she felt welling inside her.

And here was the station. Grinding and jerking and squeaking, they had stopped her there where she could look with a peculiar acuteness upon the dingy yellow bricks again. It was different. They had added a long shed. But the essentials after twelve years were the same. She buttoned her coat and stepped out into the smoke-smelling aisle, nameless figures ahead of her. What did they matter? She pushed ahead, the cool damp air against her hot cheek, the conductor's hand under her arm. There was Lise—a sleepy familiar face in the hubbub below.

"Hello, Lise!"

"Madame Soneeah!" Lise breathed out all the syllables elaborately, as always. They patted each other tearfully, standing there clear of the passing to and fro.

"Well, is the Chalmers running?"

"Ah yes, Madame Soneeah—that O'Brien he is waiting all proud with the curtains against the rain and a lot of nice dark people standing looking at it!"

Sonie laughed a sound of pure happiness.

"Get someone to bring the bags," she commanded. "Let's go— let's go *home!*"

3

The wet streets, the early morning streets, stirring sleepily. She gazed exhilarated through the rain curtains from the back seat. It was all as she had remembered it. All the same, but changed— stretched, telescoped, narrowed, distorted, all at once. The square still there, but the ancient, decrepit courthouse a prisoner among its moth-eaten oaks and magnolias. The buildings—the new post office with the neoclassic front that hadn't been there before—leaned about it, towering and snobbish, as though enduring the presence of a tombstone! Looking at it there flashed across her memory all the other important geography of her life—the Champs-Elysées, the boulevard at Cannes, Madison Avenue, Nob Hill in San Francisco— but not one of them had what this shabby place held for her. She drank it up as they exploded down Bay Street. Bay Street in the memory so wide, so new, under its elms. What a difference a scant twelve years could make! It looked old and worn too. Silly that she had never noticed it on her last visit. Time. Time. Time. What an imponderable factor. Certainly *she* did not feel so different! It had no right to change so! One thing was unchanging—fixed in its orbit, immutably. She counted six signs with the Royle & Company mark on them. She looked at them and turned her eyes ahead. She was too

340

tired to unravel the knot that included Brant. Brant long lost—long forgotten and put aside, gone to China somewhere. In the hospital she recalled reading that he had come home again.

Here was her house at last. The gravel driveway curving up through the sloping lawn to the brick dwelling that had at one time been such an astonishing thing. All new and all hers, with twenty rooms! She felt kindly toward it now. The shrubbery had grown up and the house had retired behind it as though withdrawing from the fact that Bay Street had changed. This stretch of it was certainly no longer exclusive. She thought wryly that time had caught up with her house and made it old-fashioned. The grounds of the fine dwellings across the way—the Carters' and the Smiths'—had become the sites for a lot of gleaming new bungalows. Well, one couldn't complain. Twelve years was, after all, twelve years.

She got down under her own porte-cochere and went in. Cool, empty, and preserved. She delighted in that. She had never thought to delight in anything so stable as polished hardwood floors, a remembered chair being in its place. But now this day had a special meaning.

She spent a week getting the house in order and staffing it. How often did she think of Mrs. Rose during that seven days—poor Mrs. Rose who had gone home to Indiana weeping when she had closed up the Madison Avenue house years ago, Mrs. Rose whose epitaph was a letter from a relation . . . to think of that warm, sentimental, generous person who had been like a sister-mother to her dying out in a place called St. Paul, Indiana. Who on earth had ever heard of St. Paul, Indiana? But here in this house she was still a real presence. The picture of Hope at the turn of the staircase that Mrs. Rose had always admired tearfully, the arborvitae she had planted on the front lawn. They were all ghosts of that pleasant, bosomy person so wrapped up with a part of the past—Maple Street and Madison Avenue. What a gap, but how close together in memory! Sonie reveled in sentimentality as she ordered her house.

But that task was soon finished. She had thought to remain resting in pleasant oblivion for an indefinite period. But the *Herald* was full of her presence. Reading the notes on the society page, she felt almost like an ancient monument and grinned at her shocked vanity. Can forty be that old? They write about my being here as though I were a hundred. Well, I suppose I seem that to a lot of people who never knew—and there must be lots of them now! They called. Some of those she had known. It would have been rather dreadful if she hadn't been amused. It was like a continuously bad drawing-room comedy from a past day. Of course she enjoyed playing her part to the hilt. Mrs. Talbot Graham nee Lipik. At home on Wednesday afternoon. She returned their calls, arriving magnificently with

O'Brien and the Chalmers. She exchanged the pattern of stiff clichés and fled back to Bay Street again. It amused and excited her for a while—as the playing of any part had excited her. But it was not enough. It was not what she had come back to haven, to Kingsmont, for. She put her affairs in order, called on Mr. Turner (that ancient bag of wind!) at the bank, opened an account at Lawson & Royle, and endured a dinner with Sam Royle and Roberta at the same old house on Elm Street. The Royles had never moved. Sam, dried-up in his success as a leading citizen and philanthropist of Kingsmont—a revolting skeleton at the head of the table with nothing left but the suggestive whisper and the parched mouth full of ancient teeth. And Roberta a true ghost, gibbering in fits and starts like a madwoman, with no talk except that which concerned her daughter, off now at a private school in Raleigh. Well, it had been depressing. But she had done her duty. She did not force it again.

But after a month or so, her innate vitality betrayed her. She had to have more than just the casual round of the town's sedate society (how funny it was to be a secure part of that drab round!). She began to interest herself in the activities of various ladies' societies. Not because they offered anything in particular, but because she could not content herself with absolute privacy. She had to get out. She became restless with returning health. She wandered pointlessly about the city. She joined the Methodist church and connected herself with its feminine organizations. She visited the factory section on a committee and felt a fool when they progressed along Maple Street, squalid and nameless now under its factory walls. She began to have O'Brien drive her out and leave her in some obscure corner of town to wander back home as best she could. He looked askance and hurt, but she gave him no satisfaction. She enjoyed those forays. Wandering about those familiar—and now new and strange—byways of her memory, smartly dressed and hatted, parasol against the hot summer sun, the pince-nez on the slim gold chain pinned to her solid bosom, she found that being a woman of wealth and position gave her a peculiar and special leeway when it came to looking up the past. Very few recognized her, because the past had used a scythe. It had obliterated all the old faces or taken them away. She found some old workers at the factories who remembered her and would engage in a stiff, embarrassed exchange with her about the "old days." But it was not satisfactory. It left her even more restless than she had been before. Hitherto she had been content to leave everything to chance, the casual and astonished meeting, the delighted, false or not, recognition, the colloquy, formless, without beginning or ending, the sterile memories that did not include her.

One morning she got up with a feeling of determination. After breakfast, which she always had in bed now, she dressed and ordered the car. She had O'Brien drive her to the courthouse square. When there was a place between the wagons and buggies that still made Kingsmont, for all its wide growth, look like a country town, she had him stop and told him to wait. He was content because he was immediately surrounded by a crowd of small boys and old men to whom a vehicle that ran without a horse was still a thing of astonishment. She wandered away unnoticed toward the west border of the square. But it wasn't there. A large new office building stood in its place. She hadn't noticed it particularly before, because her thoughts had not been bent that way. But she felt a pang, deep and cutting, to see that the old Soldier's Saloon had vanished as completely as though it had never existed. It got her blood up. She cornered a sweating policeman.

"Officer, there used to be a saloon there between that stationery shop and that meat market. I'm an old resident here, but I haven't been around in a long time and I'm trying to find out about all the changes, you know."

The man looked at this personable lady—she was somebody and he had better take no chances! He scratched his head, lifting the hot hat.

"Why yes, ma'am," he drawled, "you mean ol' Ed Huggerston's place. Why, he moved around there on Rice Street 'bout five years ago, I believe."

"Thank you, officer."

She left him and crossed the square toward the top of Rice Street, her head erect, glinting still with the subdued flame of her hair beneath the wide heavy hat, her parasol beating crisply against the pavement.

4

"Why, Sonie," he said, wringing her hand hard with both his old, fragile ones, and speaking in the tone of frail astonishment. "Why, Sonie, sit down—please!"

They were in the family room, dingy and empty, with the marble-topped tables and the buzzing sound of flies and the smell of sawdust and hops. She sat down at the table opposite him, placing the parasol in the next chair and her reticule on the marble top. She took a fan out of it and began to wave it at her face. It was awfully hot. She had almost forgotten how hot Carolina could be. But she was enjoying the rediscovery. She looked at the old man opposite her, clean, thin, and wispy.

"Ed," she accused, "you've moved."

"Had to. They tore down the old building, y'know. Couldn't stand in the way of progress. An' this town's growing, Sonie. Never

343

saw the like of it. A regular city now. Six times as big as it was when I was a boy. And all because of cigarettes—would you believe it! More cigarettes made here than any place in the world. Hey—" he grinned at her—"I'm forgettin' my manners. Can I offer you somethin', a glass of beer or some sweet wine? I know it's mighty early in the day—"

She smiled at him, pushing the veil up from her chin.

"Thank you, Ed. What was it I used to come to you for years ago and get in the bucket for the boarders down on Maple Street?"

"A pail of lager," he said with delight. "Why, Sonie, I can remember as clear as day you comin' to the back entrance no bigger than a grasshopper—"

"I'll have a glass of lager, thank you, Ed."

He was delighted.

"Joe!" he called over his shoulder. Then he leaned forward confidentially. "My sister's boy runs the business now. I just hang around to talk to the old customers."

A weedy young man in a soiled apron popped in at the door. "You call, Uncle Ed?"

"Joe, I want you to meet an old friend. Mrs.—Mrs. Graham, this is my nephew."

Sonie nodded and smiled.

"Pleased t'meet ya, Mrs. Graham," responded the young man all in a breath, and looked at the old man.

"Joe, bring Mrs. Graham a glass of our best Milwaukee Pilsner," said Ed, looking at Sonie. "And bring me a glass of my regular."

"Still buttermilk, Ed?" said Sonie.

"The same!" he agreed, laughing, the fragile, careful sign of enjoyment.

The young man at the door raised his eyebrows, wiped his hands on the apron, and disappeared. Sonie looked at Ed. He seemed even thinner and more blurred without her glasses. How old he had got! Time *was* a treacherous element. Outside the door she had entered there was a great sound of big wooden wheels thundering over the cobbles. She grimaced. Ed shook his head in the blur at her.

"You've been away too long, Sonie," he said above the noise. "You've forgotten the racket a tobacco van makes on the way to the warehouses."

"Yes," she agreed, "I've been away too long."

"You're lookin' as handsome as ever. Would have known you anywhere."

"Now, Ed," she said, shaking her head at him, "you needn't try any fancy talk with me. I'm a nice settled, comfortable, middle-aged woman and there's no use your tryin' to make me feel otherwise."

"But you haven't really changed," he protested. "I'm the old one

344

in this party. Be seventy-two come Nevember," he said proudly. "Right livin's what does it an' don't let anyone tell you otherwise!"

"You're still as full of the old get-up-an-go as ever," she agreed. Joe came in with a tray then and set a tall glass with its foaming head before her and a squat glass of buttermilk before his uncle. He wiped the table with his apron, nodded at them, and went out again. They raised their glasses and sipped and looked at each other.

"Sonie," said Ed, wiping his mustache, "I read in the papers about you bein' in town and openin' up your house an' all, but I didn't think to see you."

"Ed, what are you talkin' about?" She picked up the fan again and began waving it before her face. "Did you think I'd ever get so high and mighty that I would forget my old friends?"

He shook his head and blushed. "No, I didn't really, Sonie—but I knew I couldn't get up the nerve to come out on Bay Street an' see you an' talk over old times. I wouldn't have felt comfortable."

"That's why I came to see you this morning," she said, and sipped at the beer again. "I've still got those roses you gave me, Ed."

He blushed again. An old man's blush. Pink like a baby under the clean delicate skin.

"And I've still got them post cards you sent me from New York and Europe—Paris and all them foreign places."

"Ed," she said, "I've been away so long and everything is so strange and so many people are gone—"

"Where's Rosie MacAllister?" he said, still looking at his glass. "She was a fine figure of a woman."

"Ach! Mrs. Rose," she said, and felt her eyes blur even more. "Mrs. Rose went home to Indiana years ago, Ed. She—she passed on spring before last. I've missed her, Ed."

"I bet you have," said the old man solemnly. He raised his glass with a trembling hand. "I always thought Rosie was the best good-hearted woman that ever lived in this town. You know," he continued, not looking at her with the watery blue eyes, "I'm gettin' so old that I've begun to feel that I'm the only one left that remembers anything about how things used to be here."

It was a confidence and it embarrassed him further. He took another deep drink to cover it. She looked at him sympathetically and waited. After a moment he set it down, wiped his mustache, and continued:

"There aren't many left, and all I know about them is what I read in the papers now. Look at Brant Royle. . . ." He paused. She opened her reticule carefully and took out a handkerchief and dabbed at her cheeks. It was so hot! But the mention of that name moved her in spite of all the years, all the time.

"What about Brant Royle?" she asked casually.

"He's not been around in years. I guess you knew him as well as anyone did," he said, looking at her directly. "A cold, mean man, if ever I saw one, but full of big things. Look what he has done! The whole cigarette industry." He waved an eloquent old hand. "Where would we all be this day without him, I ask you? And yet there he's been away all these years—ten, twelve—and the younger generation don't know no more about him than they do of the statue of the Confederate soldier up there in front of the courthouse. An' him away off there in Chiny somewhere makin' more business for himself. He couldn't help that, I reckon, wherever he was. But he's got too big for Carolina. Always was, I guess. I read now that he's come back. Married some Englishwoman and has got two children. I don't guess we folks down here are worth his notice any more. Got to live like a high-and-mighty in a big house up there in New York. Why, I can't count the times I've shoveled him out o' the front door of the old saloon up there on the square, drunk as a lord and lookin' like Satan on wheels, not sayin' anything. He had a demon in him."

She looked at Ed curiously. Under all his words he was telling her he knew about herself and Brant. They had all known once. She had made no secret of it. He was being tactful now. She felt tender toward him. More tender than she had felt toward anyone in a long time.

"Ed," she said, leaning her elbows on the table top, "that's why I came down here this morning and looked you up. I've been away so long myself there's no one left. I wanted to get the news about everyone. I knew you would know." He flushed again with pleasure. "What about all the old gang—the people that we used to know down on Maple Street before it became a place for factories? Where have they all gone? Chris Malley I know is still out there in the East. He'll stay. He was more than half Chinese to begin with. Born that way. It suits him. I've heard from him now and then. Mrs. Pearl, Mrs. Rose—all gone. But what about poor old John Barton? He married Major Singleton's daughter years ago. I read it in the papers myself. I've tried to keep up. . . ."

"Ah yes, Sonie," he said, "I remember how good you used to be to that Barton man. A strange feller if ever I saw one. All to himself. No friends, but I remember him with those long legs of hisn—and that queer old-fashioned Yankee way of talkin'. Gave us all a turn when he up and got the Major's daughter. . . ."

He paused and nodded to himself, buried in his thoughts. She waited, looking hard at him.

"You wouldn't believe it," he said after a pause, "but they went away like everybody else. Detroit, I believe. Somethin' about makin' motorcars. Anyway, he must have lost all his money, because they came back here 'bout five years ago. Like homin' pigeons. I expect

346

it was her as much as it was *him*. Anyway they slipped back into town without anyone knowin' it. You'd never know they was here except I used to see him now and then up around the feed-and-grain store gettin' supplies like any other farmer. She was always a high-and-mighty person, an' they'd come down considerable in the world —an' there was this piece of land he'd bought years ago when he was flush, just an old tobacco farm. But you'd never see *her*. She kept to herself like she had always. No more than when she had lived up there at the old house on the hill. . . ."

He retired again into his own private memories. She did not mind his garrulousness. She was hungry and sad for what he was saying. This was what she had come down for this morning. Mrs. Talbot Graham in her motorcar with a chauffeur sitting at the stained marble-topped table in the back room of a saloon. She waited for him to go on.

"He died last winter," he said.

That moved her. One more cipher gone into darkness. One more finger touch on the surface of the past shifted, removed. John Barton dead and buried and she had not thought of him for a dozen years or more. It had not mattered before. Or it had not seemed to matter as it did now, because that empty space in the pattern of her memory shocked her, because memory was a thing that should not be assaulted by time and change. She felt guilty, deeply guilty, and hungry. She had not thought much of this man, this figure—not so much in himself, but surrounded by all the things that were vividly a part of the past.

"Ach, Ed, I'm sorry to hear that," she said. "And Mrs. Barton—"

She left it suspended. He would know, sitting there opposite her. She was amazed at herself. Even she didn't know what it all still meant to her. But it meant an awful lot. And John—that poor lost soul. Couldn't even finish a sentence without choking himself. She owed something to him. She felt full of pity for him—full of pity for all the ghosts of the past. And that included herself. They were due some homage.

"You mean Major Singleton's daughter," said Ed in a bemused voice. "I don't know. I guess she's still tryin' to carry on out there. Queer woman. . . ."

She took a deep draught from her glass and dabbed at her mouth. "Ed," she said, "I think I ought to go out and see her now that I'm home once more. Johnny Barton used to be a particular friend of mine."

"Yeah, Sonie—we all used to wonder at the trouble you took with that man. Talkin' to him and seein' him about—but you were always a good one, Sonie, really good. Folks aren't like that nowadays. Pushin' an' shovin' an' no respect for their betters."

347

"Where is this place that Johnny Barton had, Ed? I've got a big need in me, Ed," she said candidly, "to talk with the living, even the dead if I could, the folks that knew me and that I knew long ago."

"I know, I know," he agreed, and wagged his head. "Feel that way myself sometimes. . . . What did you ask me just now?"

"Where is the Barton place, Ed?"

"Oh yes. I've never been out there myself, but it seems to me—" he scratched his old man's pate, covered thinly by the white, cottony locks—"I've heard tell that they have a hundred and fifty acres down on the South Pelham Road—'bout five miles south o' town."

"Ed," she said, "thank you. Why don't you come out Bay Street and see me sometime? My front door's always open."

He nodded and smiled. "I'm gettin' on, Sonie," he said. "I don't stir about much nowadays. But I'll come an' see that big house of yours one o' these days. I've been by it many a time an' told people whose it was, y'know."

"Ed, we old friends have got to keep in touch. Thank you for the beer. It was nice to have a talk with you." She got up and put the fan in the reticule. He looked at the sawdust on the floor, an old man wagging his head and lost to anything but ancient and confused memories.

"Sonie, it's been a pleasure—you're welcome for a glass of beer any time—you know that." He pulled himself erect by an effort and stood leaning on the soiled table. A fly lit on his forehead and he brushed at it. She smiled at him, snapped her gloves, and picked up the parasol. She felt sad, but she knew what she was going to do now. The very thought that there was some point for the day filled her with the old clanging energy. It was something at last. It was a relief.

"Thank you, Ed." She extended her hand, gloved and suave. It made her feel almost young, that fragile tentative paw placed within her grasp. She grasped it gently.

"You'll come again and talk with me, won't you, Sonie?" he said, looking at her with the faded eyes as though he could read assurance from her face.

"Of course, Ed Huggerston—what do you think!"

She pushed the swinging doors aside and stepped out into the blast of heat. My, it was hot! She debated whether she should raise the parasol or not. Her clothes were not fitted for this climate. She would have to go down to Lawson & Royle tomorrow and see about some good cotton ready-mades. She decided not to raise the parasol. She beat it hard against the pavement and reeled the pince-nez out of the little gold locket and clamped them firmly on her nose. If one needed glasses to see, one should wear them. It had been pure vanity not to put them on before Ed Huggerston. He had known her when. . . .

She marched like a legion up the busy side street to the square. She noticed that they made way for her—the people who passed her. Well now, why shouldn't they? She was as much a part of these stones, these buildings, these streets full of the ghosts and happenings of her memory, as the old courthouse itself. I don't have to bother any more. For the first time she began to recognize the freedom that came with admitted age. She had never thought of herself as old—and she wasn't, she could feel the good, healthy blood beat strongly in her veins—but she had come to that time in her life when she could stop pretending to worry about all those foolish, selfish, youthful, vain things that had once been so important. Now all that mattered was doing what she pleased—not what anyone else *thought* pleased her. There was a vast difference. She smiled to herself and felt better and more active than she had in months. She knew now that coming downtown and looking up old Ed had been a good impulse. She saluted her instinct. It had never failed her from the beginning. . . . And poor old Johnny Barton dead . . . the stranger, the lost man . . . dying down here under this alien, blazing, uncaring Carolina sun.

The Chalmers, sleek and polished, a stranger among all the wagons at the curb, was still surrounded by a group of loiterers and children. O'Brien in his visored cap and gloves leaned majestically against one fender and gestured in an oracular way.

"O'Brien," she said, pushing her way through the little group. They gave her free passage, respectfully touching their hats. "O'Brien, how are our tires?"

He opened the door to the back seat elaborately.

"Mrs. Graham," he said—and she knew that he was addressing his audience as much as he was addressing her—"Mrs. Graham, they are in A-number-one condition!"

She set her foot on the running board, lifting her skirt and peering at him over the pince-nez.

"Will they take us on a little trip now? I want to go out in the country."

"Couldn't be better—couldn't possibly be better, and we've got a world of gasoline, ma'am. Filled her up this morning."

He closed the door behind her and pulled at his gloves. This was still all for the audience standing gaping on the sidewalk.

"O'Brien," she said, leaning on her parasol in the back seat, "find out how we can get on the road to South Pelham."

"Why yes, ma'am," he said, and settled his visored cap. He didn't ask her how far or how long. None of the irking questions. He

349

had accepted the charge. She could see it in the pride of his stubby Irish face. That was one the reasons she had kept him and sent him three thousand miles across the continent to stay with this irascible vehicle that had contrary motor troubles and totally unpredictable tires. They always carried three spares strapped to the side instead of the ordinary two. Practically, there flashed across her mind in that moment while he was grinding at the crank and the car was shaking under her: It will be dusty—don't you remember?—the land is dusty and the roads under the green trees do not know rubber tires much . . . and I haven't a duster. Well, what of it? It would do her good to get a little dirty for a change—so long it had been since she had felt the balm of carelessness and the touch of earth, clean earth, gritting on her skin. The motor exploded into life and shook her. She could see the faces on the pavement, white concentrated faces, stubble-bearded, smooth young faces—the same faces that had always been there. They belonged to the courthouse as much as the faded dry old trees. She raised her gloved hand and waved to them as they left the curb. It was a salute to many things that pleased her, many things that were the treasures, the private treasures, of the past—the past that was really past and only lived in her head, in old Ed Huggerston's head.

CHAPTER NINETEEN

I

The forenoon was silent. Or it seemed to be, with that mysterious listening stillness that falls on an open place, a field, lying on a slope under vast sunlight and a pale hot sky. The woman stood alone in the field, a part of the stillness, gazing down at the fringe of forest —sumac, sweet gum, oak, and pine, they closed this stretching place about like walls, hid it and kept it secret from the rest of the universe. She stood erect between two rows of tall tobacco plants, so that she seemed caught and held, a truncated thing in the sea of broad leaves washing thickly about her. She was not doing anything. Her arms were folded flatly under her bosom and the faded cotton dress that enclosed her gave her no shape or definition. A slat bonnet hung half off her head. Her face with the fine bones stretching against the taut weathered skin hung forward a little. Without energy, it was an attitude of obstinate inertness. The dark eyes, shadowed about the sockets with an indelible coloration that was beyond weariness, looked ahead of her over the thick surface of spreading leaves with an expression of intent vacuity. She was not looking at anything. Under the bland surface of the heat there hung another level of sound, subtle and harsh—the eternal chittering of cicada and cricket, of all the mysterious inhabitants of leaf and grass. And beyond her at the edge of a field two crows quarreled and fluttered in a stark dead tree. She listened to them and nodded her head, a little smile playing about the thin line of her mouth. And from them her eyes cut up into the sky, where a long wheeling speck of black—a buzzard —hung suspended against the hazy, empty sky. She watched it as though it meant something to her.

She brushed at her forehead, where a thin wisp of lifeless, graying hair hung down, and then she looked with interest at her hand, turning it from back to palm before her eyes. Was that her hand, this reddened, worn, cracked, old woman's hand? She was always coming upon some part of herself with this feeling of shock and discovery, as though time had left her but had gone on using her till she no longer recognized herself. Yes, it was her hand. She folded it again under her other arm like—like any worn farm woman. Because that's what I am—a farm woman. Her pale lips said the three words without sound. A farm woman. That's what she had been for a long time. And this was her land, her field, that she was standing in now. She looked up and over the spreading green that washed silently about her with a kind of empty astonishment in which there was neither discovery nor understanding. This is my field and this green is tobacco. And then she asked herself the two awful questions that pushed upon her so often now of late, day and night: Where am I? Who am I? She shivered under the sun and pulled her head up higher. It's because this is so strange, she thought, comforting herself, all of it—tobacco, earth, cawing crows. But no one has ever known except myself how strange. I have never let *them* know. I have kept my head up! But beyond that she began to try to find the simple reason, the immediate answer. Why am I standing here now, what did I come here for? The fact that she must wait here silently for that answer filled her with more terror than anything else. And it was a terror that hung blacker and blacker so that she could not put it off with the fact of her pride. That pride was worn, old, a cold refuge to cling to. If I could only think, now . . . I must think. . . .

She dropped her eyes to the nearest thing—the rows of tobacco —and under its flagrant green she saw the leaves hanging and withering against the stalk, withered in a strange vegetable agony. Ah yes, it was the wilt—the wilt was in the crop again this year. Mr. Bettis had told her when he came up to the house this morning with Simon, "I'm afraid the wilt has got in the south field again, ma'am." "Oh, has it, Mr. Bettis?" And when the house was swept and the furniture polished (because she polished it every day now—the sideboard, the hall mirror, the two chairs), she put on her bonnet and came down alone to see. And that was why she was here now. She turned in the row with a stiff, awkward movement back toward the house. She knew now why she had found herself standing there in the hot emptiness. Her mouth tightened again with an expression of remote scorn. The south field has the wilt . . . it will be a poor crop again this year . . . it was a poor crop last year. She thought of this almost with satisfaction. And then as she gazed up the low row toward the weathered farmhouse, the barn, and the buildings crouched under the little grove of old trees she was struck again with the feeling of terror. It seemed so far from her. Thousands of miles. In a flash the green impersonality surrounding her, and lying between her and the house, seemed vastly sinister. They were flames, diseased, green flames. She was caught in the midst of them to be consumed under the hot implacable sun with crows crying in the distance. The terror became panic, blind and overpowering. Instead of walking back up the row she began to run, holding her skirts tightly away from the aisle of leaves, those sick and dying green things reaching out from their stalks, clutching and caressing. The whole field seemed to tilt and swim under her feet so that she staggered. She moaned, because she felt that she might fall and go down drowning in that endless crevasse between the tobacco plants—be lost forever.

"Simon! . . . Simon!" she called ahead of her in a dry keening voice, and heard the crows answer from down the field. But nothing else. Would she never reach the yard and the house? They swam in the heat miles and miles away. But she went on running till at last she burst out from the edge of the field upon a dusty pathway running along the kitchen garden. Some chickens squawked. They exploded from beneath her feet and ran crazily in among the cucumber vines and a row of dying tomato plants. She stopped at the sight of them and giggled, pressing the fingers of one hand hard against her mouth. Why, I'm all right, she thought. What on earth am I running for? I should not have gone so far down the field. In the middle of the day, too. Whatever possessed me! And I'm all hot and weak . . . wet under my arms, my skin feeling like a slick melon under the cloth . . . disgusting! No lady sweats—*no indeed, no lady sweats!* She jerked the bonnet up on her head again, pulling her neck up tight, and walked steadily up the yard between the old corncrib and the barn to the foot of the back steps and stopped. The smells of the yard, the feathery smell, the hot sour smell of clabber and manure, rose like a miasma thickly about her. It sickened her a little. Why, she thought, I've been smelling it forever and ever and it still sickens me.

"Simon! . . . Simon!"

She heard her voice, querulous and complaining, call the name again. But why am I calling Simon? The house was silent. She stood staring up at the worn, gray farmhouse. So empty, so deserted-looking. How hideous it is, she thought, how common—my house! And she began to giggle again, the hopeless, horrid little sound. But why doesn't someone answer? She began to feel that perhaps there was no one—that it was really empty and had always been empty and she was the only one there, imprisoned, deserted, at the end of a continuing nightmare of sun and field and sagging, rotting farmhouse.

"*Simon!*"

She screamed now. And then a Negress, enormously fat and old, shambled out on the porch above her. She carried a dented metal pot full of apples. A knife stuck out of one black fist. She wheezed and panted as she leaned her bulk against the porch railing.

"Why—that you callin', Miss Meg?" she said crossly, mumbling the words over empty gums. "You know Simon ain' heah. Simon's down to Mr. Bettis's with Lil Jim. What you want?"

The woman at the foot of the sagging steps nodded, pressing her hand against her mouth.

"Yes, yes, I forgot."

She was so relieved with happiness at seeing the face, the black pouchy face, above her that she couldn't think. Why, that's Relda. Is that the way Relda looks? She went on nodding her head.

"Miss Meg," said the black woman in the mumbling, cross voice, "come in heah out of that sun. What are you doin'? You oughta have bettah sense than to go wanderin' round like that."

"But James," said the woman standing in the yard. "I must see James."

"Cose, cose, he'll be back come dinnertime. You come on in heah."

"All right, Relda," she said in the meek, thin voice, and came slowly up the stair. "All right, but he's been gone a long time. I want to see him as soon as he comes in. I have something I must speak to him about."

She stopped on the porch and looked commanding, the dark eyes flashing out of the gaunt face. The Negress padded to her and took her by the arm.

"Go on now an' set yohself down an' rest. I'll bring yoh somethin' cool to drink," she muttered crossly. "Wanderin' round in this hot sun—I decleah!" She allowed herself to be propelled to the door. "You go sit on the poach—the sun's round to this side now."

She said nothing. Just nodded and went on into the hallway alone. It was dim and narrow and smelled of coal oil. At the mirror stand she stopped. It stood crowding the space, gleaming and rich with polished wood, at the foot of the little rickety stairway that crawled up the bare wall to the rooms above. She ran her fingers over the mahogany lovingly. No dust. As beautiful as it had always been. She smiled and then saw that there was a face smiling back at her. Not smiling exactly but grimacing out of a haunted countenance. Why, who is that? she thought indignantly. Strangers wandering around my house. And then she stopped and put her hand to her mouth again. Why, it's me. She nodded at the image, the graceless, stiff-necked bobbing. Overhead came a creaking of boards, a woody, restless sound.

"Cousin Tabby?" she whispered, turning her head upward. "You want something?"

She waited and everything was quiet—except somewhere a fly was buzzing in the shadows. She frowned then. Ah no, what can I be thinking of? Cousin Tabby has been dead and gone all these years. Now what on earth could have made me do that? The sun, that's it. The sun! I've been out in the sun too long. I must go somewhere and sit down very quietly and then James will come, and everything will be all right. But she felt exhausted leaning against the mirror stand. That piece of furniture by its very presence, a grotesque thing really in this empty, bare farmhouse, reassured her that she was not dreaming, not lost. Go sit on the porch, that was what Relda had said. Yes. She must rest a little—then she would feel all right. She mustn't let all those people think she was tired. That she could no longer stand up against them. She had stood up against them so long that a little weakness now was not going to shame her before them. They were waiting there outside the door to jeer at her, to look at her curiously. It would be easier to slip into the parlor and sit where they couldn't see her. She crossed to the open door and leaned against the jamb. But this wasn't the parlor— this little room, this hideous, shambly, bare little space with the two horsehair chairs the only thing that she knew. And then, too, she had never run away. She had put her head up against them all these years.

She took off the bonnet with slow, blind movements and dropped it on the little cane-bottomed chair just inside. I will go on the porch like Relda said. And I will sit where they can all see me and see that I am still here and not caring about them. She pushed open the rickety screen door and stepped out on the porch. It did not even shock her any more to know that there were no tall, white columns, no long stretch of floor—just the bare worn planks and two sagging rockers and the yard, devoid of grass—just some heavy red dahlias nodding in the sun. The little narrow pathway bordered with rocks leading down to the gate that wouldn't close and the little roadway that led nowhere beyond. She pulled her head high and walked carefully over to one of the rockers and sat down. She did not rock, but sat and stared out across the little yard

354

in an attitude of prideful patience—waiting. The heavy brooding silence closed about her.

It was only gradually that she became aware of the splutter and roar of the motorcar approaching out of the heated stillness. She could not even think how long she had been hearing it. And then the strange black vehicle slid along the fence, grotesque and panting. It stopped just short of the half-opened gate. She sat looking at it with astonishment—not shock, but a kind of gaping surprise that had no thought in it. It was only when she saw the figure of the woman step out, helped by a fancily uniformed man, that she began to feel the ache at the base of her neck. She must have been holding it too still, too high—it was such an effort nowadays.

The woman by the car was coming through her gate, walking energetically up her pathway—a slight, active figure under a broad-brimmed hat. She got up out of the rocking chair and walked to the head of the steps watching her. The approaching woman smiled—a wide, friendly, questioning smile. She plucked at her bosom among the rows of rich ruffles and with a little scooping gesture placed some glasses on her short nose.

"Is this the Barton place?" asked the visitor in a crisp, polite voice.

The woman on the porch crossed her hands over the faded cotton dress in the gesture of patience and nodded slowly.

"Yes," she said, "yes, it is."

"I wonder if I might see Mrs. Barton," said the woman on the pathway. There fell a sudden silence full of the buzzing hum, the fly and insect sounds, in the yard, the sound of the sun beating downward. The woman on the porch went on nodding slowly. She had never stopped.

"Why, yes," she said in the astonished voice. "Yes, I am Mrs. Barton."

2

Sonie, sitting in the rocking chair, thought out of the shock, So this is Major Singleton's daughter—this is the one, this gaunt specter in the poor dress and the coarse, graying hair . . . Margaret Singleton, this derelict . . . the one Brant Royle . . . And she felt pity well over her in a wave. No one should have this happen to him. Not even a criminal. This ruin, this lost thing, this ghost sitting opposite her and talking in the tired, precise voice and looking at her out of the fierce dark eyes as though waiting for a blow to strike her. It made Sonie fiercely uncomfortable. She had come out on this impulsive journey to find something, to pay some small homage to the past and her own sense of emptiness—but she had not thought

355

to meet with this. It was an incredible, unbelievable thing. Ol' Major Singleton's daughter—the legendary creature in a castle on a hill. . . . What had happened in all these years to leave nothing at the end but this?

"I know that this is an intrusion," she was saying in the brisk, strained voice, "and that we have never met. . . . But I used to live in Kingsmont and have come back again, you know. And I didn't hear until today that Mr. Barton had passed away. I used to know him years ago. I was a friend of his—and I just wanted to pay my respects."

My, how lame I sound! she thought. But thank God I can babble on like this. Maybe it will ease up things, and she went on thinking: We meet at last—and this is what it is like. I never knew that other woman, and now she has disappeared. This is what happens. . . .

"Mr. Barton—oh yes," said the faded, gaunt figure in the chair, the dark eyes blazing unfalteringly at Sonie. "Mr. Barton died in March. The doctor said it was typhoid fever, but I don't know—"

"I don't know whether John ever even mentioned my name. You see, I hadn't seen him since long before I was married, but he used to know me as Sonia Lipik—but my friends all called me Sonie. Now I'm just plain Mrs. Graham. Mrs. Talbot Graham. My husband is dead now, too."

"Lipik," said the woman, and nodded. "Oh yes—I believe I have heard that name somewhere." She began to rock slowly, a wondering expression coming over the weathered features. "Well, Mrs. Lipik, it is very kind of you to come. I'm sure I appreciate it. A friend of Mr. Barton's—" The tired voice, precise still, cultivated —the voice of someone else—trailed off.

"I would have come sooner," continued Sonie, rushing into the silence, "but I hadn't heard. I've been away a long time—and one loses track, you know."

She was beginning to feel uncomfortable. There was something about this meeting beyond the shock, something in the remoteness of the other woman that made her feel strange. She began to regret the impulse that had brought her to this meeting. But she had always been an impulsive fool! She would just have to see it through. Thank God O'Brien was out there with the car and she could simply walk out of this and go home whenever she wanted to. But she was not going to let it panic her. She would do as well as she could what she had come to do and then get away and not bother any more. But she could not help feeling some sense of guilt riding under her uneasiness. It was terrible that time could blot out whole facts in one's memory. (And what did one have but what one remembered?) And what had time done to this woman? That was the thing. Here she, Sonie, rode grandly up in a silly Chalmers; and here was this woman who had lived on an eminence, unreal and princesslike, over all her childhood, sitting faded and worn—a husk on a run-down farm. It was too incredible!

"Yes," John Barton's widow said. "One does lose track. I haven't been to Kingsmont for years. You might think that strange with just a few miles to go—" the fierce dark eyes swept Sonie's face— "but they are cruel there—and they have destroyed the town. Nobody but cruel people would do a thing like that. I have not gone back among them, but I have never lowered my head to them either!"

Why, she's mad, stark-mad, thought Sonie. That's why I have been so uncomfortable. The poor creature is out of her head.

"Of course," she said a little desperately, and removed the pince-nez nervously from her nose, reeling them back into the locket. I must get away as soon as possible. This is more than I bargained for. I should feel triumphant, but I can't. It is just terrible. She felt a sense of personal outrage. If time was going to do a thing like this, it should hide it. She felt cheated of all the reason for the pain she had suffered because of this woman—not what she was now, but the thing she had been. She could not feel anything but pity and horror before this poor ghost. It drained hate of its treasure, the thing that one had fed on for so long, and made it empty and worthless. This is the woman Brant Royle loved; this is the woman who held the whip between us. No, no, she could not face it without its making a whole part of her knowledge and belief grotesque and incredible.

"I hope you won't think I am simply prying," she went on, thinking that her fool mouth was running on with the speeches she had rehearsed during the ride, but which now sounded like the questions of a zany before this figure in the hideous, sagging dress—but she couldn't stop. She had to keep on talking. "Because I didn't come to intrude, but when I heard that John had married and gone away to the North again it didn't occur to me that he would ever come back. He never seemed to belong down here in the South."

The woman nodded in slow agreement and then suddenly leaned toward Sonie, looking sidewise out of the dark eyes as though she did not want to be overheard.

"They ruined him in Detroit," she said with a kind of satisfaction, closing her mouth thinly on the statement. "Simply ruined him, robbed him of all his money. He didn't have a chance. But then there were no gentlemen among them—no gentlemen at all. Just trashy thieves and Yankees. I told him they would just take his money and throw him out—and they did. And when they did we had to come back here, because he wanted to grow tobacco. We've always grown tobacco, you know, in my family . . . finest tobacco in the county . . . my father fought in the war . . ."

"Ah yes," said Sonie helplessly, "Major Jim—I used to see him

357

riding down by the warehouses when I was a little girl. I remember he wore a gold ring and it shone when he flicked the reins. He was a fine-looking man."

The figure opposite her still leaned out of the chair tensely.

"They ruined him too," she said in her cold precise voice. "Those Yankees and that trash—killed him. They would have killed me too if I hadn't been stronger. You see, I wouldn't let my head down to them. . . . I never will!"

She leaned back then and began to rock slowly, nodding primly over her thoughts. Then she said calmly, like an afterthought:

"I'm not being very hospitable, and I hope you will forgive me, Mrs. Lipik. But this is the busy time of the year. They're going to pick in a day or so. And it's a fine crop. We've always had a way with tobacco, you know—in my family. Well, my servants are all quite busy, or I could offer you some refreshment."

"Thank you very much," murmured Sonie. "Very kind of you, but please don't bother."

She tensed herself to get up. It was time to bring this parody of a visit to a close. And as she gathered herself to do something positive about it there were suddenly voices in the roadway. She heard O'Brien's soft rumble and a child's excited treble. Almost at the same moment the woman in the rocker stood up, tensely and proudly, and looked out across the yard. It was an extraordinary and compelling transformation. For a moment Sonie could only look at her. The face was at once calm and alive and beautiful. And the body denied the plain, worn dress. By some alchemy implicit in her attitude as she stood there, it became a regal garment.

"James," called the woman clearly. "James—I've been waiting for you."

Sonie turned her eyes down the yard now. There was a Negro, rather old and stooped, standing by the car bowing and grinning at O'Brien. And between them she saw over the ruined fence a small, tousled head—black hair just showing.

"James!" the warm, vibrant cry came from the woman again. And then the faces in the roadway turned toward the house. Then Sonie saw the small boy come sedately through the gate, walking with the gravity of a grownup in his faded jeans. Up the pathway to the porch. He was thin, fine-drawn, and the face was sweet and grave—a child's face (Sonie judged in that moment that he must be ten or twelve) but with a maturity in the features, a level wondering gaze out of the startling blue eyes. It was a face that looked at things and thought about what it saw.

"My son!" announced the woman standing there waiting. It was not for the child but for Sonie. And the way she said it made Sonie feel that all that had been before this moment was just a bad dream.

358

The boy trotted obediently up the steps. He looked at the visitor candidly and without surprise, and nodded. Sonie felt a flash of delight and curiosity run over her. She put on her pince-nez again. So this was Johnny Barton's son. She felt almost that she was in the presence of some delightful miracle. Here was something, a possibility that she had never even considered.

"Mother," said the boy, a little breathlessly, "it's a motorcar!"

"Come here," commanded the woman. When he stepped obediently to her she took his face between her hands with a gesture at once immensely prideful and tender. She looked at him for a long time hungrily, then raised her eyes to Sonie.

"He is a Singleton—all Singleton," she said deliberately. "My grandfather had blue eyes. James, this is Mrs. Lipik—mind your manners!"

He turned to Sonie again and gravely extended a dirty hand. Sonie took it.

"How do you do, James," she said, looking at him searchingly. She did not even mind being called Mrs. Lipik any more.

"Fine, thank you," answered the child in the grave, precise treble. "Is that your motorcar?"

"Yes. Do you like it?"

He nodded and stared out into the roadway with the blue, dark-lashed eyes. Sonie was charmed with him. The whole day seemed to have been retrieved from disintegration and horror by the fact of this small boy—so concentrated on his own thoughts, so old-fashioned and mannered in his speech and attitude. He was too thin, though; very likely didn't get enough to eat, she decided practically. How could he in this shambling ruin of a house surrounded by and cared for by nothing but doddering Negroes and an unbalanced parent. It was a miracle that he had survived at all.

"It is a beautiful car," the boy was saying. "I saw three motor-cars in Kingsmont last Saturday. Someday I would like to make something useful and beautiful like a motorcar."

"You are your father's son," chuckled Sonie with approval. "I used to know your father—I was just telling your mother—and your father was forever making things."

"He was nice—my father—but he got sick and died." The child's precise voice was without any emotion. He was simply stating an interesting fact. "He used to make me things before he died. He made me a real water mill and we dammed the branch up and it ground up acorns. That was when I was real little—" he frowned —"but he made me a lot of other things too."

His mother, standing behind him, made a fierce, pointless gesture in the air before her face as though she were brushing at an insect.

"But they took it all away from him—trash and Yankees," she said in the frail, harsh voice. She put her fingers against her mouth and nodded. "Trash and Yankees."

The child seemed to notice nothing shocking in this behavior. He turned and listened to his mother politely and then faced Sonie. She felt the hot discomfort rising in her again. Now, because of the boy, it seemed worse. She also began to feel angry, as she always did when a situation baffled her. She started to say something to break the silence, but before she could open her mouth the other woman, with an erratic sudden movement, leaned out over the porch railing.

"Simon!" she called in the flat, shrill voice. "Simon, come here immediately!"

The old Negro talking to O'Brien in the roadway nodded and answered, "Yes'm, Miss Meg—I'm comin'."

He came up the path, bent and limping but with a kind of patient dignity in his bearing. His bald dome with the grizzled fringe glistened in the sun. The woman went on talking to him as he came.

"Whatever can have possessed you, Simon—don't you see we have guests? Go tell Relda to set another place for dinner immediately!"

She turned from him then with the curious abruptness. She stared with the dark, smoldering glance from the boy to Sonie and covered the little thin and meaningless smile with her finger tips.

"Yes'm, Miss Meg." The old Negro walked stiffly out of sight around the corner of the porch. It was not till he was gone that it swept over Sonie what had been said.

"No—no, thank you, Mrs. Barton," she protested, bobbing up briskly out of the rocker. She was so upset that she forgot her reticule and it fell with a little jingling of its contents to the floor. "It's very nice of you, but I really must get back to town. I only meant to drop in for a little visit to pay my respects, you know."

Sonie reeled and unreeled the chain on the pince-nez with agitated fingers. She saw that the boy had picked up her purse and was standing holding it out to her politely. She smiled then.

"Thank you," she said, "thank both of you. You must come and see me sometime when you are in town, Mrs. Barton. It would be nice—"

"Thank you!" the woman interrupted her flatly and shook her head vehemently. "But I never go into town any more. You see, they all talk about me behind my back—they want to humble me. But I won't be humbled. No indeed, I can't have that!"

Sonie felt anger and pity churn about in her again. It was impossible. She really must get away. She couldn't bear it another five minutes. And if the Chalmers got tempermental, as it often did, and O'Brien had to do a lot of fiddling about under the hood and

360

churning with the crank (which he so adored to do!) while she sat there in the back seat—why, she would simply *discharge* him! She knew she was beginning to think a little hysterically and hated it. She fixed a smile on her face. Thank God! she thought, I'm still able to act a little.

"Well, good-by then, Mrs. Barton," she said warmly. The woman did not reply. She nodded her head once and then held it high and stiff, looking blankly at Sonie as though she was no longer there. Sonie turned to the boy and offered her gloved hand.

"Good-by, James." He shook her hand gravely. There was such poise and calm in him that she felt amazed once more. "Don't you ever come into Kingsmont?" she asked impulsively.

"Yes, ma'am. Every Saturday with Mr. Bettis—and sometimes on Wednesday too."

"Well, maybe you will come to see me, James—and maybe your mother wouldn't mind if I took you for a little ride in my motorcar. Would you like that?"

"Yes, ma'am," he said, and the blue eyes flashed and glowed at her. She smiled and nodded at him and went down the steps. She walked briskly to the road, holding up her skirts from the dust. O'Brien helped her in and she settled back on the seat stiffly staring ahead of her. But the Chalmers seemed in a hurry to be off, too. It started almost immediately with the big shaking roar that she always considered so ridiculously demonstrative. She turned then and waved her hand to the woman and the boy on the porch. Neither of them responded. They stood exactly as she had left them, staring back at her.

Ah, what a joy it was to be moving, even though the roadbed made her teeth rattle. The dust began to rise and sift in upon her. She welcomed it and breathed deeply; she felt soiled. The dust seemed clean by comparison. Ach, Sonie, my girl, she thought, you always can manage to get yourself into some kind of mess even now after all these years! But she grinned at herself and felt younger than she had in months. Well, at least I've been now and done my duty.

But during all that dusty, hot ride through the still August noon back to Kingsmont she felt uncomfortable. She couldn't pass this experience off by saying simply that she had done something sleazy in the way of a "duty." It was a feeling of guilt that came troubling her, and she could not shrug it off. The eyes of the woman continued to haunt her. Why, she looked a thousand years old, she kept repeating crossly. I would never have recognized her—and she can't be more than a year or so older than me. I *know* because I remember how she *used* to look. And poor Johnny Barton—married to her all these years and now lost forever. Johnny Barton buried in the shadows of his own strange soul, the stranger who had stumbled in upon

361

them and made them all rich and had gone on stumbling down into deeper and deeper obscurity. Sonie shook her head and sighed. It was thinking of him that was partly responsible for this feeling of annoying guilt. Ach, don't be a fool, Sonie, what could you have done? But— Here she stopped stock-still among her thoughts and pulled herself erect in the seat. She swayed with the car and felt the hot wind beat on her cheeks. But there is something I can do! she whispered, and beat with a determined fist upon her lap. Of course. What a fool I've been! It's what I've been thinking about for the last quarter of an hour without knowing it. That child . . . Johnny's boy. . . . Something's *got* to be done about that boy—yes indeed, and I'm the one to do it.

Her thoughts went racing happily ahead then with the car. They were formless, disconnected, and fell into no meaning or plan yet, but they were energetic and positive. She grinned at herself again and reaching up, gave the wide hat an insolent shove so that it leaned rakishly over her forehead. This was more like herself—why, she hadn't felt this good in years!

3

She went on feeling good. It was almost as though she had been asleep for a long time and was now awake. Here was something positive to do, to work for, to focus her considerable energies upon. It transformed the whole world. She had come back to Kingsmont simply as a place of refuge. But now that was all changed. She had found her place again. The world seemed suddenly something she belonged to instead of something she remembered. She went about her house with a foolish high heart that astonished her—and all because of a child's face. She was honest enough to realize that all this went deeper than just what she could grasp. Like all active, sane people, she was motivated profoundly by sentiment—and she knew that her thinking set off by this encounter with John Barton's son was colored by more motives than the obvious. She was making her peace with her life. This was her chance. And it was almost as though she had come back to the crude ugly bustling city of her origin because her instinct knew that she would find what she was looking for. In being honest she tried to see if it was only because she was a childless woman, unfulfilled. But she knew that was too easy an answer. It went deeper than that. It went far into the fathoms of the past and her feeling that she must be honest and pay her debts. . . .

In the first wave of her discovery she sat down and planned in detail how she could help young James. If the woman was mad—or half-mad—there were state institutions; she could call it to the attention of the authorities and remove the child bodily. Then she swore at herself for being a fool again. Such an obvious and easy course would never do. The skeins were too tangled between the boy and his mother. She might ruin everything with the first step—just because the woman had acted strange. . . . She had always been under the shadow of eccentricity—that would not be enough. And the boy, becoming a kind of warm obsession, a focus, in her thoughts and feelings, was worth more careful planning than that. She must move slowly. Let her common sense, the thing in her that she had always trusted, reveal the right way. So she decided to do nothing for the present, just to possess herself with patience. He said he came into town on Saturday, but in the meantime she could not keep herself from haunting the places where the farm wagon with him in it, the blue eyes and the grave old-young face, might be discovered.

Saturday came at last. She had O'Brien take her down to the courthouse square early. She had some business at the bank that made her presence all right, even if he did not come. The thought filled her with a kind of panic that surprised her. Why, I am acting like a woman in love, she thought, putting on the pince-nez, that badge of respectability and solidity. How silly of me! But just the same she was not surprised when she came out of the bank that morning and energetically walking around the square, came at last upon his face under an old felt hat. It was just as she had expected. It had a kind of finality that reassured her. He sat in the old buckboard with the two dusty mules, alone. She walked to the edge of the pavement.

"Hello there, Jim," she said.

The boy's blue eyes swung upon her. His face was streaked. He had been weeping, but the mask of gravity preserved it intact.

"How-d'y-do, ma'am," he responded.

"I've been looking for you. You said you came in on Saturday, you know."

He nodded. "Yes, ma'am."

"Haven't you got a handkerchief?" she said. "Your face is a mess."

"No, ma'am."

"Well, here," she said, and stepped down between the wagons till she stood below him. She dug into her reticule and pulled out the folded square of fresh, scented linen. He took it from her and wiped blindly at his eyes, still looking at her.

"What's the matter, Jim?"

"It's the wilt," he said quietly; "it's got my field too now."

She didn't know what he was talking about, but she knew that it was something important. He handed the handkerchief back to her.

363

"I was going to make a good crop this year," he said, "but the wilt got it."

"I'm sorry, Jim," she said, being cheerful.

"But it oughtn't to be like that, y'know, Mrs.—" he searched for her name—"Mrs. Lipik. There ought to be some way of stopping it. It's all over the county this year, Mr. Bettis says. What I want to know is why there were one, two plants in every row of my field that it didn't get. There's a reason for that. Maybe it would be a good thing for someone to find out. Maybe I could find out about it myself someday."

Why, of course, she thought, he's talkin' about tobacco. I should have known. His crop—their crop—has gone bad. He was looking at her, but his child's face was concentrated and removed.

"Jim," she said, "I haven't got the motorcar with me today, but would you like to step across the square there to the drugstore and have some ice cream—and we could talk about your tobacco. . . ."

She waited with a pang of apprehension. Everything seemed to hang in the balance.

"I don't think Mr. Bettis would mind. He's gone to the bank," he said, looking across the milling people, the passing carts, the electric trolleys clanging by.

"Well, come along, then. I need some ice cream myself."

He let himself down from the seat in one economical movement that placed him beside her on the cobbles. They walked back to the sidewalk and he patted a mule's head and clucked, passing his hands down the reins tied to the hitching rail. Then he joined her and they walked side by side across the old square under the trees—neither looking at the other. All Sonie could think of was that it was just as she had expected, and that she was filled with happiness.

They entered the drugstore and sat down at one of the tables. When the boy in the apron came to them she ordered two chocolate ice-cream sodas with whipped cream. Then they settled back like a couple of old cronies and looked out at the procession milling beyond the wide opening of the drugstore.

"Jim," she said casually, being careful with her voice, "who is Mr. Bettis?"

He frowned. "He works the tobacco in shares for Mother," he said. "He worked for my father."

"Oh, I see," she went on casually, studying the table top where a fly crawled across the gleaming enamel. "What's Mr. Bettis doing at the bank?"

"Oh, he nearly always calls at the bank. We have to get money, you know. Mother tells him how much and he has to go in and get the men at the bank to lend it to him. Mother says we can always pay it back."

He said it as easily and as unconcernedly as though stating the time of day. It fell like a plummet into her thinking. She filed it away for future reference. The soda clerk came up then and set the tall drinks before them and they took the straws between their lips, looking at each other over the glass rim. She felt perfectly comfortable now. Nothing was being forced. He had accepted her. This was the only way to do it.

"Jim," she said, "if you don't mind, my name is not Mrs. *Lipik*, but Mrs. Graham, and I used to live in Kingsmont a long time ago. I've been away. I think your mother just didn't hear me right."

"Oh, that's all right," he said, and sucked greedily through his straw. "Mother isn't well—she's sick a lot of the time. She was sick before Father died."

He said it casually with the terrible flat directness of a child. It was so impersonal and yet it told her so much. Then he raised the blue eyes and smiled, his mouth still puckered about the straw.

"Mrs. Graham," he said, and she grinned and winked back at him. "You know I hope you didn't mind my crying." He continued stirring at his glass. "But it always makes me cry when things die. It seems such a bad thing for them to die—and it's bad for the people who grow them."

"Certainly, Jim, I understand exactly—I've cried over things myself."

"You have?"

"Of course. I wasn't always able to do very much about it, but I always tried. Didn't you say back there in the wagon that you thought someone ought to find out about what was killing your tobacco? I think it would be a fine thing if someone did. Because anything that is an enemy of tobacco is an enemy of this state, and the men who grow tobacco!"

"Yes, ma'am." He nodded again, the slow nod, the grave considered gesture that so moved and charmed her. "That's right, Mrs. —er—Graham."

He smiled suddenly, pleased with remembering her name. Sonie glowed all over like a schoolgirl.

"Maybe you'll be the one who'll find it out, Jim."

"Maybe so." He nodded again with the concentrated expression, thinking deeply within himself. "I would like to. It would be better, doing that—or as good—as being smart like my father was."

"Indeed it would, Jim!" she agreed fervently. She didn't know why she said it so fervently. But the presence of this child compelled her in a way that she did not stop to consider. They both fell silent and content, finishing their sodas and looking out into the crowded hot Saturday-morning street. Then they got up and she paid for the refreshment. Wordlessly they went out into the square again and began to walk slowly back to the wagon. She did not press the point now that she had gained it. She felt instinctively that this tenuous understanding between them could not ever be forced. They walked in silence till they came to the hitching post and the wagon. Mr. Bettis was not back from the bank, because it was still empty. He climbed in and sat gravely in the hot sunlight. He did not bother her with a lot of polite thanks for the entertainment. It thrilled her that he didn't, because it was an admission of their intimacy.

"Jim," she said from the sidewalk, "will you be coming into town on Wednesday?"

"I don't know—maybe."

"Well, I'll be looking for you. And if you can get Mr. Bettis to let you come out to my house, we'll take a ride in the motorcar."

He nodded, and the blue eyes gleamed warmly at her under the absurd old hat. "All right, ma'am; thank you, ma'am."

And that was all. They nodded warmly to each other. No nonsense of chattering prolongation. She gestured to him and walked away down the side of the square feeling very happy and content and wondering if the soda was going to disagree with her. She didn't like sweet things this early in the day. Then she smiled and shook her head and walked briskly around to the bank. She had something to do, something very definite. It had formed itself clearly in her mind while she sat with him in the drugstore. She crossed over and entered the bank. Passing down the row of tellers' and bookkeepers' windows, she stopped at a desk. A young man, smooth and suave with a superior air, sat there looking learnedly at a pile of papers.

"I would like to see the manager," she said. "Just tell him it's Mrs. Graham—he'll see me."

He looked up at her and the superior mask changed immediately to the expression of servility with which she was so familiar. She had always scorned and mocked it all her life. But she was pleased with the power she had now. It could make the change in this efficient (no doubt) nincompoop's expression like magic.

"Ah, Mrs. *Graham*," he said in the professional voice. "Of course, let me just go and see, Mrs. Graham."

He returned in a minute, holding the door. She nodded thanks as she went in. It was a scene she was familiar with, had been familiar with for years—New York, Paris, San Francisco—this cubicle with the man in the expensive suit, the desk, the papers, the air of impregnable security; it could be any of those places. She felt perfectly at home. She knew the man behind the desk—whatever the name. She knew this office intimately, although she had never set foot in it before.

"Mrs. Graham," said the man, rising in greeting. He gestured toward the chair opposite him. "Won't you sit down?"

She nodded and disposed herself. It was as hard and expensive-feeling as she had always remembered a score of similar chairs.

"Mr.—?" She surveyed the man coolly.

"Pendleton, Mrs. Graham—and I must say it's a pleasure. I had read with a great deal of interest that you were back in town. And I am delighted to be of whatever service I can."

"Mr. Pendleton," she said, "I do not want to take up your time on this busy morning, but there is something that I believe you can help me with." He waited with his head inclined toward her politely. "There has been a man here this morning to borrow some money—a Mr. Bettis, I believe."

He rocked back in his chair and put his finger tips together. He looked gravely at the desk.

"Yes, ma'am, he was—just a few minutes ago, to be exact." He shook his head and pursed his mouth.

"Mr. Pendleton, did you lend him the money?"

"Yes," he said, continuing to study the desk top.

"On what security, Mr. Pendleton?"

He cleared his throat. She looked at him.

"I know what I am asking may not be exactly ethical, but I am concerned, because it concerns the family of an old friend of mine."

"To be perfectly frank with you, Mrs. Graham," he began, with that air of ponderous unction and superiority that had always irked her. Why, she thought, do they all act like high priests just because they have to fool with the mysteries of money and finance? "To be perfectly frank—and I would not divulge this to anyone else, because it is really very awkward and painful, particularly for Mr. Randolph, our president—"

"Well now," she said impatiently, and fixed him with her pince-nez, "let's not waste time, Mr. Pendleton."

"You see, it's an old and sad story, Mrs. Graham. Mr. Bettis comes in here and borrows money, supposedly on some land that Mrs. Barton owns. That land was mortgaged and overmortgaged years ago, but Mrs. Barton is the daughter of an old family here in town, and Mr. Randolph out of pure sentiment has been carrying her all these years. Why, I don't know what they could have done without it," he said, raising his eyes piously. What an insufferable, superior ass! thought Sonie, looking at him grimly.

"Yes?" she said sharply.

"Well, it just won't do—and I *know* Mr. Randolph is getting tired of going on and on year after year like this. I really do admire him. Fine man, Mrs. Graham—excellent citizen—but there has to be a stopping point somewhere. I reluctantly, very reluctantly, let Mr.

Bettis have another hundred dollars this morning. I authorized it, as a matter of fact, just before you came in. Why, the total must run into the thousands after all these years! And of course Mr. Randolph has let Mrs. Barton—she was Major Singleton's daughter, you may know?—go on believing that he is taking notes against her property. Philanthropy, pure philanthropy, and sentiment for the sake of an old friend. You don't find many men as generous nowadays, Mrs. Graham." He looked across at her severely.

"Mr. Pendleton," she said, fixing his stare in her own—"by the way, are you related to the Pendletons who had the old factory years ago down below the warehouses on West Street?"

The man almost smirked at her in his smugness. "My paternal uncle, Mrs. Graham," he said. "Fine family."

She wished she could reach out and slap his face a bit. What a horrible creature! She had met a thousand like him. She had merely forgotten how contemptible they were.

"I thought so," she said, and leaned toward him. "Mr. Pendleton, I have come here on a very private matter and I know I can trust to your discretion." He waited unctuously, and she delighted in continuing as though addressing a menial: "You can tell Mr. Randolph that he doesn't have to bother about the Bartons any longer. I'm assuming that responsibility for personal reasons, into which I do not wish to go. Just let Mr. Bettis or Mrs. Barton or anyone authorized to represent them come in here and borrow whatever they need in the same way they have been doing. My only provision is that they must under no circumstances know—any more than they have known about Mr. Randolph's charity, as you so kindly put it. But I want them to have any amount they need whenever they need it. My credit is good, I think."

"Of course, of course." He was nodding, actually groveling before her. Contemptible creature! She was really quite nauseated.

"And I insist upon liquidating all the notes Mr. Randolph holds to date. I want everything handled out of my account from now on. Do you understand, Mr. Pendleton?" He continued to nod like a fatuous mannequin. She got up from the chair. "Well, if we understand each other, I won't take up any more of your time," she said, removing the pince-nez. He rose and bobbed before her. She would not endure anything more from him. "Arrange it in whatever way is convenient to Mr. Randolph and the bank. I shall expect an accounting each month and that is all. Thank you and good day, Mr. Pendleton. I shall very likely see you again."

He rushed to the door and opened it for her. For some reason she thought of Mama. Mama would have spit on him, she thought. She grinned and went briskly out through the building into the sunlight.

The square looked wonderful. It was full of a sudden magic that she had been looking for hungrily. This was what she had come all these years and all these miles for. It was good, wonderfully good, to be alive and looking at it. She breathed deeply and felt the old, heavy smell of the tobacco rush into her nostrils as though smelling it for the first time. She *liked* this place! It was wonderful to be home. Now, when is Wednesday? He might come on Wednesday, she thought. Ach, you are such an eternal fool, Sonie Lipik! But her whole body thrummed with happiness as she walked briskly through the moving crowd to the corner.

4

She saw him on Wednesday and they went for a ride in the Chalmers.

She was to see him—when weather, illness, and space did not make it impossible—at least once a week for the rest of her life. It was the most absorbing and completely satisfying relationship she had ever experienced. She often looked at herself in one of the mirrors that adorned the big handsome house out on Bay Street and saw the image of herself, mature, erect, energetic—the competent widow and matron, the member of the *older* generation, with the red hair, carefully dyed (because it remained becoming to her and the narrow green eyes)—a pleasing image, one which gratified her. It had on it for her the history of all her life until now. And now here she was—the woman, the *being*, alone, past the great struggle, honored, accepted, autocratic, returned—and still astonishing to herself. She knew that she was alive, competent, an object of envy. Time and experience had moved her through several worlds. But essentially she was still the same Sonie Lipik. A being she quarreled with, fussed at, caressed and spoiled, but enjoyed. Perhaps it was because her essential energy and tolerance, her down-to-earth recognition of the requirements and mystery of living, had never deserted her. The fact of herself might present certain dilemmas and perplexities at any given hour, but her honest, steady, green-eyed, skeptical gaze held true through passion and sentiment. The image looked, grinned, and shrugged its shoulders at her.

Just what about this new entanglement with this waif, this child, James Barton?

She attacked it directly, face forward—as she had always approached anything that meant something essential to her. It also meant that in approaching it she did not employ all the knowing polish and technique of relationships that she had learned in her life. She had never been a fool—foolish perhaps, many times, but never a fool. Carefully considered, she brought all her attention and forces to bear on this relationship with a child. She recognized early that she was not simply filling the emptiness that she felt; that she was not pouring on him the hungry need of a childless woman. No, she thought immediately, I am not the motherly sort—and don't try to fool yourself, Sonie Lipik. Her feeling for this sudden relationship with the boy went deeper than that. She could not unravel all its reasons and she had sense enough not to try. You simply got lost then. She must always have her finger on the pulse of the main stream somewhere. And this boy—this grave, blue-eyed child, the son of the past—was simply *that*. Any sentiment was simply gratuitous. What she felt in this she knew to be authentic, however tentative and unformed. She respected it deeply. And because she respected it she proceeded with caution.

It was well that they had met during the summer. He was free. And because he was free she got to know him in their meetings. From those encounters, so grave and formal and so masculinely terse, she gradually built up the picture of his brief past and its essential quality. She quickly discovered that, contrary to her romantic and emotional concern, his strange and terrible environment was not strange and terrible to him. He took it as it was. John Barton had been his father, but he was remembered in the boy's mind as a few sparse and kindly acts. The mother was mentioned with feeling always, but with nebulous respect. Sonie discovered early that his visits, the events that brought him within her orbit, were things that he accepted not because he enjoyed coming to Kingsmont, but because he had recognized a deeper responsibility. There was fine stuff in him. It had been marked with integrity at birth, and the fact of poverty, insecurity, the terrible wash of weather and the arbitrary caprice of growing things, had left no mark on his lone childish pride and dignity. That fascinated her more than she could ever admit. He was so complete. He needed no one, because he had always had some fundamental and fixed concern that admitted of no sophistry.

She saw his poverty always clean and shaped by the spirit within him. And in seeing it she had to pay homage to his forebears. Here was the essential element that had made leaders, had governed the mysterious regions of wealth and power—old Major Singleton, the shadowy mother, those creatures of another world—resurgent in this boy. She respected that enormously and never violated it. She learned early that he did not like the city.

One Wednesday when he came to her house—driving the mules up the curved driveway of the house, stopping them under the porte-cochere as though he came in a dashing phaeton—after a grave exchange over milk and cookies they had gone into town borne in the admired Chalmers. She had discovered that he had never seen the factories where the tobacco found its reason for being.

"You mean, Jim," she had said, "no one has taken you down into Jamaica to show you what has made this city what it is?"

"No, ma'am."

"You like raising tobacco, don't you?"

"Yes, ma'am, I sure *do!*"

"Well, you ought to see the big cigarette factories, then. My father used to work in one of the first of them."

"He did, Mrs. Graham?" he said, crowding the last of the cooky into his mouth.

"He certainly *did*," she said sharply; "he was the best cigarette roller in his day. I even worked there long ago myself."

His mouth stopped moving and he looked at her open-eyed over the big ornate dining-room table where they sat.

"You mean your father worked in the factories, and you did too, Mrs. Graham?"

"Of course," she said. "Why not? A lot of people did and still do. You should know that. Look, Jim," she said after a moment, "would you mind not calling me Mrs. Graham?"

"No, ma'am."

"All right. You let me call you Jim, don't you?" He nodded and brushed the crumbs away. "I'm your friend now, aren't I?" She held herself very still while she looked at the table. This was another step forward. She had not planned on taking it here. It was her intuition, her basic, animal impulse that always plunged her forward.

"You certainly are," he said fervently.

"Then call me Sonie, please. All my friends, my *real* friends, call me Sonie."

He did not seem surprised or embarrassed by this demand. She was delighted anew by his equanimity. It thrilled her in a personal way as though she had been responsible for it. He paused only a moment.

"All right, Sonie," he said. And that was that. From that day he never called her anything else.

"All right, that's settled," she said. "You've finished your cooky. Let's go down and see the factories."

They did. She made the patient O'Brien let them out at the head of Rice Street and they walked down, side by side in the hot afternoon sun, into Jamaica Town, through the rows of dwellings, through the rich smell of poverty—animal and human—the cries, the movement, the unchanging violent energy. The years could never take away their hold on her. This eternal excitement behind the drabness of brick wall and offal.

"That's it—Royle and Company," gesturing toward the long block of building. "The biggest cigarette factory in the world. That's where all the tobacco you grow and all the tobacco any farmer in

371

this state grows finally finds a place—if it's good tobacco," she added. And wondered why she said it so severely.

"Yes," he said. "I've seen it from up the street at the warehouse when Mr. Bettis and I brought in the crop come market time. . . ." His voice trailed off. She glanced at him. He wasn't looking at the factory. He was looking at some children playing and quarreling in the gutter across from them—dirty, thin, squabbling little animals. One was crying bitterly and the others were dancing about it and jeering.

"Well, Jim, don't you think it's impressive? It's one of the land-marks of the state."

"No," he said, "I think it's ugly. I couldn't stand to be near it. It's so closed-up!"

She could have hugged him then. It was a flood of pure feeling. If she had been in the habit of crying she would have let the tears fall heedlessly there before God and everybody.

"Why, Jim," she said, because she could say nothing else.

"I hate closed-up places, Sonie." He continued looking at the brawling children across the cobbled street. "There aren't any trees. There isn't any sky or anything growing. I like to be near things growing. I don't think I could ever live here in town. Too close and big."

"Why, Jim!" she said, and bit her tongue. She was going to say more. But good sense made her cautious. Also what he had said had suddenly opened a floodgate of memories, of hates and loves within herself. She looked at the dirty brats with new eyes. Why, *I* was one of them once, locked-up, imprisoned. She was seeing them through this strange child's eyes. It was a naked revelation. She felt that she had been blind all her life. From that day she came to regard James Barton, the little boy, as a talisman—a being fated somehow to dis-cover the mystery and the sum of her life to her.

After their walk through Jamaica and the factory district she could not get the picture of those children out of her mind, because those children, impersonal, disgusting little waifs that they were, became images of staggering import in her mind. And when James was gone she went to the new telephone that had been installed in her house only the week before and called some people. She called many people. People with names all along the top of the list. She had a long conversation, full of all the persuasiveness and guile that she could bring to it—with the Mayor (a being she had never laid eyes on; but he must bend to her will now, because her mind was set).

"Why, yes, Mrs. Graham, I think you are perfectly right—we have certainly neglected our public and social duty on that score—a most worthy object, we'll call a meeting with the factory managers and councilmen—"

"Now Mr. Mayor," she had said in the new, scornful, business-like voice, "there's no expense on anybody's part except my own. *I* want to do it. I'm footing the bill for a least a quarter of a million dollars. That's the way I feel about it. And if all your politicians and factory managers don't see it the way I do—I don't care, because I can assure you that it *will* be done. Because I'll do it!"

"Most generous, Mrs. Graham, most generous." The old familiar voice of the world of men coming out of the earpiece. She curled her lip.

"I mean it, Mr. Mayor," she said.

And she did. The creation of the much-praised social project that was to be known as the Graham Memorial Settlement House and park, carved out of the crass, inert ugliness of Jamaica Town, began with that conversation. She stirred up the whole community before she had finished. And when she was lauded and praised on every side, honored by state politicians and the papers both in the town and abroad for her efforts in behalf of the factory children, she accepted it simply, graciously, thinking all the while of a small boy's face—a face thin and brown with the touch of sun and space, of a place that he loved—and the blue eyes looking at those lost and dirty children. Those children who were the children of her youth, pitiful strangers in her eyes. She knew that she had redeemed herself in the eyes of whatever heaven she thought of, and won the accolade of her own approval, when she took him down to Jamaica Town again months later and showed him the new building and the new grounds where the shrieking children swarmed. Let the city, the state honor her. . . .

"I think they can breathe good now, Sonie," he said. And that was all. That was enough. Whenever she heard anyone talk about the Graham Foundation as one of the pioneering social works in the South in the years afterward, she smiled. Let them think that the smile was the expression of a notably active and gracious citizen—an expression of great simplicity and humility. She knew that it was a little homage for John Barton's son.

And so the years slipped by. She was an honored person—respected and catered to by all the moving swarm of the town's continuing growth, dirty and energetic among its factories and warehouses. She could look at it all now with humor and compassion. Impatience had died out of her along with hunger and restlessness. She could take on age, be a public monument, and enjoy it. . . . She was through with the world of friends and enemies. She could move among them still smartly dressed, go up to New York once in a while and have the *Herald* note it in elaborate prose, open her old-fashioned house on Bay Street once or twice a year to entertainment, lend her name to worthy committees and movement—in short, be as honest and as active as she chose. And it was all possible because of Jim Barton—Jim Barton, the little boy in patched jeans sitting opposite her and answering questions in her ornate parlor, Jim Barton the awkward adolescent, with the same grave blue eyes coming in to town to go to the high school—and sometimes coming out to see *her* and ask her some questions. . . . And then all of a sudden there he was, the young man—the stubbornness, the integrity, intact—sitting in the same chair, in the same room where he had come first from the wagon driven under the porte-cochere. The same, but a man now with his own path to follow—the essence of him unchanged by the years of toil and sweat among the tobacco rows, unchanged by the cruel, scrimping life of poverty. Unchanged even by that shadowy thing in a cotton dress who was his mother and whom he had never disparaged nor complained about through all the years while she sank into deeper shadows—clinging, but not dying. The long waste of it had always angered Sonie, but she had never once mentioned it. She was too wise for that! Just as she was too wise ever to ask how he was getting on, where the rations were coming from, how the crop was doing. . . . Because she knew. The Kingsmont Bank & Trust sent her a punctilious monthly statement. He might find out someday—but it would be too late.

"Well, Jim," she was saying on this afternoon, "what are you going to do now?"

He glanced out the window and the light fell across his face. She observed with satisfaction: He's going to be a fairly good-looking man, too, presentable—not too good-looking, because he doesn't care a bit. I like that.

"I've been thinking it over," he said in the slow bass that was now his voice.

"Are you still set on going back to the farm for good?"

"No, Sonie." He shook his head—the dark, young man's head thick with unruly hair.

"Well, *what?* It's time you were deciding. I've always told you that if you wanted to go to college I would let you have the money."

"And I've always told you, ma'am, that if I went to school I wouldn't be in debt to you. I don't like being in debt to anyone, but I am going to college!"

She was excited by this. She held her composure—the staid, warm, elderly woman's mask that she had put together for this part of her life.

"Good! Well, how are you going to manage it?"

She had to sit very still, because this was hurting. She had never imagined that it could hurt like this or that she was still vulnerable to life. But here he was declaring he was going away—because that was what it amounted to—and that statement, simple, definite, the declaration of his maturity that she rejoiced in, she felt as a pain. She was cross at herself for the thickness in her foolish throat. He was taking a long time about answering her, but she was used to that, too. She had become accustomed to—no, dependent upon—so many subtle, indefinable things about him; and they belonged peculiarly and privately to her in a way that he—no one—could ever know, or should know. Ach, how long ago had she made the promise to herself that she would never become involved with another human being so that they could hurt her? And here she was perilously back on the edge of that dangerous territory.

"Sonie, I've got it all figured out. I don't just want to go to college. I've known that all along. I want to go where I can learn something that will help me do some good. I want to be able to do some good here in this county, in this state."

"Don't talk all around it," she said impatiently. "You've got it all set. I know you!"

"All right. I'm going where they will teach me more about tobacco," he said simply.

She threw back her head then and laughed heartily. The light glinted on the indestructible red hair. He looked solemnly at her.

"Ach, Jim—excuse me," she said, and wiped her eyes, "but I can't help it! You come out solemnly as though you were telling me something special and unusual, and here we are face to face with the eternal tobacco again. But I'm not laughing at *you*—you know that. It just seems the one thing all of us can never get away from no matter how far or how fast we run!"

"I don't want to run away from it," he said. "It needs someone to run it. It needs help. It needs someone to find out a lot of things. . . . I've been offered a scholarship at A. and M. in chemistry. If I work hard I maybe can keep it for the whole four years."

"You mean, after all this, that you are just going down a few miles to Raleigh?" She shook her head laughingly at him. Only to Raleigh, she was thinking, why, that's not far at all! O'Brien and I can drive down that far any day.

"Where else would I go to find out what I want?" he asked humorlessly. "The Royle Foundation has set up the best experimental work on tobacco in the whole world and A. and M. is where the Royle Foundation is."

She felt as if he had drawn her up short on a rein. She said as calmly as she could, because she felt at that moment a great force, an irony, a fate—whatever you might name it—working out its inevitable pattern. It was too monstrously good that this boy should

375

come under Brant Royle's fancy charity to the industry and the state.
She said:

"Of course, Jim, I think it's a fine thing. Remember I told you
that a long time ago."

"Of course I remember," he said shortly. "Why should I forget
it, Sonie?"

"Nothing, nothing—don't be cross with me, now," she said, looking hard at him, aching over him, firmly suppressing the sense of
loss. "And I don't want any nonsense about being in debt to anyone
if that includes me and any little thing I may happen to send to you
while you are down there. Do you hear me, young man? You've
known me too long now and we are too old friends to parade that
kind of pride between us."

"No, ma'am, Sonie," he said, "I won't."

They smiled at each other. For no reason at all she wanted to
break down and cry. But she went on smiling.

CHAPTER TWENTY

I

The big man on the terrace looked down across the sweep of
lawn and grunted with satisfaction. It was no particular satisfaction;
it was just part of the ritual of the day—that he should come out here
on the terrace, look down across the shrubbery, the Italianate fountains, the workmen in the distance, and grunt before he went in to
his breakfast. The morning rolled goldenly about him and the big
house behind him. Sunlight struck the cypresses, the rows of hedges,
caught the long curve of the road that swept down under the fold
of the land. It caught and gilded spectacularly the granite, frozen
female figure with one arm uplifted, the hand cupped, in the basin
of the fountain a hundred yards away. Nothing like it outside the
Medici Gardens. That's what the papers had all said so often, when
they were first built, that he had begun to believe it himself. Well,
they had cost enough. Three hundred thousand dollars. Of course
that was an exaggeration, but it was near enough to the truth for him
to take a particular satisfaction in it.

The terrace stretched a hundred feet on either side of him,
flagged with imported stones. Behind him reared the elaborate silver-
gray stone façade, mullioned windows, green copper gutters (especially made in England), gargoyles under the eaves from a French
abbey, slated gables, carved granite frames—a whole architectural
phantasmagoria that had been the subject of more newsprint than he
cared to remember. It wasn't a house. It was a monument—built,

gathered, carved, out of his energy, his will to make a fitting place for his life. It was twenty years now. Twenty years a-building, twenty years of the most expensive architects and construction. He rocked on his heels, moved the unlighted cigar from one corner of his mouth to the other and thought: I can see the river, but not well enough. That means that the river cannot see my house—I had them move a whole hill so I could see that river and it could see my house. Twenty years has made a difference. Look at all those trees that have grown up. I'll have to have it all landscaped again. . . .

"Hey, you!" he called to a workman pulling a ladder among the carved yews (brought all the way from Kent). The man looked up and stopped, touching his hat respectfully. "Hey, where's Mr. Pelham?"

The man scratched under his cap. "He's down by the greenhouses, I think, sir."

"Well, go get him for me. I want to see him when I've finished breakfast."

"Yes, sir!"

He'd tell Pelham to get after that overgrown hill right away. Keep them busy through the fall. Might cost a hundred thousand. He thought suddenly with the clear honesty that came to him in these mornings alone: This is my castle, known everywhere, the place where I live, the things I have made with twenty years of my life—China, the South, to the contrary. But I still bother with it, fuss with it, press it, shape it, like it was something that mattered. He knew he didn't really like it. The only thing that had kept him at it was the fact that the world all saw him barricaded like a giant within it—remote, fearsome. It was a mandarin gesture only, a thing of *face*. They expected it of him. They prostrated themselves before *it*—not *him*—but the fact of power and riches that he had become. He sometimes felt that he was no longer human, a creature of aging flesh and blood, but a prisoner to this creation of his. He had to live up to it continually. He growled in his throat and turned to the big Gothic doorway twenty feet behind him across the flags. Well, I wanted it, made it—I can't snivel now.

He crossed the space, his hands clasped behind him, his head thrust out a little beyond the heavy, bowed shoulders—a big man dressed richly and soberly in black. It astonished him to think that he was considered old. But he was. Sixty-six was not exactly a spring chicken any more. The twinge in his left thigh often impressed that upon him. But he still had in him more than any of the swarming, grasping world out there beyond this confine of lawns and gardens. He clamped his teeth on the cigar and entered the door. A houseman, discreet, shadowy, acknowledged his presence with a bow just inside the hallway.

"Your breakfast is ready, Mr. Royle."

He nodded and passed into the big quiet place where the marble stairway mounted majestically out of it, where the tapestries, the Ming vases, the huge Persian rug, lived like articles in an exhibition. The servant cleared his throat behind him. He turned to the man. What now?

"Sir, beg pardon, sir."

"Well?"

The servant stood before him—an abstract figure of professional hauteur and humility. He was so used to it that again it was only a symbol. He frowned over the thought that he didn't know this serving creature. Just a faceless individual, a permanent factor like the leaden gargoyles under the eaves outside, but completely inhuman. . . . Maybe I've got to be really inhuman myself. . . .

"I thought you would like to know, sir—Mr. Rudolph"—(Rudolph was the butler)—"Mr. Rudolph asked me to advise you that Mr. Randall arrived last night and will be breakfasting with you."

So Randall was back. Without warning, as usual. The thought of his son was suddenly distasteful. Randall was always turning up unannounced. The big man scowled and pressed his feeling down. After all, servant or not, this man must not be aware of any disruption. He nodded peremptorily and strode through the vast drawing room at his left. It irritated him more than he could admit that Randy should pop up now. He had no right to burst in and out, insolently and helter-skelter, safe in the knowledge that he was immune as *his* son. He didn't want to breakfast with Randall. It was an outrage, a disruption of the ponderous pattern of his life. Something had happened. Something was always happening with this boy, this child of his—this thin and insolent creature who squirmed about on the fringes of his life. Why couldn't he stay put? Why couldn't he be planted like one of the tall yews out there on the lawn, be cut and pruned and shaped as he saw fit—be really *his* son? He paused in the center of the drawing room, a little shocked that he should think of this product of his loins, this fact of dynasty, in conjunction with an inanimate shrubbery; but it was true. And when the son did not concur it angered him in a blind, irrational way. He should stay put. After all, by God, he'd sweated and spent his life's blood showing the world that he could make things out of nothing, had made it sway to the left or the right according to his least whim or bidding. He stopped, chewing fiercely at the cigar. It was an outrage that he, at this time of his life, should have to deal continually with the irritations of one of his possessions. Because Randall was one of his possessions—son or no—and he would be the first to admit that! Here, again, was the perverse element that dogged his days, ate like a canker at the center of his monumental sense of self-satisfaction. It

378

was elusive, a poison that he could not endure. He glared before him, a big, stolid figure of a man standing in the middle of a big room like a museum.

His eyes fell on the portrait, full-length, gilt-framed, of a woman. It hung over the huge stone-carved fireplace. A thin, pale woman, rather pretty, lost among the swirling velvet and rich textures of the composition. Poor Liz! He looked at her image with strange compassion. Even in the painting she seemed weak, lost, and frightened. The Honorable Elizabeth Inverlock—Mrs. Brant Royle. Well, he had loved her, worshiped her, surrounded her with all the things that he thought worthy of her. But, like everything else, she had eluded him. Maybe it was because he had been too drunk with the idea that he —a man out of the hot fields of Carolina, a poor boy who had made his way to the top—could have a girl from the old aristocracy of a parent country, the real thing, as his wife! That was a mystery beyond any passion. But Liz had eluded him. She had retired into the background of his energy from the very beginning. She had simply been something that was taken out, admired, paraded, and then put back among the Chinese mahogany, the Venetian chests, the French tapestries—something that belonged to him. Well, there hadn't been much blood in Liz from the outset. Too frail to match his energy, his voracious will to build, make, dominate; she had been lost in that. To the end a well-kept, elaborately surrounded furnishing—now here she was, an expensive portrait by that French feller hung over an expensive fireplace. . . .

Thinking of his son waiting at breakfast in the dining room beyond, he recalled Randall's birth—not for any special reason, but because she had shocked him then. Helen, the first child, was two years old and surrounded in an Oriental splendor of amahs and padding servants in the house. By then he had got over the fact that the first child was only a girl. She had become his daughter—Brant Royle's daughter—by then. Something beyond any disparagement. Liz had almost died with her. Then there came this second birth. And that had really finished her. He had always felt that this woman, his wife, had given up not because the fact of bearing children was a difficult thing, but because she did not want to stay in the framework of his making. He remembered the little bundle, red and squirming, presented to him, and his going to the bedside, the odor of the anesthetic still close in the room. . . .

"Liz," he had said, glowing with triumph, "it's a boy! You have made me very happy. We'll name him after your father, Liz—Randall. What do you think of that?"

The wan figure under the sheets, the worn pretty face on the pillow with the shadowed eyes. She flinched shockingly at the sound of his voice.

"Ahhh!" she wailed. "It's only because it's a boy, Brant. It doesn't mean anything else to you really, does it? Well, I've done it now—maybe I can rest." And then she had added in the English speech that he had always admired. "Poor little Helen—poor little thing!" Then she turned away from him. Nothing that he had protested had got anything else out of her. He had hated her then. Hated her mostly for becoming a stranger, something not *his*. He didn't know what she was talking about. Well, Liz had been dead for a dozen years. But her portrait here could still make him think, trouble him. He grunted and shifted his big shoulders under the black coat, the heavy neck swelling over the stiff collar. I'm tired of this place. Need to get away. Maybe go over to Europe in the fall. . . .

He strode into the dining room. It was huge, on a scale with the rest of the house. A long stretch of parquet floor, crimson draperies in the long windows, the glitter of the chandelier over the table. The table a long expanse of polished surface with two chairs set, one at the end nearest him and one at the far end. In that chair someone sat with cutlery and china in disarray before him, papers, letters, scattered among the dishes—a newspaper hiding him now. Rudolph, the butler, that impeccable, sardonic liveried man, pulled the chair aside for him. . . .

2

"Morning, Randall," Brant said, seating himself. The paper crashed down. The young man jumped to his feet, his pale-blond hair precisely in place, his sallow face (just plain unhealthy, Brant thought; always took after Liz!) with the big jutting nose, the thin, faltering mouth, and the bright shifting eyes. Brant felt a sense of weariness and distaste come over him. Somehow his son looked like Samuel Royle in that moment—he had never remarked it before. Well, he's my son!

"Ah—good morning, Father," said Randall, blinking at him. "Hope I'm not inconveniencing you barging in like this."

There was an expression of craft and knowingness on the young man's face that rubbed Brant raw. It was just the way Randall looked. He mustn't lose his temper. That wouldn't do any good. Randall would end up simply looking secretly and disparagingly down his nose, that expression of weak contempt, and nothing would have been learned or gained. But then nothing very much in their relationship had ever found a common footing. He thought again, as Rudolph reverently filled the coffee cup at his plate, that he needed to get away. He'd narrowed his life too long. Closed it up. The bread had gone stale.

"Randall," he said, looking at the younger man, "I thought you were happy in Cincinnati."

"Well, I won't keep you in suspense. Pearson and Smith and I didn't quite agree, Father—if you know what I mean." Randall cocked a derisive, pale eye down the length of the table. "So if you're going to jump on me, let's get it over with so we can get on to the business of what you are going to have me do next. I'd like to run down to little old New York before lunch. I've got some business. . . ." He opened the newspaper he had been reading and glanced through it. Brant felt the blood rising in him. Randall was really intolerable without trying to be. He seemed to be outdoing himself on this occasion. There was an air about him, knowing, complacent—as though he, not Brant, was in command of the situation. This was the third job he had left since college—for what real reasons he, Brant, would receive a full account later. Brant had always counted on that air of guile, hoping that beyond that in this boy of his there was buried some talent linked with his own genius. There was something there; that he knew. Randall had aplomb, knowingness—like the narrow shrewdness, the shiftiness, of Samuel. But there was nothing of the wide sweep, the intuitive feel and audacity for a big design, that lay in him. It was wrong, perhaps, to expect it. He would have to try again. He was willing to have infinite patience with this son of his.

"No, Randy," he said, stirring the coffee, "you're starting with the wrong idea, son. I'm not going to jump on you. You're a grown man. I've tried to let you find your own corner. I'm willing again—as I have been in the past—to give you any advantage you need when you have made a choice."

Randy's mouth flickered with a smile and he bowed politely over his paper.

"Thank you very much, Father. I must say you've always tried. Well, we can try again. I'll find something eventually—you've been very generous with me. There's no hurry, is there? I'll look around for a while as usual. And then, as usual, you'll find some sort of answer and I'll go at it again. It's a pity, isn't it, Father—such a waste of your time. But then"—he shrugged his narrow, almost feminine shoulders under the well-tailored coat—"I'm not the man you are, never will be, and as I have told you, there's no use my trying."

Brant, taking strong gulps of the coffee, felt that it wasn't all anger in him for his son. He felt a strong wave of affection; but the emotion had nothing to do with the present situation any more than it had to do with any of Randy's life at all. He always found himself saying, This is my son—*my* son, and by God you'll have to accept him.

"Randall," he said, "don't act like a child with me. I am not angry with you. . . ."

"Good. Then we can finish breakfast in peace, sir. I'm not trying to make you angry with me. I just think we might as well face the facts."

"Look here. I've been facing a lot more facts in the past year than you have all your life, Randall. Don't try to tell me about facts."

"Now, Father, that's what I'm talking about. Absolute waste of time to get angry. We've been through all of it before. It's just going to take time, and after all I admire you enormously—I have all my life. But I'm not you. There's no use trying to make me you. I've got my potentialities, I know that, but I just haven't found my niche!"

"You're taking a damned long time finding it. The world doesn't wait."

"Oh, Father, you're not going to go into that lecture about time and money, now, are you? Spare us both. Because you know as well as I do that being your son, I can afford any amount of both!"

Brant glared at his cup. The insolent puppy! Randall had always behaved in this patronizing manner, as though his son enjoyed making him angry. Well, he would not give him the pleasure this morning. He didn't feel up to it. His sense of age and unrest growing with this day was already too much for him. He did not want to add to it. When the time came, he knew that Randall would do as he commanded. This was all just fuss and fury—a stupid stretching of his clever little muscles. He would bow humbly and accept in time. To that extent he understood his son. In the end the other would accede, with the expression of sidewise, sly submission.

"We'll talk no more about this now, Randall," he said sharply, and began buttering his toast.

"Very well, Father," the other replied, and retired behind the newspaper. Silence fell upon the big room, broken only by the sound of his crunching on the toast, by the silent, impersonal movement of Rudolph from behind the chair to hand him the marmalade from the sideboard. The sunlight poured in discreetly through the tall curtained windows, and outside in the summer day Brant could hear the clattering hum of a grass-cutter passing down one of the slopes toward the river. The room felt icily unreal, even with the August day burning along the river outside. He suddenly flung down his cup, clashing it in the saucer. Down the table, the paper lowered and the questioning, mocking gaze of the young man flickered across to him.

"Oh, I beg pardon, sir," he said, folding the paper and putting it aside. "Excuse my bad manner. . . . Some more coffee, Rudolph, please." Rudolph slid noiselessly to him and leaned with the silver pot. Randall looked brightly and politely at his cup. "Had quite a bit of mail waiting for me this morning, you know," he continued in a conversational tone. "Surprised me. Most of it the usual, but there was a letter from Helen." He picked up an envelope from the untidy pile by his place. "Always surprises me to hear from Helen."

Brant grunted. "What's so surprising about hearing from Helen? She's your sister, isn't she?" he said with heavy sarcasm.

Randall's small mouth jerked briefly into a smile as he toyed with the envelope.

"I don't know. It always surprises me to find that she is my sister —after all I've seen very little of her, y'know. We don't have much in common, never have. I've never liked meek women. Helen was born meek. Meek and stubborn."

"Don't talk a lot of foolishness about your sister, Randall!"

"Oh, I beg your pardon, sir. I didn't mean it in any personal way. Objective observation—purely objective!" He turned the flickering half-scornful gaze from his father back to the envelope in his hand. "Well, anyway she writes a fairly dull letter. Dutiful, you know. I never seem to have the time to answer, but she always writes. Once a month. I've been hearing from her for years!" He shook his head in a kind of half-humorous amazement.

"Well," growled Brant, "get on with it! What does she have to say? I heard from her last week myself."

"Oh, nothing exciting. Just a lot of staid, unimaginative comment about our beloved English cousins, and this house and that she has visited, and how things seem to be brightening up over there for the first time since the war." He threw the envelope down on the table and began to examine the nails of his hand. "It's a pity, but I don't think Helen has any talent for that kind of life—all this expensive schooling and traveling about. She's tried, because she's a more dutiful child than I am, but she doesn't really like it. And to think of all these years of fancy governesses and traveling companions, all the advantages she's had—and no real talent for it. Now me, I would have known what to do with all that."

"What are you talkin' 'bout now, Randy?"

It came to him in a flash then that he did not like this man, his son—this posturing, knowing creature who sat down the table from him. In fact he had never liked him. All his feelings for the boy had been founded on sentiment. And the sentiment was not created on a human basis but simply on his sense of ownership, of possession. By virtue of the same fact he knew also that he could never easily rid himself of Randall. The same sense of this stranger being *his*, of his prideful possession—like this great ornate castle, no more and no less—made him eternally committed. He could never escape, no matter what he felt. It was part of a deeper thing and not subject to the sway of passing judgments and emotions.

383

Randall was still examining his hands, his lids lowered over the small bright eyes. He looked completely feline. Brant wiped his mouth on the napkin.

"Well?"

"You've spent all this time trying to make a big businessman out of me and you've done the same thing with Helen trying to make a big social success out of her, haven't you? Well, neither of us has given you much of a dividend on your investment yet, have we? Now suppose you had started the other way around. Sent me to do what Helen has been trying to do in her poor way all over Europe—over in England with all those fancy in-laws, Mother's people, standing dutifully by. I rather think I would have enjoyed it. I like a good splash, I like expensive people. Helen doesn't. Helen's just as big a failure now as I am."

"What a damn lot of hogwash you talk, Randy. Your sister has never once complained to me about anything. She could if she wanted to—"

"Certainly, certainly," said the younger man, leaning back in his chair and staring at the ceiling. "I said she's meek—dutiful, I expect is a better way of putting it. But she hasn't had much chance to be otherwise. But you mark my words, sir, I said Helen is stubborn, obstinate—remember we were in the same nursery together for a long time, and I know! She's been living like a medieval princess in a big, fancy, emancipated world. But once she finds out something she really wants, look out! She's like you, Father, to that degree, whether you know it or not, and one of these days it's going to crop out. I think she'll surprise you. I still say I'm not at all temperamentally unsympathetic with my sister, but I do know *that* in her. Maybe she should have gone into business, instead of me," he said musingly toward the carved plaster of the ceiling high above him, "who knows?"

"Randall," said Brant furiously, "I don't know what in hell you're talkin' about. I only know you're talkin' too much—*as usual!* Go on back to your paper and leave me be."

"Certainly, Father!"

Randall picked up the paper and began reading it, turning the pages, cocking his glance in an elaborate, half-amused way. Brant motioned for his cup to be filled again. Something was all wrong this morning. He hadn't felt so restless and empty in many a day. To be honest, he knew that Randall's presence wasn't totally responsible for it. It was merely aggravating something, some personal dissatisfaction, in him. Then there was the fact of age—he clung to that for a moment: there was too much distance between him and his children, too many years. Why, he was almost old enough to be their grandparent. But that was one of the prices you had to pay when you had spent most of your life making a world. Maybe it was his fault; perhaps he ought to try a little harder to bridge the gap instead of quarreling like this.

"I must say the news is unexciting these days. Mr. Coolidge has signed another bill," said Randall from his end of the table in a mild voice. "That's getting to be a bad habit with him—get him into trouble." He turned a page and sighed. "The market seems to be getting steadier anyway—you're doing all right. South Eastern Utilities up two points since yesterday. How do you do it, Father?"

Brant grunted in response. The question was purely a rhetorical one. He was tired of this breakfast. It was not agreeing with him, frugal in content as it had been. His stomach felt dull, a heavy entity resting lumpishly against the edge of the table. He pushed back in his chair.

"Speaking of reading the paper"—Randall picked up another journal at his side—"I've got a copy of the *Kingsmont*, North Carolina, *Herald* here. They put it in with my mail by mistake—do you still read it? I remember you used to."

"I don't read any newspapers much any more—no time," said Brant, only half listening.

"Well, I got quite interested in it this morning. And it occurred to me that it was strange that you've never taken Helen and me, or sent us, down there to look over the old family stamping grounds. I know you've never kept us from going, but you've never even mentioned the possibility as long as I can remember. Consequently, North Carolina has always been an exaggerated and mysterious name in my mind—almost exotic; and I feel quite sure that I would find all that provincial bustling industry, all that business of cigarettes, boring in the extreme—if I really ever had to *be* there. It's certainly not my dish of tea. But—" He picked up the paper and began running his eye up and down the columns. Brant watched him tightly. He felt strangely tense, hating, really hating Randall then more than he had ever hated him before. It was making him feel sick. Randall continued casually, obliviously:

"But I find that I know a lot about the names and places they write about here. All sorts of people I have heard you mention keep cropping up—and of course there's always an item about Uncle Samuel and Aunt Berta. Gives me a real old-fashioned family feeling. There's a notice that Cousin Tina has gone visiting in Palm Beach. Now the little I know of Tina has never led me to think of her in any sentimental way, but being a *Southern* cousin always gives me a pleasant sensation of being connected with magnolias and juleps when I see her name in print." He snickered. "And there's a lot of news about the tobacco crop for this year. I really must see what one

385

looks like sometime, you know—due regard for my bread and butter, and all that. There's a fine account of a scandal in the highway commissioner's office. . . ."

Brant was hardly listening any more. He could only think: Have I come to this? A creature of gold, embedded in sacred power so that I can make a factory, light a city, change the lives of half a million people just by speaking briefly over a telephone—the world hating, fearing, honoring me whenever I choose to show my face—and all it amounts to is that I must sit alone, vastly and ultimately alone, in this cold room and hear a despicable little nincompoop who is, incidentally, but eternally, my own flesh and blood, mock me with the name of Kingsmont. . . . Kingsmont. . . . Twenty years now and he had bitterly, steadfastly locked it off from himself—a wasteland obstinately held banished, a name in confidential reports, production charts, financial statements.

"And the obituaries," Randall was saying. "What a lot of odd things you run across in all those little death notices. There's one here, for instance, about a recently deceased gentleman named Prenski—*Prenski*, sounds Russian—and right below it one about a Mrs. Barton whose funeral took place last Wednesday. Barton—Barton? Isn't that the name of that unfortunate gentleman who sold you the cigarette machine? No relation here, I suppose, but it goes on at much length about Mrs. Barton being the daughter of one of the oldest tobacco families in the state—Singletons. Now, of all the names I've heard you mention, all the stories you've told either to me or in my presence, I don't remember any Singletons, but 'old tobacco family'—there's something about it that brings all my Rebel romanticism to the fore. . . ."

So she was dead, Brant thought dully. He had never really believed that it could be true. She was finished—cut off from his hate or his abiding passion forever. Why, he had buried her twenty years or more ago, finally and absolutely, and found his peace elsewhere. But it was a lie. He was no more free now in the face of the ultimate fact of death than he had been in the toils of his own sickness. A lot of people had died. Pete Henry, Liz, Pa—all of them. He had been able to accept that. But Margaret was dead. He felt as though a knife had been thrust into the core of his unrest and twisted, filling him with a blinding, reasonless, aching need. This was the last act between them. And it had been accomplished far away without him as witness. But it could not be just finished without him. If it killed him he would have to go. . . .

"Did you say Singleton, Randall?" he heard his voice asking.

" 'Nee Singleton,' it reads, 'only daughter of Major James Singleton,' et cetera, et cetera. Did you know them?"

"Yes, I knew them."

"Well, if it was anyone connected with the sacred cigarette industry I felt reasonably sure that you—"

"Randall," he said carefully, "does it say when she died?"

"No—just the usual funeral notice, and rather sparse at that."

Brant pushed himself up from the table and stood leaning on it looking across at the wall beyond Randall's head. The young man glanced up at him curiously, the paper still open in his hands.

"Randall," he said again, and in his mind he was thinking with agonizing clarity: I am old—I know it now; I'm finished—they've all gone off and left me, escaped me. "Randall, go send Mr. Wyatt up to my room, and then go up and pack your things again, if you've unpacked them."

"Oh"—the younger man's face paled under the sly mockery—"are you kicking me out? Come, Father, let's be reasonable."

"I'm going down to North Carolina as soon as I can get to New York," Brant continued through a stiff mouth. "I'm taking you with me."

Randall's expression relaxed. Any surprise he might be feeling was completely hidden now. Only his shrewd eyes darted momentarily about the room through sheer habit. But he said calmly:

"Certainly, Father. I'm already looking forward to it—should be rather fun!"

CHAPTER TWENTY-ONE

I

He told the Negro chauffeur to stop the car at the side of the dusty road and stepped out into the hot afternoon. Twenty-five years, and this was one place that had not changed. Just another country road with old wagon ruts tunneling through trees and deserted fields and blanketed in the shimmering heavy silence of summer. He was pleased with the accuracy of his memory, because he had been a young man when last he passed this place—a young man in a wagon. Now it was Sam's big black Buick and Sam's chauffeur borrowed for the afternoon. He had been surprised only by the shortness of the journey. Two miles from town was no longer the distance it had once been. Nor was it even two miles really. They had left a new suburb not a quarter of a mile back where they had turned off. Kingsmont had gone right on growing without him.

"I'll be back in a few minutes," he told the Negro on the front seat.

The chauffeur nodded and touched his hat, watching him as he walked away. Now that the moment had come he felt a little hollow and weak. That damned cold had kept him locked up at the hotel for more than two weeks after he and Randall had arrived. Two weeks of fretting and fuming, of formal visitations from Sam and Berta, from the company managers, the homage of the business to this ancient monarch—because that was what he was to them now. No friends, no familiar faces, no one who really cared a jot in hell. And here the awesome legend had suddenly turned up after twenty-five years. He couldn't blame them, but he had endured them with bad grace. Majesty could afford all the bad grace it wanted. They were not surprised by it. Well, he had rid himself of them at least for this afternoon, sent Randall off with the man from the Maple Street manufactory to look at a shipment of Turkish leaf. And here he was alone on the last lap of his mysterious personal journey. As he remembered it, the clump of old cedars was to the left of him off the road there. He walked stolidly toward it, gratefully feeling the hot sun on his back. The cold had left him feeling a little frail and feverish. There was no doubt about it, he was getting old. And this journey this afternoon was the craziest thing he had ever done, perhaps in all his history. But he could no more keep from doing it, finishing it finally at last, than he had been able to keep from doing all the other things that had branded him as strange. He was alone. He had always been alone. It was peculiarly fitting that he should accomplish this alone.

He turned up a cut in the bank—barely a track, weedy and overgrown, carved out of a tangle of blackberry and honeysuckle. He was breathing a bit heavily when he got to the top of the little rise and felt himself enclosed by vines and growth. He suddenly took his cigar from his mouth and threw it into the grass. It seemed more fitting. Then he stopped with a blind feeling of rage and despair. He was not alone, after all. A mule was tied to one of the cedars, and a young man in his shirt sleeves was silently raking among the little company of gray headstones, weathered and lichened, and covered by grass. The mule and the young man turned and looked at him. He glared back—and felt a fool for glaring.

"Good afternoon, sir." It did not sound like the voice of a farmer. It was pleasant, direct, unquestioning. Brant pulled himself together and approached him. He stopped at the barrier of the old rusty wrought-iron fence, and grabbed at two of the points for support. He managed to nod.

"I've come to pay my respects to Mrs. Barton. I wasn't here for her funeral—just got into town." He blurted it all out harshly.

The young man nodded and wiped his face with his sleeve.

"Very nice of you, sir," he said gently and gravely. He began raking the rubbish into a neat pile with slow, easy strokes. Brant could not look away from him. Why did he feel he had seen this

388

strange young farmer before? What was there about the tanned face, the black hair, the clear blue eyes? For the first time he felt awkward—an intruder. What could he say now? Even now came the old sense of blind fate working against him. It was ruining even this moment. . . .

"I haven't been able to get back here since the funeral myself to clean up," the young man was saying in an easy conversational tone. "This is a busy time of the year for a tobacco farmer. But I took off a little this afternoon to come over. You see, no one's taken much notice of this old place for a long time."

There was nothing in his tone or manner to indicate that he found Brant's presence extraordinary. Becoming calmer himself, Brant found this young man singularly attractive. He tore his eyes away and looked down at the fresh mound at last. Looking at it he felt no pain. He didn't know exactly what he had expected. But that bare, raw little elevation of smooth earth meant absolutely nothing. He felt as though a tremendous weight had been lifted from him—a wild sense of relief and freedom. Here at the end of the long tangled dark journey were the platitudes of silence and peace. He could stop fighting now—stop struggling at least, beating at one of the walls. In him there rose a silent cry compounded of both joy and sadness. He knew he was an old man. If he had only suspected before, he knew now that he would walk away an old man. Hollow, fragile—a stranger. But he was closer now to these old enemies than he had ever been before. They could not hurt him any more. Under the lichen mottling the headstone nearest him he read: James Randolph Singleton . . . Born 1840 . . . Died . . . He saw that the young man was watching him with a grave blue stare.

"I knew Mrs. Barton's father too," Brant said gruffly.

"You did, sir!" The young man smiled suddenly and warmly. "I didn't have the honor. He died a long time before I was born. But I've heard a lot about him. Mother always made me look up to Grandfather more than anyone else."

Brant felt the afternoon reel and grind to a halt around him. This was why this farmer had held his attention from the moment he had seen him! This man was her son—the dark brows, the intense blue eyes, the stubborn chin.

"I'm sorry," he said at last in a voice surprisingly calm, "I didn't realize you were a member of the family, sir."

The young man smiled again, leaning on the handle of the rake, a kind of stolid dignity about his body. He wasn't tall. But Major Jim had been short—and dignified too.

"Yes, I guess I'm the last one left, in this county, at least. In spite of my father's name, Mother always tried to make me feel that I was a Singleton. Funny, I never could see what particular difference it made."

He was so at ease, so un-self-conscious, that Brant felt the shock drain out of him. There was something about this youngster, beyond the fact of who he was, that continued to attract him. He felt a hunger to prolong the conversation.

"The Singletons were a great name in tobacco, sir."

"Well, I'm afraid we've no great name any more now, but we're still mixed up in tobacco." He said it without any bitterness; he wasn't even being humorous, Brant realized. He was just stating it in a quiet, serene voice. "My father was, too. He was really an inventor, I suppose. They used to say he made the machine that made Kingsmont. And then my grandfather was a tobacco manufacturer, and here am I at the other end of the picture—a grower of sorts, but I'm not complaining!"

"I can see you aren't, sir." Brant smiled for the first time and took a cigar out of his inner pocket and bit off the end. "I used to complain all the time myself. I was born on a farm just east of here. I hated being a slave to tobacco."

"Oh, then you're a tobacco man, too?"

"I have some connections with the business." Brant put the cigar in its accustomed corner of his mouth. "And, one way or another, I have always had a personal interest in pretty nearly everything to do with tobacco."

"It's the *only* thing I'm interested in," said the boy, walking to the mule. "You said you hated once being a slave to tobacco. Well, you must know yourself that raising tobacco is one of the damnedest, most delicate, backbreaking jobs a man ever takes on—yet there are thousands of people around here whose lives are dependent on whether it grows well or not. Well, we've come quite a way, I think, since the day you had to farm it—quite a long way—toward making the cussed tobacco plant a more dependable factor. If we can lick all the illnesses, the pests and diseases, evolve a plant that will simply stand up against all of them right on through, season after season— then we've taken most of the backbreak, not to mention the heartbreak, out of the slavery for the tobacco farmer. That's why I'm interested in tobacco—I've had my back broken."

He had taken a piece of twine out of his pocket and lashed the rake to the saddle while he was speaking. Brant said:

"Well, sir, this is very interesting, what you tell me, but I'm a little confused. You don't talk like a farmer."

The boy glanced sidewise over the mule's rump. He was smiling and there was a slight blush under the tan. For all his show of poise, thought Brant, he's shy—shy as they come.

"No, I don't guess I do. Dr. Carr down at A. and M. said I was born talking like a damned pedant, and I'm at my worst when I get to talking about tobacco!" He began to loosen the mule's reins from the branch of the cedar. He was going, and Brant did not want him to go just yet.

"This seems hardly the occasion or the place to talk about this, sir. But I'm interested—very much interested. If you aren't farming, what is it you do do?"

"Nothing spectacular," he said, stopping the mule near Brant. "I run a tobacco experimental station on a farm near here, that's all."

"I see. I don't want to keep you now. But I'm in Kingsmont for an indefinite period. Would you consider it an intrusion if I came down someday and had a look at what you are doing?"

The tanned, square face flushed again. The youngster was deeply pleased.

"Not at all, sir! There's nothing I like better than showing someone what we are trying to do. But I warn you I'll very likely bore you to death."

He swung himself up on the mule and smiled, the shy curve on the serious mouth.

"I'll take a chance on that," said Brant.

"Don't say I didn't warn you, then!" The mule started to walk slowly and Brant, hands thrust behind him, walked with them. There was something mutely warm and companionable in the moment. He had never experienced this with Randall. As they reached the roadway the boy turned in the saddle and tipped the weather-beaten felt hat.

"Good-by," said Brant. They nodded at each other. The boy turned the mule's head to the left and kicked at its sides. They trotted solemnly up the road away from where the car was parked. Brant watched them, chewing on his cigar. The cloud of dust thickened under the mule's hoofs till they turned the curve. He stood there for a moment in the blazing sun. He felt oddly excited and exhausted by this encounter. He couldn't get the boy out of his mind. Margaret's boy. . . . It was as though she had waited all these long years to show him that simply by her dying he could not free himself from the tangled skeins that bound him to the Singletons. It was finished, damn it all to hell! he assured himself. I knew it was finished for all time when I looked on her grave up there under the trees. Why can't you leave me in peace? What am I getting mixed up in now? Why did I tell him I'd come? I was born a damned fool! I haven't the slightest idea of doing that; I'm through with getting myself cluttered up with something else—I just want to be quiet and rest. He stamped back down the road to the waiting car and got in, feeling dizzy and confused—maybe that cold had left him weaker than he had reckoned on.

"Let's go back to town, boy," he said, slumping back into the seat.

The ride was quickly over. Through it he remained buried behind his scowling, angry face. When the car entered the square, he roused himself suddenly and growled at the Negro:

"Boy, don't take me back to the hotel. Turn up Hill Street there. I'll tell you where to stop."

The car obediently turned up the old familiar thoroughfare. He sat watching it flow grimly past. He hadn't meant to do this. He couldn't tell why he was doing it now. It had come upon him in a flash—like a solution. Some force deep under his confusion and sickness had made the decision for him. Now that it had been taken he felt almost calm. Here at least was something certain and unchanging.

"Boy, pull up at the gate in that fence."

The car stopped. The Negro came to open the door for him, but he was already standing on the sidewalk searching deep in his trouser pockets for the keys. The keys that had never been used but had stayed in his pocket like a talisman through all these years. He found them and pulled them out, searching them over between his fingers.

"Now go on down to the hotel," he said over his shoulder, "and pick up my baggage and bring it up here. I'll phone down to them."

"Yassuh!"

Hearing the car wheel away, he walked to the gate and unlocked it. It clanged softly behind him. Well, here they were at last, he and the house—all that was left—both of them unchanged. He had never changed; this was a passion not subject to the wear of time. And the house, the trees, the grass, were precisely as they had always been because he had barricaded it against the outside world, seen that it was preserved for just this very moment, when he felt free to come to it—and feel safe, safe at last.

Outside the fence Hill Street, full of noisy commerce, the din of traffic, flowed past and around the edges of the little island where he stood. Oblivious of it, he began to walk up the gravel path—a deliberate, old man's walk, heavy, implacable. . . .

2

After that first month he scarcely left the house, except to take an occasional ride down to the factory. He seemed enormously content just to stay where he was. He walked about the house, through all the rooms, delighting in the fact that the smallest one of them pleased him more than all of that great expensive pile he had left up there on the Hudson. But *that* was a joke, and he was perhaps the only one who knew it. He grinned fiercely to himself, thinking

392

what was being rumored in Kingsmont, how incredible that he should choose after all these years to come back to the town and close himself up in that old house right in the midst of the dirtiest, shabbiest business quarter—Negro tenements to the north of it and the red-light district only two blocks away over in the Oak Street section. He could almost hear them saying it: Old now, worth millions —he can afford to be crazy! They had to drive past and stare from their cars at the iron fence, at the yardmen watering that astonishing fresh stretch of lawn; at the pair of glossy young thoroughbreds brought down to inhabit the old stable being taken out for exercise by the groom; at the big Packard sitting black and sleek in the driveway, its running board against the old carriage block. Well, let them look their fill—they'd get used to it soon enough. He knew them *well!* In the meantime he would often sit in a rocker on the porch in plain view and rock, chew on his cigar, spit when it pleased him out upon the lawn, and stare fiercely back at them.

The heat didn't bother him, the oily, garbagy stench from the busy street, nor the inhuman, incessant noise of the tobacco vans coming up and down the hill day and night. And now with no trees left on Hill Street, he could see right down to the courthouse below him in the square. It was a period of great peace and content for him . . . the feeling of the house, the servants, the horses about him . . . really like a home for the first time in all of his life. In that he had not been disappointed. Everything else had shifted and changed under his hands. This hadn't. He even began to accept Randy. Randall had come forth himself with the suggestion that since he was here in Kingsmont it might be a good thing for him to learn something about the business. He seemed very happily occupied with his work in the sales office of Lyman & Holt Company, manufacturers of Gilt Bond cigarettes—one of the biggest sellers in the country. He didn't even seem to mind moving into the house with Brant, and Brant felt a strange gratitude for his presence; no matter what reservations he might have about the essential weakness or strength of the boy, the idea of his *son* being in this particular house with him warmed him profoundly. All these years he had never had the feeling of a *family.* This was what it was like. He often thought of cabling Helen and telling her to come on home. But some new shyness in him, some apprehension for his present state of content, made him put it off—delay it till a better moment. There was no hurry—no need to hurry ever again.

It was in the flush of this feeling of well-being, of bland benevolence and health, that he thought of the agony and the feeling of illness that had preceded it. That strange suspended meeting in the little forgotten burial ground under the cedars. The serious and shy young man, Margaret Singleton's son. . . . It seemed foolish to him now that he had ever thought it meant anything more than just what had been said and done that afternoon. And that had been nothing more than a chance encounter between two utter strangers.

But he couldn't slough off all the scars of the past as easily as he supposed. Much as he tried to put it aside as the days passed, the memory of that meeting returned to haunt him more and more. The face of Margaret's son stood before him every time he looked at Randall. It ate at his peace of mind. The ghosts of the past would not let him alone. They must always pursue him like furies, proposing enigmas, mysterious comparisons between what he had wanted and what he had gained—the old, sick sense that he was being cheated and colossally fooled, that the meaning of his whole life (if it had any meaning) had completely eluded him and now all he was enjoying was a very small fool's paradise. He began to think of nothing else. It seeped back into him like an old familiar poison. He snarled at the servants, quarreled bitterly with Randall, and stalked scowling and bewildered about the house.

There came a morning when he ordered the car, clapped the old-fashioned bowler on his head, and directed the chauffeur to drive out the South Pelham Road. . . .

3

He stood in the yard between the gray old house and the neat white group of outbuildings, and there was a tobacco-curing barn down beyond near the edge of the field, with the leaning shed, and the cut wood stacked and ready beneath it. Next month they would begin the curing, and the skies in the dark, late summer night would look down on the glowing stove mouths and the sprawled men, eating and drinking and talking through the long dark hours while the leaf turned golden in the careful heat—it had been many a long year. . . . He felt a pang of nostalgia flow to him from this place. Not that he hadn't seen hundreds of them—not that this farmyard was specifically like any of them, but it stirred up the odds and ends of happiness that had been the only heritage from his hard youth. This could have been the house, the yard, the tobacco farm—the only difference being that this had an unnatural neatness, a clean rectitude and precision, that made it seem almost like a theatrical setting.

The man was approaching him now, bareheaded, from between two of the outbuildings. He had remembered the face acutely—the dark hair, the serious broad face.

"Hello, sir."

"You don't remember me, do you?"

"Of course—you're the gentleman I talked to that afternoon out at the old burial place."

394

"That's right. I thought I'd come out this morning and take you up on your offer."

"Well, of course I'm pleased and honored." So humorless and grave and steady he was standing there. "Let's have a look at the special plantings. You see, this is a question of genetics really—that and soil prophylaxis. My special interest is resistant strains right now. If you'll just come along—"

Brant followed him, thinking with wonder that there had been no gap between. This moment might easily be the moment after he had watched the mule disappear down the empty roadway.

The two men went down into a field of tobacco. They passed between the two rows, the broad back of the young man ahead of him. He was talking continually in the grave voice. Brant wasn't really listening as he followed ploddingly. He heard only a lot of words—*plant-bed sanitation . . . rhizoctonia . . . sore shank . . . wilt . . . black shank*—some of them familiar words out of the past, some of them just words. His concentration was on the man himself. Not on what he was saying, but on the feel of attraction, of solid, implacable vitality flowing out of the turn of the neck, the tanned forearm as it fingered a leaf delicately and commented on some special detail.

". . . Most of us feel that we can lick the problem only by developing plants which are inherently resistant to any single disease or complex of diseases. This half-acre has been planted with a special seed of my own, purposely cultivated for two seasons in succession in contaminated soil—it's stood up against it without a failure. Look there in that patch, those two rows." Brant obediently shifted his gaze, two stretching rows of graying, withered leaves on the stalks. The blue gaze, passionate, concentrated. "Those are plants from the common seed of this variety. . . . Look at 'em—dead as doornails, a hazard to the whole economy. That's the kind of chance *you* took when you grew tobacco, sir—that's the kind of chance we aren't going to have to take much longer!"

The words became a blur—something distant and apart from thought. Who the hell cared about the tobacco plant, the tobacco industry, the poor damned farmer? What he, Brant, cared about and drank in thirstily was the sound of this voice. This concentrated, passionate, selfless voice, *dedicated*—where had he ever heard the sound of it before? Because he *had*. . . . His thoughts swarmed around it, and then suddenly it was all clear—this was he *himself*, the blue-shirted back walking ahead of him, this was his voice speaking to him over the hard, young shoulder, full of excitement, caring about something deeply. Oh, the boy, the lost dark being drowned in the wash of time, lost in the mindless drive. He had lost that voice and sought for it the rest of his life—only to find it at last in *her* son.

This man should have come out of his own want, his passion, his loins, and what did he have out of his crying? A credit good for twenty million dollars, but he had lost the good, the positive shaping thing long ago—and this man had it.

"Damned interesting, Mr. Barton," he said. "Damned interesting."

"Let's go back up to the yard again. I've made a kind of laboratory out of what used to be the old barn." The young man turned and brushed apologetically past him, reversing their direction back toward the house. "I think you might be interested in some things I've found by analysis."

"Certainly," Brant said. "What is this about now—"

But he was blind again except to his own obsession, his want and need of what Margaret's son had pure and simple—a birthright, the thing that he had long ago lost. It focused the sickness, the fury of old resentment, in him. He could only grasp that and hold onto it as the only real thing, the terrible, remorseless seed in him—and here he was only the high lord of twenty million dollars. This young man was set against him because he lived and thought and *was* simply and completely what he had always wanted to be. He could not bear it any more now than he had been able to twenty—no, thirty—years ago. He hated him. He would destroy him if he had a weapon in his hand—drag him down with him to the deepest pit of hell, Pa's hell—because his whole life could not match what this boy, this shy, passionate young man, held the secret to!

The next half-hour passed in a blur. They went into one of the buildings. He lent a grave ear to a dissertation among some test tubes, some labeled jars set on a shelf, some gleaming apparatus, some charts. He was introduced to a couple of other young, bright-faced men—one in overalls, one in a laboratory apron—who followed their progress silently and reverently listening to the boy. . . .

"Mr. Barton," Brant said out of all of it, "I gather from your conversation that you went to the State Agricultural College."

"You are correct, sir. Received my M.S. there in biochemistry."

"But what puzzles me, Mr. Barton, is that fact that all you have shown me indicates some special financing. Who or what is putting up the money for all this experimentation—surely not the State of North Carolina alone?"

The blue eyes, the concentrated brown face, turned to him. Margaret Singleton's son shook his head.

"You are perfectly right, sir. The state is aiding in this work as best it can, but any work like this has to have special funds—and even that is never adequate."

"Special funds?"

"Certainly. I would have had to stop two years ago, half-finished, if the Royle Foundation at A. and M. hadn't come across with aid for our work. Mr. Royle has always been generous to the industry that he made."

Of course, thought Brant, Mr. Royle has always been generous —I have known it all along. Aloud he asked:

"And you mean that without the help this Foundation affords you your work would be crippled?"

The young man smiled, a small smile.

"I'm afraid I would simply have to go back to making a living farming and let the improvement of the tobacco plant go to hell— without the help of the Foundation."

"It seems a shame that such necessary work should hang on such an uncertain factor." Brant hoped the irony he felt would not betray him.

"I know, sir. If only we could make *them* see—the manufacturers' world, I mean—see that it is to their advantage to improve the sources of their raw material. . . . Why, I've proposed a half-dozen plans. . . ." He went on eagerly talking and Brant was no longer hearing him. He was feeling still. He had the key for evil or good again—the symbol of power. It was never absent. By a flick of his finger he could obliterate this boy, ruin him, crush him out. That was all he needed. It was strange how calm he felt of a sudden. He could go back to Hill Street and rock on the porch and look down on Kingsmont, at peace in his house. . . .

"Mr. Barton," he said when they stood again in the clean bare yard, "this has been a most instructive and interesting morning. I cannot express my appreciation to you for it. Perhaps I can be in a position to further your work one of these days—I have friends, connections—" How cynical, how petty this all was. And he knew it. And he thought with a little shudder of agony, I can't help it—this is what it means to have sold yourself down the river—forever.

"That is very generous of you," said the young man, the calm, undying fruit of the enemy tree! "Please come again. I've enjoyed talking with you. I'm sure you could give me some ideas I haven't thought about."

It wasn't until he was in the car and a mile or so down the country road that he realized that the other man had gone through these two meetings without ever realizing that he was Brant Royle. He wasn't interested, this boy, in who or what he or anyone was. He was interested only in the precious, minute seed that held the fate of an economy in its microscopic black pod. He grimly relished the situation. He would not have to go back again ever now. He need not be haunted by the blue eyes, the integrity, the lost *him*. It was all answered now—as everything had always been answered, ultimately: Can I have it? If not, I can buy or destroy it. As simple as that. It had worked before, he knew that it still worked. He almost felt vigorous again, pleased with this consistency—he had not betrayed himself, shilly-shallied; he had had moments, but he would never try to wander off the old path again. He would just hew straight into the mouth of hell from now on—and be damned to the rest of them! He had been untrue to most things, but this he would be true to till the end—it was the only religion, the only philosophy, he knew.

He got out in the driveway and strode across the gravel with more energy than he had felt in a month. He wasn't dead yet—not by a long shot! Randall was standing on the porch waiting for him. Sly, supercilious, the air of malice, always implicit, glistening on his surface.

"Well, sir! You're almighty early home for lunch. Have they dispensed with your services down at Lyman and Holt already?" Brant growled as he mounted the steps.

Randall rubbed his hands in the falsely apologetic gesture and smiled with the weak mouth, his big nose drawing to one side.

"Now, Father, not so fast—I'm afraid you jump to conclusions, as usual!" He looked up under the pale brows at Brant, a crouching, almost apprehensive glance. "I came out here to warn you. You have a little surprise in store for you, so you might as well take advantage of this moment to prepare yourself for it."

"All right, Randy, don't try to enjoy it too much." Brant threw the stub end of his cigar out onto the lawn. "What is it?"

"It gives me peculiar and amazed pleasure, Father, to inform you that Helen arrived in town an hour ago—unannounced, and what is more amazing, *completely alone*. She now awaits your pleasure, trembling, no doubt, at her temerity."

"Randy, that smart-aleck talk may amuse some people. It doesn't me. Where is your sister?"

"She was sitting in the—er—south parlor, I think you call it. I left her a moment ago when I heard the car coming in."

Randall's face was a picture of malicious triumph. He looked at the nails on one thin, nervous hand in a characteristic gesture. Brant snorted at him in supreme disgust. Things were really getting back to normal again. The little dream was over! He strode in at the front door, slamming it after him. . . .

4

He paused inside the doorway and glanced across the old, gentle room. She sat rather awkwardly. She looked ungainly in the chair. Apprehensive was the word. She had been born with no gumption, always crawling about with that frightened air, that warding-off-the-blow look—when there had never been any blow coming. It always brought every bit of scornful cruelty in him rushing to the surface. And yet she was his flesh and blood—his daughter.

"Well, Helen," he said, planting his feet on the rug, "I must say I'm surprised."

"Hello, Father."

She had a nice voice. He had always acknowledged that. Gentle, pitched low. She rose from the chair. She was tall. Her height was the only physical evidence about her that he could relate to himself. Other than that she was thin, bony, and awkward. He had always considered her a perennial colt. He was pleased to see that the tweed suit, well cut, became her. In spite of everything she had always had a kind of elusive style. She got that from poor Liz, not from him. She was not pretty. The mouth was too small and pale, but it and the chin had character. The broad nose too. Even the eyes, undistinguished in color as they were, sat well above the long pale cheeks. Perhaps her really distinguishing feature was the pale-blond hair, heavy and sleek and caught severely in a big knot at the back of her neck. He surveyed her as she stood before him, and then took the cigar out of his mouth.

"Is Miss Bardon with you?" he demanded curtly.

"No."

She did not flinch under his gaze. Just stood there respectfully, her long hands clasped in front of her. This startled him a bit.

"Why not? Is she sick, or dead, or has something happened to her that I haven't heard about? Salaried traveling companions do not disappear." He was speaking with more sarcasm than he felt. It was the voice he always associated with Helen. She did not appear to notice it.

"Won't you sit down, Father? I want to talk with you if you will let me."

He scowled in amazement. This was certainly a new tone in her. "I'm perfectly comfortable on my feet!"

"All right. Do you mind if *I* sit down?"

"Don't beat about the bush, Helen. Why are you here? Where is Miss Bardon?"

She sat down again. In spite of the little awkwardness, she looked contained and composed. Her chin was set a little more obstinately than usual. That was all.

"I dismissed Miss Bardon."

"Hmm! That's very interesting. I don't remember you writing me about any such intention."

"I didn't. I decided it by myself."

He continued to hear her unbelievingly. What had happened in the six months since he had last seen her?

"Helen, I don't find any of this very funny. If you've got anything sensible to say, say it."

"That's what I came here to do, Father. I came all the way from Gidden's Square, Kensington, to say it." She was looking at him with the curiously obstinate expression, her long face a little tilted. "Do you know how old I am, Father?"

This line of attack confused him for a moment. It was completely unexpected. In fact, the whole interview was running counter to precedent.

"How old you are?" he growled. "Of course I know—what the devil difference does it make?"

"I thought not," she said. "One of the things I came here to say was that I'm nearly twenty-four years old, that I hate traveling around, that I want to come some place and stay for a while, and I don't need a nurse or a governess or a companion any more. I think I can take care of myself."

"Oh, so," he said, scowling darkly at her, "you've decided this all for yourself, have you? Well, let me remind you of the fact that the nurses and the governesses that you have been provided with were not just for your convenience. Lot of snobbish nonsense, I fully realize—but you aren't just anybody. You're the daughter of a very rich man, a potential heir to millions, and you've always got to have somebody to look after what the world looks at. You're *my* daughter!"

"Am I?" she said. "I'd like to believe that was true."

"Helen, of all the ridiculous things!" he exploded angrily, and then lowered his voice. The house still made him self-conscious. "You're not making much sense."

"Please, Father, I'm tired. I didn't just come here without a reason—certainly not to provoke you. I guess it will be hard for you to understand why I really came."

The honest pleading in her tone embarrassed him. He grunted and walked to the window. He stood there with his back to her looking out into the sunlit yard.

"You've got to admit," he said without turning, "that you didn't give me much warning."

"I couldn't. There wasn't really time after I decided. And if I had just written to you I'm sure you wouldn't have understood."

She paused. He grunted again.

"Well—what is it?"

"It's really very simple—that's why it will be difficult to believe. Nothing has happened to me, there has been no accident, no one has tried to assault or kidnap me—nothing has happened except that I am tired of being a name, a person rushed around all over everywhere simply because I am your daughter."

400

"You don't find that satisfactory?" he interrupted sarcastically. "I'm sorry. I thought I had been doing the right thing by you."

"Oh, I'm not blaming you!" she protested mildly to his back. "You've done everything, given me everything—maybe that's the trouble. But I think what I want most of all now—and no one, not even you can give me that—is to know who *I* am. Perhaps I want to be *your* daughter, not the daughter of someone called Brant Royle."

In the midst of his outrage with her, his amazement, he was deeply touched by this. But it was hard for him to change in a moment.

"So you pop in here this morning. What do you want *me* to do, Helen?"

"Nothing," she said. "Nothing at all. I don't want anybody to do anything at all. That's what I'm so sick of. I just want you to let me stay here quiet and out of the way for a while till I get straightened out with myself. I would have done it before, but I couldn't bear the thought of just going back to New York—all those rooms! You may not believe it, but it has frightened me ever since I can remember. Randy wrote me after you both came down here and told me about your moving into this old house. And the fact that you and Randy were together in a different house in a different place made me feel horribly lonely where I was. I wanted to be where you were, if you would let me." She sat in the chair, twisting the long thin hands slowly in her lap. Her voice was low, but he could sense emotion beating under it like a captive thing. Not looking at her now, he knew that she was someone he had never seen or known. But it was his daughter—a real person, somebody with a little steel in her that he had never expected. Maybe there were a lot of other things. . . .

"Helen," he growled over the clamped cigar, "don't talk like a damned fool! What a question for *you* to ask—can you stay!"

"Well, Father, may I?"

She asked it simply, obstinately. It made him cross all over again. He was *not* going to be forced into a direct acquiescence.

"Where have they put your bags?" he said.

"I'm afraid the servants were a little upset—they didn't know what to do about me. Randall came because I telephoned him at his office. He had them put me in that nice small room at the end of the hall upstairs. . . ." She hesitated and waited for him.

"Well," he said, "you'd better go get settled. They'll be calling us in to dinner in a little while."

"Thank you, Father!"

He heard her get up and come to stand behind him. It was a peculiarly poignant moment. Neither of them knew what to do. There was no history of demonstrativeness between them. She

401

waited, and then crossed to the hall door. She paused there, half-turning back.

"Father," she said, her voice full of happiness, but shy, "Father, I like your house!"

He did not turn from the window even then. He was stubborn. He was old and he was not used to giving in—to *anyone*.

"Thank you," he growled. And that was all. He did not see her smile at him, warmly and hesitantly. It almost made her long, sad face beautiful. But he stood there listening to her go all the way up the stairs—neatly, precisely, one step after another.

He stared out the window and wondered where Randall had taken himself. Very likely lurking out there on the porch somewhere, relishing this row with Helen. Well, there hadn't been a row! He felt pleased and warmed to the core. It had been a very successful morning, all told. His visit to the farm, Helen's turning up. The house, he felt, was complete now, really complete at last. Everybody was in it!

CHAPTER TWENTY-TWO

I

It was a season of content for Brant. At least, it was the first time he had felt a modicum of peace working between him and the universe. He settled into it cautiously, apprehensively, through that fall following Helen's appearance. It held on through the winter and into the spring.

He began to feel very intensely about his daughter. It was a hidden, bound, reluctant emotion. And because he could not believe it or give it countenance, he fought it more openly than he would have ordinarily. He had the sense to see that what he was enjoying was not only this discovery of his daughter, however grudgingly, but it was the fact of a whole truth in his life—a meeting point between him and his existence—that had no meaning to anyone except himself. Helen was simply part of that truth. Here he was, the great old man, the recognized genius, the fountainhead of the whole industry, come home to roost. Here were the town, the factories, the thunder of commerce moving to and fro over the face of a land that had always challenged him more than any other—all of it the creation of his energy, his relentless dream. He could sit on his porch now and look down over it all and feel the fields washing over the rolling earth, out of the pines, up to his personal achievement. When the weather turned cold he could still sit at the front-parlor window, cigar between his teeth, and look down at it spread out before him like a final and cosmic report—a testament to his life. He knew that because he at last stood, walked, slept, and ate within the confines of the house that his life had taken on a special color and warmth that glowed deeply within him. A feeling that he had pursued the whole world round and never found till he decided to put away the old recalcitrant bitterness, the hard anger and sense of outrage against this land, this town, this cluster of energy and people. He had left it—run away from it, abjured it for almost a quarter of a century. And here, after all this torment, he sat in a chair on an old porch or at a window and looked upon it and felt for the first time no need to run, to press, to crush, to hold, and show them all!

Now, here was his daughter. . . . Helen had been no more than any of the other achievements a personal thing—a factor that could move him. As his daughter she had always commanded the concern that he held for anything that was *his*. She must be the best, the most costly, the most admired, the most thickly surrounded with the things *he* was able to give her. A cipher only. Not a person. Now she appeared mysteriously, full-blown, a person, a force governed by thoughts, passions, needs about which he had no inkling. It was a revealing experience, this trying to know someone else!

It pained him that he could not communicate his new feeling for her except in the old language of a dog growling. He observed her ceaselessly out of the corner of his eye. Her comings and goings took on a special personal concern. She had been so long something that he had accepted—a thing surrounded by a panoply of guardians, companions, nurses, travel and show, an entry in his checkbook or a photograph in a paper—that now to have her with him under this special roof, this old house isolated on a hill, took on a painful and special importance. He began to want to know her better—to know what she liked to eat, the clothes she liked to wear, the food that pleased her at the table, the activities that attracted her. But it had to be a slow process. A process attacked obliquely, almost humbly.

They had nothing in common to ease the situation. She was in the house. She wanted to be there. She came and went according to the dictates of an order that he did not attempt to question or criticize, because it might disturb the tenuous understanding he felt developing between them. It was a feeling that could not be borne out by any positive evidence. Something she said at dinner, when he and she and Randall ate solemnly in the old dining room, something she asked him about one of the horses or about some old name that came up in the conversation.

In this he was as shy and inarticulate as she. They were like two strangers, met for the first time, trying to find a way to talk to each other. She did not help him. She remained in the blond, thin air that was her element. In spite of this, as the winter wore on he began to think her handsome, distinguished. Unconsciously he bequeathed to her all the attributes that he had admired most in poor Liz, that lost ghost of a wife.

He pressed nothing with her. Ordered nothing, interfered in nothing. With Randall it was just the opposite. Randall he could not understand, nor ever could. Randall possessed all the qualities that would forever move him to disparage their possessor. And so he treated his son like a pawn, interfered with his decisions, badgered him. He could not help himself. Randall squirmed, bowed, twisted under his thumb. He could feel Randall hating him, purposely goading him, slipping in sidewise to his attention. It often shocked him to know that Randall stood before the world as *his* son. And then all the old demons of his pride came out of hiding and forced him to acknowledge this effete, mocking stranger as his own. Blatantly, crudely, in many awkward ways he forced Randall to the attention of his employers. He paraded him about through the factories on one of his inspection forays, talking about him in loud, enthusiastic tones. But he did not like Randall—he could never like him—and Randall knew it. It intensified the malice, the empty bitterness, in the younger man. And having no object, no release, it began to fasten on his sister.

Brant merely watched the city accept his presence and that of his children. He refused to mix with the importuning society that beat at him. He did not have to do that any more than he had ever done it—except when it suited his purposes. But he watched with interest his daughter and son acknowledged as the prime prizes in the provincial game. Randall took it—the hostesses, the parties, the entertainments—with the ease of an old hand. Helen still went into it awkwardly and slowly. Brant Royle's daughter! He saw her accept their invitations, go to the meetings of the societies, accept the invitations, be escorted by bright youngsters who saw in her only the fact that she was his daughter. She had no graces, no special and startling beauty. Only the name of Royle and a certain obstinate distinction that was uniquely hers.

He watched her move through the winter trying to find a place. He saw her recoil slowly again into herself. That hurt him for her because he did not know how to help her, and she seemed so lonely. He brooded over her, locked in his glowering silence. The only thing that warmed him continually was the feeling that she was grateful for his silence, grateful for any further sign in him of tenderness.

She joined the societies of young women, she went to their affairs, she was mentioned regularly in the papers. But she did it with an air of dutiful resignation—as though fulfilling some obligation.

"Helen, where is it you're off to tonight?"

404

"The Piedmont Club's benefit dance, Father."

"Do you really want to go, Helen?"

"Why, yes, Father—of course."

"You don't look very excited at the prospect—although I like that new dress. Blue becomes you."

"Do you really like it, Father? I got it last year in London. I always thought it too elaborate for me."

"Not at all; very becoming, very becoming!"

"Thank you, Father!" The pale long face lighted up for a moment. It became alive.

He yearned over her. "You seem to go to a great many of this sort of thing."

"Certainly—they expect it of me!"

That was all. They expected it of her.

As the winter passed he saw her drop imperceptibly out of this stream of activity. She had done her duty. She did not seem particularly happy or unhappy. She really looked lost. She began to go about more by herself. Generally it was on little journeys and forays down into town, shopping—or just for rides in one of the two cars. That was the way the town saw her. A pale face slumped against the car cushions riding past. That's Helen Royle, the millionaire's daughter—he *owns* this town. . . .

It was either the car or one of the colts that he had brought down from Kentucky to grace the old stable. Riding was one activity that really pleased her. Almost any afternoon, if the weather was not too raw, she could be seen beautifully dressed in riding clothes, slim and erect, cantering along one of the outlying roads where the city dwindled into the country. She looked particularly alone mounted on the young horse—isolated and remote as she rode by. A severe being, untouchable and completely correct. Watching her pass, a fleeting image in the tailored tweed riding habit, the city thought she was exactly as she ought to be. They took a kind of abstract pride in her. They thought it only right that she was always followed at a discreet distance by a Negro groom on another horse. After all, she was Brant Royle's daughter!

It was on a February afternoon, rather late in a gray day hung with chill and the threat of sleet, that Helen, returning along the old South Pelham Road—one of her favorite rides (since it avoided most of the city and had long stretches of flat empty clay track for the horse)—heard a car approaching her from the rear. She did not notice it at first. But it came up behind her slowly and she heard a voice calling her name.

"Miss Royle, O Miss Royle!"

The car proceeded beyond her. It was an old-fashioned sedan, well kept and polished. A chauffeur was driving and there was someone in the back seat who waved a gloved hand at her. The car drew up at the side of the road. She came up to it with some misgivings, because this was precisely the sort of thing she had been avoiding. All these importunities, these cooing voices, these voracious ladies who wanted her to do things, or come to things, or assist at things. . . . She halted the horse, her face polite but cold. The car window was lowered and the face of an elderly woman—sixty or thereabouts —rather ugly but distinguished and energetic under the wrinkles, looked out at her with bright eyes. Helen noticed that she wore earrings and a smart hat, too—both a little extravagant for the woman's age.

"I know this is as rude as all get-out," said the woman in a warm, hoarse voice, "but you'll just have to ignore it. I saw you riding ahead of me and I thought this was as good a time as any. You don't know me from Adam. There isn't the slightest reason for your knowing me except that I like the way you ride a horse and that I used to know your father real well."

"Oh, I see," said Helen coolly. She smiled in spite of herself. There was something about the energy and the frankness of this older person that warmed her.

"Now look here, m'dear," said the lady, shaking a gloved finger, "let's not have any misunderstanding. I don't want anything from you, but, as I said, I knew your father a long time ago, and—well, let's be honest about it, I've read about you and seen you at a distance all winter, and I was just curious to know you."

Helen laughed. It was the first time she had laughed so frankly and openly in a long time. "Well," she said, "excuse me! I didn't mean to be rude—but I hope I measure up."

"Don't be a fool, m'dear," grinned the lady in the car. "How could you measure up to anything in five minutes? I'm Mrs. Talbot Graham. . . . You haven't been in Kingsmont long, and you may or may not have heard about me. I'm one of the landmarks of this city, although I've done my best to disparage the honor! Insulting foolishness. I'm old enough to be rude about it." She winked outrageously at Helen. "Age has a lot of compensations—being as rude as you like is one of 'em!"

Helen laughed again. She could not help herself, and she was delighted. "I beg your pardon."

"Ach! laugh while you can. I don't blame you," exclaimed the lady in the car. "I'm a funny, eccentric, talkative, curious woman— and now that I've seen you I think I'm going to like you, in spite of your father!"

The colt stamped and pawed restlessly at the roadway. Helen patted his neck soothingly.

"You don't like my father?" she said, feeling suddenly a little stiff.

"Honey," and the occupant of the back seat threw her a mocking glance out of the bright eyes, "I haven't spoken to him in twenty-five years—and that's something of a record for me, if you *knew* me! Well, anyway I used to know him better than anyone in this whole wide world. But we have an old quarrel. I don't hold it against you —poor dear!"

"That's generous of you," said Helen shortly.

"Now don't get all up against me on account of that. *That* has nothing to do with you. I said I think I'm going to like you. Oh, this is no place to conduct a civil conversation! Why don't you drop by and see me sometime when you have nothing better to do? I won't bite you, and I won't ask you to meet anybody. I'm selfish. I'm also cranky and won't take *no* for an answer—and it won't benefit you a bit to get angry with me. It isn't worth it."

"That's very nice of you, Mrs. Graham, but—"

"No *ifs, ands,* or *buts*. It's settled, then. If you haven't a lot of gallivanting about or horse-riding to do, why don't you have tea with me? *Tea*—what a horrid little word! I've loathed it all my life. Wretched drink, too. Won't bother you with a drop of it if you don't like it. This Thursday, then, around four? You'll come? If you don't want to stay, you can leave whenever you please and I won't think a thing of it. One thing, though." She lowered her voice and grinned —she had beautiful teeth. "Don't say anything to your father about where you are going. He wouldn't like it!"

Helen felt herself in a maze of warm confusion. She smiled. "I won't—" she began before she could think.

"Good, good! I'll be looking for you—not a word to your father, understand! This is between you and me! Get along, O'Brien, with this decrepit wagon—*if* you can make it start!"

This last was addressed to the chauffeur, who turned a red, indignant countenance to her, scowled, and put his foot on the starter. The motor responded with a roar. He looked triumphantly at her.

"Indeed, Mrs. Graham," he yelled above it. "Decrepit *indeed!*"

The lady glanced from him to Helen with an intimate look that included the girl on the horse. The car lurched forward. A little white glove fluttered from the window.

Helen watched them disappear down the road. She heard the groom's horse stamping behind her. She had forgotten all about him. She wondered how long he had been waiting there. But the face of the young Negro was respectful, uncommunicative. Helen dug her heels into the warm flanks and let the reins go. The horse plunged under her and tore down the road. She let him have his head as far as

407

he wished to go. She felt exhilarated and excited by the little encounter, abrupt and startling as it had been. Thursday . . . Thursday . . . Thursday . . . She heard the thundering hoofs booming the word out on the damp clay of the road.

2

Helen went on Thursday. She had to look up the address in the telephone directory, but she didn't really mind. It was all part of the excited air of conspiracy that moved her. She felt almost like a little girl again when she left the house and got into the car. It was as though she was embarking on a voyage of discovery—her life had allowed so little of discovery!

She went that Thursday afternoon. And she went many other afternoons, always slipping away in an atmosphere of excited secrecy —although as far as she could see no one in the house paid any more attention to her going than it had to anything that she did. No matter whether it was a simple sortie down into town to purchase hairpins or a comb, or a gift handkerchief for her cousins in England, or to have lunch at the hotel with Clementine Royle (that spoiled and wide-eyed young lady who personified in her shrieking, pouting manner everything that offended Helen, first cousin or not!). She was grateful for once that her simple function as a new relation in her family permitted her this protection and obscurity. She did not mind the obscurity. She cherished it more and more. She had endured much by being Brant Royle's daughter, and for most of it she had no talent. She often seemed a terrifying ghost to herself, a thing measured out in newsprint, an awkward face, smudged and unrecognizable among other smirking unrecognizable faces on the society pages of two continents. She had come to Kingsmont, fled there like a refugee into an unknown land, hoping, like a creature in the last extremity, to find a kind of sanctuary. A sanctuary from everyone—the nurses, the governesses, the fancy traveling companions, the people whom she had had to meet; they had surrounded her from the time she could first remember. She had needed a refuge from the feeling that she was not a creature of flesh and bone but some strange feminine extension of that strange and terrible parent thundering behind a curtain, an unknown giant.

And so she had come to Kingsmont like a soul in torment. Inarticulate, shy, with no desire for the robes of grandeur inevitably thrust upon her. But she had found Kingsmont too waiting like a beast of prey for her. No different from a dozen other places in her wanderings. But in spite of it she had gained some security. That was precious. It was something she had desired passionately, like a parched man in a desert. The security of being at last, in some meas-

408

ure, herself—*Helen*. Not Helen Royle, or anyone. Just plain *Helen*. Out of her habitual acquiescence to the importunities that beat at her—the notes, the requests, the dutiful visits, the parties, the faceless young men who called and took her out—she had begun to believe that she might clutch at the edge of something like real humanity and happiness here in this struggling, dingy, raw, and vigorous Southern land, about which she knew nothing, but before which she humbly stood and hoped. Brant she still found terrifying. An image, a looming shadow that she could only recognize, battle, and reach out to mutely, hoping for some sign that would make her feel that he saw her not as that ghostly thing, *his* daughter, but simply as herself come face to face with him. Here she felt thwarted again. And beneath her failure with him moved the deep waters of her profound resentment. Resentment not because of the things he had done to and for her, but for the things that he had *never* done.

She had no illusions about herself as a physical object. She accepted her plainness, her social awkwardness. She bitterly scorned the journalistic prose that hid these truths behind meretricious words. . . . "The distinguished Miss Helen Royle, daughter of Mr. Brant Royle, president of . . . Attending were Miss Helen Royle, daughter of Brant Royle . . ." It went on endlessly, the feverish cry of an empty hunt. She had been resigned to it for years. Privately she was no longer willing to accept or to read it. It only emphasized her wild sense of unreality. So she had come fleeing to this unknown quantity named Kingsmont. . . . And in spite of everything—in spite of recognizing that all the things she had fled from formed here to enclose her again—she had gained a kind of fragile peace. Her father, her brother. She had come unbidden and openly to both of them. She desired desperately to touch them—to have them reach out and touch her and make her feel that she was cherished for herself. And what had she found? Not hostility. Worse. A dark blank wall of smiles, frowns, the eternal façades surrounding even the simplest events of a day's living. Brant remained immured behind his own separate and dark fury. Randall remained all glib irony, all elusive sidewise glance. Her brother had his own life. She sensed almost a hatred in him as though she had forced herself, intruded, into a life already awry and bitter; she questioned him desperately about his work, all the things that he seemed interested in. He would not believe that she was any more real or that she wanted to know and love him. Her encounters with Brant left her frozen. From them she retired into a region of sheer obstinateness without form or object or reason. And so she found herself alone at last. Alone as she had always been. Her only solace was the realization that if she had to be alone she would rather be alone *here* with these objects of her hungry searching than anywhere else. And if they sought to drive her

409

off, there was the strength in her that would not let them. She could stay and endure. . . . And then she had met this startling elderly woman—Mrs. Graham, Sonie Graham, what a name! She went to tea.

"Honey," Sonie had said at that first meeting when they sat in the dim plushy drawing room of the brick house, the windows gray with the winter afternoon outside, "honey, let's understand each other right away. Look, you don't want tea. There isn't a drop of tea in the house. Let's have a cocktail. Lise makes a good dry Martini that warms my bones. You like Martinis, I hope?"

"Why, yes—yes, of course," she had said, and didn't know why. She had never had a cocktail in her life, not because there had been any lack of opportunity but simply that the idea had never seemed sufficiently interesting.

"Of course you would—you've got good common sense. I knew that from the moment I yelled at you out the car window. Something about the way you sat on that fool, capering horse. Style, real style—that's difficult on a horse! Hey, Bellers!" she yelled toward the dining room, and winked broadly at Helen. She sat so straight, so sparkling with life, that Helen felt dazed. The butler appeared, a dim figure in the doorway—but with an air of enjoying being a butler in this house.

"Bellers," Sonie continued, not looking at him but at Helen with that searching speculative glance, "Bellers, run upstairs—and I mean *run*—and rout Lise out of her dotage and tell her I want some Martinis, d'y' hear?"

"Of course, ma'am."

Sonie grimaced again at Helen and waited until he had gone.

"He loathes me, honey, simply loathes me. Had him for ten years and that's why he stays. He thinks I'm the most nouveau-riche creature he has ever come across—nouveau riche at my age!" She leaned forward, straight and vibrant, toward the girl. "I just don't have to pretend any more, honey, that's all. Age has its compensations, let me tell you! Do you mind my calling you honey? I'll stop if it bothers you."

"Why, not at all, Mrs. Graham, if you want to."

"Good girl! Humor an old woman. Well, not so old—not ancient, anyway! I have a name. It's something that they used to call me all the time when I was a little chit of a thing, prancing about Maple Street. I find it slipping out all over the place nowadays. Well, when we get to know each other better and you feel comfortable with me I'll make you call me Sonie. Don't bother about it now—later."

And so they had their cocktails, sipping them and looking at each other comfortably over the slim-stemmed glasses in the big,

410

fussy drawing room. Helen felt the bloom of unexpected happiness flood softly through her. She could not explain it. She did not even try to. She simply sat and listened to this garrulous, elaborately dressed lady who demanded nothing of her, asked her no questions, but ran on and on in her warm husky voice, pulling at the eyeglasses strung to her erect, firm bosom, patting her absurd dyed hair. In any other setting she, Mrs. Graham, might have seemed an eccentric monstrosity, a phenomenon. But here she was right, irresistible. Helen found herself listening, hungrily and gratefully. Here was someone who looked upon her out of a wrinkled, too carefully made-up face! A face full of humor and vitality for all its age, the green eyes still alive and bright with energy and interest—a laughing, honest face that saw nothing of her, Helen Royle, the mythical, unreal shadow surrounded by millions of dollars, factories, securities, the child of a legend. This woman saw her as a living human being, an awkward, thin girl with a good face, good bones under the pale skin, good eyes back of the shyness, the pale, rich hair—saw her as she was and asked no questions, made no surmises, insisted upon no intrusions. Made her feel, in short, like someone who walked in her own right upon the earth. It was a new and gratifying experience. Whatever else might develop in her relationship with this woman, she would forever be profoundly grateful for that. It was the one thing she had sought everywhere. It was somehow humbling that she had to discover it here with a virtual stranger. She felt, beyond all the words, the parabolas, of the monologue so energetically woven about her, that she was in the presence of an honest spirit, one which had lived a great deal, and had acquired the final grandeur of complete and terrible honesty.

"Honey," Mrs. Graham was saying, looking accusingly at the empty cocktail glass in her fine hand—so tense and capable and expressive, "I don't know what you have heard about me already, or you may not have heard anything. But let me say this right here and now. The papers yell respectfully when I happen to move about and stir up a fuss one way or another—and I *do* stir up fusses, can't help it—the papers say that I'm Mrs. Talbot Graham. But don't you believe it. Don't believe one little word of it—and I know you don't, because I can see you've been through *that* mill. Because what I am *really* is just plain little ol' Sonie Lipik from Maple Street. Now I expect you don't even know about Maple Street. Your father owns a big factory down there. But I'll take you with me one of these days and show you how Maple Street used to be. I'll show you the old school and where the Vitcheks—oh well, listen to me go on. All I want to say is that I'm no better than I ought to be and I'm perfectly proud of it. Which is more than I can say of a lot of other people around here. They won't have said much about me, only that I

411

began as the daughter of a boardinghouse keeper. They don't dare say more, the poor fools! because I know more interesting things about most of *them*. But I'm not a bit afraid of having been a girl from a boardinghouse. Some of them came from far worse beginnings. And the worse the beginnings, honey, the bigger the house, the sillier the front with all those big gates and lawns and servants and cars. I know they don't fool you, but no matter what they have told you, just remember that I'm not trying to live up to anything or anyone—just myself. And fool that I've been, many a time, I've always known what *kind* of fool. Here—this glass is dry as July!"

She leaned back and called hoarsely over her shoulder, "Bellers! Stop eavesdropping and tell Lise to make up some more cocktails. This is a special occasion. You'll just have to get used to me," she continued confidentially, lowering her voice to Helen. "I'm sentimental, horribly, disgustingly sentimental, and I like to make an occasion of anything that pleases me. This afternoon pleases me. The fact that you came here on my invitation pleases me—*you* please me!"

Helen met this feeling the blood flush hotly in her face. This woman was so terrifyingly direct and honest! Perhaps it was such an honesty that she had been looking for.

"Mrs. Graham, you're most awfully kind—"

"Honey, for goodness sake stop all that formality—I haven't got time for it. In fact, call me Sonie, will you? Only my friends—and they are few—call me Sonie. It flatters me. And I've never really liked the other—*Mrs. Graham!*"

"All right," said Helen, feeling more reckless than she had ever felt in her twenty-four years, "all right—Sonie!"

"Ach! That's what I like to hear. Shocks you a bit, doesn't it? Well, don't let it—although I like having it shock you for the moment. Not many people call me Sonie nowadays—there aren't many left who have the privilege, and they're buried around in odd corners. None of this hoity-toity grabbing crowd. *They* call me Mrs. Graham, yes, ma'am! and they prance and scrape and bow and show a proper consideration, or there's a big row, believe you me!"

The erect figure in the stiff green dress, with the old-fashioned boned collar high about the wrinkled neck, bowed toward her. Helen nodded back and smiled. It was a moment of complete and precious intimacy.

The winter passed like that. Measured out in Thursdays. Betweentimes she proceeded along the route of the old, curtained, surrounded life—occasionally going forth into the town, riding the roan colt violently out in the chill, lunching with Uncle Sam (that withered, uncomfortably squirming individual, the First Citizen!) and Aunt Berta, or going shopping with Tina and listening to her cousin's condescending gabble about New York, and the Florida season, and the boys who had come down from Princeton. It was all written off as something to be endured, something that had become completely unreal. These guarded, treasured escapes—taking one of the cars (when they were available), manufacturing stiff evasions for Randall when he poked and pried mercilessly at her, hurrying out the front door, leaving the big, isolated house with its muffled air, the overhanging shadow of her father, no matter where he was—in the parlor, upstairs or downtown in his office—or plunging awkwardly down Hill Street past the grimy shops and dingy brick fronts till she could reach the trolley stop at Bay Street.

She liked this last way best of all. Going alone and unattended. Waiting for the little impersonal jangling car. Taking out her nickel and presenting it to the conductor, sitting down on the hard seat beside a dowdy housewife or a little girl, nose plastered against the window, or a middle-aged office clerk, correctly dressed, but tired, bent on some journey in the afternoon. The getting-out at last and the walk up the long block past the iron fences, the old shrubbery, till she could turn into the curving driveway, walk up it and present herself safe at last under the brick porte-cochere and place her finger upon the bell. Then at last the plushy parlor set about with its gilt-framed pictures of Venetian scenes, of Hope, with a lyre, sitting blindfolded on an impossible rock, the good imitation Chippendale chairs, the heavy mahogany Grand Rapids table with the awful claw feet—all of them come to mean more than anything she had ever had or known. They and the figure, energetic under its parody of extreme respectability, the pince-nez on the active chain, the sequins on the corsage, the glittering jewelry, that advanced to meet her each time.

"Honey, take off that awful hat!" The warm, immediate voice assuming charge from the very moment of Helen's entrance. "Is that the kind of thing they let you wear up there at Hill House? They ought to know better. You with that fine head of hair. Real blond hair. Now take my old mop. It began red. Real red, I want you to know, no matter what they've told you. I dye it now. Have for years. Why shouldn't I? Red was always becoming to me. Whether or not it makes me look a fright now makes no difference. *I* still think of it as becoming to me—and that, after all, is what matters!"

No one else. Just the two of them sitting there and talking. Whether true or not, the older woman always gave her the feeling that her appearance was a thing of special and unique importance. That she, Helen, was a person necessary—no, demanded! During that winter she got from the other woman a whole picture of the past of Kingsmont, of people, of the factories and the farmers coming into town on week ends. It almost had the flavor of a fairy tale that she had heard as a child, remote and golden. And in hearing it she began to want to know the reality and to be glad that she was where she was so that she could without special effort mingle with these things when they came about—the eternal, immutable face of this country that she was discovering.

She listened to the other woman. Gave herself over passively and gratefully. But she realized that in the gush of words and revelations Sonie was subtly sounding her out, testing her, prying out all of her history bit by bit. A question thrown in here and there in the midst of the flood, catching Helen off guard, so that she answered honestly and frankly without thinking. She did not mind, because she felt always that she was safe. For some reason she did not dare to fathom, Sonie liked her. That was more than enough. She, in turn, gradually pieced together a picture of the other's life. The little girl down among the factories in the boardinghouse (she made a special lone pilgrimage herself to see Maple Street), the handsome young woman forced into bright being, respected and disparaged in the same breath. The triumphant young woman rich with the sudden wealth that her father, Brant Royle, had brought to the tobacco world; the strange hiatus in Europe; the little journey into the spangled world of the theater (Sonie had pictorial evidence here, faded, posturing faces pasted into a thick book). They bent their heads together—the orangy, frowsy red and the sleek blond—over the yellowed pages and smiled sidewise at each other. Helen had the feeling that the older woman was letting her in on a colossal joke, a warm and human hoax that had been perpetrated. Something that had been enjoyed intensely when it had happened, but understood and put away. A whole history of rich things that had been taken and used with complete honesty, appreciated for their worth, but never allowed to scar or twist the essential vitality of this vulgar, sophisticated lady whom she thought of now as her only friend in the world.

Through it all she was intensely aware of Sonie's tact. It lay under all the bustling, ceaseless energy. With it Helen began to soften, to want to know more than she asked. It was a voyage of discovery and encounters, a river of exciting flotsam and jetsam. Sonie's conversation poured out upon her all she was trying to find out, all the things that had made her father, driven him away, brought him back. . . . She was aware of the care Sonie took not to drag Brant's name into their meetings. But there came a day at last—no considered preamble, no careful leading—when it just came inconsequentially out of the conversation. . . .

"Honey," Sonie said, and twined some blue beads roped about her neck, "honey, your father was a magnificent creature when I first knew him, no matter what you see him as now. And he was an impossible man. I'll be honest with you—I knew him about as well as a person could know such a wild, possessed country boy who had a fire in his brain. But I've been sort of wild that way myself all my life. Shopping around, y'know. But I knew the real thing when I saw it. Someday I'll tell you all about your father and me. This isn't the right time. The fact is that we are both fools—stubborn, crazy. Look here, I'm bothering you with an old quarrel, so old I don't remember just exactly what I felt about it except I knew the way he was going didn't suit me. Well, anyway we cut off from each other, and that was after, long after, Johnny Barton came wandering in here amongst us—*long after*. I haven't told you about Johnny Barton, have I? Well, give me time. *He,* poor excuse for a man that he was, really made this town, this industry, all the fat, busy, money-grabbing town that we live in. Well, that story's for some other time. The thing that I want you to know is that age and experience can give you some tolerance from the outside looking in, but it can't change what's in the heart of you. Look at your father there, and *me* here—twenty-five years nearly and we're still so all-out proud that we can't say 'How-d'y-do, let's sit down and forget all this stupidity!' No, not for a minute. He sits up there sulking in that old house that he worshiped when he was a boy and I crawl around down here and set my mouth and say I'll never make the first move. Silly, just plain silly, but I can no more do anything about it now than he can—even if he wants to—and I'm not any more sure what *it* is now than I ever was. The fact remains—and it should cheer you, because you've got all your life ahead of you—the fact remains that age and getting some little sense in you about things never set you free from your pride, your little stupid ties. Remember *that* when the time comes for you to question yourself. And remember a funny old woman who had a lot to say on the subject and no cure for the ill!"

"Sonie," Helen said in the hesitant voice still, "Sonie, did Father make it so difficult for you—"

"Ach! honey, he could no more help it than breathe. Don't you worry about *that*. He's not done too well by you, for that matter—but then he doesn't know it. God help him, he's not done so well by himself, the big, blind bear that he is! Now, let's not bother ourselves about your father. I want to know why you aren't going to the church your uncle built in memory of the old man, your grandfather. I don't go myself, but don't think I don't hear about everything that goes on, particularly about the people I have an eye on. . . ."

"I went when I first came," Helen protested eagerly. "I *really* tried, but I just couldn't bear them looking at me and whispering—you know. . . ."

"Of course, honey, of course I know, and I'm proud of you that

415

you haven't let yourself be shoved in with the rest of this dog-eat-dog set of money snobs that swarms over Kingsmont. But it doesn't matter a hoot in Hades. I'm just as big a sinner myself, not even a good old-fashioned Sunday believer, in spite of the settlement house and all those things. We're out of their reach; they can't scratch us (much as they would like, the silly lot of them!). They let me alone and call me eccentric. They let you alone because you're Brant Royle's daughter and the niece of Mr. Samuel Royle—and there's the hospital and the First Methodist Church and the Royle Agricultural Foundation over at the college near Raleigh, and all the rest of it. Sops for our blessed consciences, cake to the crowd we've walked all over—and a hope that we've made some kind of compromise with the hereafter. And they all have to respect it, because they would like to do the same thing themselves. In fact, they act like they've done it anyway, in *our* names—which is perhaps more true than we like to think about, the poor, desperate fools that they are! Here! Your glass has been empty for the last ten minutes. Let me call Lise—"

"No, thank you, Sonie. Really I've had quite enough—don't bother about me. But if you—"

It could have been any of a dozen of their meetings, as patterned and as certain as the hour. It was also the happiest thing Helen had ever experienced in all her life. She began to feel that here, from this woman, so bound up in the mystery of her forebears and those lost lives, she was receiving all the warmth, all the richness of human contact, that she had hungered for and never had. Here was mother, sister, friend, all in one—and something much more. She treasured it with increasing passion, guarded it fervently, took more and more precautions to protect the fact of its existence.

Then there came the afternoon—sometime very late in the winter, so late that the lawn was newly green outside and the elms across the street from Sonie's windows looked like thick smudges of chartreuse—there came the afternoon when they sat as they had always sat when they were in Sonie's house, relaxed and comfortable, talking and listening in complete understanding with the world outside shut away, a distant thing—almost an unreality for the moment. And then there had come the knock at the door. Not the bell, but a big, grand firm clamor on the brass knocker. Sonie sat bolt upright, frowning. She put her glass down on the table. . . .

"Ach, who's that now? Nobody calls on me any more. They know better. Now do you suppose one of those ignorant salesmen has come wandering in at my gate?"

Bellers stalked in from the dining room, casting his habitual expression of sour resentment in their direction as he passed toward the front hall.

"Bellers," called Sonie over her shoulder, "don't let them get you involved in a lot of polite exchanges now—send them away, the lady of the house is definitely not at home!"

She winked at Helen and settled back into her chair. But the sound of the door opening had been followed by a young bass voice.

"Afternoon, Bellers."

"Afternoon, sir."

"I know this is unusual, Bellers, but is Mrs. Graham at home?"

Sonie's body relaxed in the plush chair. She smiled and shrugged at Helen, enigmatically, woman to woman.

"Bellers," she called loudly, "don't try to pretend. Come on in here, Jim!"

She got up then. Helen watched her, feeling suddenly cold and apprehensive. This had never happened before. There had never been an intruder. She watched Sonie cross quickly to the hall doorway and hold out her hand to a young man—a square-set young man with a grin on his face.

"Jim, what are you doing in town today?"

"I'm sorry, Sonie," he was saying, looking at her with the warm, grave face, the shy smile, pleased and intimate, "I wouldn't have done it, except that I was in to see Tredwell down at the hardware store about a shipment, and got through earlier than I had expected. I just thought I'd run out here and see how you were. Do you mind?"

"Of course I mind! You know I don't like surprises! But stop standing there like a yokel and come on in!"

Helen felt still and alone. There was such intimacy under their words, such old understanding and liking, that she felt closed out. She sat carefully looking at her thin hands, meticulously folded in her lap.

"Helen—I'm sorry." It was Sonie's voice bearing down upon her. "But now that he's here, there's nothing I can do about him. Jim, this is my old friend Helen Royle."

He came to her with the square face, the blue, remote gaze that made her eyes falter. He held out his hand.

"How do you do," he said, shaking her lax hand. "I'm one of Sonie's *old* friends, too—but I don't expect she would admit it."

And then he smiled again suddenly and the blue eyes, the stubborn, concentrated face, lit up. It accepted and compelled her with its shy directness. He is uncertain, too, she divined in a flash; he is alone. She lifted her face and smiled back at him. She saw then, with a strange thrill of joy, that there was nothing in him that had been changed or colored by the sound of the name "Royle." She might have been Smith or Jones or something from a remote land for all he appeared to notice. It did not interest him. And because she saw that what he had heard meant nothing to him, she felt the blood come

417

back into her, the ease of breath, braced. . . . She released her hand and sat back again into the chair looking at him.

"I'm not such an old friend," she heard herself saying, "I'm really a newcomer to Kingsmont. I don't know anything. Sonie is trying to educate me."

"Well, you've come to the right place!" He looked solemnly back at Sonie standing in the doorway. "Sonie, I hope you've told her *everything*."

Sonie patted the back of her hair, rattled her beads, and answered him with an oddly young, coquettish glance.

"Of course I have," she assured him in the husky voice full of playful innuendoes. "Well, practically everything."

"Even about me?" he asked, and Helen could see that he did not mean it jokingly. He was in earnest. Everything was in earnest about this man.

"About *you*, Jim?" said Sonie, leaning elaborately over the back of her recently vacated chair. "I haven't even mentioned your name. Helen isn't interested in the diseases of the tobacco plant, I hope, or any of that business about the situation of the tobacco farmer in the economy, so don't spoil this afternoon with another one of your lectures."

"Oh, but I am!" Helen burst out. She felt astounded at herself. She had never intended saying anything of the kind. It had just come out of her in the moment. She felt the blood crimson her face and shifted in her chair. The intense blue gaze of the young man swung down upon her again. He wasn't a distinguished-looking young man, but there was such compelling honesty, such integrity and concentration, in that look that she welcomed it. She was like a drunkard sipping a new brew.

"You are?" he questioned quietly. "What do you want to know about it?"

"I don't know," she answered weakly—and hated the falling sound of it. "I know you'll think I'm just—making conversation. But I don't know anything about tobacco. I've been nearly half a year in North Carolina and I haven't learned anything about it. Does that make me sound silly?"

"Ach! Helen," snorted Sonie behind her chair, "you're just like all of us—and *he*, he won't know what I'm talking about, of course, but *you* do, and I'm delighted with you, honey!"

"I've got a place near town and we'll be laying out the plant bed soon," he said, ignoring the interruption. "Have you ever seen a plant bed?"

"No," said Helen, shaking her head slowly and looking helplessly at him. "A plant bed? I'm afraid—"

"Well," he said eagerly, going beyond her in a swift flight, leaving her behind in his interest, "it's this way. . . . It's a kind of wonderful ceremony observed in thousands of little corners of this state. It's the beginning of the whole process, before spring, even—the little clearing in a pine grove, staked out, burnt over, the ashes of last year's leaves, a testimony and assurance that the new seed will have a chance—and it's a little seed, the littlest seed you've ever put your eyes on: *the tobacco seed!* It needs a particular ground, virginal and uncontaminated, for its beginnings; because it holds, at that moment, all the wealth of this state, of Kingsmont—all the income of thousands of farmers spread out over this belt of the state."

"God save us!" said Sonie. "We're off. Helen, I'm sorry, but life is like this when Jim is around. Life is a great big ridiculous green plant. Fat green leaves with awful diseases—but he'll fill your ears as long as you can bear listening. Look here, Jim, we're having a cocktail like civilized humans. Are you going to have your same brew? Because if you are I've got to go out and stir up the kitchen a bit."

"Sonie, don't bother about my coffee," he said, looking not at her but at Helen.

"Bother—what arrogant children you men are!" She left them, clashing her beads irritably, and went out beyond into the dining room.

"Now in preparing the plant bed for the tobacco seed," continued the young man, the grave and concentrated young man pacing up and down the rug before her. He stopped for a moment to glance out the window toward the street. She scarcely heard him. She was thinking: Tobacco! What a strange and lovely word. Particularly the way he said it now. She scarcely heard any of the rest he was saying. She could only look shyly and helplessly at him, walking up and down, not noticing her. She was an ear, a thing to listen. . . .

Sonie, coming back into the room some ten minutes later, paused on the threshold and looked at them, isolated in her big room. The young man leaning over the chair, the thin figure of the young woman stretching up to him. . . . Even in the failing afternoon light the tableau struck her. It held her stock-still. And as she stood there, she experienced a sharp pang—it was a moment of pure envy and jealousy. She was too old for jealousy. She was past *that*. She would not admit it now. She shrugged her shoulders; they had not even noticed that she had returned. And then suddenly looking on them there suspended, unaware, she had a feeling of compensation, of ironic rightness. These two people, of all the people on earth, were meeting under her roof! She was filled with a sense of perverse satisfaction. She appreciated deeply the irony, and that she alone was witness to it!

419

"Well, look now, look now," he was saying. (Sonie could hear him plainly.) "What you need to do is come out and see it. I can show you better than just talk about it. You ought to see it, you know —anybody living here in the midst of it ought to see and try to understand it from the beginning to the end. Now my place is just a few miles out. Would you like to come out—if you can arrange it, of course—and let me show you what I've been doing?"

"Yes, of course." Helen's clipped, nervous voice, so earnest, so naked, now waiting on him. "I'd like to very much, if it won't be too much trouble. . . . "

"Trouble, ma'am! It would be a pleasure any time during the week you could come—"

"Jim," interrupted Sonie, walking deliberately into the room. Running the old beads over and over again between her fingers, she hoped that her face had learned after all these years not to reveal what she felt. "Jim, your coffee will be here in a minute."

3

How hot the August afternoon beat upon her! How wonderfully blazing—flame upon flame, glancing across the bare, beaten yard to the edge of the old trees, throwing flat still light upon still light out of a pale-blue sky from the white farmhouse across to the old white-washed outbuildings and then up to the sky again. She had never endured a Southern summer before. It was a new experience. She found its discomforts not at all terrifying. There seemed something quite impersonal, immutable, and serene about this Carolina countryside pinioned in this blazing element. House, tobacco field, stretching; great hovering tree; the empty stillness. It was like nothing in all her cottony, plush-insulated life. No, *this* was not exotic. It was an acknowledged manifestation. It was something that lay recognizable against her eyes and against her blood.

She stood, a slim quiet figure, at the center of the deserted yard looking down toward the placid green of the tobacco field and thinking with a wild feeling of joy: Why am I here? When did I first come here? Why have I continued to come? Fascinating questions that had only one answer. An answer that she did not dare examine because it was already a part of her breath. She wanted only to submerge herself in the feeling of happiness, of blind direction. . . .

He took a long time coming. He always did. She smoothed the crisp, starched white piqué of her summer skirt, and blushed a little to think how she had taken time over the choice of her blouse, a sheer batiste, long at the sleeve, high at the neck. She had bought it in France ages ago—last year—but it was fresh, deceptively simple, flattering to her ungenerous bosom. . . . How female I really am! she

420

thought with a kind of warm disparagement. It was not really disparagement, only recognition of the truth. She gave a hitch to the curved straw brim of her hat and squinted her eyes down toward the tobacco field, concentrating—not thinking about herself or anything.

There is a tobacco field, those tall plants with the big green leaves hanging heavy and outward from the stalk, one after another. Row upon countless row of them—not only here but miles and miles of them all over this country—springing straight upward from the gray, sandy earth. And they all look exactly alike and they all mean something quite beautiful beyond what they are intended for, those perfect, green plants! He's quite right (she nodded under the brim of the wide straw hat), quite right. In that green leaf, in all those rows, lies the magic that has made all those factories possible, all those houses, all that money, all those little white-wrapped cigarettes. They *are* this world! Yes, he was quite right—those blue eyes blazing could never be wrong, they had no capacity for anything except their vision. They admitted of no distraction. That was the only thing she found in any way terrifying; the thing that nibbled at the edge of her glow, her happiness. He was stubborn, arbitrary, concentrated, and humorless. She tallied them all off and cried wildly: It doesn't matter! He would be difficult, forever remote, with that terrible, concentrated, *selfless* selfishness that brooked no interruption. I don't care, I don't care! she chanted standing there with the lost smile curving her small pale mouth, facing the tobacco field. . . .

"Helen!"

His voice hailed her up the pathway along the field. She saw him now, walking steadily toward her, wiping his face with a soiled kerchief. He was naked to the waist because he had been in the fields and it was hot. His square, spare torso glistened brownly under the sun. He was completely unaware of his nakedness. He stopped before her with the light in his eyes, the light that she could never really believe had anything to do with her. She could not even feel any special deference to his nakedness. He was like no other man she had ever known in her limited experience. She had never thought much about men or love except in a conventional sense. The physical presence had always been something blurred and faceless, something in correct dress with a correct voice, escorting, deferring to, that ephemeral quality known as Helen Royle. *This* golden creature, polished with perspiration over his burned hide, this elusive and at the same time solid young man with the wonderful eyes who never saw her . . . She accepted it now. She knew it would be like that forever, no matter what.

"Should I have come or not?" she said, looking squarely at him, her hand at her throat in an unconscious gesture of defense.

421

"You *are* a one!" he said, rubbing his forearm and looking at the earth between his dusty shoes. There was always something shy, elusive, and at the same time pleading in his gestures toward her. "Why shouldn't you have come, Helen?"

"I don't know. I've been out here all through the summer learning about tobacco, and now it's all finished, I expect I haven't any excuse to come!"

She looked at him like a suppliant, the long, fine fingers of one hand playing with the cloth of her shirtwaist. He watched the hand resting on the sleeve. She saw the blood color the tan on his face, as though her hand there had touched something mysterious in him.

"Of course you should have come!" he said. "You couldn't have come a better day. That south quarter of the little field I showed you—remember?—the one I planted in the spring with the new seed . . . well, it's stood up against *everything*. The patch next to it is lying in the rows, riddled with black shank, but the other is the finest upstanding tobacco you ever saw. Not a blemish! Do you know what *that* means?"

"No," she laughed. "I'm the one who's learning, you know. What does it mean?"

She watched him carefully. He stood so independent and alone before her in the dust of the yard. Oh, Jim, oh, Jim, what does it mean—not your tobacco, not the green plant, but *you* and *I*—you the man, I the lost woman looking at you—what do *we* mean under this hot summer sky? Do you even see me here? Her head inclined toward him, her pale unpretty face sober and watchful. He was not looking at her. He was searching that private distance of his, that unknown landscape, that geography she could never invade. It was almost like a hostile land, that separate vision of his.

"It means," he said stolidly, the words careful, serious, "that if I can manage to run through next season, I'll have something that will make a difference to the farmers in this state!"

"Next season?" she asked brightly, continuing the conversation as if it really mattered to her. "What do you mean *if* you can manage next season?"

"I mean plenty. Frankly, Helen, I'm on my last legs—my credit has run out. The gentlemen in the Agriculture Department think I'm a fool, a crazy fool, as usual. If the Foundation didn't come through I don't know where I'd be. I'd just have to stop and go work in a factory or something!" He smiled—the brilliant shy smile—directly at her. It was almost as though he had reached out and touched her. She felt hot and weak. . . .

"Oh *no*, Jim—after all you've done! They can't let all your work go to waste now."

"You're wrong. *Of course* they can! After all, I'm a long-term investment at best, and I've been long enough about it as far as they're concerned. They've sunk a lot of money in me—me and my sweating over the perfect tobacco plant."

"But they won't let you down now!" she cried. "When you've got this far—"

"This far!" he said scornfully. "What are my experiments, my plants, to anyone except to me and Marshall and the one or two others who slave here with me? My friends down the road take their crop, cured and in hands, bring it into the warehouse in September, and sell it. They've done it for years. Their fathers did it before them. They think they're doing all right as long as they are able to bring home some little token of a year's labor. Well, they think I'm an educated crank sweating out here in one or two fields with my fancy tobacco. Why shouldn't they? They know that tobacco will be grown a long time after they and I have gone into our graves; they know that cigarettes will be made in Kingsmont and other cities as always."

He stopped and scowled. It was a new and bitter note for him.

"But Jim, can't you keep on in spite of it? They need you."

"Sure they need me, but I have to use the money of the rich to help *them*. I guess that's only right—as long as the rich don't mind my using their money for my little experiments."

"You mean the Foundation?"

She dared not look at him. He had never given the slightest indication that he saw her in the light of her name or connected her in any way with the money that had helped him. But he *must* know. He could not help knowing. Still, his face was as it had been at their first meeting—sober, concentrated, looking at that secret, inner vision that did not include her.

"Yes, I'm afraid I mean the Foundation. Thank God for the Foundation!" He laughed briefly.

"Come along!" he said. She had become accustomed to that flat, impersonal command. "Let's go have a look at my *good* tobacco! You're nice, Helen, to turn up like this. I need someone to talk to today."

He reached out and took her by the arm, turning her down the pathway. She felt will-less, lost under his touch.

He drew her with him down the path of sun along the field. She could only feel his hand under her arm. The sun, the sky, the hot still smell of green growing that surrounded them, was a presence.

"It's awfully hot. Will you be all right?" he said, looking down anxiously at her.

"Don't be silly, Jim!" she answered, and pulled at the brim of her hat. Her thoughts raced along with them. Three months! she was thinking—or nearly three months—since he came into Sonie's parlor and spoke to me. Time—weeks, days, months—what does it matter?

What matters, she answered herself honestly, is that he wants to show me this stalwart, mysterious, adamant plant of his growing in a field. What matters is that all else that has ever happened to me in my life means nothing to me beside *this*. . . . Walking in the dust under the cruel sun close beside this stubborn stranger full of pride in the thing he is trying to do. Pride, that's it. He has terrible, remorseless pride. . . . But I am lost, forever lost, knowing it. In spite of it, I would have had to run here this afternoon, unbidden, mocked at, and unashamed simply to look on this blue-eyed pride—this pride that looks at me and hardly knows I am here. . . .

They cut down into the field between the tall rows of leafy green. It was beautiful. So regular, so intact, so proud. The plants were like him in a way. Impersonal, delicate, complete, each healthy plant standing in its place in the long row. She was the stranger—something that must come down among them only to observe.

"This is just the regular planting," he said, marching ahead of her. "We'll take a good crop off this! You haven't seen a harvesting yet, have you?"

"No, Jim. I've only been here since spring."

"I'm always forgetting," he chuckled over his shoulder. "I've got such a one-track mind that it's hard for me to believe there are people who have never grown tobacco!"

He threw back the dark tousled hair and laughed one of his rare laughs. It was a special sound. A sound awkward and without true humor.

"Well, you haven't seen anything yet! It's a wonderful, backbreaking time of the year for the farmers in this part of the world. Picking the leaves—you'll have to see their hands breaking the leaves off, swiftly, accurately. Putting them down on the sled with the slow mule plodding down the row. And then there is the best yet—the curing barns." He paused and shook his head.

"What?" she said weakly, not wanting him to stop, wanting only to hear the sound of his eager, deep voice.

"The best yet, the curing—the old log curing barns with the folks staying up all night singing, and the women bringing food down from the house and the fire in the furnace blazing out in the night. It's a good time, Helen, you must see it!"

"Oh, I want to, Jim!"

He turned his head and looked at her. She met it openly, and then reached out and caressed a wide green leaf. She felt again blind and defenseless under his sudden and special gaze.

"Well, here it is," he said, "the results of five years' work."

She looked about her over the leafy surface level with her shoulder. She wanted to appear as though she had received a revelation. But here were only tobacco leaves, millions of them under the sun.

424

How could she tell him alone that she wanted most desperately to be a part of whatever was *close* to him?

"It's beautiful, Jim!" she cried. She hated herself. It was so inexpressive and banal. She could do nothing but look at *him*, the beautiful, naked back, the brown skin, the solid muscles made of this earth, this sun, this labor—the solid, separate invincibility of him! She was glad that he had turned away and was sweeping the field with an eager, questioning eye. The arc of that glance rested around him like a benediction.

"That's it," he said quietly, "not a weak plant. . . . But just look over there—not even five yards away!"

She followed the sweep of his arm obediently. A few rows beyond them, the green solidity fell away abruptly as though a giant had taken a scythe and cut a narrow swath through the field. They stood so close that it was with an effort she could see the long lines, five rows of them. Grayed, wilted stalks drunkenly bent and dried. Corrupted, ruined things, blasted upon the earth. She felt a sudden compassion for them in the midst of all this burgeoning, this arrogant and challenging green. She could not help feeling an identity with them. If she had been left as she had been—a lost plant withering? . . . She was still lost, in a way, but she had found something, *someone*, who had warmed and made her whole life meaningful. The poor plants had not achieved that. Diseased and forsaken, they had died. And that was all there was to it. . . .

"Jim," she said, looking at the edge of his profile, "Jim, how dreadful for them."

"What do you mean?" he said, puzzled. "They had the same chance. Both seeds planted in the same ground. One came out of it victorious."

"I know—I think it's wonderful. Your fine plant and everything. Don't bother about me—I can't talk very intelligently about all these things, as you do. I understand what you say. I love to hear you talk about them. You make tobacco sound like something strange and wonderful—something to be cherished, guarded, worked over." She did not say that she wished passionately that she was a tobacco plant under his hand. An absurd and shameful concept. But it *was* true—oh, how true it was! She could feel her very bones melt and change into sap, stem, and broad-veined leaf under that square tense brown hand.

"Helen," he said, turning back to her, "I'm glad you came this afternoon. I needed someone to talk to!"

Someone to talk to, she thought, is that all? Is that all I am—no more than someone to talk to?

"I'm glad about your new tobacco, Jim," she said. "I'm glad because it means so much to you."

He looked at her with the sudden hot expression, remote and

encompassing her as though he were looking at her for the first time. It was the look that she could not endure.

"Come on," he said. "This sun's too hot. I am a thoughtless fool for dragging you down here in the middle of the afternoon. I've been out here working since daybreak. I hadn't realized how tired I am —makes me mad when I get tired. There's so much to be done."

"There always is," she agreed, not knowing why she said it.

"Let's get out of the sun."

They cut across the rows, passing carefully between the tall, impersonal green stalks. She felt them cling gently against her sides. The touch of those leaves excited her. Here under the wide sky, in this hot, silent space of green, she felt Jim's nearness more acutely than ever before. Without understanding how, she sensed a piercing intimacy. She *knew* he felt some of it too.

"Look," he said, pointing across the field, "there's Marshall and the boys. I ought to be down there with 'em."

Far below them, over the sea of leaves, she saw minute human heads moving along the rows. They bent and nodded, lost in a sea of green, dazzled and remote under the sun. James reached back and caught her hand and pulled her with him to the edge of the field. A great red oak hung there, its trunk rough and broad, its limbs stretching out and up and shutting out the sky. She felt the dry pop of acorns under her feet. It was still out there in the sunlight. But here was a different stillness, cut off, suspended. She let herself be pulled passively along till they stood against the trunk of the old tree, side by side, looking back.

"They didn't see me," he said tenderly. "They think I'm at the house. Funny that I should care—I do, but I'm tired."

"Why don't you rest, then?"

He turned the blue gaze from the field to her. He smiled, the serious mouth tender.

"Thank you," he said and squatted down against the tree.

She leaned back gratefully against the trunk, feeling his presence almost with a sense of despair. She had not meant it this way. She had not come out all this way from Kingsmont on this afternoon knowing this. But it was true. . . . He doesn't even know I'm here, *really*—he'll never know.

"Helen," he said, speaking toward the field of tobacco and drawing circles with his finger in the dust, "dear Helen—"

"What?" she said, and waited, her palms against the tree.

"It means a great deal to me to have you here this afternoon."

"I'm glad, Jim."

"Helen, you don't know what it's meant to me all these weeks —your coming out here and listening to me talk, talk, and letting me show you—"

426

"Jim, you know who I am, don't you? I'm not—"

"Yes," he said and his head fell back against the rough bark, "I know. You're Mr. Brant Royle's daughter."

"Does it make any difference?"

"Why should it?"

"I don't know. I was afraid—"

"Helen—Helen—" His brown bare arm reached up to her. She met his hand with hers. They remained clasped, tensely, palm to palm.

"Jim," she said in a small, distant voice, "does it matter that I live now in your grandfather's house?"

"Hill House," he said, and shook his dark head. "What was Hill House ever to me? Something my mother talked about! *This* is my home! Of *course* it doesn't matter—it matters only because I like to think of you living there."

"Ah, Jim!"

The arm pulled her irresistibly downward, impelling her to give way. She sank beside him. He turned his face up to her and, as she descended, he pulled her face to his. Their mouths met, softly, passionately. The earth swung under her for that moment. Then he released her. All she could see was the blue eyes warmly smiling.

"There!" he said. "It's taken me a long time—but I've done it at last. Good, sweet, *dearest* Helen!"

All she could think of was how warm he felt, how precious his skin under her touch, the strong clear odor of his body. *Ah, Jim, Jim!* she cried silently to herself. But all she could do was to reach up with a hand and touch his mouth, his good strong mouth. She had never felt so happy, and she had never felt so sad.

"Does it seem so strange?" he asked.

"No," she managed to answer dumbly.

"I've known it for a long time—almost from the time I saw you sitting there all stiff and shy in Sonie's house." He sighed. "Well, it isn't going to be easy ever, Helen, you and me—we might as well know that from the beginning. But I love you, will always love you, no matter what pain I cause you or myself. That's all there is to it!"

He smiled again, the hesitant, little-boy smile. But his voice was terribly serious. She felt herself tremble under the truth of those words. She could not see the future. She did not even dare try to look at it. But she knew that he had spoken the truth for both of them. No matter if the world and their lives could be arranged so that there was no shadow of an obstacle—it would *never* be easy, no. She smiled back at him, frightened, and at the same time so deeply happy that she would have this tree under which they sat this afternoon preserved without past or future, forever as it was.

"Jim," she said, "Jim, you're tired."

427

She pulled his head against her shoulder and felt it drop there heavy—wonderful, precious weight! She knew then that this was unique, this moment, that its substance would never *be* again. No matter how long she lived, nor what happened to her. It was running out from beneath her, disappearing, breaking up while she tasted it. She embraced his head suddenly and fiercely against her thin breast. . . .

"Helen . . . Helen," he murmured drowsily, and kissed the wrist against his mouth. It was a long moment. A more timeless moment than when their mouths had met. The old tree bent over them. She looked down at his face. It was hidden against her, childlike, the eyes closed. She felt against her the slow, calm ebb and flow of his breath. He was asleep suddenly, like a child. She brushed her cheek cautiously against his tumbled hair and smiled. She dropped her eyes and looked at him—all of him, as though she could consume and preserve him as he was at that very hour. . . . Ah, Jim, Jim! she cried again silently, the note of despair poignantly within her, because she was flooded with a profound sadness and wisdom. No matter what, it will never be like this again—never, never. . . .

They rested thus against the tree, warmly close, for a long time. The afternoon slid by. Wide-eyed and hypersensitive to every creak of the world about her—the sharp break of a twig, the drill of a wasp in the bark behind her, buzzing, buzzing at his hidden labor. The strident cry of a jay in the tree beyond where they sat, the distant, pigmy call of a human voice down beyond the field. . . . It was all so separate and yet so filled with meaning of which she had no real knowledge, nor would ever have knowledge of again in her life. She recognized that. She accepted it.

He stirred at last in her arms; the fine, male torso—so unconscious and given over to her keeping—began to separate, to dissociate itself from her. The division tore at her like an agony. He sat up, shook his head blindly, opened his eyes, and looked at her. Then he leaned forward and kissed her again.

"I went to sleep," he said with a kind of wonder.

"Yes," she said, and smiled. He smiled back.

"Excuse me please—awful manners!"

"I didn't mind," she said gravely. "I could look at you all to myself without you or anyone else bothering me."

"Well," he said, half jokingly, half deeply serious, "did you get scared? Did you change your mind? I'm just a farmer you know, and you're—"

"Jim!" she said, and put her hand full against his mouth. She was really frightened. "Jim, what are you saying—please—"

He clutched her hand in both of his and pulled her upright with him. They stood looking solemnly, even a little sadly, at each other.

428

"Helen," he said, "I must go have a talk with your father."

"No—please—"

"We must be sensible about this. It may sound silly, old-fashioned, but I must go talk to your father—about a lot of things."

"Please, Jim—not, not yet."

"Why? There's nothing gained by putting it off. The sooner the better."

"But it's so soon, there's time—"

"No. I want to marry you, and this is the only way I know of going about it."

"Jim, dearest Jim, I love you more than anything for wanting to do it—but *must* you? Isn't it all right like it is?"

He shook his head and looked out into the day away from her face. "It may seem funny, but this is the way I have to do it."

She smiled and patted his cheek, turning his face to her again. "You're *really* awfully old-fashioned, aren't you?"

He frowned then, his jaw set. "Maybe so."

"And you're stubborn too, aren't you—terribly stubborn?"

"Yes," he admitted, and grinned warmly, "I'm stubborn."

He took her arm and turned her toward the field and they walked silently out toward the rows in the direction of the house again.

CHAPTER TWENTY-THREE

I

The feeling that he was a visitor grew upon Brant throughout the summer. He watched the old seasonal green cover the town beyond Hill Street (he could observe it so intimately, so privately from the porch). He saw it spread into the distance under the heat haze, violent and mysterious. It included factory stack, building, the curled break of a housetop; it was a mysterious extension that had no definition. It ran toward a horizon he could never see. He sat and rocked and rocked, chewing on his endless cigar and glowering, his chin sunk upon his broad chest. As a young man he had loved and wooed this land and this town with a white-hot passion. Not simply because it had been his birthplace. Not even because it had challenged him deeply or flung him off time and time again. Not even because he had subdued it at last, placed it in bonds by his energy and will. Beaten and subdued, it had always eluded him. He had had to throw it off in the end and go away for twenty-odd years, rush far around the earth. Just to be able to come back like this in the end and sit on the porch of the old house under the nice old trees and see a couple of boys coming down the sidewalk—one with a stick clattering along the iron uprights of the fence. He could hear one of them saying in a merciless adolescent baritone:

"Yeah, that's where ol' B. Royle lives now—ol' B. Royle!" They turned their faces toward the house. They saw the figure sitting alone on the porch, whooped with crazy laughter, and charged off down the hill past the ice plant. Brant smiled grimly after them. Ol' B. Royle—that's what he had become. A fearsome letter of the alphabet! It implied something ancient and historical. He rather liked it. It flattered him. They were all still afraid of him. By God, they'd better be!

And even though he had achieved a sort of truce at last, he was haunted by a feeling of oppressive loneliness. He realized that he was reluctant to leave Kingsmont, even though his habits, the business of his far-spread empire, still clamored at him. He remained because here in Hill House he felt less driven, less *deserted!* How he had feared his coming to this house, as though he would expose himself to the final disappointment! But in this *one* thing he had been right. It had retained none of its ghosts. There was no aura of the Singletons, no trace of the past, left in this dwelling to trouble him. It was simply and entirely *his.* His as nothing—man or beast or business—had ever been. So he did not really mind being alone as long as he was in this last citadel. To the world outside he remained the grand old man of the tobacco world, bowed to, crawled to, fawned upon. Each weekday he drove down majestically to the office kept sacred for him all these years. He had to make several short trips up East when the pressure from certain quarters grew a little querulous. But he always returned hurriedly with a feeling that he was coming back to *his* house, to *his* daughter Helen, even to Randall.

The machinery of his enterprises had long been running on its ponderous impetus. And although he kept a fierce and exacting eye on it, manipulating and ordering its course, it was just habit—the testy pride of an old work horse. But he knew it now, and knowing it made him feel mellow. He still had the energy. But he was tired. He only wanted to hold onto this warmth, this strange calm that he felt in the season. He realized, too, that in achieving this he had concentrated his security in a few, dangerously few, factors—the house particularly, and the shy, unspoken relationship with his daughter. Even in Randall—the young man whom he could never really respect but who held his grudging and jealous attention, because he was his *son,* and, more than that, because Randall was weak and would always need him. He desired thirstily to be needed. And the desire itself had muffled some of the old hurt and anger, quieted the restless

430

beast in him that drove him forever onward—even now when there was no reason to go onward.

It had warmed his relations with other men, too. He often walked home from his office so that he could stop along the way and talk with some old doorman at one of the warehouses, or at the stand on the courthouse corner engage the ancient newsboy in a long discussion of politics and the weather. Chance encounters with bright youngsters, brash and energetic and full of the keen look of hunters, the new generation of businessmen in the tobacco country and in Kingsmont, afforded him particular delight. He would discourse tersely with them, give them advice, and feel warmed by their respect, their genuine awe and gratitude at this simplicity in him.

He knew that Helen was happy. He watched her jealously. Saw her leading her quiet, uncommunicative life in the house throughout the summer. He liked having her drive about in his car, having her ride the horse so well. He recognized the warmth in her quiet voice, the expression surprised in her eyes when they met in the course of the day. It pleased him to think that he was perhaps, in some measure, responsible for that happiness. But he had to proceed carefully with her. She was so fiercely private about everything she did. He had kept his hands severely off, not wanting to frighten her by any move that might make her feel that he was trying to order her life for her. He could not see where their relationship was leading them, but he was content to let it develop slowly in this atmosphere of formality. He would have to give her time after all these years. He would have to give himself time.

Randall, on the other hand, as the months passed, sought him out, brought all his worries and problems to him, consulted him interminably. But Randall was doing all right. He had his friends and his circles of activities outside the office. Brant got frequent reports on his progress. Randall was turning out to be a very capable man in the business. But Brant could not help feeling in Randall's catering to him, in his son's ever respectful attitude, something that rang false. He could not put his finger on it. But he blamed it on his own ignorance of the boy. No matter what he felt, he was determined to give *his* son as much help as he could. He continued to be patient, supporting Randall, cajoling him, guiding him. At the same time, he was almost humble with Helen, interfering with her in no way. It was quite enough to know that she was there—that she had come and had continued to stay because she evidently wanted to stay. Under no compulsion—and *that* was important! He did not care much what the city thought. He had always, in the last analysis, been arrogant with Kingsmont. Now, since it concerned *his* daughter and *his* son, they would have to accept them, no matter what *they* thought of the three people living up at Hill House!

431

Yes, he mellowed and slowed down that year, but he had by no means stopped. Two projects occupied his immediate energies, especially during that summer: one, the construction of the vast new wing on the Royle Memorial Hospital; the other, the launching of the new and revived City Realty Company. He and Sam had owned a controlling interest in the old company for years. The new organization had purchased a city block just north of the square, razed it, knocked out all the little run-down stores and the granary and decrepit warehouses. A new issue of stock had refinanced the old company. The City Realty was erecting the town's first skyscraper. Brant had thought from the first days of his return that it was time someone was giving the city a *real* building. He heard himself alternately lauded as a farsighted citizen and condemned as an old pirate! It didn't matter. He discounted both blame and acclaim. They no longer meant anything to him in the way that the act of *doing,* making, had come to mean. Maybe it was foolish. Maybe he and a lot of the others would lose some money. But that again was not the point. Money had long ago ceased to be a point. He paid a daily call at the hospital to badger the directors or to argue with the engineers. Then he would (either walking or driving in the Packard, as it suited him) travel across town and repeat the process on the site of the new building. Tall and massive, the big, almost bald head thrust a little forward, he stood chewing the eternal cigar and growling at the usually harrassed men standing respectfully grouped about him. When he had to go to New York or to Chicago for a few days, detailed reports were sent to him both by telephone and by letter. He thoroughly enjoyed himself. He hadn't felt healthier in years. The old stomach trouble that had begun to plague him during the years in China, the infirmity that had caused him no little discomfort and left him with the gnawing fear, disappeared almost completely that summer. He slowed down. He was doing something he liked to do, he almost convinced himself that he was happy.

Toward the middle of September, when the local tobacco market was about a half a month old and the big warehouses down toward Jamaica Town still echoed daily to the cry of the auctioneer, he came back from a trip to New York, where he had gone to attend a meeting of the Tobacco Board of Foreign Trade. He had stopped over in Washington for a conference with Washburn, the senior Senator from North Carolina, and had taken a train that put him in Kingsmont at four in the afternoon. It was an awkward in-between hour, and he had the car take him down to the factory. He told the chauffeur he would walk home. He had not expected either Helen or Randall to meet him. They were busy about their own affairs, and he would have been almost shocked if either of his children had turned up on this occasion. He found himself deeply pleased, how-

432

ever, while he was finishing going over some reports to have his son come into the office unannounced.

"Hello, Father, nice trip?"

"All right, I guess. What are you doing down here? I heard you were out of town." Brant cleared his throat and frowned at the figures on the paper in front of him.

"Oh, I just got back from a little inspection with Tom Shelby—we had to check over the Townshend warehouses this afternoon. Finished earlier than we had expected. Heard you were back, so I thought I'd stop by and walk home with you. You are walking?"

"Certainly," growled Brant, without looking up.

"Do you mind?"

"Don't be a fool! Of course I'd like to have you walk home with me."

"Thanks, Father."

Brant watched obliquely while Randall walked to the window and looked out. Randall looked very spruce, even with his thinness, the shoulders narrow and slightly stooped. Yes, there was a kind of distinction about him. Brant felt weak with gratitude toward his son in that moment. He wondered anew what essential quality there was in *his* son that always put him off. . . .

"I'll be ready in a minute," he said. "Just finishing with these daily reports."

"Don't hurry, Father. Anyone who can bury himself in *that* kind of reading matter with *that* air of absorption is due all the time he needs!"

There it was. Always the note of malice. Well, he supposed he deserved it. What had Randall or anyone else of his blood ever known of him? He threw the papers down on the desk with a grunt and smiled unwillingly. His cigar was a chewed stump. He threw it savagely and accurately into the old polished brass spittoon and reached into his pocket for another. He bit at the end mechanically and moistened it with his tongue.

"If you don't mind, Father," said Randall, observing him out of the narrow face with the overlarge nose, "it has always seemed eccentric—your smoking cigars, you know! You've spent millions making the rest of us smoke your cigarettes—" He stopped and looked at Brant with that glance, half derision, half childish puzzlement. Why, it's funny, thought Brant, he looked like Pete Henry used to look at me, although they're not a thing alike—absurd!

But he felt further warmed by this flash.

"Hell, Randall," he boomed happily, getting up, "never could stand the damn things!"

"I beg your pardon!"

433

Then Randall threw back his lean, blond skull. The bare room clattered with his high, whinnying laughter. Brant grinned unwillingly above his cigar and grabbed his hat from the tree. He felt good.

"I want to go across to see how the building's doing."

They both knew to what "the building" referred. That vast, clangorous, skeleton structure rising bone by bone up into the limpid sky over beyond the square—so high already that the city could not help looking at it.

"Of course, Father," said Randall, struggling to keep step with him.

Brant wished suddenly and passionately that Randall and Helen would address him otherwise. This impersonal, cold title: *Father.* It always held him off at a distance, an insulated, formal entity. But even while he hungered for something closer, he recognized the justice of it. He had to admit that he would have been outraged if either of them had suddenly said "Pa!" *Pa. . . . Oh, Pa* echoed down his life!

They crossed the square through the late-afternoon traffic and cut down beyond the new Citizens Trust Company, the florist, the cleaner and dyer, Randolph's Book & Stationery Shoppe. . . . They were there. The high board fence, the shelter over the sidewalk. The machinery, the packed clay and debris. He stopped, and Randall stopped with him, across the street from it. Brant's eyes moved upward over all that massive steel, that delicate skeleton of his will reached up into the lovely afternoon sky. An antlike figure swung out upon a thread, waved a minute arm against engulfing space. Brant smiled. His mouth dragged sidewise over the cigar.

"She's comin' along, comin' along!" he said, not to anyone in particular. Just to his sense of well-being.

"Amazing, Father, really amazing how much they've done. I can't keep up with them."

"They're doin' all right. I hope the hospital is doin' as well. I'll run down there first thing in the mornin'."

"They couldn't help it," Randall assured him, looking up into the sky beyond his big nose.

"Now what d'you mean, Randall?"

"Simple, Father. Here's a whole building industry swarming over a problem, pushing something up higher than anything else they've seen around here. There're plenty of men, plenty of *know-how*, but the thing that makes it really grow is that Mr. Brant Royle is standing off here and looking at it!"

"You're the world's damnedest fool, son!"

But he didn't mean it. He felt only happiness. Here was the young man at his side speaking familiar platitudes. He had heard them a thousand times from a thousand adulatory lips. He could not

434

permit them to mean on this occasion only another expected congratulation. Even knowing and feeling all he did about Randall. He took Randall by the arm.

They walked on through the late autumn afternoon, warm, friendly. The day seemed spiced with an edge of cold that made Brant's blood quicken. He closed his eyes on this happiness. He could not really believe it. Somewhere there lay a flaw that he would have to put his foot on, a wound he would have to accept. This could not last.

They turned up Hill Street. Hill Street, so ugly and forlorn and plain. All its contours, its grandeur, a thing only of memory—a shabby, noisy, dirty wayfare. Only his house at the top to redeem it.

"How's Helen been?" he said, striding slower upon the incline.

"Helen? Oh, fine, I suppose. I don't see her often, y'know. At breakfast now and then. She's got her own life."

"Do you think she really likes it here, Randall? I mean living up here at the house, the town, and everything?"

"Oh, Helen's all right, perfectly all right."

There was something triumphant in Randall's tone that made Brant glance at the other's face.

"Now what d'you mean?"

"Nothing, Father; why, nothing at all."

"Sure you mean something—come on! I know you that well!" He saw the hateful expression of malice flash across Randall's face.

"You know, Father, I think we underestimate my nice sister, you and I."

"I don't know what you're talking about!"

"Of course not, Father! I just mean that Helen's got depths we've never suspected. She interests me, y'know, really interests me. I never could really believe all the smug, docile meekness she hides behind."

"Randall—"

"Patience, Father. I just mean that she's gone ahead making some kind of very fine life for herself behind all that. I've observed her pretty thoroughly this summer, and I must say she's begun to fascinate me. She's been going out on her own and finding out about the world. I admire her for it!"

"Listen, Randall, I don't like your tone."

"For instance, she's got interested in growing tobacco."

"Growing tobacco!"

"Now, Father, you can hardly blame her for that. After all, it's in the blood."

Brant felt his face grow tight. He wanted to reach out and strike Randall. He passionately hated this air of quiet malignance. He walked slower.

435

"Randall, stop talking around the subject. What are you trying to tell me about your sister?"

"Oh, nothing very exciting. I thought you would be interested to know, though, that she has been showing an unusual interest in a little experimental farm—I believe that's what they call it—about two miles out of town. Goes there every other day or so. I don't know the place, but Tom Shelby was telling me this afternoon that he met her there only last week, while he was down on some business with the man who runs the farm."

The street and the afternoon seemed to darken and constrict about Brant. He felt his stride falter, and pushed ahead.

"Who is this Shelby?"

"You know, Father—Mr. Hiram Shelby's boy. He's the chemist in charge of the laboratory at the factory."

"Yes," said Brant, "I know him. Well, what of it?"

"Nothing—not a thing. I just thought it curious, this interest of Helen's. Has she ever spoken about it to you?"

"No, I can't say she has. She'll bring it up when it suits her."

"Of course, but I thought it might interest you to know ahead of time. In fact, *that* doesn't interest me nearly so much as another fact about her activities here."

"Now what?"

"She moves in strange and wonderful ways. I never thought of her as the social type, did you? And she's not. Definitely not. But she's managed somehow to get intimate with one of the most interesting people in town."

"Helen is a Royle. She shouldn't have any trouble meeting whom she likes."

"Ordinarily not, of course. I agree with you. But this is a harder nut to crack. She's become a crony, it seems, of a Mrs. Talbot Graham out on Bay Street since this spring."

"Mrs. Graham?"

Brant could feel Randall's flickering glance upon him. He plowed ahead, stony-faced. Graham—Graham? The name meant nothing. . . .

"A grande dame, Father, with a long local history—practically not to be seen except by royal command. I've heard a lot about her and I've asked around for more, because she really is a marvelous old lady. Like something out of a book, y'know. Used to live down in the slums as a girl. And now after running over half the world she's settled down here. Sentiment, of course—she's really facing down to an interesting past!"

"What past? Why do you talk all around? What are you trying to say, Randall?"

Even as he asked it he knew that history, fate—whatever he

436

wanted to call it—was crowding down upon him; finding him out in his sanctuary. Mrs. Graham? The name chimed and chimed, half-remembered but half-remembered with an acute and special knowledge.

"You are impatient as usual, Father."

"I *am* not."

"Pardon, sir. I meant to say—well, it seems that this Mrs. Graham with whom Helen has struck up an intimacy has a very interesting history, a history that includes, of all people, *you,* Father!"

"Me?" he growled, and then snarled in the old arrogant way, "Me—a lot of people include me in their history."

"Certainly, Father, you *are* pretty much the history of this place, aren't you? That's what I've liked about being here, y'know. Running down all the old family tracks, seeing what and who made what. This lady, from what I have been able to resurrect out of aged gossip, ran a boardinghouse of colorful reputation in the old days."

"The old days," Brant said, and could not stop his tongue. "What do you or anybody, you youngsters, know about the *old* days? *She* didn't—it was her mother!"

He was betrayed. He could not believe his own voice. The past was *not* the past. It lay immediately behind a thin shell of the present. He had not expected this. He had expected any number of imponderables since he had set foot in Kingsmont, but here—bitingly, unavoidably, out of the mouth of his son—came this shadowy, smirking accusation. The whole structure of his content began to crumble. He could not bear it.

"Oh, then you know who I'm talking about?"

Randall's voice, once again the stranger's voice. Removing, effacing with one petty, cynical gesture all that he had embraced the past few months—he had been fooling himself. In that moment he felt the blackest reaches of his personal hell close triumphantly down upon him. It was with a terrible effort that he held back some violent and positive gesture, some movement that would destroy this pursuing angel.

"Well," he temporized, and raged inside, "I think I know who you are talking about now."

"Fabulous, simply fabulous—dyed red hair, lots of jewelry, horrible brick house behind a lot of shrubbery—was born with a kind of Russian name, Lipinsky or something."

"Lipik," corrected Brant, barking out the two clean syllables. Of course, of course, it was perfectly right that *she* should be here. Only his stubbornness, the high realm in which he moved, had allowed him the luxury of this special ignorance. She must be an old woman now, well on—and she was like an irrepressible cork on the surface of his life. She bobbed up. Always. He must have seen her passing a hundred times during the summer and never known it was she—an old woman. He could not imagine her being old!

"Ah yes, that's it—Lipik," Randall was saying with relish. They were at the last block. "Thank you, Father. I told Tom Shelby you'd know if anyone knew what the truth was."

"The truth, Randall," he said stiffly over the cigar, "is what you or anyone else wants to make it. Mrs. Graham is a very remarkable woman."

"Oh, I agree, Father! Completely—that's why I've been trying for months to meet her, to get in her house, without success. But here is Helen—quiet, meek Helen—pulling the wool over our eyes and getting in where none of the rest of us can."

"Randall," said Brant, looking straight ahead of him (the iron gates), "Randall, why do you hate your sister?"

"Hate Helen?" The breathless, elaborately insincere voice at his side answering him. "Why, Father, what a question! I don't hate Helen. You flatter me. I don't even *know* Helen, I just envy her because she has some magic that will gain her access to these mysteries!"

"Damn it, Randall," he said, and flung the gate open, "mysteries, old ladies—what a lot of absolute hogwash you talk!"

"I beg your pardon, Father."

"Oh, shut up!"

He walked ahead, striding up the walk, up the steps, and to the porch. Inside he handed his hat to the Negro and stomped into the parlor. Even there he could not escape hearing Randall go upstairs, padding neatly like a discreet animal, to his room—his lair.

He was alone in the parlor. The afternoon streamed in at the windows. He walked back and forth before those elegant apertures. Outside lay the gracious green, the trees in the yard. Faithful guards to the last. Whether it was he or ol' Major Jim. They shut it all out for both of them. For the first time he began to understand that shadowy symbol out of his past—that really ridiculous, overhated little man. He understood now some of Major Jim's bewilderment, the thing that must have made him march up and down, up and down, this cool, remote room. You could not escape from your life nor from yourself—ever. The world never allowed you a real hiding place. You met yourself, the dark furies that pursued you from the birth hour, here in the inner sanctum—the place that you had gained by the finger tips of a whole life—and they found you out.

The minutes ticked away. The house knew he was there. It had that hushed air, that sound of muffled activity, which he had always heard with an inner grin of comfort. But there was no comfort in it for him now.

He heard the footsteps on the porch at last. The front screen door opened. The precise, quick sound of her crossing in the dim hallway. He walked to the door. "Helen!" He uttered the name brusquely into space.

She turned at the foot of the stairs. He felt sickened with that turn. The ghost suddenly at the foot of the stairs—the dark hair, the enigmatic face, that lost face, gone down into dust, a grave by a forgotten road, hung over with cedars and the slow effacement of brambles and honeysuckle vines. . . .

"Hello, Father! Did you have a nice trip?"

He had never heard her voice so warm, so alive. Maybe it had been this way before, but only now had he ears to hear it. Every creak in the wall would have a special and terrible meaning now.

"Helen, thank you, yes—have you a moment?"

"Certainly. I was just going up to get ready for dinner."

"Come in here, Helen, I want to talk to you."

"Of course, Father."

The obstinate meekness. Something flared anew within him. Hypocrite! She had kept this all from him. Meek voice—the voice of betrayal. She came obediently to a window, her thin figure, the erect backbone under the clothes, the severe hat. He could not endure them!

"Yes, Father."

"Helen, I won't keep you. . . . I understand you have been visiting a Mrs. Graham."

"Yes, Father."

No apology in her voice. No anything. Just flat admission.

"I would prefer that you didn't."

"I don't understand, Father."

"It doesn't matter whether you understand or not. I haven't interfered with your life here until now. This I *demand* of you!"

She was silent. He watched her from his pacing up and down. She did not move at the window. She only seemed to change, to become crystallized, obdurate.

"I'm sorry, Father, but I can't accept that."

He stopped then on the rug, stone-still. "You mean you won't obey me?"

"I mean that Mrs. Graham is my friend. I don't know why you request this of me, but I can't accept it."

In spite of himself he felt a little flame of admiration run through him for this woman, this unknown entity who happened to be his daughter. She had no fear in her when it came to the essentials. The essentials were here. Here in both of them. Angry, blindly angry, as he was, perversely he appreciated her at that moment more than he had ever appreciated her.

439

"Helen, if you can't, if you must be disobedient—"

"It's not a question of disobedience, is it, Father?"

He could not escape this. Whether she knew it or not she had asked it in this question.

"No, that's right. I'm just asking that you do what I request. Sometime I'll explain why, but now—"

"It's getting late, Father, if you don't mind—"

"I do mind! I want your answer *now!*"

All the swelling rage, the forces, black and nameless, leapt up in him. It was like it had always been when something stood against him—no matter what. He could not bear it. His daughter, the world of business, he charged blackly against them all. The challenge must be met, conquered, subdued. She turned to him then in the window, faceless. A tense black outline, framed.

"I'm sorry," she said in the quiet, *maddening* voice, "but I can give you no other answer than I have. And since you insist that I stay away—"

"Well?"

"I might as well include in this conversation something else that you had better know. I hadn't intended doing it now. I had thought to find some better time for it. But I expect there will never be a better time—or a worse either." Her voice, disembodied, scraped against his fury. He planted his feet wide and glared in her direction motionless. Waiting. "There is somebody whom you don't know, Father—he is coming to see you about me."

"About you?"

"I know that sounds silly. But it's true. I can't keep him from doing it even though I know it's useless. But he wants to talk to you, and I think you ought to be prepared for it. It's only fair. It's fair— but it won't change anything. No matter what you say to him or what he says to you. He wants to marry me, I don't know why"— her voice faltered in the calm, deliberate course—"and I am going to marry him."

The terrifying feeling that the last defense between him and the long years was breaking up, finally and utterly, in this room, on the rug beneath his feet, the feeling that had begun with Randall's chatter on the hill—a deep, sonorous toll—beat soundlessly upon him, engulfed him. It had nothing to do with Helen, and yet it had everything to do with these things that she was saying. It wasn't that he didn't understand the plain words—it was more than that. It was the fact that he would have to face the truth that stalked him behind those words.

"Marry whom—if I may ask?"

How formal his sarcasm! How artificial his speech! That was what the years had done to him. He could no longer even talk like

440

the real being in him. This was the big country boy, the boy with the dusty, broken shoes, speaking.

"You don't know him, yet. He's not somebody you would be likely to meet," she continued.

"What's his name?" he demanded. He didn't need the answer. He knew it, because it was inevitable—could be no other.

"James Barton," she said into the dimming room, and it swirled into deeper blackness for him. He had not escaped. He could never escape.

"I see," he said in the hard voice. Ah, he didn't want to be hard. He never wanted to be hard again. He was tired. But the wheel of his life ground on, bearing him on its iron rims. "I think I've come across him. Working on tobacco, isn't he?"

"Yes," she said. And for the first time there was a kind of fear in her voice.

"Helen," he said cruelly, savoring the cruelty, "you've been here nearly a year. I lived here thirty years. And tobacco—everything about it—has been my business. *Of course* I know this James Barton!"

They were silent. Each looking across the darkness at the other.

"That's all I wanted to say, Father," she said, her voice dropping the words one by one into the space between them.

"So this farmer is coming to see me—about marrying you?"

"If you want to put it that way."

She was miles away from him. She had retired across all the unused years, separated herself finally and completely. He knew he had lost her then.

"Have you thought about this—what it means?"

"Yes, Father. I've thought an awful lot."

"Why didn't you come to me before?"

"I wanted to. I wanted to talk to somebody," she burst out, and then enclosed her speech in the protective rigidity. "But I didn't have anyone, you know."

He felt crushed under the terrible indictment of that. But he would not admit it. He would not admit it even in the clay they carried to the burying ground. He held before him only the raging flame of rebellion. Now even his own flesh rose against him—his daughter, this girl.

"So he's coming to see me—about you?"

"Yes."

"And what am I supposed to say?"

"I don't know," she said sadly, and the sadness did not include him. "I tried to tell him—"

"He's evidently a young man of character," he said glibly, "an

441

opportunist—but he's in no position to ask you. Why, Helen, it won't work, no matter what he has to say."

"I'm sorry, Father, but I'll be honest with you—as I've tried to be ever since I came here. I don't know either whether it will work or not. . . . I'm terribly confused in my own mind. The only thing I know is that he is the first person who has ever been gentle with me—told me he loved me. And beyond that, if it means a mess, I'm willing to accept it, because I love him."

She said it so honestly that the very words, beyond their implication, pierced down into him. She had never said "I love you, Father," to him!

"Listen," he said, "you are my daughter, and over and beyond that you are heir to the thing that makes this land run. Do you think this man, this grubber in a tobacco field, cares any more—"

"I'm sorry, Father," she interrupted sharply. "This is no good. I'm tired. Let's talk about it later."

"What do you mean by later? You've already decided, haven't you—with or without my participation?"

"That's true," she admitted, and he saw her shoulders slump.

"I'll talk to him—sure, I'll talk to him when he comes. When will that be?"

"I don't know—but he'll come. Not to your office. That would be against his principles. He'll come here, to the house."

"His grandfather used to live here, you know."

She shrugged. "That doesn't make any difference." She sounded weary and resigned. "That hasn't anything to do with it."

"All right, Helen. I'm dead-set against it. You know that, don't you?"

"I knew you would be," she said calmly, "but it doesn't really make any difference—I'd still go with him."

"You're talking crazy," he said. "Now look here—you're a grown-up woman, you know it won't work—"

"Father," she interrupted in the sad, calm voice, "I know all he will say to you when he comes here. I know all you will say to him. You will both be right. It won't work, as you have already told me, but still I've got to have him, in spite of being Helen Royle—in spite of belonging to the cigarette industry!"

This shocked him into silence. What did she mean? What did she dare mean? He brushed it aside in his smoldering resentment.

"Well," he said, "say what you want to, there are things that must be considered—"

"Oh, I know—I *know!*" she cried out. "I knew them before I was born! If you will excuse me now, Father—"

"Well, if you know all this," he bellowed in blind rage, uncaring of the house about them, uncaring of the whole world save the two

442

of them, "what makes you think you have a chance in hell—?" He clamped his mouth shut.

She remained still for a moment. The soft evening thickened in the parlor. Outside on Hill Street a horn tooted, a strident, distant voice. She moved then. She walked straight to the hallway. There she stopped and half-turned—and still she was an outline, faceless, remote. . . .

"Because he wants me," she said. And then she walked out into the hallway. He stood rooted to the carpet and heard her feet pacing up the old stairs. Always footsteps on those stairs, fatal, obdurate, rhythmic sounds falling away, leaving him alone.

2

He did not see her the next morning. He went and came as usual, following out the inflexible pattern. But it was an annoyance. All his thoughts were suddenly wrapped around this slim, plain girl. He could think of nothing else. Not just her physical being, but the fact that she had stood up and defied him. No one, nothing, had ever gainsaid him and lived.

He made token visits to the new buildings and then he crouched in the back seat of the car while it carried him smoothly out Bay Street past Sonie's house. Sonie, Sonie, Sonie . . . *She* had no business turning up here like this. They had called it quits so long ago. It was an effort to remember how or when. All that remained was the slight, the bitterness. She had failed him when he needed her most. But that was long ago. He was haunted by a storm of memories. He could not look out his office window without seeing the ghostly outlines of the old street—the house with the dark front porch and him standing outside the old screen door waiting and then the hoarse, warm voice—Sonie. . . .

Well, he had thrown that over, used it, trampled it under him as he had the old manufacturing crowd, the Pendletons—but why list them? They made no understandable pattern. There was Barton —the rest had not returned. They were nothing. But Sonie, that hopeless, feeble man, John Barton—all the rest who had fallen under him and been forgotten lay forgotten, but these two came up again, rising out of the confused broil and tumble of the past—relentlessly.

The day came at last. And when it came it was a relief for him to see, as he rolled into the driveway in the back seat of the Packard, the figure in the neat, unpressed suit waiting stolidly on the porch. He knew instantly who it was.

"Well, Mr. Barton, this is a surprise."

"It's nice of you to remember me, sir. I didn't know your name

443

when you came out to the farm that day last year. I didn't think to ask. But I found out later."

Simple, devastating statement devoid of surprise. The blue, concentrated stare fell upon him undiminished.

"Hope you haven't been waiting long—won't you come in?"

"Thank you, sir."

The ceremony of the door. The ceremony of the taking off of hats. The boy kept his, clasped solidly in his two hands. They went into the parlor.

"Sit down, Mr. Barton."

"If you don't mind, sir, I'd prefer standing."

Where had he heard those very same words? They swooped down upon him in a shattering echo. Why, they had been said in this same room! He had stood there—Major Singleton had come in the door. This was the ultimate irony. He thought, I'm getting old and full of fancies—*this* is too much!

"Suit yourself!" he said bluntly.

The blue stare received the rudeness with no sign of disturbance. Brant occupied a long moment taking out a fresh cigar, preparing it, and placing it in his mouth. He felt savage, excited. This was what he needed, the face-to-face! He could deal with this.

"Mr. Barton, I've made inquiries about you since I saw your work—very interesting. You have the respect of a good many learned people in this state. For myself, I can say that I am pleased that the Foundation's money has served some real purpose. I was on a farm myself once—I think I told you."

"Yes, sir, I remember. It's good of you to say these things. I don't think what I've managed to do could have been done without the Foundation."

"Well, there have to be all sorts of us, don't they?—the businessman, the manufacturer, and you up at the other end, the scientist —all of us working together, eh?"

"I like to think of it that way, sir."

This formal reiteration he found suddenly unnerving. Sir, *sir*—

"I used to know your grandfather, Major Singleton," he said abruptly.

"That's right, sir. I think you told me once before."

Brant was impatient with this preamble. It was stretching itself out beyond endurance. And yet he felt compelled to respect it.

"This was his home," he said. "Fine house. I liked it so much I didn't let them tear it down."

The boy looked curiously around the room. There was no sentiment in that survey. It looked, catalogued, accepted, and discarded all in a glance. Brant felt cheated. It put him on the defensive. What

444

was more, it put him in the position of defending the past. There should have been more reverence in that look, more recognition.

"You know, sir," said James in the firm, young bass, "this is the first time I've ever set foot in this house."

"Well, well," said Brant, holding the figure across the room tightly in his gaze. "That's funny, y'know. Think of that! First time."

His blade was out, sharpened on his agony and hate. He felt it. How could this other man standing stolidly at ease opposite him not feel it? Sonie . . . Margaret . . . John Barton . . . the horrible roll call, living and dead . . . and here was this man, this square, contained, dark young man whom he had met first at the side of a grave with a mule standing against a cedar tree. . . . This was the boy whom he could have admired—have worshiped and placed all his gains before—if he had been *his* son (as he should have been). But because he could not, because there was the true fruit of his loins, the son, his life had given him Randall, he hated this young man.

"I've always wanted to see the inside, you know," James Barton continued in the tranquil bass voice.

"I hope you aren't disappointed."

"Disappointed?" The broad, tanned forehead creased. "Why should I be, sir? It all seems very nice."

Brant before the fireplace felt his bones curdle.

"Nice?" he said. "Mr. Barton, what can I do for you?"

There it was—out in the open, flat, straight to the point. The boy breathed deeply.

"Mr. Royle, I've come to see you about your daughter."

"I'm way ahead of you, Mr. Barton. Let's not waste time. You want to marry Helen?"

"Yes, sir."

"All right, I'm curious to know why you've come to see me, then. Isn't this something between you and Helen?"

"Of course, sir, but I thought it only right that I speak to you."

"I find that very flattering of you. It's rare in this day and time. What do you want of me? Just to say 'go ahead'?"

"I just felt you ought to know, sir."

"I hate to take the wind out of your sails, but I know already."

"Well, Mr. Royle, I know all the things that are against it. It's plain presumption of me. Helen insists it makes no difference. I'm a farmer, you know, really—just a farmer in spite of my experiments and laboratory work. I have nothing to offer her in place of all this." He gestured suddenly into the space offered by the room. "But I do love her—and will honor her, sir!"

There was no apology in this old-fashioned statement. It was said as humorlessly, as compellingly, as anything Brant had ever had said in his presence.

445

"Listen, young man," he said in his most dictatorial tone. "For your information, I've already talked this over with Helen. She's a woman and she's been protected, expensively protected, against the world—you know that?"

"Yes, sir."

"All right, I shan't beat about the bush with you. I don't mind her being in love with you and wanting to marry you. I don't mind your feeling the same way about her. But Helen—no matter what you or she thinks—is not fit for the kind of life you have to offer her. It wouldn't be worth a cent after a month. I *know* her—and I lived your kind of life when I was a boy. It's no different anywhere. Helen doesn't realize that—"

"Aren't you underestimating her, sir?"

"Maybe so, maybe so, but what I'm not underestimating is the thing she has to live up to in this state. She's going to come into a big inheritance one of these days. Her name is Royle and that carries certain obligations, not only here but pretty near all over the world. All I'm trying to say—apart from you and me—and I'm trying to be fair, is that Helen can't marry a dirt farmer, whether he's a graduate in chemistry from A. and M. or not."

"I understand you, sir, but I don't think that matters to her."

"Look, it doesn't make a damn bit of difference whether it matters to you or to her; what matters is what it will mean a month after you've made the vows. And because of Helen it matters to me. I'm not a snob. I grew right out of the yellow earth of this county myself. I know what it means to sweat. I'm not throwing you down on that. I'm just saying that you've got to see things as they are—and Helen isn't like they are!"

The square, standing figure remained quiet. The dark head inclined politely. The face was set, obdurate, expressionless. Brant plunged on. He didn't want an interruption. His words gave him a feeling of complete assurance.

"Look here, I've no objection at all to your marrying my daughter, but let's be practical about it. You've done good work out there on the farm and for the State Agricultural Bureau. Why couldn't you do as much good here in town where we are? Think about it. I can put you in a place, any place you see fit—one of the laboratories down at the factories. You could head the whole experimental works—maybe find out a better way to make cigarette tobacco hold the right amount of moisture. It's a problem we haven't licked yet. I've had the best men in the world working on it—"

"No—thank you, sir." The hard young voice was as flat as a blow.

"Don't you understand me? I'm offering you a sensible way out of this predicament."

446

"Sorry, sir, I couldn't possibly accept. I know where my work lies. I've known it since I was knee-high. And if Helen is going to be with me—that's where it is!"

"You mean you want to stay out there slaving in that field for a possible improvement in the tobacco plant? You're a damned fool!"

"I've been called that before, sir, but it hasn't changed my mind."

Brant felt the blood rush tight about his face. Didn't this young idiot know what he was being offered? Did he realize *who* he was standing up against?

"Look here," he said deliberately, "don't you know that the only reason you're able to keep going on your little projects is because I—not just anybody, but *I*—put up the money for the Foundation?"

James rewarded him by flushing at last. It was not a flush of anger, more of astonishment.

"Yes, sir," he said in the maddeningly polite voice, "I—"

"All right; since I give, you ought to know I can cut it off like a faucet any time I see fit. What'll happen to your precious experiments then? Look, I'm not trying to blackmail you, but if you continue to be foolish, I don't mind employing that method a bit." He sounded jovial, almost friendly, for a moment.

The boy shook his head. He did not smile. His square face was almost pale.

"I'm sorry, Mr. Royle; neither you nor anyone else can make me change my mind about the kind of work I want to do. I'm afraid you can't scare me by saying you'll remove the support of the Foundation. I'll beg, borrow, or steal to keep my work going, with or without the Foundation, so it's no use."

His face was without emotion. He looked at Brant steadily. The square jaw was perhaps a little more set, the mouth a tighter line.

"All right, Mr. Barton," Brant said, and felt his rage shake and sicken him. There was a kind of terror in it, too. He had passionately desired this meeting so that he could reassure himself that he still held the power. Instead, this man stood opposite him obdurate, immovable, not a shattered victim but a nemesislike figure. This is Margaret's son . . . John Barton's son . . . Major Singleton's grandson! The names rolled louder and louder in and out among his thoughts. He swayed ponderously on his heels, feeling dizzy. The horrible sense of dark, inscrutable inevitability that had been closing in upon him during the past few days was piercingly certain at this moment. All of it somehow manifest and concentrated in this quiet young man standing across the rug from him. If only he could have cried out then, voiced in some way the unendurability of this final recognition—I cannot escape! . . . *There is no escaping ever!* The great wheel had swung full round. It would go on silently, heaving,

447

turning, and he could not halt it, because he was damned, bound fast upon it—*he had always been bound fast to it.*

"All right, Mr. Barton," he repeated in a voice suddenly tight and hoarse. "You have very likely heard I am a hard man, a mean man, a man who stops at nothing, pays any price to get what he wants. Well, sir, it's true, every damned word of it. I'm that and more. If you and my daughter set yourselves against me in this, I will do everything I can to make it impossible for you—and I *can.* If you don't know it now, you will soon find out. I've lived a long time, Mr. Barton—"

He cut off suddenly under the steady blue gaze. It was calm, without fear, as if these words meant nothing. The innocence, the ignorance, of that look. . . . Why, the man didn't even know what he, Brant, was talking about! It was the ultimate, devastating affront.

"Good afternoon, Mr. Barton!"

James Barton shook his head once then. It was a gesture of wonderment, almost of compassion.

"I'm sorry, sir."

Sorry, sir . . . Sorry, sir . . . *Sorry, sir!*—the words echoed endlessly and insanely about the room. Brant felt his teeth meet through the remains of his cigar.

"Good afternoon, Mr. Barton!"

The hoarse, animal-like bellow of agony broke out of him shockingly. James Barton inclined his head courteously and, turning, walked out of the room.

He did not move. He did not dare move. He heard the front door quietly open, quietly shut again. The strong steady footsteps crossing the porch, going down the steps—down, down. . . . He had a feeling that those five familiar wooden steps had extended themselves nightmarishly . . . he could still hear the feet descending them. . . .

He lived a terrible moment before he realized that it was not the same feet nor the same stairs. Someone was coming down into the hall from above. He knew then, even before she stopped in the frame of the doorway—the slim, awkward, flat young woman's body, the pale straight hair lying severely on the head. He turned his eyes to her then. She stood, almost fragile in the light streaming in at the windows from the dying summer afternoon, and looked at him. Ah, Helen, daughter, he thought, it's you. . . . It has to be *you* now. . . .

He saw then that she was holding a hat—a round little hemisphere of straw with childish ribbon ends falling from it—holding it gently in the narrow, long-fingered hands. She had never appeared so weak, so defenseless, so precious as she did in that moment.

"Hello, Helen," he said carefully, "I'm sorry—I didn't know you were in the house."

"I didn't go out this afternoon," she said, turning the little hat around and around between her hands. Her voice was quite colorless, remote. "I was supposed to drop by at Aunt Berta's at three—I forgot. I forgot till I heard the car come in."

The old house, the room, the hallway, fell away into silence between them. The moments ticked by in infinitesimal segments. They looked and looked at each other.

"You heard, then?" he said, at last.

"Yes. Everything." Her tone was almost apologetic. "I was at the top of the stairs. I didn't mean to—I suppose I should have gone away, back into my room." She stopped and lifted her head. "No. I should have come down here then. I knew it, but I couldn't move. I just stood there against the wall listening. I was frightened—just as I have always been."

"Well?" he said.

"Nothing," she said. "I'm just not frightened now—that's all."

"Is that all you've got to say?"

"What else is there to say?"

She looked at him with curious, remote directness. He could not bear it. He dropped his gaze to the little hat.

"Are you going somewhere?"

"Of course."

"Where—if you don't mind my asking?" He could not stop the black, bitter voice coming out of him. He was caught. He had to go on and on. . . . The dark wheel continued to turn. . . .

"I'm going to find Jim."

To find Jim . . . to find Jim . . . The silence widened, mawed between them. She turned then slowly away from him to the hall.

"Helen," he said, "Helen, if you go now—you know you can't come back."

He saw the narrow shoulders straighten. She turned again and came back through the doorway, walking deliberately until she stood only a few feet away. Her eyes were wide, her arms stiff and tense against her sides.

"Come back?" she whispered, and it was a sound full of amazement. "Do you think I'd want to come back *here?* This is a beautiful house. I've been almost happy here. But you've ruined it, poisoned it. I came here to find a home. I've never had a home in my life—"

"Helen!"

"Let me finish. I hadn't meant to talk—to say anything to you.

I've never been able to say anything to *you. Who are you?* My father? I told you when I came here, uninvited, that I'd come to try to find out who *I* was—who the thing everybody called Helen Royle, Brant Royle's daughter, was. And the only way I could was to find you because I needed you. You let me come, you let me stay. How grateful I was to you for that! I almost began to believe that I could find a way to you, because I began to feel that I belonged—was not just someone drifting around lost and unrecognized in your background. But you couldn't even make me feel that this was really home, that I belonged here. *You've never given me anything!*"

He reeled blindly under that naked cry of accusation. She caught her breath, and then continued in the soft, wondering voice.

"But I know why now," she said, turning her head to the window as though she could no longer bear looking at him. "It's not just me. You don't know how to give. You just know how to own, hold, crush. I just happened to be your daughter. I might as well have been a dog, a car, a piece of furniture—well kept, surrounded with the very best that money could buy, exhibited on occasion, or just referred to in passing, something that could feed your terrible pride when you needed it, not a thing of flesh and blood, your flesh and blood, but *your* daughter—a thing to be moved about, ignored, to spend money on"—a shudder shook her—"something abject, nameless, horrible! . . . Because I know the truth about you now. I could not really face it or make myself believe it till I stood upstairs there a while ago. I think I've known it for a long time, but the fright of being in the presence of something evil—really and completely evil—and not being able to face the real truth of it is a thing that can hold you. I wonder now if you even know what I am talking about?"

"You really hate me—despise me, don't you?"

She turned from the window then and looked at him. It was the face of a stranger again, smoothed and remote under the blond hair.

"Hate you?" She shook her head. "I don't think so. I just know that whatever you do you can never touch or hurt me again. I'm free of you and all the things I thought I wanted so desperately from you. I don't need you any more—you don't hate something you don't need."

She lifted the hat and set it carefully on her head, pushing it down precisely into place, the long fingers tucking at her hair. It was a gesture full of terrible finality—more terrible because of its simplicity. Again he stood voiceless watching the figure walking away from him. They had all been walking away from him—not just this afternoon, but all his life!

The door closing—the feet retreating down the steps—down.

450

down . . . The unbearable and ghostly refrain. . . . But this was not nightmare. This was true. She had stood there and said it all—and she had walked away leaving him rocking slowly, almost imperceptibly, back and forth on his heels. . . . She had walked away. . . .

He moaned suddenly and ran heavily, like a man bleeding to death, to the nearest front window. He crashed into a chair and did not feel it. He caught at the long drapery and held to it gratefully as he stared out into the yard. The path to the gate was serenely empty under the old trees.

A motor van came roaring down the curve into Hill Street. He caught a glimpse of the flat eternal mustard-colored piles under the edge of the tarpaulin as it passed. This was August. The market would be opening in another week . . . tobacco . . . the slow tide, impersonal, resistless, was beginning to flow in. . . . Another van roared by as he stood there looking. It was an old familiar sound become diabolical. He raised his fists and beat them against his ears.

He knew now. He was deserted, utterly, finally—beaten to his knees.

And he knew too that there was no longer the strength in him, or the will, to fight it. . . .

4

The afternoon blazed and died. The yard filled with darkness. The traffic noises along Hill Street became more muted and distant. Lights began to glow in the buildings. The raw, bluish glare of the street light just beyond the gate flashed out and a little swarm of insects began to gather and dance under it. And still he sat in the chair in the window, a heavy, sunken figure. He held a fresh cigar in the fingers of his right hand. He had never put it in his mouth. But he knew what he had to do now. He had only to wait until the strength came back into him.

No one came near him. Even the servants were shut away in the secure order of their activities. And the house, even the house, had deserted him. It lay a thick, strange shell about him—suffering his presence. That, in a way, was the worst of all. He could somehow manage to breathe if the house let him stay. Once—and once only—there flared in him a moment of rebellion, a last gasp of will to escape. He started halfway from the chair to go and find Randall. Anything would be better than sitting here alone under the slow, tearing throb of his agony—if he could just talk with someone, about anything, for a little while. . . . And then he sat down again. Randall wasn't even in town, he'd been gone up to Danville since Wednesday. He almost smiled then at himself. How could he ever

451

have thought that there would be even a moment's respite? You are bound on the wheel . . . there is never any escape. . . .

He heard Jeff, the Negro butler, come silently into the room behind him and begin turning on the lights. He was desperately grateful for that little orderly formality going on near him. He warmed himself at it and while he did it he knew that the moment had come. He could wait no longer. A kind of dead calm flooded him. He felt fragile, gentle, and full of a strange humility.

"Will you be dinin' in this evenin', Mr. Royle, suh?" The considerate servant's voice behind him in the doorway.

"No, Jeff." How gentle and weak his voice came out of him— the voice of illness. "Thank you. I'm going downtown tonight."

"Very good, suh."

He waited till the soft servant footsteps died beyond hearing. Then he got up slowly, hitched his coat about his shoulders, and walked into the hall. His hat—the black, old-fashioned bowler—lay there on the table. He picked it up and set it on his head. As he did so his hand went toward the button on the wall. It was a gesture of habit: that button was wired especially to a bell out back in the part of the old stable that acted as the garage now. He pulled his hand away. Call now for Charles and the car? Not this time. Not for this journey. There was only one way he could make it—and that was humbly and alone.

He opened the front door and closed it carefully behind him. He went down the walk putting one foot deliberately in front of the other. By the time he reached the gate and passed through it out into the street he was walking with an increasingly plodding strength, his hands clasped behind him, the cigar in his mouth, head and eyes bent forward. . . .

CHAPTER TWENTY-FOUR

I

He stood in the unknown hallway at last handing the bowler to the gaunt butler. He watched as the servant, his face creased and sour, placed the hat on the tree. He didn't know what time it was. He didn't really care. The important fact was that he had got here, he had rung the bell under the porte-cochere, and he had been admitted. The man turned back to him with a resigned, insulted expression and started to speak as though about to address something faintly disgusting on the floor at his feet.

"For heaven's sake—who is it, Bellers?"

The voice was cross. But it was still imperiously full of the old hoarse energy. He did not wait for the butler to answer. He plodded past him to the door and stopped.

"Hello, Sonie," he said.

She stood alone in the warm, overfurnished room. One hand rested lightly on a chair back and on it there was a great, glowing ring the color of grass. For a moment he could see nothing but the big ring and the slant cat eyes—the remembered eyes—in the broad face. It was exactly the same, yet different, subtly different. The angles and planes had been blurred. Twenty-five years had changed her some. He did not know what he had expected, but it shocked him a little to realize that she had managed time as she had managed everything else in her life—with humor and to her advantage. It was implicit in every detail of her as she stood there, from the too-red hair down the generous bust, the still trim waist under the dark-green dinner gown. There were even earrings, and more beads than he had ever remembered about her throat. She did not move or say anything for a moment. She simply stood and looked at him. Then she pulled among the beads on her chest and popped some glasses on her nose. At the same time her other hand went up back of her head to pat her hair. He almost smiled then. That one small gesture made him so grateful that he could almost have wept. The narrow eyes behind the pince-nez swept him with a glance of hostile examination.

"I should have known it," she said crisply. "You didn't weather very well, did you?"

"Sonie," he said humbly—let her say anything she wanted to; he was prepared to accept it, "can I come in?"

"After—how long has it been now? I wondered which of us would have to give in first." There was a subtle hint of mockery on the wide, expertly rouged mouth. It was a subtly histrionic expression. Even now she could no more help being a little of the play-actor with him than breathing. She waved an arm toward a chair. The gesture was accompanied by a muffled jangling and tinkling. She still covers her arms with those damned bracelets, he noted.

"Won't you sit down?" The invitation was made in an elaborately artificial voice.

"Thanks," he said, coming into the room and sinking carefully into the chair. He waited, expected to hear the hoarse derisive laugh break over him. But she said nothing. She did not even move. Just stood there by the other chair looking at him with narrowed, glittering eyes. He bent forward in the chair, looking humbly toward the floor.

"I came here tonight to ask a little favor of you."

She chuckled dryly.

"Ach! I was right. I knew it the minute you stood there," she

453

said triumphantly. "Twenty-five years hasn't changed you a bit really. I'm pretty sure why you are here, too!"

"Sonie, is my daughter—is Helen here with you?"

"She is." Her voice had become terse and cold. She was not going to make it any easier for him, but he hadn't expected her to.

"I'd like to see her for a few minutes. There are some things I must say to her."

"Haven't you said enough to her already?"

He shook his head slowly and looked up at her. His face was pasty-white. The dark eyes were bloodshot, but there was no mistaking the hot and desperate plea in them. His hands hung down between his knees, one of them clutched the other in little spasms. . . .

"No, I haven't said enough to her," he continued in the quiet, dogged voice. "I've said too much, maybe—but not enough."

"You've always done that to everybody."

"Yeah, I know. Can I see Helen, Sonie? I won't take long."

She stood rattling the beads between her fingers for a long moment. Her face was inscrutable. It neither affirmed nor denied. Then she tossed the elaborate coiffure upward with a decisive movement.

"Bellers!" she shouted full-throated, her eyes still on Brant. "You always managed to come at the wrong time," she said. "And too late."

"I don't know what you mean, Sonie."

"Ach! Of course not, you poor man, that's the trouble. You've always been so busy trying to run the world—or giving money away—you never really found out what *anything* meant." She broke off and shouted over his head. "Bellers! Damn that pompous fool. . . . " She began to pace a little, up and down, irritably.

How grateful he was for this little display of impatience in her. It was so warm, so human, so like her! He was starved. He gulped it down shamelessly.

"You haven't changed much, Sonie."

"You mean my temper?" She stopped short in her pacing, turned her head to him, and grinned for the first time. "No, and that's not the only thing that hasn't changed. Why didn't I tell you five minutes ago to run along and not bother us? I should have. You've forfeited every right I can think of for being allowed to come in here tonight. It'll only make more trouble. I know that. I've known it ever since I laid eyes on you over thirty years ago. But look at me"—she shrugged her shoulders and began pacing again, up and down—"as big a fool as ever—at my age! First time you turn up I let you in, and I'm going to do what you ask. Ach!—once in my life, only once, I had enough sense to say *no* to you."

She was furious. Watching her he could only feel thankful that she—anybody—still felt enough toward him to be angry.

454

"I remember, Sonie," he said quietly.

She stopped short then and looked full at him, biting her lip. Her forehead creased with a little flash of pain. Then she uttered an exclamation of disgust—whether at him or herself, he could not tell—and turned away. She began again to pace the three or four steps toward the other chair and the three or four back. The warm, rich glow from a table lamp shone over her dress. The garment looked alive as she moved. She stopped again in the center of the rug and cocked her head on one side.

"When I said that *no*," she continued in a calmer voice, "I knew I had done a sensible thing at last. I'd watched you walk all over, use, and destroy a lot of other people—not that any one of them had ever meant anything particular to you except as stuff to feed that big black pride of yours. Well, I knew then that you weren't going to be able to destroy me, anyway. I saved myself. I said some of these things to you then if you remember."

"Yes, I do." He nodded slowly, unable to look away from her.

"I was young then, and I was hurt. I didn't know whether what I was saying was right or not. There were some moments afterward —and this may please you—that were bad for me, because, you see, I never could quite get rid of you. Oh yes, I've watched you, read about you, followed what you were doing, saw you go right on up where you'd been headed all the time. Don't ask me why—I don't know myself. Never will. Maybe it's just because I got in the habit a long time ago of wondering about you and *hoping* for something— I don't know what—to come out in you. Or maybe I was just hoping to see the time when you'd be forced down on your knees by somebody or *something.*"

"Sonie, if you please," he broke out in the tired, dumb voice, "I'd like to see my daughter."

She turned to him, halted and suspended—as though she had been caught in mid-air. She rolled her eyes toward the ceiling and threw up her palms.

"Ach! Of course—there I go! This wasn't the time, but it had to be said—took twenty-five years." She shook her head in wonder at herself. It hurt her to see him then. She could not let it hurt her. She grabbed the beads and strode toward the hallway.

"Bellers! For heaven's sake!" There was a pause. Brant felt that pause behind him as a substance, a thing of solidity. "Well," her voice continued, "you've been long enough about it. I could have gone myself!"

"Madam?" The disparaging, bodiless voice of the servant was suddenly there.

"Bellers, if Mr. and *Mrs.* Barton have finished their coffee, ask them to come in here, please!"

455

"Very good, ma'am!"

The beads rattled behind him. *Mr. and Mrs. Barton.* . . . Brant examined the deliberate announcement—because it was an announcement. It had been done, then. How soon or how late, it didn't matter. He felt cold, almost shivering, as he sat there. He had been sweating from his walk when he had come to the door, but he could see the long curtains hanging listless in the windows across the room. They were lace curtains, tea-colored—where had he seen them before? Lace curtains and Sonie . . . Maple Street. . . . There was no breeze. It was a breathless evening. After all, it was August. . . .

Sonie crossed back into the room.

"She did it, then," he said, more to himself than to her. "I don't mind, but it was just this afternoon—"

"I told you you were too late," she said in a voice full of hard triumph. She was standing by the chair, waiting now, facing the door. "I told you—"

"Yeah, you told me. It doesn't matter—I didn't come here because of that."

They waited in the still, breathless room. Each of them immobile in his place. There was nothing more to say—or perhaps there was everything to say. He heard their steps, muffled on the thick carpet, coming into the room. He stood up, a ponderous, painful movement. They swam into his sight like children, standing side by side, still shy, still awkward. James in the unpressed suit. She in the skirt and waist in which she had walked out the door.

"Hello, Helen—Mr. Barton."

"Hello, Father," she replied. Her voice was cool, remote, unyielding. It was no more than he had expected.

"Will you sit down for a minute please, Helen?" he said humbly.

She looked at him, adamant. Then she seated herself on the small settee, hands folded primly in her lap like a schoolgirl. The young man remained standing, solid, bland, looking down at Helen.

"If you will excuse me—" said Sonie, starting to cross between them.

Brant raised a hand fumblingly at the air.

"No, Sonie, I'd like you to stay. I want all of you to stay. What I've got to say concerns all of you."

She fell back against the chair, watching him. James Barton seated himself stiffly on the settee beside Helen. He took one of her hands in his. The three pairs of eyes fell upon Brant, quiet and waiting. He did not sit down himself. He stood, his hands clasped behind him, the big shoulders bowed, his own glance upon the rug, as though he found some new talisman, some strength, in the convolutions of the floral pattern winding out beneath his feet.

"What I've got to say won't take long, Helen; and now that I'm here to say it I don't have any real good way of putting it into words. But no matter how I say it, I'm afraid you won't believe it. I can't blame you for that—still, in spite of everything, I've got to say it."

He fell silent. Helen said stiffly from the settee:

"All right, Father. We're listening. What is it?"

For a long moment he just stood looking at a big maroon rose framed between his feet. Then he began speaking, slowly, carefully:

"I just came here to tell you—all the things I said this afternoon to you, to both of you, they weren't true, they were wrong." He looked at the rug and clasped and unclasped his hands behind his back. It was an agony, not only inside of him, but a pain of not having the words at his command. He looked at the two people on the settee beseechingly. They sat, their hands joined, looking woodenly, stolidly at him out of a kind of abstract happiness. They couldn't help him. He couldn't expect anything from them now. "This is hard for me to say—not because I don't want to say it, Helen, but because I don't know how to say it. But I was wrong, dead-wrong— been wrong for a long time. I don't ask you to forgive me. I don't ask anything really of you. But you're my daughter, and whether you can believe it or not, I can't stand to have you go away from me now, wherever you are going—to have you leave me without giving me a chance to open a door to you somewhere. Right now I'd do anything—crawl to you if you wanted me to—just to have you say you'd try to let me love you—not have you, make you, do anything, I wouldn't touch you—but just let me love you and be in a place where you could feel that you—you and Mr. Barton—could call on me when you needed somebody to help. You said that you didn't need me any more. That hurt—that hurt *bad*. I don't ask you to try to love me, but I'd like you to need me sometimes. I'd like you to feel that there was something I had that you could use—" He faltered and shook his head blindly.

"Father," she said, her face pale and set, her mouth straight and cold around the words. "Father, I'm sorry, but there are too many things standing between you and me. There's nothing I can say now. What do you want me to say?"

"I don't know, Helen," he went on, shaking his head. "I wish I did. I only know I had to come out here tonight and say this to you —even though it's a mean thing to make you face on your—your wedding day. I'm sorry. . . ."

"Father"—she looked from the boy beside her to Sonie standing still holding her beads—"you, Jim—and Sonie—I haven't anything to say. I've said it all already. I can't change all that in a flash. I can't say it's all right, Father, because it isn't. . . . Or if it ever will be all right, it'll take a long time. I've got to have time. . . ."

"Yeah—yeah, I know!"

He gestured almost peremptorily—a gesture with the ghostly vestiges of directors' and board meetings. It was the only gesture he knew.

"Helen, you can have all the time you want. All I ask is that you don't cut me out cold. That you and your—husband let me be a little part of whatever you make of your lives. That you give me just a little chance to make you want me to be a part of whatever you are doing."

It was so strange, so solemn, with the four of them there—and the two of them talking, intensely, across to each other, like creatures fighting for their very lives.

"How can I say anything?" said Helen. "I've already said all I can say. You can't change it now. I can't change it yet. Because that's the way I feel—you made me feel that way. Maybe after a while—"

"I'm not asking for anything now, anything. I just want you to say you'll let me hope for something with you sometime in the future."

"No—no." She flared up then, fiercely. It was a cry that went through his vitals. "I can't promise you or give you anything! I thought we were finished—done." She hid her face in her hands. "I don't want to argue with you tonight!"

Silence fell like a blow into the room. All of them—standing or sitting where they were under the lamp glow, under the plushy, late-summer air that pervaded the room—felt it enclose them.

"All right, Helen," said Brant in the mild voice, "all right."

"I'm sorry—" She broke off and shook her head blindly.

"I don't blame you," he went on, because he couldn't stop yet, "but I came here to say it—I had to say it—" He faltered and then added, almost to himself, "before I could ever go home again to Hill Street."

No one said anything. They just looked at him, a creature incomprehensible, and alien. He endured it in silence and then pulled himself ponderously out of the chair. He nodded his head slowly and formally in the direction of Sonie, standing running the green beads through her fingers and watching him.

"I thank you, Sonie. . . ."

She made no response, no sign of any kind. He started to go, then half-turned back to the girl on the settee.

"Helen, what about your things—your clothes? You'll need them."

She acknowledged this with a stiff nod. "Yes—I'll send for them tomorrow if I may," she whispered.

"Of course."

He looked once more at them sitting there, the young man and

458

the young woman, frozen, shy, and implacable—immensely implacable.

"Good evening," he said. He walked out of the room and into the hallway. He didn't need anyone to show him the way out. But before he reached the door the tall figure of the butler stepped from the shadows, like a disdainful jack-in-the-box. He extended the bowler politely.

"Your hat, sir. Shall I call a cab?"

He put the hat on and reached in his coat for a cigar.

"No," he said gruffly, "I won't need one."

He put the cigar—the comforting gesture, the familiar rich taste of the tobacco—in his mouth. The door opened. He walked through it out into the night.

2

He felt bruised and weak—a creature hollow, and more than half beaten to the earth. But beyond that, deep in him, there began to be a kind of peace. He had abased himself. He had been denied and shut out. Well, he had done all he could do. A sort of pride—an ashy remnant of the old thing—began to rise in him. It was cool and frail, but it gave him something to hold to. He wasn't completely lost. The little pride was something he could still cling to—depend upon.

He walked out into the wide stretch of suburban Bay Street— the dark reaches of lawn and shrubbery, the houses withdrawn, shut in behind the glow of their windows.

He had walked all the way out. All the way. It must have been a mile or more. But that was all right. To use himself physically was what he had needed. At least it was part of it. Now that he had made this first step in his penance the best he knew how, he was exhausted. He didn't feel equal to the journey back . . . back where? The house . . . He put it out of his thoughts. He was afraid to face it. But he stopped a block away near a street light, a lone dark figure humped at the shoulders looking at his own feet, waiting. . . .

About a quarter of an hour passed before a streetcar came rumbling down around the curve headed toward town. He stepped out and it ground protestingly to a halt. Mounting it, he thought that he didn't even know how much it cost, the fare—he who owned all of them, supplied the power that ran them, didn't even know the fare! This was the final admission, the final humiliation, he thought. He stepped up into it.

"What's the fare?"

"Five cents," said the conductor, tiredly closing the door behind him and pulling on the bell cord. There was a strident clang over-

459

head and the car lurched forward under him. He found a nickel and handed it over and went down the narrow, swaying aisle. He found an empty place. It was wonderful just to sit there alone feeling the darkness rush by him, pushing a little cool wind against his face. No head turned to him. There were five or six in the car. They didn't know who he was. Brant Royle! Who was he? They were as deeply buried in their loneliness, as lost and separate, as he. Passengers crossing a kind of eternal Styx. He began to wish that he could travel on endlessly like this. Unknown, unsought-for, unaccused. He had a feeling that no one, nothing, could touch or hurt or shatter him as long as he sat on this hard straw-woven seat—obliterated. He sat and chewed the cigar and watched the busy, bright city spring up about the progress of the car. . . . Just beyond Elm Street he reached up and pulled the bell cord. He would get off at the square. He was not alone. A man and a woman, talking together in hard, low voices preceded him down the steps to the street. The car clanged impersonally beyond them, turning the corner at the square. The three of them stood poised, hesitant, stranded. The woman laughed and and she and her companion crossed the foot of Hill Street in the direction of the movie house. Its lighted marquee glittered feverishly midway down the block. Brant watched the man and woman depart as though he would have liked to go with them. They at least were human flesh, warm and breathing. They had some place they were going. He had no place. . . .

He stood for a long time on the corner chewing his cigar, feeling the inhabitants of the square—slowed and thinned by night—ebb and flow before and about him. A newsboy thrust a paper at him— thrust a mocking, gamin face under a cap up toward his—"Papeh!— Mornin' *Herald!*"

Oh, good little newsboy! he thought. Where did you come from? Where are you going? . . . Stay a while—don't leave me.

"Sure," he said in the humble voice. "How much?"

"How much?" said the child's voice, astonished. "You jokin'? *Herald's* always been three cents!"

"Here," he said. "Give me one."

He gave the boy a quarter and took the folded paper. The urchin began to search among a jingle in his pocket.

"Keep the change, son," he said.

"Thanks" was the curtly enthusiastic reply. It had a note that he recognized deep in him. Under the casual formality was the sound of predatory scrambling—the voice of all the merciless, ruthless, bitter anguish to get on in the world. . . .

Without a backward glance he fled from it, clutching the folded paper under his arm. He walked stiffly down the side of the square. He did not consciously choose a way, but he found himself at last

460

passing through the dark, thick, fish-fry, Negro stretch of Rice Street —his feet pounded hard and lone on the cooling pavement. The night pressed close and hot, breaking out upon him the smell of horse dung, pine, and tobacco—always, eternally, tobacco. The bright leaf which at that moment in the night was being watched and tended, heated and colored, in all the little glowing barns spread over the countryside. He had been born with the smell of it in his nostrils. It was something that had never changed in his life, the single stable element—that golden bright leaf. . . .

He hurried on, stalking down the darkness, and came at last to the factory block. There was his factory. The long gleaming tiers of windows glowing in the night, the hum of machinery roaring endlessly—in darkness as well as day. He had set those wheels to running, they were still running. . . . They were more permanent, more safe, than he at the moment. He walked to the steps of the office. He even reached in his pocket for the key. Am I completely crazy, he thought, to go up there to the bare room with the desk *now*? Is it because this is the last place . . . the only place . . . buried under the ghosts of a million hands, a million miles of tobacco plants, a million turning wheels? The factory roared steadily on and on above him. He looked at it and turned back over the way he had come. He was hurrying now—trying to escape. It was as blind an action as he had ever known. He was at the bottom of the pit. He could not run, only walk step by step all the way back to the square, cross it, reach the sidewalk at the foot of Hill Street. . . .

Climbing the old, dark incline was to him suddenly like climbing a treadmill of all his days. Under him his feet sounded like the feet of a tired beast pacing across the waste places of the earth. Serene and utterly removed, the night floated above him and the city. About him the blank, empty faces of buildings leaned—the scattered faces of humans hurrying, weaving, strolling, in an unreality of street lights and plunging shadows; the lost wail and cry of a car, a truck grinding down past him into farther reaches of darkness. Had all of this ever been a part of him? Had he *really* helped to make this, drag it clangorously into being? It was like dust in his mouth, choking him. . . .

Fragments swam into his thoughts, unrelated, unconsidered— Shall I call a cab, sir? . . . call a cab . . . call a cab . . . That was a million miles behind him and here he was walking savagely and nakedly into the night, the still handsome head of him thrust out defiantly against the darkness like an ancient, indomitable bull . . . wounded, but undefeated . . . *call a cab*? Christ! He still had his own two feet under him, and they alone had carried him upright through many a heaven and many a hell in his time. But now, he considered grimly, in this hour, those two fateful old continents are

461

lost to me, those familiar old lands with their thunder of wings. Walk? . . . Of course I can walk . . . even though it means that I have to walk through the sudden and immense vacuum with no hand reaching to hold me up, to keep me from falling, with no knowledge but that I have sinned long, I have tried to confess. . . . The far, faint music of invisible hounds, diabolically noiseless, nosed his trail from the skies. They've caught you at last, Brant Royle, cornered you, run you to earth. . . . Evoke Corporal Smart, the slim first cigarette, evoke Mason's Best, Buckingham, Treasure, Paul Harris—all of them, the long glittering list, stretching around the earth, wrapped by your hands. . . . Call upon the hospital . . . the Foundation . . . the park with the lake and the swan and the iron swings for little children . . . summon them up to answer for you. . . .

He put his face toward the end—concentrated the last thought, the last ounce of his energy, upon gaining the top where safety, where the last and ultimate sanctuary, lay waiting for him . . . the blood and memories, the wood, the clean white columns, the gracious forgiving structure . . . the house. His heart, lean, stripped, and youthful, raced on ahead—only his feet moved slowly one after the other, automatons, worn and unhurried. . . . And as he went it seemed that several others were with him, surrounding him, ahead of him, figures of himself . . . in ragged jeans and bare, dusty feet . . . in the first store-bought suit, tight, unyielding . . . in the bowler hat . . . the Bond Street clothes—all of them panting in a like desperation, the several ghostly heads thrust forward at the same dogged angle, all of them racing to sanctuary. . . .

He was there. His own gate opened and let him in. He paused for a moment, hearing his breath sob out of his throat. He leaned back against the hard, impersonal iron, his eyes running on, tracing the length of the walk, up the broad steps, drinking in the whole proud, remote façade—proud, yes, *and* remote even after fifty-odd years of his passion. He walked toward it—an old lover, an old enemy, in this hour. . . . But it was with humility and gratitude. He could still feel its earth under his feet, he still had the assurance that *it*, at least, was there—and that it was *his!* He wheeled on the top step of the porch, a creature at bay. Beaten? . . . Finished? . . . Brant Royle? He pierced the darkness over the city, glaring fiercely into the night. . . .

Below him the gate opened. A figure stood in it, black, nameless, and hesitant. It was a woman. She closed the gate and came purposefully up the pathway. Where had he seen her before, the enigmatic, inescapable figure stepping toward him out of the shadows and into the light?

"Brant," she said. Her voice was low, almost shy.

"All right," he said roughly. "What do you want?"

"You big fool!" she said. "Going off there from the house walking, no car. I've spent the last hour or more running up and down Bay Street—and a lot of other places—just looking for you. I finally just landed and had O'Brien park outside there in the street until you came. I knew you hadn't come—I could tell by the house. . . ."

"What do you want, Sonie?"

The figure, faceless still, an outline at the foot of the steps, raised arms toward the black blob of a hat, resetting it.

"What do I want? Ach, what a question! I got worried about you after you left the house. I thought I'd better repay your call. It may seem sort of sudden—but after all it's been twenty-five years!"

Her voice was so young, so dark and warm. Twenty-five years. . . . He could see her—full, young, and vibrant . . . the body he had touched, held, known . . . twenty-five years. . . .

"Well, come on up on the porch—don't stand there like a—"

"Like a what?" She marched up the steps then, outraged. "I didn't come all the way up here and wait just to quarrel with you, Brant."

"Listen, Sonie," he growled at her out of the corner of his mouth. He felt as though the darkness had opened—that there were stars somewhere. He did not try and question it. "I'm tired . . . I don't feel like fighting either—any more, ever."

"Look at him!" she implored the porch, the trees, the night. "The same black, bumbling, stupid idiot of a bear that he always was!"

She stood a little behind him and apart. They both were silent, gazing down over the town. It was velvet splashed with jewels. Little twinkling clusters, glows, blinking signs—the hotel, red and amber—the sign on two of the factories down in Jamaica Town . . . Royle & Company . . . Royle & Company. There was something remote yet friendly about it, reaching toward them in the annealing, the healing darkness. . . .

"What do you want, Sonie?" he said again after a while, not turning or looking toward her, his legs planted, his face toward the city.

She did not answer at once. But she came up close without touching him. He could hear the jewelry jingling, could smell the heavy scent. She was still bedecked and bedizened—at her age! he snorted. But he began to feel warm, desperately warm, inside. . . .

"Look here," she commanded, "I don't want anything. I saw

you tonight at my house for the first time in a long time. And I said a lot of hard things to you—you needed them said. I heard you say some things too—things I'd never thought to hear out of your mouth. And I saw you go away. . . ."

"Well?" he rumbled.

"Nothing," she said in the warm, hoarse voice, that old voice that had suffered neither change nor loss with the years. "But I thought someone ought to come up and tell you that you hadn't said everything—that I hadn't said everything, bone-true as all of it was."

"If you want to make fun of me, Sonie, you've come at the wrong—"

"Shut up!" she said crossly. "You never would listen to anybody. Look, Brant Royle, I saw you go out of my house as I had never expected to see you while I stood up in my shoes—with your tail between your legs! You were whipped and you knew it—but, more important than that, you said it out loud, and you said it to somebody about something that you had found at last meant more than everything you'd set up for yourself in the face of the world. I must say *that* gave me a big shock! What's more, I couldn't resist it—and more than that, I couldn't have you going out from us believing about yourself and about your life what you seemed set on believing—that everything you'd spent your life for was worthless, that you were lost, disowned."

"Well, isn't it pretty much that way, Sonie?"

"No, *no*," she said fiercely. "Ach, I could beat your stubborn, stupid ears at this minute! But I swore I wouldn't lose my temper ever again with you—I won't this time. You've got what was coming to you, in a way, at last. Listen, Brant, you can't ask of the world what you've asked of it and not expect to pay *something*."

"No? I've paid plenty all my life."

"I'm sure of that. And you got what you wanted."

"How do you know I got what I wanted?" he demanded, setting his teeth. He reached in his coat pocket for the comforting cigar.

"Well, didn't you? You worked an almighty long time for it."

His thoughts were a warm, grateful confusion at that moment as he bit off the end of the tobacco and spat it out into the darkness. It was so *good* to have that angry, prying voice poking out of the darkness at him, tired, utterly weary, and empty as he felt. He heard the bracelets jingle again. How many years were lost, gone, irreplaceable. . . .

"Sure I worked," he admitted, gripping the cigar between his teeth. "I slaved more than anybody. I got everything—*everything* that I set out to get . . . and not one thing I really wanted. They

464

all got away from me, every single one of them—except this house. . . ."

"You mean this place—ol' Major Jim's place?"

"Yeah, I mean *this* place. An' if you laugh I'll throttle you, old as you are, and be glad of it!"

"I'm not laughing."

"I couldn't even have a real son of my own. I have Randy, sure! But who is he? Somebody with my name. Helen—" He broke off and chewed the cigar.

"I said you had to pay," she said quietly. "All of us do—you, me, every poor soul of us! But I can't stand you talking like a fool. And that's what you're talking like—and feeling almighty sorry for yourself, aren't you? You're talking like you've got nothing for your money—made nothing!"

"Well," he said again, "have I?"

"Of course, you damned idiot!—you always did make me curse you. Now listen to me." She snorted indignantly at herself. "You had a daughter—a good, nice girl, because I know her better than you do —but you didn't know you had her, or that it made any difference, until it was too late. I told you you were always too late. There were always too many other things between you and the breath and blood of life. But that doesn't mean that it's done, that it's finished."

"After tonight—isn't it?"

"Are you dead already? No, it isn't finished as long as you want it out of that slow, late heart of yours. It'll take time . . . *sure*. What do you expect? But you've taken your time about coming around to the truth. You've got to give her and Jim a little time, too. It's going to be hard uphill work every inch of the way—but you've never been afraid of work."

"Is this why you've come all the way up here tonight—to say this?"

"Yes, part-way—part-way, I wanted to make you stand up like I remember you, and stop moaning—it isn't at all becoming to you. I want you to look around you and recognize *what* you've really accomplished in spite of yourself. Of course you've done plenty of mean, bad things. But you've done a lot of big, wonderful things. When I first saw you in the doorway of the warehouse down on Maple Street, I saw something—a kind of wonder and goodness in you, a thing that you never would let see the light of day, because there was so much you had against *your* world. But I've never forgotten that wonder. No matter what else has happened between us. I always believed in that part of you—and I haven't been wrong. Well, look, you ol' fool—look down there below you!"

She stepped close beside him and he saw her arm dart out toward the whole spreading night below them. He looked. . . .

465

Kingsmont—that ephemeral, rich, pulsing, mysterious quantity sprawled outward into a sea of black. And beyond it he could feel the fields, the woods, the great mysterious pattern of the inhabited state, the earth, wash up around them in silent waves. He had cleared those fields, sweated in those rows, sprung that green plant into life, harnessed that river, enriched every hamlet and farm, gladdened the hearts of many simple men nameless to him. Now he could understand what it really meant. It thrilled him. He filled his lungs full of the warm night air. The trees in the yard bent over him. They were friendly. They understood. They were wise—so much wiser than he had ever been. And she was wiser than all of them. His eye caught again upon the little cluster of lights blinking at him out of the far darkness—Royle & Company . . . Royle & Company . . . Royle & Company. He looked at it as though he had never seen it or those words before. They were beautiful. They stated and restated a sturdy affirmation against the great black, against all the lost ruin of the past, against all time and despair. . . .

"Sonie," he said—and reached an arm out blindly to her.

He still was afraid to turn his head. He felt too shy and new and naked standing there. . . .

She peered at him, trying to trace out his profile. She started to reach for the pince-nez on her breast. Ach, this was no time for specs! They couldn't help. She slipped an arm through his and shook it gently. It was a warm and friendly touch—just a little sad. It said between them all there was to be said for the time, the bitterness, the years, that had flown away. He bent the big, stalwart, indomitable head down toward her. She could see no feature. All of his face was curtained and hidden in night. But she didn't need to see, because she already knew—had known for long years—every line, mark, shape of that countenance. She grinned up at him in the darkness, the old, wide-mouthed, mocking grin. She couldn't see, but she could feel the grim mouth curl—halfway only, as it had always done—in response. It was years . . . years . . . years since she had seen that elusive, tender, remote thing on that mouth. . . .

"You're a good gal, Sonie Lipik," he said in the deep, tired voice. "A good gal!"

"Yes," she said, nodding her head, the proud old head, "I always was!"

466